THE ILIAD

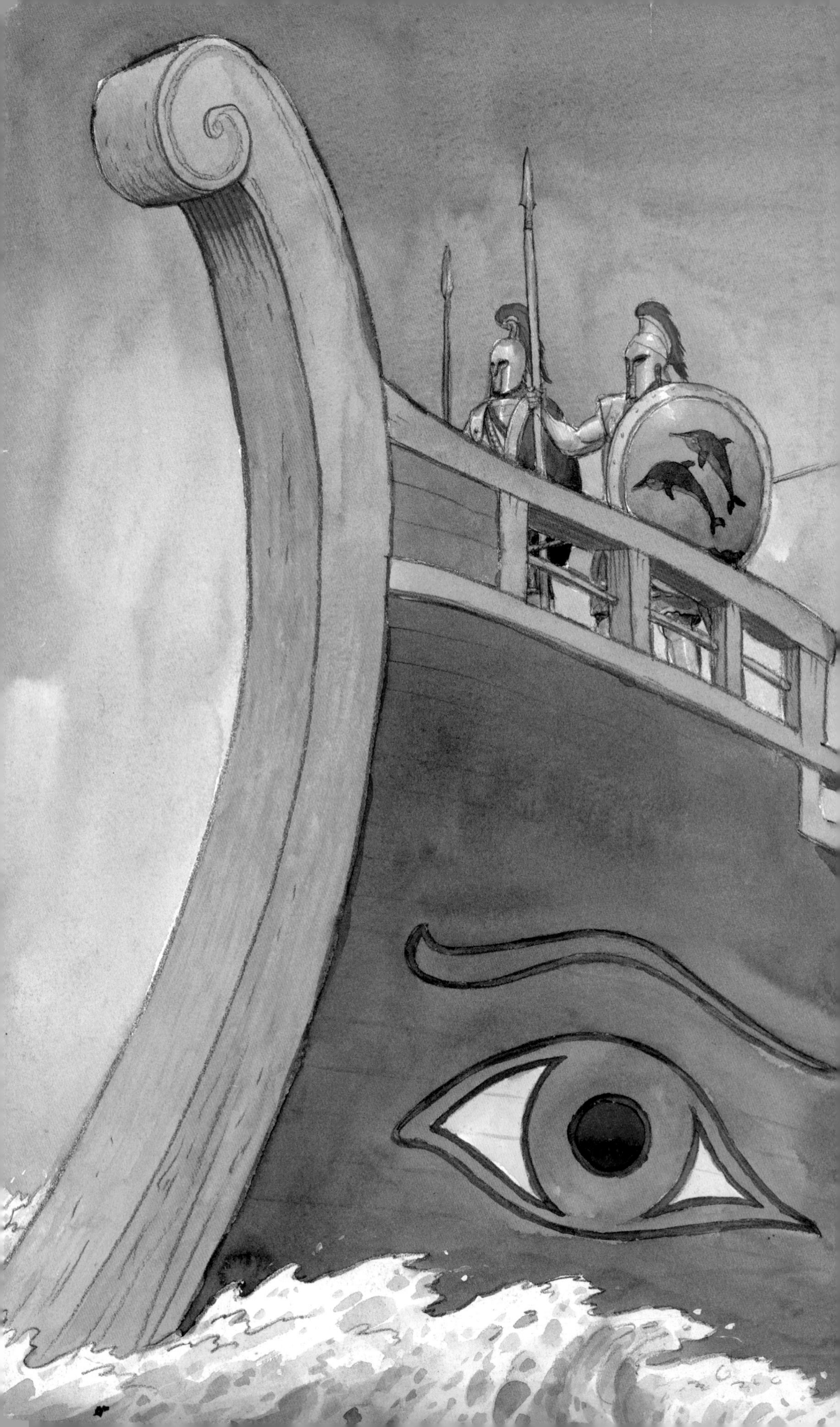

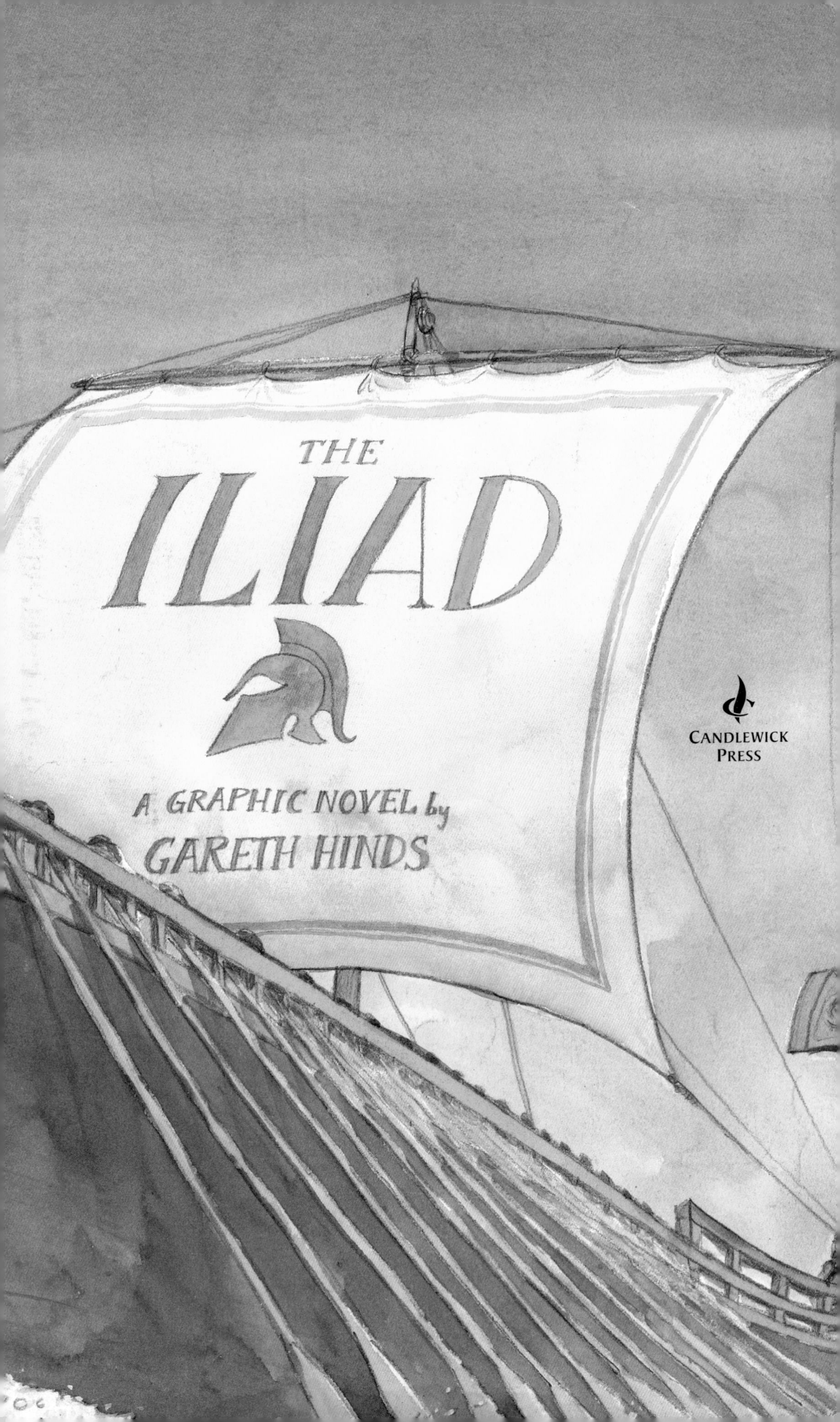
THE
ILIAD
A GRAPHIC NOVEL by
GARETH HINDS

CANDLEWICK
PRESS

IMPORTANT ACHAEANS (GREEKS)

AGAMEMNON
Son of Atreus
High King of
Mycenae

MENELAUS
Son of Atreus
King of Sparta

ODYSSEUS
Son of Laertes
King of Ithaca

ACHILLES
Son of Peleus
Leader of the
Myrmidons

PATROCLUS
Son of
Menoetius

"LITTLE" AJAX
Son of Oileus
Prince of Locris

"GREAT" AJAX
Son of Telamon
Prince of Salamis

NESTOR
Son of Neleus
King of Pylos

DIOMEDES
Son of Tydeus
King of Argos

TEUCER
Son of Telamon
Half-brother of Ajax

The initial letter of each captain's name is subtly worked into their breastplate and/or helmet. This and their unique shield decoration should help you tell them apart.

Important Trojans

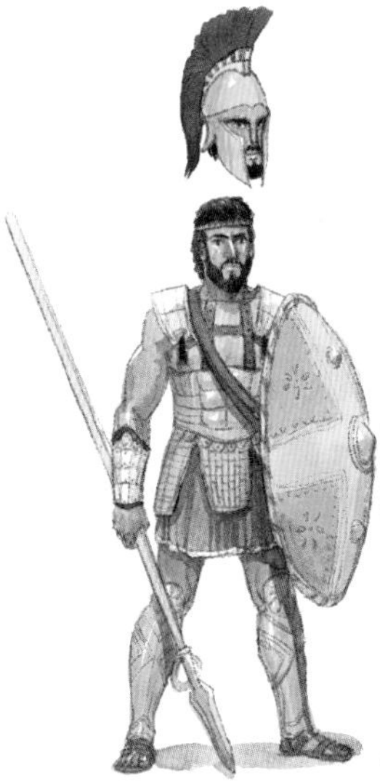

Hector
Son of Priam
Prince of Troy

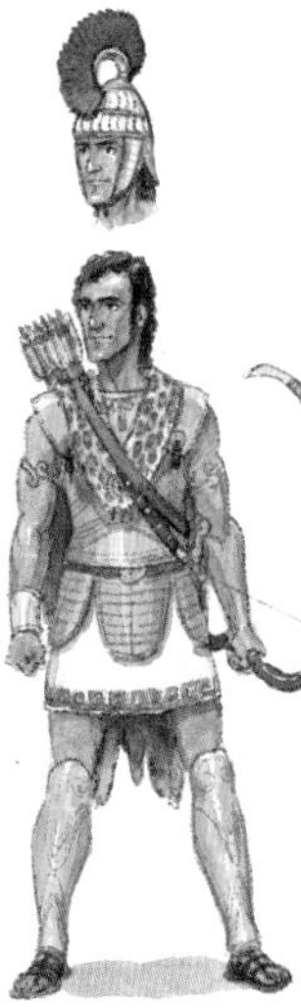

Paris
Son of Priam
Prince of Troy

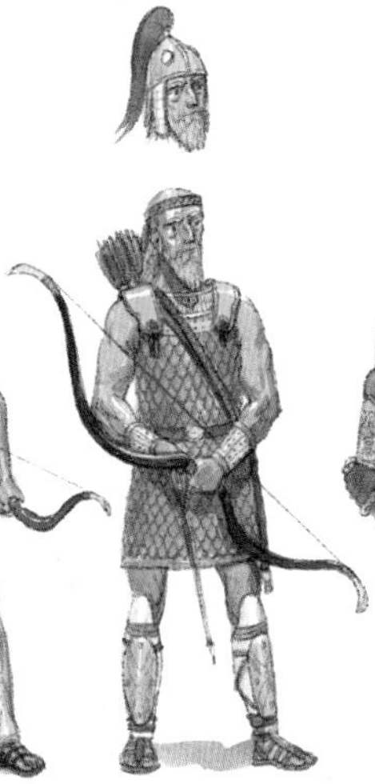

Pandarus
Son of Lycaon
Leader of the Zeleans

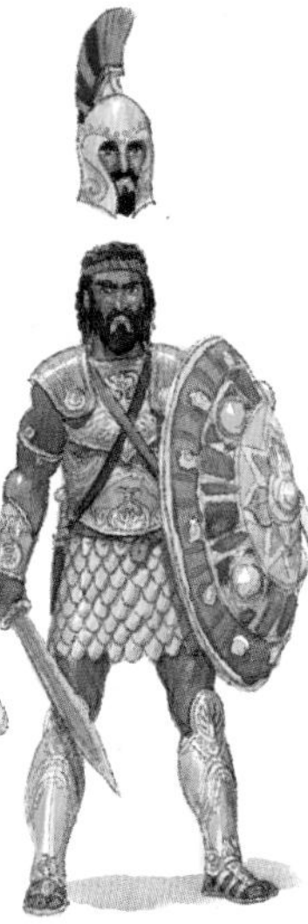

Sarpedon
Son of Zeus
King of Lycia

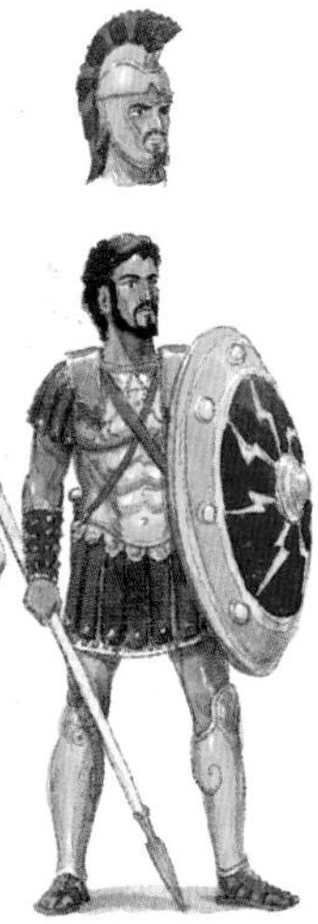

Aeneas
Son of Aphrodite
Leader of the Dardanians

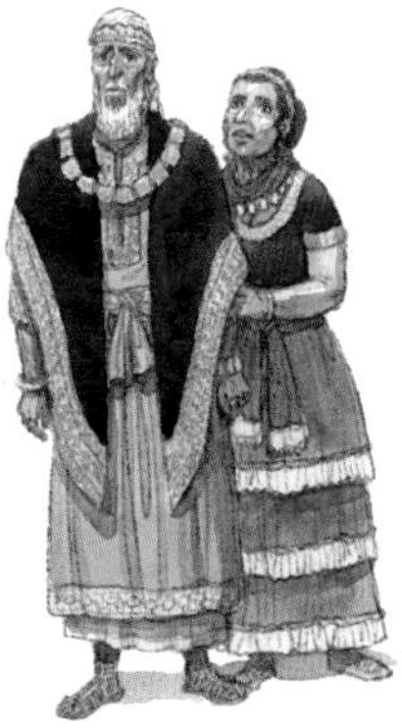

Priam and Hecuba
King and Queen of Troy

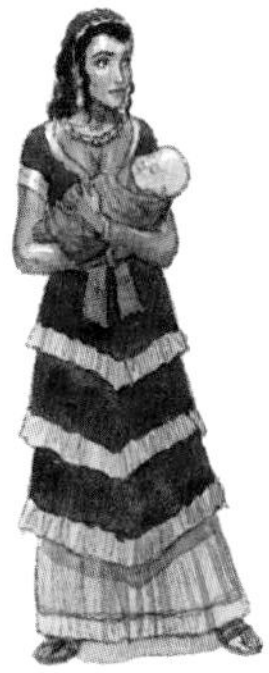

Andromache and Scamandrius
Wife and Son of Hector

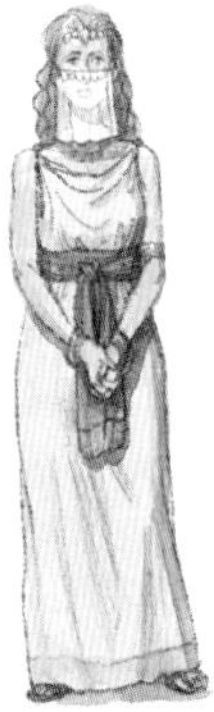

Helen
Daughter of Zeus
Wife of Menelaus

The Gods

(Top row: children of the Titans; bottom row: children of Zeus)

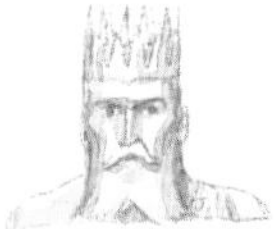

Zeus
God of Lightning
Chief of the Gods

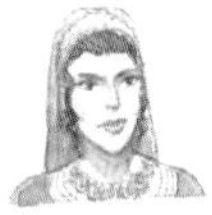

Hera
Goddess of Family
Wife of Zeus

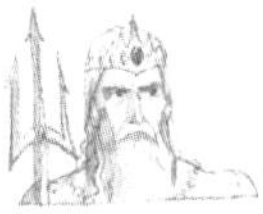

Poseidon
God of the Ocean

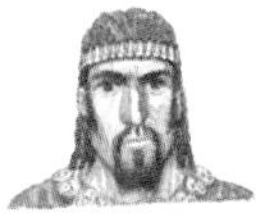

Hades
God of the Underworld

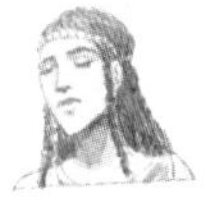

Thetis
Goddess of the Sea
Mother of Achilles

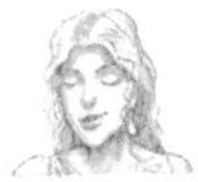

Aphrodite
Goddess of Love

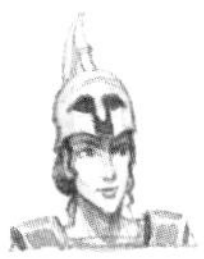

Athena
Goddess of Wisdom, Craft, and Battle

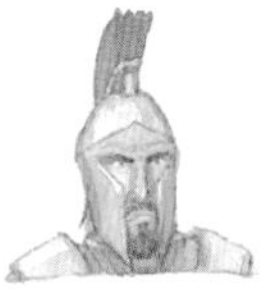

Ares
God of War

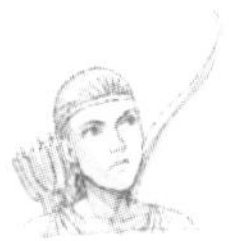

Artemis
Goddess of Hunting
Sister of Apollo

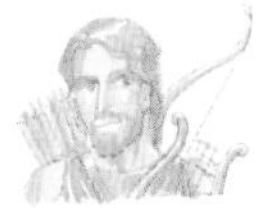

Apollo
God of the Sun and Medicine

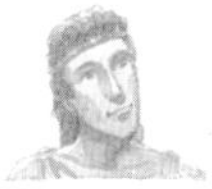

Hermes
God of Trickery and Messengers

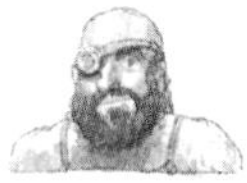

Hephaestus
God of Fire

Prologue

This is not the story of the Trojan War. Or at least not the whole story.

In *The Iliad,* Homer relates events that took place in the tenth and final year of that war, centering on a feud between the warrior Achilles and the leader of the Greek forces, King Agamemnon. It does not tell the whole story of how the war started, or how it ended.

The Trojan War was fought probably sometime around the twelfth century B.C.E. (the late Bronze Age) between the people of Troy, on the west coast of Turkey, and the Achaeans — a loose alliance of city-states in and around Greece (nobody used the names Turkey or Greece at the time). The Achaeans were also sometimes called the Argives or the Danaans, just to confuse you.

The war was fought over a woman. Or possibly an apple, or a lot of gold, or control of trade routes. Here's what supposedly happened: the two mightiest gods, Zeus and Poseidon, were both attracted to a sea-nymph named Thetis. But Zeus received a prophecy that Thetis would bear a son far more powerful than his father. Nobody wanted to see how powerful that son would be if he was fathered by a god, so a marriage was hastily arranged between Thetis and a mortal adventurer named Peleus (a companion of the legendary Heracles).

The gods all came to their wedding and gave them priceless gifts, such as a pair of immortal horses and a magnificent spear and suit of armor. The goddess Eris (Strife or Discord) wasn't invited to the wedding, but she showed up anyway. She rolled a golden apple into the midst of the party, with the words "For the fairest" written on it. This resulted in a beauty contest between Hera, Athena, and

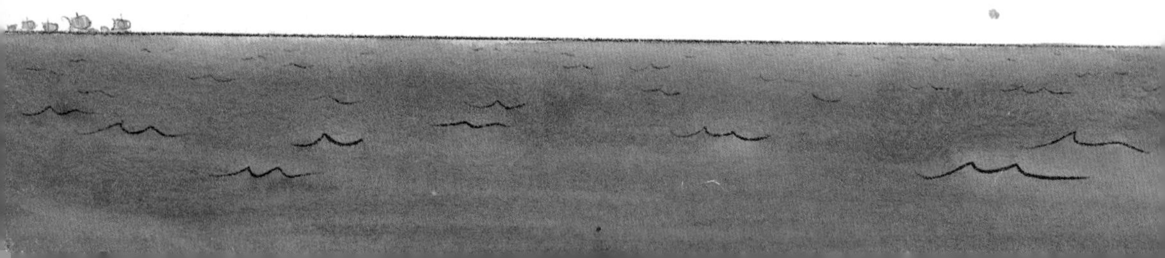

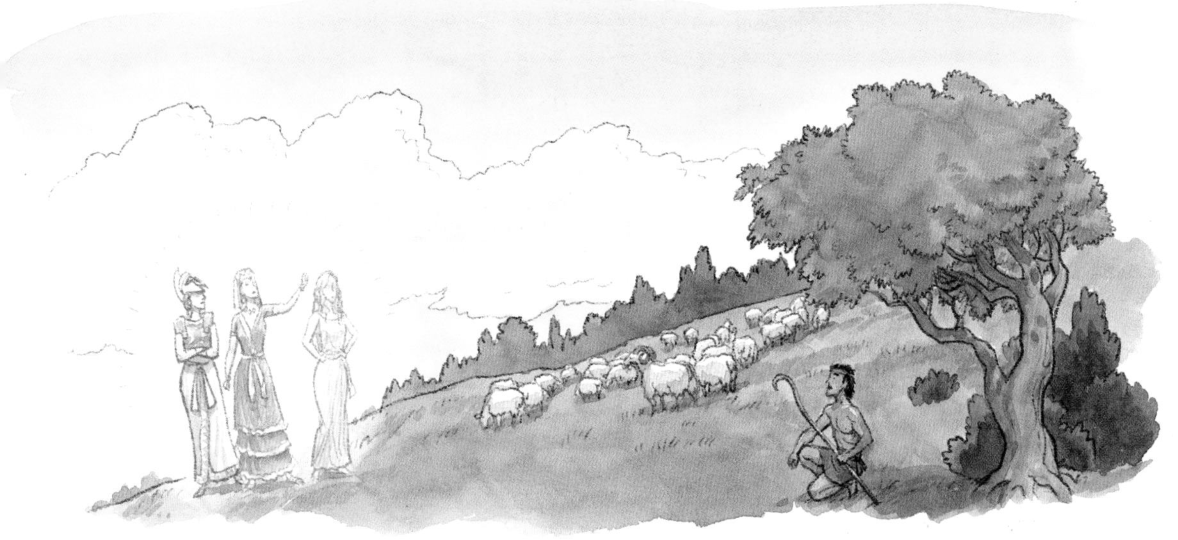

Aphrodite, each of whom thought she was the fairest, and this contest was judged by the (un)lucky Paris, prince of Troy. At first he said he couldn't choose, but then the goddesses started offering him gifts, and Aphrodite won by promising him the most beautiful woman in the world: Helen, daughter of Zeus and Leda. She neglected to mention that Helen was already married. Also, by choosing Aphrodite, Paris made Athena and Hera his enemies forever.

Most of the Achaean leaders had been suitors of Helen years before. During that courtship, all of them had sworn an oath to defend whoever won her hand. The winner turned out to be Menelaus, King of Sparta.

So when Aphrodite helped Paris seduce Helen and steal her away, Menelaus and his brother, Agamemnon (King of Mycenae), called in the oaths of all the Achaean leaders, and they all set sail for Troy to claim Helen (along with the gold she'd taken with her and the loot they hoped to plunder from Troy, plus command of the best trade routes between Asia and the Mediterranean).

As for Peleus and Thetis, they did have a son. His name was Achilles.

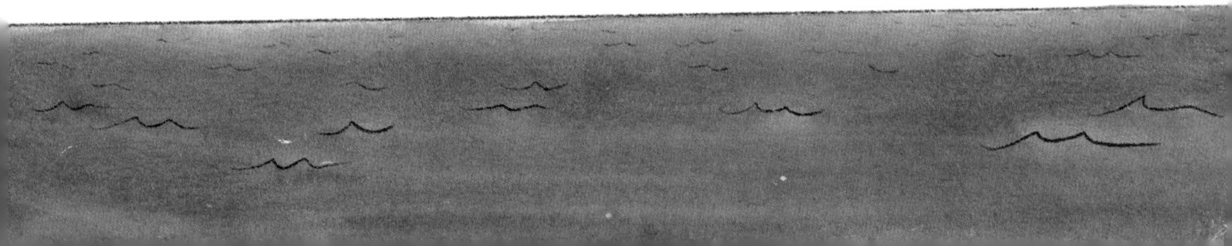

Book 1

RAGE. Sing to me, O Muse, of the rage of Achilles, fiercest of all the Achaean warriors who sailed to Troy. His anger at King Agamemnon cost the Achaeans countless losses, sending the souls of many strong men down to Death.

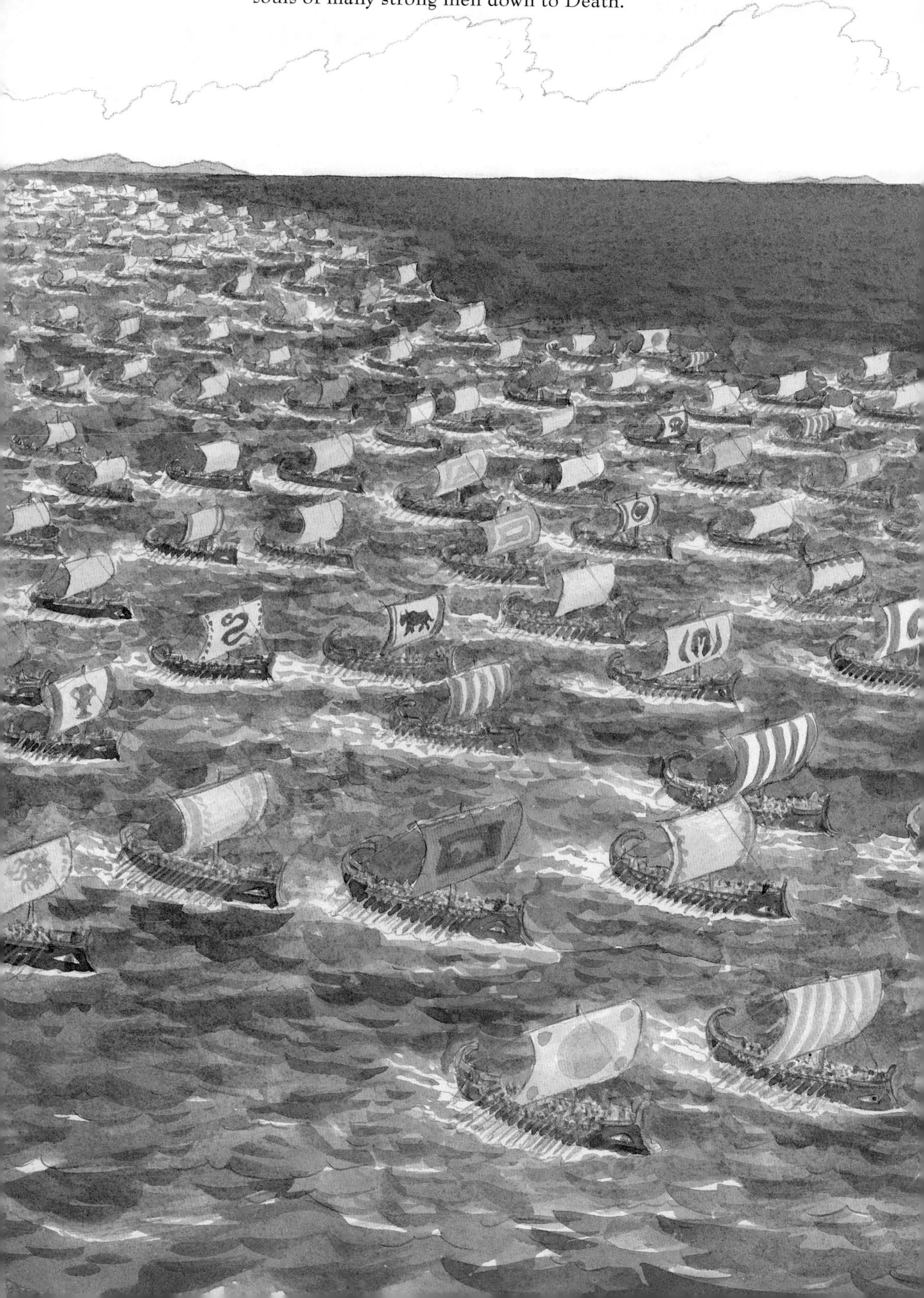

They went to sack the city, to topple its towers and take back Helen of Sparta. Agamemnon led that mighty army across the sea to Troy, blackening the waves with an endless fleet of ships.

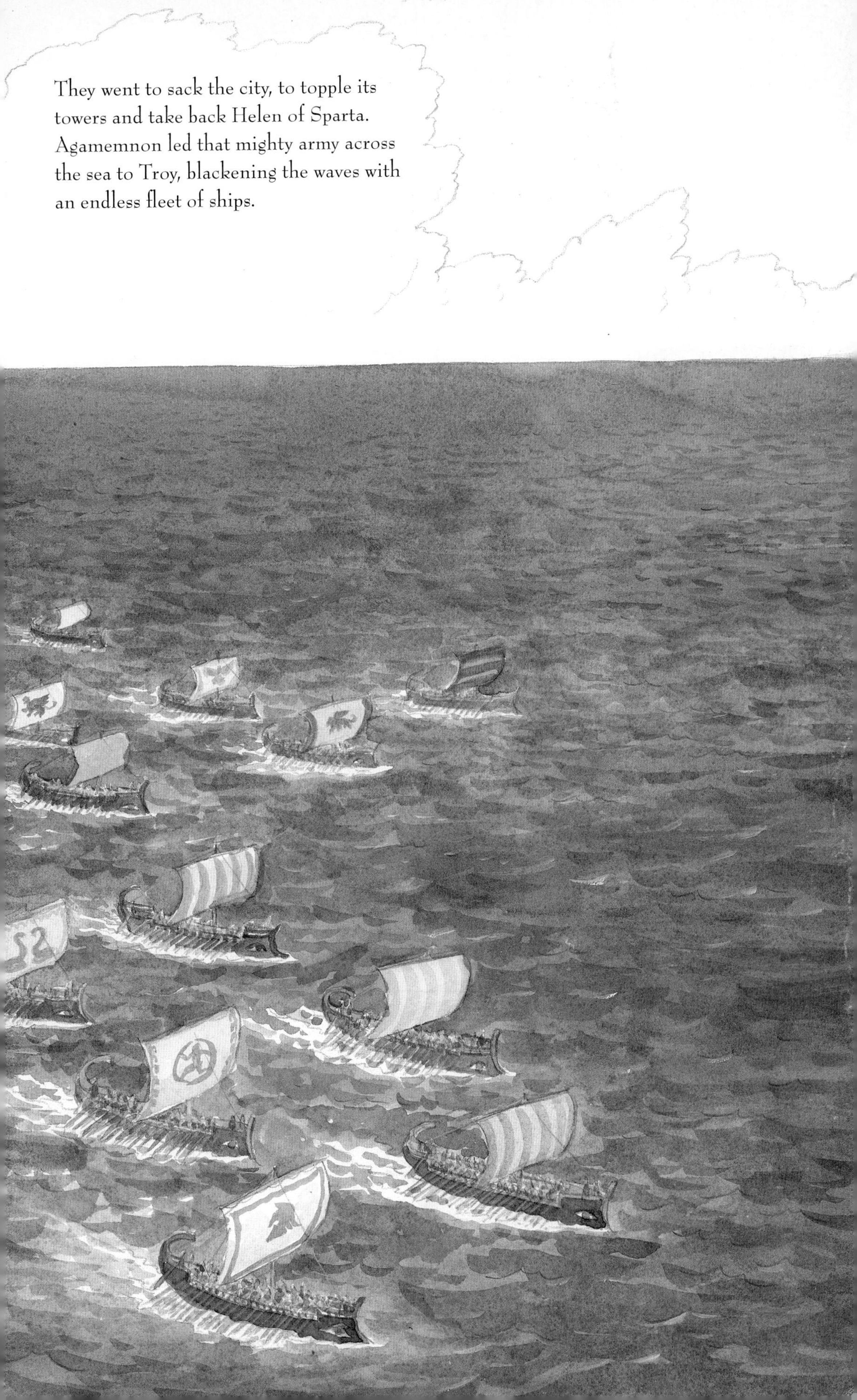

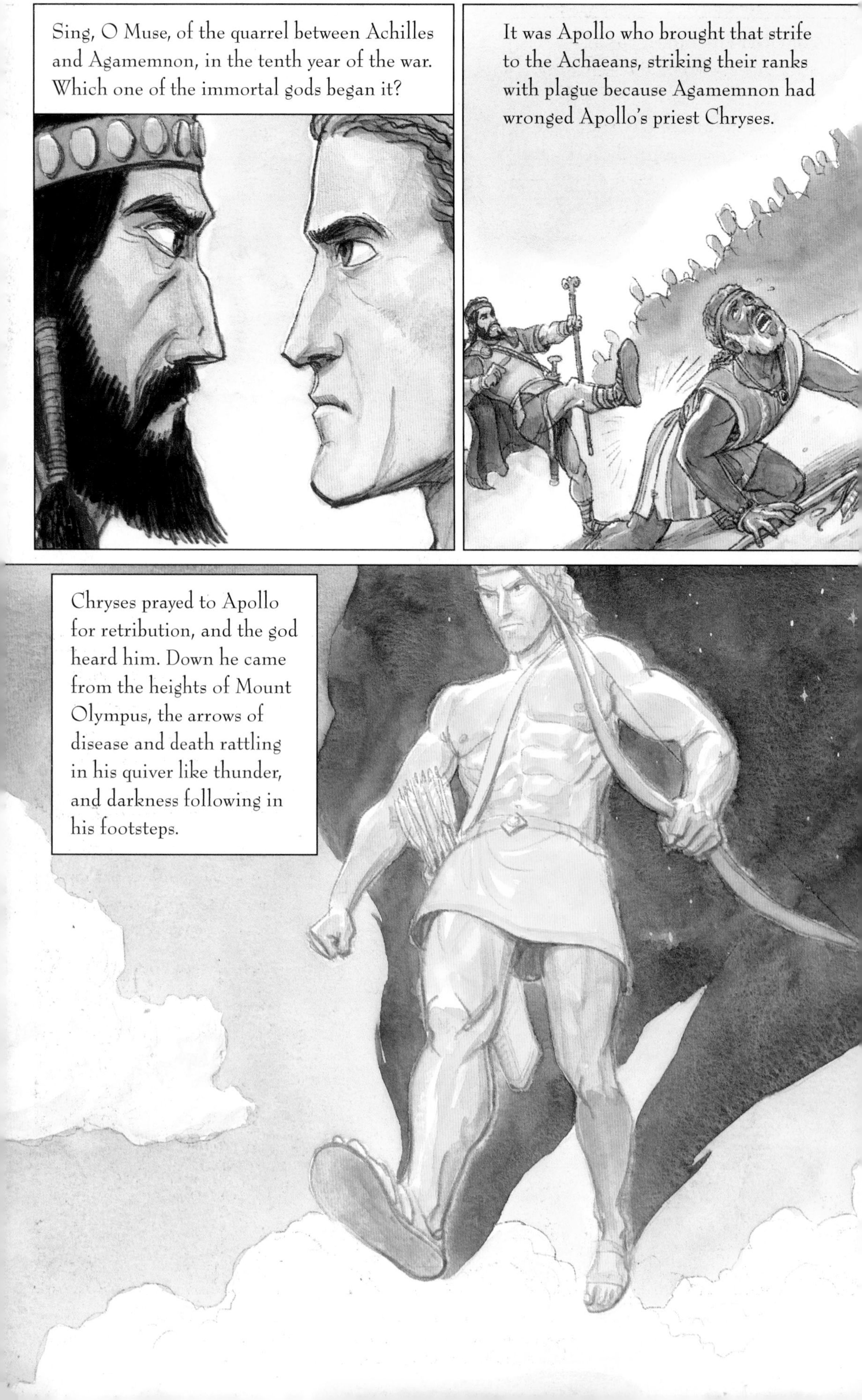
Sing, O Muse, of the quarrel between Achilles and Agamemnon, in the tenth year of the war. Which one of the immortal gods began it?
It was Apollo who brought that strife to the Achaeans, striking their ranks with plague because Agamemnon had wronged Apollo's priest Chryses.
Chryses prayed to Apollo for retribution, and the god heard him. Down he came from the heights of Mount Olympus, the arrows of disease and death rattling in his quiver like thunder, and darkness following in his footsteps.

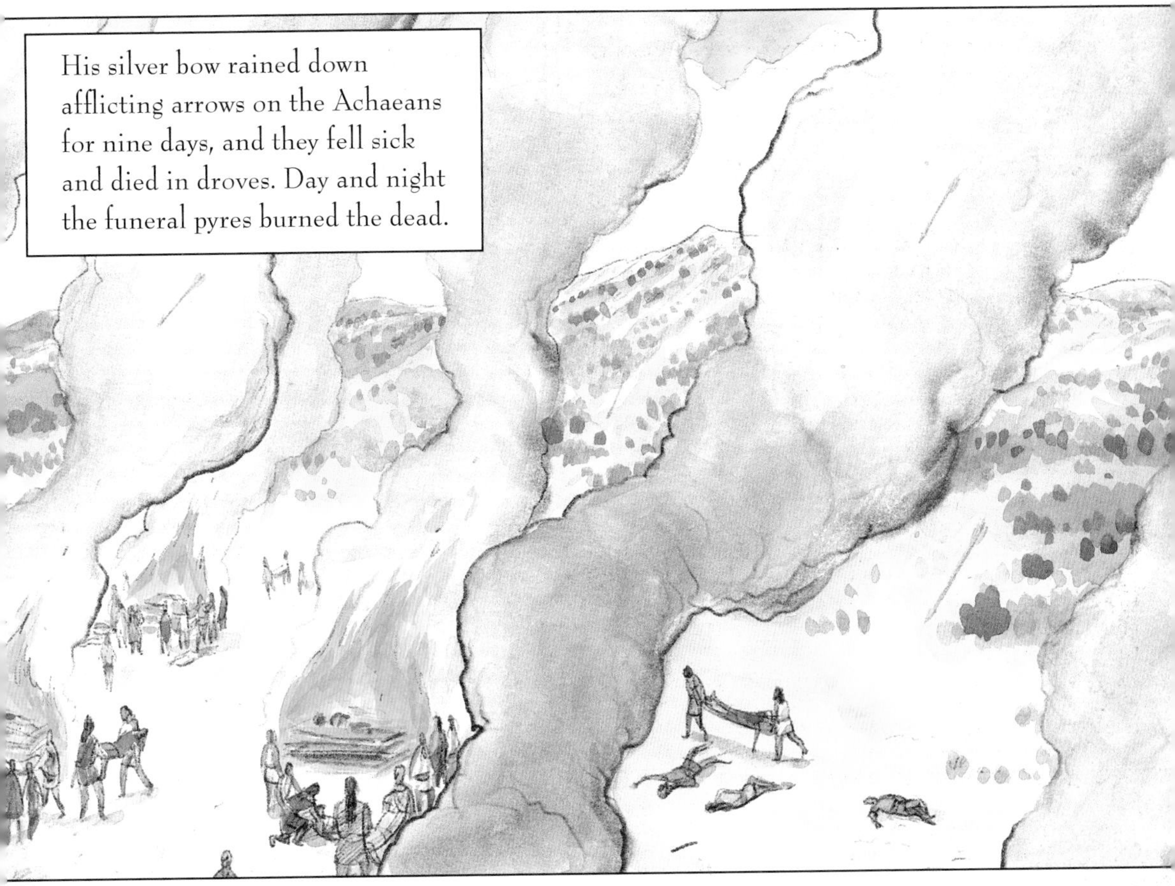
His silver bow rained down afflicting arrows on the Achaeans for nine days, and they fell sick and died in droves. Day and night the funeral pyres burned the dead.

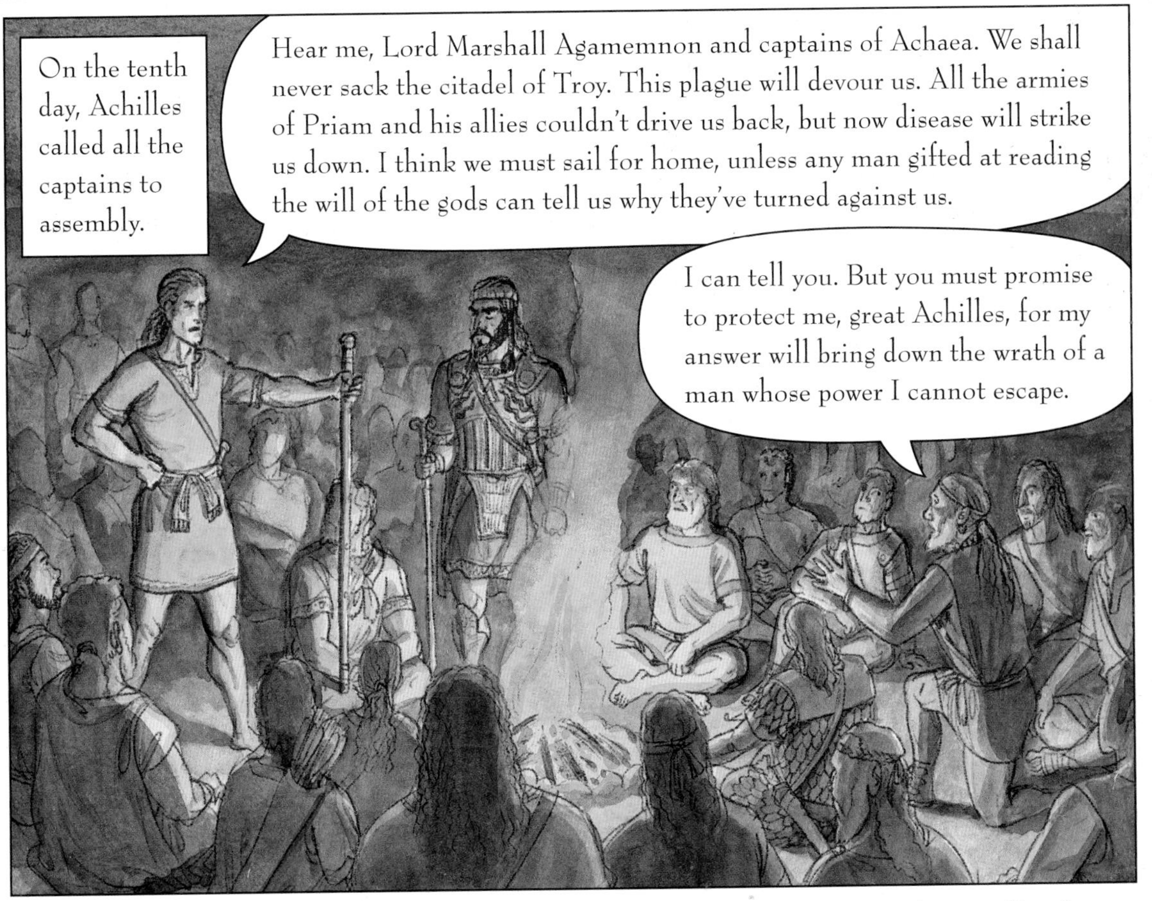
On the tenth day, Achilles called all the captains to assembly.
Hear me, Lord Marshall Agamemnon and captains of Achaea. We shall never sack the citadel of Troy. This plague will devour us. All the armies of Priam and his allies couldn't drive us back, but now disease will strike us down. I think we must sail for home, unless any man gifted at reading the will of the gods can tell us why they've turned against us.
I can tell you. But you must promise to protect me, great Achilles, for my answer will bring down the wrath of a man whose power I cannot escape.

The sceptre Achilles is holding represents permission to speak in assembly and was passed around so that only one person spoke at a time. Agamemnon also has a sceptre, which marks his authority as High King of the Achaeans.

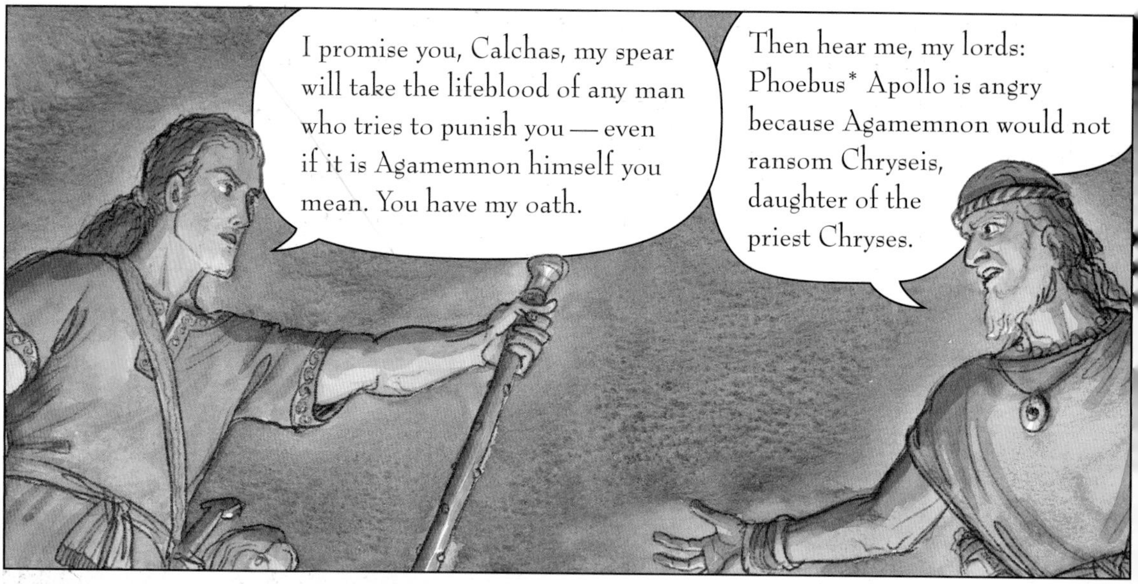
I promise you, Calchas, my spear will take the lifeblood of any man who tries to punish you — even if it is Agamemnon himself you mean. You have my oath.
Then hear me, my lords: Phoebus* Apollo is angry because Agamemnon would not ransom Chryseis, daughter of the priest Chryses.

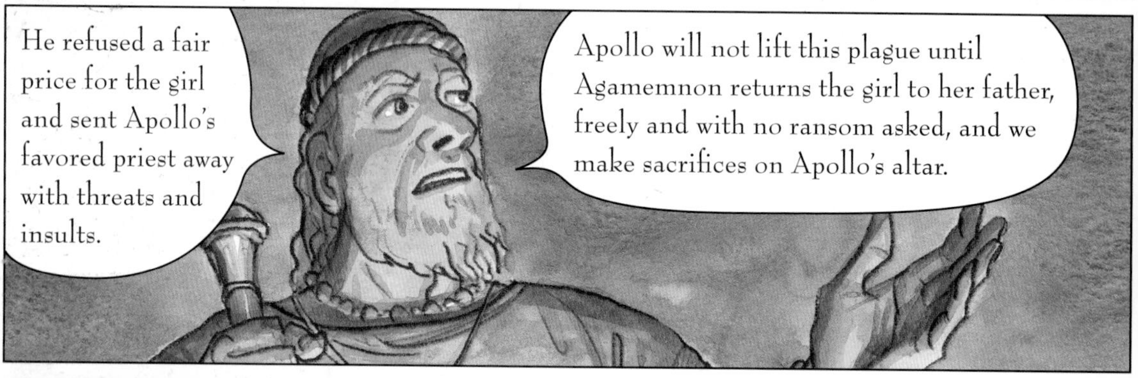
He refused a fair price for the girl and sent Apollo's favored priest away with threats and insults.
Apollo will not lift this plague until Agamemnon returns the girl to her father, freely and with no ransom asked, and we make sacrifices on Apollo's altar.

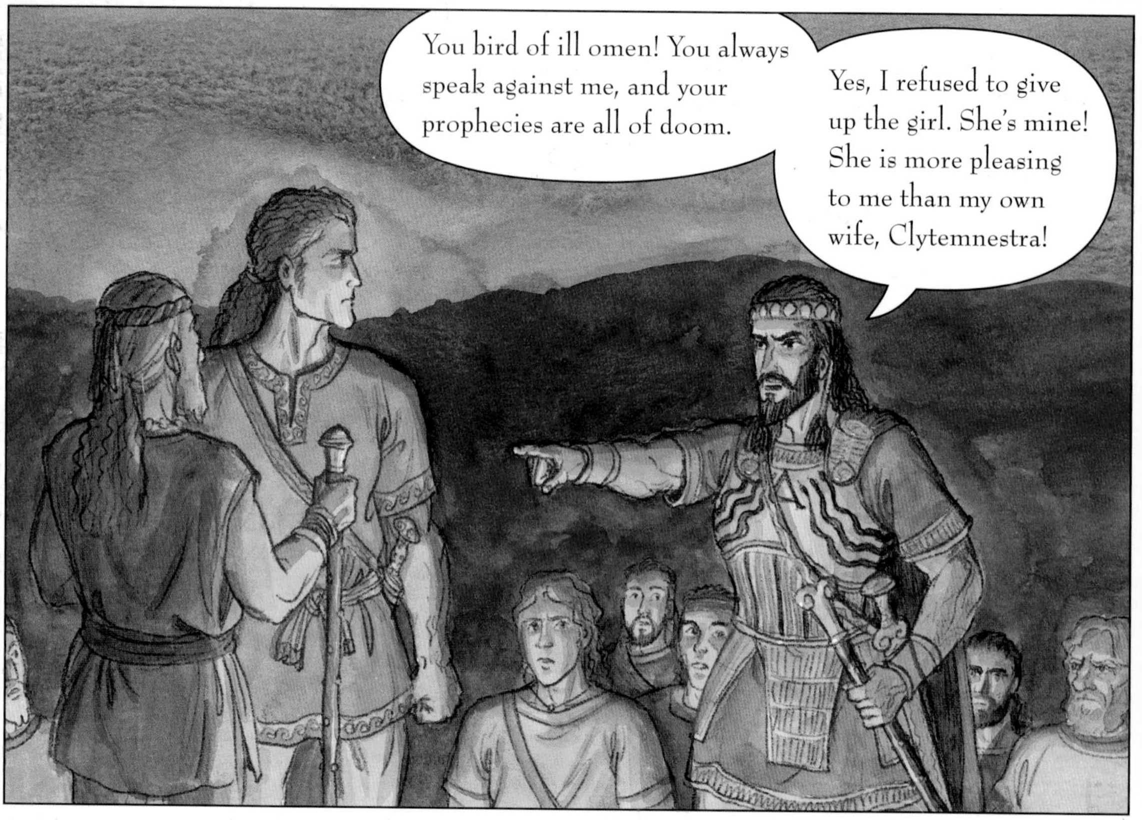
You bird of ill omen! You always speak against me, and your prophecies are all of doom.
Yes, I refused to give up the girl. She's mine! She is more pleasing to me than my own wife, Clytemnestra!

*A popular nickname for Apollo, *Phoebus* means "bright."

And yet, if it is true Apollo brings this plague, then I will give Chryseis up to appease the god and save the army.

But heed me: I must have another woman in her place! How would it look if I of all men, the Lord Marshall, lost my prize?

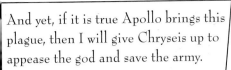

All the spoils of war have been shared out. What woman shall be offered up to satisfy your pride, Agamemnon?

Perhaps I will have *your* woman, Achilles. Or Odysseus's, or Ajax's, or any one I choose! That man may choke with rage, but let him! I will take his prize to replace mine.

Who shall it be. . .?

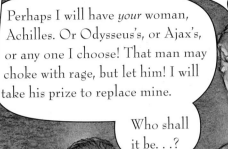

Well, there's time to choose later. Let's waste no more time now — take Chryseis back to her father at once, and make offerings to Phoebus Apollo.

You overbearing, shameless, greedy fool! How can any man obey you in battle after you threaten to take from us by force what was given fairly?

I have no quarrel with the Trojans. They've done nothing to me. I came here to fight on your behalf, to help your brother retrieve his wife. Is this how you reward me?

I've done your will, fought harder in the field than you ever have, sacked city after city.* Yet each time you take the lion's share of plunder!

Well, I've had enough. This time I'll sail for home, and leave you here to face the killing spear of Hector.

* The Achaeans attacked many lesser cities allied with Troy. The prisoners they captured, both men and women, became slaves (though they might be ransomed or could buy their freedom back.) Slaves were among the most valued prizes divvied up with the other "spoils of war."

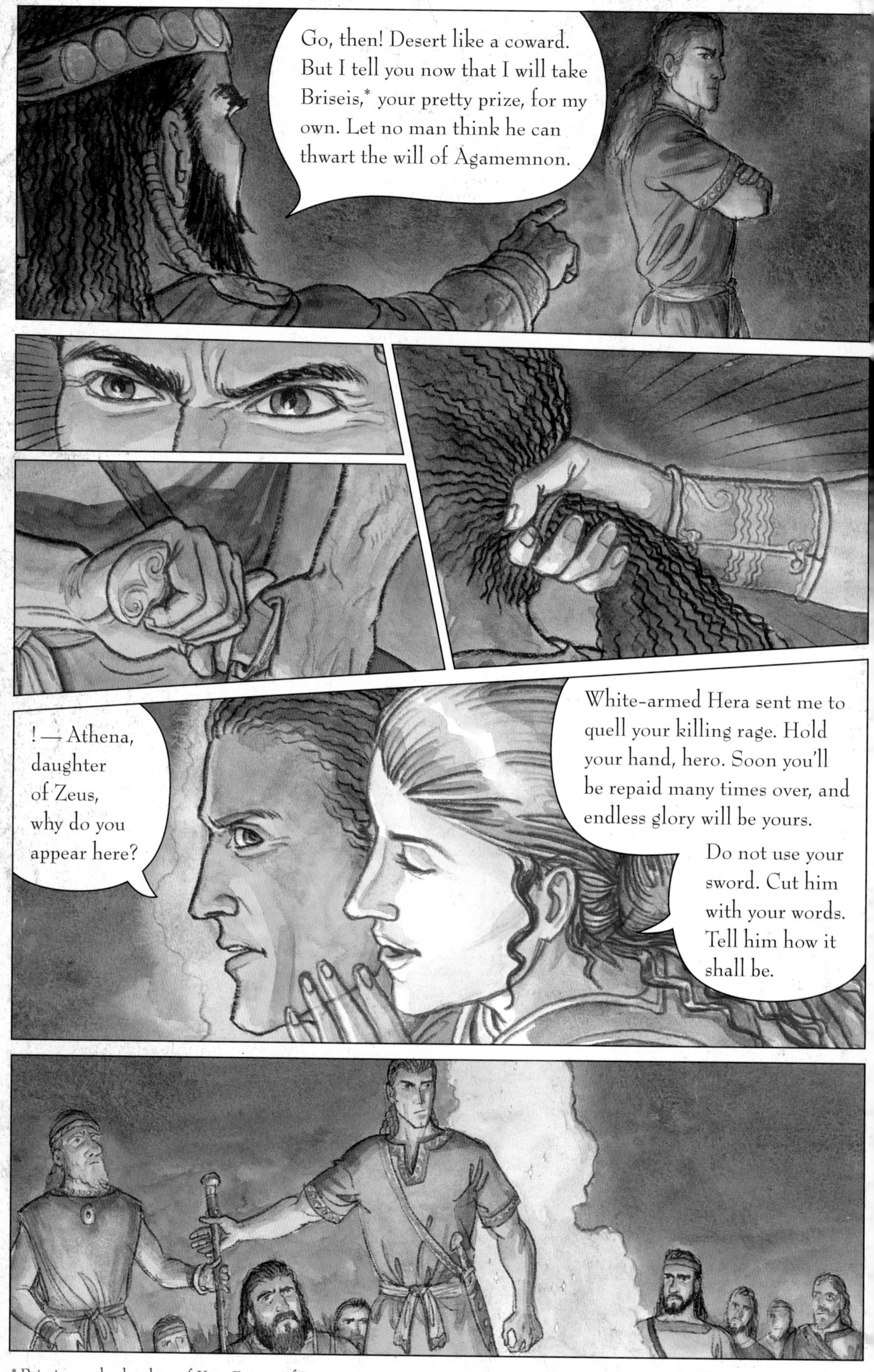
Go, then! Desert like a coward. But I tell you now that I will take Briseis,* your pretty prize, for my own. Let no man think he can thwart the will of Agamemnon.
!— Athena, daughter of Zeus, why do you appear here?
White-armed Hera sent me to quell your killing rage. Hold your hand, hero. Soon you'll be repaid many times over, and endless glory will be yours.
Do not use your sword. Cut him with your words. Tell him how it shall be.

* Briseis was the daughter of King Briseus of Lyrnessus, an ally of Troy. Achilles captured the city, killed her husband and brothers, and kept her as a prize of war.

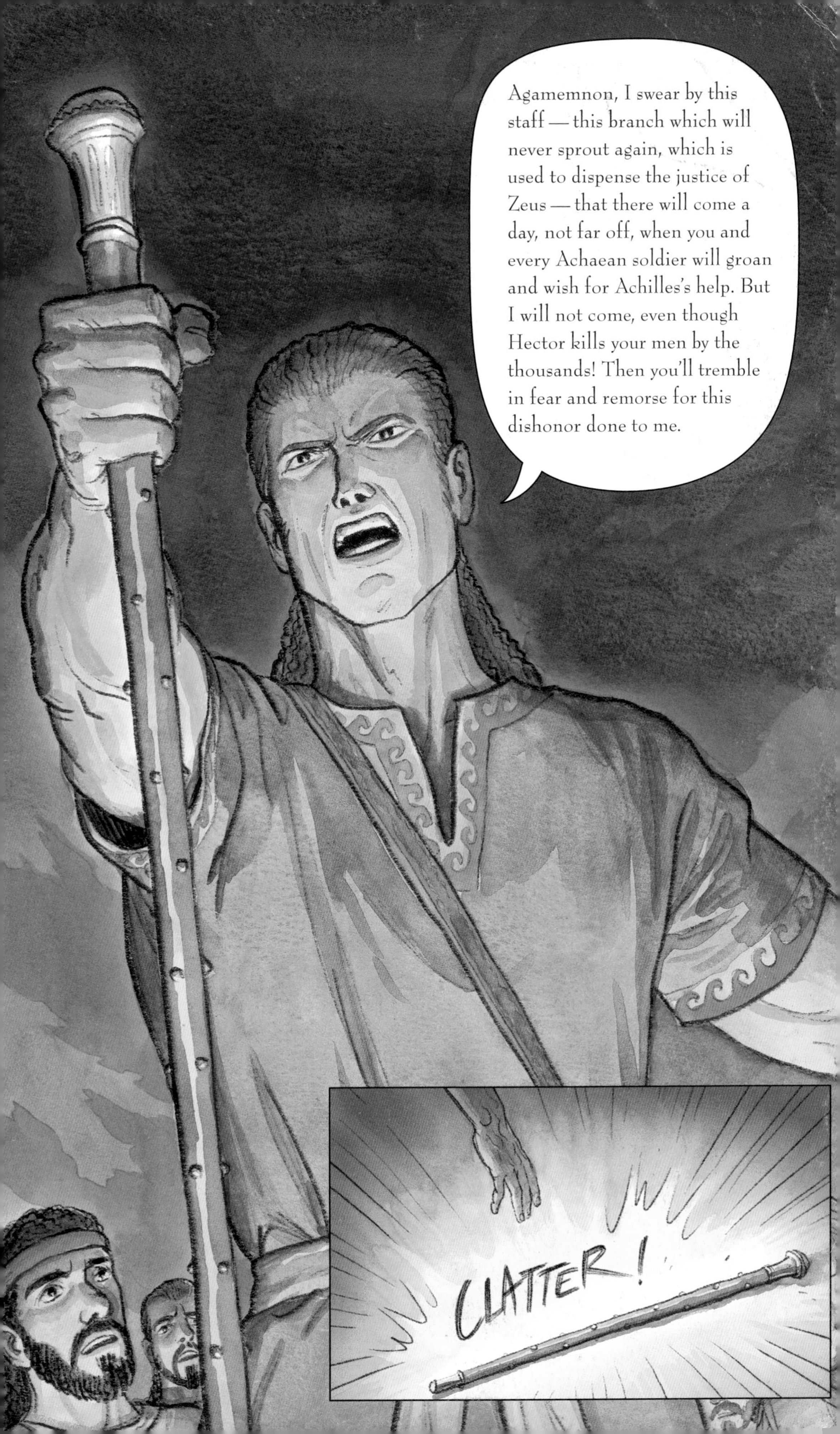

Agamemnon, I swear by this staff — this branch which will never sprout again, which is used to dispense the justice of Zeus — that there will come a day, not far off, when you and every Achaean soldier will groan and wish for Achilles's help. But I will not come, even though Hector kills your men by the thousands! Then you'll tremble in fear and remorse for this dishonor done to me.
CLATTER!

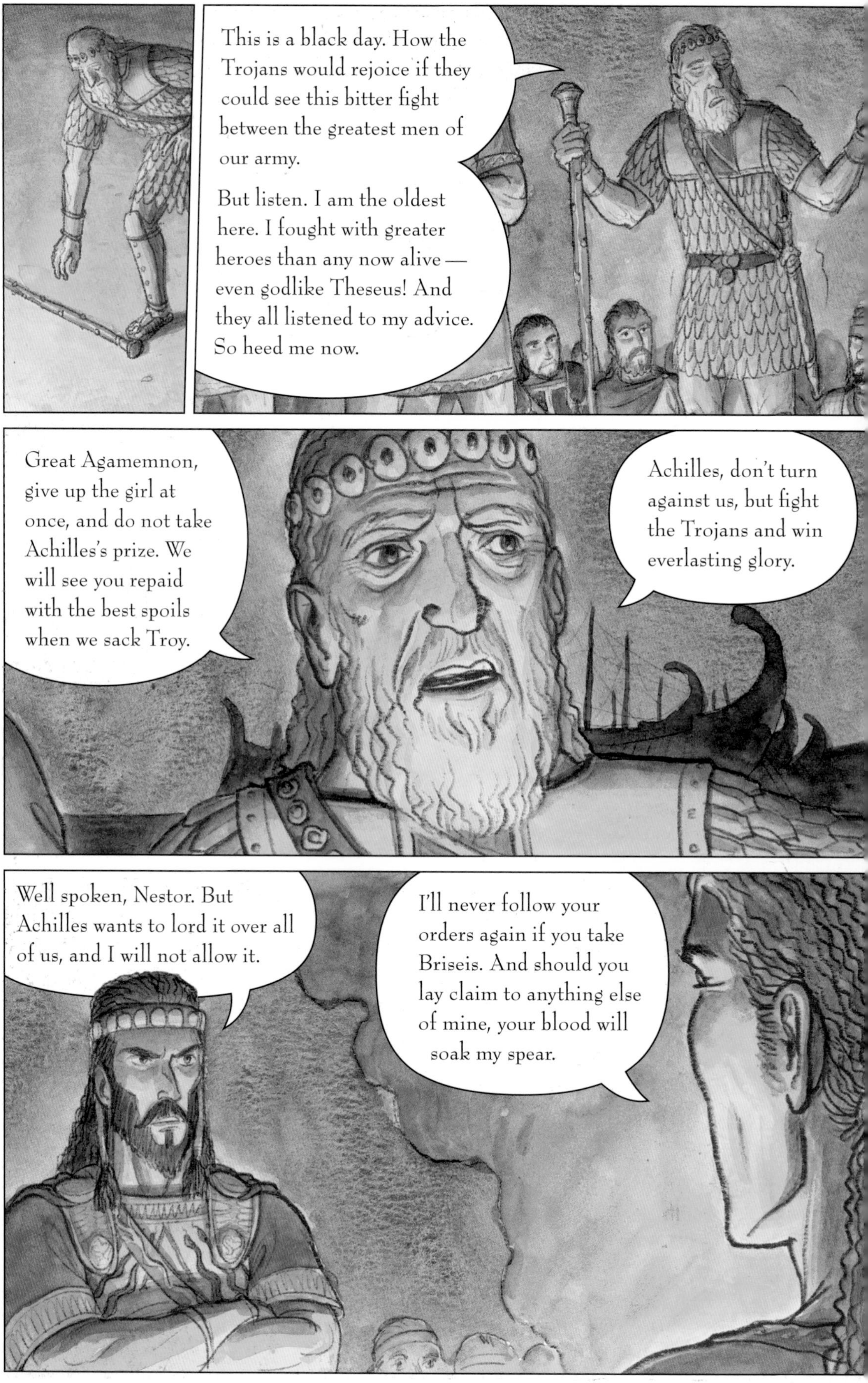
This is a black day. How the Trojans would rejoice if they could see this bitter fight between the greatest men of our army.
But listen. I am the oldest here. I fought with greater heroes than any now alive — even godlike Theseus! And they all listened to my advice. So heed me now.
Great Agamemnon, give up the girl at once, and do not take Achilles's prize. We will see you repaid with the best spoils when we sack Troy.
Achilles, don't turn against us, but fight the Trojans and win everlasting glory.
Well spoken, Nestor. But Achilles wants to lord it over all of us, and I will not allow it.
I'll never follow your orders again if you take Briseis. And should you lay claim to anything else of mine, your blood will soak my spear.

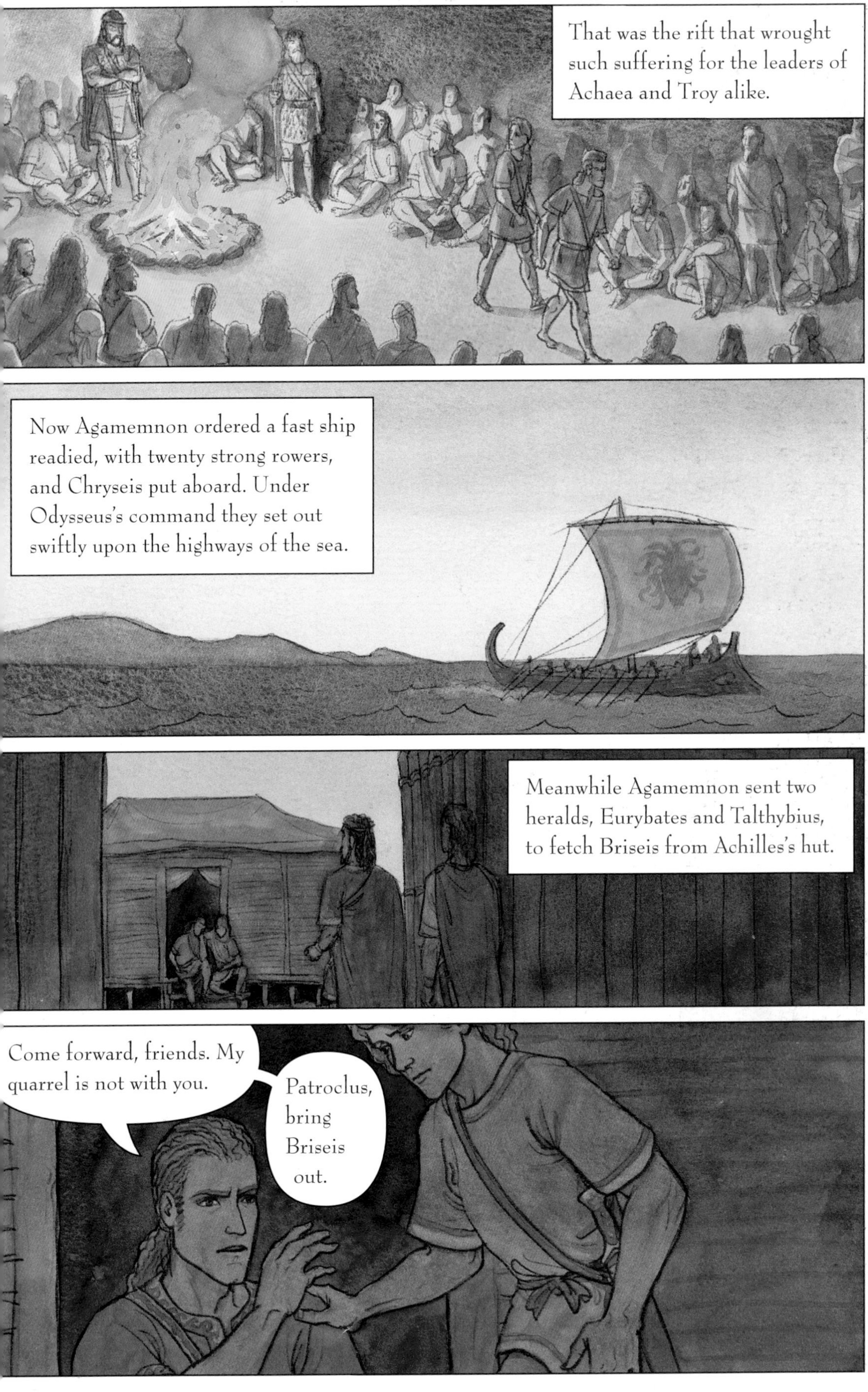
That was the rift that wrought such suffering for the leaders of Achaea and Troy alike.
Now Agamemnon ordered a fast ship readied, with twenty strong rowers, and Chryseis put aboard. Under Odysseus's command they set out swiftly upon the highways of the sea.
Meanwhile Agamemnon sent two heralds, Eurybates and Talthybius, to fetch Briseis from Achilles's hut.
Come forward, friends. My quarrel is not with you.
Patroclus, bring Briseis out.

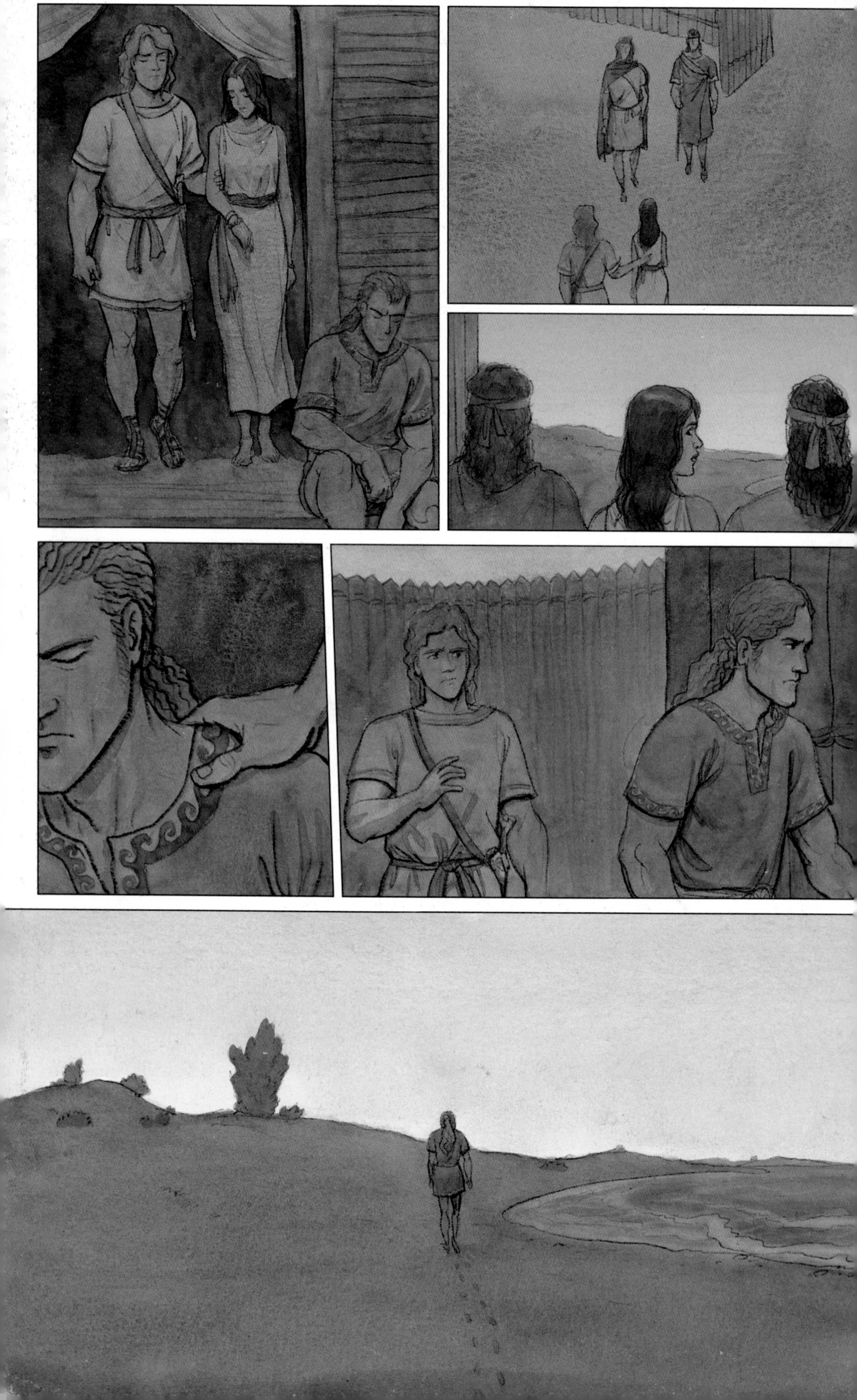

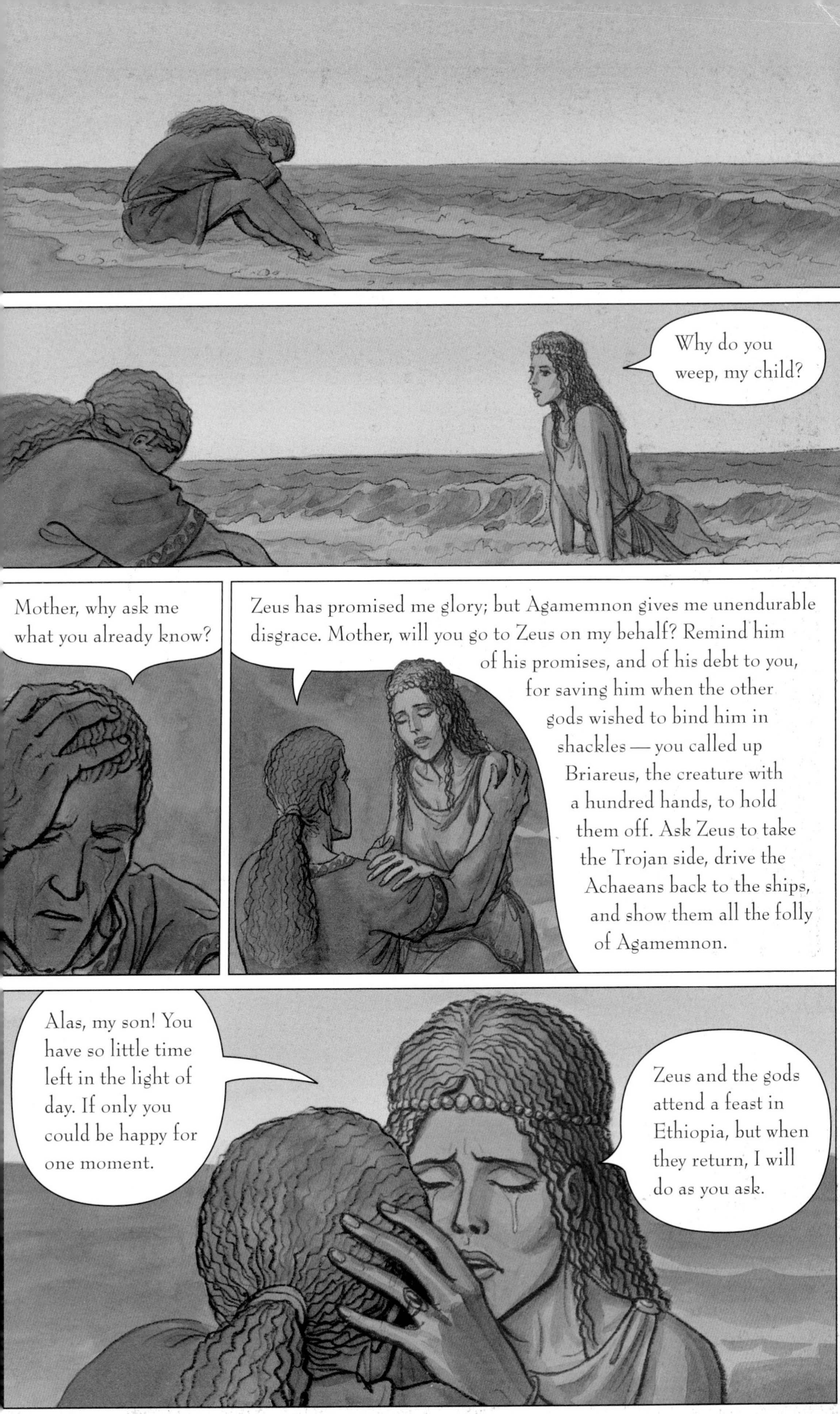
Why do you weep, my child?
Mother, why ask me what you already know?
Zeus has promised me glory; but Agamemnon gives me unendurable disgrace. Mother, will you go to Zeus on my behalf? Remind him of his promises, and of his debt to you, for saving him when the other gods wished to bind him in shackles — you called up Briareus, the creature with a hundred hands, to hold them off. Ask Zeus to take the Trojan side, drive the Achaeans back to the ships, and show them all the folly of Agamemnon.
Alas, my son! You have so little time left in the light of day. If only you could be happy for one moment.
Zeus and the gods attend a feast in Ethiopia, but when they return, I will do as you ask.

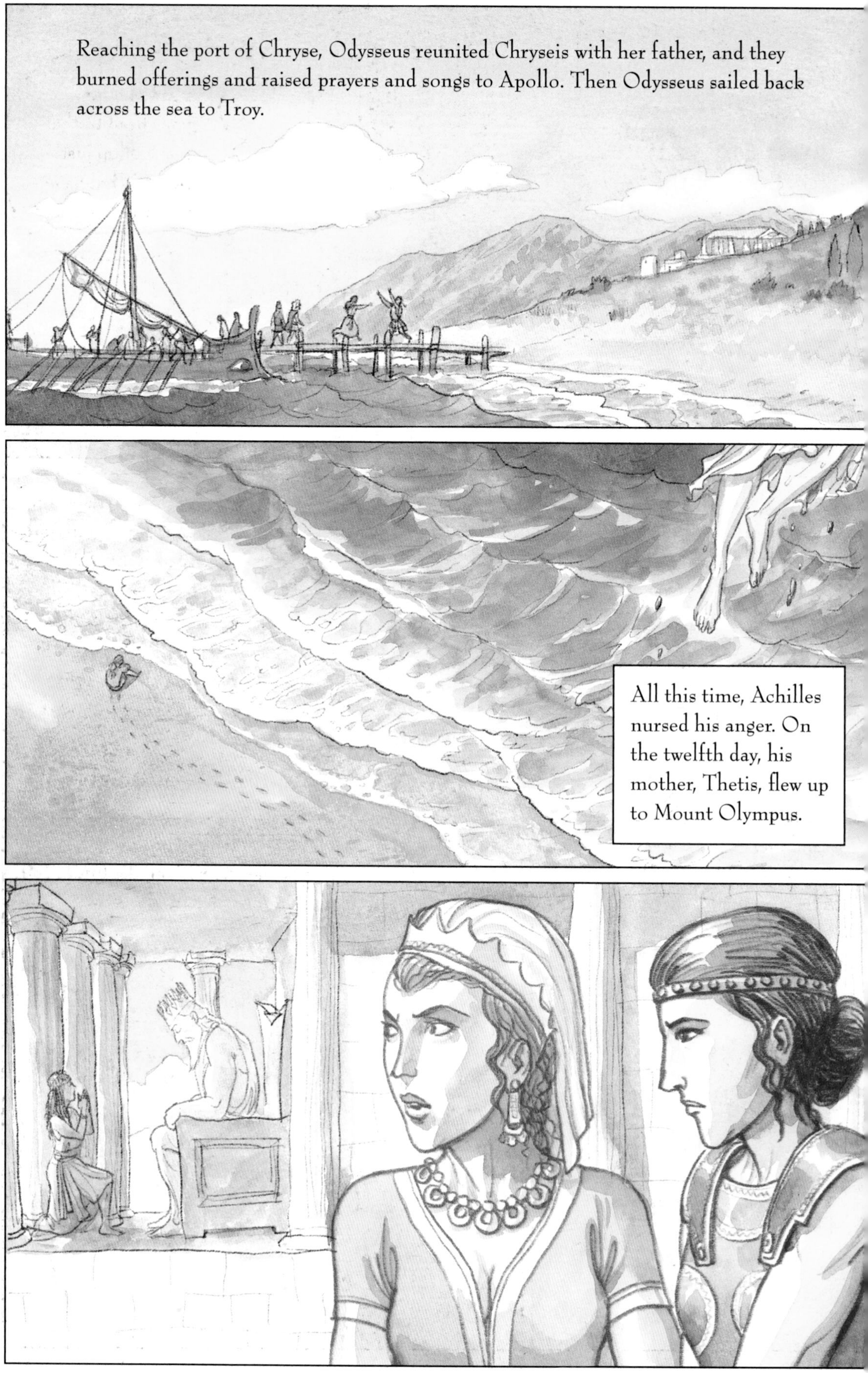
Reaching the port of Chryse, Odysseus reunited Chryseis with her father, and they burned offerings and raised prayers and songs to Apollo. Then Odysseus sailed back across the sea to Troy.
All this time, Achilles nursed his anger. On the twelfth day, his mother, Thetis, flew up to Mount Olympus.

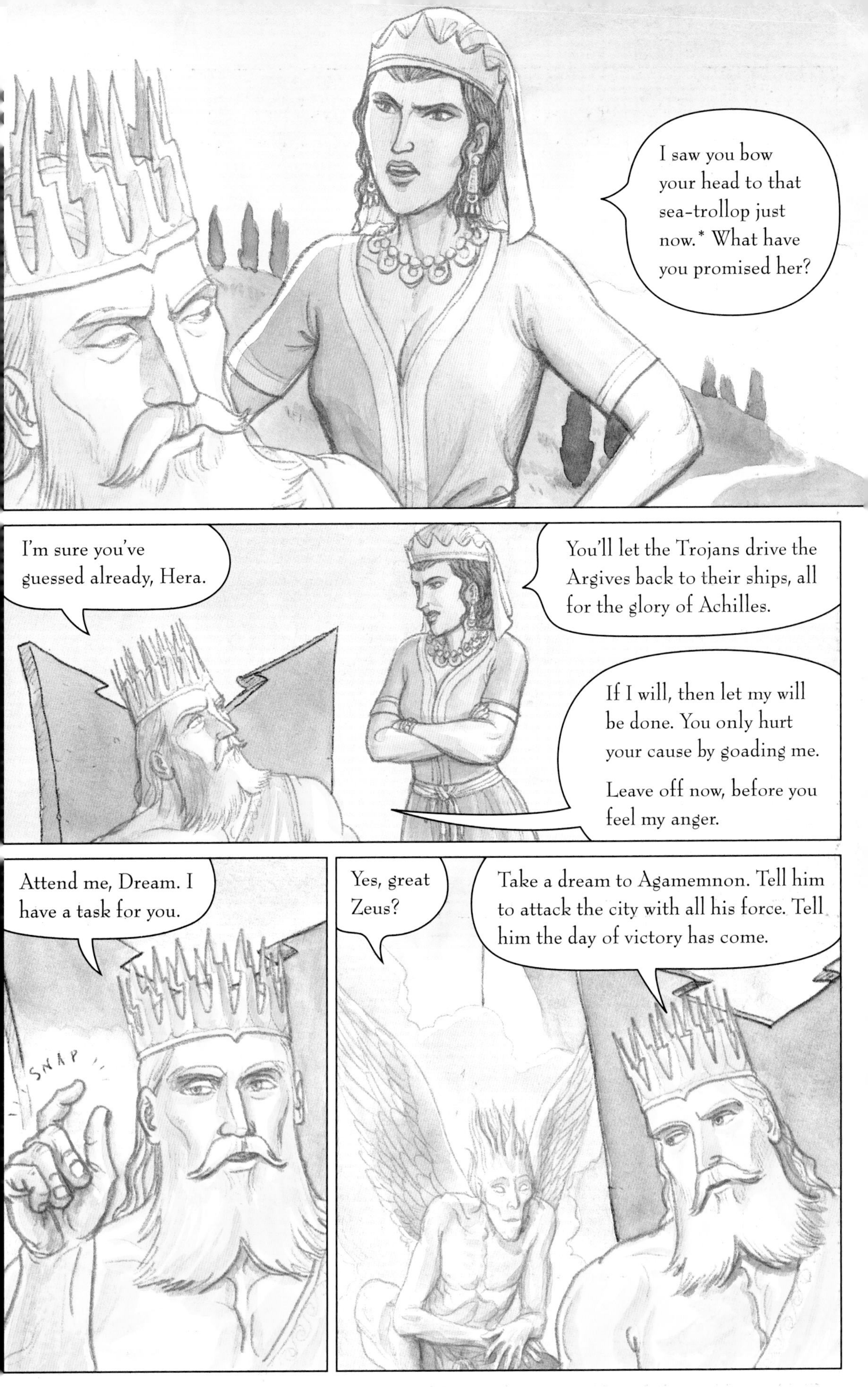
I saw you bow your head to that sea-trollop just now.* What have you promised her?
I'm sure you've guessed already, Hera.
You'll let the Trojans drive the Argives back to their ships, all for the glory of Achilles.
If I will, then let my will be done. You only hurt your cause by goading me.
Leave off now, before you feel my anger.
Attend me, Dream. I have a task for you.
SNAP
Yes, great Zeus?
Take a dream to Agamemnon. Tell him to attack the city with all his force. Tell him the day of victory has come.

* If Zeus bowed his head when making a promise, it was said to be an unbreakable vow.

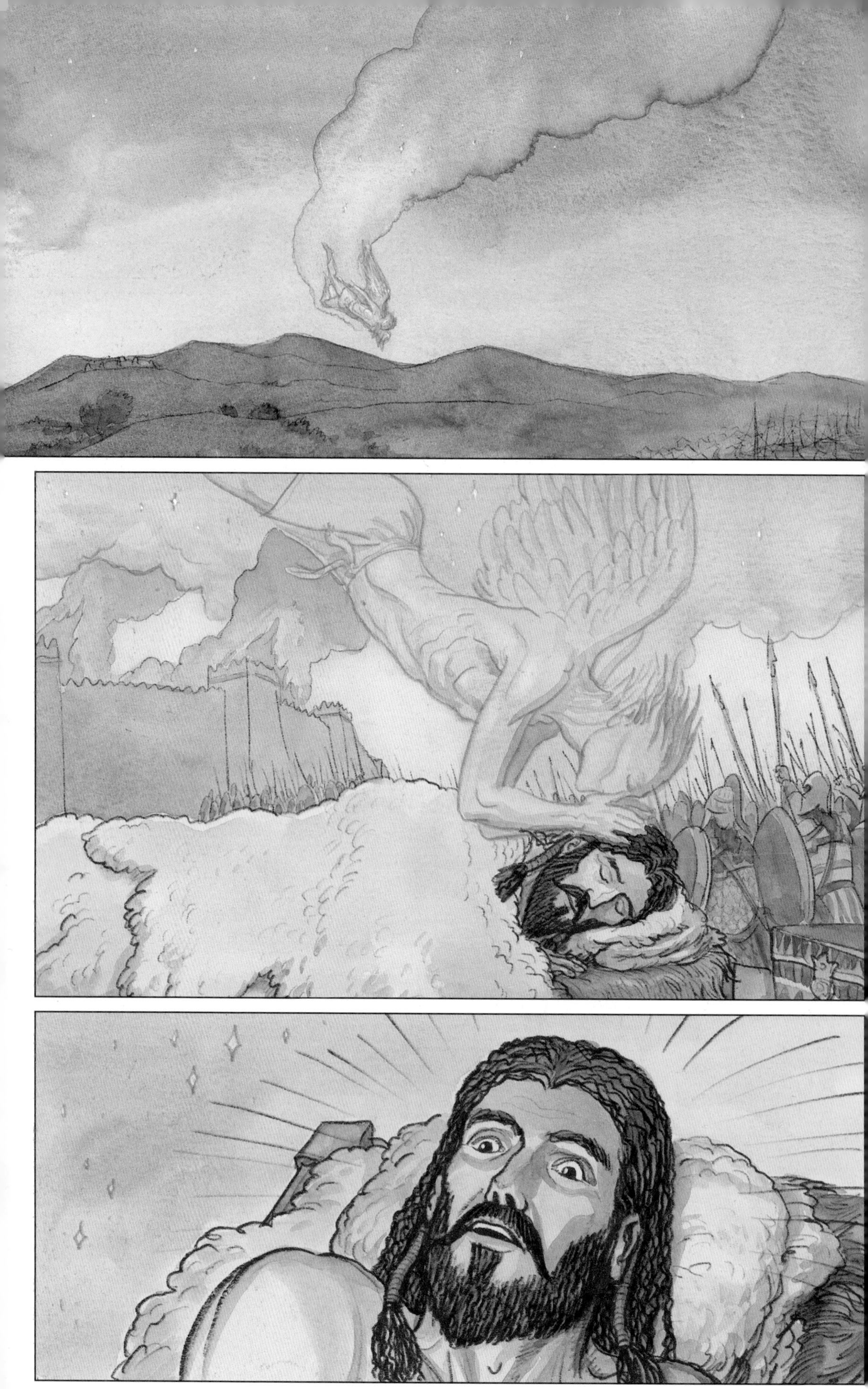

Book 2 — The Armies

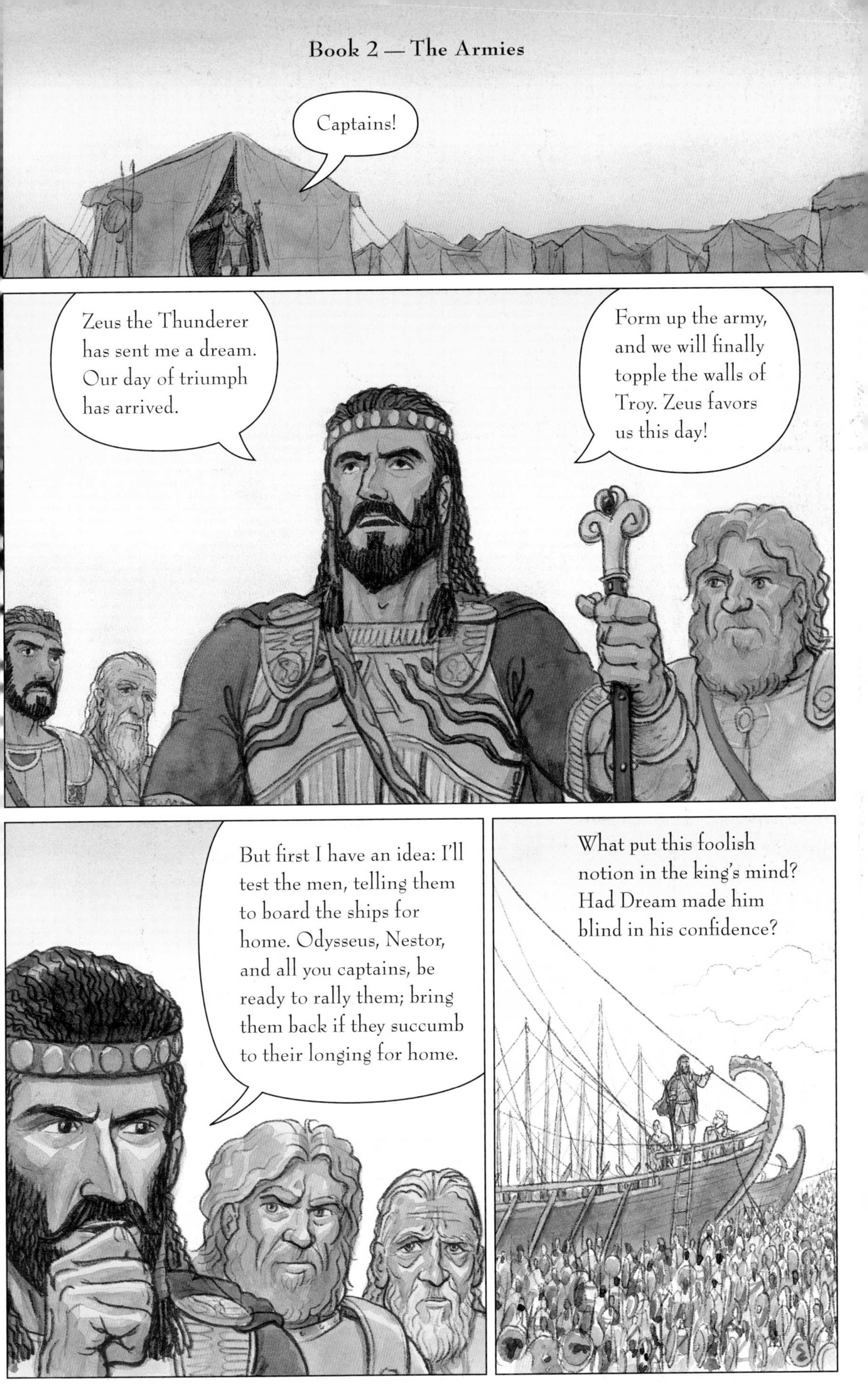
Captains!
Zeus the Thunderer has sent me a dream. Our day of triumph has arrived.
Form up the army, and we will finally topple the walls of Troy. Zeus favors us this day!
But first I have an idea: I'll test the men, telling them to board the ships for home. Odysseus, Nestor, and all you captains, be ready to rally them; bring them back if they succumb to their longing for home.
What put this foolish notion in the king's mind? Had Dream made him blind in his confidence?

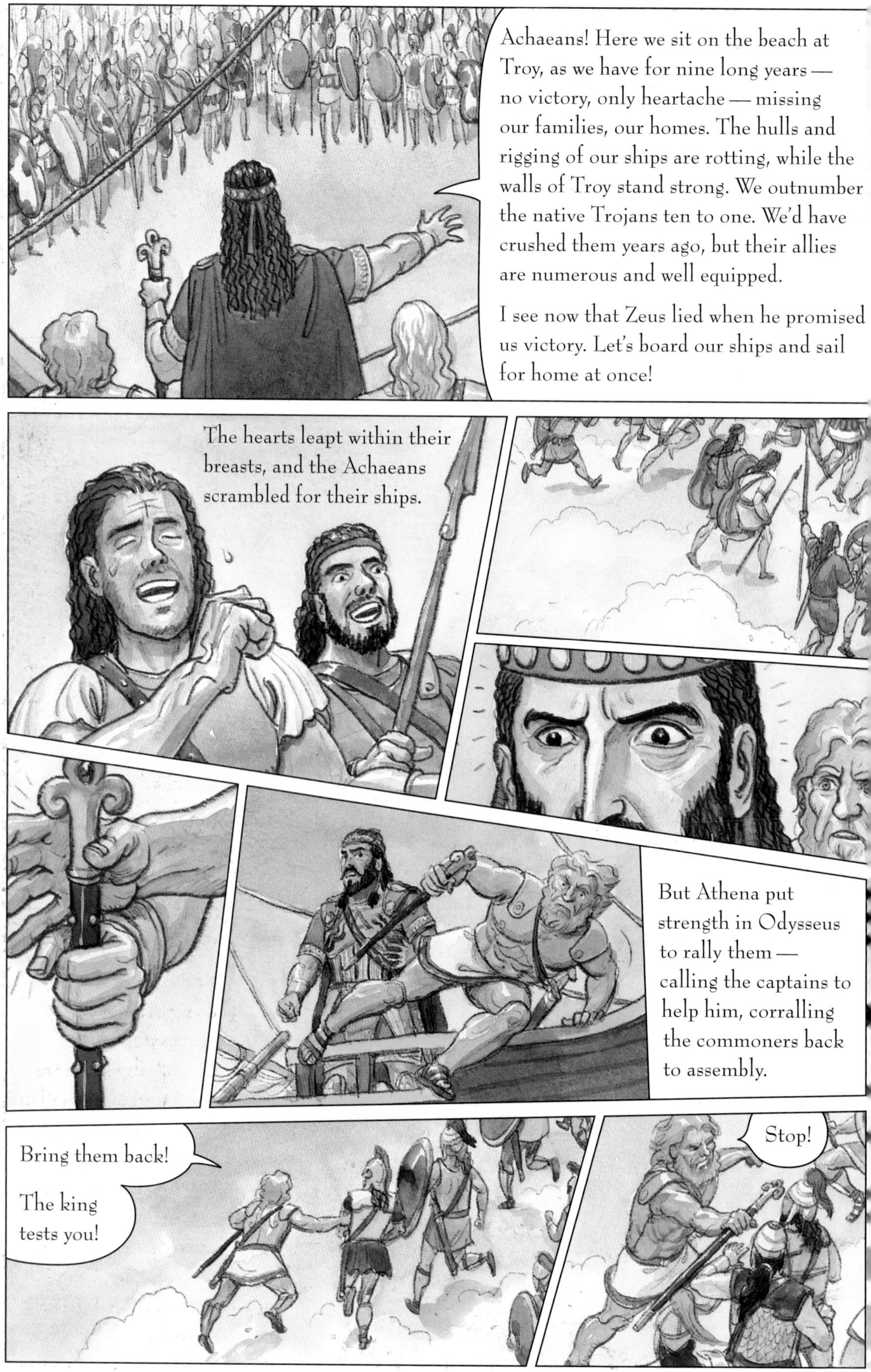
Achaeans! Here we sit on the beach at Troy, as we have for nine long years — no victory, only heartache — missing our families, our homes. The hulls and rigging of our ships are rotting, while the walls of Troy stand strong. We outnumber the native Trojans ten to one. We'd have crushed them years ago, but their allies are numerous and well equipped.
I see now that Zeus lied when he promised us victory. Let's board our ships and sail for home at once!
The hearts leapt within their breasts, and the Achaeans scrambled for their ships.
But Athena put strength in Odysseus to rally them — calling the captains to help him, corralling the commoners back to assembly.
Bring them back!
The king tests you!
Stop!

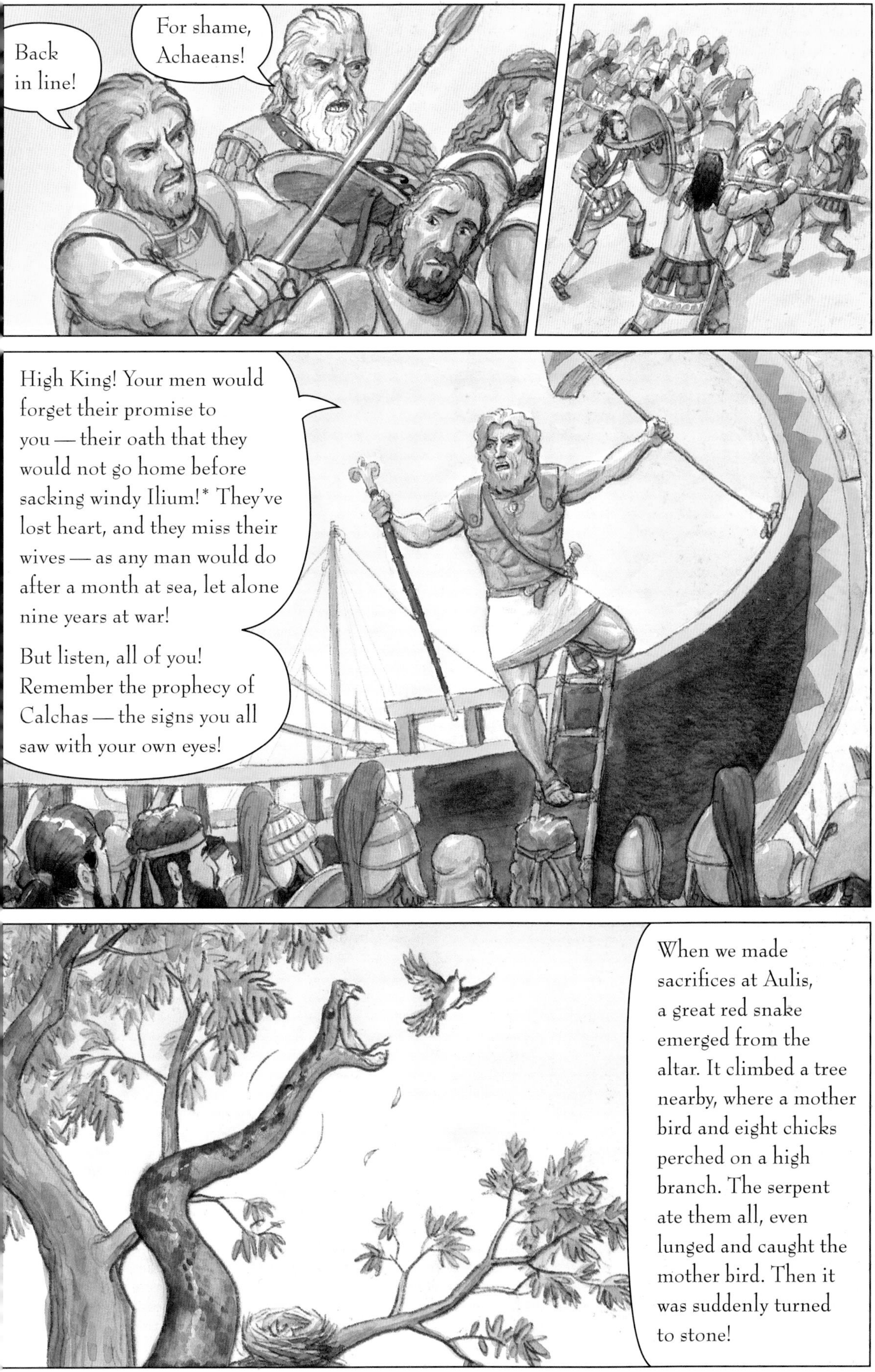
Back in line!
For shame, Achaeans!
High King! Your men would forget their promise to you — their oath that they would not go home before sacking windy Ilium!* They've lost heart, and they miss their wives — as any man would do after a month at sea, let alone nine years at war!
But listen, all of you! Remember the prophecy of Calchas — the signs you all saw with your own eyes!
When we made sacrifices at Aulis, a great red snake emerged from the altar. It climbed a tree nearby, where a mother bird and eight chicks perched on a high branch. The serpent ate them all, even lunged and caught the mother bird. Then it was suddenly turned to stone!

* Troy is also known as Ilium, Ilion, and Ilios, in honor of its founder King Ilos. *The Iliad* means, roughly, "the Song of Ilium."

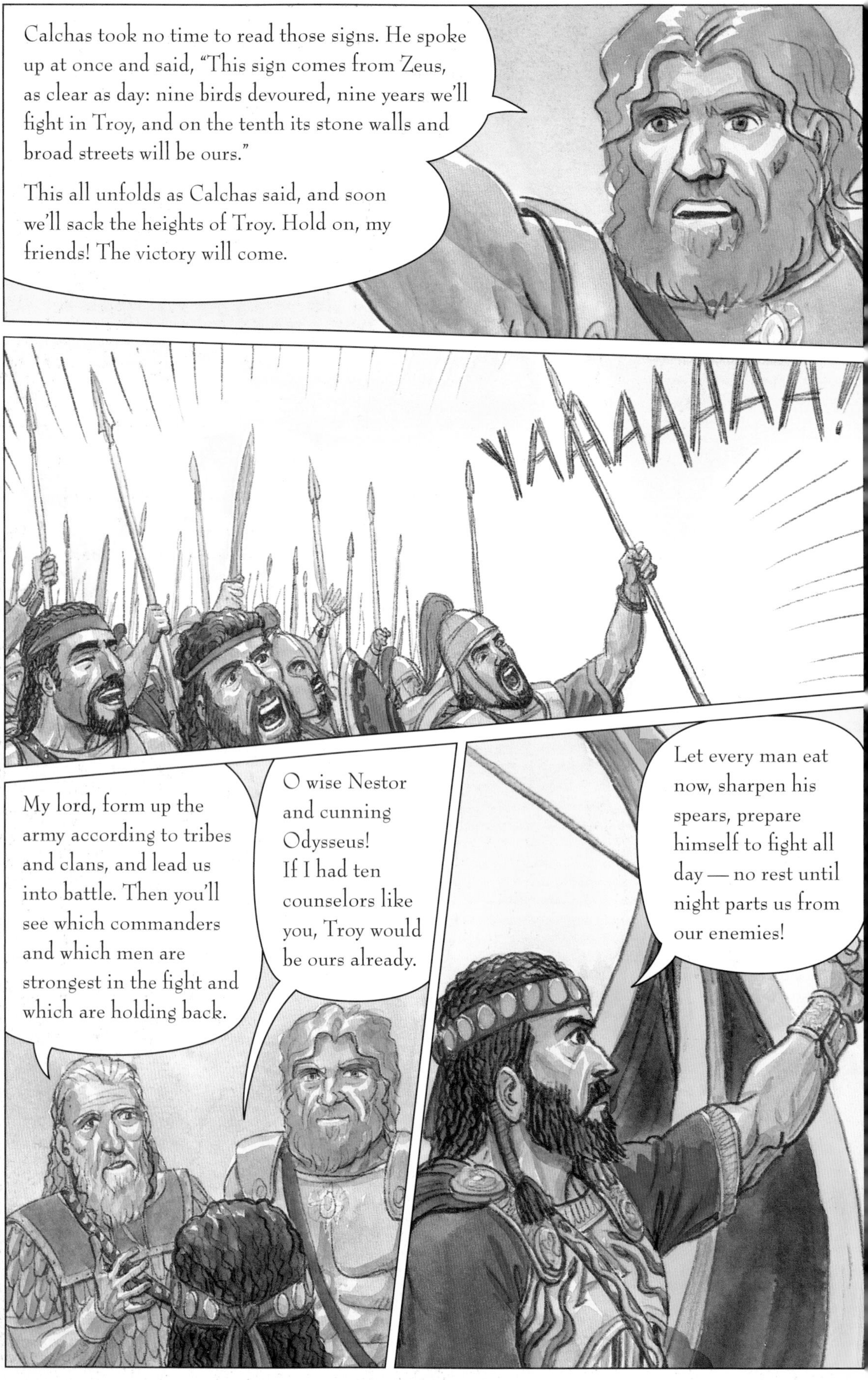

Calchas took no time to read those signs. He spoke up at once and said, "This sign comes from Zeus, as clear as day: nine birds devoured, nine years we'll fight in Troy, and on the tenth its stone walls and broad streets will be ours."
This all unfolds as Calchas said, and soon we'll sack the heights of Troy. Hold on, my friends! The victory will come.
YAAAAAAA!
My lord, form up the army according to tribes and clans, and lead us into battle. Then you'll see which commanders and which men are strongest in the fight and which are holding back.
O wise Nestor and cunning Odysseus! If I had ten counselors like you, Troy would be ours already.
Let every man eat now, sharpen his spears, prepare himself to fight all day — no rest until night parts us from our enemies!

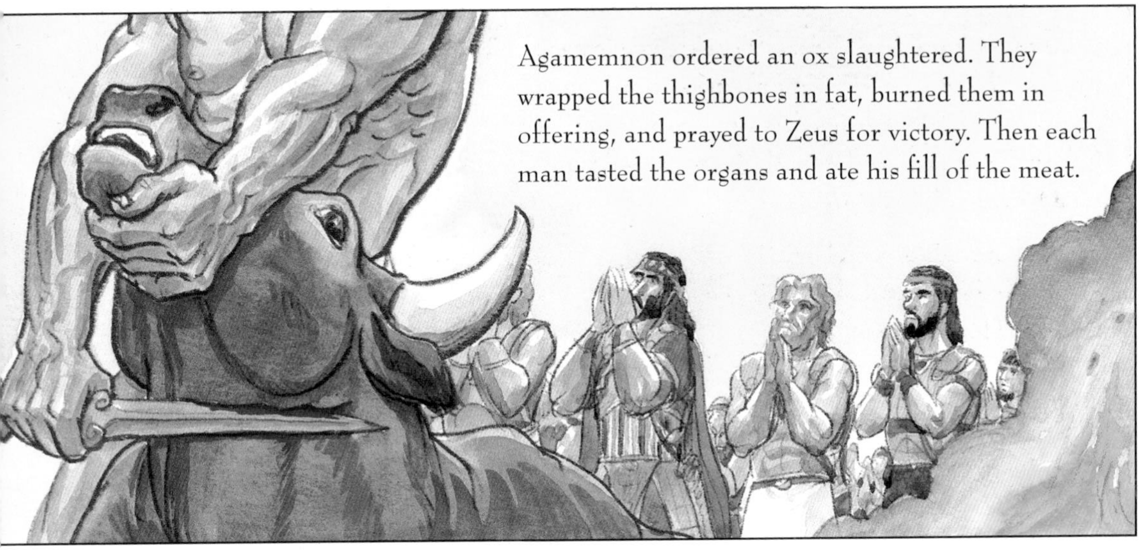

Agamemnon ordered an ox slaughtered. They wrapped the thighbones in fat, burned them in offering, and prayed to Zeus for victory. Then each man tasted the organs and ate his fill of the meat.

Then the heralds called the army to muster on the open plain.

O Muses who look down from high Olympus, how shall I describe that mighty host of men who poured out from the ships, like the great flocks of migrating birds that take wing in the meadows by the stream of Caÿster — as numerous as the leaves of a forest.

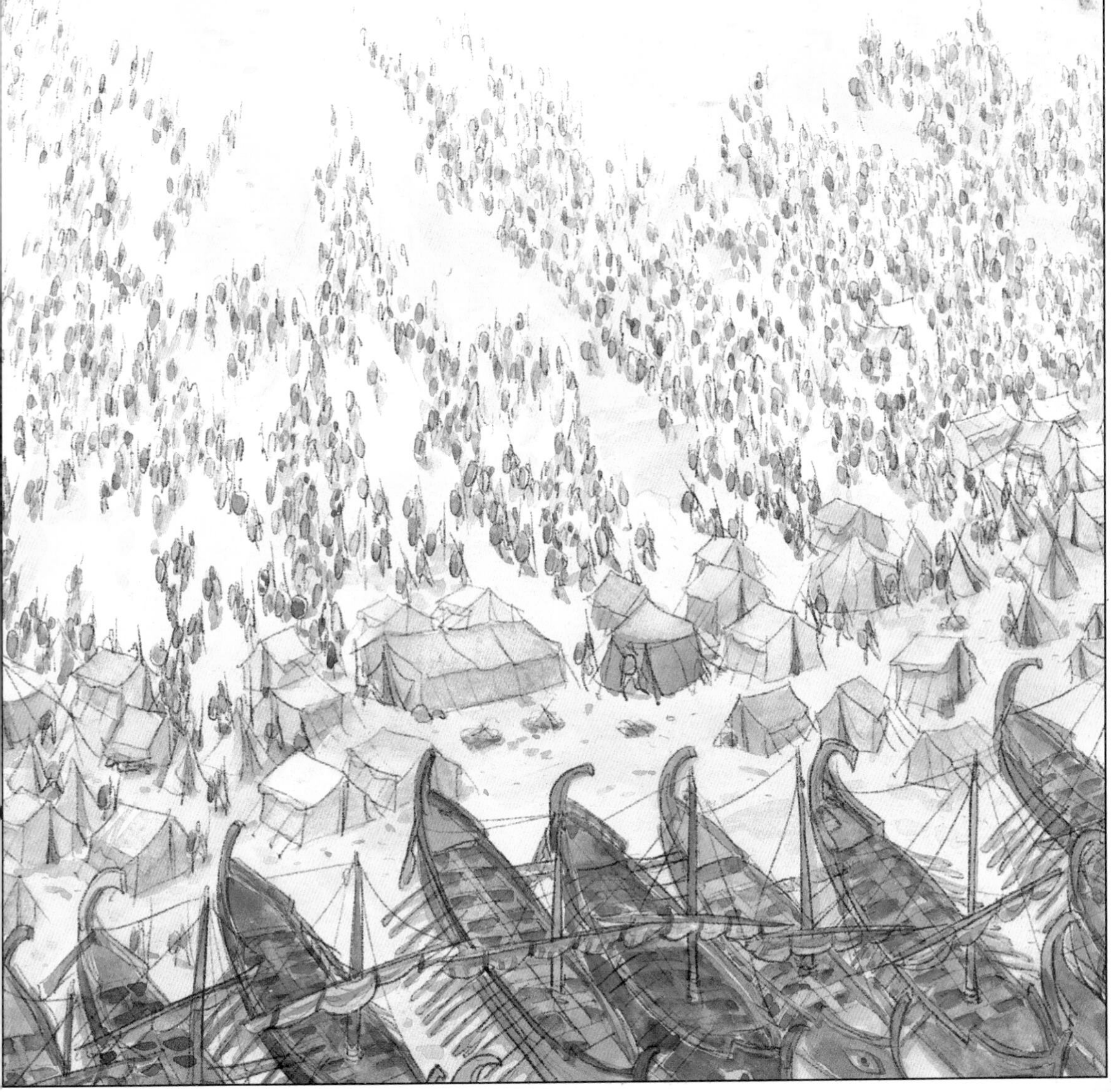

I could never name all the rank and file, but tell me, O Muse: who were the captains, the heroes who led each company in battle?

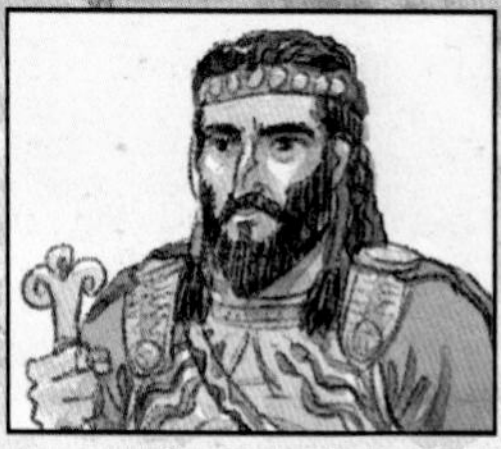

From the mighty citadel of Mycenae, High King Agamemnon brought 100 ships.

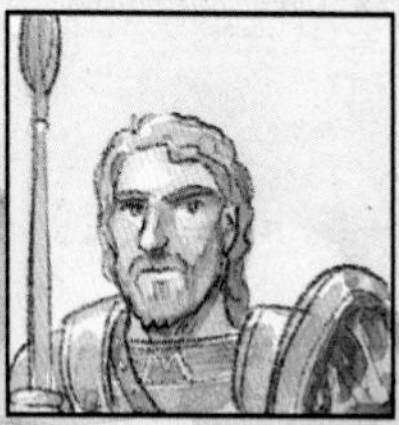

From Sparta came Agamemnon's brother, Menelaus, lord of the war-cry and husband of Helen. 60 ships.

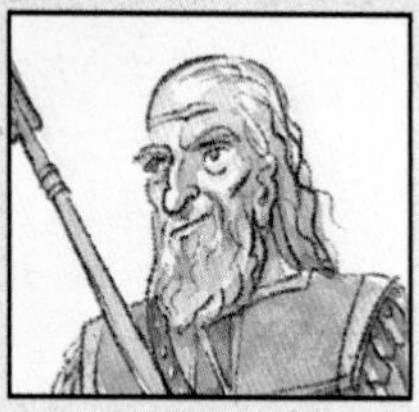

Men of Pylos, led by the wily charioteer Nestor of Gerenia. 90 ships.

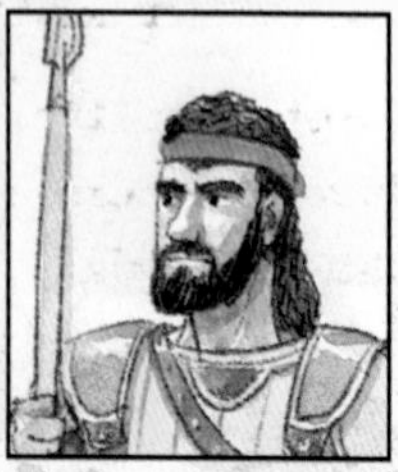

From the stallion land of Argos came Diomedes and his lieutenants Sthenelus and Euryalus, with 80 ships.

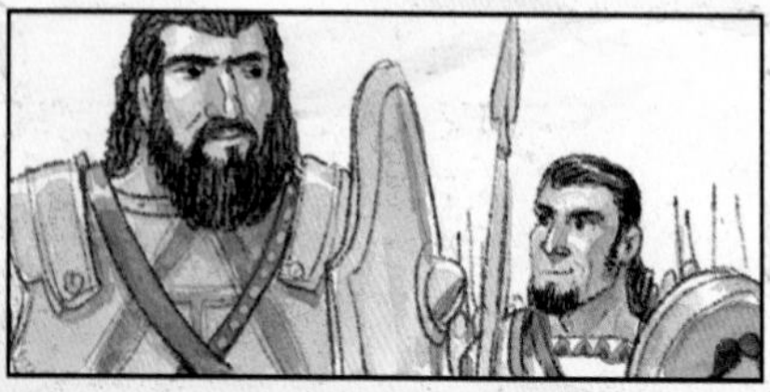

The giant Ajax, son of Telamon, brought 12 ships from Salamis, with 120 fighting men in each, and beached them at one end of the line, where the greatest danger lay.

Beside him were the Locrians, led by "Little" Ajax, son of Oileus — little by comparison with Telamonian Ajax, but no man had more skill with a spear. He brought 40 ships.

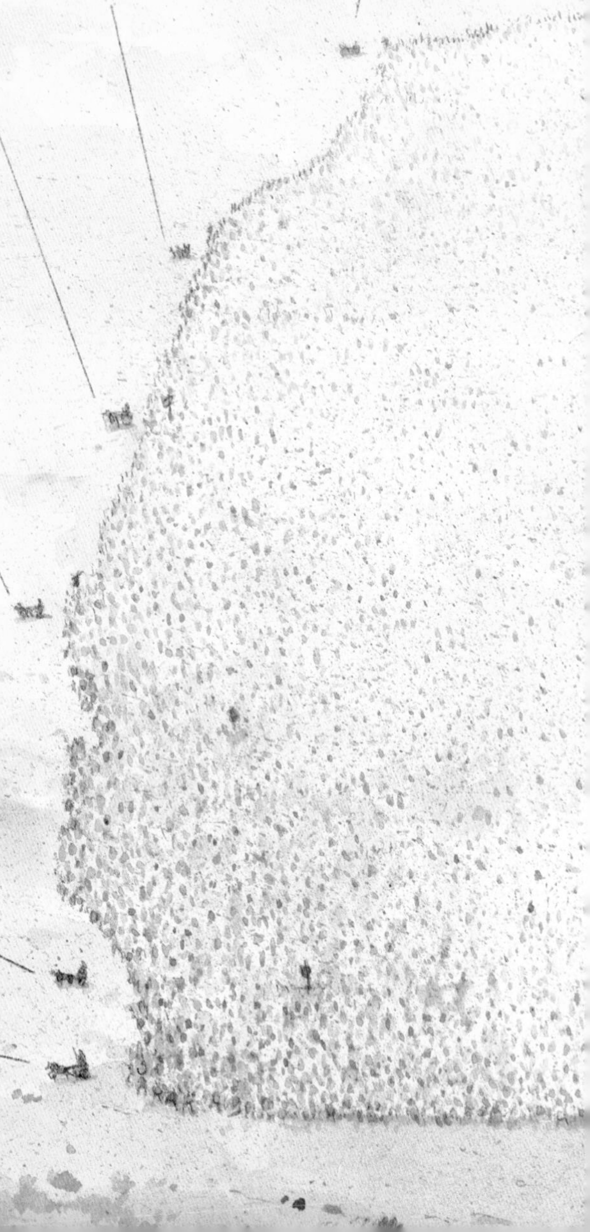
N

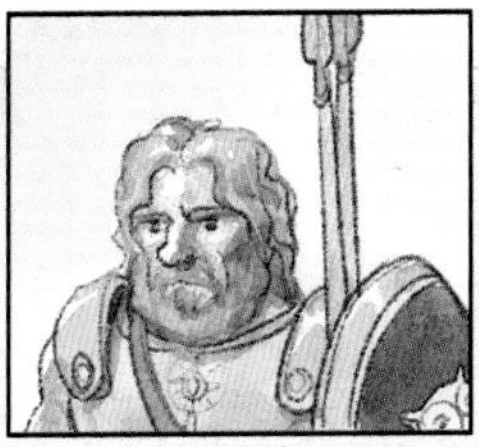

Odysseus led the proud Cephallenians of Ithaca, Neriton, Zacynthus, and Samos. 12 ships.

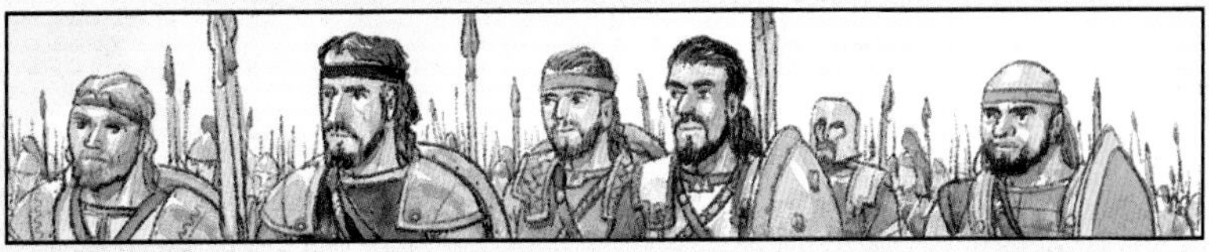

Tlepolemus, son of Heracles, brought 9 ships from Rhodes.

Idomeneus of Crete. 80 ships.

Podalirius and Machaon, sons of the healer Asclepius, brought 30 ships.

Agapenor of Arcadia. 60 ships.

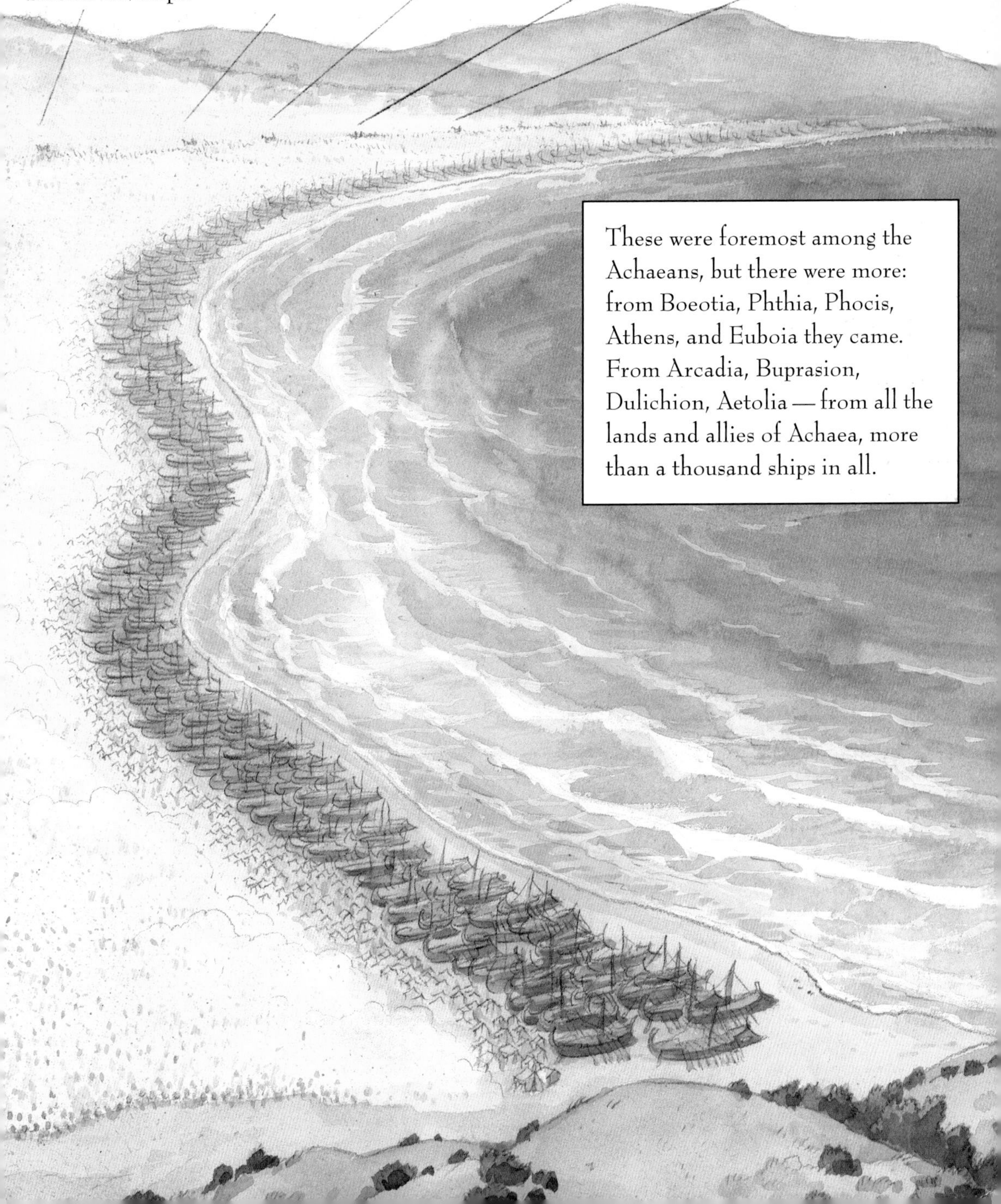

These were foremost among the Achaeans, but there were more: from Boeotia, Phthia, Phocis, Athens, and Euboia they came. From Arcadia, Buprasion, Dulichion, Aetolia — from all the lands and allies of Achaea, more than a thousand ships in all.

On they flowed, rank on rank, to the plain before the Scamander River, and the earth resounded with the tramp of marching men and horses' hooves. The captains in their chariots rode ahead of their soldiers, armor flashing, horsehair plumes nodding grimly above their helms.

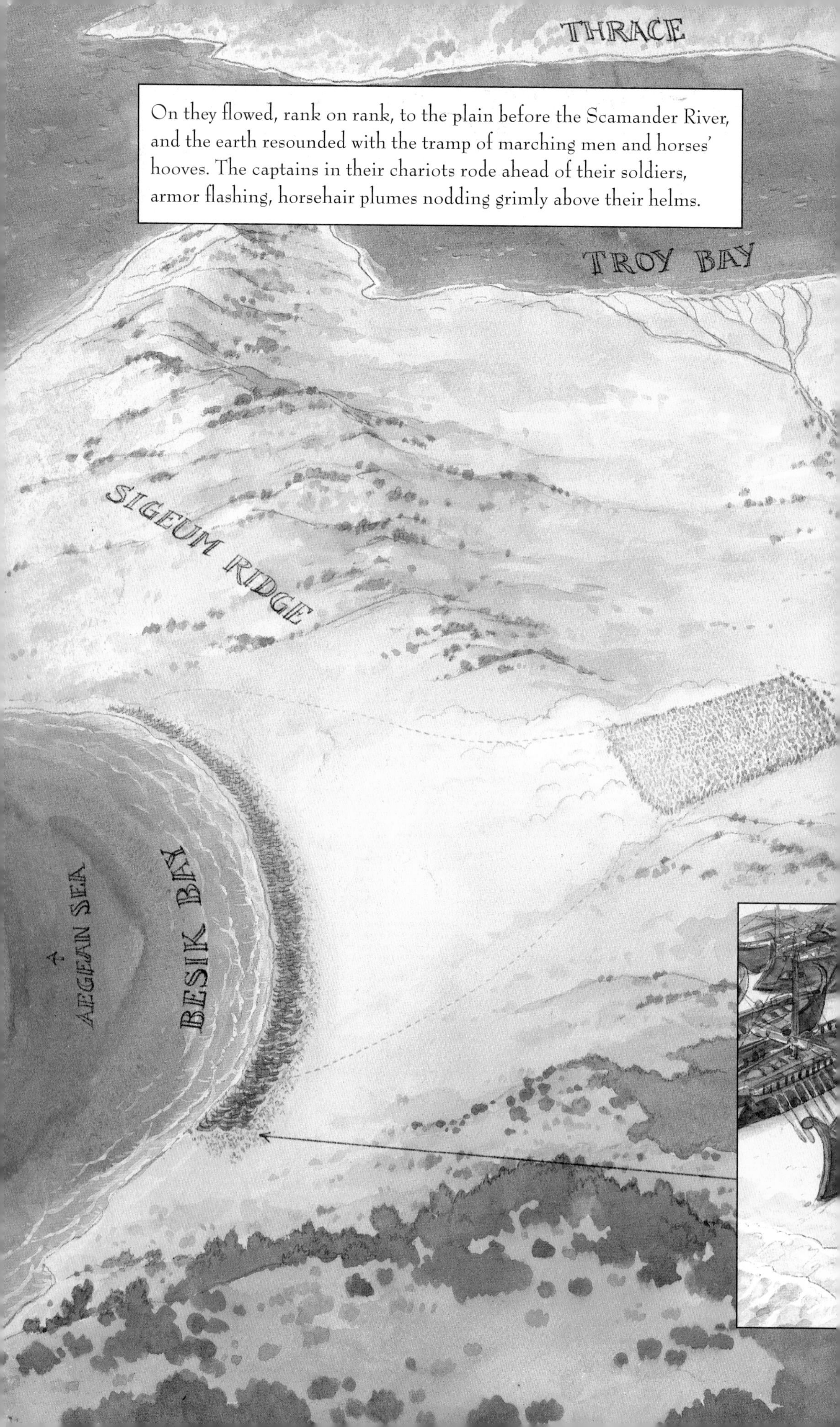
THRACE
TROY BAY
SIGEUM RIDGE
BESIK BAY
AEGEAN SEA

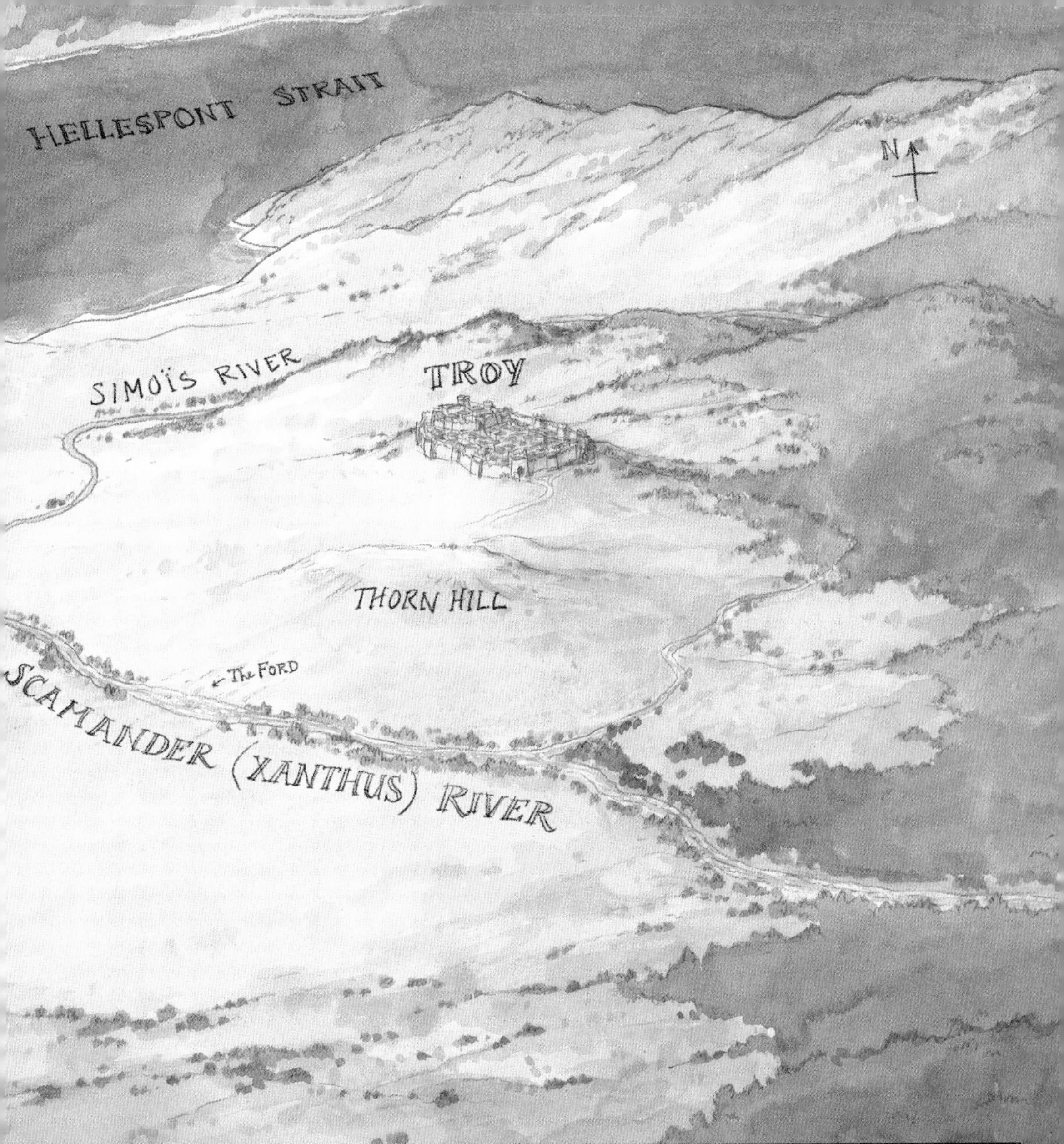
HELLESPONT STRAIT
N
SIMOÏS RIVER
TROY
THORN HILL
The FORD
SCAMANDER (XANTHUS) RIVER

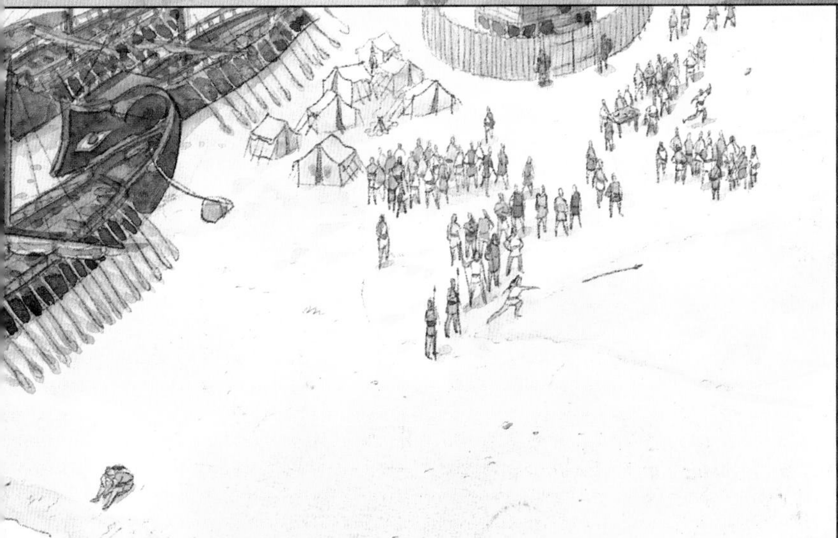

Only the mighty Achilles stayed back now, just as he had threatened. He had brought fifty ships of fierce Myrmidons, but now they idly tossed discs and spears on the beach while their commander pined for Briseis and nursed his anger at Agamemnon.

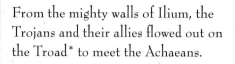

From the mighty walls of Ilium, the Trojans and their allies flowed out on the Troad* to meet the Achaeans.

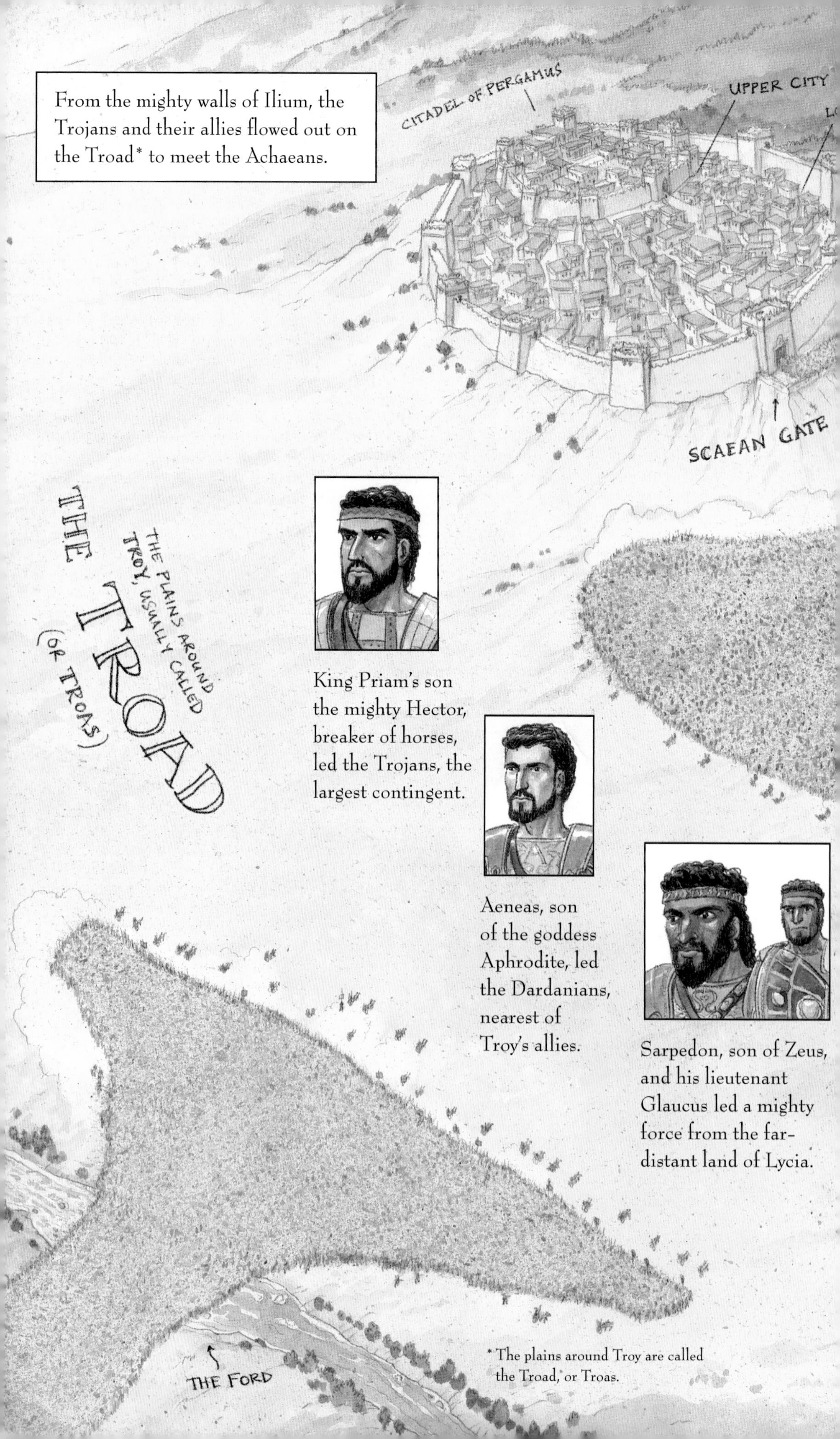

CITADEL OF PERGAMUS

UPPER CITY

SCAEAN GATE

THE TROAD (OR TROAS)

THE PLAINS AROUND TROY, USUALLY CALLED

King Priam's son the mighty Hector, breaker of horses, led the Trojans, the largest contingent.

Aeneas, son of the goddess Aphrodite, led the Dardanians, nearest of Troy's allies.

Sarpedon, son of Zeus, and his lieutenant Glaucus led a mighty force from the far-distant land of Lycia.

THE FORD

* The plains around Troy are called the Troad, or Troas.

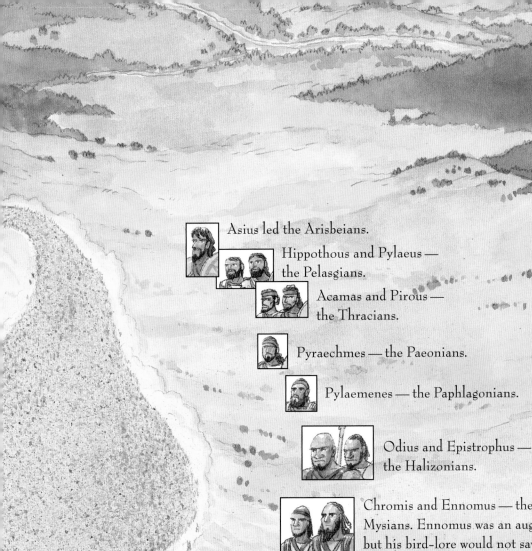

Asius led the Arisbeians.

Hippothous and Pylaeus —
the Pelasgians.

Acamas and Pirous —
the Thracians.

Pyraechmes — the Paeonians.

Pylaemenes — the Paphlagonians.

Odius and Epistrophus —
the Halizonians.

Chromis and Ennomus — the
Mysians. Ennomus was an augur,*
but his bird-lore would not save
him from the hands of Achilles.

Phorcys and Ascanius —
the Phrygians.

Nastes led the Carians.

The men of Adresteia
and Apaesus were
led by Adrestus and
Amphius, sons of
the seer Merops. He
begged them not to
go but could not turn
them from their fate.

The men of
Zelea were led
by the famous
archer Pandarus.

*An *augur* is someone who predicts the
future based on the flight of birds.

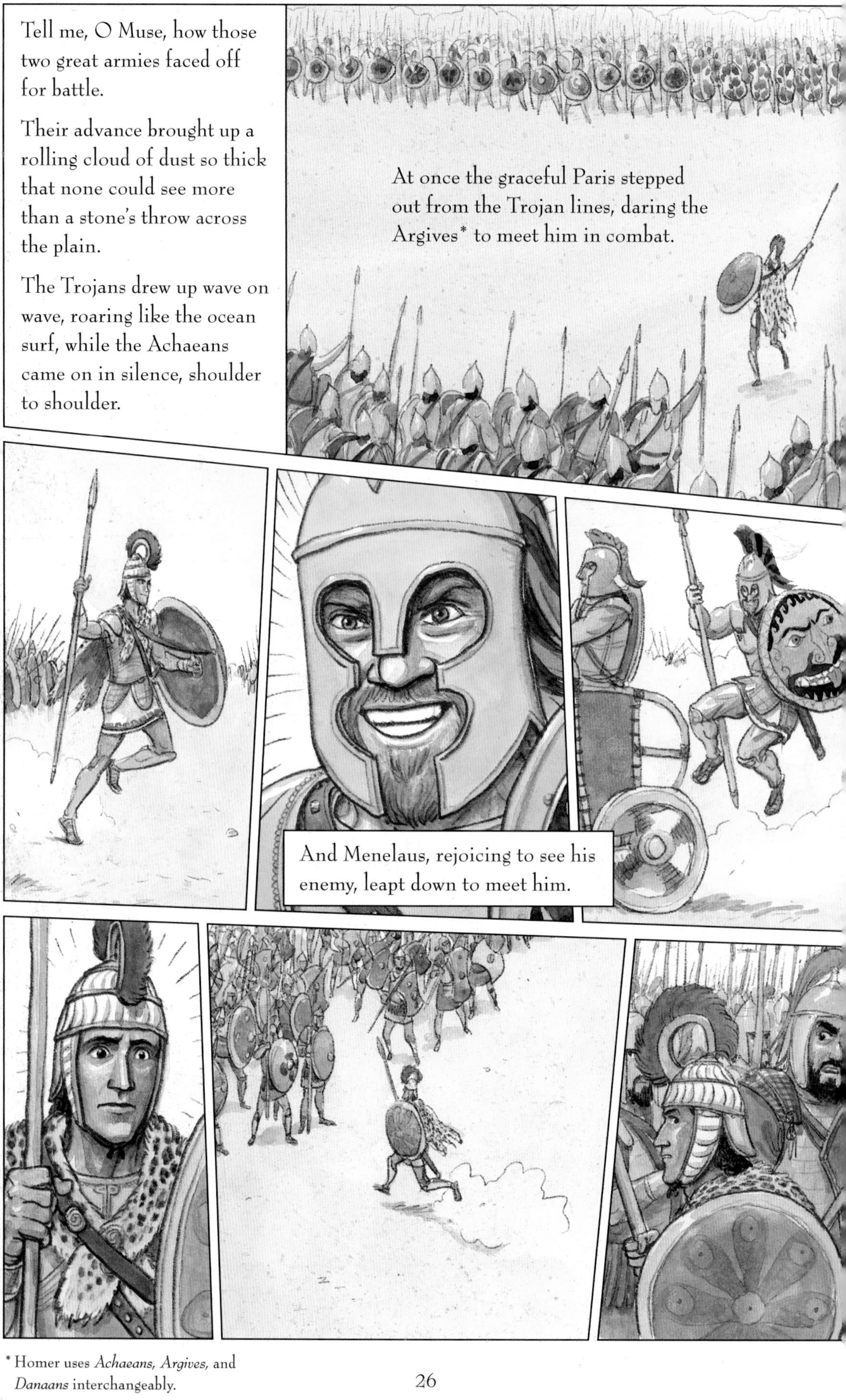
Tell me, O Muse, how those two great armies faced off for battle.
Their advance brought up a rolling cloud of dust so thick that none could see more than a stone's throw across the plain.
The Trojans drew up wave on wave, roaring like the ocean surf, while the Achaeans came on in silence, shoulder to shoulder.
At once the graceful Paris stepped out from the Trojan lines, daring the Argives* to meet him in combat.
And Menelaus, rejoicing to see his enemy, leapt down to meet him.

* Homer uses *Achaeans, Argives,* and *Danaans* interchangeably.

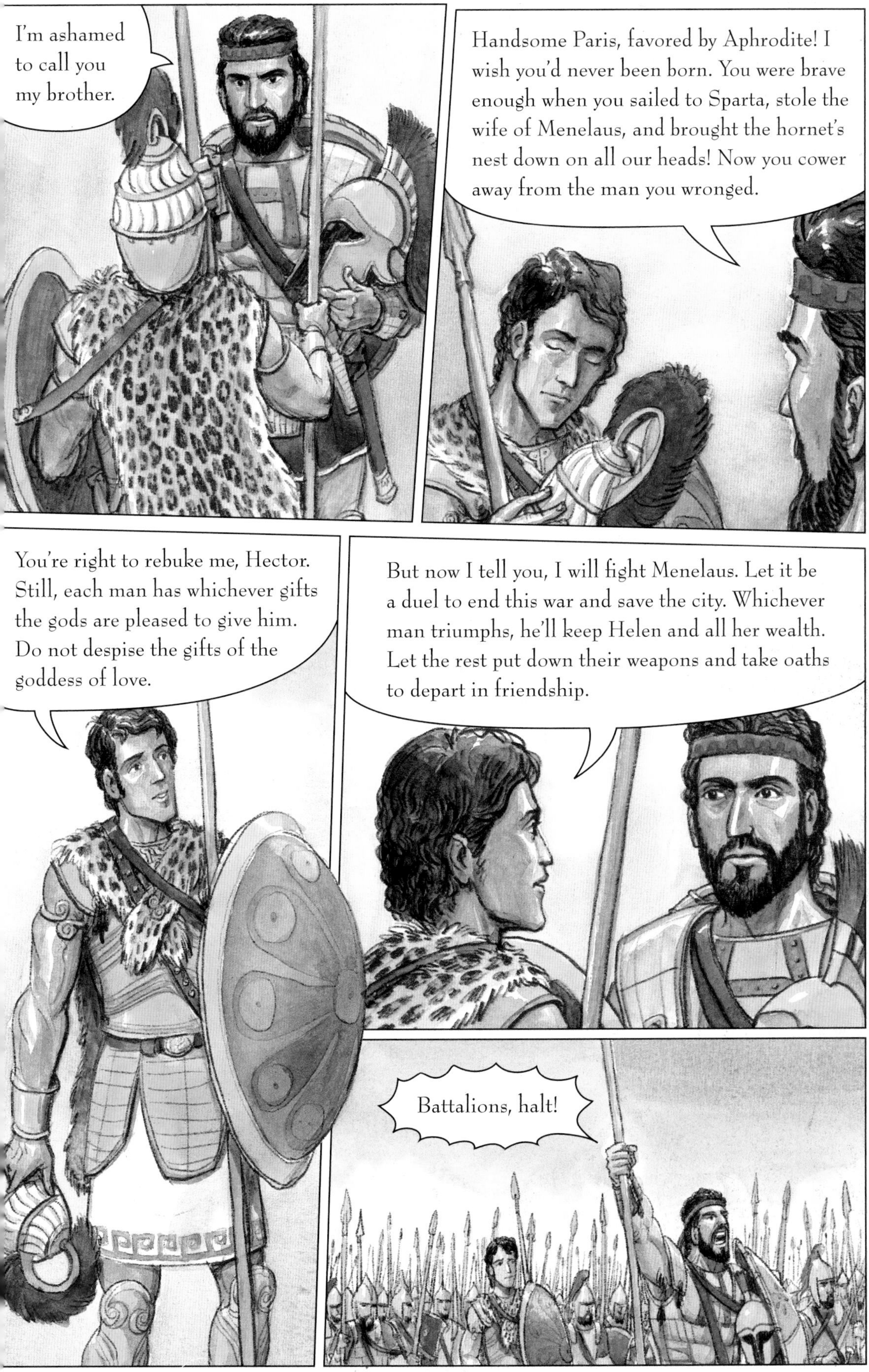
I'm ashamed to call you my brother.
Handsome Paris, favored by Aphrodite! I wish you'd never been born. You were brave enough when you sailed to Sparta, stole the wife of Menelaus, and brought the hornet's nest down on all our heads! Now you cower away from the man you wronged.
You're right to rebuke me, Hector. Still, each man has whichever gifts the gods are pleased to give him. Do not despise the gifts of the goddess of love.
But now I tell you, I will fight Menelaus. Let it be a duel to end this war and save the city. Whichever man triumphs, he'll keep Helen and all her wealth. Let the rest put down their weapons and take oaths to depart in friendship.
Battalions, halt!

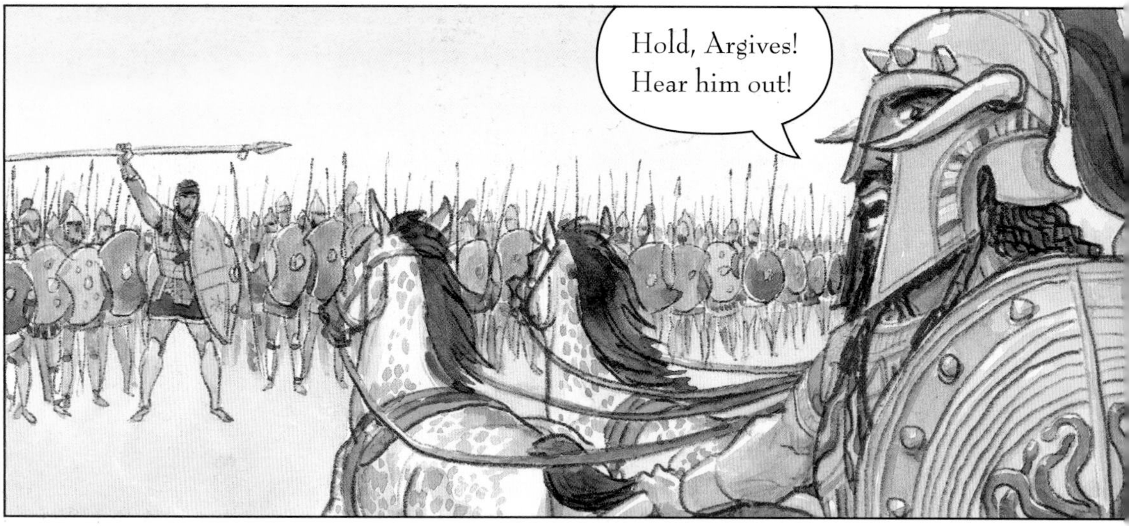
Hold, Argives! Hear him out!

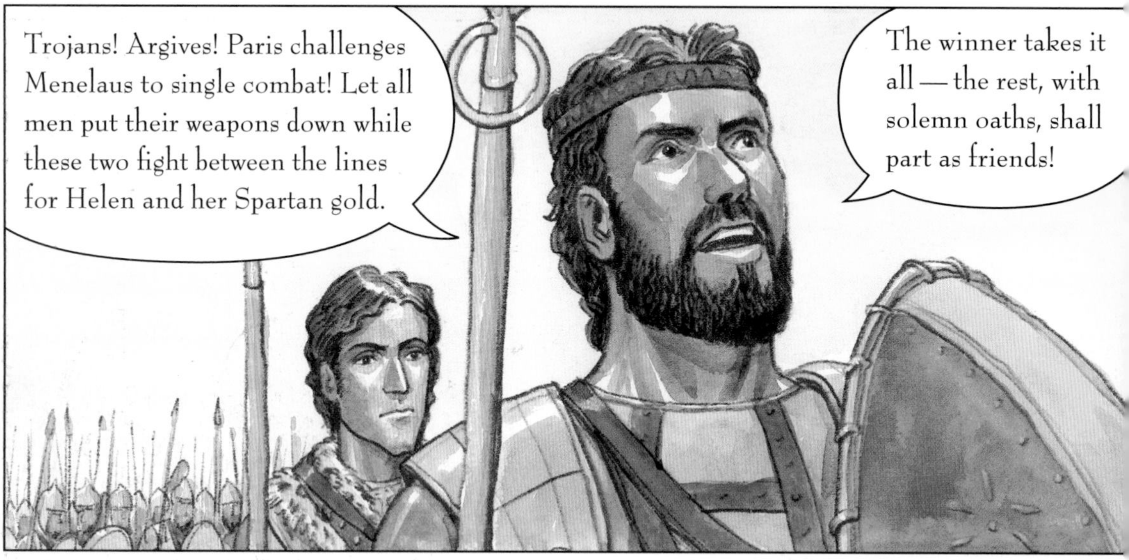
Trojans! Argives! Paris challenges Menelaus to single combat! Let all men put their weapons down while these two fight between the lines for Helen and her Spartan gold.
The winner takes it all — the rest, with solemn oaths, shall part as friends!

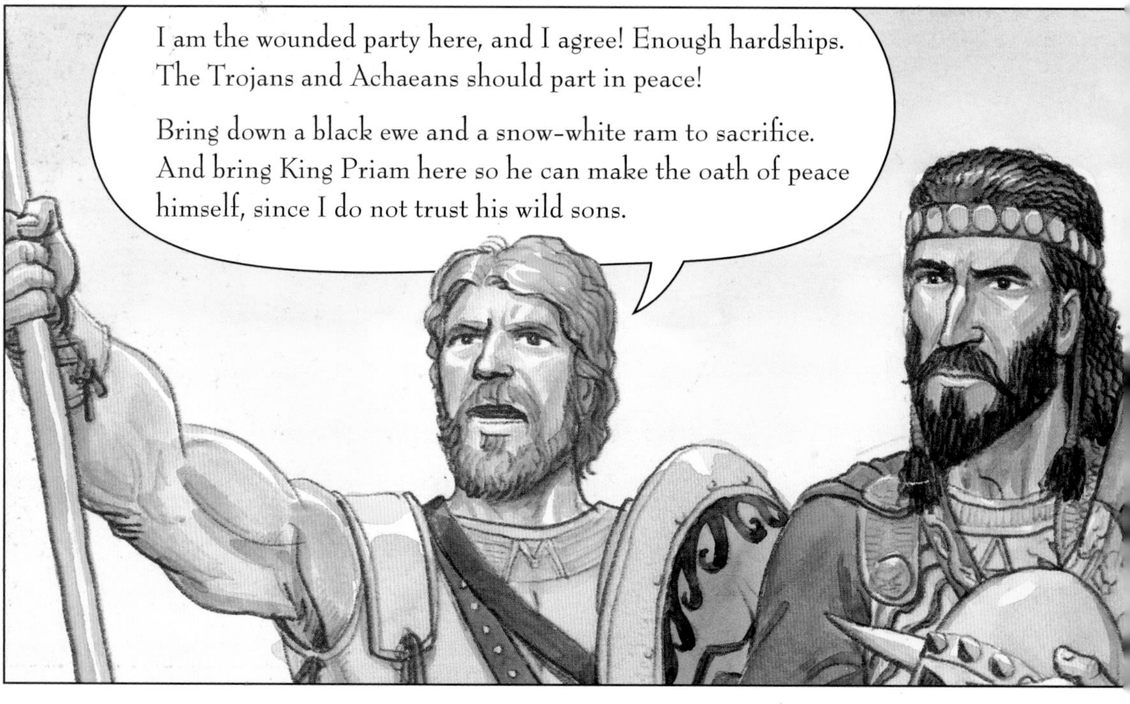
I am the wounded party here, and I agree! Enough hardships. The Trojans and Achaeans should part in peace!
Bring down a black ewe and a snow-white ram to sacrifice. And bring King Priam here so he can make the oath of peace himself, since I do not trust his wild sons.

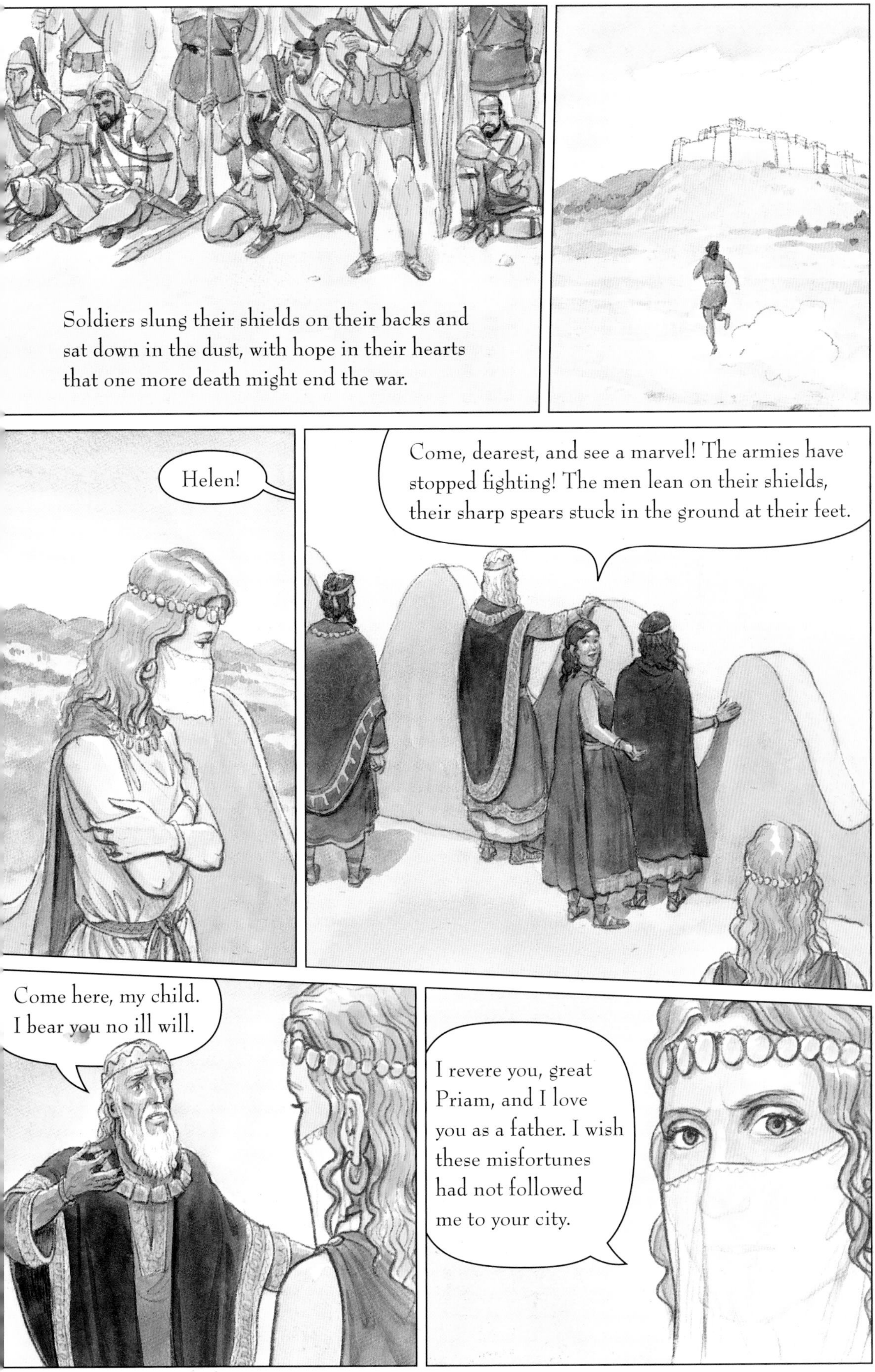
Soldiers slung their shields on their backs and sat down in the dust, with hope in their hearts that one more death might end the war.
Helen!
Come, dearest, and see a marvel! The armies have stopped fighting! The men lean on their shields, their sharp spears stuck in the ground at their feet.
Come here, my child. I bear you no ill will.
I revere you, great Priam, and I love you as a father. I wish these misfortunes had not followed me to your city.

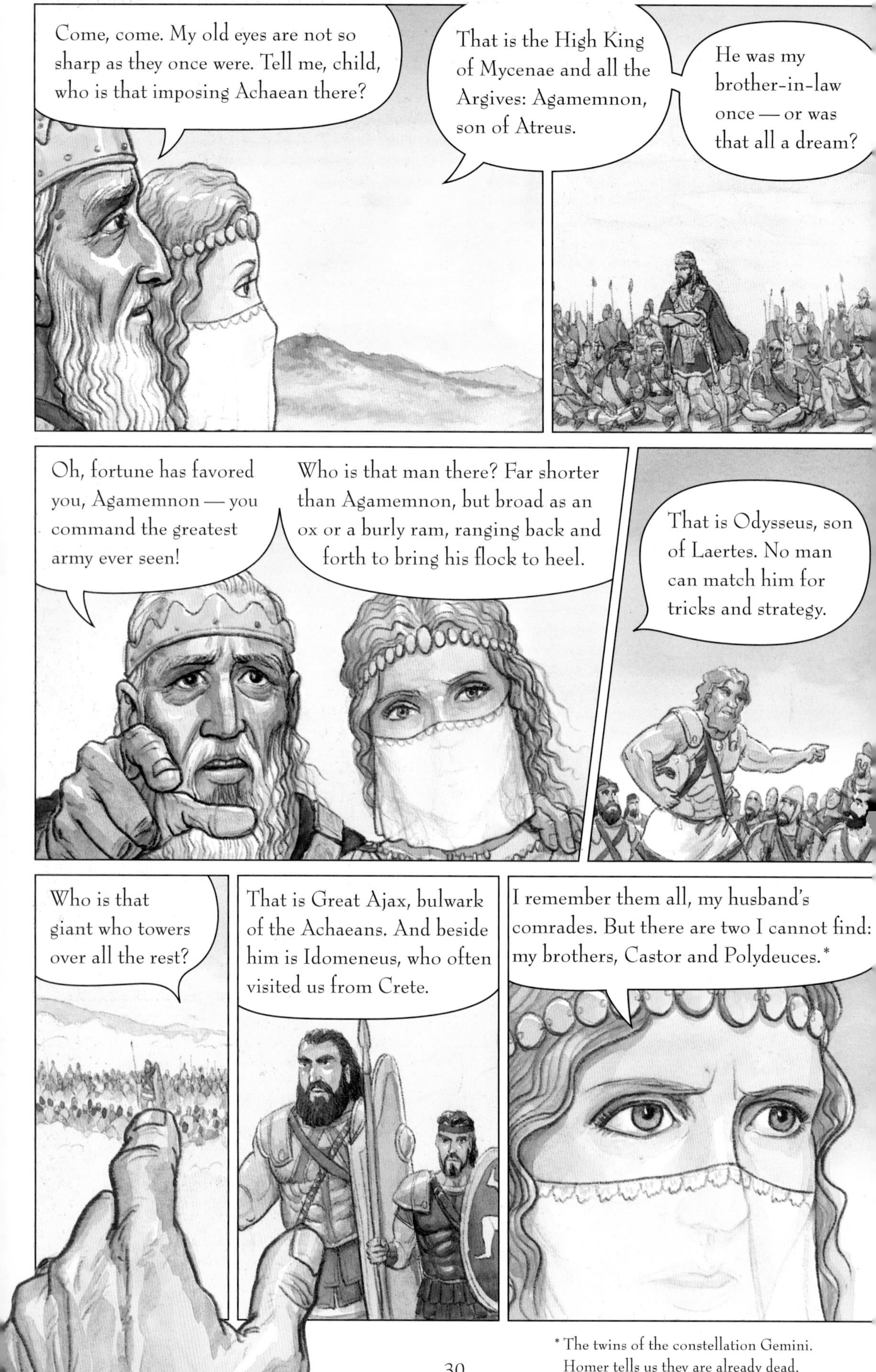
Come, come. My old eyes are not so sharp as they once were. Tell me, child, who is that imposing Achaean there?
That is the High King of Mycenae and all the Argives: Agamemnon, son of Atreus.
He was my brother-in-law once — or was that all a dream?
Oh, fortune has favored you, Agamemnon — you command the greatest army ever seen!
Who is that man there? Far shorter than Agamemnon, but broad as an ox or a burly ram, ranging back and forth to bring his flock to heel.
That is Odysseus, son of Laertes. No man can match him for tricks and strategy.
Who is that giant who towers over all the rest?
That is Great Ajax, bulwark of the Achaeans. And beside him is Idomeneus, who often visited us from Crete.
I remember them all, my husband's comrades. But there are two I cannot find: my brothers, Castor and Polydeuces.*

* The twins of the constellation Gemini. Homer tells us they are already dead.

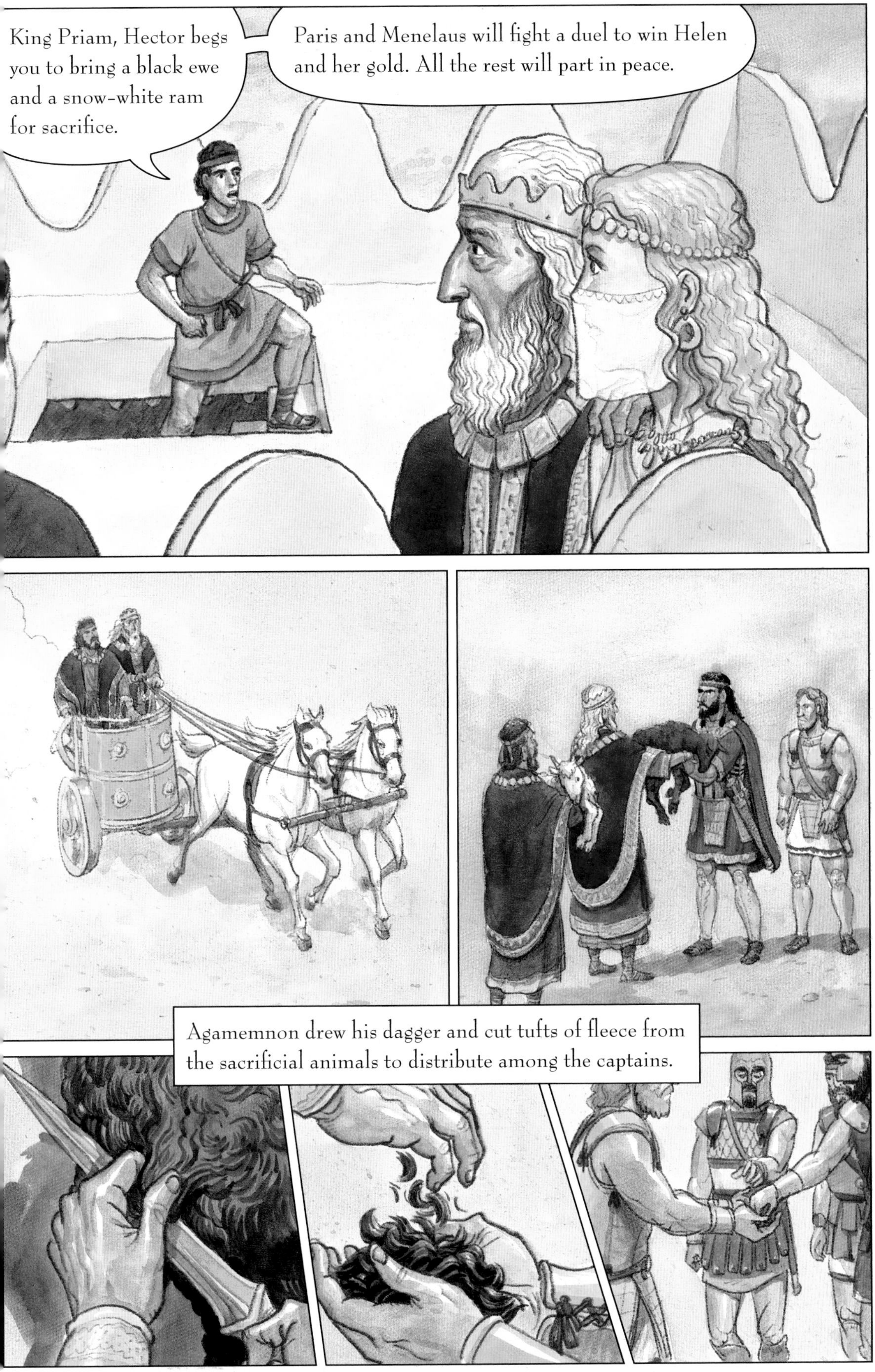
King Priam, Hector begs you to bring a black ewe and a snow-white ram for sacrifice.
Paris and Menelaus will fight a duel to win Helen and her gold. All the rest will part in peace.
Agamemnon drew his dagger and cut tufts of fleece from the sacrificial animals to distribute among the captains.

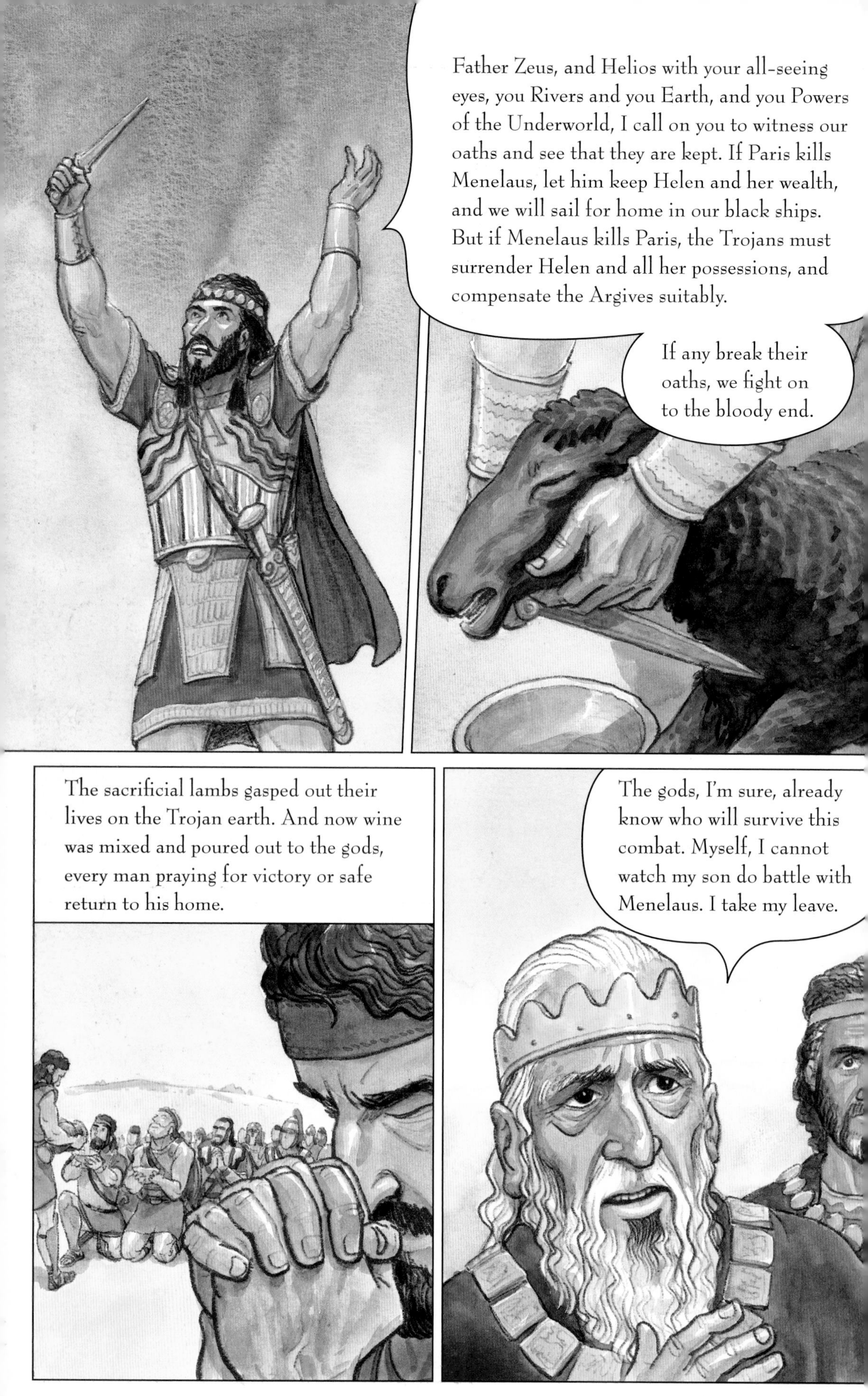
Father Zeus, and Helios with your all-seeing eyes, you Rivers and you Earth, and you Powers of the Underworld, I call on you to witness our oaths and see that they are kept. If Paris kills Menelaus, let him keep Helen and her wealth, and we will sail for home in our black ships. But if Menelaus kills Paris, the Trojans must surrender Helen and all her possessions, and compensate the Argives suitably.
If any break their oaths, we fight on to the bloody end.
The sacrificial lambs gasped out their lives on the Trojan earth. And now wine was mixed and poured out to the gods, every man praying for victory or safe return to his home.
The gods, I'm sure, already know who will survive this combat. Myself, I cannot watch my son do battle with Menelaus. I take my leave.

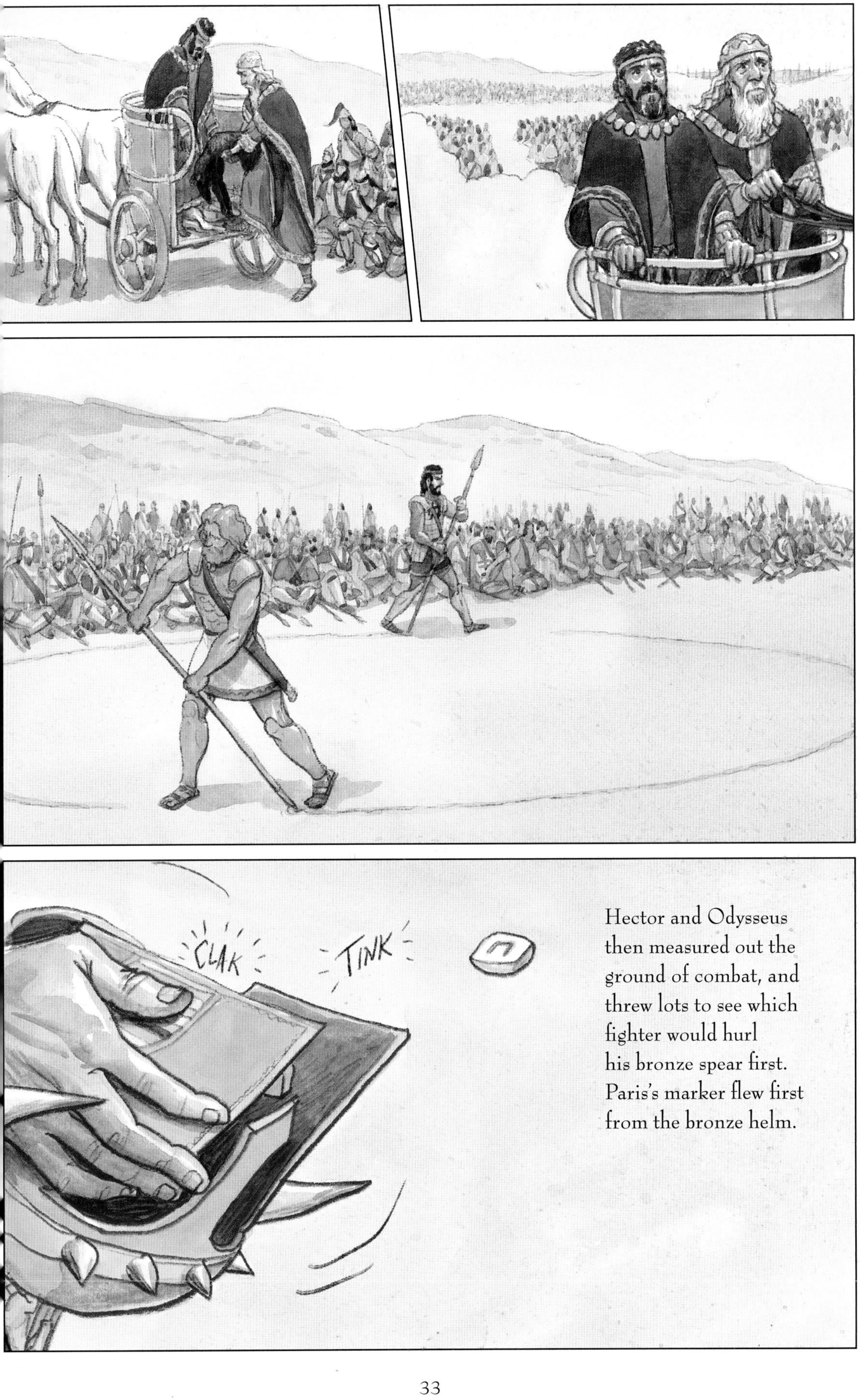
CLAK
TINK
Hector and Odysseus then measured out the ground of combat, and threw lots to see which fighter would hurl his bronze spear first. Paris's marker flew first from the bronze helm.

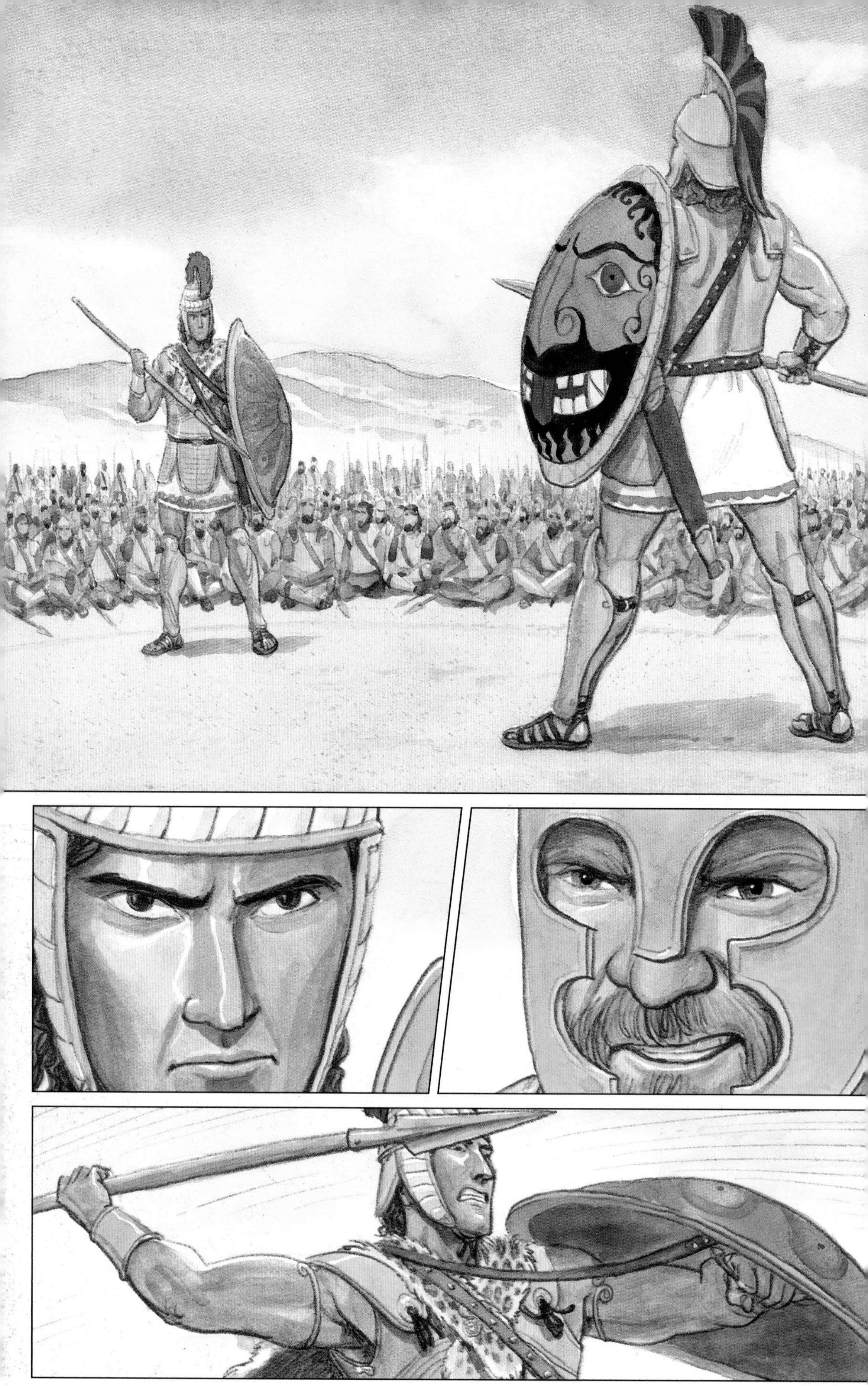

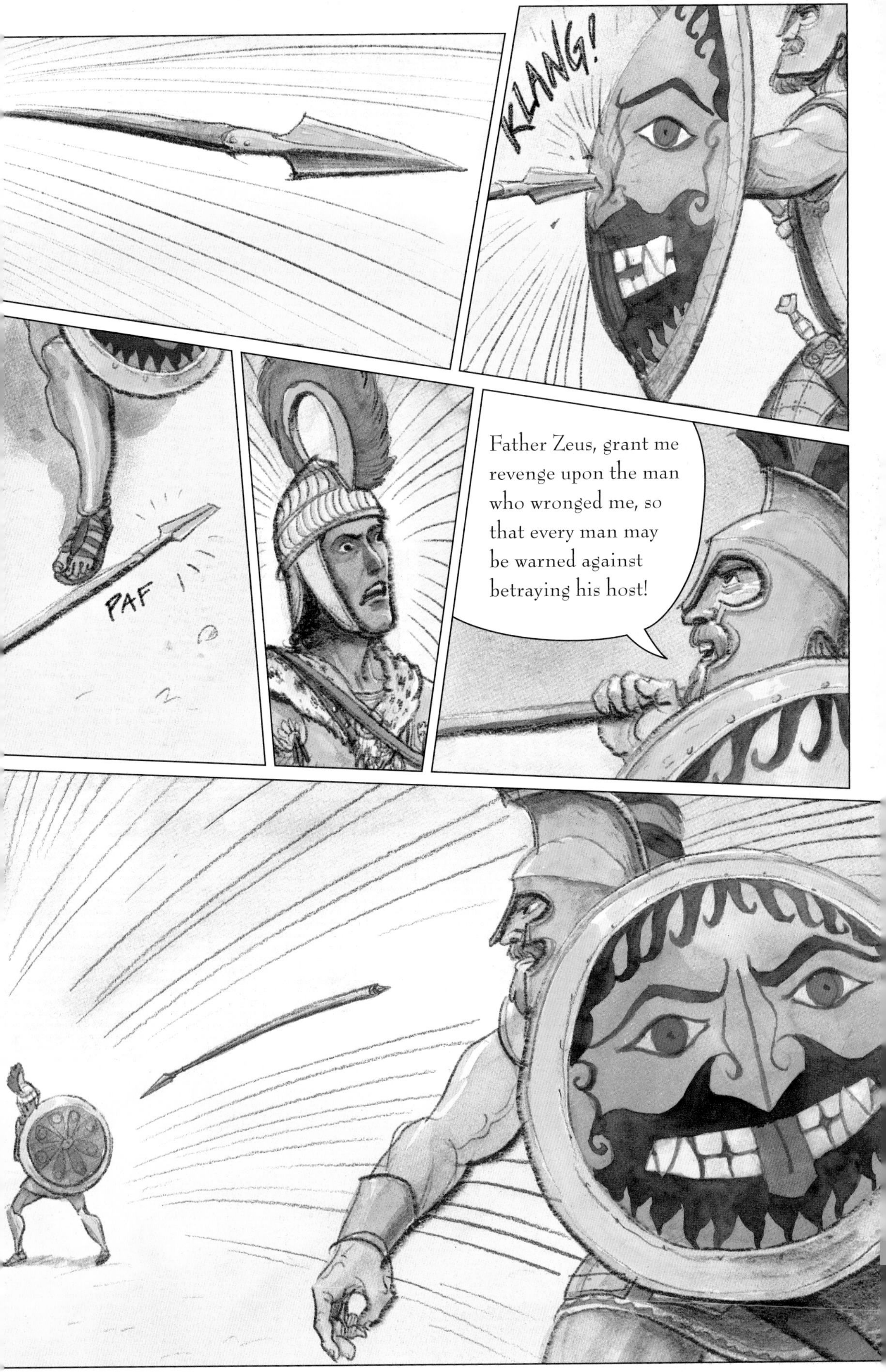
KLANG!
PAF
Father Zeus, grant me revenge upon the man who wronged me, so that every man may be warned against betraying his host!

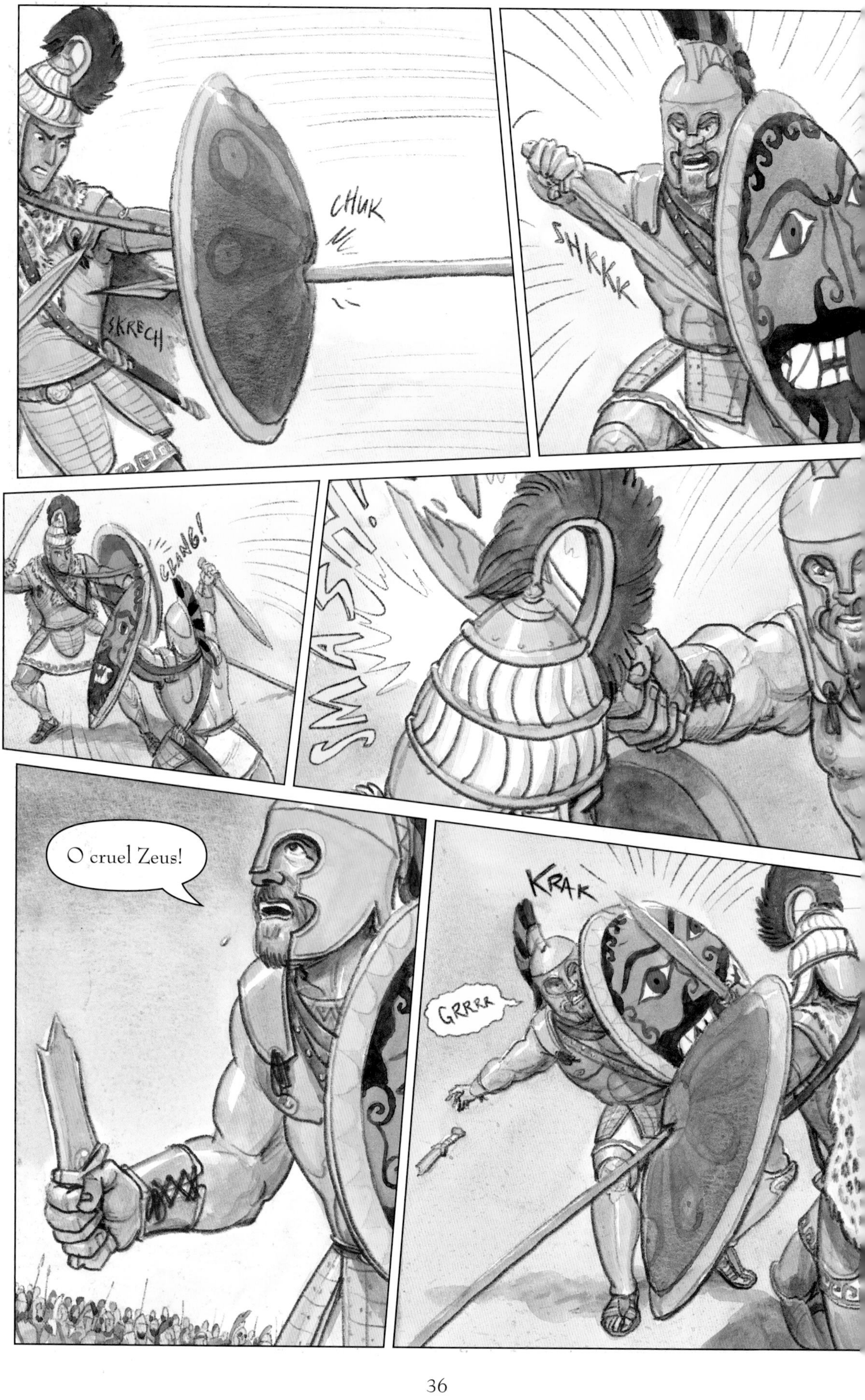
CHUK
SKRECH
SHKKKK
CLANG!
SMASH!
O cruel Zeus!
KRAK
GRRRR

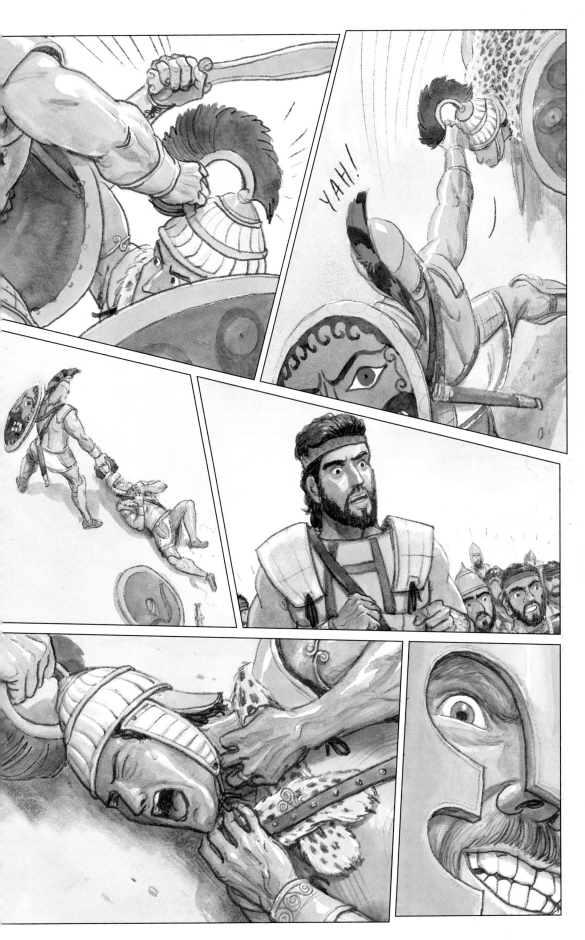

YAH!

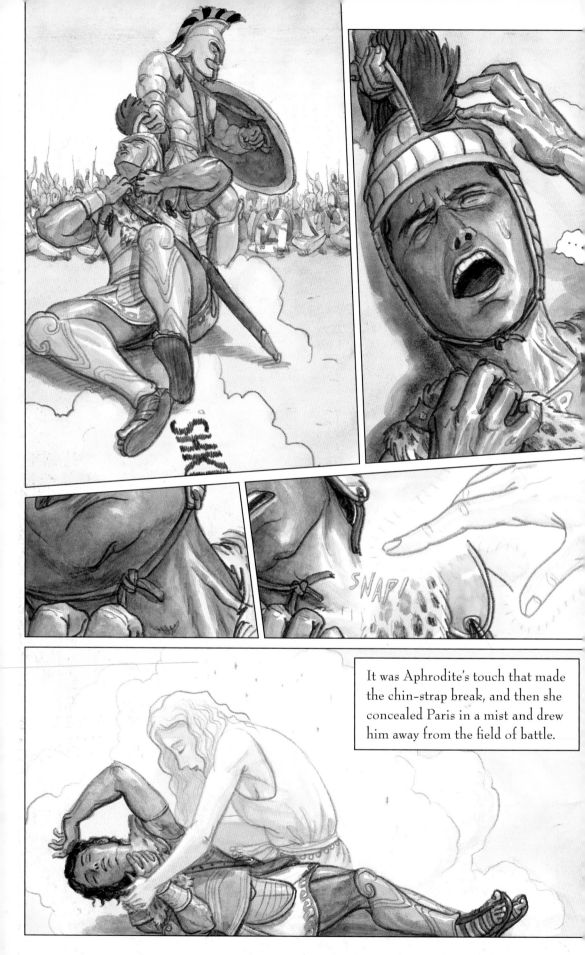

It was Aphrodite's touch that made the chin-strap break, and then she concealed Paris in a mist and drew him away from the field of battle.

SHK

SNAP!

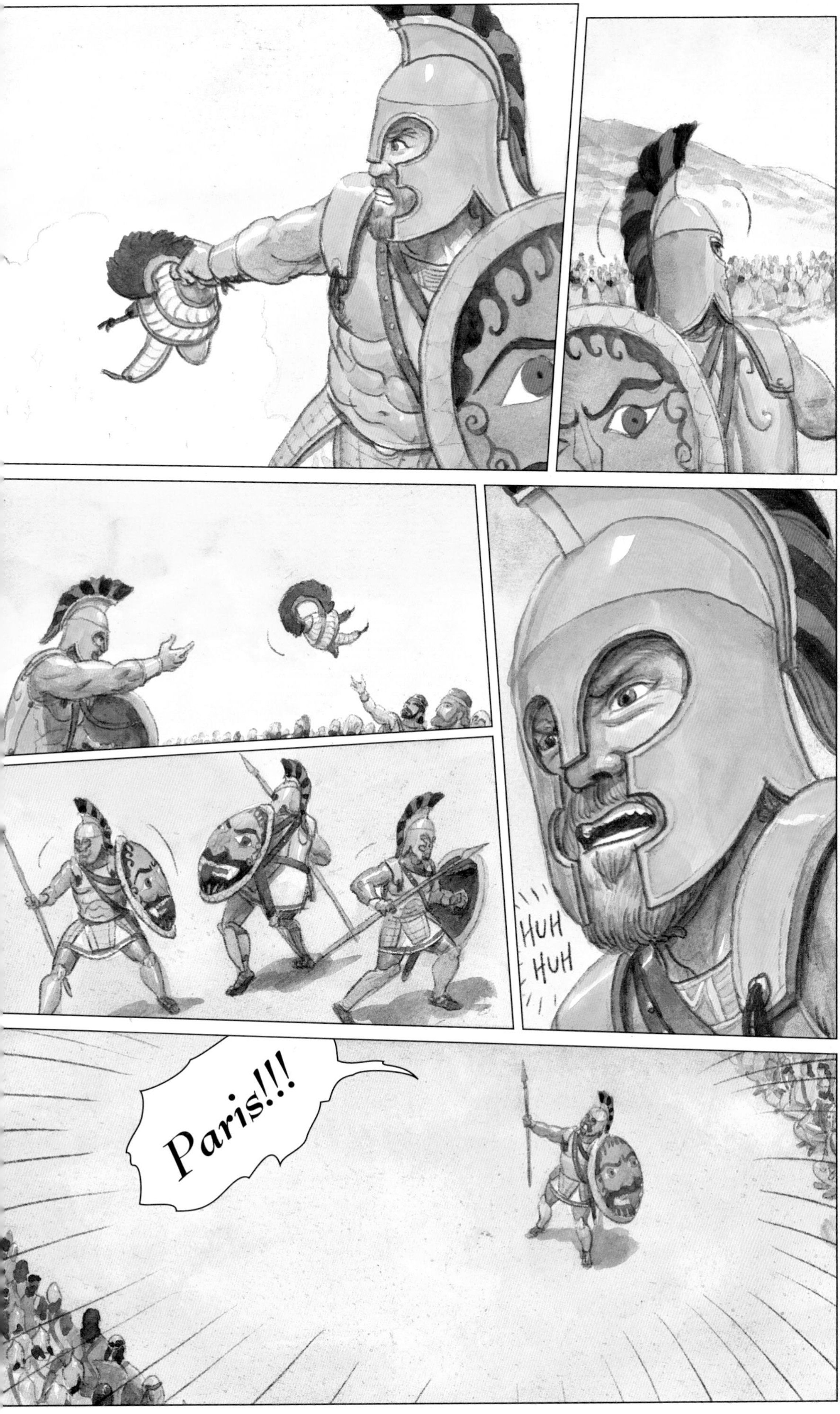
HUH
HUH
Paris!!!

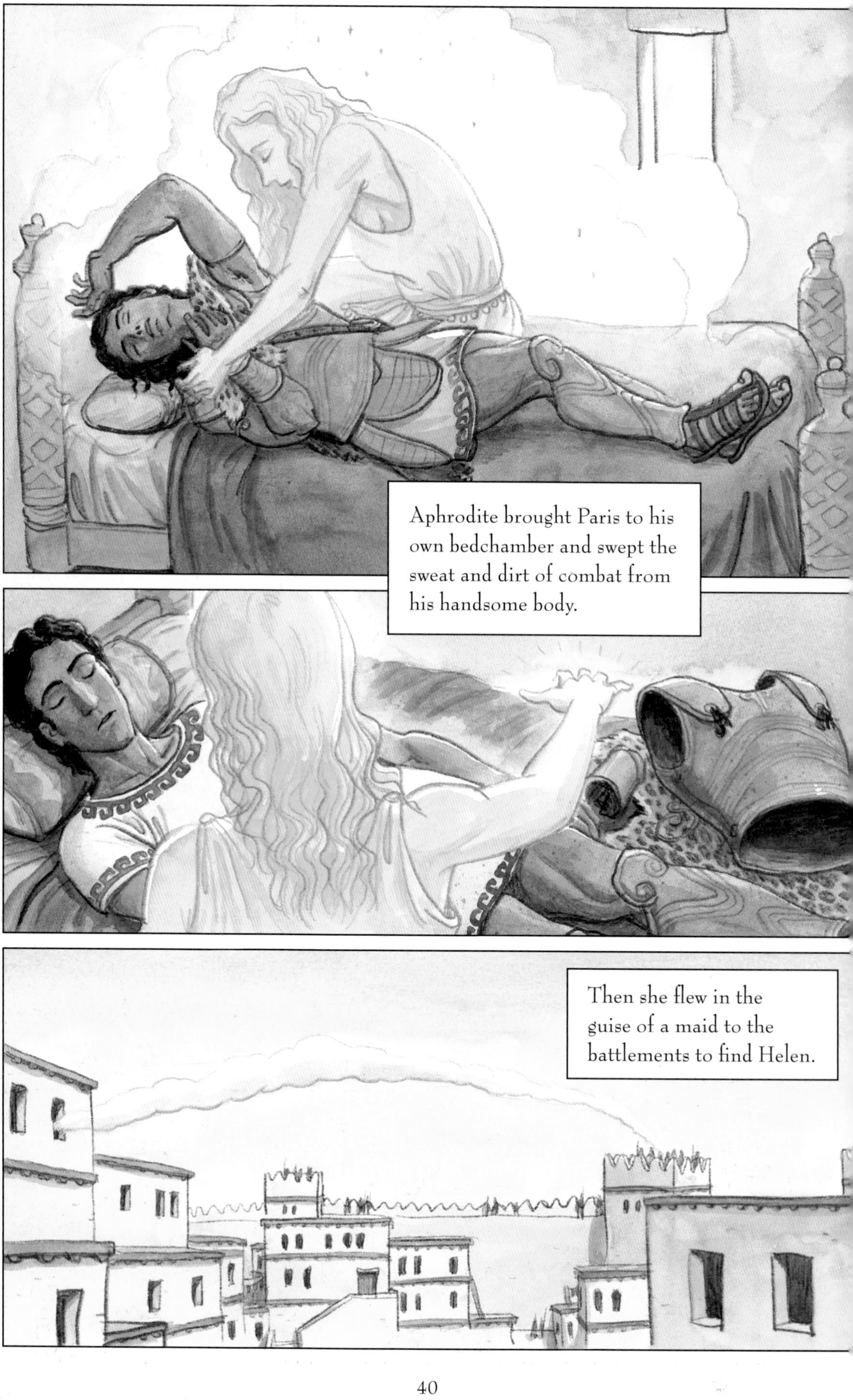
Aphrodite brought Paris to his own bedchamber and swept the sweat and dirt of combat from his handsome body.
Then she flew in the guise of a maid to the battlements to find Helen.

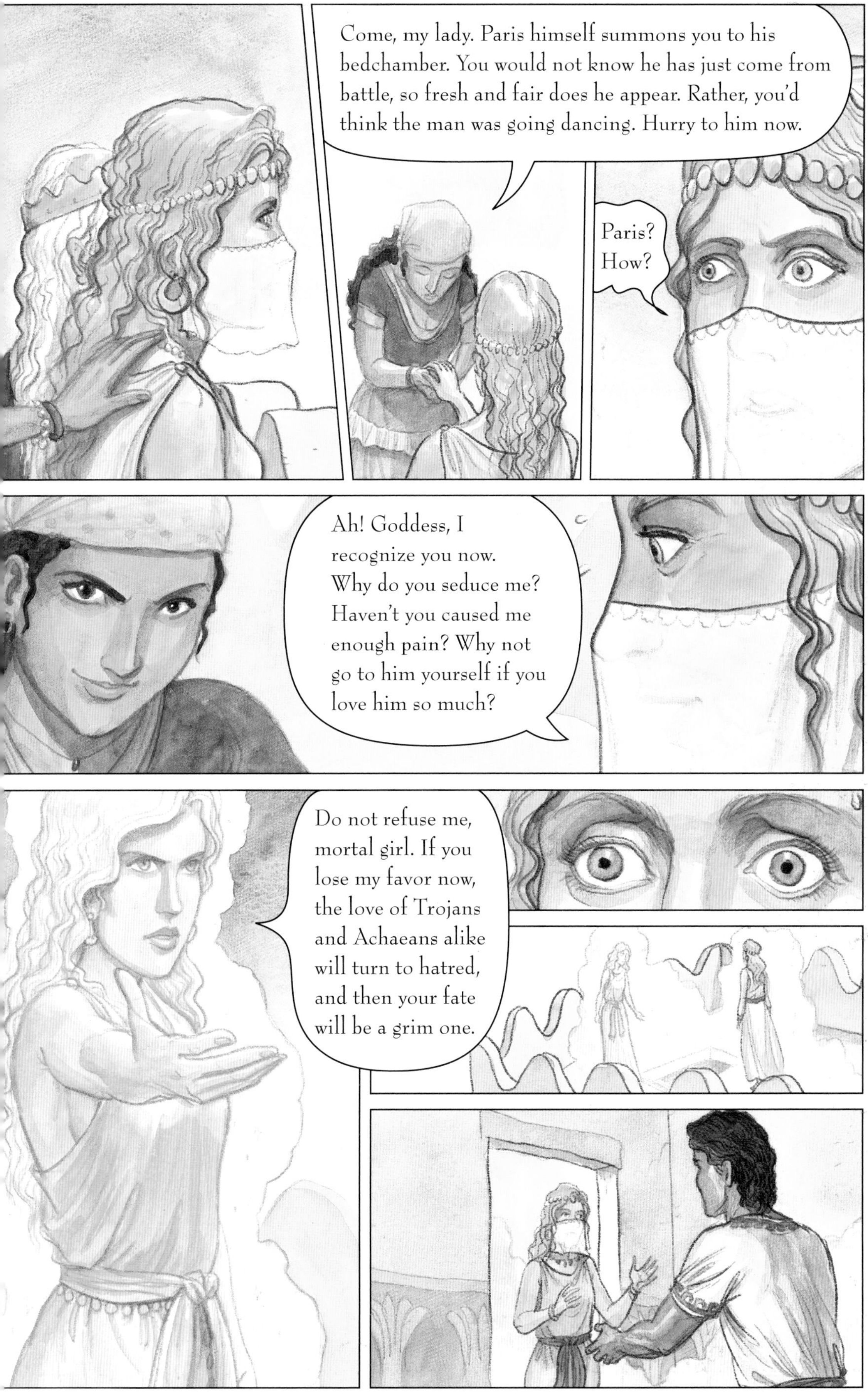
Come, my lady. Paris himself summons you to his bedchamber. You would not know he has just come from battle, so fresh and fair does he appear. Rather, you'd think the man was going dancing. Hurry to him now.
Paris? How?
Ah! Goddess, I recognize you now. Why do you seduce me? Haven't you caused me enough pain? Why not go to him yourself if you love him so much?
Do not refuse me, mortal girl. If you lose my favor now, the love of Trojans and Achaeans alike will turn to hatred, and then your fate will be a grim one.

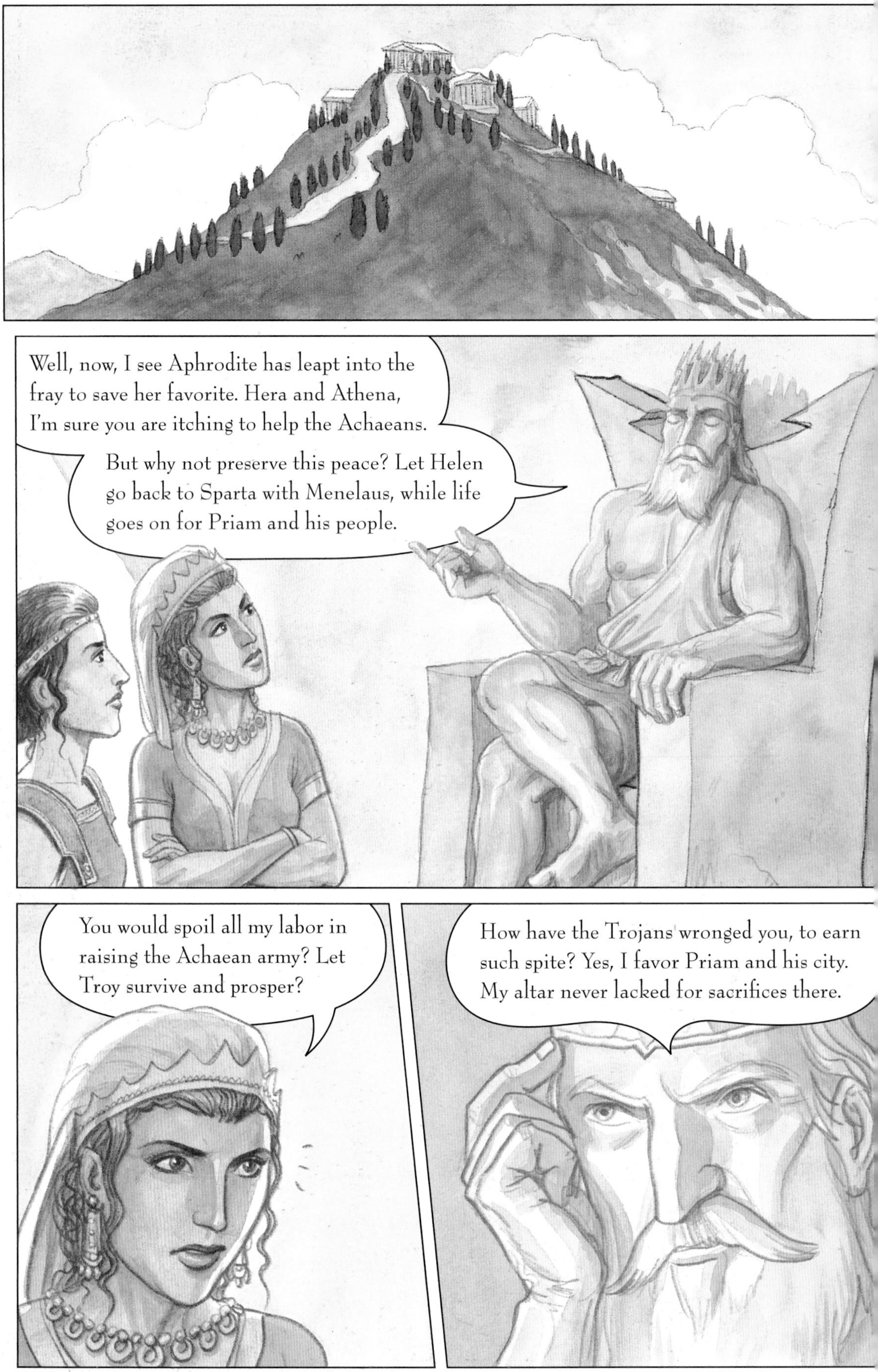
Well, now, I see Aphrodite has leapt into the fray to save her favorite. Hera and Athena, I'm sure you are itching to help the Achaeans.
But why not preserve this peace? Let Helen go back to Sparta with Menelaus, while life goes on for Priam and his people.
You would spoil all my labor in raising the Achaean army? Let Troy survive and prosper?
How have the Trojans wronged you, to earn such spite? Yes, I favor Priam and his city. My altar never lacked for sacrifices there.

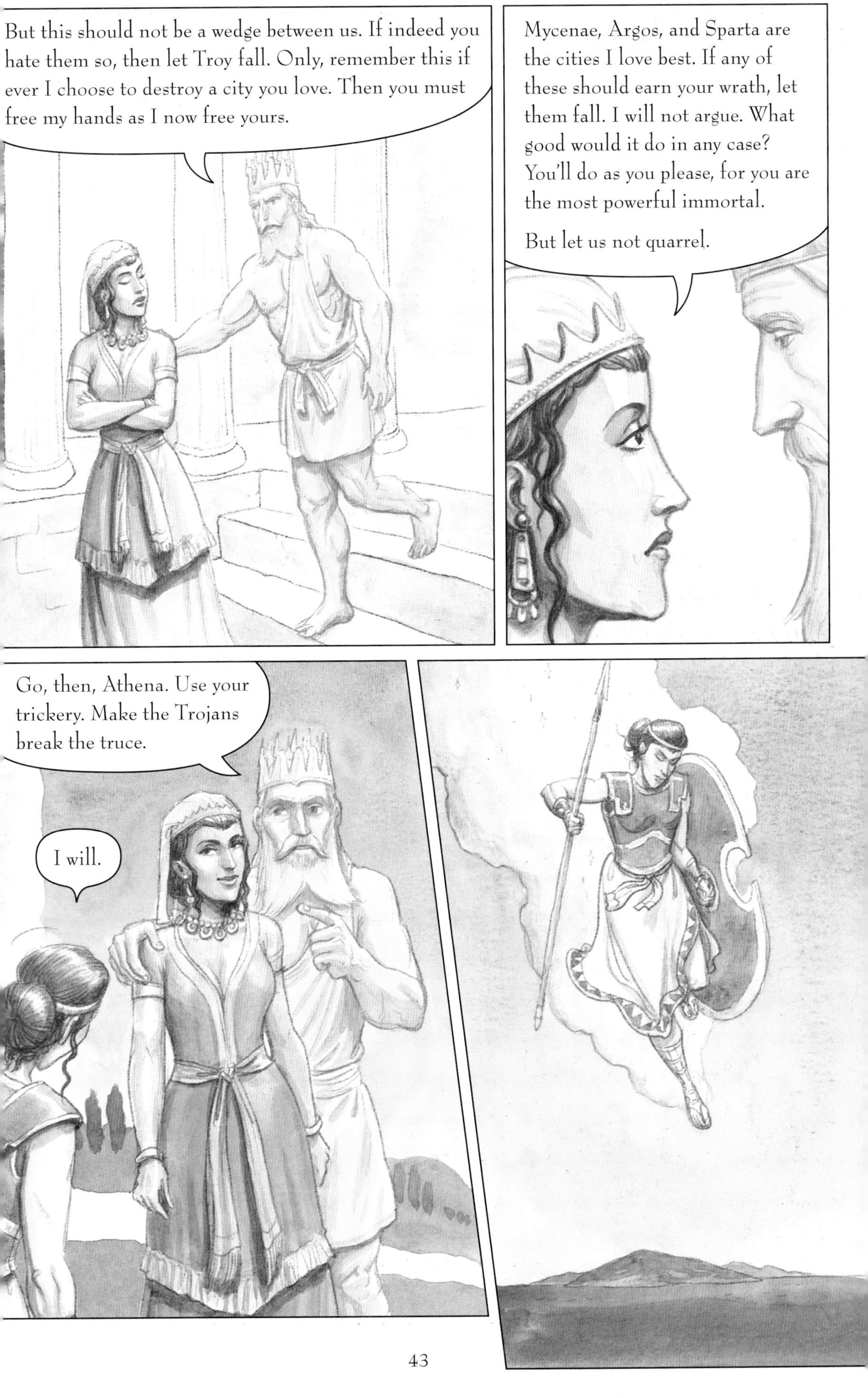

But this should not be a wedge between us. If indeed you hate them so, then let Troy fall. Only, remember this if ever I choose to destroy a city you love. Then you must free my hands as I now free yours.
Mycenae, Argos, and Sparta are the cities I love best. If any of these should earn your wrath, let them fall. I will not argue. What good would it do in any case? You'll do as you please, for you are the most powerful immortal.
But let us not quarrel.
Go, then, Athena. Use your trickery. Make the Trojans break the truce.
I will.

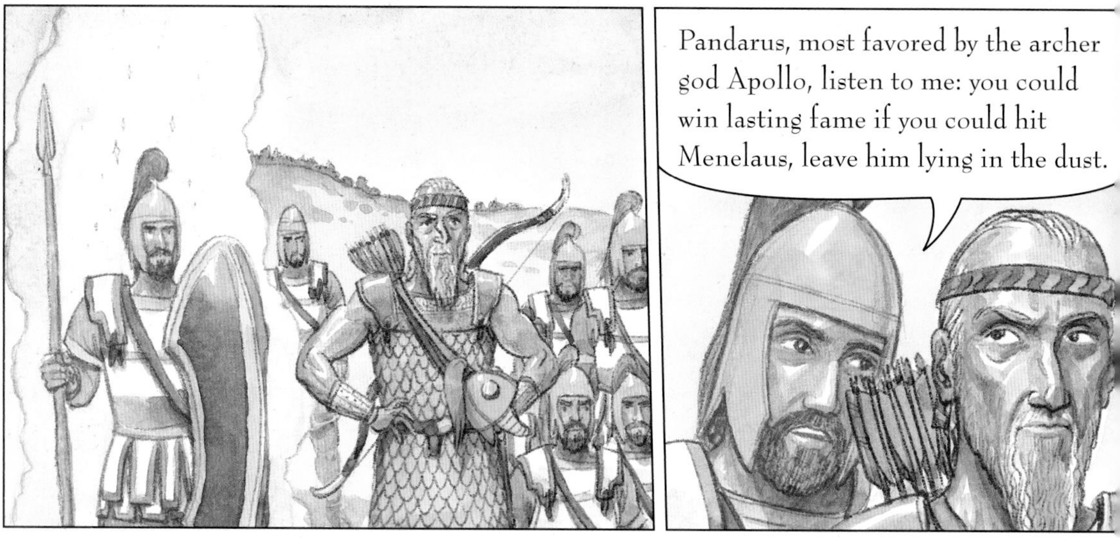
Pandarus, most favored by the archer god Apollo, listen to me: you could win lasting fame if you could hit Menelaus, leave him lying in the dust.

Pandarus's bow was made from the horns of an ibex he had killed, hiding in the mountain crags — he'd hit it cleanly in the chest and brought it down. The horns were four feet long, and he'd cut and fitted them in strips to make a mighty bow tipped with gold. Now silently he prayed to Apollo, promised a hecatomb* of first-born lambs, and drew an arrow, newly made and razor-sharp.

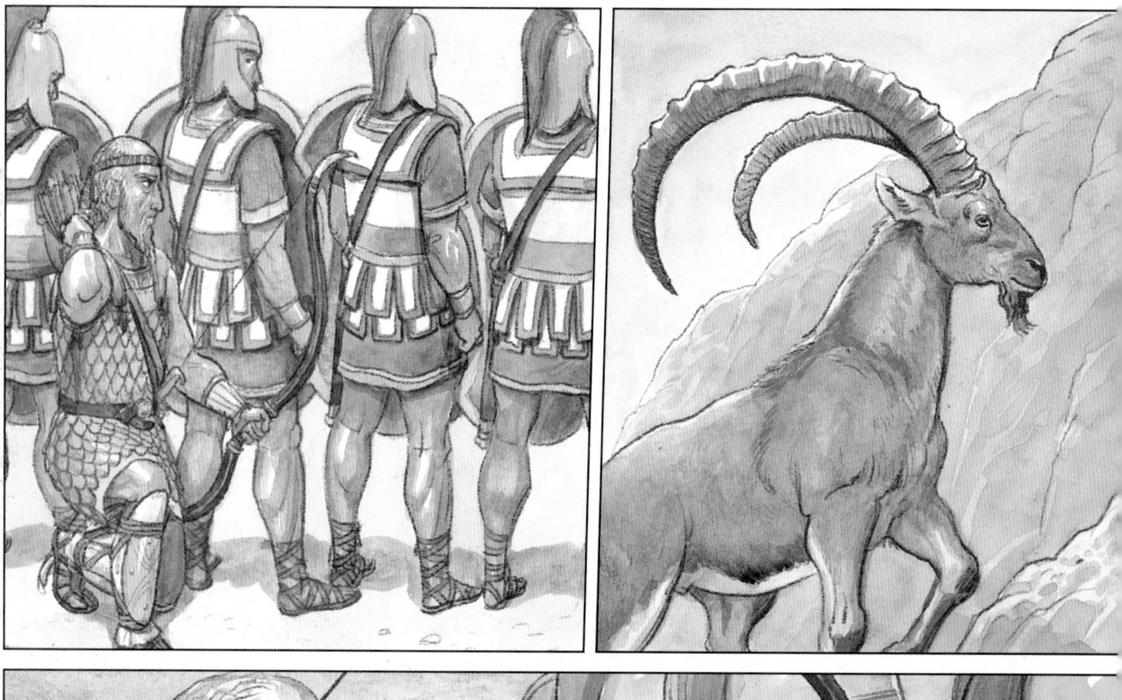

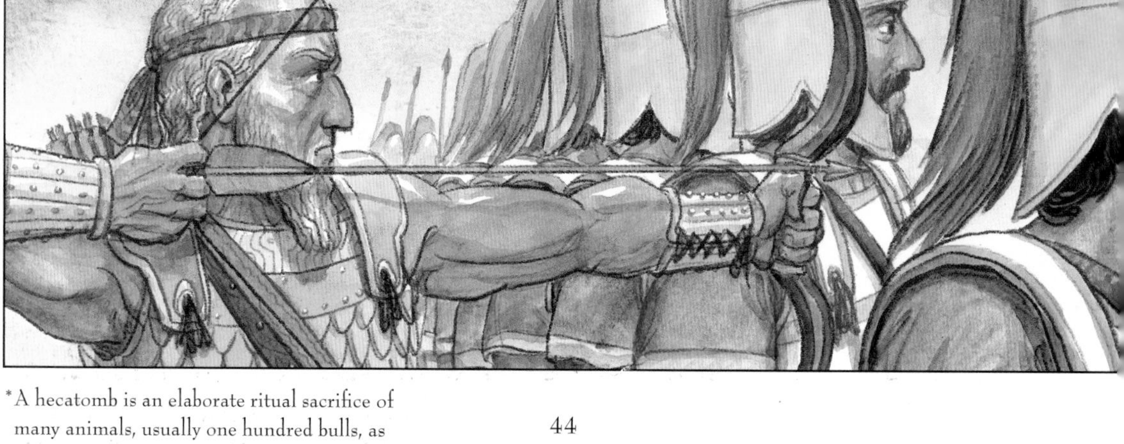

*A hecatomb is an elaborate ritual sacrifice of many animals, usually one hundred bulls, as seen in Book 3 of *The Odyssey*.

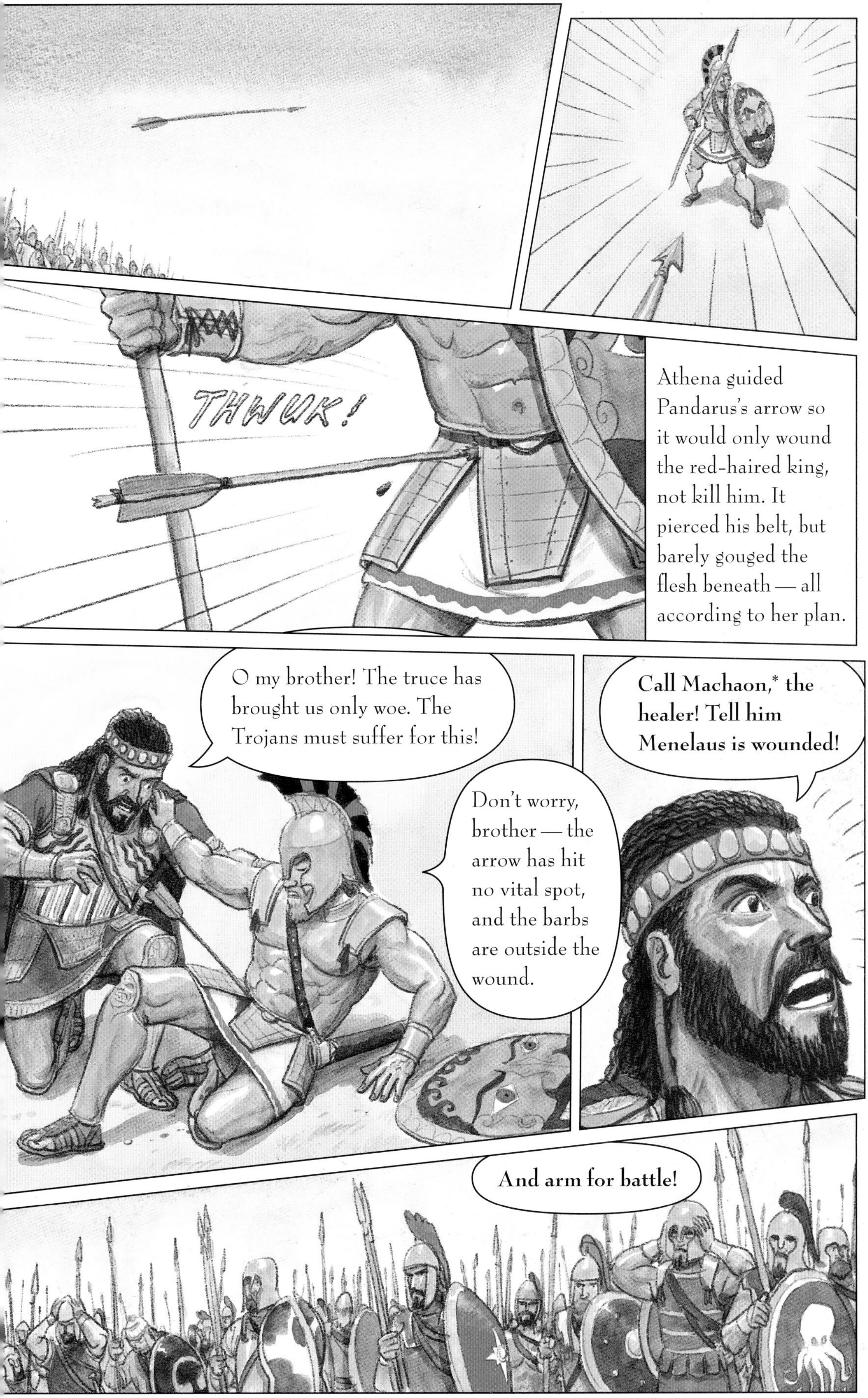
THWUK!
Athena guided Pandarus's arrow so it would only wound the red-haired king, not kill him. It pierced his belt, but barely gouged the flesh beneath — all according to her plan.
O my brother! The truce has brought us only woe. The Trojans must suffer for this!
Don't worry, brother — the arrow has hit no vital spot, and the barbs are outside the wound.
Call Machaon,* the healer! Tell him Menelaus is wounded!
And arm for battle!

* Machaon is the son of Asclepius, the most revered healer in Greek history and mythology.

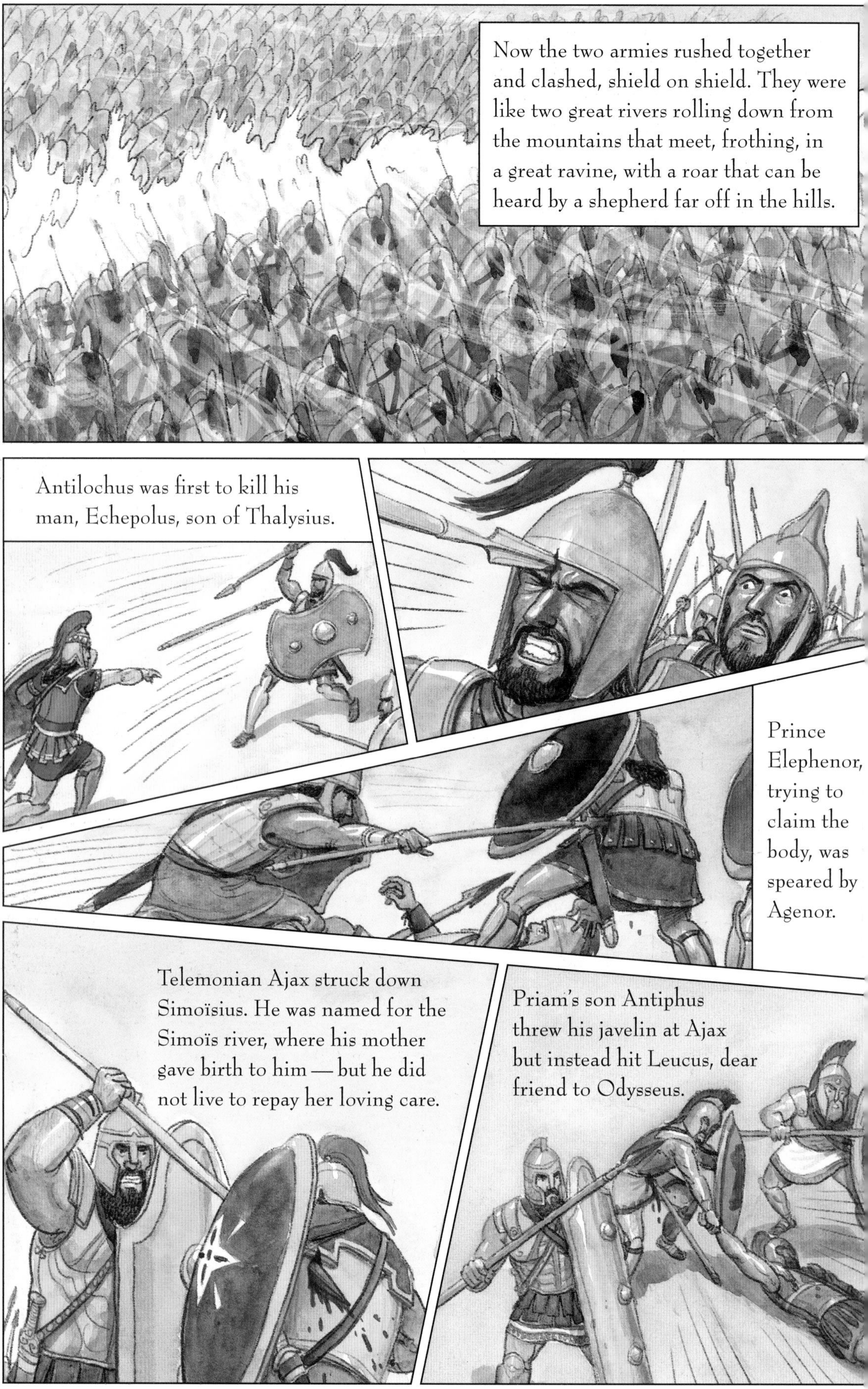
Now the two armies rushed together and clashed, shield on shield. They were like two great rivers rolling down from the mountains that meet, frothing, in a great ravine, with a roar that can be heard by a shepherd far off in the hills.
Antilochus was first to kill his man, Echepolus, son of Thalysius.
Prince Elephenor, trying to claim the body, was speared by Agenor.
Telemonian Ajax struck down Simoïsius. He was named for the Simoïs river, where his mother gave birth to him — but he did not live to repay her loving care.
Priam's son Antiphus threw his javelin at Ajax but instead hit Leucus, dear friend to Odysseus.

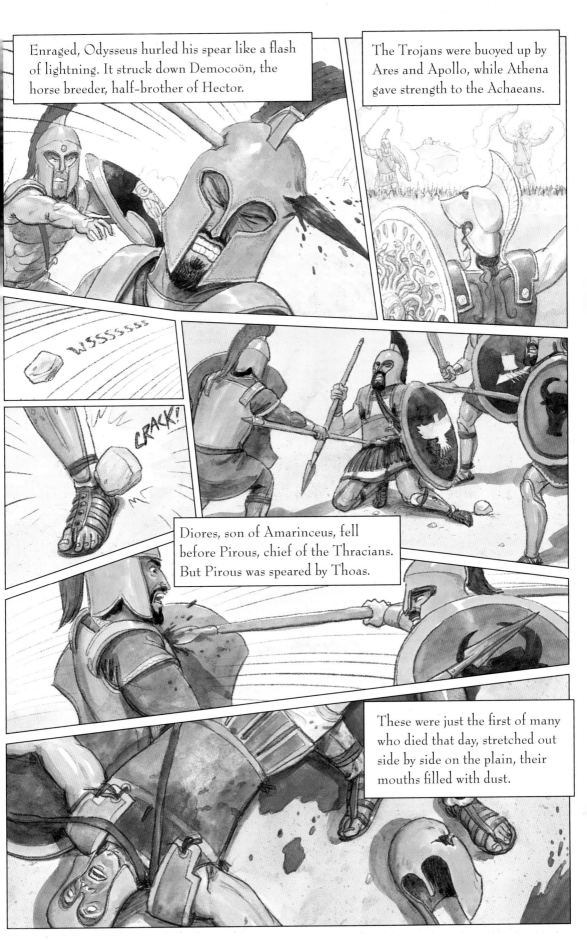

Enraged, Odysseus hurled his spear like a flash of lightning. It struck down Democoön, the horse breeder, half-brother of Hector.

The Trojans were buoyed up by Ares and Apollo, while Athena gave strength to the Achaeans.

WSSSSSS

CRACK!

Diores, son of Amarinceus, fell before Pirous, chief of the Thracians. But Pirous was speared by Thoas.

These were just the first of many who died that day, stretched out side by side on the plain, their mouths filled with dust.

The Achaeans advanced, and Trojans fighters fell:

Phaestus, son of Borus.

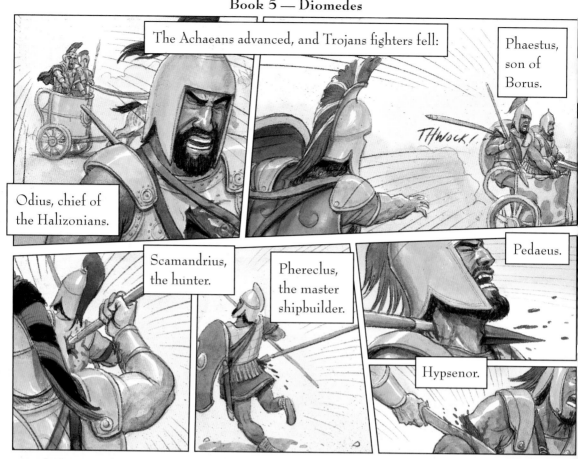

Odius, chief of the Halizonians.

Scamandrius, the hunter.

Phereclus, the master shipbuilder.

Pedaeus.

Hypsenor.

THWOCK!

Athena chose Diomedes, son of Tydeus, for glory that day.

First he killed Phegeus, son of Dares.

He seized Phegeus's fine chariot, and his comrade Sthenelus took the reins.

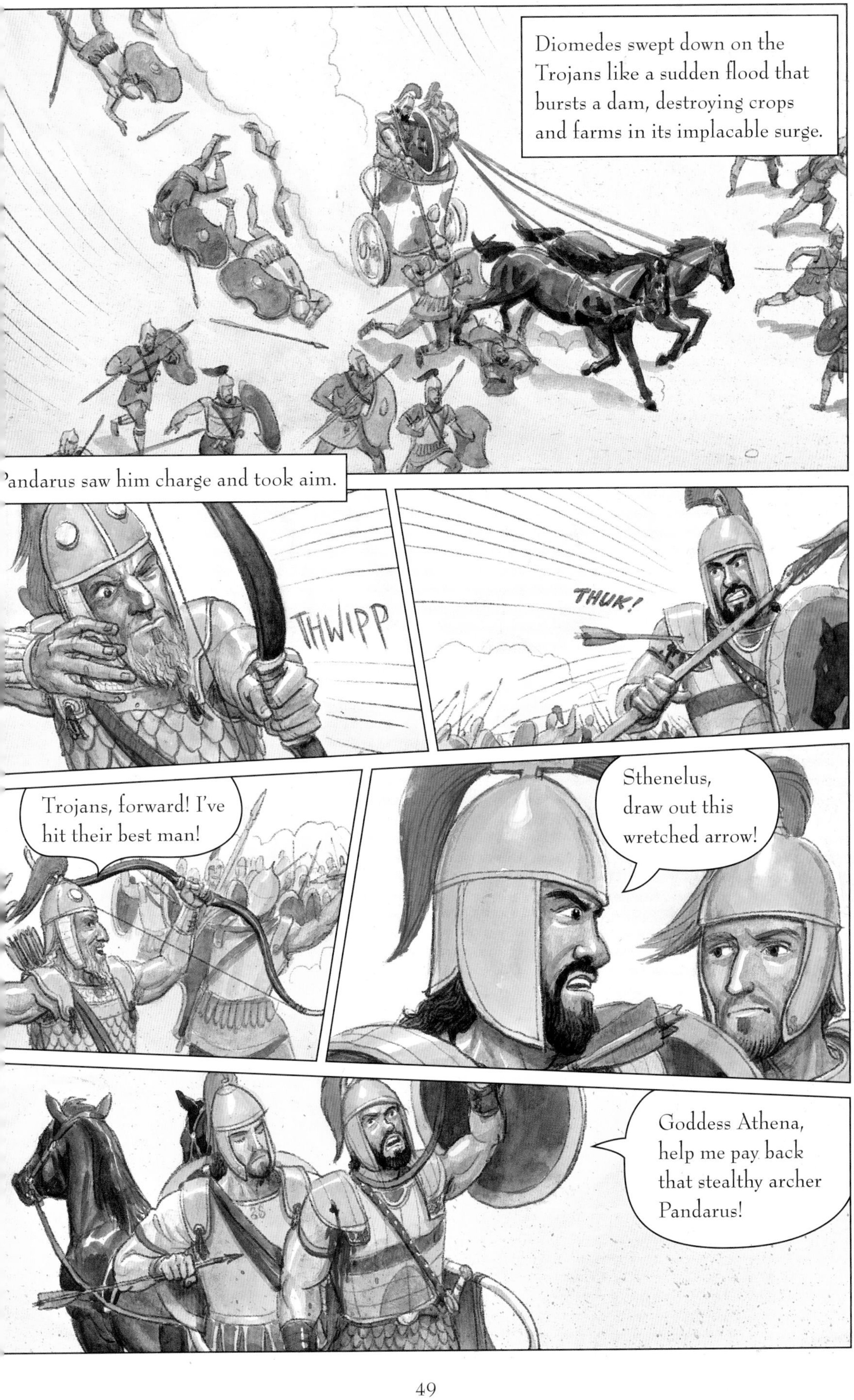
Diomedes swept down on the Trojans like a sudden flood that bursts a dam, destroying crops and farms in its implacable surge.
Pandarus saw him charge and took aim.
THWIPP
THUK!
Trojans, forward! I've hit their best man!
Sthenelus, draw out this wretched arrow!
Goddess Athena, help me pay back that stealthy archer Pandarus!

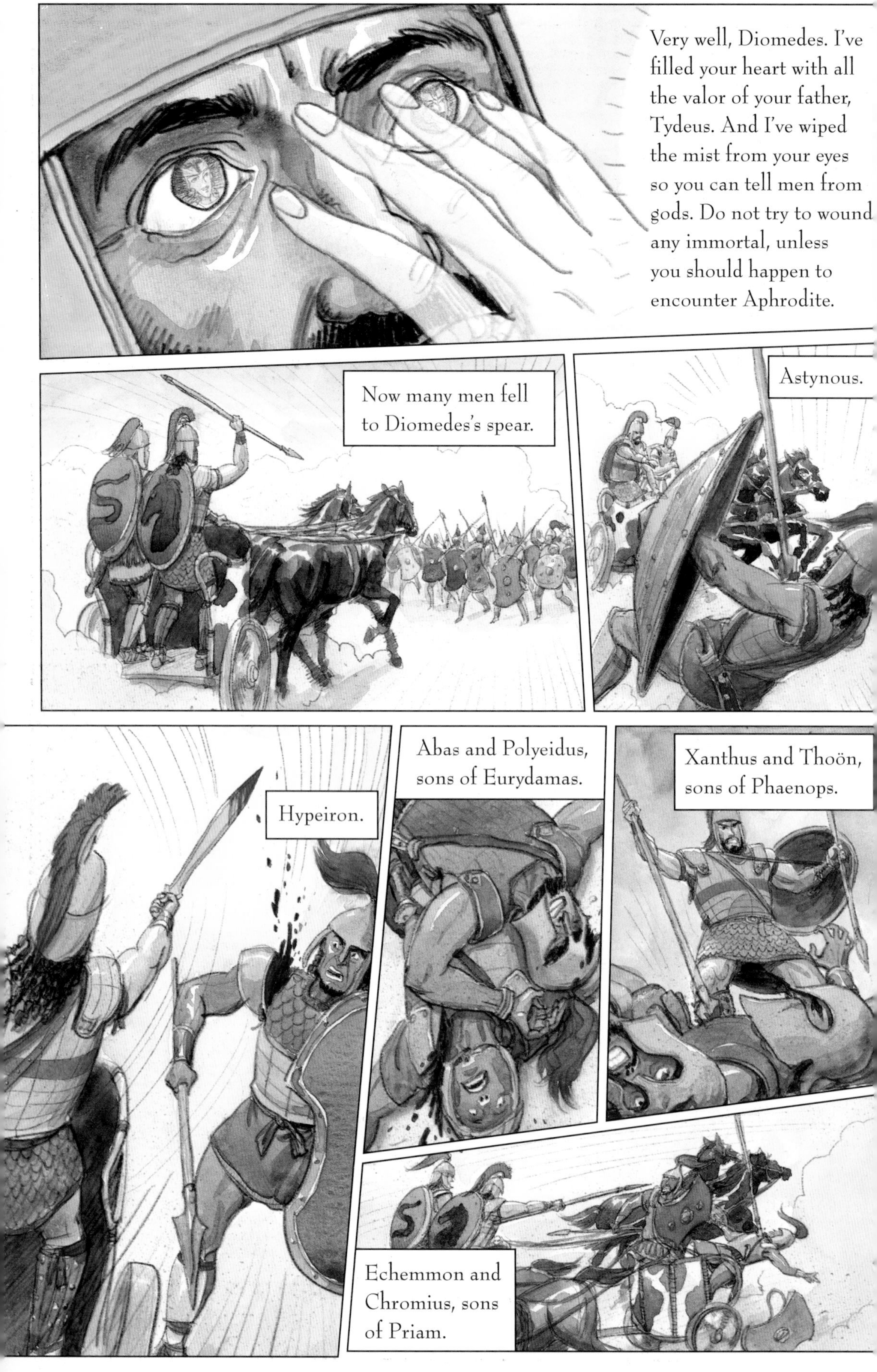
Very well, Diomedes. I've filled your heart with all the valor of your father, Tydeus. And I've wiped the mist from your eyes so you can tell men from gods. Do not try to wound any immortal, unless you should happen to encounter Aphrodite.
Now many men fell to Diomedes's spear.
Astynous.
Hypeiron.
Abas and Polyeidus, sons of Eurydamas.
Xanthus and Thoön, sons of Phaenops.
Echemmon and Chromius, sons of Priam.

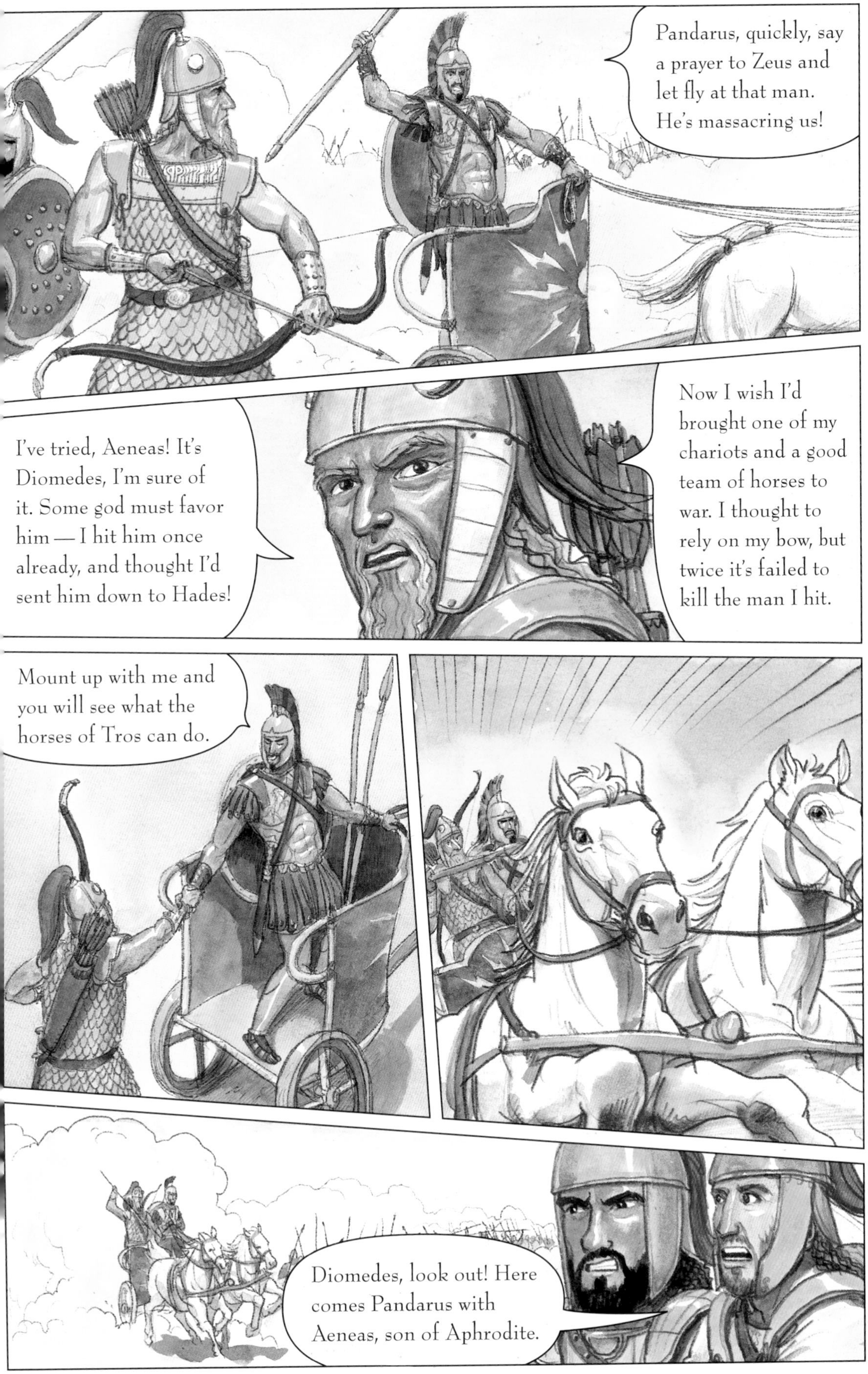

Pandarus, quickly, say a prayer to Zeus and let fly at that man. He's massacring us!
I've tried, Aeneas! It's Diomedes, I'm sure of it. Some god must favor him — I hit him once already, and thought I'd sent him down to Hades!
Now I wish I'd brought one of my chariots and a good team of horses to war. I thought to rely on my bow, but twice it's failed to kill the man I hit.
Mount up with me and you will see what the horses of Tros can do.
Diomedes, look out! Here comes Pandarus with Aeneas, son of Aphrodite.

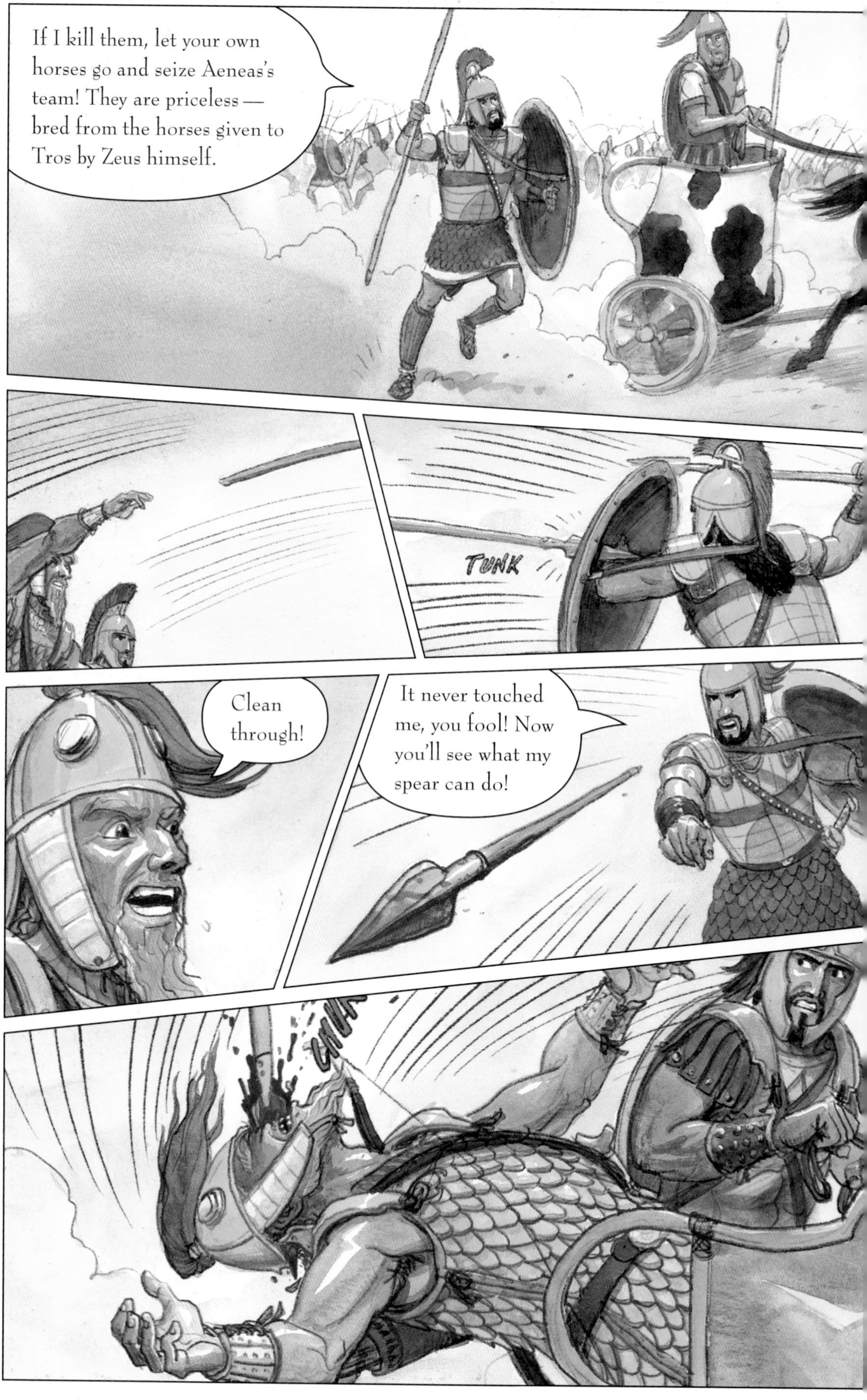
If I kill them, let your own horses go and seize Aeneas's team! They are priceless — bred from the horses given to Tros by Zeus himself.
TUNK
Clean through!
It never touched me, you fool! Now you'll see what my spear can do!

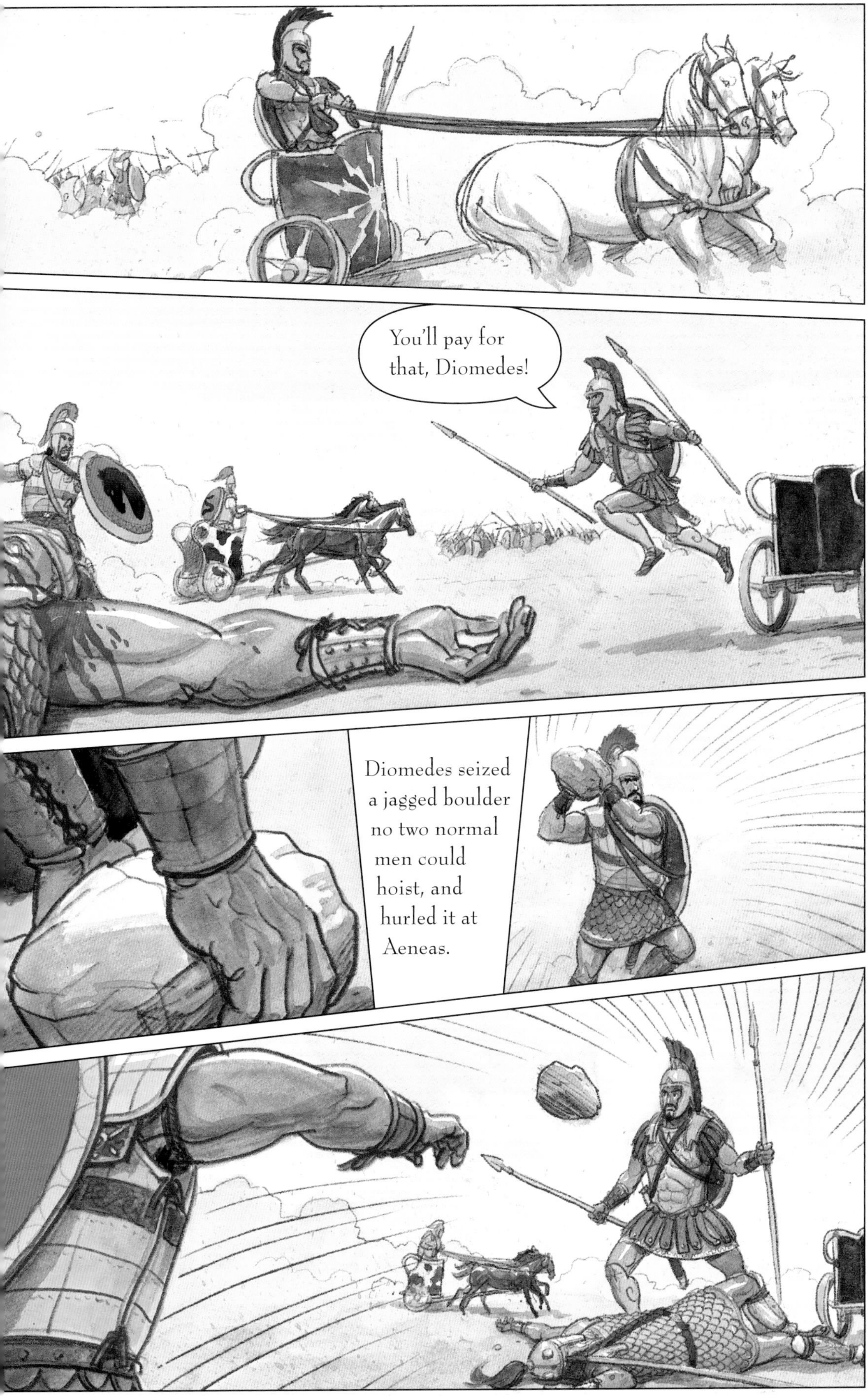
You'll pay for that, Diomedes!
Diomedes seized a jagged boulder no two normal men could hoist, and hurled it at Aeneas.

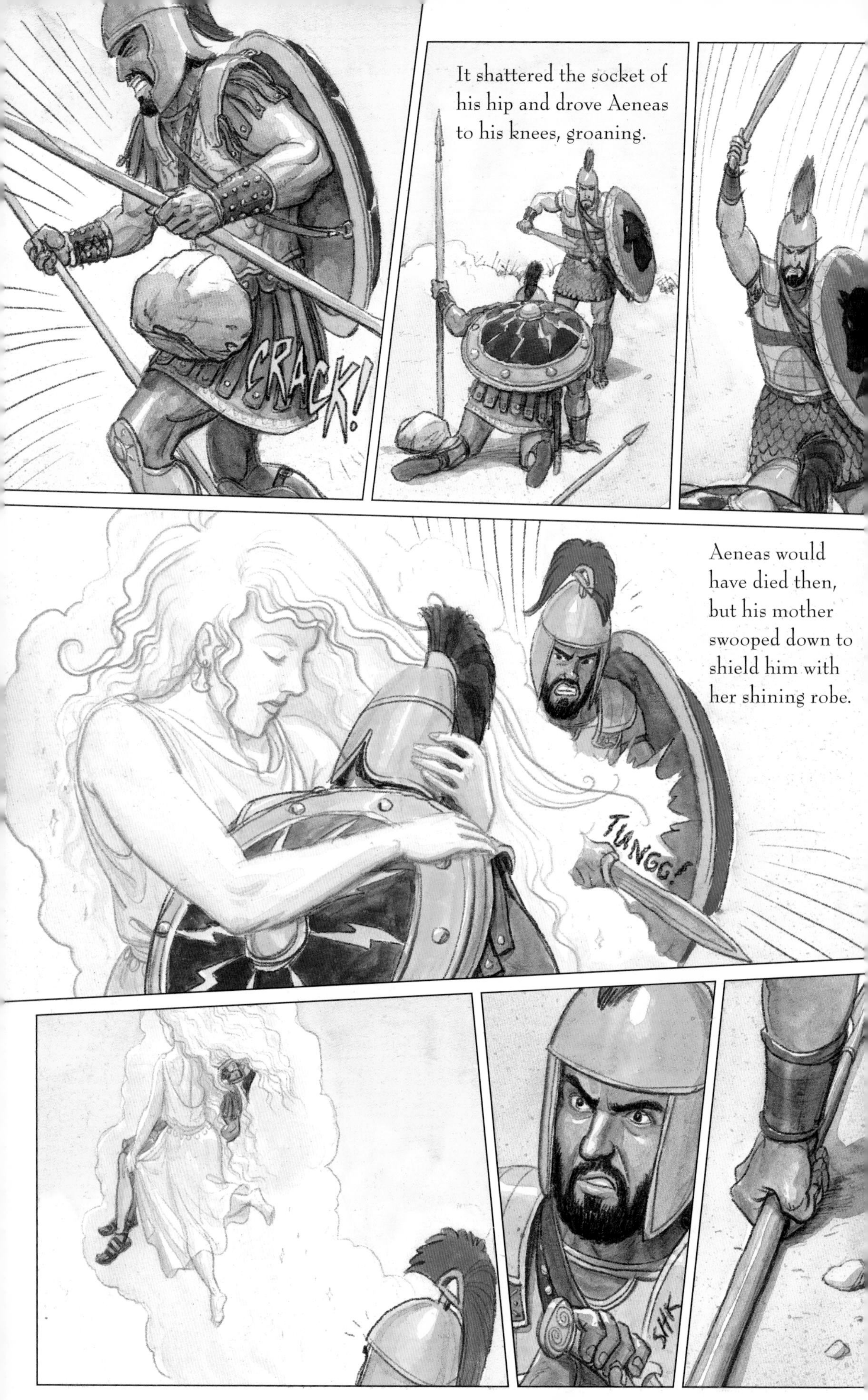
CRACK!
It shattered the socket of his hip and drove Aeneas to his knees, groaning.
Aeneas would have died then, but his mother swooped down to shield him with her shining robe.
TUNGG!
SHK

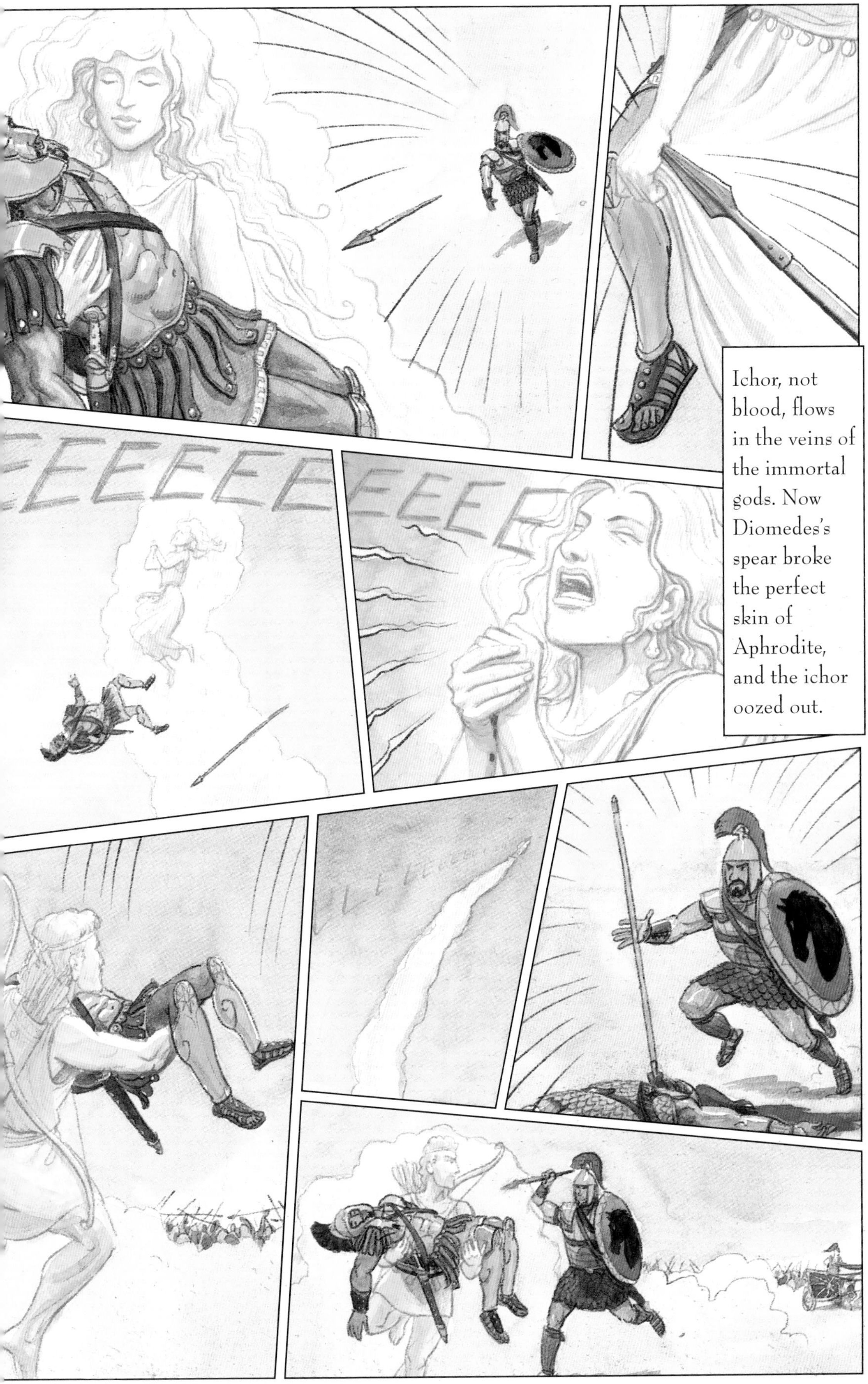
Ichor, not blood, flows in the veins of the immortal gods. Now Diomedes's spear broke the perfect skin of Aphrodite, and the ichor oozed out.

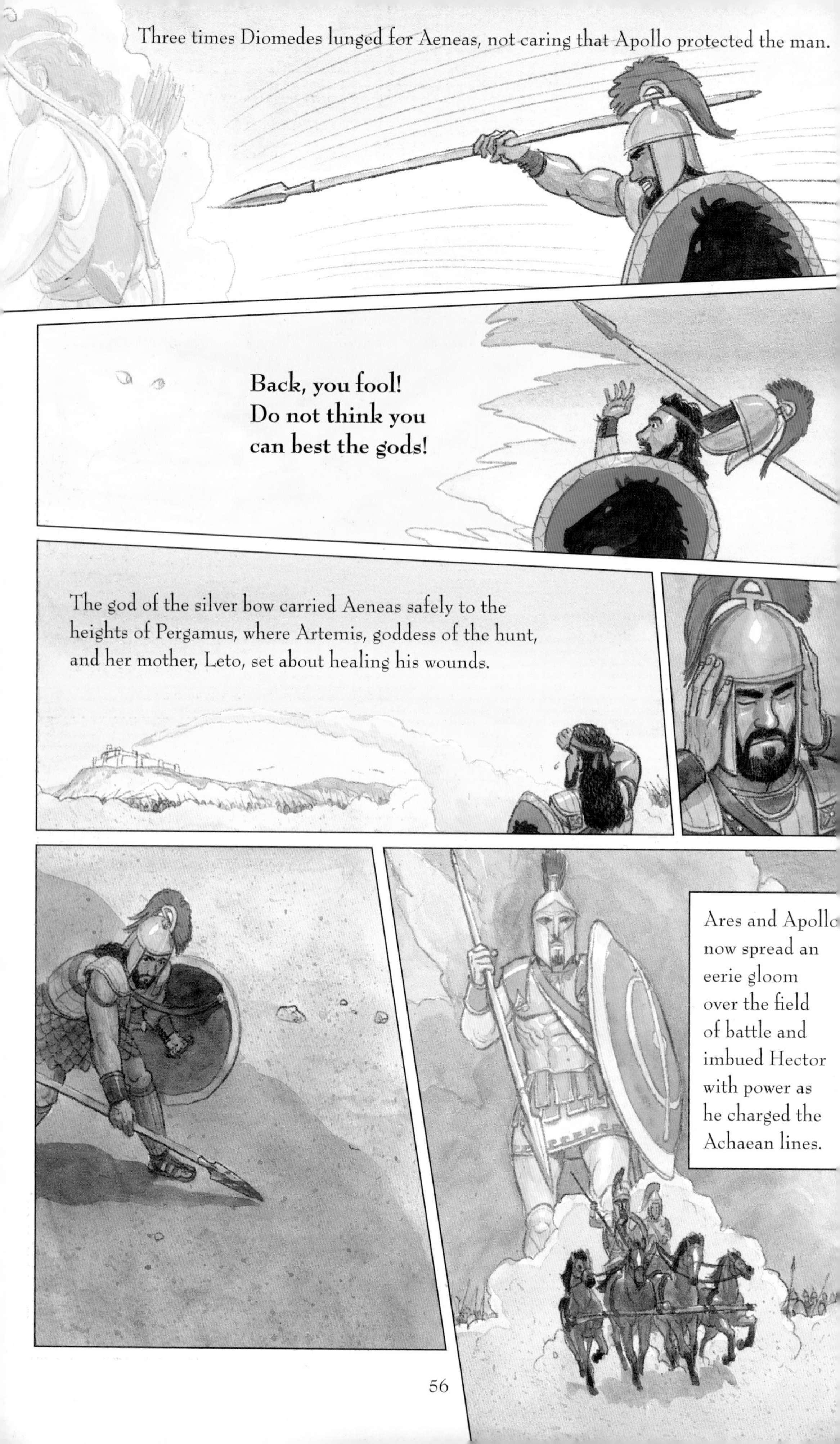
Three times Diomedes lunged for Aeneas, not caring that Apollo protected the man.
Back, you fool! Do not think you can best the gods!
The god of the silver bow carried Aeneas safely to the heights of Pergamus, where Artemis, goddess of the hunt, and her mother, Leto, set about healing his wounds.
Ares and Apollo now spread an eerie gloom over the field of battle and imbued Hector with power as he charged the Achaean lines.

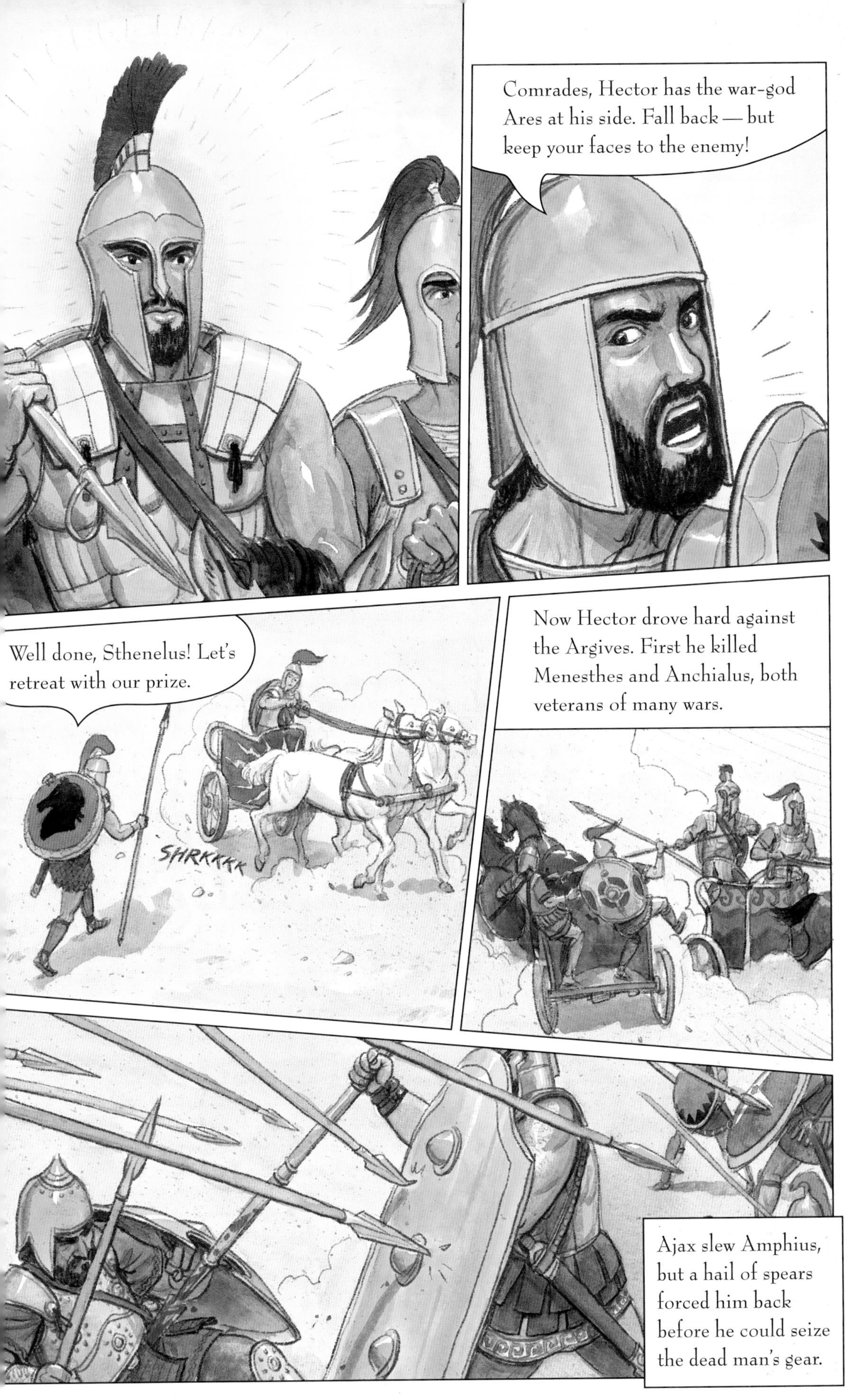
Comrades, Hector has the war-god Ares at his side. Fall back — but keep your faces to the enemy!
Well done, Sthenelus! Let's retreat with our prize.
SHRKKKK
Now Hector drove hard against the Argives. First he killed Menesthes and Anchialus, both veterans of many wars.
Ajax slew Amphius, but a hail of spears forced him back before he could seize the dead man's gear.

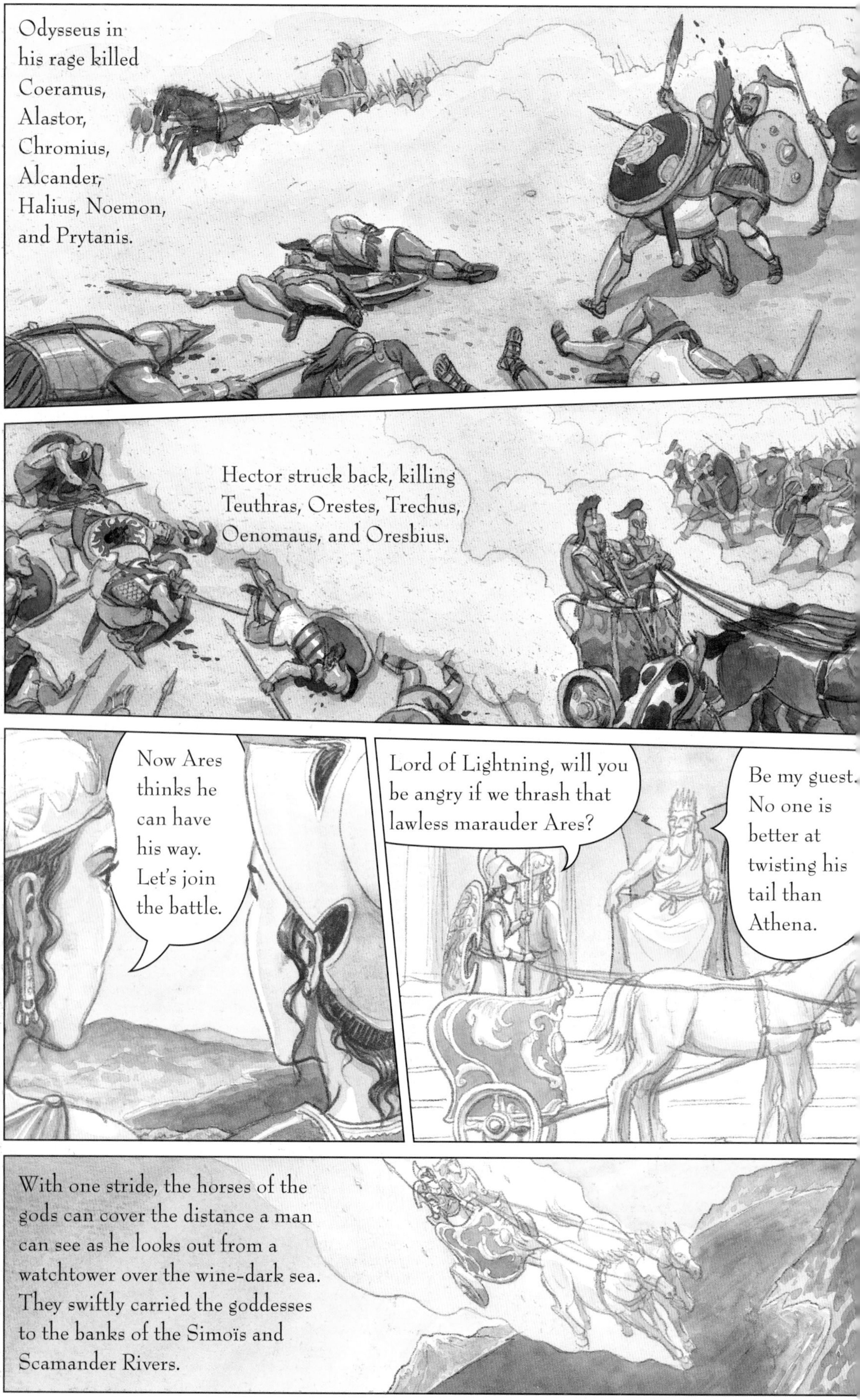
Odysseus in his rage killed Coeranus, Alastor, Chromius, Alcander, Halius, Noemon, and Prytanis.
Hector struck back, killing Teuthras, Orestes, Trechus, Oenomaus, and Oresbius.
Now Ares thinks he can have his way. Let's join the battle.
Lord of Lightning, will you be angry if we thrash that lawless marauder Ares?
Be my guest. No one is better at twisting his tail than Athena.
With one stride, the horses of the gods can cover the distance a man can see as he looks out from a watchtower over the wine-dark sea. They swiftly carried the goddesses to the banks of the Simoïs and Scamander Rivers.

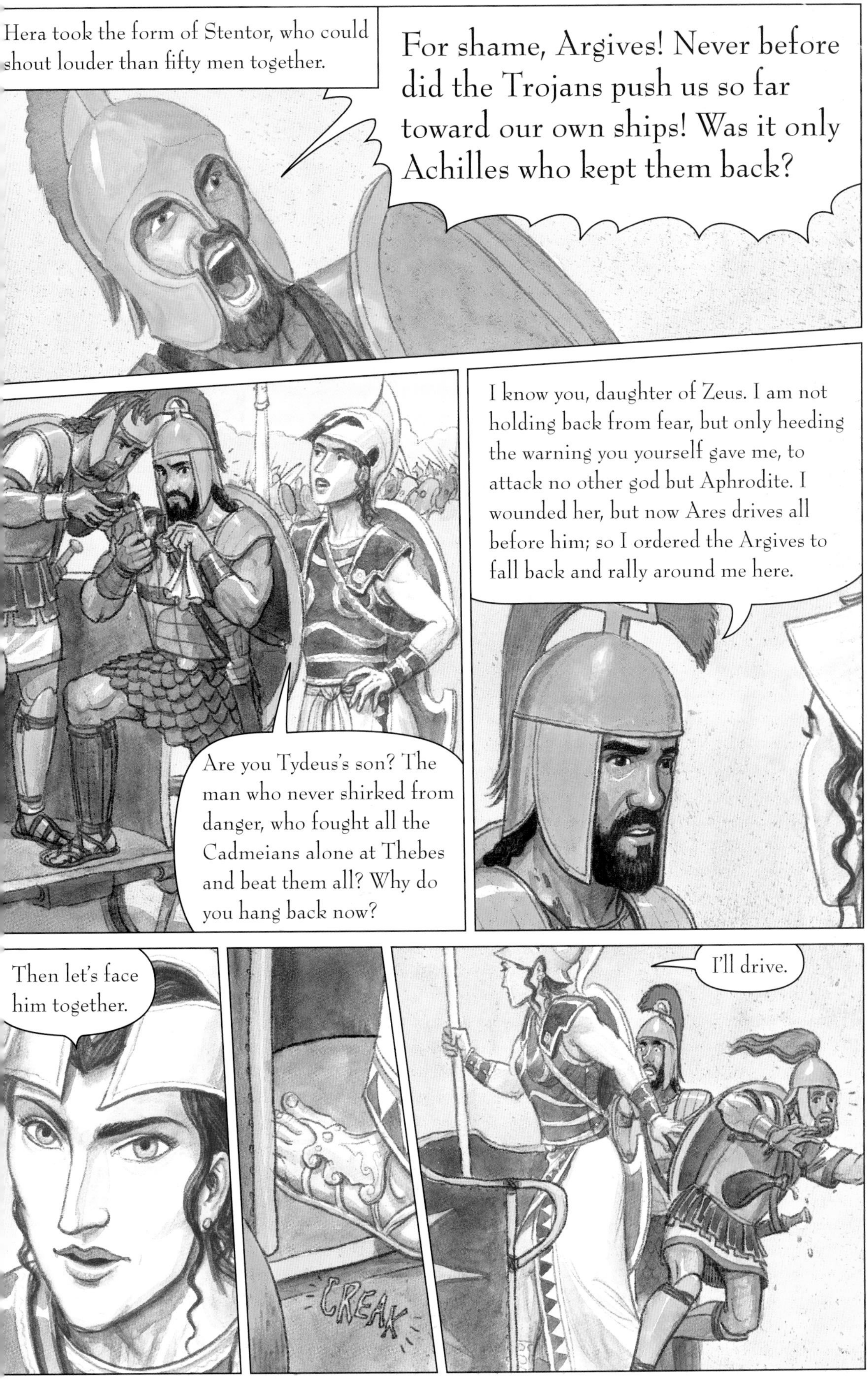
Hera took the form of Stentor, who could shout louder than fifty men together.
For shame, Argives! Never before did the Trojans push us so far toward our own ships! Was it only Achilles who kept them back?
Are you Tydeus's son? The man who never shirked from danger, who fought all the Cadmeians alone at Thebes and beat them all? Why do you hang back now?
I know you, daughter of Zeus. I am not holding back from fear, but only heeding the warning you yourself gave me, to attack no other god but Aphrodite. I wounded her, but now Ares drives all before him; so I ordered the Argives to fall back and rally around me here.
Then let's face him together.
CREAK
I'll drive.

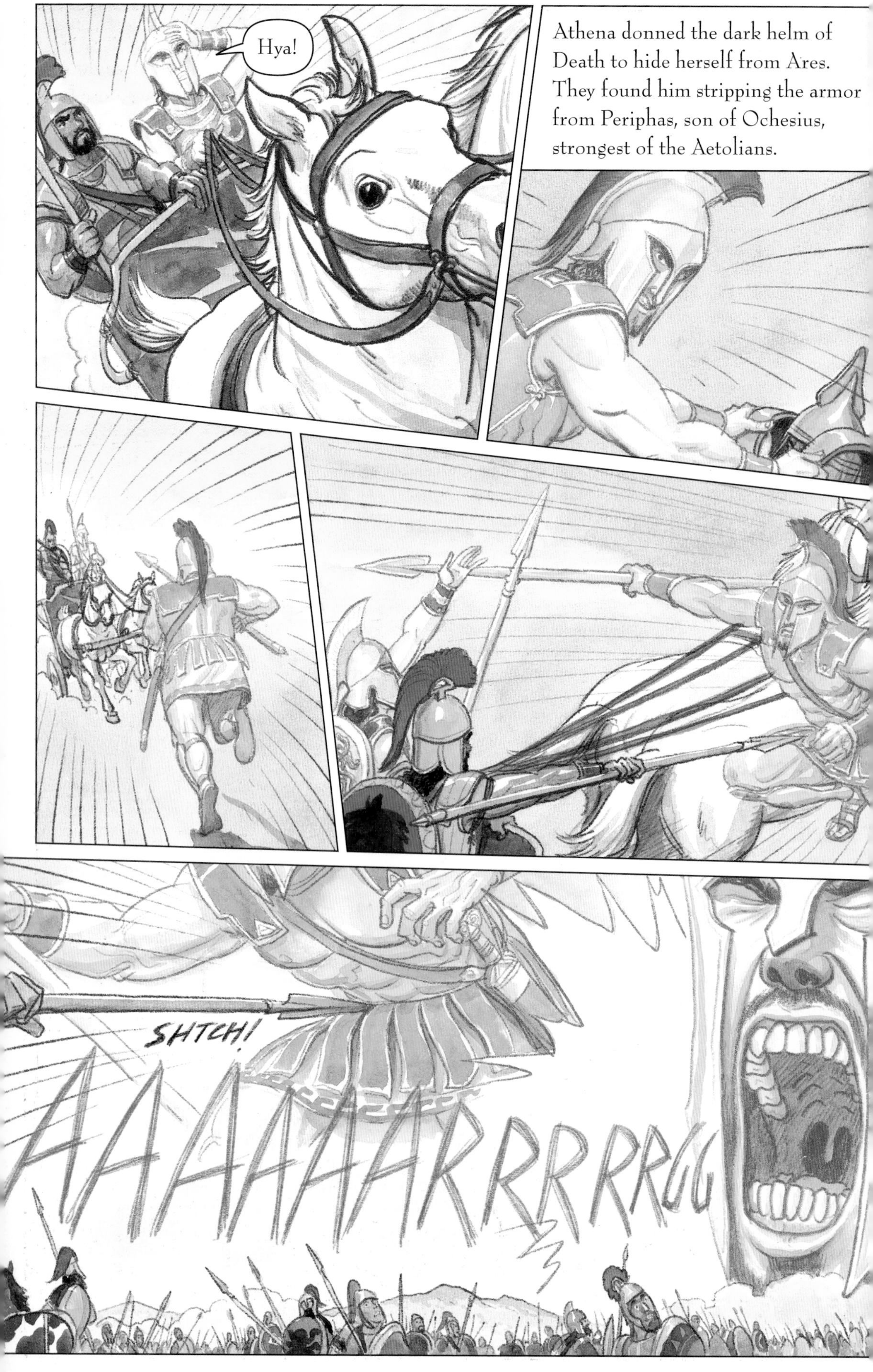
Hya!
Athena donned the dark helm of Death to hide herself from Ares. They found him stripping the armor from Periphas, son of Ochesius, strongest of the Aetolians.
SHTCH!
AAAAAARRRRRGG

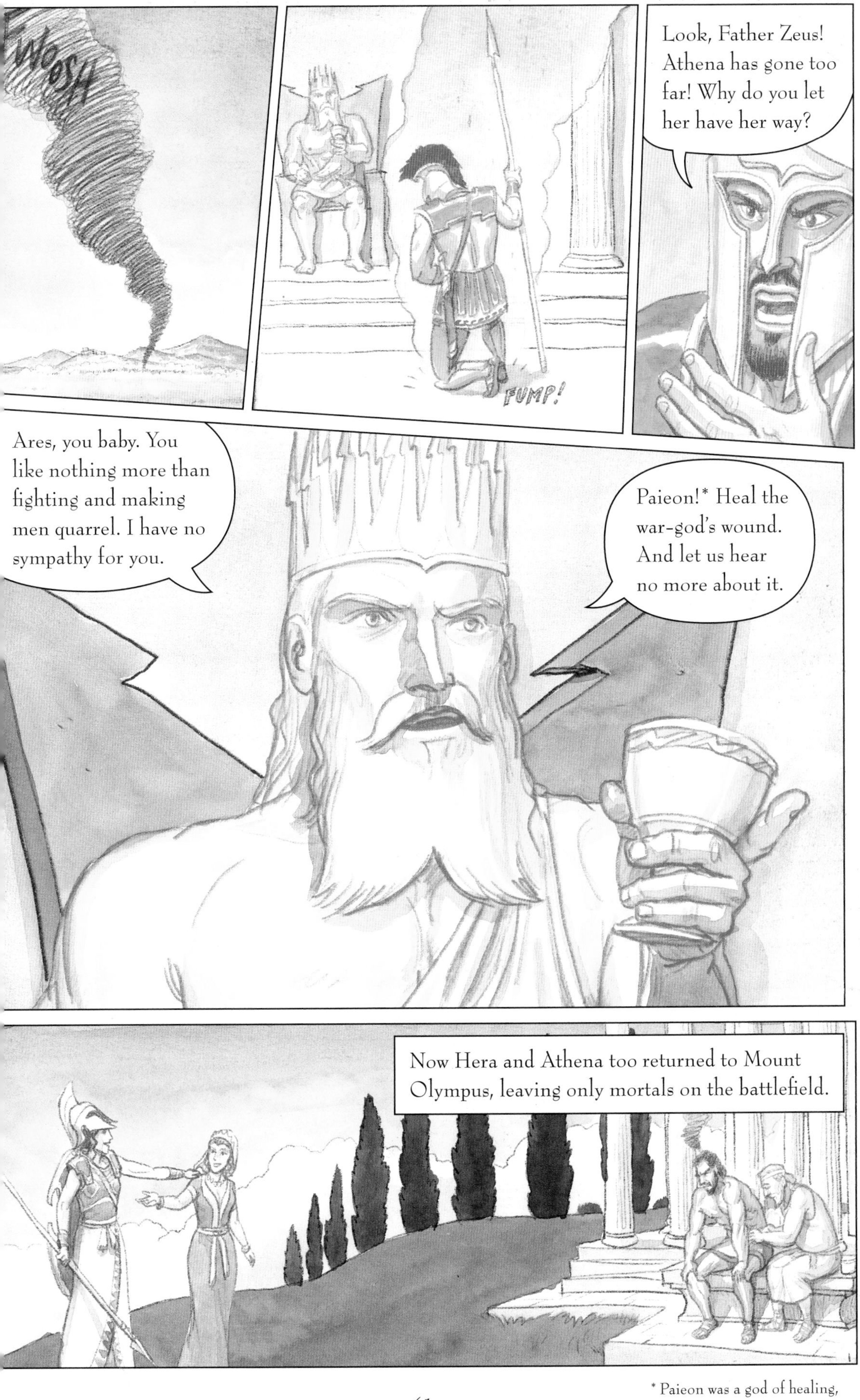
WOOSH
FUMP!
Look, Father Zeus! Athena has gone too far! Why do you let her have her way?
Ares, you baby. You like nothing more than fighting and making men quarrel. I have no sympathy for you.
Paieon!* Heal the war-god's wound. And let us hear no more about it.
Now Hera and Athena too returned to Mount Olympus, leaving only mortals on the battlefield.

* Paieon was a god of healing, rarely named in Greek myth.

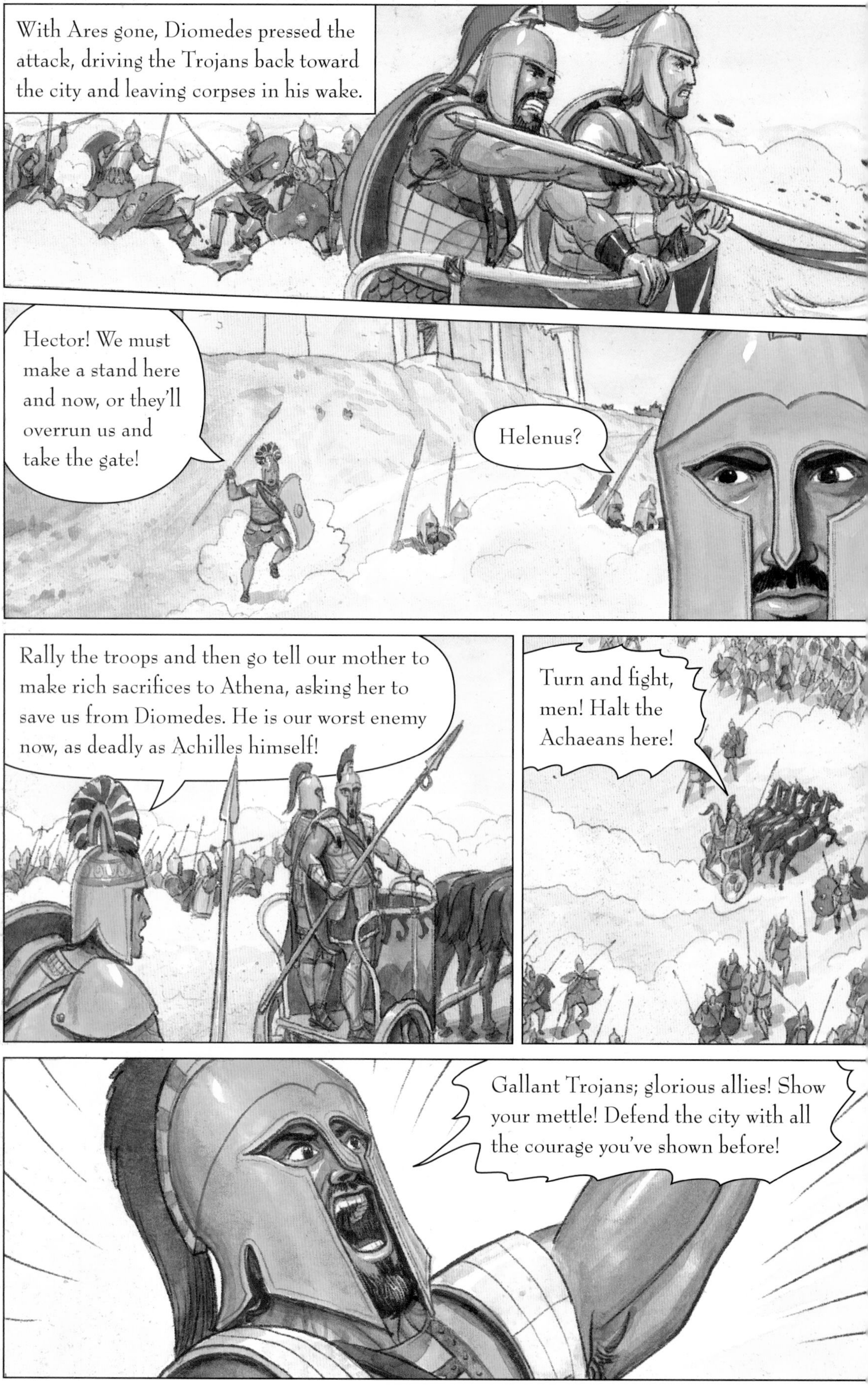
With Ares gone, Diomedes pressed the attack, driving the Trojans back toward the city and leaving corpses in his wake.
Hector! We must make a stand here and now, or they'll overrun us and take the gate!
Helenus?
Rally the troops and then go tell our mother to make rich sacrifices to Athena, asking her to save us from Diomedes. He is our worst enemy now, as deadly as Achilles himself!
Turn and fight, men! Halt the Achaeans here!
Gallant Trojans; glorious allies! Show your mettle! Defend the city with all the courage you've shown before!

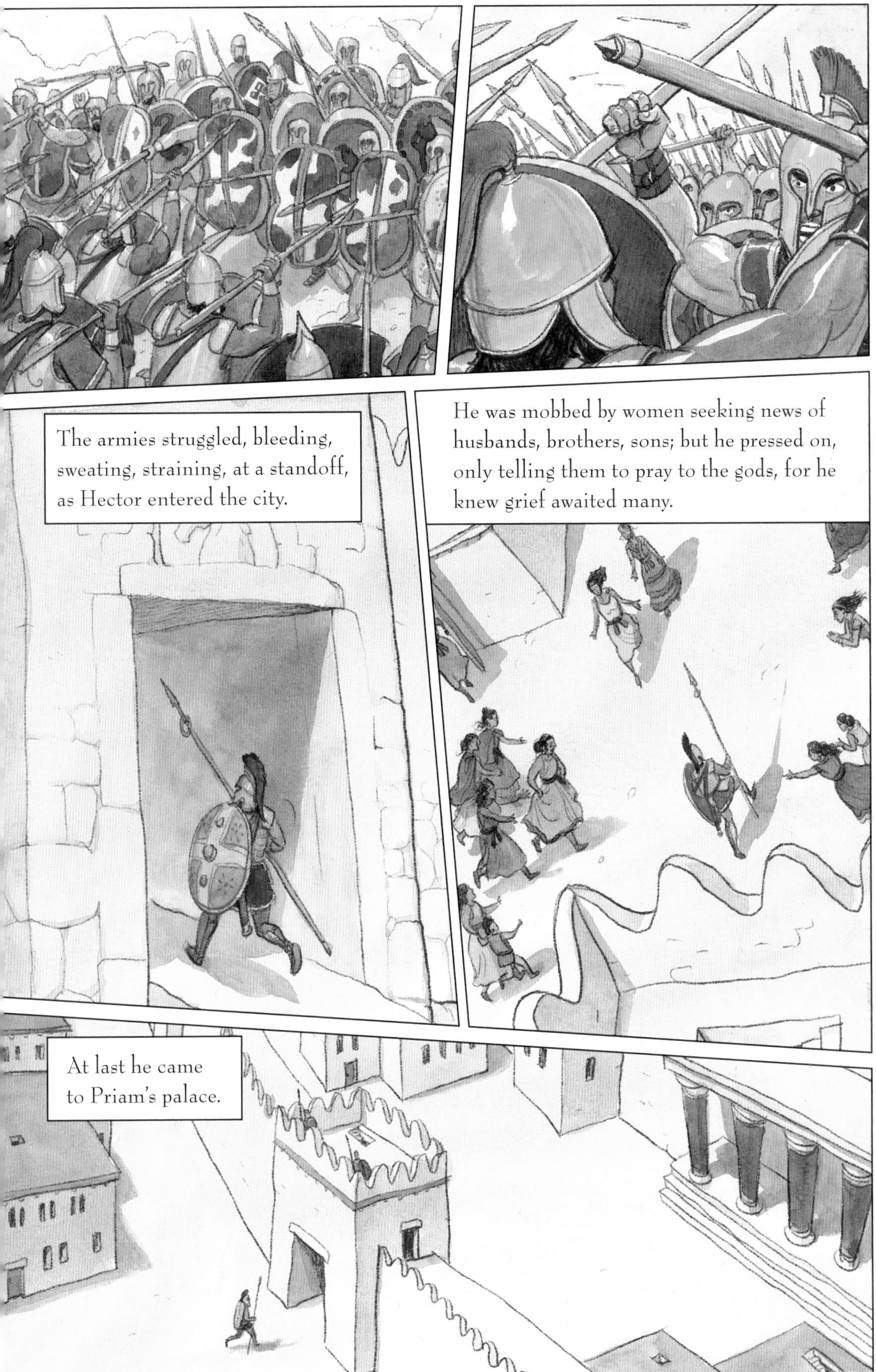
The armies struggled, bleeding, sweating, straining, at a standoff, as Hector entered the city.
He was mobbed by women seeking news of husbands, brothers, sons; but he pressed on, only telling them to pray to the gods, for he knew grief awaited many.
At last he came to Priam's palace.

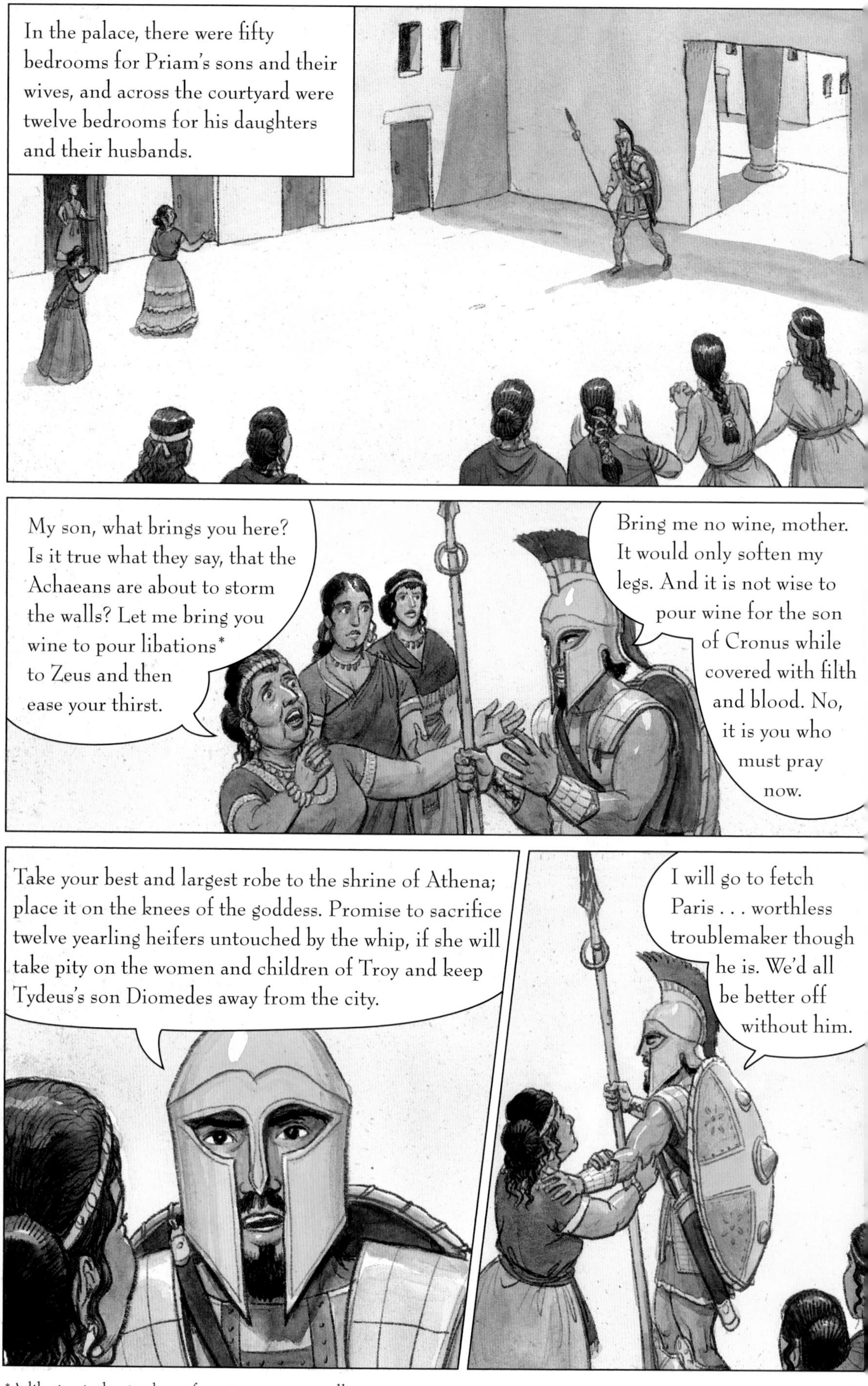
In the palace, there were fifty bedrooms for Priam's sons and their wives, and across the courtyard were twelve bedrooms for his daughters and their husbands.
My son, what brings you here? Is it true what they say, that the Achaeans are about to storm the walls? Let me bring you wine to pour libations* to Zeus and then ease your thirst.
Bring me no wine, mother. It would only soften my legs. And it is not wise to pour wine for the son of Cronus while covered with filth and blood. No, it is you who must pray now.
Take your best and largest robe to the shrine of Athena; place it on the knees of the goddess. Promise to sacrifice twelve yearling heifers untouched by the whip, if she will take pity on the women and children of Troy and keep Tydeus's son Diomedes away from the city.
I will go to fetch Paris . . . worthless troublemaker though he is. We'd all be better off without him.

*A libation is the ritual act of pouring out part or all of a beverage, usually wine, as a sacrifice to a deity.

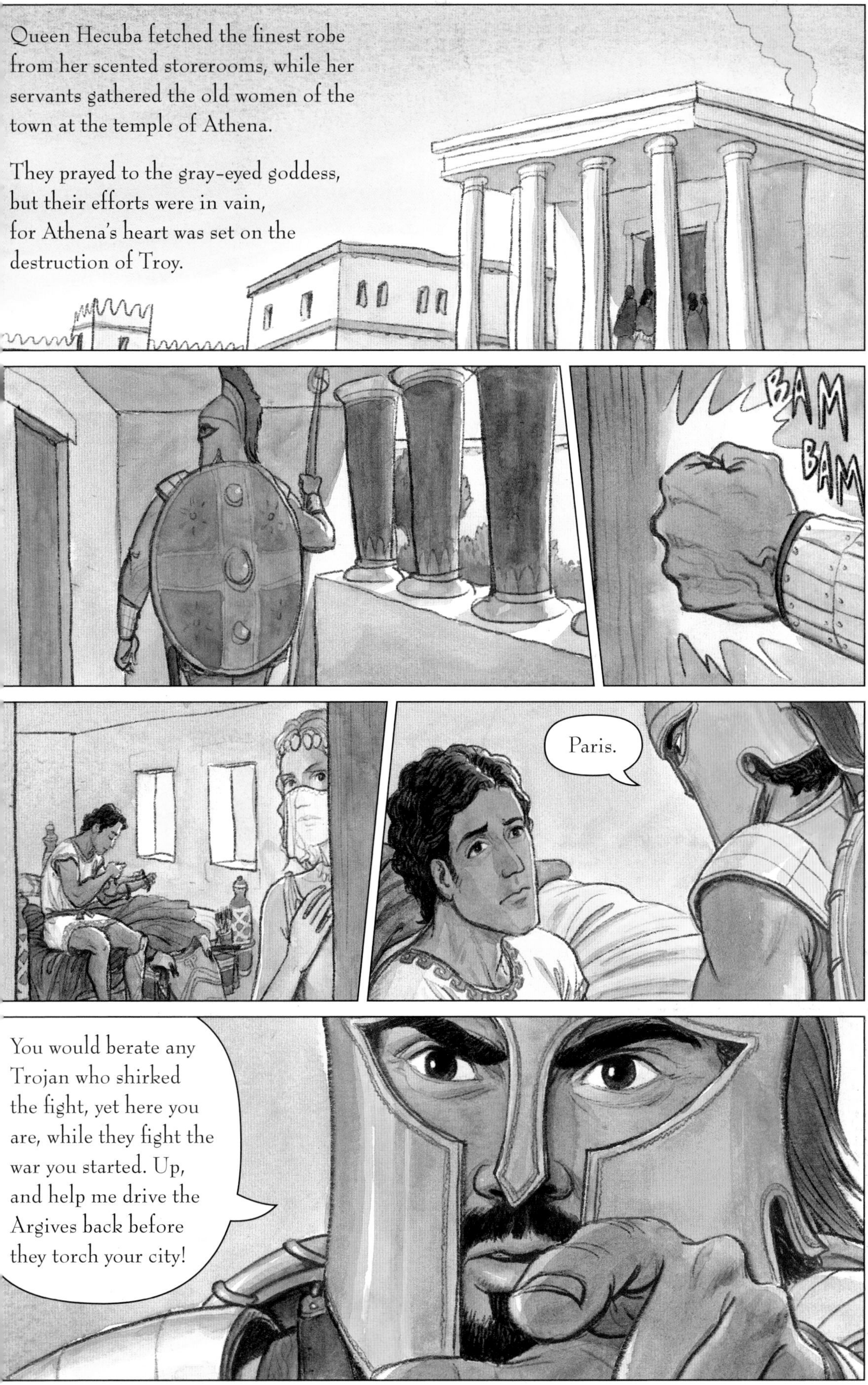
Queen Hecuba fetched the finest robe from her scented storerooms, while her servants gathered the old women of the town at the temple of Athena.
They prayed to the gray-eyed goddess, but their efforts were in vain, for Athena's heart was set on the destruction of Troy.
BAM
BAM
Paris.
You would berate any Trojan who shirked the fight, yet here you are, while they fight the war you started. Up, and help me drive the Argives back before they torch your city!

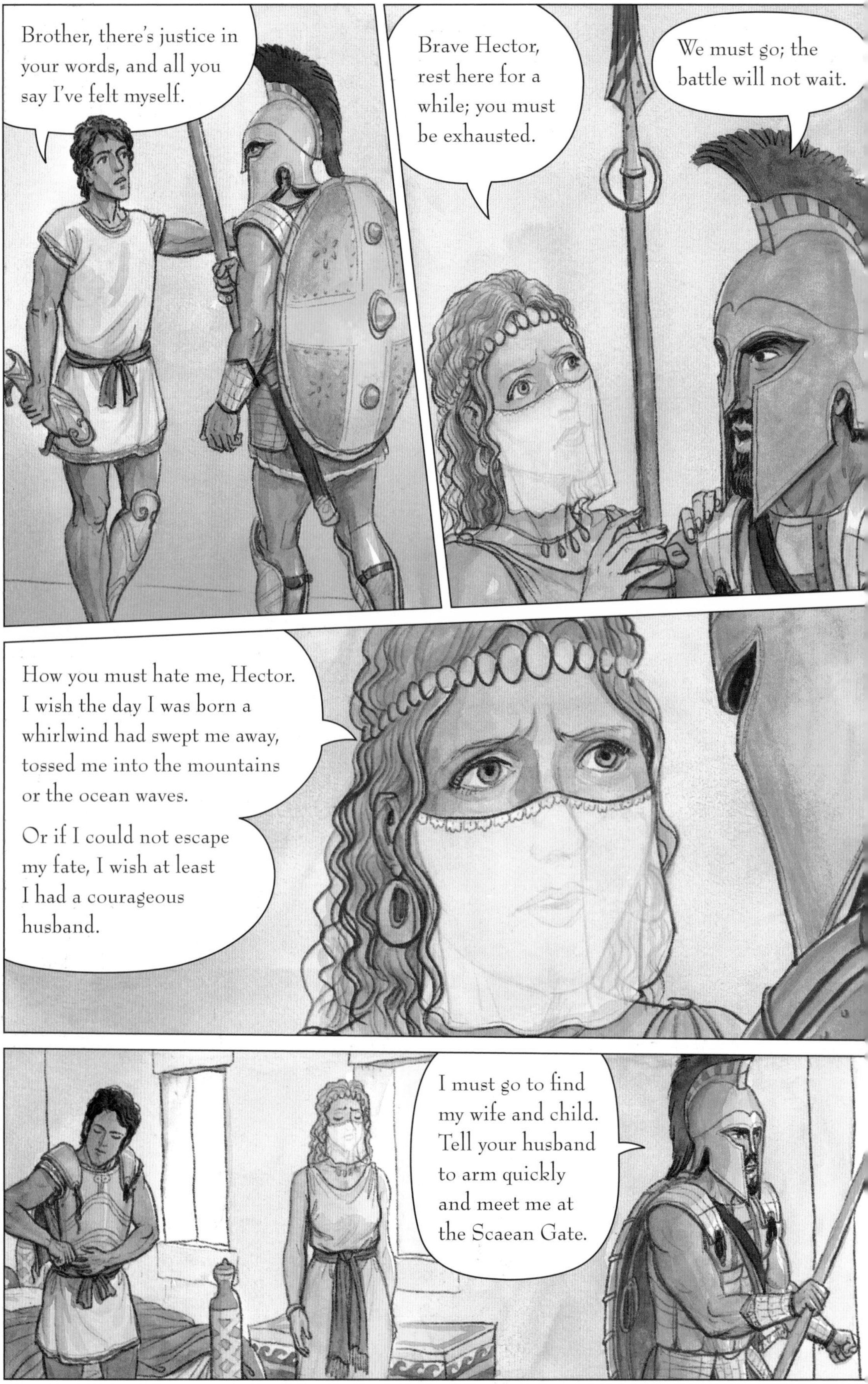
Brother, there's justice in your words, and all you say I've felt myself.
Brave Hector, rest here for a while; you must be exhausted.
We must go; the battle will not wait.
How you must hate me, Hector. I wish the day I was born a whirlwind had swept me away, tossed me into the mountains or the ocean waves.
Or if I could not escape my fate, I wish at least I had a courageous husband.
I must go to find my wife and child. Tell your husband to arm quickly and meet me at the Scaean Gate.

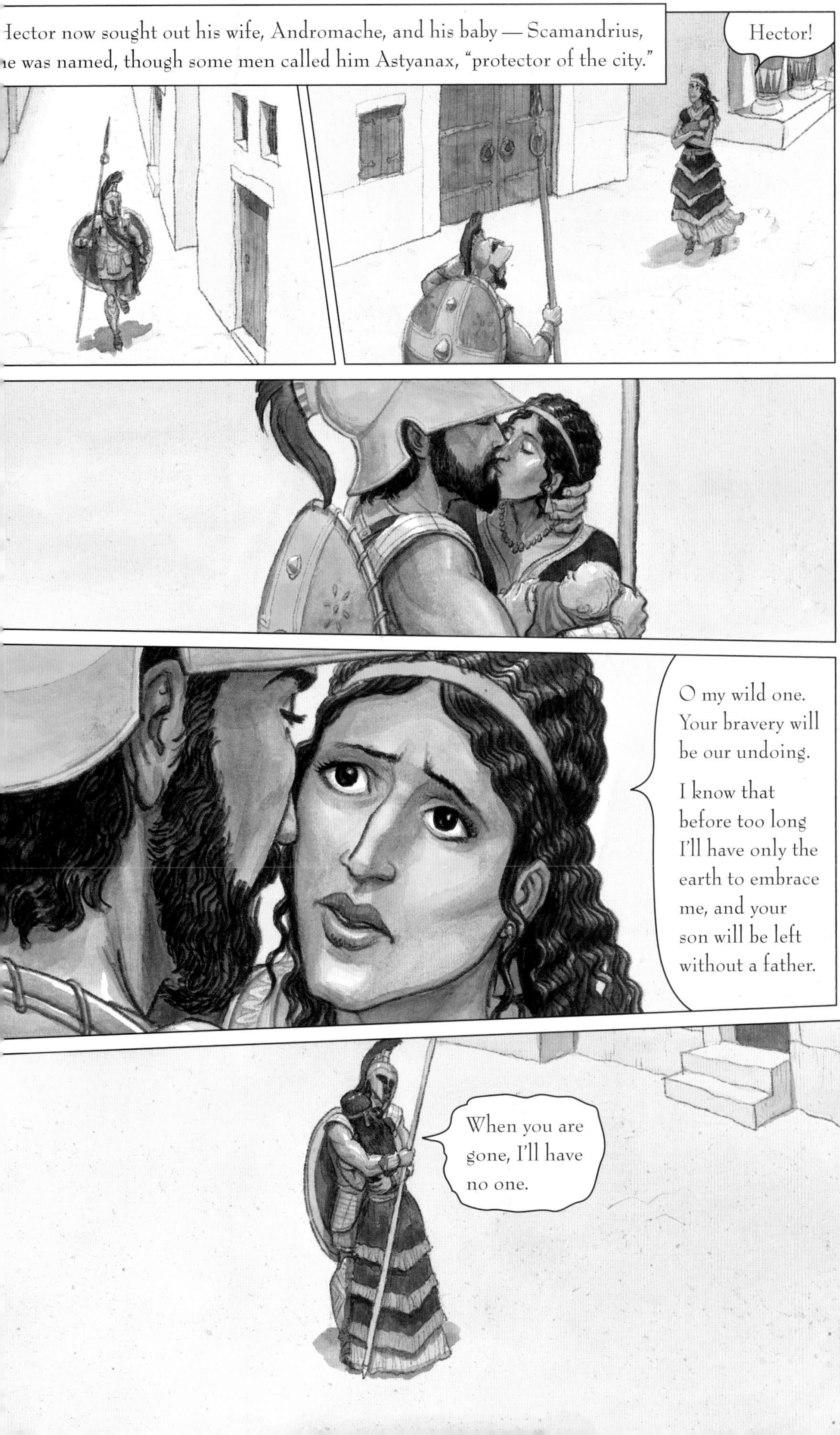
ector now sought out his wife, Andromache, and his baby — Scamandrius,
e was named, though some men called him Astyanax, "protector of the city."
Hector!
O my wild one. Your bravery will be our undoing.
I know that before too long I'll have only the earth to embrace me, and your son will be left without a father.
When you are gone, I'll have no one.

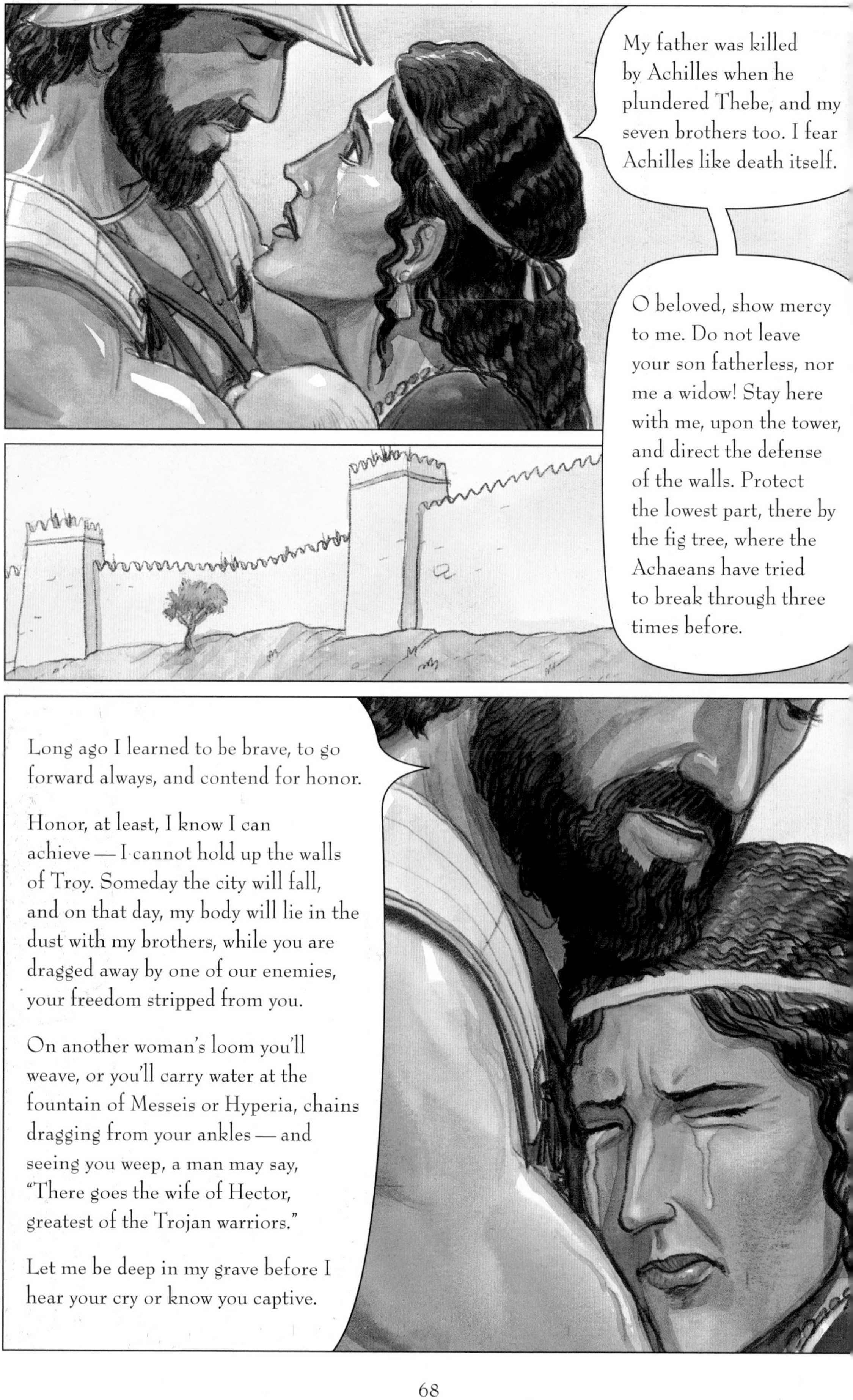

My father was killed by Achilles when he plundered Thebe, and my seven brothers too. I fear Achilles like death itself.
O beloved, show mercy to me. Do not leave your son fatherless, nor me a widow! Stay here with me, upon the tower, and direct the defense of the walls. Protect the lowest part, there by the fig tree, where the Achaeans have tried to break through three times before.
Long ago I learned to be brave, to go forward always, and contend for honor.
Honor, at least, I know I can achieve — I cannot hold up the walls of Troy. Someday the city will fall, and on that day, my body will lie in the dust with my brothers, while you are dragged away by one of our enemies, your freedom stripped from you.
On another woman's loom you'll weave, or you'll carry water at the fountain of Messeis or Hyperia, chains dragging from your ankles — and seeing you weep, a man may say, "There goes the wife of Hector, greatest of the Trojan warriors."
Let me be deep in my grave before I hear your cry or know you captive.

WAAAAAH!

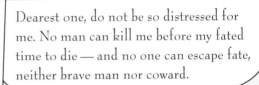

My helm frightens him.

Great Zeus, and all the gods above, may this child, my son, grow strong and brave. May he triumph in war, and rule in power here in Ilium, that someday men shall say, "He is far greater than his father!"

Dearest one, do not be so distressed for me. No man can kill me before my fated time to die — and no one can escape fate, neither brave man nor coward.

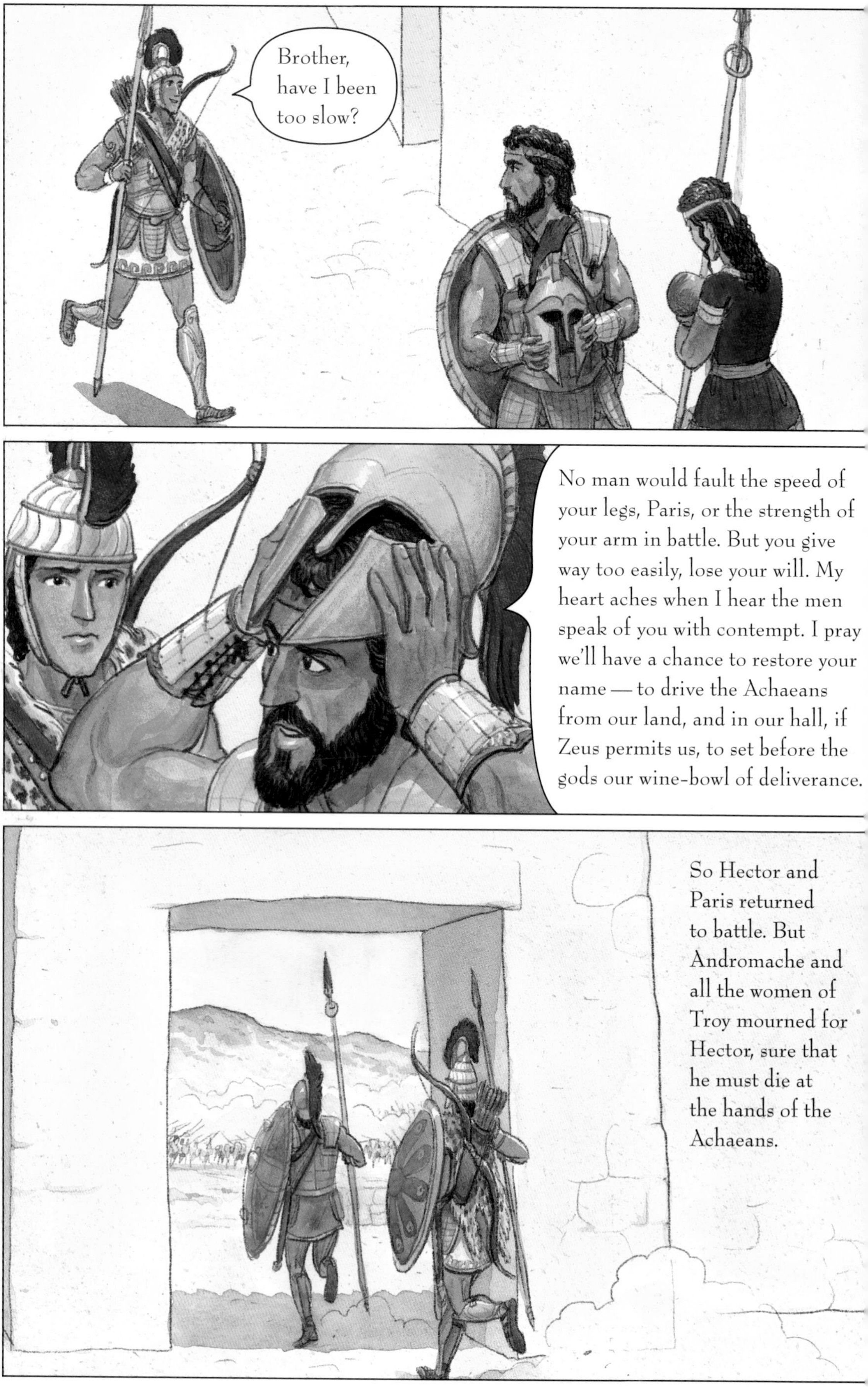
Brother, have I been too slow?
No man would fault the speed of your legs, Paris, or the strength of your arm in battle. But you give way too easily, lose your will. My heart aches when I hear the men speak of you with contempt. I pray we'll have a chance to restore your name — to drive the Achaeans from our land, and in our hall, if Zeus permits us, to set before the gods our wine-bowl of deliverance.
So Hector and Paris returned to battle. But Andromache and all the women of Troy mourned for Hector, sure that he must die at the hands of the Achaeans.

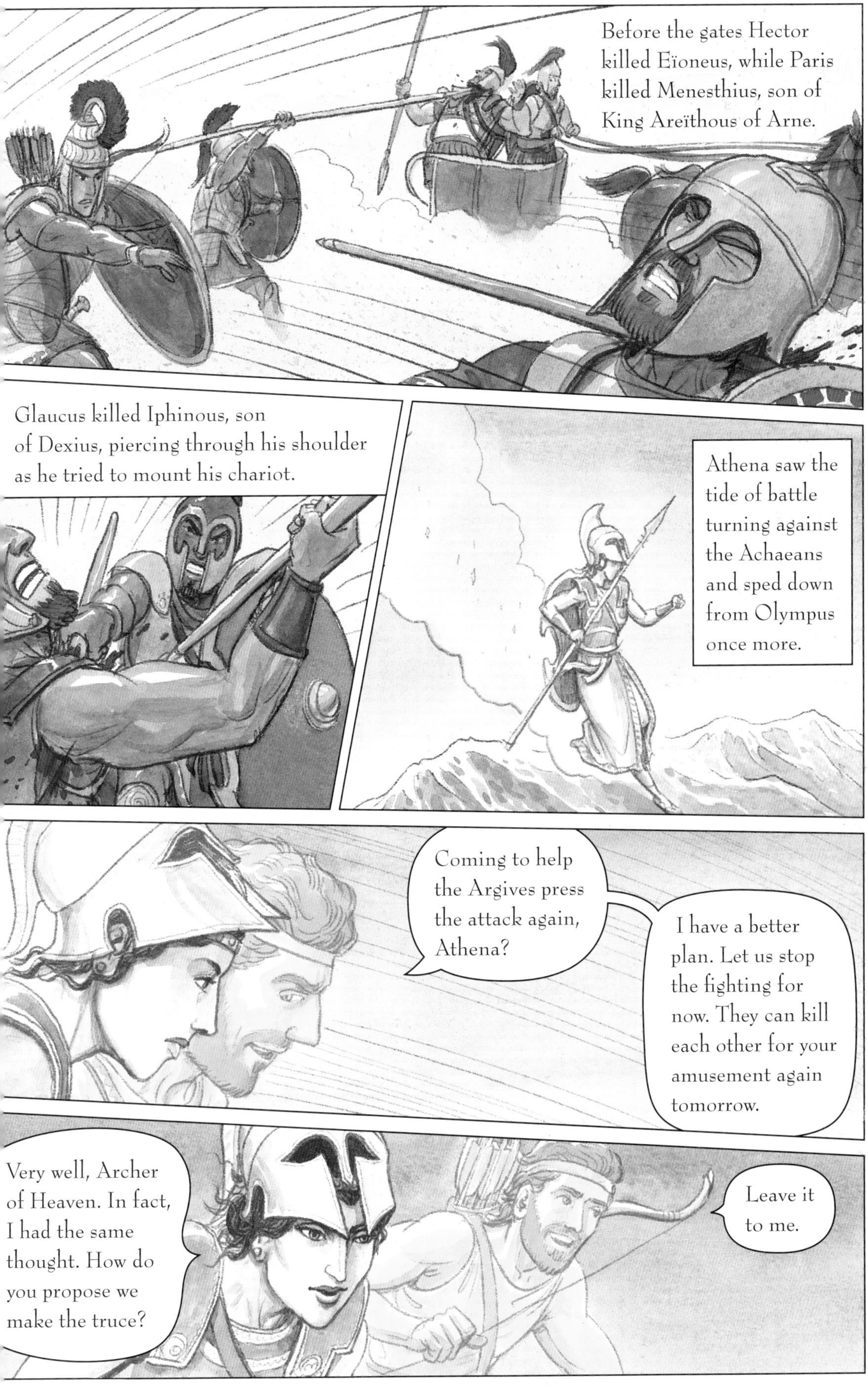
Before the gates Hector killed Eïoneus, while Paris killed Menesthius, son of King Areïthous of Arne.
Glaucus killed Iphinous, son of Dexius, piercing through his shoulder as he tried to mount his chariot.
Athena saw the tide of battle turning against the Achaeans and sped down from Olympus once more.
Coming to help the Argives press the attack again, Athena?
I have a better plan. Let us stop the fighting for now. They can kill each other for your amusement again tomorrow.
Very well, Archer of Heaven. In fact, I had the same thought. How do you propose we make the truce?
Leave it to me.

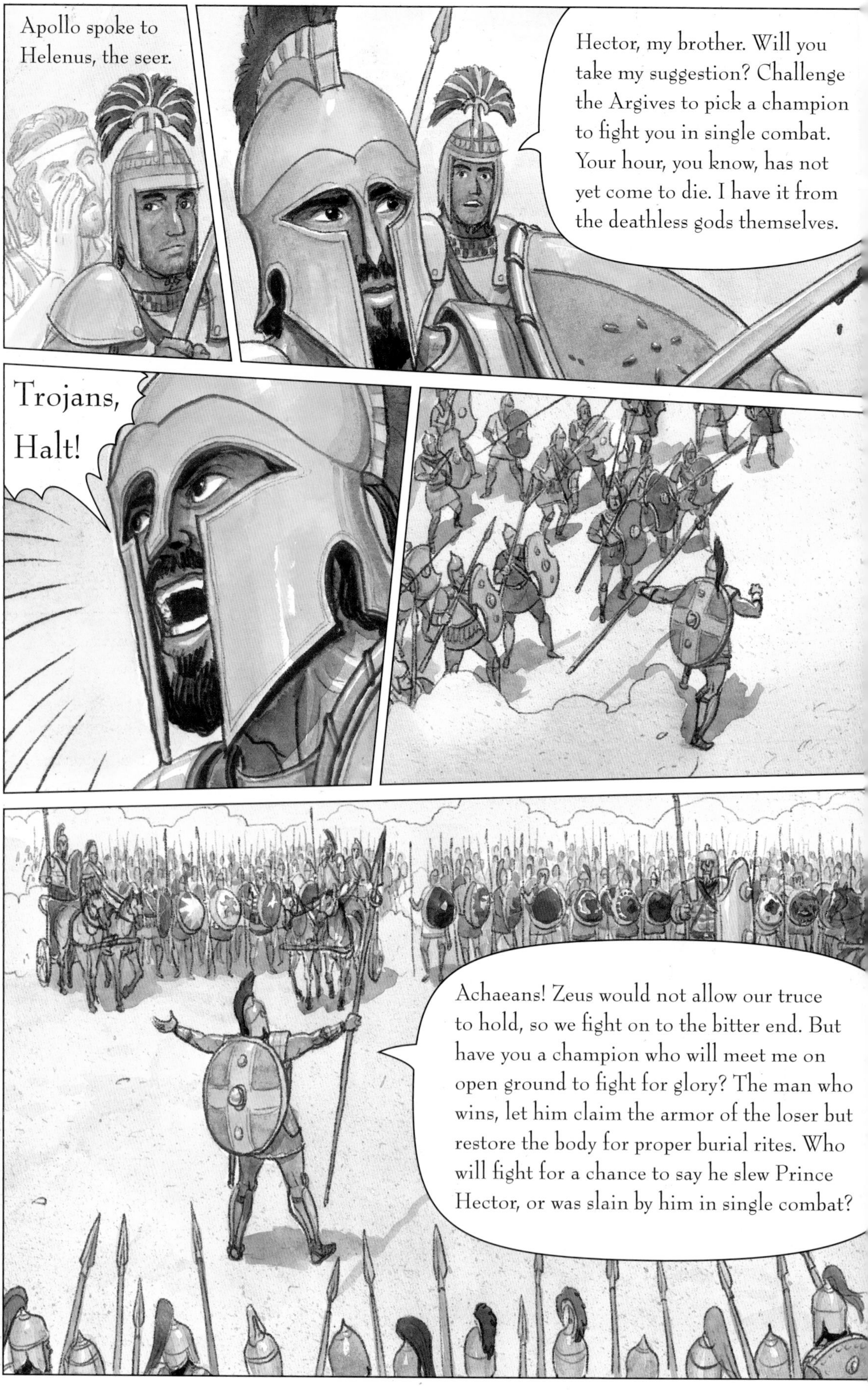

Apollo spoke to Helenus, the seer.
Hector, my brother. Will you take my suggestion? Challenge the Argives to pick a champion to fight you in single combat. Your hour, you know, has not yet come to die. I have it from the deathless gods themselves.
Trojans, Halt!
Achaeans! Zeus would not allow our truce to hold, so we fight on to the bitter end. But have you a champion who will meet me on open ground to fight for glory? The man who wins, let him claim the armor of the loser but restore the body for proper burial rites. Who will fight for a chance to say he slew Prince Hector, or was slain by him in single combat?

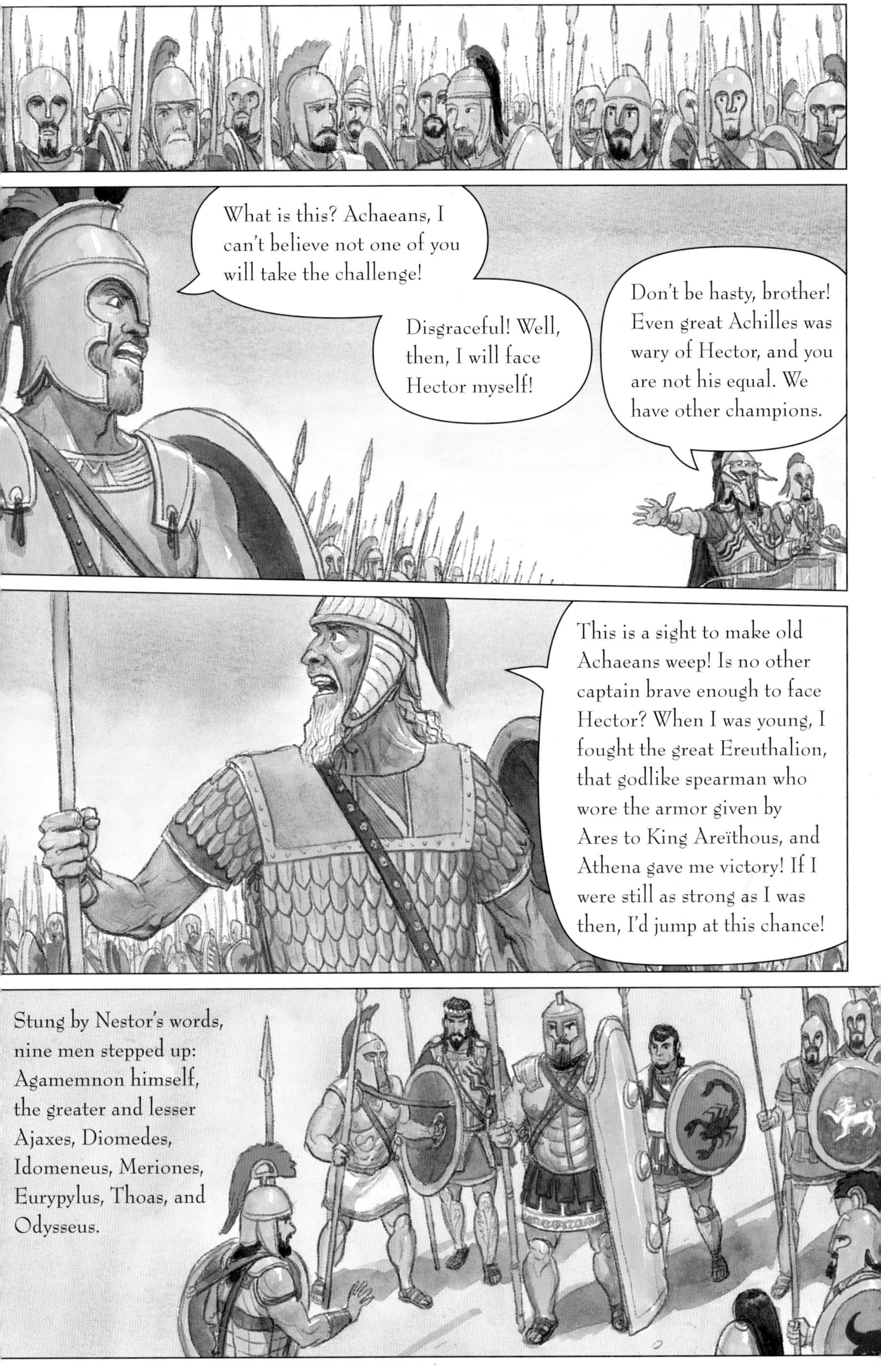
What is this? Achaeans, I can't believe not one of you will take the challenge!
Disgraceful! Well, then, I will face Hector myself!
Don't be hasty, brother! Even great Achilles was wary of Hector, and you are not his equal. We have other champions.
This is a sight to make old Achaeans weep! Is no other captain brave enough to face Hector? When I was young, I fought the great Ereuthalion, that godlike spearman who wore the armor given by Ares to King Areïthous, and Athena gave me victory! If I were still as strong as I was then, I'd jump at this chance!
Stung by Nestor's words, nine men stepped up: Agamemnon himself, the greater and lesser Ajaxes, Diomedes, Idomeneus, Meriones, Eurypylus, Thoas, and Odysseus.

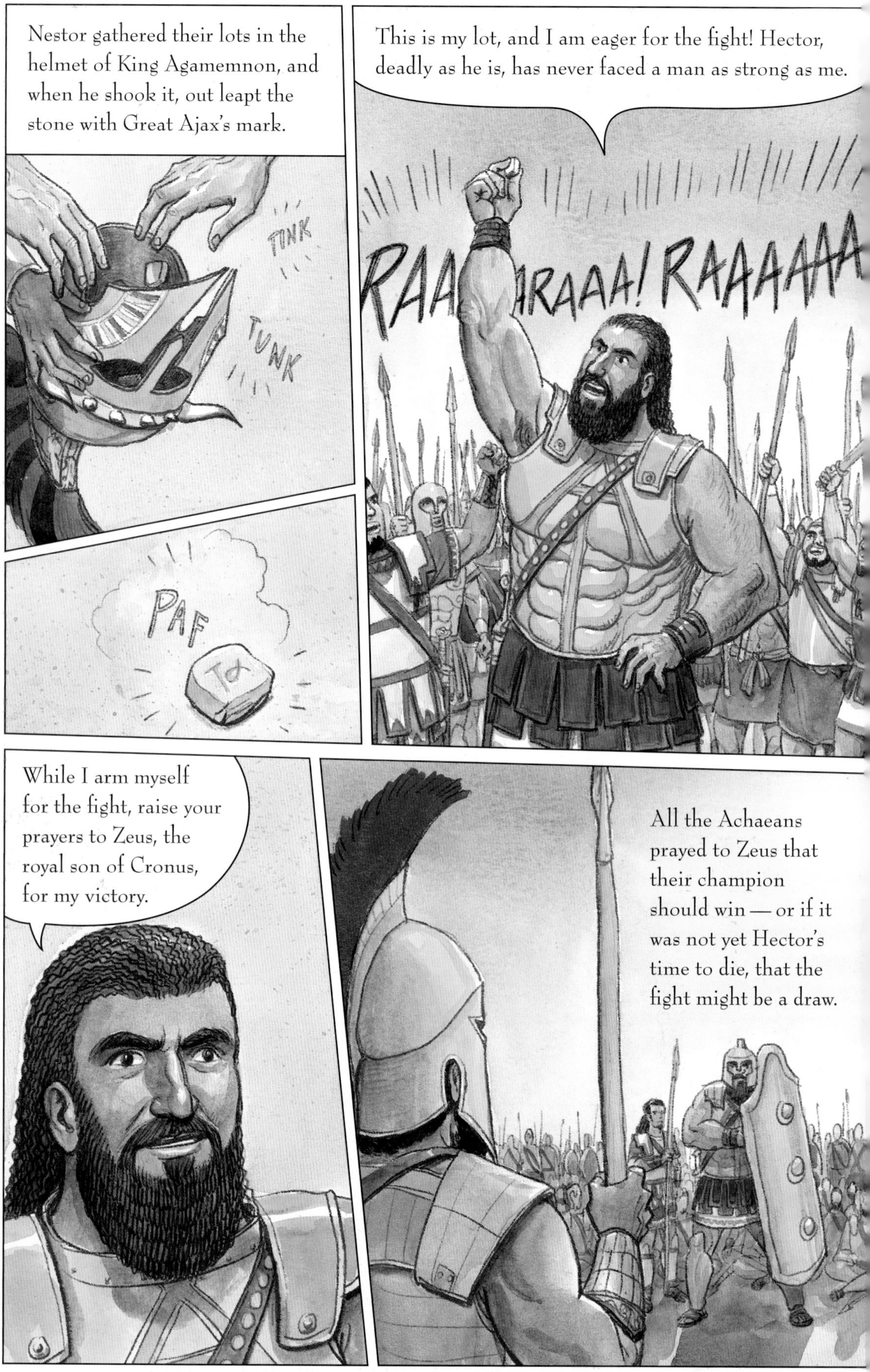
Nestor gathered their lots in the helmet of King Agamemnon, and when he shook it, out leapt the stone with Great Ajax's mark.
TINK
TUNK
PAF
This is my lot, and I am eager for the fight! Hector, deadly as he is, has never faced a man as strong as me.
RAAARAAA! RAAAAAA
While I arm myself for the fight, raise your prayers to Zeus, the royal son of Cronus, for my victory.
All the Achaeans prayed to Zeus that their champion should win — or if it was not yet Hector's time to die, that the fight might be a draw.

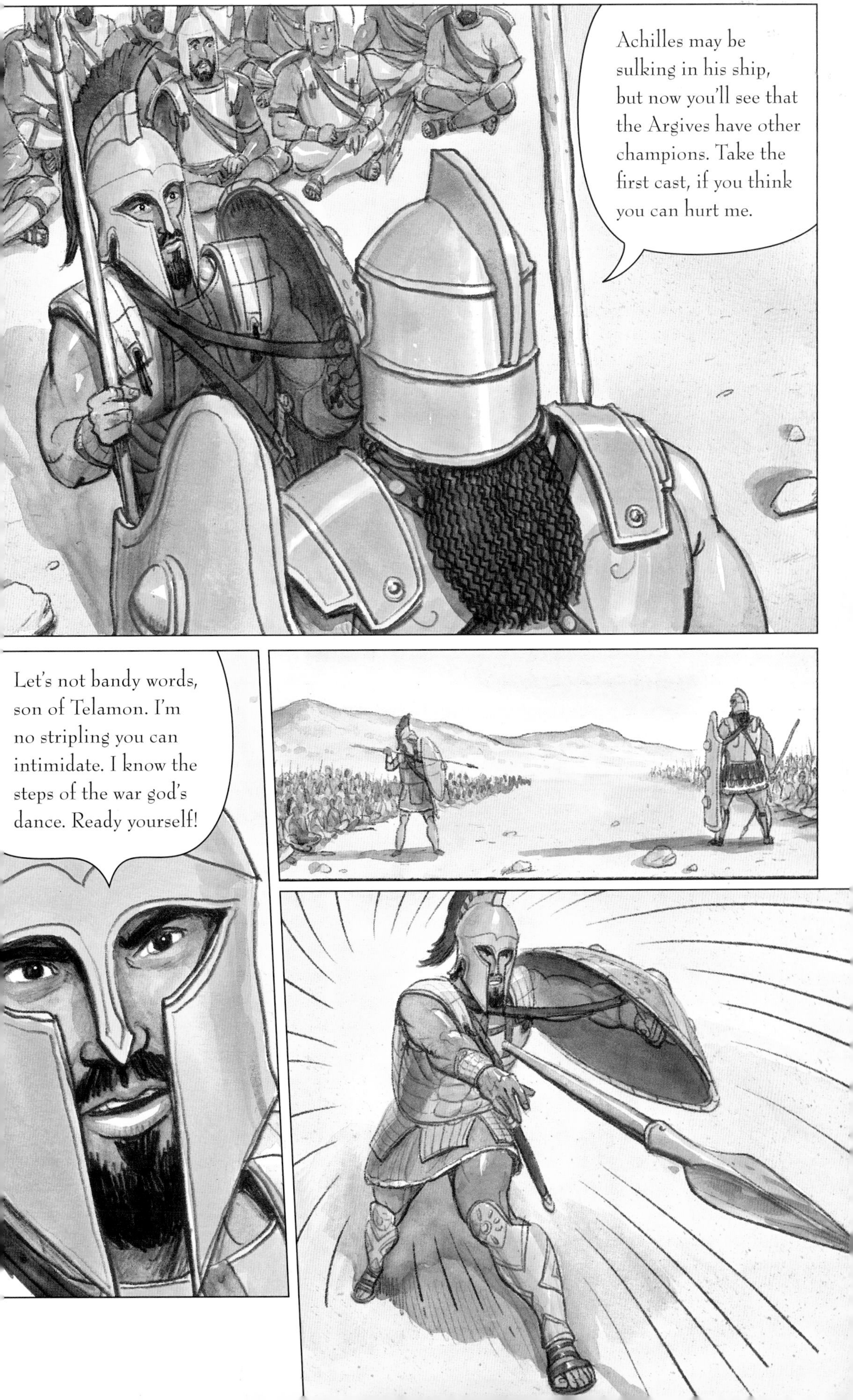
Achilles may be sulking in his ship, but now you'll see that the Argives have other champions. Take the first cast, if you think you can hurt me.
Let's not bandy words, son of Telamon. I'm no stripling you can intimidate. I know the steps of the war god's dance. Ready yourself!

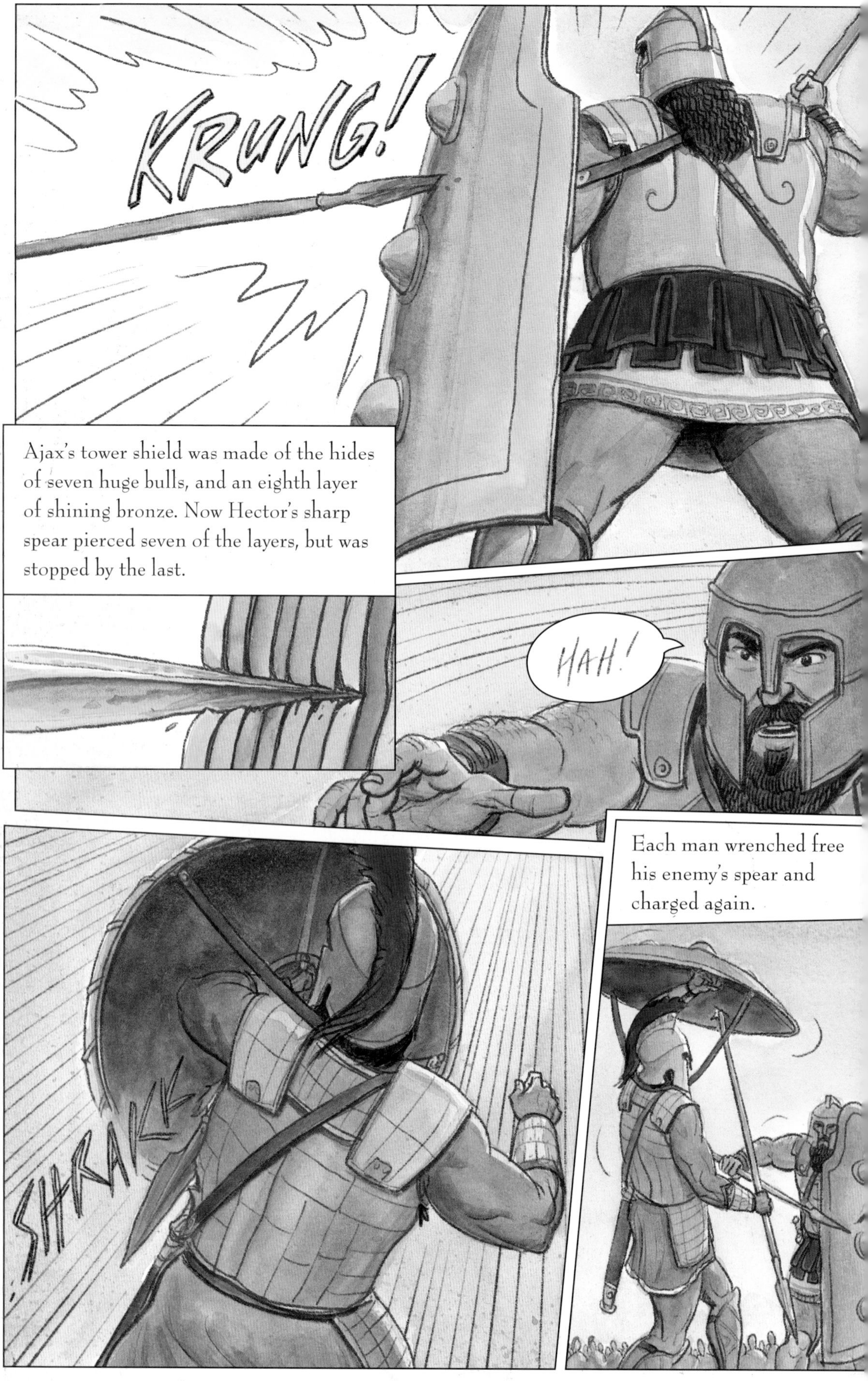
KRUNG!
Ajax's tower shield was made of the hides of seven huge bulls, and an eighth layer of shining bronze. Now Hector's sharp spear pierced seven of the layers, but was stopped by the last.
HAH!
SHRAKK
Each man wrenched free his enemy's spear and charged again.

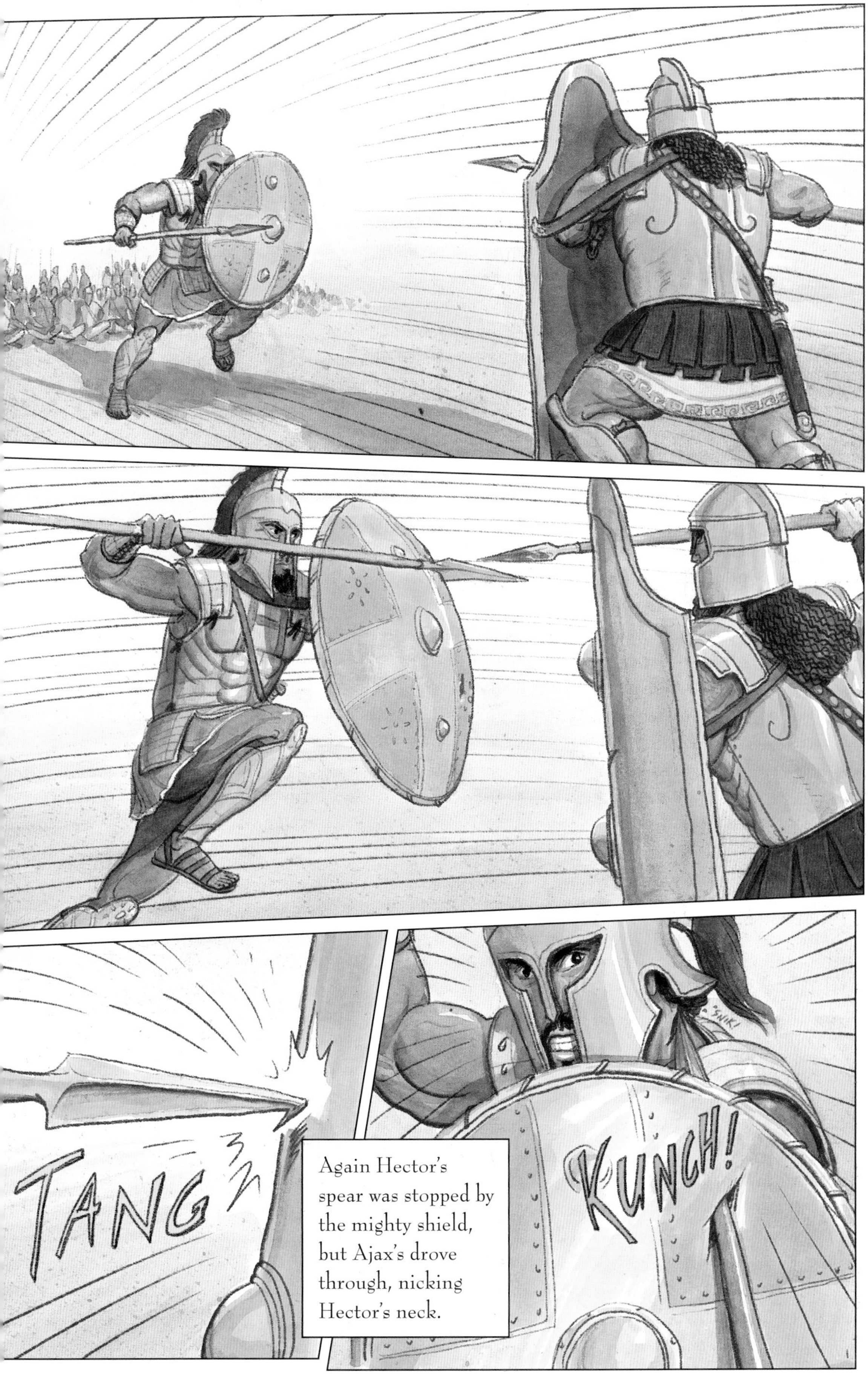
TANG
Again Hector's spear was stopped by the mighty shield, but Ajax's drove through, nicking Hector's neck.
SNIK!
KUNCH!

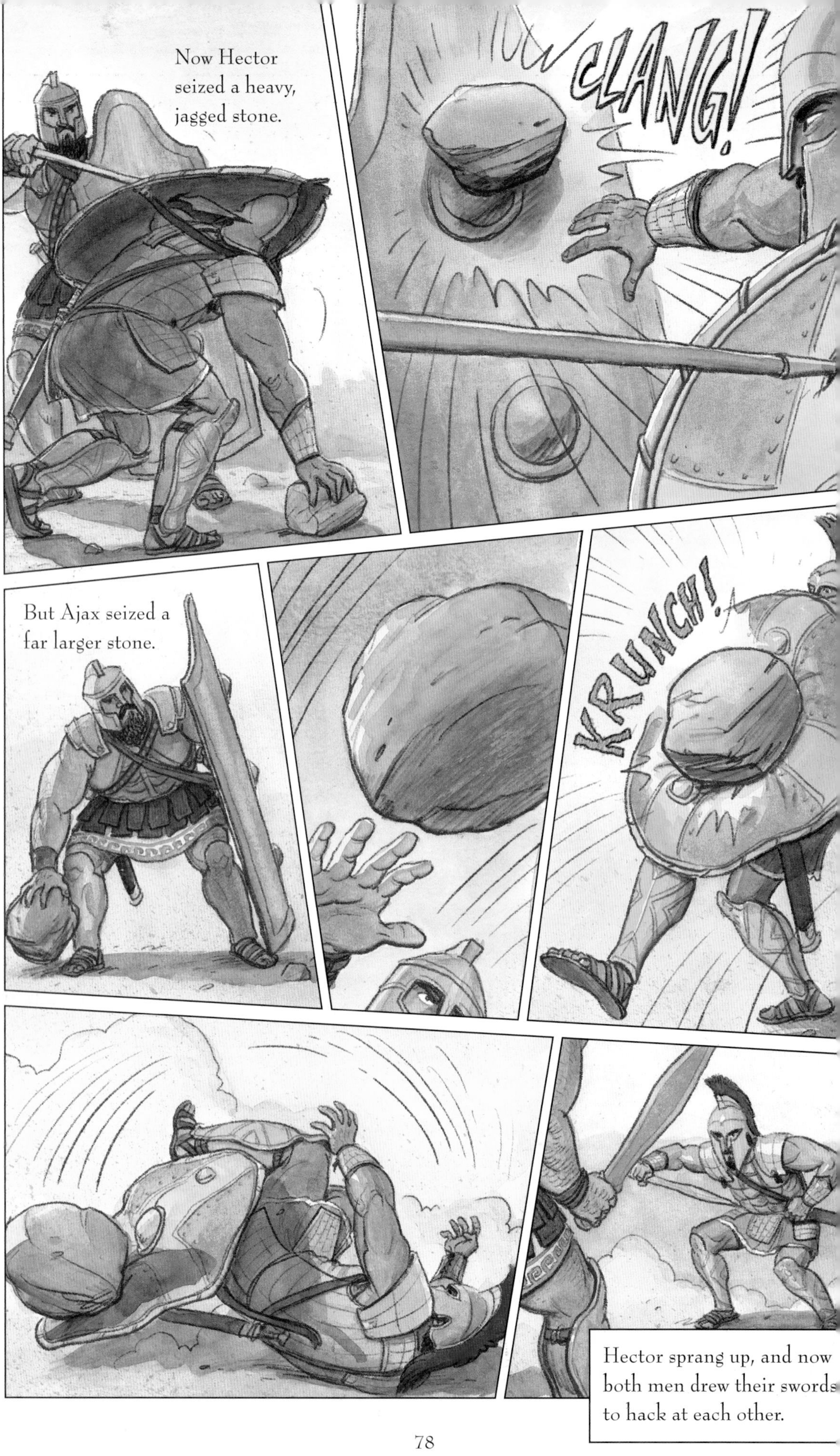
Now Hector seized a heavy, jagged stone.
CLANG!
But Ajax seized a far larger stone.
KRUNCH!
Hector sprang up, and now both men drew their swords to hack at each other.

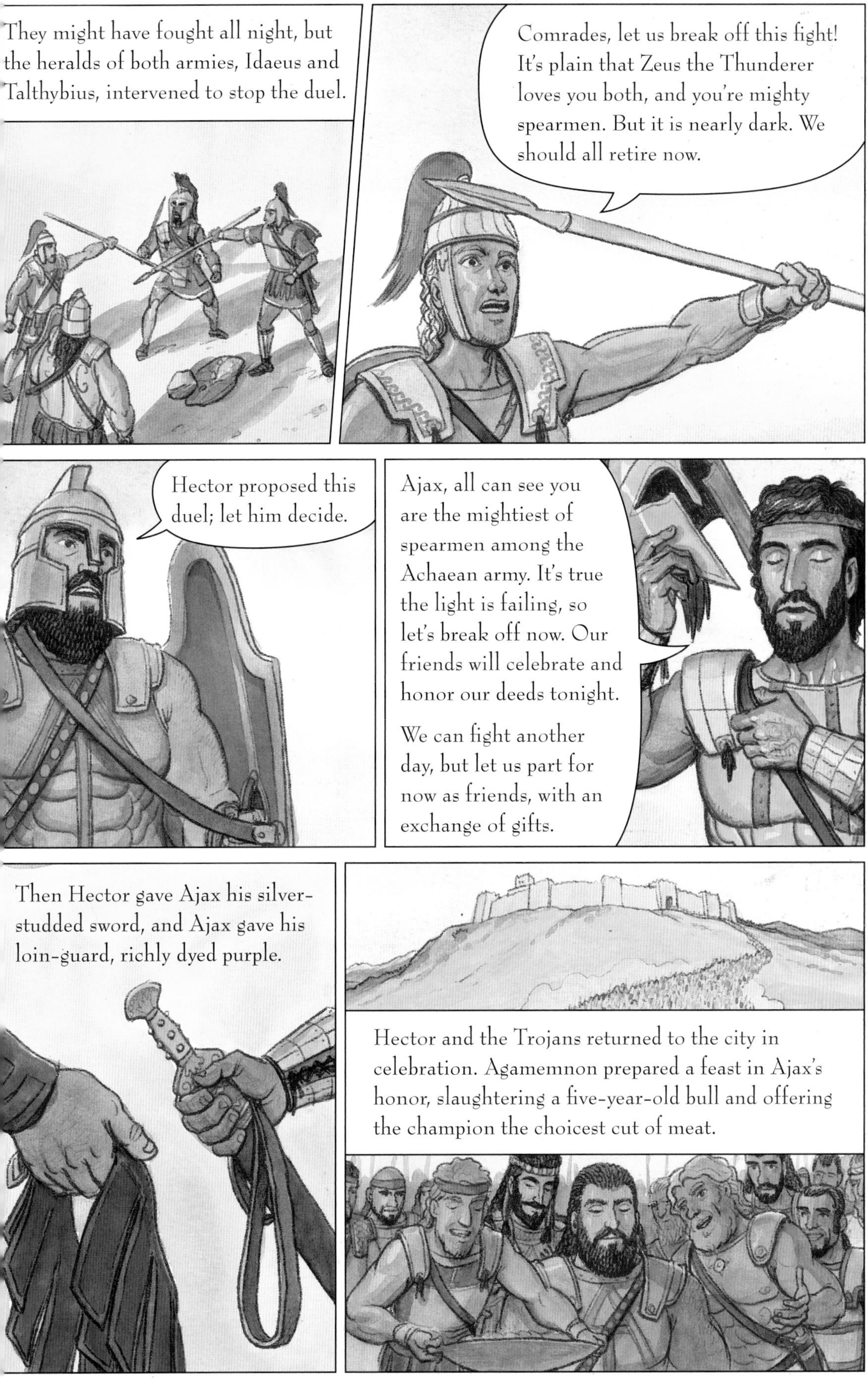
They might have fought all night, but the heralds of both armies, Idaeus and Talthybius, intervened to stop the duel.
Comrades, let us break off this fight! It's plain that Zeus the Thunderer loves you both, and you're mighty spearmen. But it is nearly dark. We should all retire now.
Hector proposed this duel; let him decide.
Ajax, all can see you are the mightiest of spearmen among the Achaean army. It's true the light is failing, so let's break off now. Our friends will celebrate and honor our deeds tonight.
We can fight another day, but let us part for now as friends, with an exchange of gifts.
Then Hector gave Ajax his silver-studded sword, and Ajax gave his loin-guard, richly dyed purple.
Hector and the Trojans returned to the city in celebration. Agamemnon prepared a feast in Ajax's honor, slaughtering a five-year-old bull and offering the champion the choicest cut of meat.

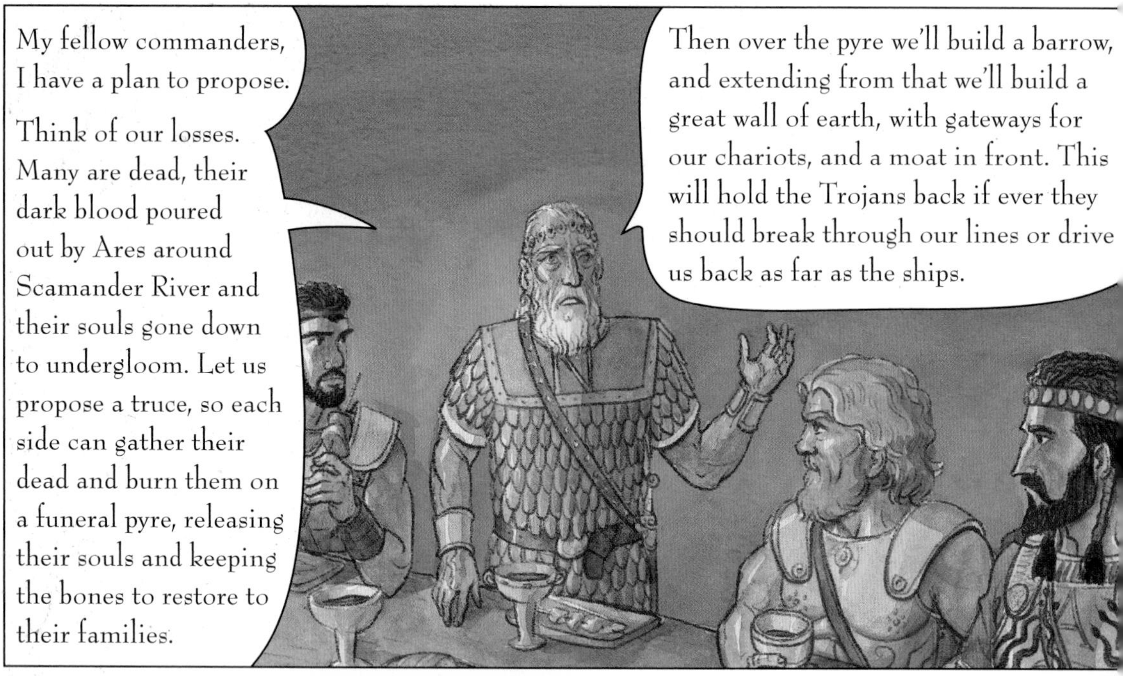
My fellow commanders, I have a plan to propose.
Think of our losses. Many are dead, their dark blood poured out by Ares around Scamander River and their souls gone down to undergloom. Let us propose a truce, so each side can gather their dead and burn them on a funeral pyre, releasing their souls and keeping the bones to restore to their families.
Then over the pyre we'll build a barrow, and extending from that we'll build a great wall of earth, with gateways for our chariots, and a moat in front. This will hold the Trojans back if ever they should break through our lines or drive us back as far as the ships.

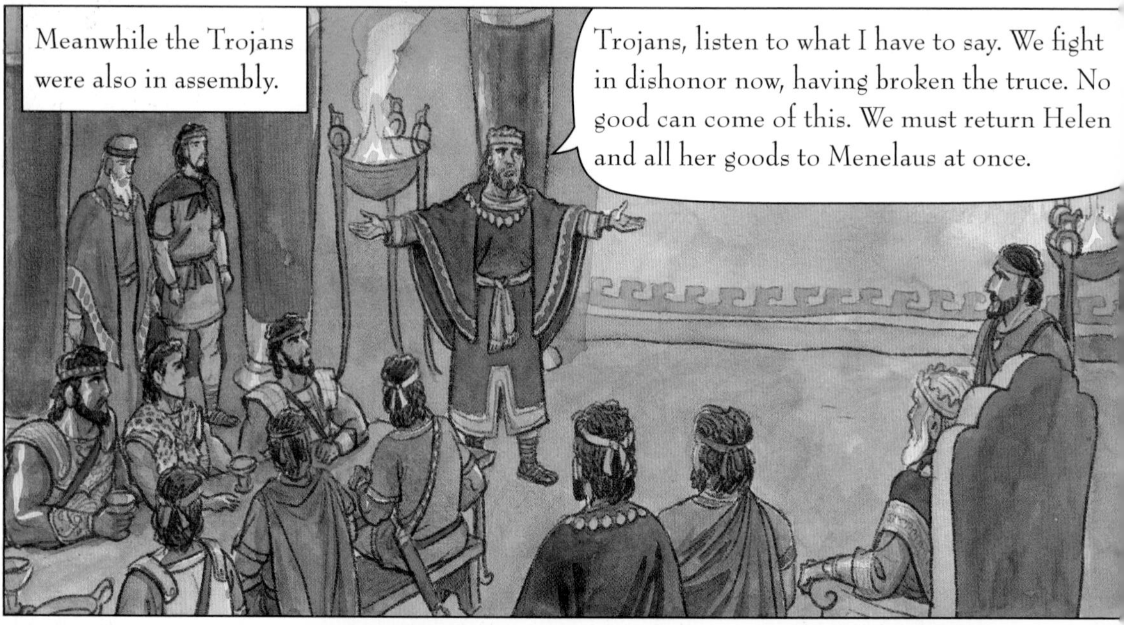
Meanwhile the Trojans were also in assembly.
Trojans, listen to what I have to say. We fight in dishonor now, having broken the truce. No good can come of this. We must return Helen and all her goods to Menelaus at once.

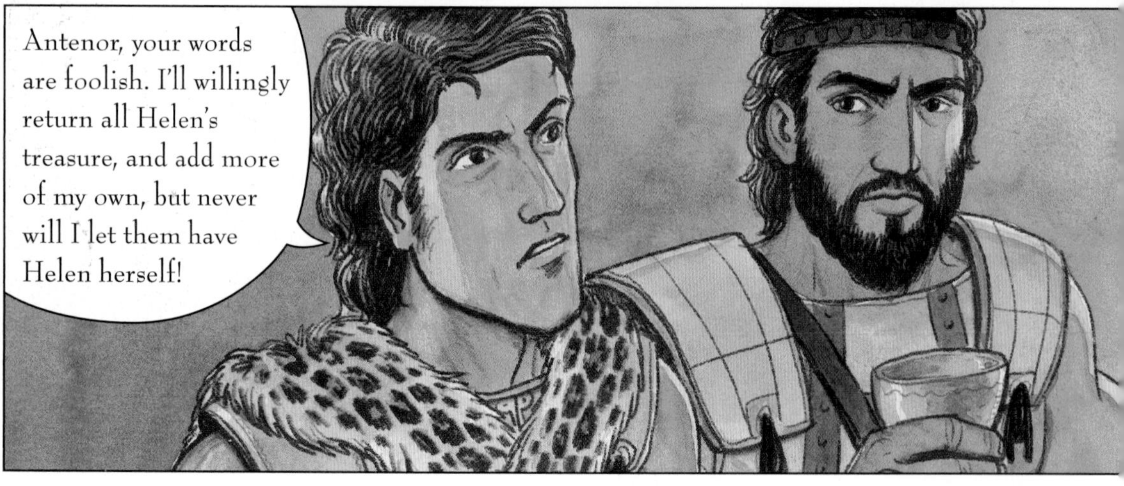
Antenor, your words are foolish. I'll willingly return all Helen's treasure, and add more of my own, but never will I let them have Helen herself!

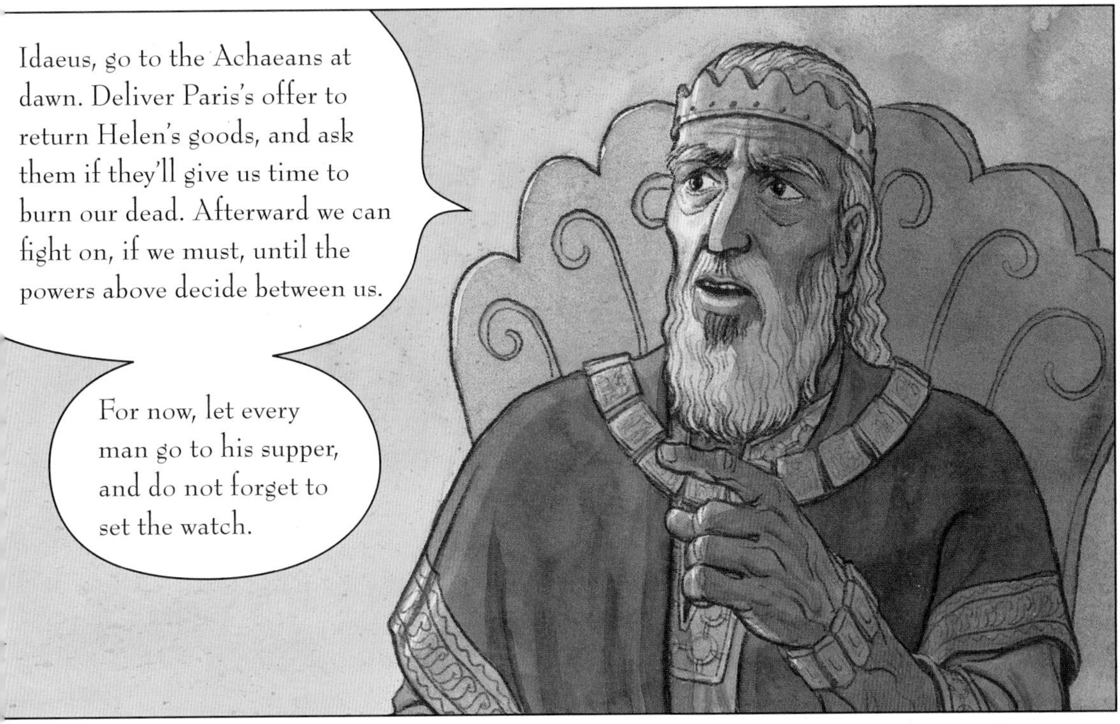
Idaeus, go to the Achaeans at dawn. Deliver Paris's offer to return Helen's goods, and ask them if they'll give us time to burn our dead. Afterward we can fight on, if we must, until the powers above decide between us.
For now, let every man go to his supper, and do not forget to set the watch.

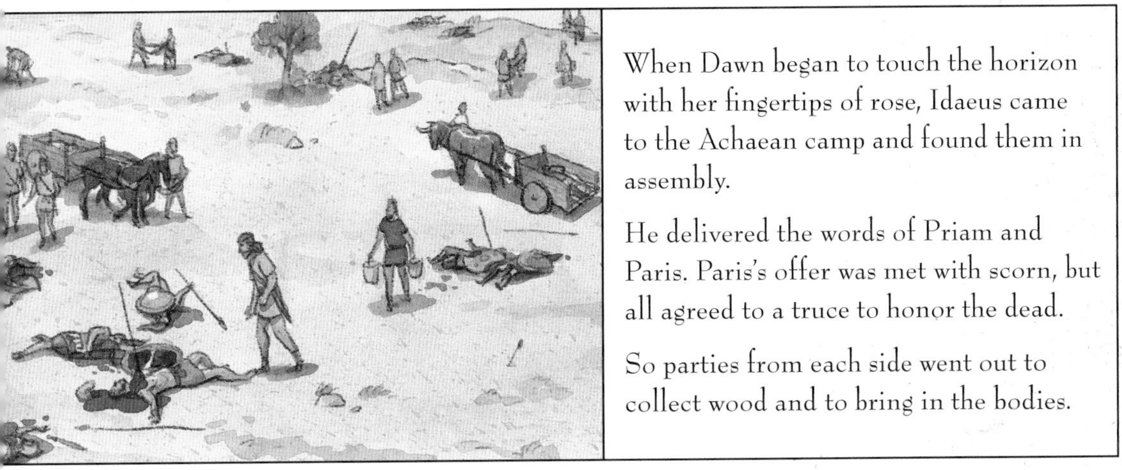
When Dawn began to touch the horizon with her fingertips of rose, Idaeus came to the Achaean camp and found them in assembly.
He delivered the words of Priam and Paris. Paris's offer was met with scorn, but all agreed to a truce to honor the dead.
So parties from each side went out to collect wood and to bring in the bodies.

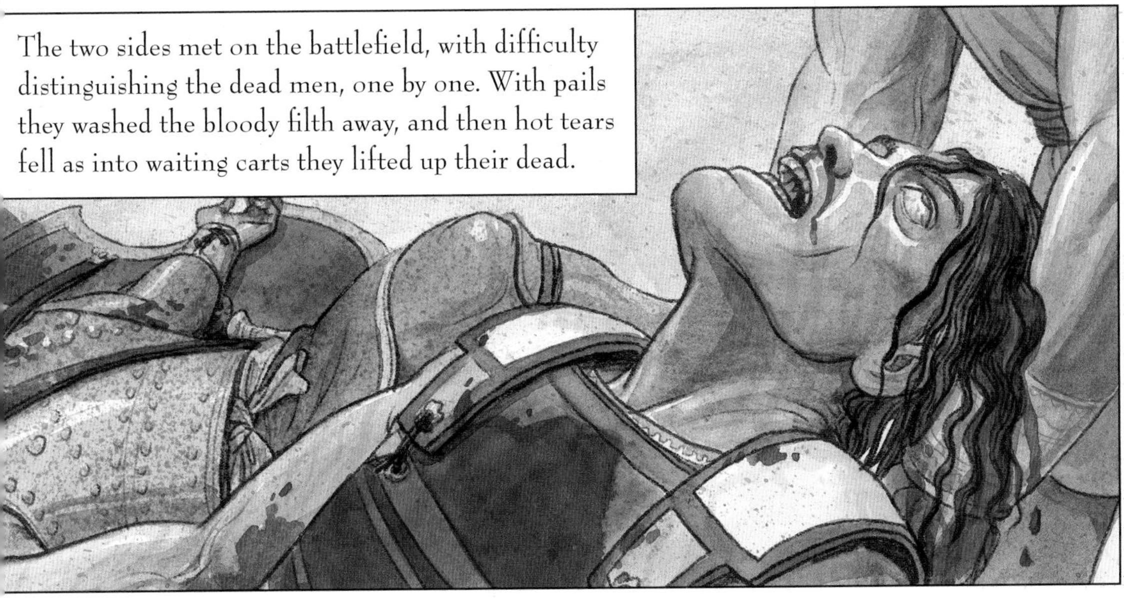
The two sides met on the battlefield, with difficulty distinguishing the dead men, one by one. With pails they washed the bloody filth away, and then hot tears fell as into waiting carts they lifted up their dead.

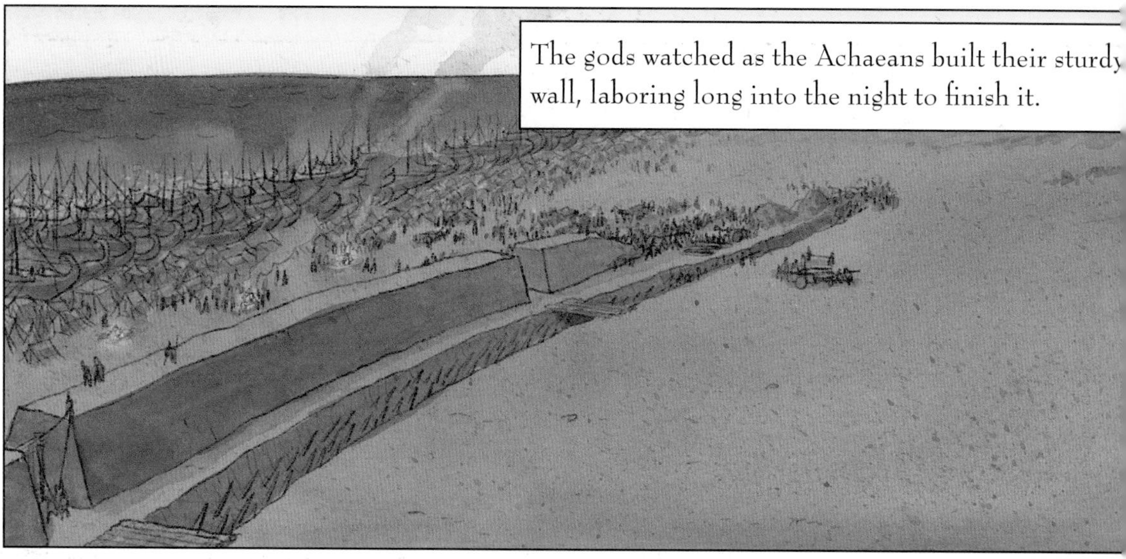
The gods watched as the Achaeans built their sturdy wall, laboring long into the night to finish it.

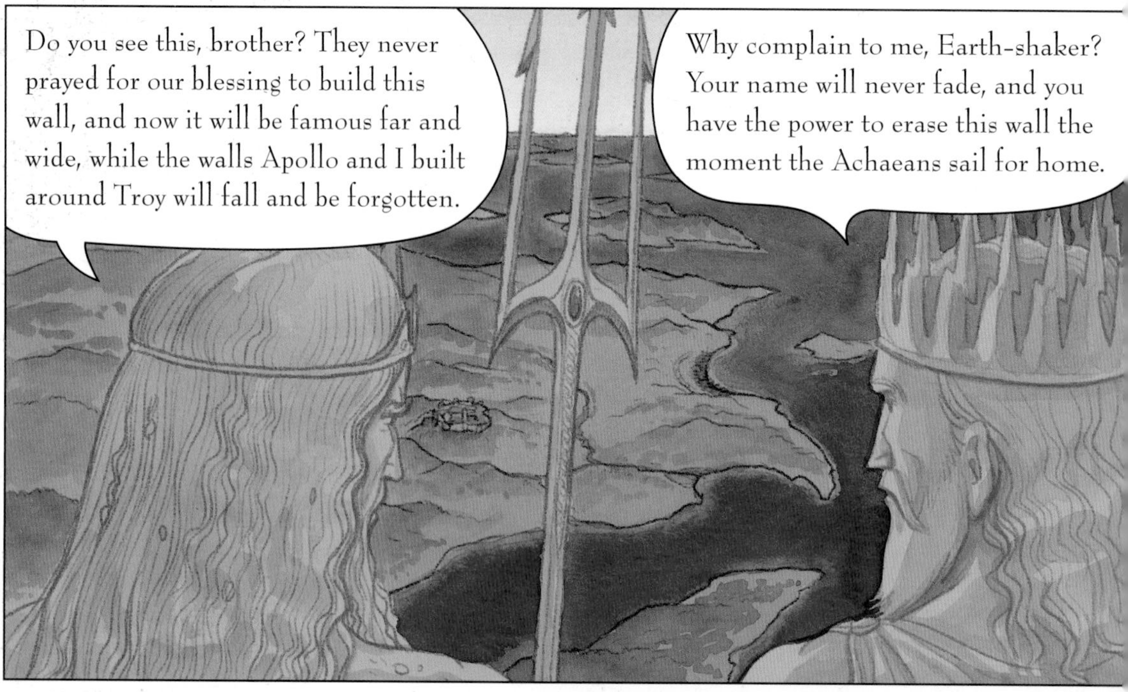
Do you see this, brother? They never prayed for our blessing to build this wall, and now it will be famous far and wide, while the walls Apollo and I built around Troy will fall and be forgotten.
Why complain to me, Earth-shaker? Your name will never fade, and you have the power to erase this wall the moment the Achaeans sail for home.

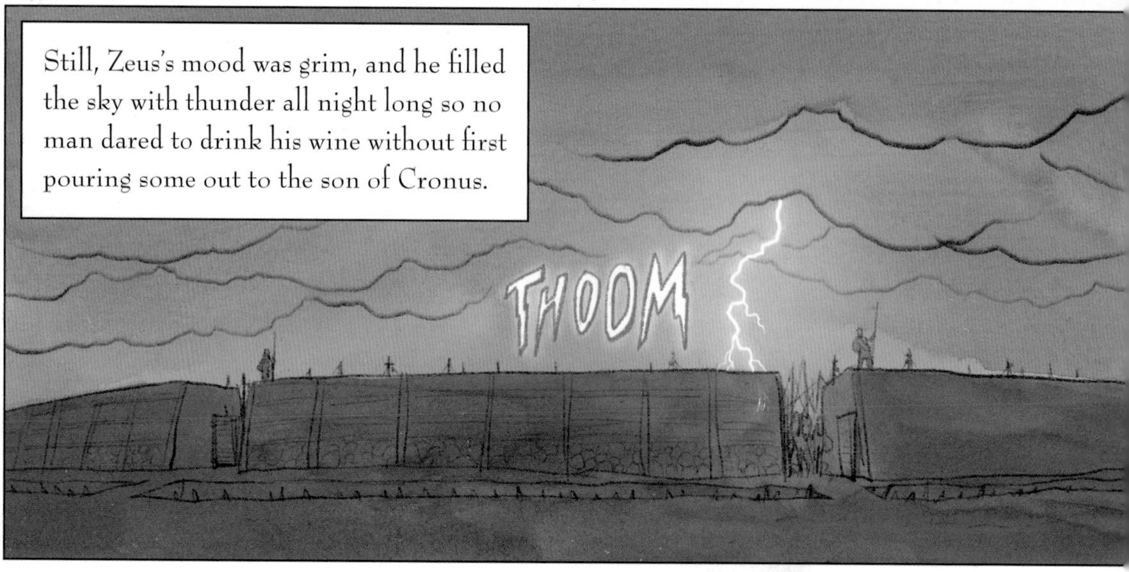
Still, Zeus's mood was grim, and he filled the sky with thunder all night long so no man dared to drink his wine without first pouring some out to the son of Cronus.
THOOM

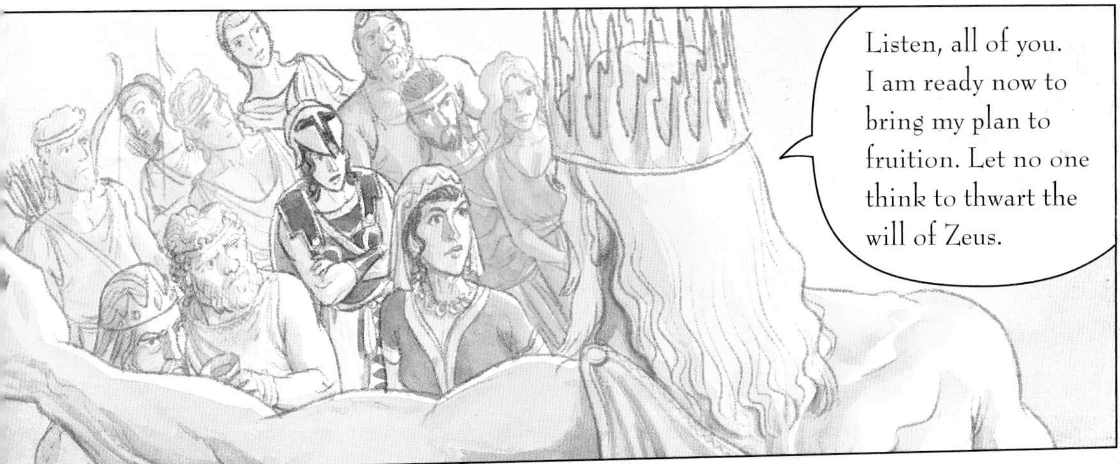
Listen, all of you. I am ready now to bring my plan to fruition. Let no one think to thwart the will of Zeus.

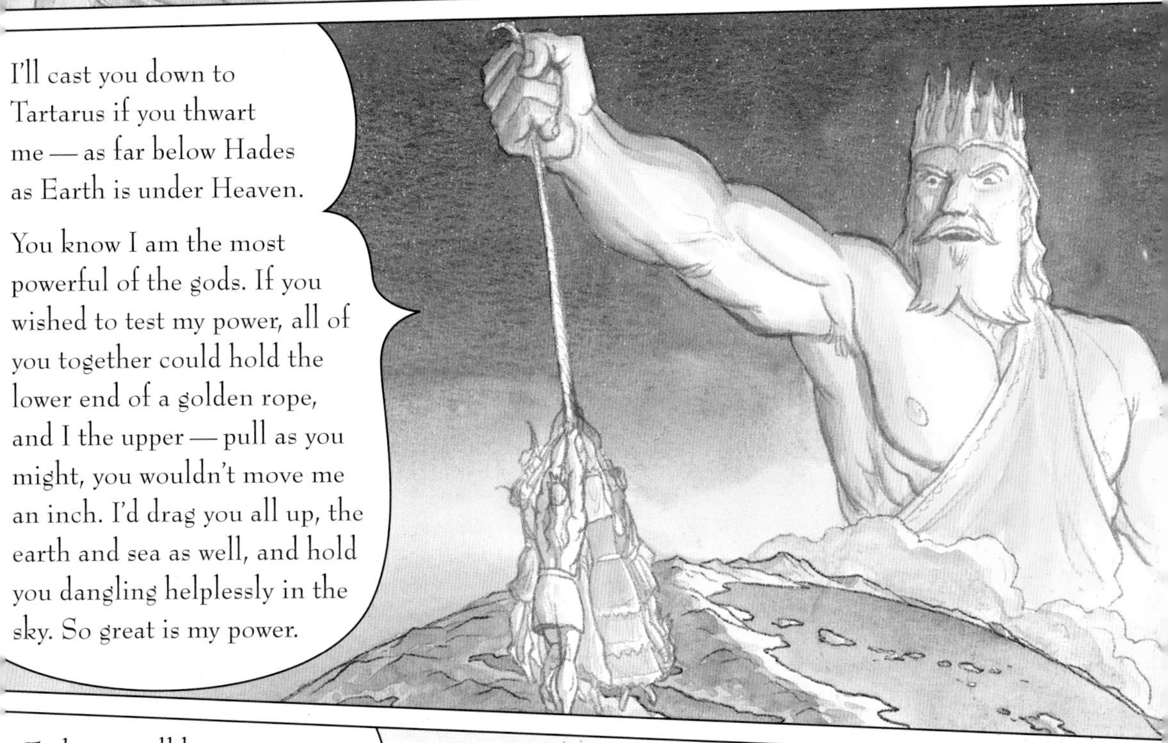
I'll cast you down to Tartarus if you thwart me — as far below Hades as Earth is under Heaven.
You know I am the most powerful of the gods. If you wished to test my power, all of you together could hold the lower end of a golden rope, and I the upper — pull as you might, you wouldn't move me an inch. I'd drag you all up, the earth and sea as well, and hold you dangling helplessly in the sky. So great is my power.

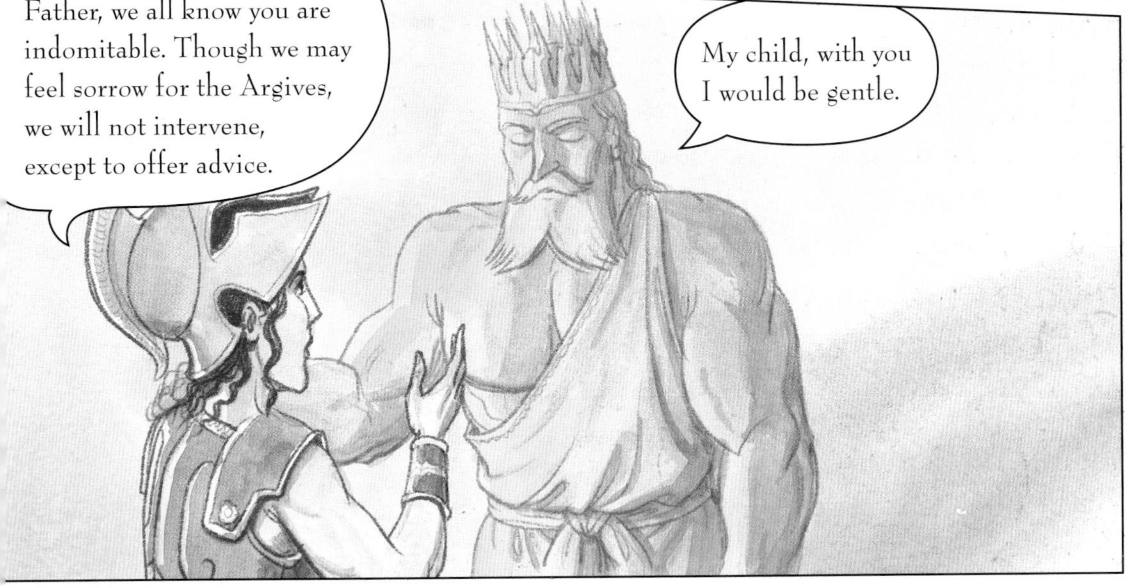
Father, we all know you are indomitable. Though we may feel sorrow for the Argives, we will not intervene, except to offer advice.
My child, with you I would be gentle.

Then Zeus harnessed his team and drove them down to his temple on Gargaron, highest peak of Mount Ida, where he would have the best view of the armies doing battle. Once more the armies poured out upon the plain and met, clashing, shield on shield, and blood darkened the dry earth.

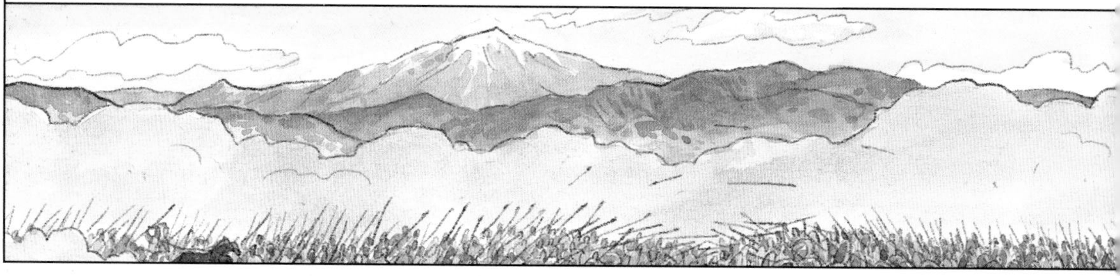

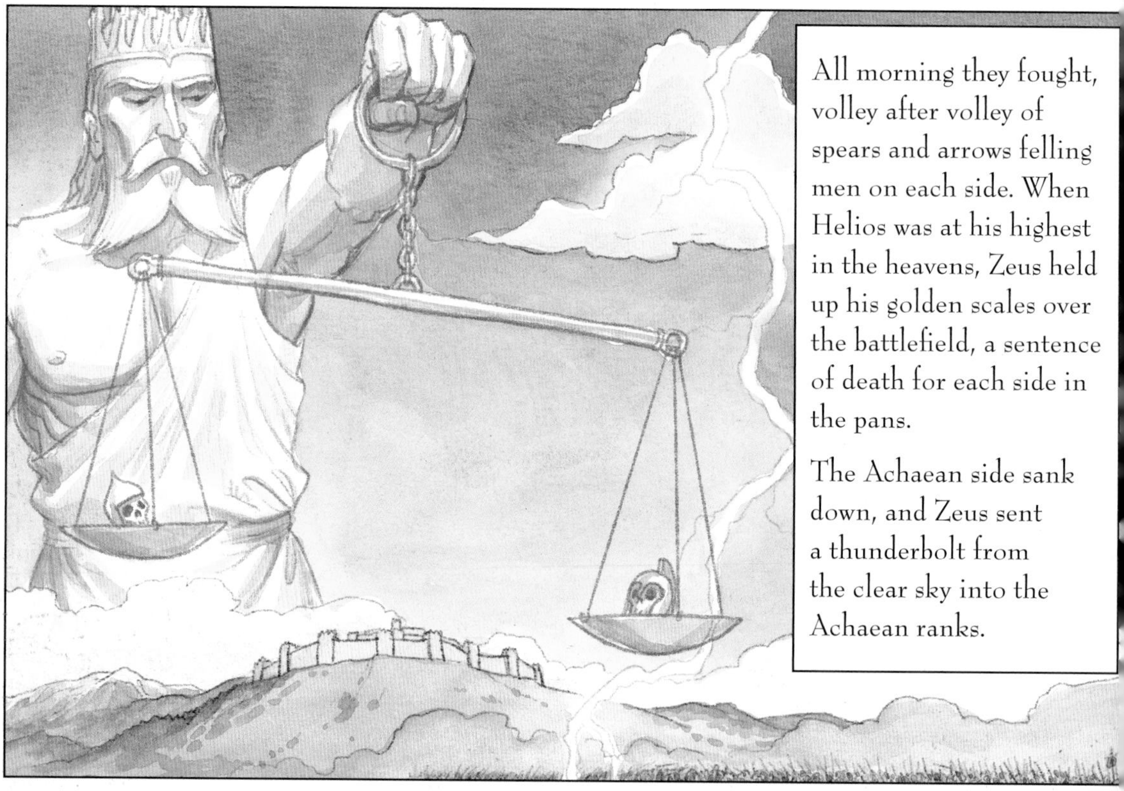
All morning they fought, volley after volley of spears and arrows felling men on each side. When Helios was at his highest in the heavens, Zeus held up his golden scales over the battlefield, a sentence of death for each side in the pans.
The Achaean side sank down, and Zeus sent a thunderbolt from the clear sky into the Achaean ranks.

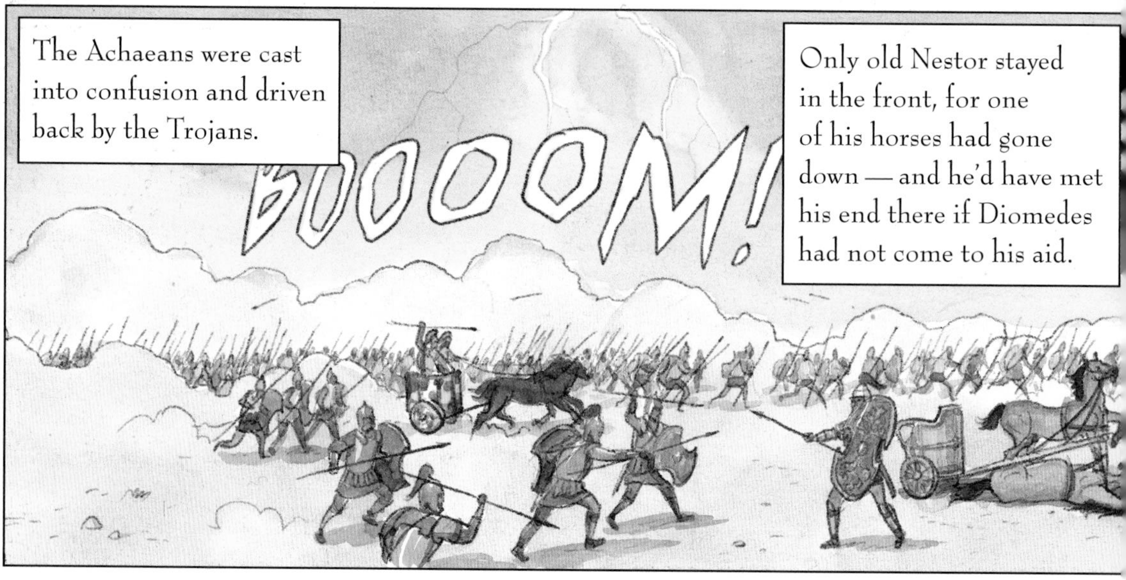
The Achaeans were cast into confusion and driven back by the Trojans.
BOOOOM!
Only old Nestor stayed in the front, for one of his horses had gone down — and he'd have met his end there if Diomedes had not come to his aid.

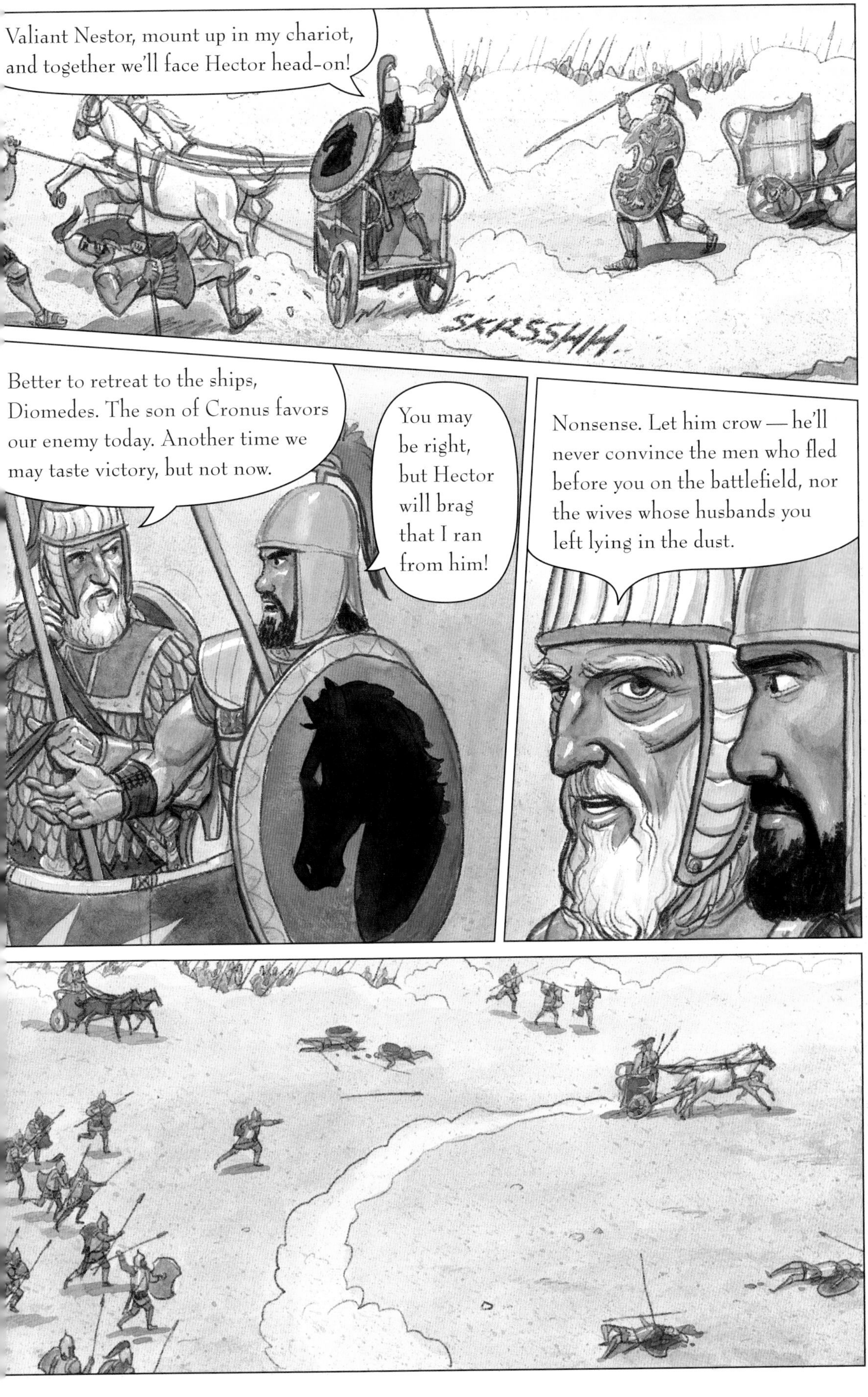
Valiant Nestor, mount up in my chariot, and together we'll face Hector head-on!
SKRSSHH.
Better to retreat to the ships, Diomedes. The son of Cronus favors our enemy today. Another time we may taste victory, but not now.
You may be right, but Hector will brag that I ran from him!
Nonsense. Let him crow — he'll never convince the men who fled before you on the battlefield, nor the wives whose husbands you left lying in the dust.

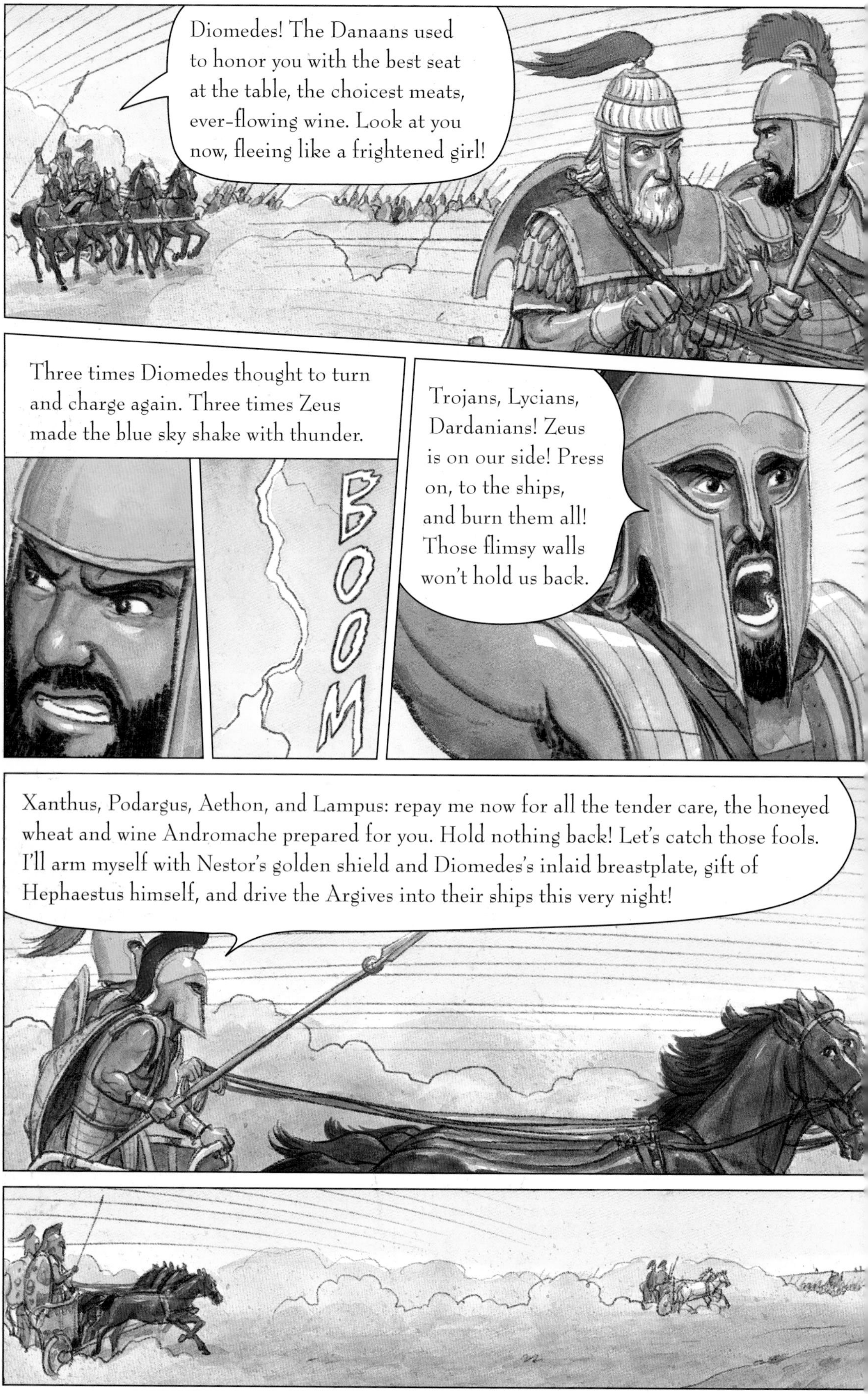

Diomedes! The Danaans used to honor you with the best seat at the table, the choicest meats, ever-flowing wine. Look at you now, fleeing like a frightened girl!
Three times Diomedes thought to turn and charge again. Three times Zeus made the blue sky shake with thunder.
BOOM
Trojans, Lycians, Dardanians! Zeus is on our side! Press on, to the ships, and burn them all! Those flimsy walls won't hold us back.
Xanthus, Podargus, Aethon, and Lampus: repay me now for all the tender care, the honeyed wheat and wine Andromache prepared for you. Hold nothing back! Let's catch those fools. I'll arm myself with Nestor's golden shield and Diomedes's inlaid breastplate, gift of Hephaestus himself, and drive the Argives into their ships this very night!

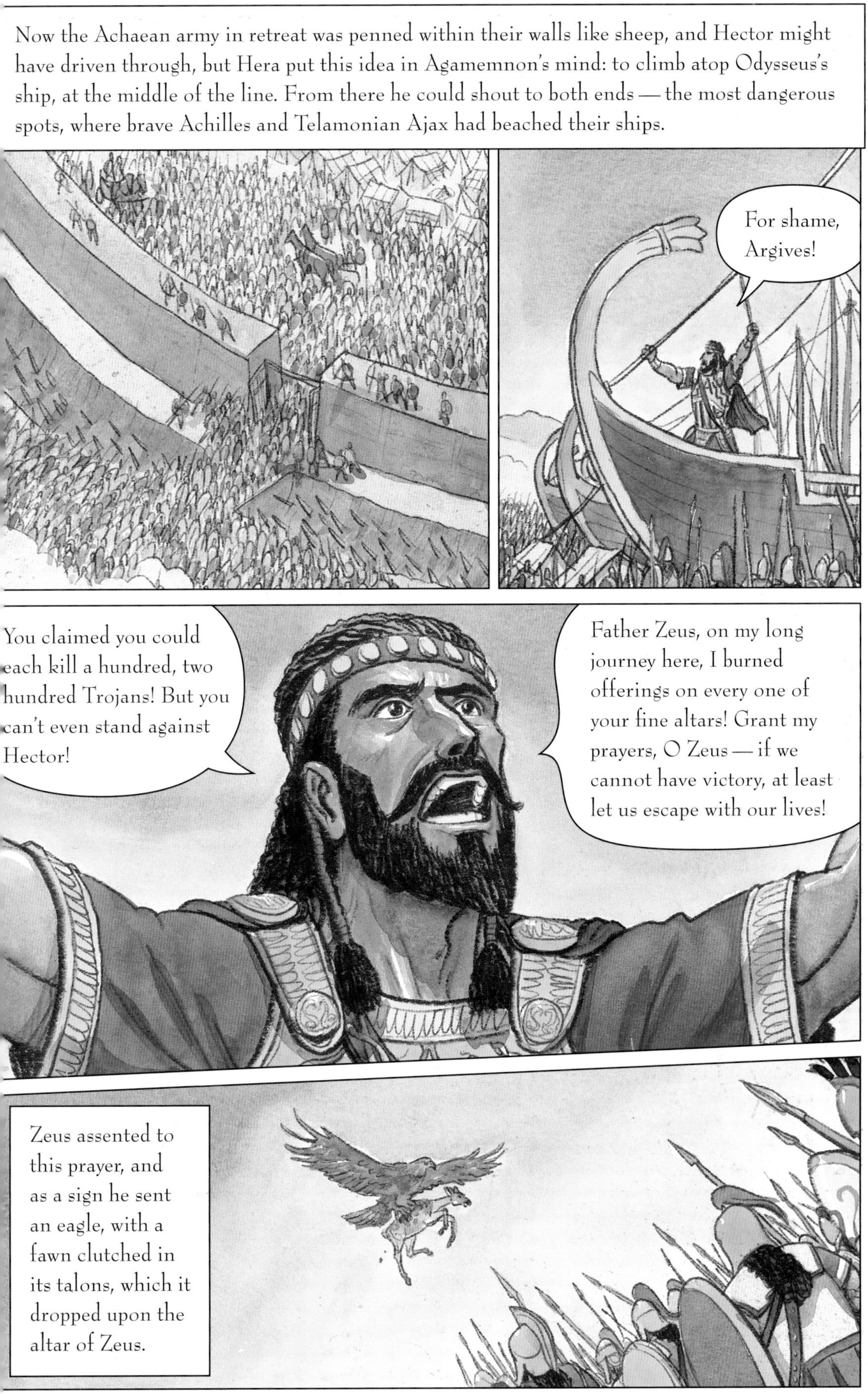
Now the Achaean army in retreat was penned within their walls like sheep, and Hector might have driven through, but Hera put this idea in Agamemnon's mind: to climb atop Odysseus's ship, at the middle of the line. From there he could shout to both ends — the most dangerous spots, where brave Achilles and Telamonian Ajax had beached their ships.
For shame, Argives!
You claimed you could each kill a hundred, two hundred Trojans! But you can't even stand against Hector!
Father Zeus, on my long journey here, I burned offerings on every one of your fine altars! Grant my prayers, O Zeus — if we cannot have victory, at least let us escape with our lives!
Zeus assented to this prayer, and as a sign he sent an eagle, with a fawn clutched in its talons, which it dropped upon the altar of Zeus.

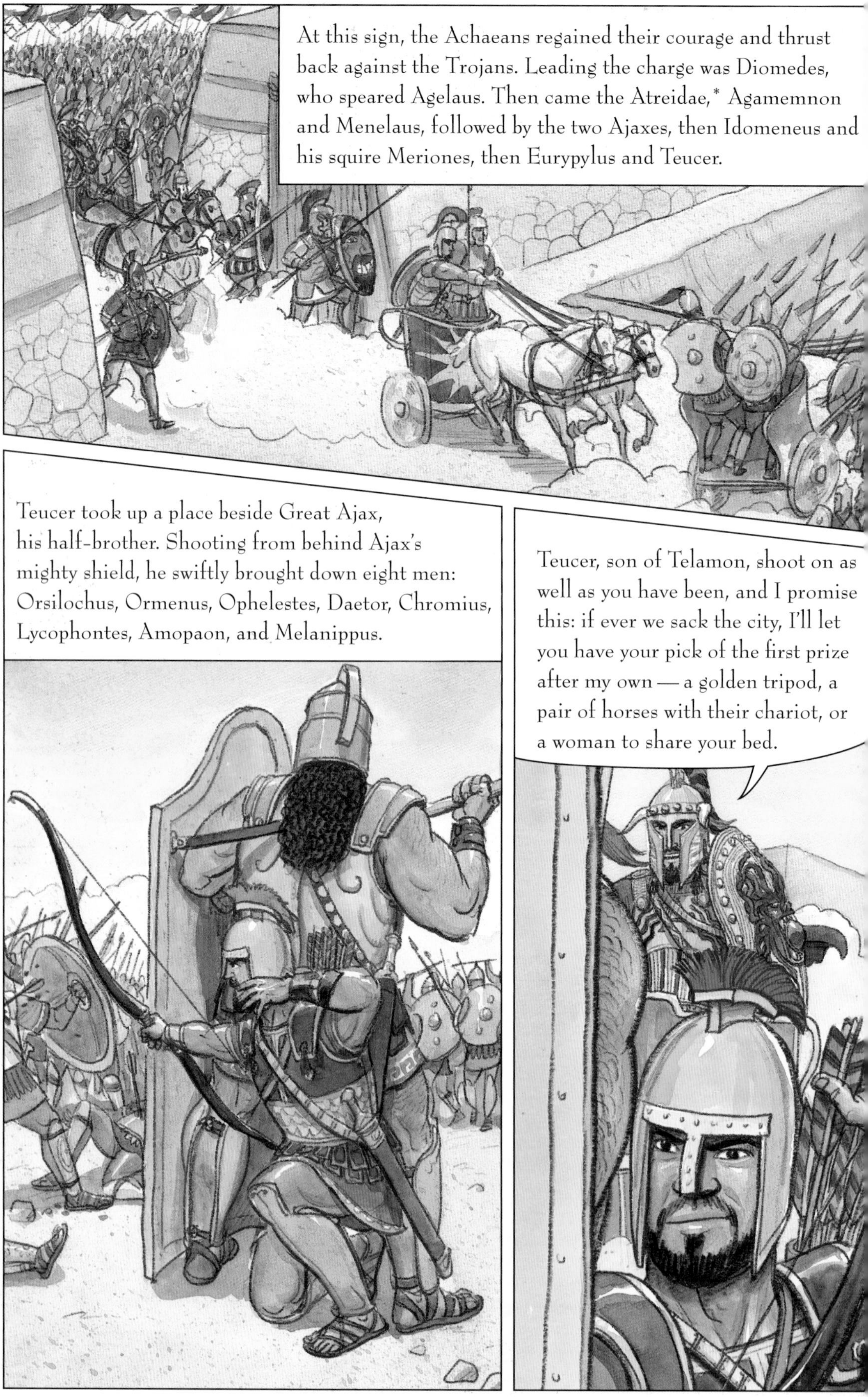
At this sign, the Achaeans regained their courage and thrust back against the Trojans. Leading the charge was Diomedes, who speared Agelaus. Then came the Atreidae,* Agamemnon and Menelaus, followed by the two Ajaxes, then Idomeneus and his squire Meriones, then Eurypylus and Teucer.
Teucer took up a place beside Great Ajax, his half-brother. Shooting from behind Ajax's mighty shield, he swiftly brought down eight men: Orsilochus, Ormenus, Ophelestes, Daetor, Chromius, Lycophontes, Amopaon, and Melanippus.
Teucer, son of Telamon, shoot on as well as you have been, and I promise this: if ever we sack the city, I'll let you have your pick of the first prize after my own — a golden tripod, a pair of horses with their chariot, or a woman to share your bed.

Atreidae means "sons of Atreus," plural of Atreides; "-ides" means "descendant of."

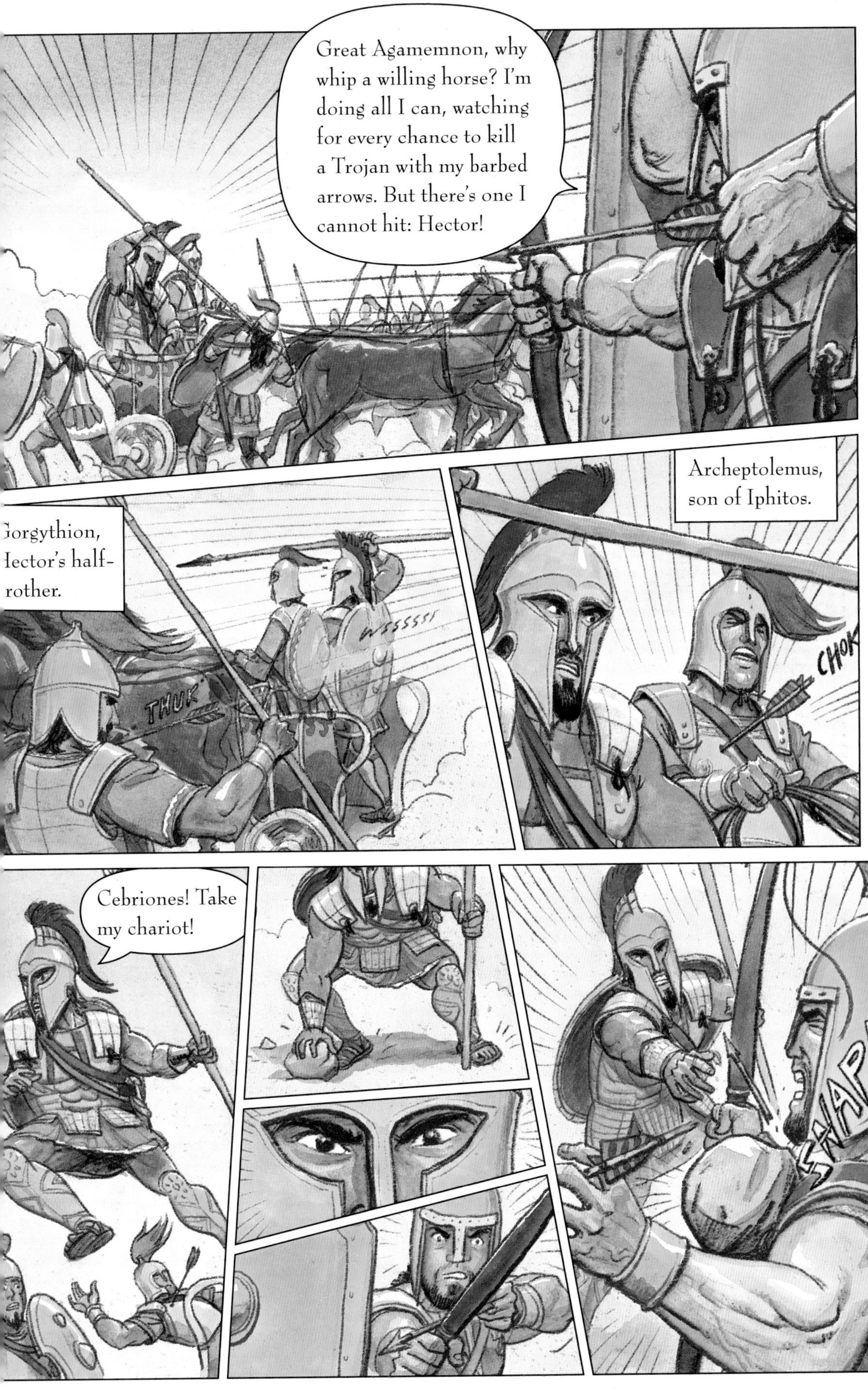
Great Agamemnon, why whip a willing horse? I'm doing all I can, watching for every chance to kill a Trojan with my barbed arrows. But there's one I cannot hit: Hector!
Gorgythion, Hector's half-brother.
THUK
WSSSSS
Archeptolemus, son of Iphitos.
Cebriones! Take my chariot!

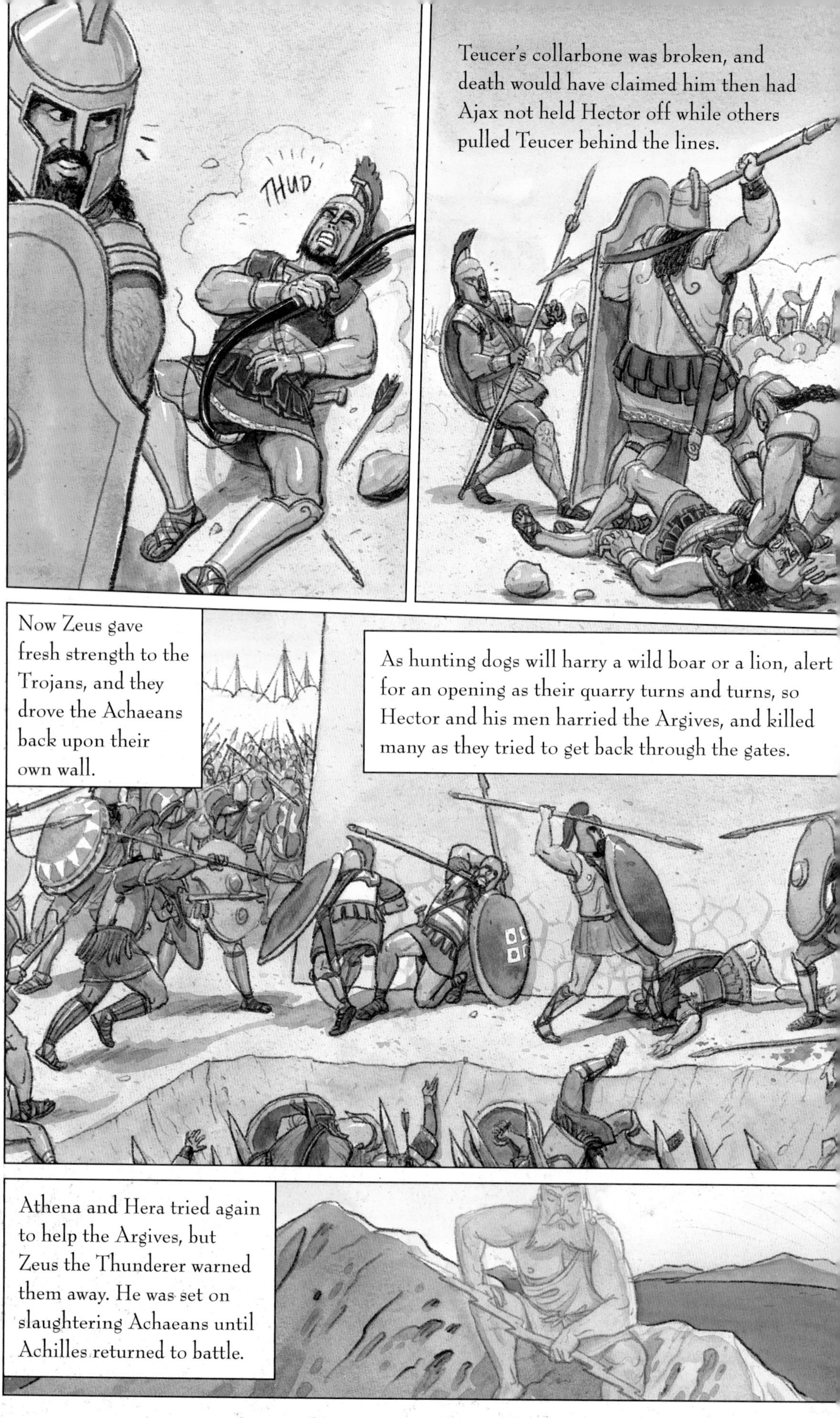
THUD
Teucer's collarbone was broken, and death would have claimed him then had Ajax not held Hector off while others pulled Teucer behind the lines.
Now Zeus gave fresh strength to the Trojans, and they drove the Achaeans back upon their own wall.
As hunting dogs will harry a wild boar or a lion, alert for an opening as their quarry turns and turns, so Hector and his men harried the Argives, and killed many as they tried to get back through the gates.
Athena and Hera tried again to help the Argives, but Zeus the Thunderer warned them away. He was set on slaughtering Achaeans until Achilles returned to battle.

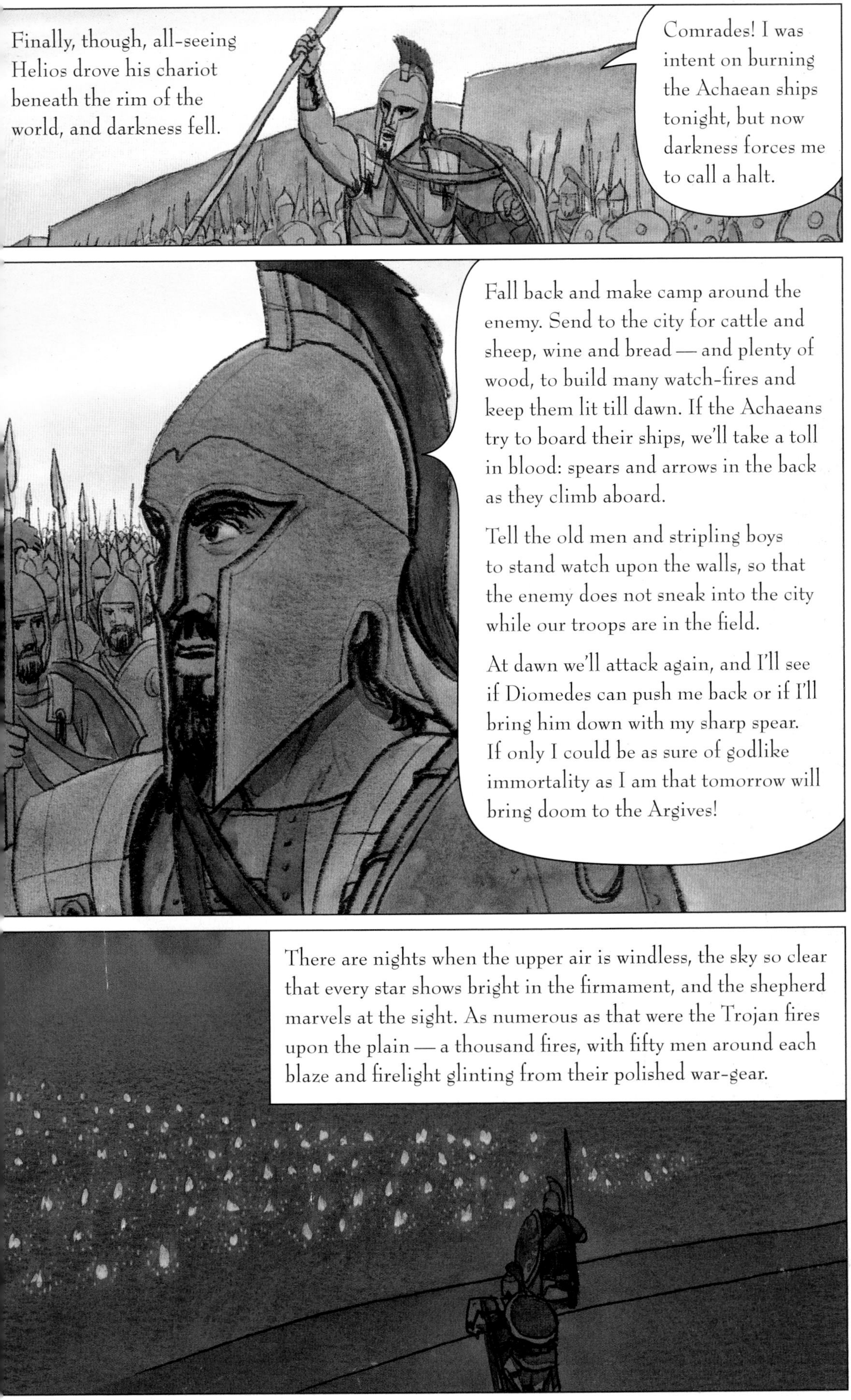

Finally, though, all-seeing Helios drove his chariot beneath the rim of the world, and darkness fell.
Comrades! I was intent on burning the Achaean ships tonight, but now darkness forces me to call a halt.
Fall back and make camp around the enemy. Send to the city for cattle and sheep, wine and bread — and plenty of wood, to build many watch-fires and keep them lit till dawn. If the Achaeans try to board their ships, we'll take a toll in blood: spears and arrows in the back as they climb aboard.
Tell the old men and stripling boys to stand watch upon the walls, so that the enemy does not sneak into the city while our troops are in the field.
At dawn we'll attack again, and I'll see if Diomedes can push me back or if I'll bring him down with my sharp spear. If only I could be as sure of godlike immortality as I am that tomorrow will bring doom to the Argives!
There are nights when the upper air is windless, the sky so clear that every star shows bright in the firmament, and the shepherd marvels at the sight. As numerous as that were the Trojan fires upon the plain — a thousand fires, with fifty men around each blaze and firelight glinting from their polished war-gear.

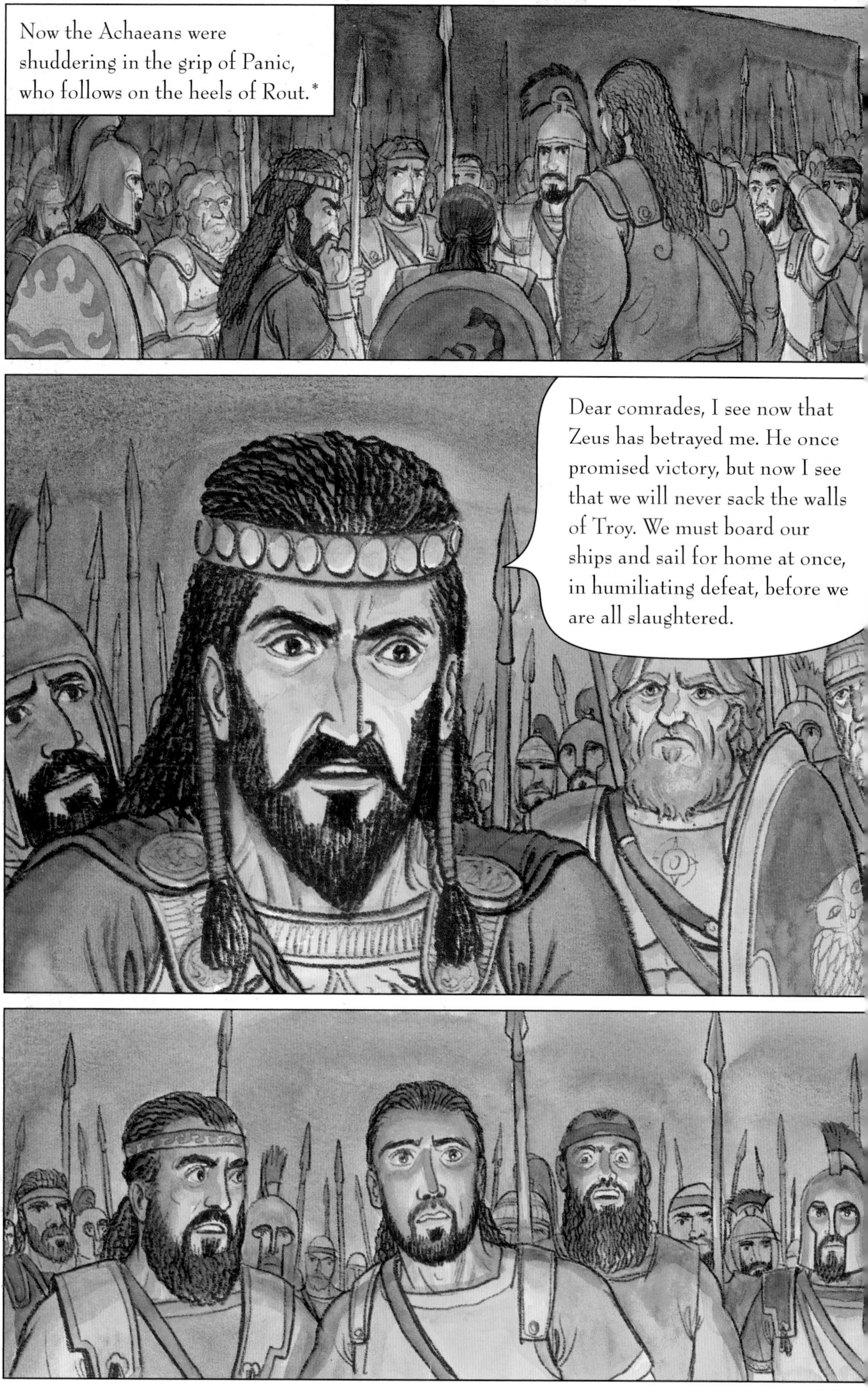
Now the Achaeans were shuddering in the grip of Panic, who follows on the heels of Rout.*
Dear comrades, I see now that Zeus has betrayed me. He once promised victory, but now I see that we will never sack the walls of Troy. We must board our ships and sail for home at once, in humiliating defeat, before we are all slaughtered.

* Panic and Rout are personified as Deimos and Phobos, sons of Ares and Aphrodite.

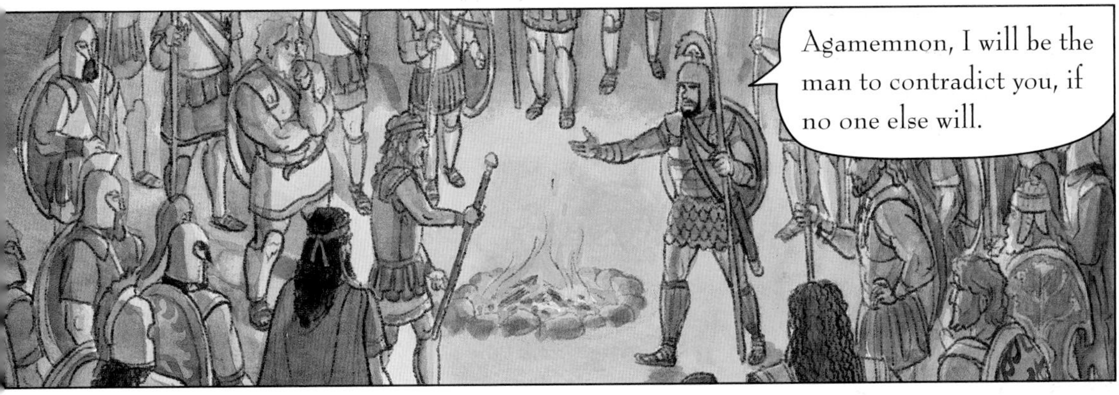
Agamemnon, I will be the man to contradict you, if no one else will.

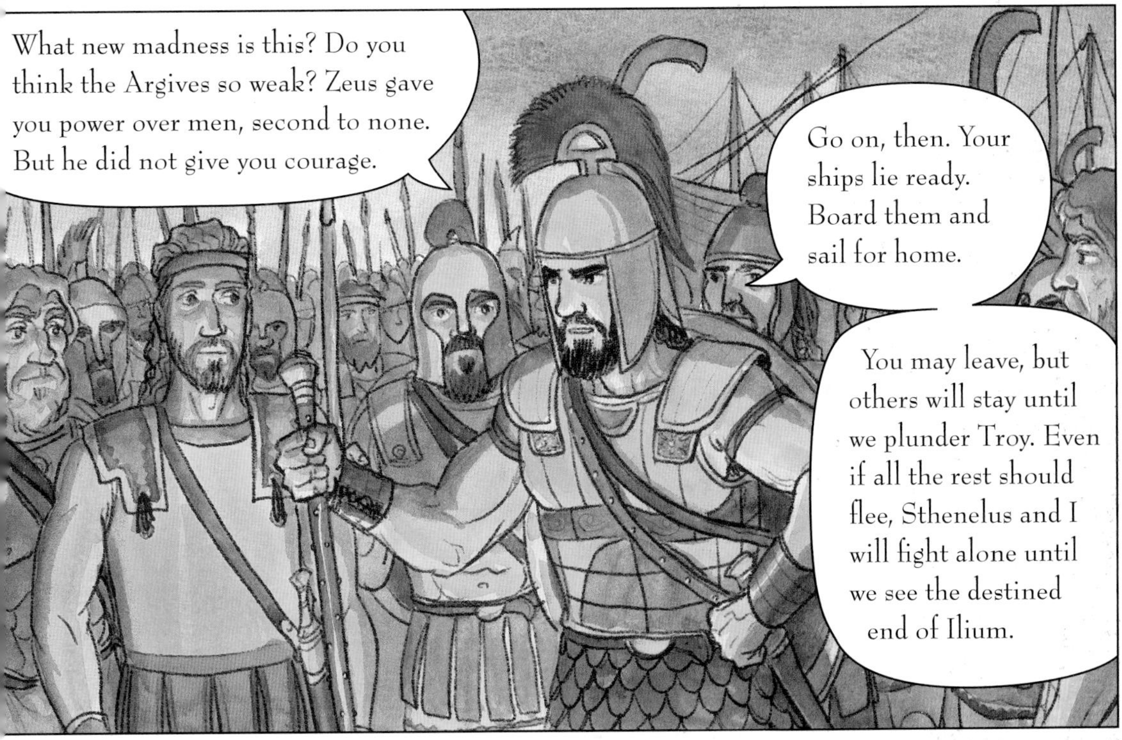
What new madness is this? Do you think the Argives so weak? Zeus gave you power over men, second to none. But he did not give you courage.
Go on, then. Your ships lie ready. Board them and sail for home.
You may leave, but others will stay until we plunder Troy. Even if all the rest should flee, Sthenelus and I will fight alone until we see the destined end of Ilium.

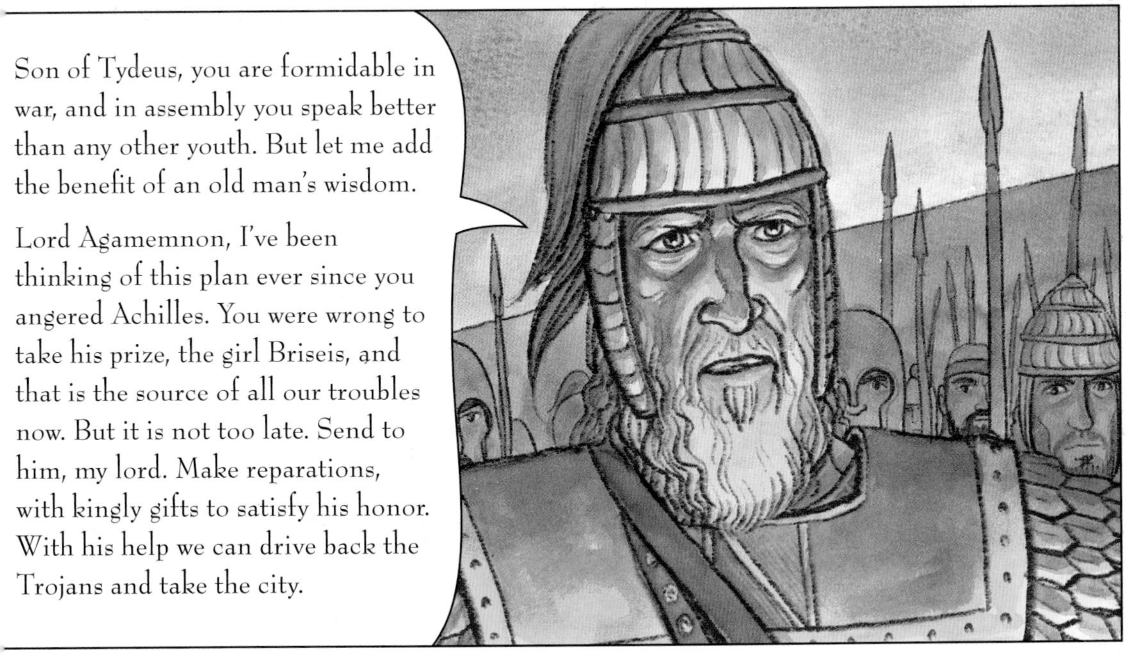
Son of Tydeus, you are formidable in war, and in assembly you speak better than any other youth. But let me add the benefit of an old man's wisdom.
Lord Agamemnon, I've been thinking of this plan ever since you angered Achilles. You were wrong to take his prize, the girl Briseis, and that is the source of all our troubles now. But it is not too late. Send to him, my lord. Make reparations, with kingly gifts to satisfy his honor. With his help we can drive back the Trojans and take the city.

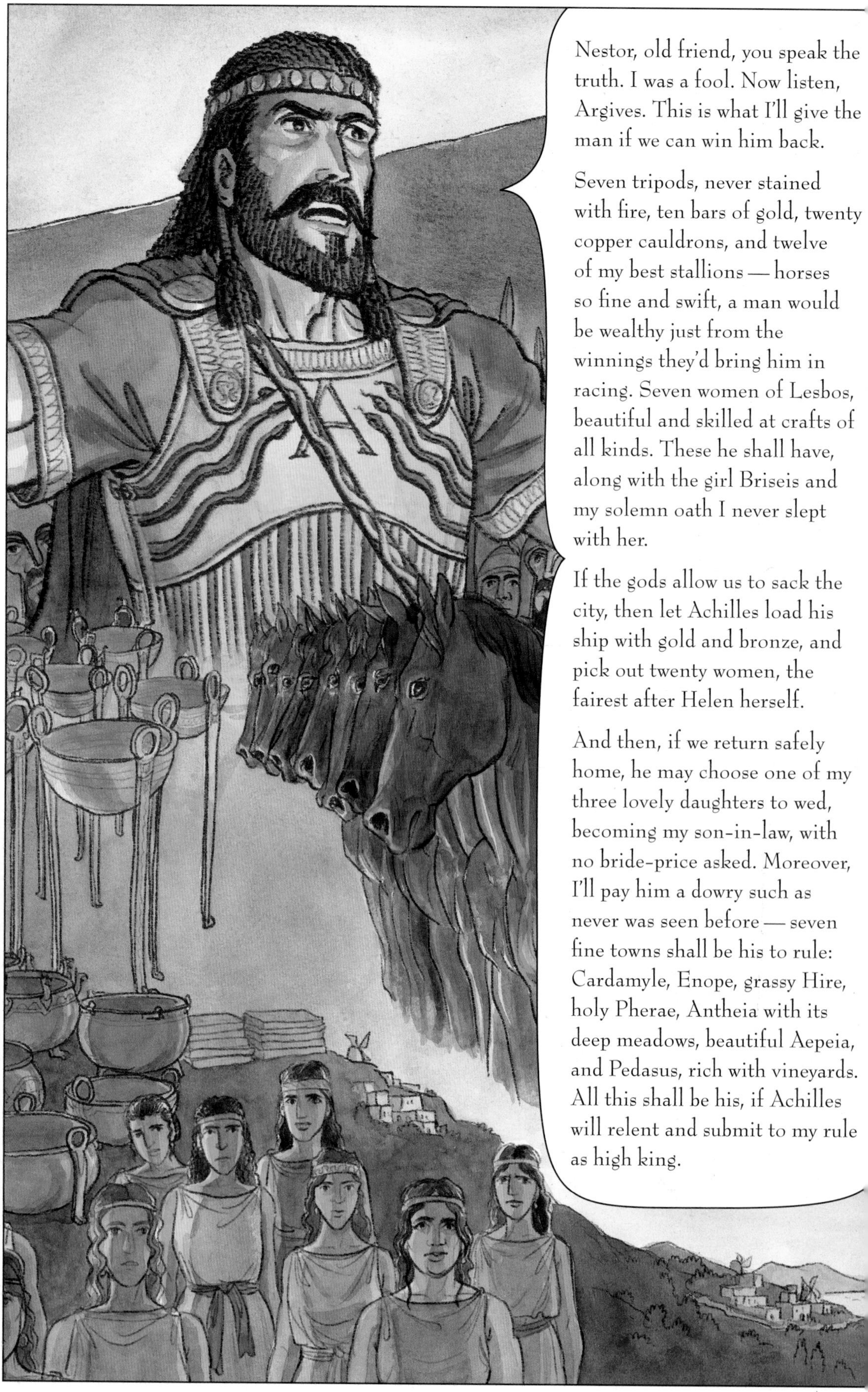
Nestor, old friend, you speak the truth. I was a fool. Now listen, Argives. This is what I'll give the man if we can win him back.
Seven tripods, never stained with fire, ten bars of gold, twenty copper cauldrons, and twelve of my best stallions — horses so fine and swift, a man would be wealthy just from the winnings they'd bring him in racing. Seven women of Lesbos, beautiful and skilled at crafts of all kinds. These he shall have, along with the girl Briseis and my solemn oath I never slept with her.
If the gods allow us to sack the city, then let Achilles load his ship with gold and bronze, and pick out twenty women, the fairest after Helen herself.
And then, if we return safely home, he may choose one of my three lovely daughters to wed, becoming my son-in-law, with no bride-price asked. Moreover, I'll pay him a dowry such as never was seen before — seven fine towns shall be his to rule: Cardamyle, Enope, grassy Hire, holy Pherae, Antheia with its deep meadows, beautiful Aepeia, and Pedasus, rich with vineyards. All this shall be his, if Achilles will relent and submit to my rule as high king.

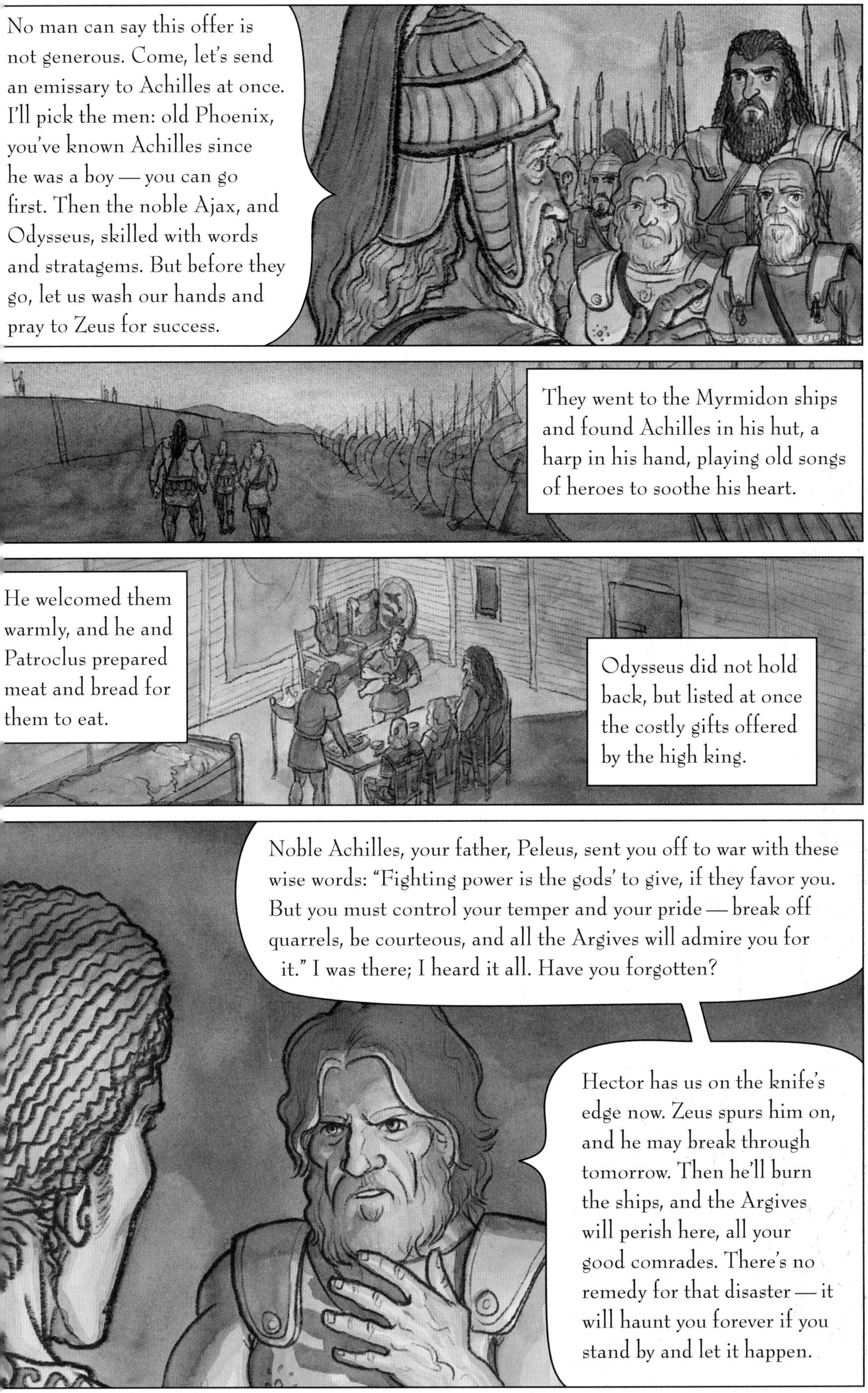
No man can say this offer is not generous. Come, let's send an emissary to Achilles at once. I'll pick the men: old Phoenix, you've known Achilles since he was a boy — you can go first. Then the noble Ajax, and Odysseus, skilled with words and stratagems. But before they go, let us wash our hands and pray to Zeus for success.
They went to the Myrmidon ships and found Achilles in his hut, a harp in his hand, playing old songs of heroes to soothe his heart.
He welcomed them warmly, and he and Patroclus prepared meat and bread for them to eat.
Odysseus did not hold back, but listed at once the costly gifts offered by the high king.
Noble Achilles, your father, Peleus, sent you off to war with these wise words: "Fighting power is the gods' to give, if they favor you. But you must control your temper and your pride — break off quarrels, be courteous, and all the Argives will admire you for it." I was there; I heard it all. Have you forgotten?
Hector has us on the knife's edge now. Zeus spurs him on, and he may break through tomorrow. Then he'll burn the ships, and the Argives will perish here, all your good comrades. There's no remedy for that disaster — it will haunt you forever if you stand by and let it happen.

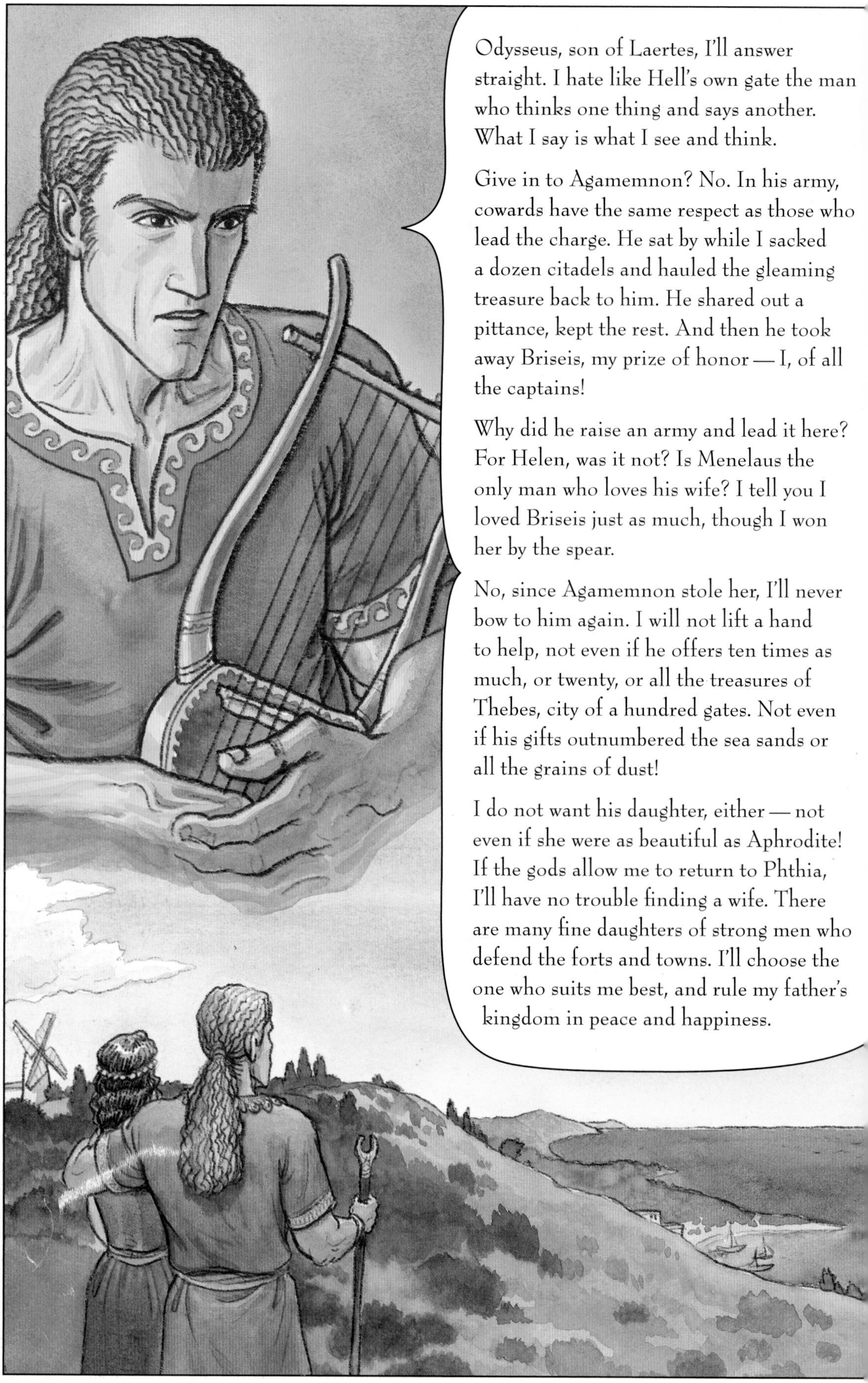
Odysseus, son of Laertes, I'll answer straight. I hate like Hell's own gate the man who thinks one thing and says another. What I say is what I see and think.
Give in to Agamemnon? No. In his army, cowards have the same respect as those who lead the charge. He sat by while I sacked a dozen citadels and hauled the gleaming treasure back to him. He shared out a pittance, kept the rest. And then he took away Briseis, my prize of honor — I, of all the captains!
Why did he raise an army and lead it here? For Helen, was it not? Is Menelaus the only man who loves his wife? I tell you I loved Briseis just as much, though I won her by the spear.
No, since Agamemnon stole her, I'll never bow to him again. I will not lift a hand to help, not even if he offers ten times as much, or twenty, or all the treasures of Thebes, city of a hundred gates. Not even if his gifts outnumbered the sea sands or all the grains of dust!
I do not want his daughter, either — not even if she were as beautiful as Aphrodite! If the gods allow me to return to Phthia, I'll have no trouble finding a wife. There are many fine daughters of strong men who defend the forts and towns. I'll choose the one who suits me best, and rule my father's kingdom in peace and happiness.

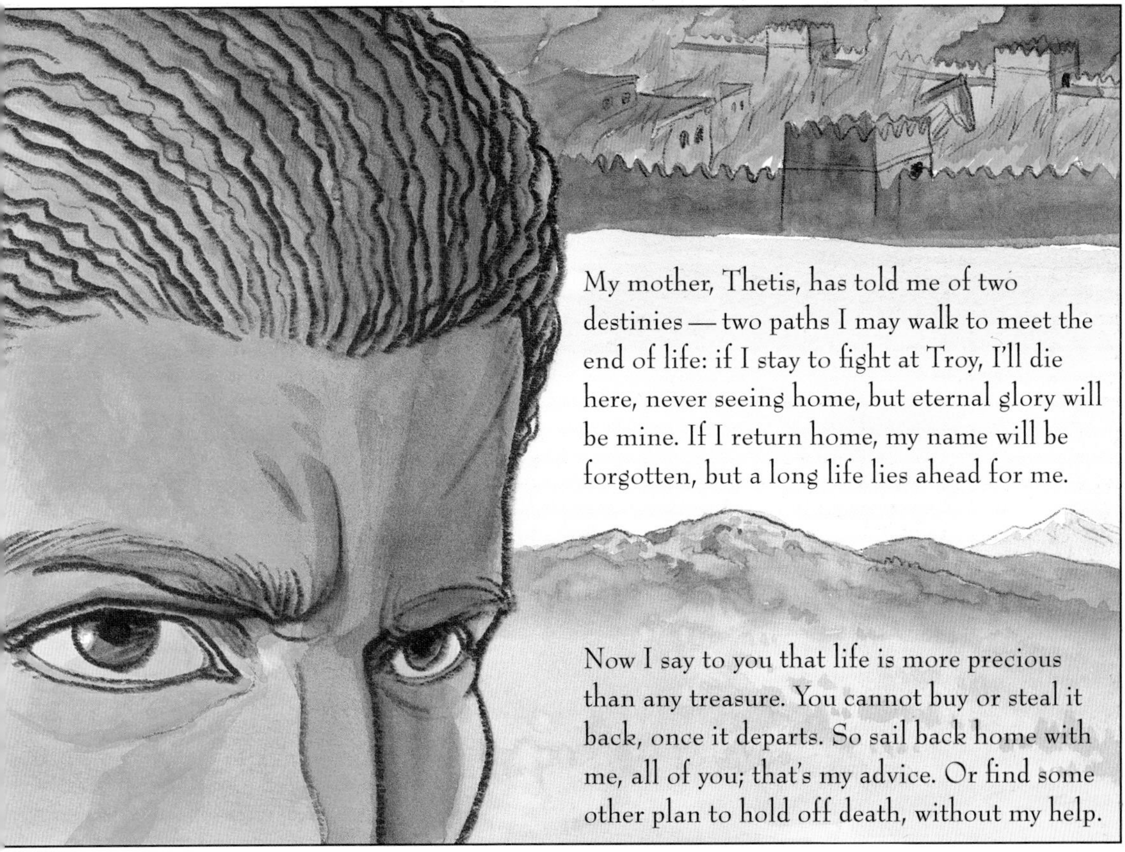
My mother, Thetis, has told me of two destinies — two paths I may walk to meet the end of life: if I stay to fight at Troy, I'll die here, never seeing home, but eternal glory will be mine. If I return home, my name will be forgotten, but a long life lies ahead for me.
Now I say to you that life is more precious than any treasure. You cannot buy or steal it back, once it departs. So sail back home with me, all of you; that's my advice. Or find some other plan to hold off death, without my help.

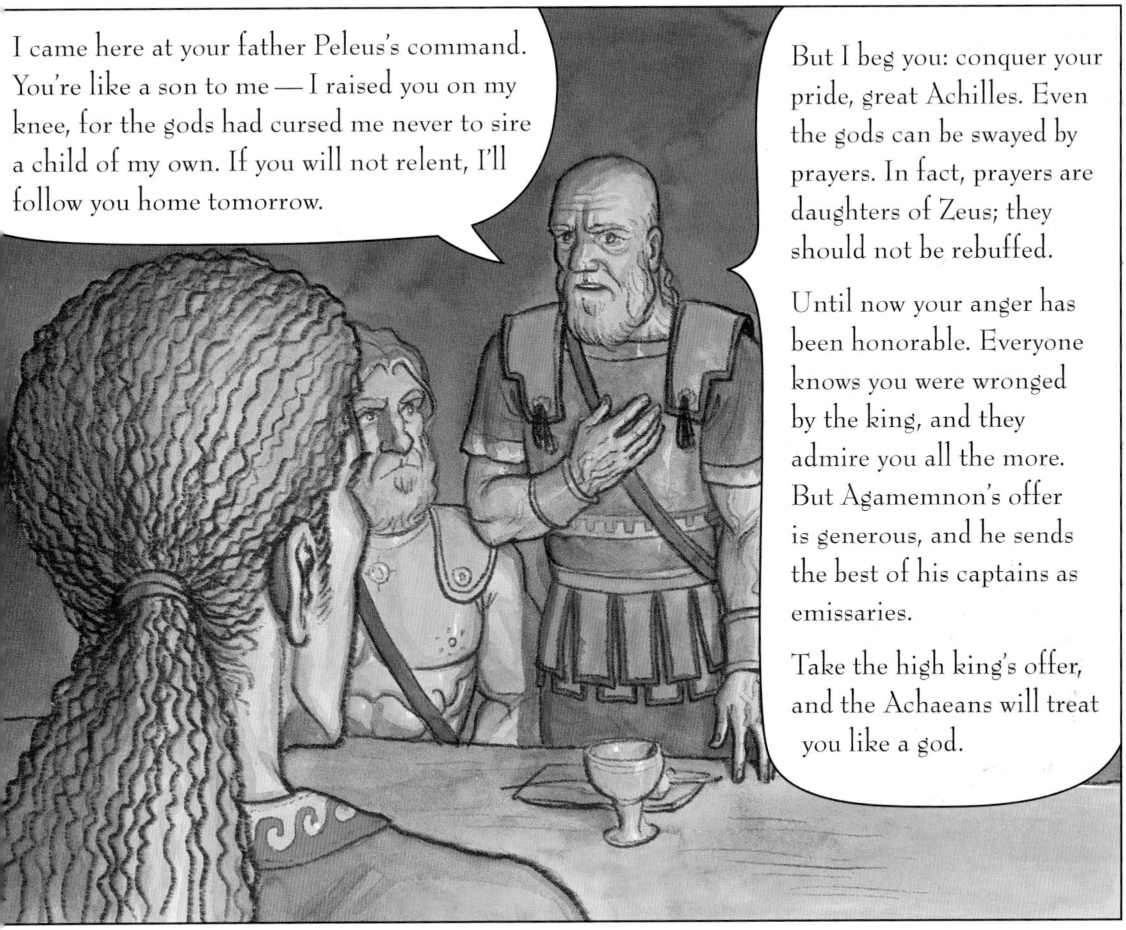
I came here at your father Peleus's command. You're like a son to me — I raised you on my knee, for the gods had cursed me never to sire a child of my own. If you will not relent, I'll follow you home tomorrow.
But I beg you: conquer your pride, great Achilles. Even the gods can be swayed by prayers. In fact, prayers are daughters of Zeus; they should not be rebuffed.
Until now your anger has been honorable. Everyone knows you were wronged by the king, and they admire you all the more. But Agamemnon's offer is generous, and he sends the best of his captains as emissaries.
Take the high king's offer, and the Achaeans will treat you like a god.

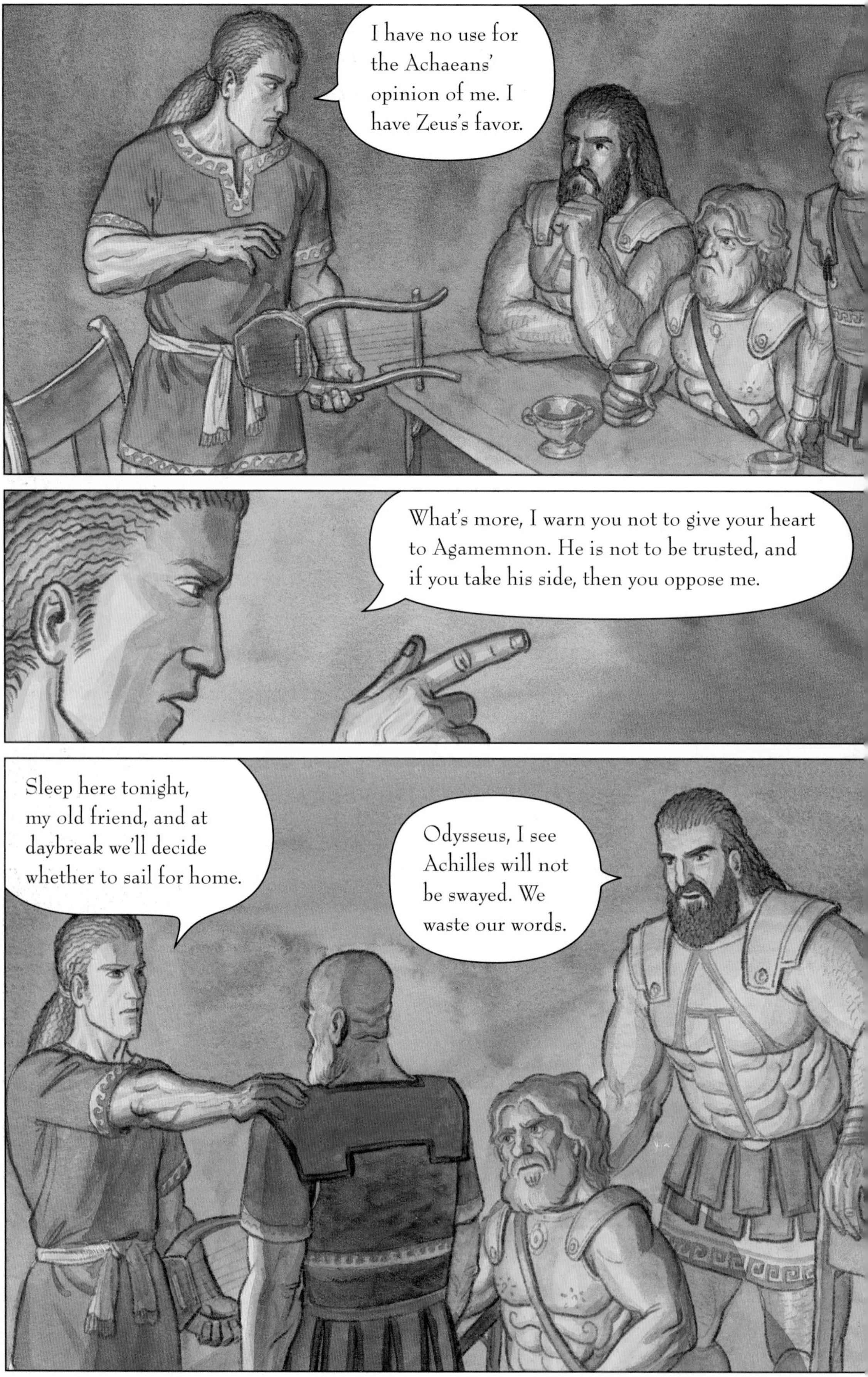
I have no use for the Achaeans' opinion of me. I have Zeus's favor.
What's more, I warn you not to give your heart to Agamemnon. He is not to be trusted, and if you take his side, then you oppose me.
Sleep here tonight, my old friend, and at daybreak we'll decide whether to sail for home.
Odysseus, I see Achilles will not be swayed. We waste our words.

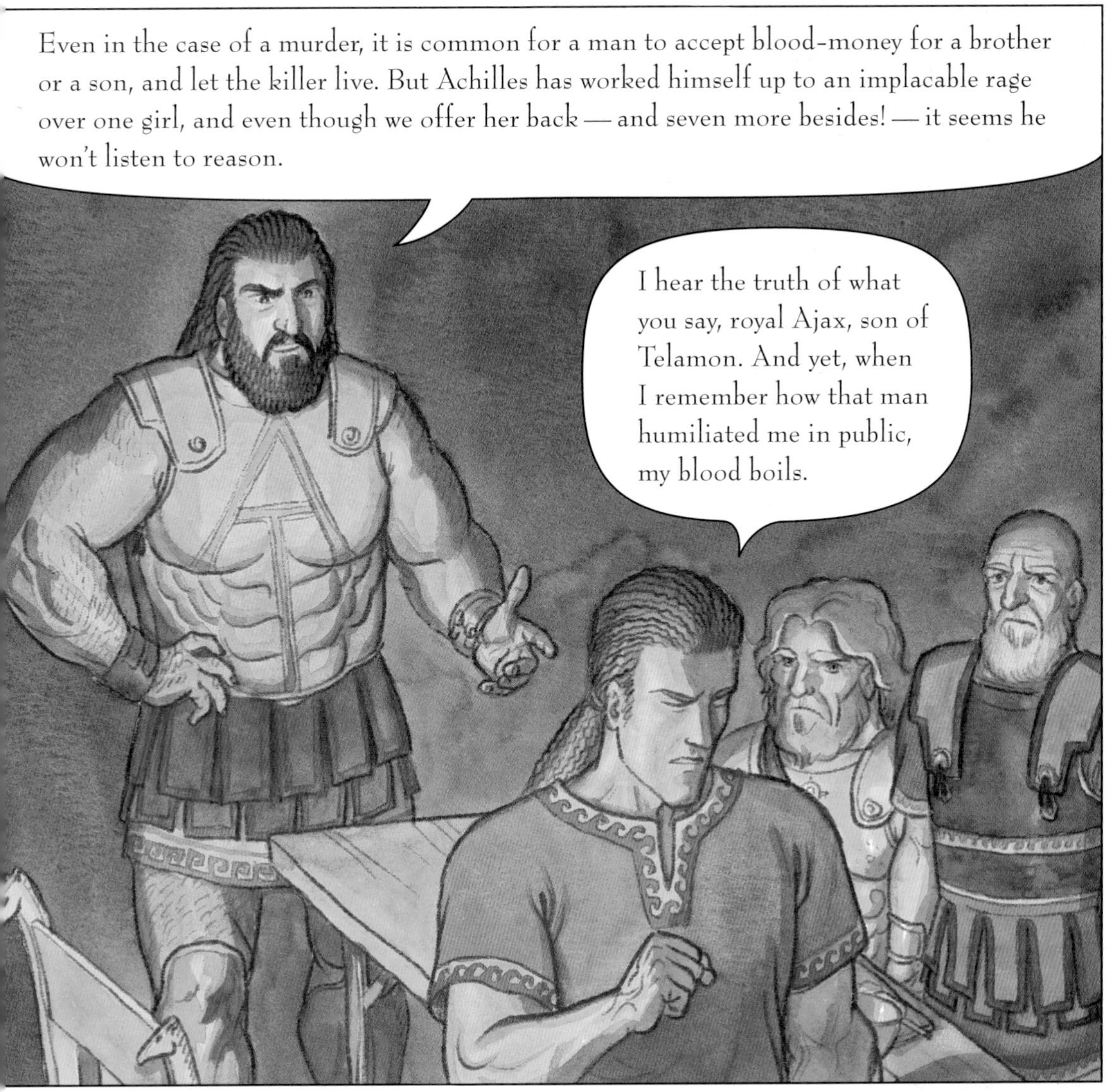
Even in the case of a murder, it is common for a man to accept blood-money for a brother or a son, and let the killer live. But Achilles has worked himself up to an implacable rage over one girl, and even though we offer her back — and seven more besides! — it seems he won't listen to reason.
I hear the truth of what you say, royal Ajax, son of Telamon. And yet, when I remember how that man humiliated me in public, my blood boils.

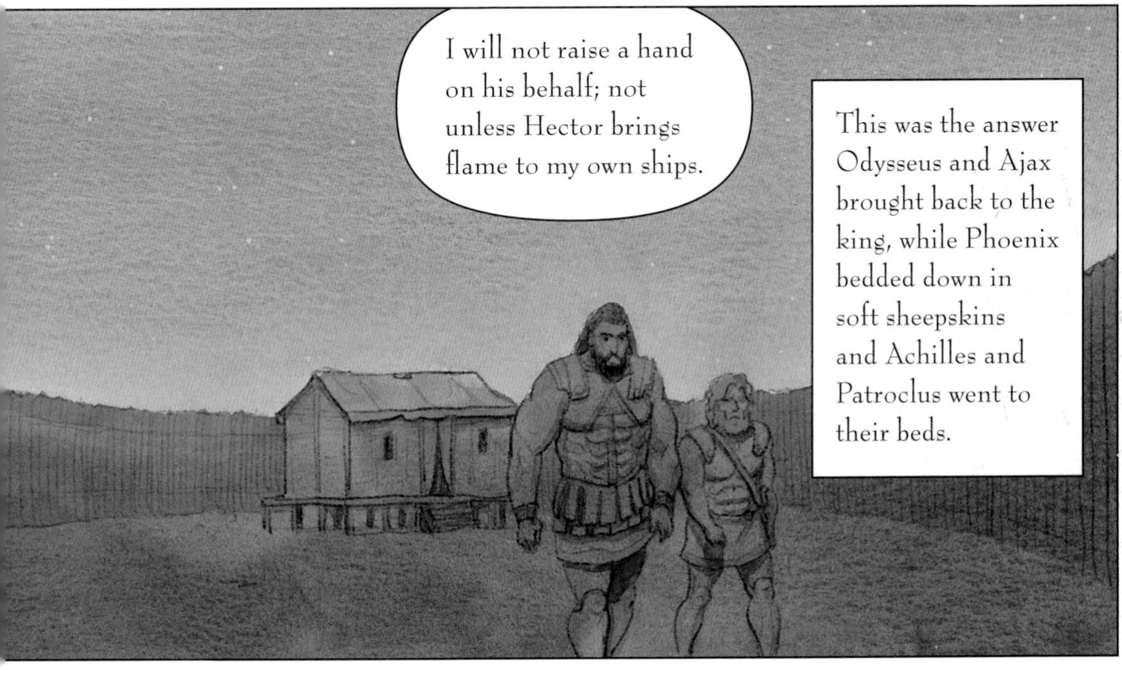
I will not raise a hand on his behalf; not unless Hector brings flame to my own ships.
This was the answer Odysseus and Ajax brought back to the king, while Phoenix bedded down in soft sheepskins and Achilles and Patroclus went to their beds.

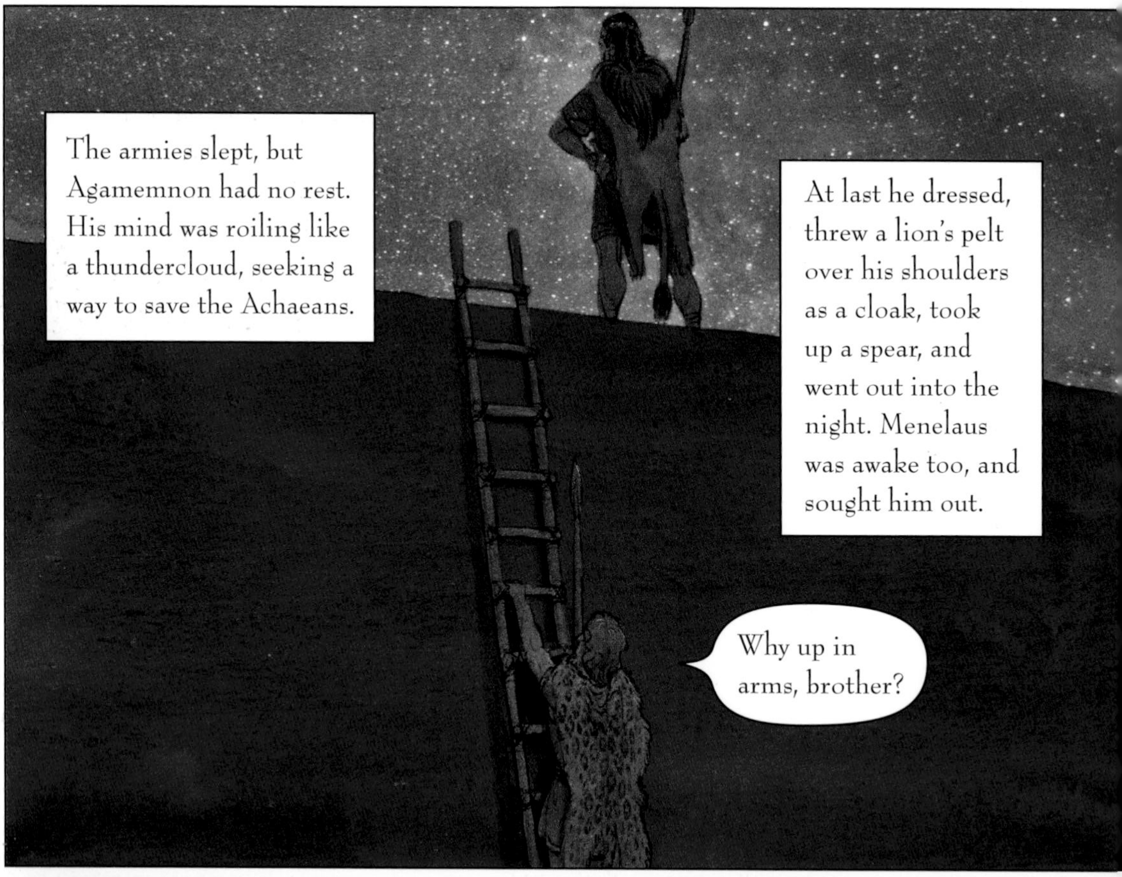
The armies slept, but Agamemnon had no rest. His mind was roiling like a thundercloud, seeking a way to save the Achaeans.
At last he dressed, threw a lion's pelt over his shoulders as a cloak, took up a spear, and went out into the night. Menelaus was awake too, and sought him out.
Why up in arms, brother?

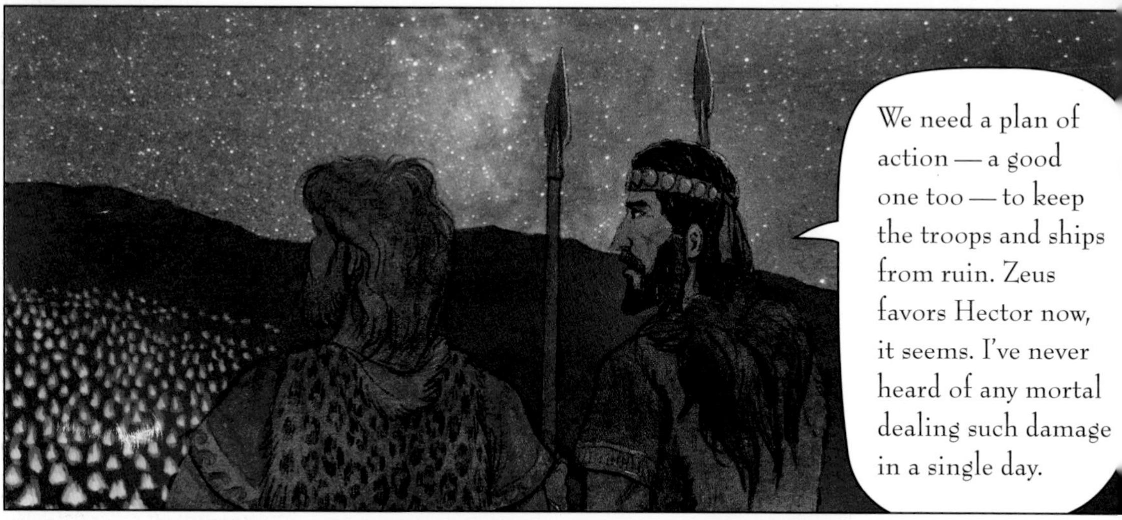
We need a plan of action — a good one too — to keep the troops and ships from ruin. Zeus favors Hector now, it seems. I've never heard of any mortal dealing such damage in a single day.

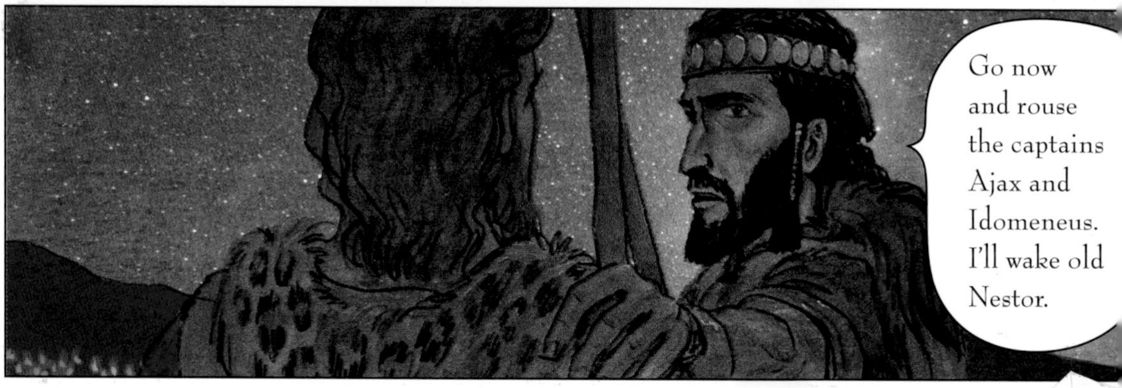
Go now and rouse the captains Ajax and Idomeneus. I'll wake old Nestor.

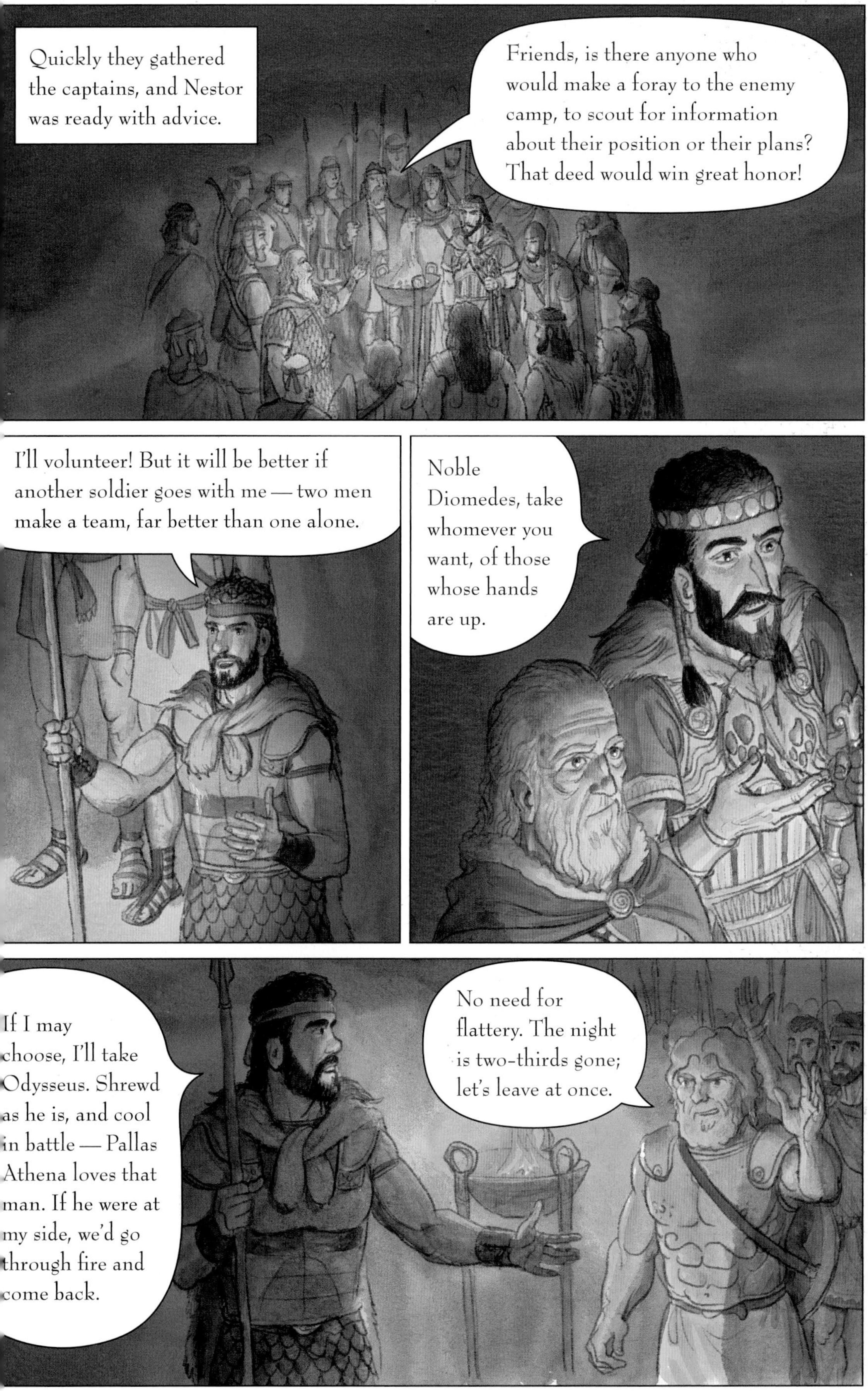
Quickly they gathered the captains, and Nestor was ready with advice.
Friends, is there anyone who would make a foray to the enemy camp, to scout for information about their position or their plans? That deed would win great honor!
I'll volunteer! But it will be better if another soldier goes with me — two men make a team, far better than one alone.
Noble Diomedes, take whomever you want, of those whose hands are up.
If I may choose, I'll take Odysseus. Shrewd as he is, and cool in battle — Pallas Athena loves that man. If he were at my side, we'd go through fire and come back.
No need for flattery. The night is two-thirds gone; let's leave at once.

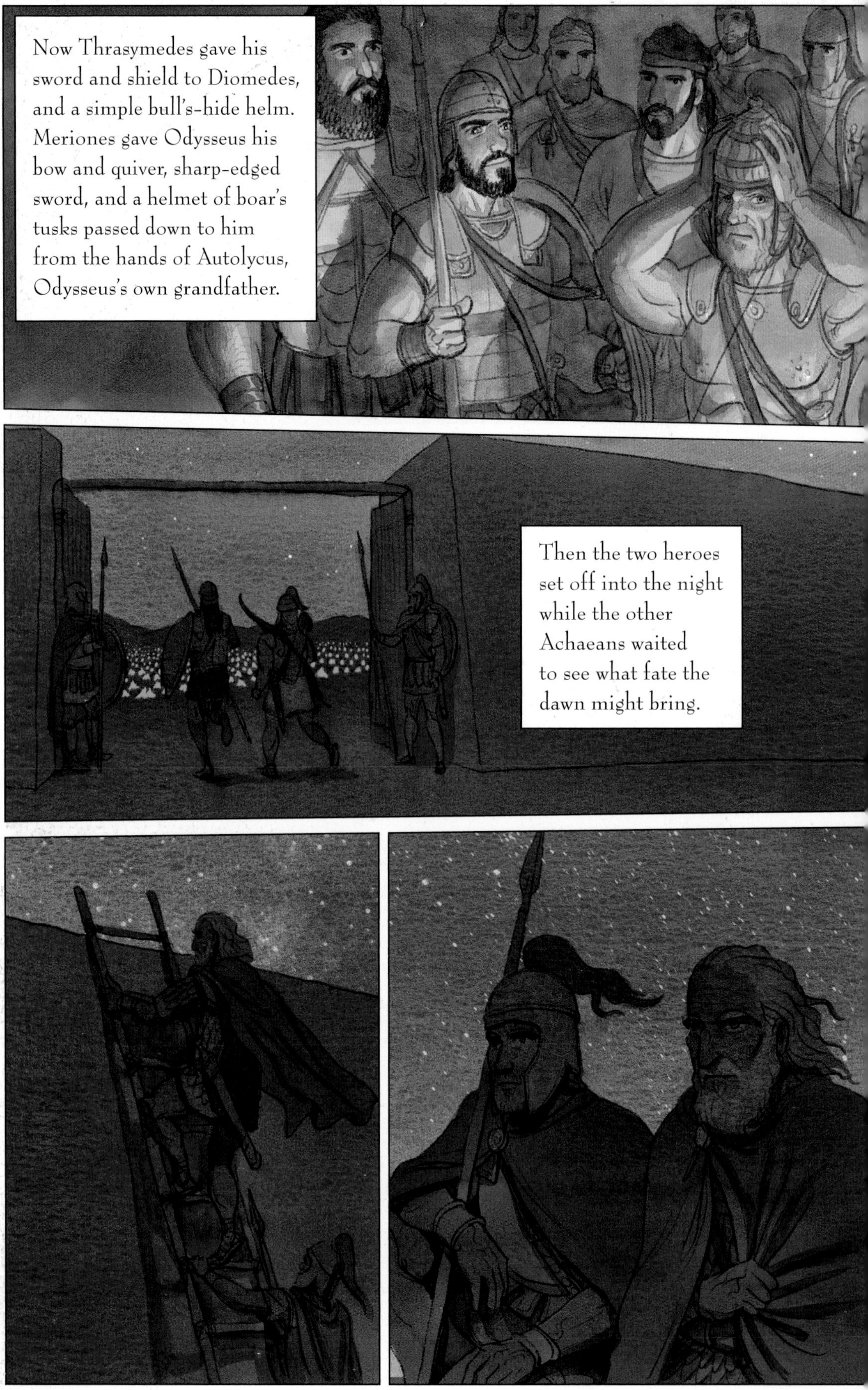
Now Thrasymedes gave his sword and shield to Diomedes, and a simple bull's-hide helm. Meriones gave Odysseus his bow and quiver, sharp-edged sword, and a helmet of boar's tusks passed down to him from the hands of Autolycus, Odysseus's own grandfather.
Then the two heroes set off into the night while the other Achaeans waited to see what fate the dawn might bring.

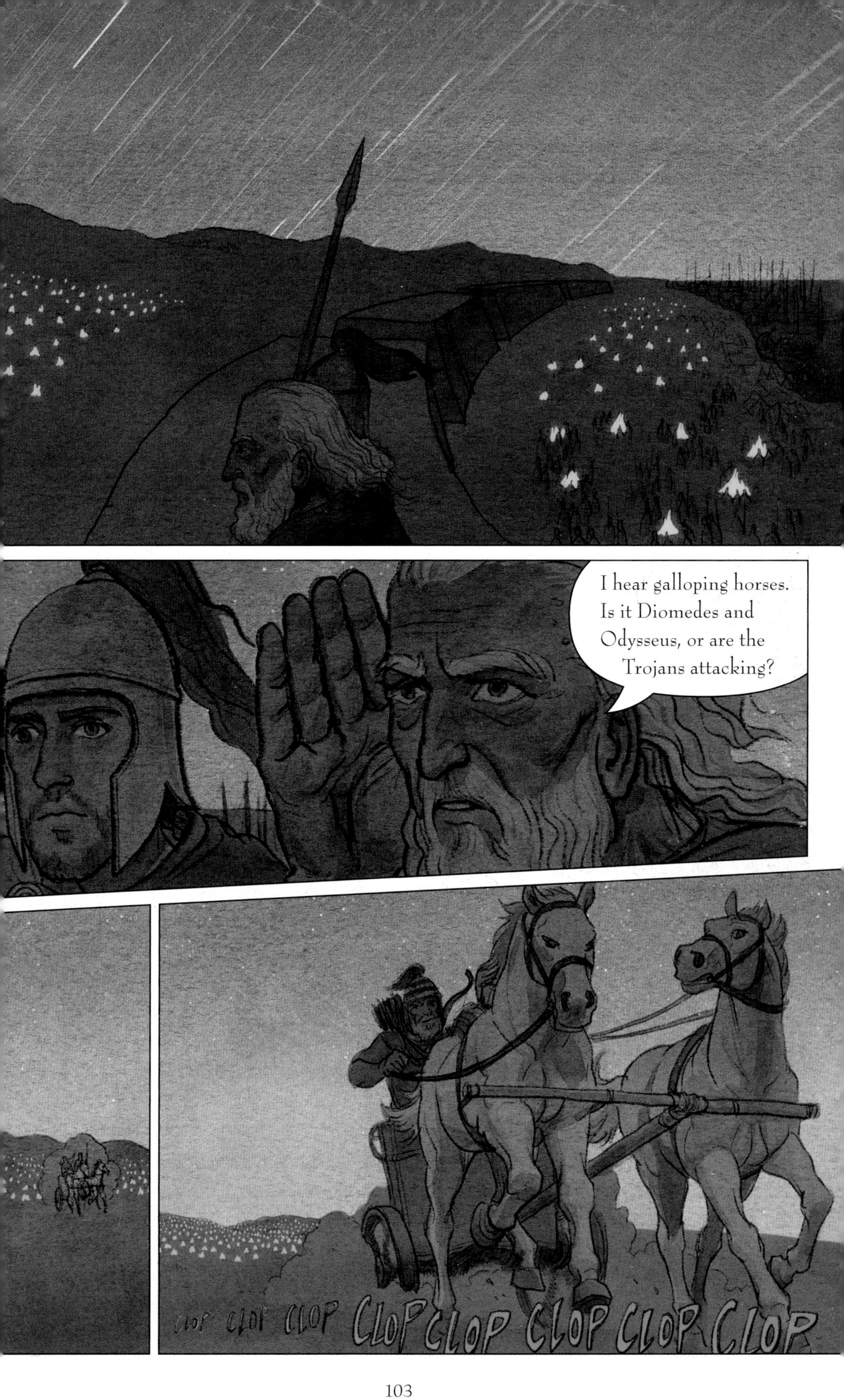
I hear galloping horses. Is it Diomedes and Odysseus, or are the Trojans attacking?
CLOP CLOP CLOP CLOP CLOP CLOP CLOP CLOP

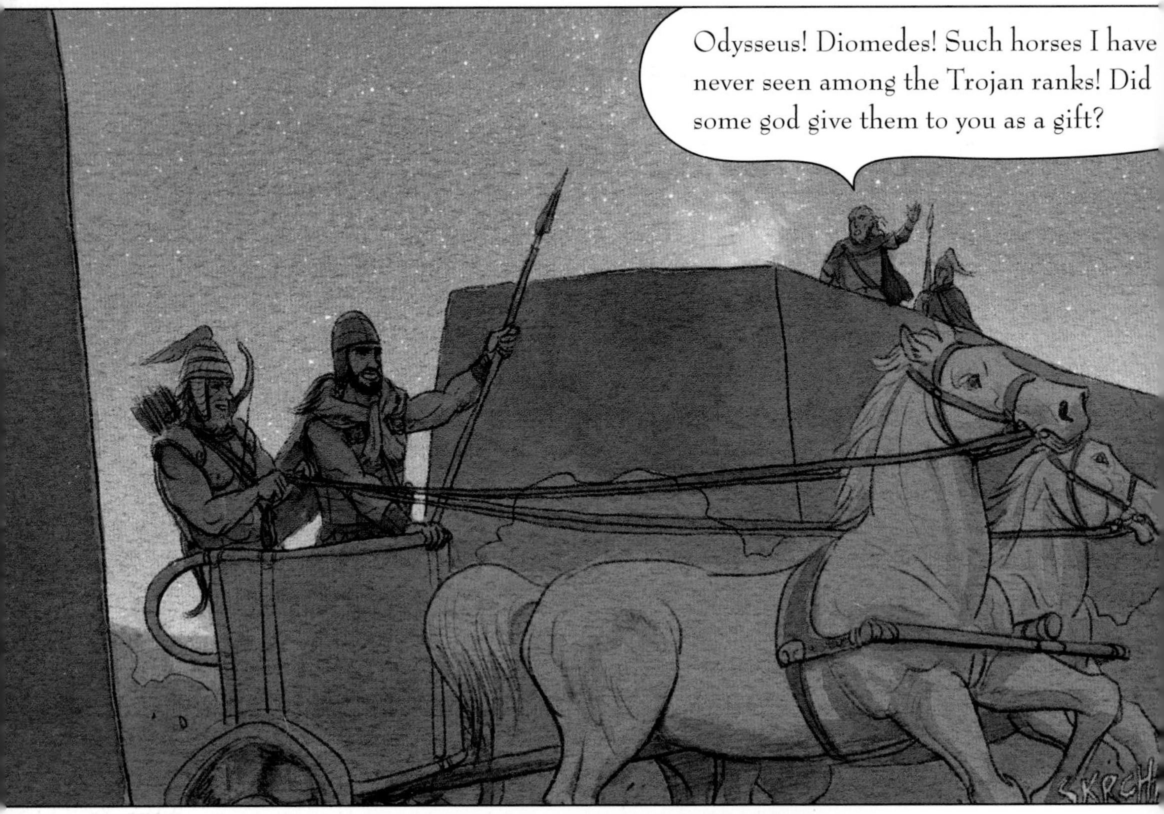
Odysseus! Diomedes! Such horses I have never seen among the Trojan ranks! Did some god give them to you as a gift?
SKRCH

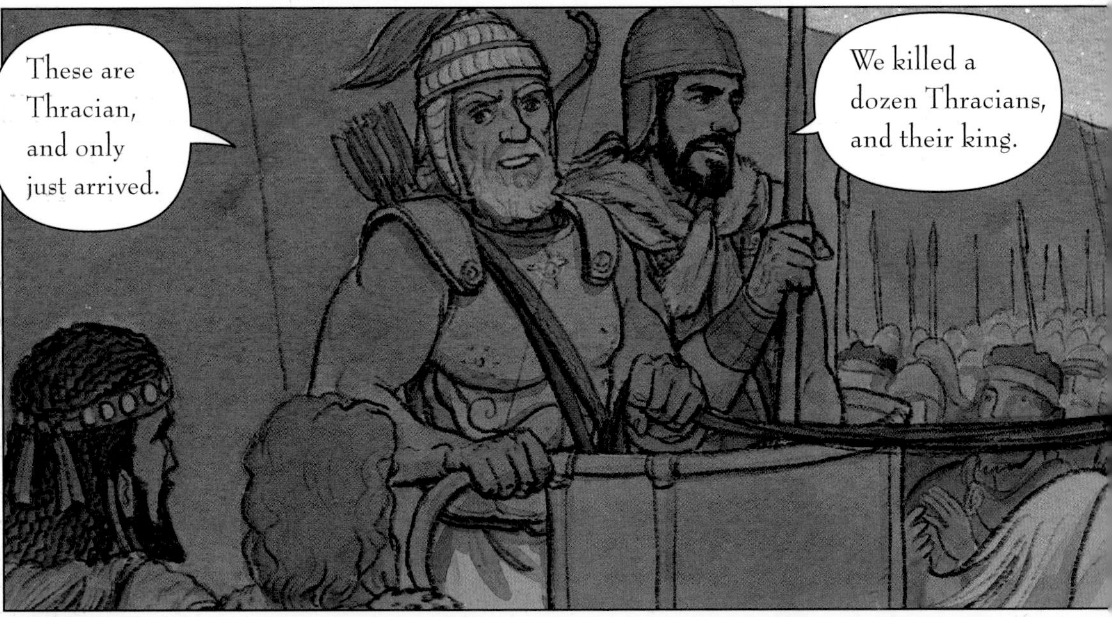
These are Thracian, and only just arrived.
We killed a dozen Thracians, and their king.

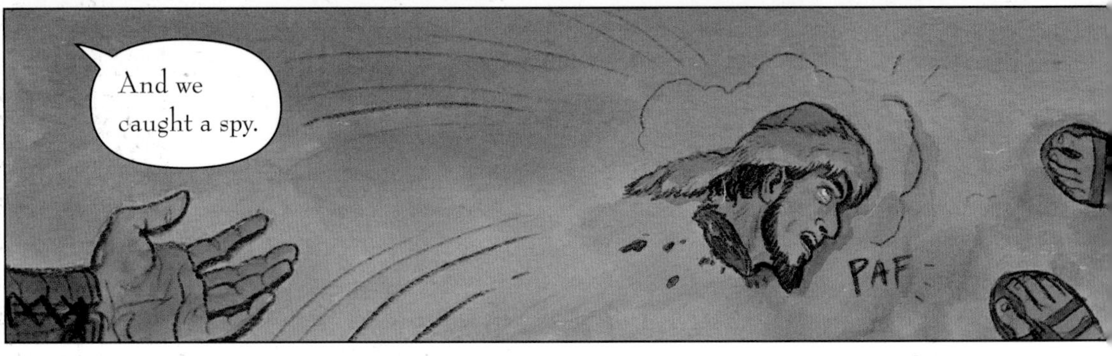
And we caught a spy.
PAF

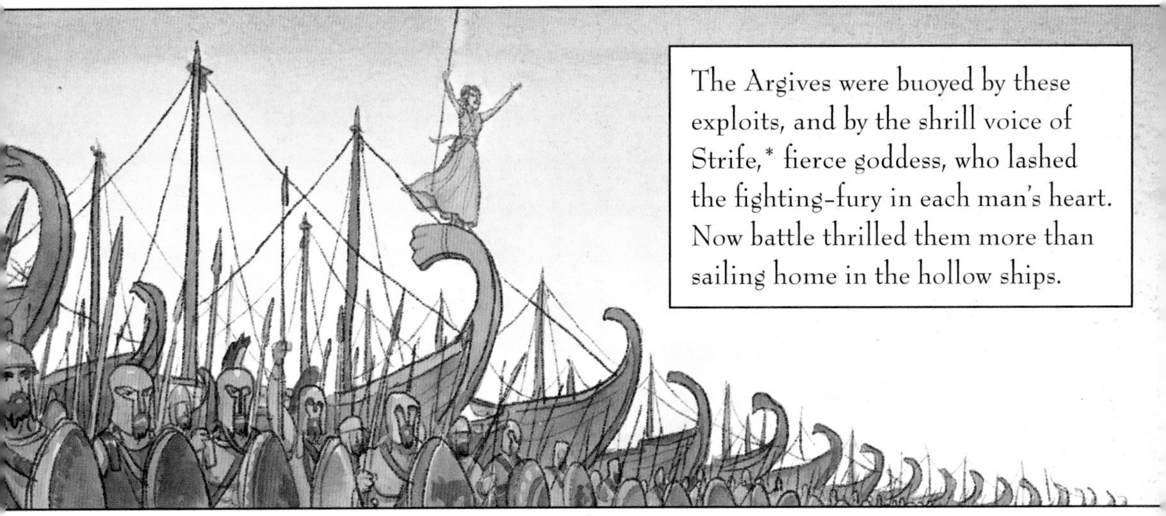
The Argives were buoyed by these exploits, and by the shrill voice of Strife,* fierce goddess, who lashed the fighting-fury in each man's heart. Now battle thrilled them more than sailing home in the hollow ships.

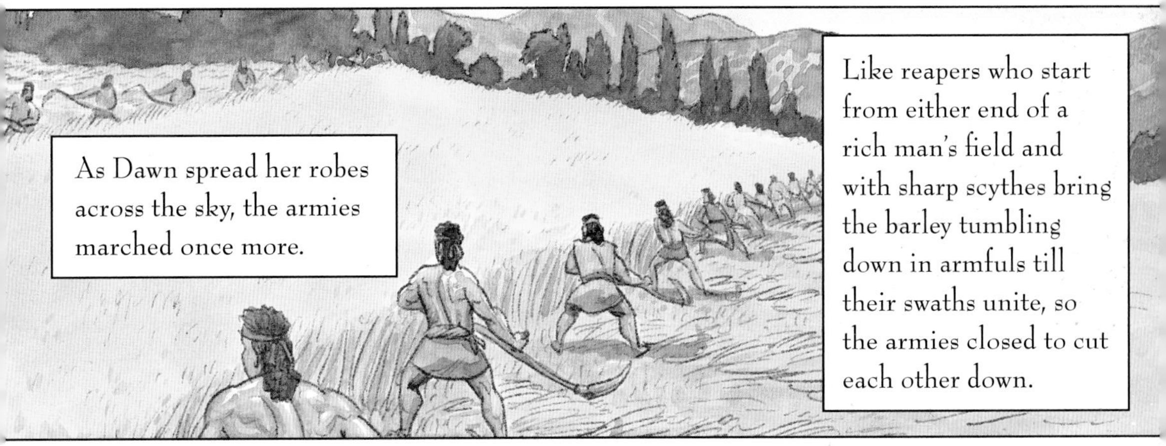
As Dawn spread her robes across the sky, the armies marched once more.
Like reapers who start from either end of a rich man's field and with sharp scythes bring the barley tumbling down in armfuls till their swaths unite, so the armies closed to cut each other down.

All morning, volley and counter-volley found their mark, and men crowded down to the house of Death. But just at the hour when a woodman felling trees in a mountain dell will stop to rest his weary arms, the Argives broke the Trojan lines. In charged Agamemnon, in front of all.

First he killed Bienor and his driver, Oileus, stripped them of their gear, and then killed Isus and Antiphus, sons of Priam.

Then Peisander and Hippolochus. They begged for their lives, but their father was a sworn enemy of Menelaus, so Agamemnon cut them down.

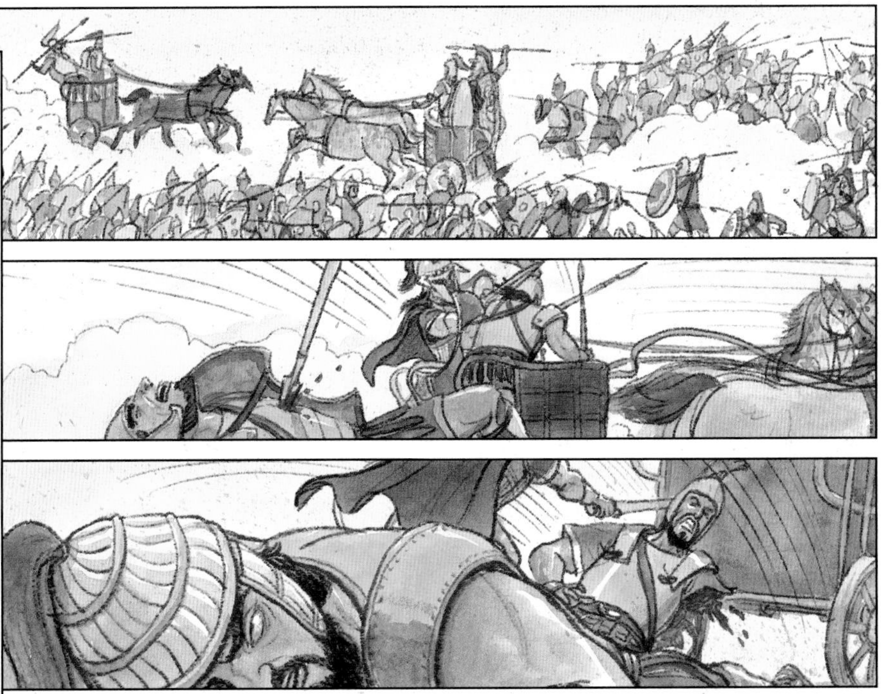

* Strife, also called Eris or Discord, is the same goddess who started the Trojan War with a golden apple, in revenge for not being invited to Peleus and Thetis's wedding.

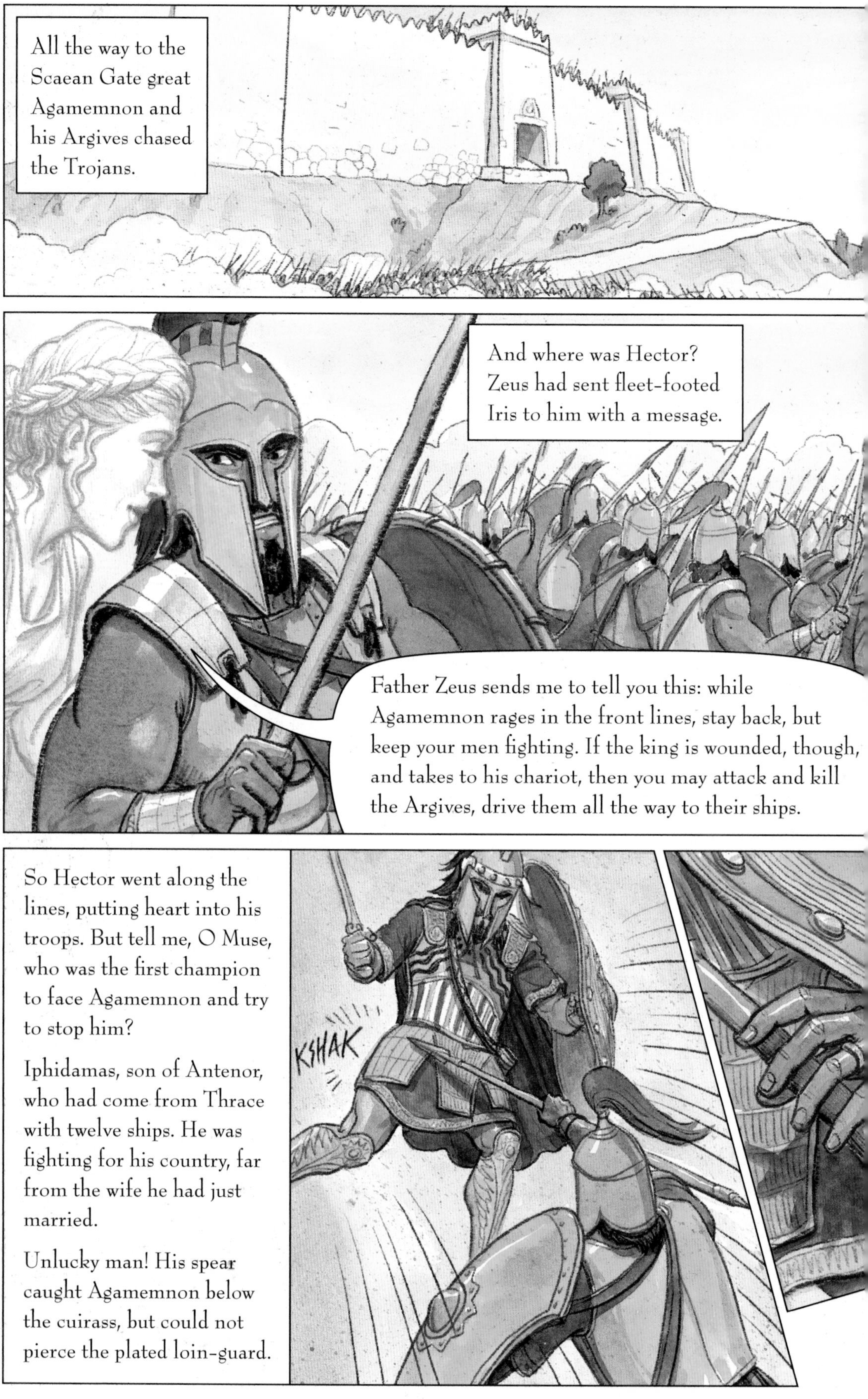
All the way to the Scaean Gate great Agamemnon and his Argives chased the Trojans.
And where was Hector? Zeus had sent fleet-footed Iris to him with a message.
Father Zeus sends me to tell you this: while Agamemnon rages in the front lines, stay back, but keep your men fighting. If the king is wounded, though, and takes to his chariot, then you may attack and kill the Argives, drive them all the way to their ships.
So Hector went along the lines, putting heart into his troops. But tell me, O Muse, who was the first champion to face Agamemnon and try to stop him?
Iphidamas, son of Antenor, who had come from Thrace with twelve ships. He was fighting for his country, far from the wife he had just married.
Unlucky man! His spear caught Agamemnon below the cuirass, but could not pierce the plated loin-guard.
KSHAK

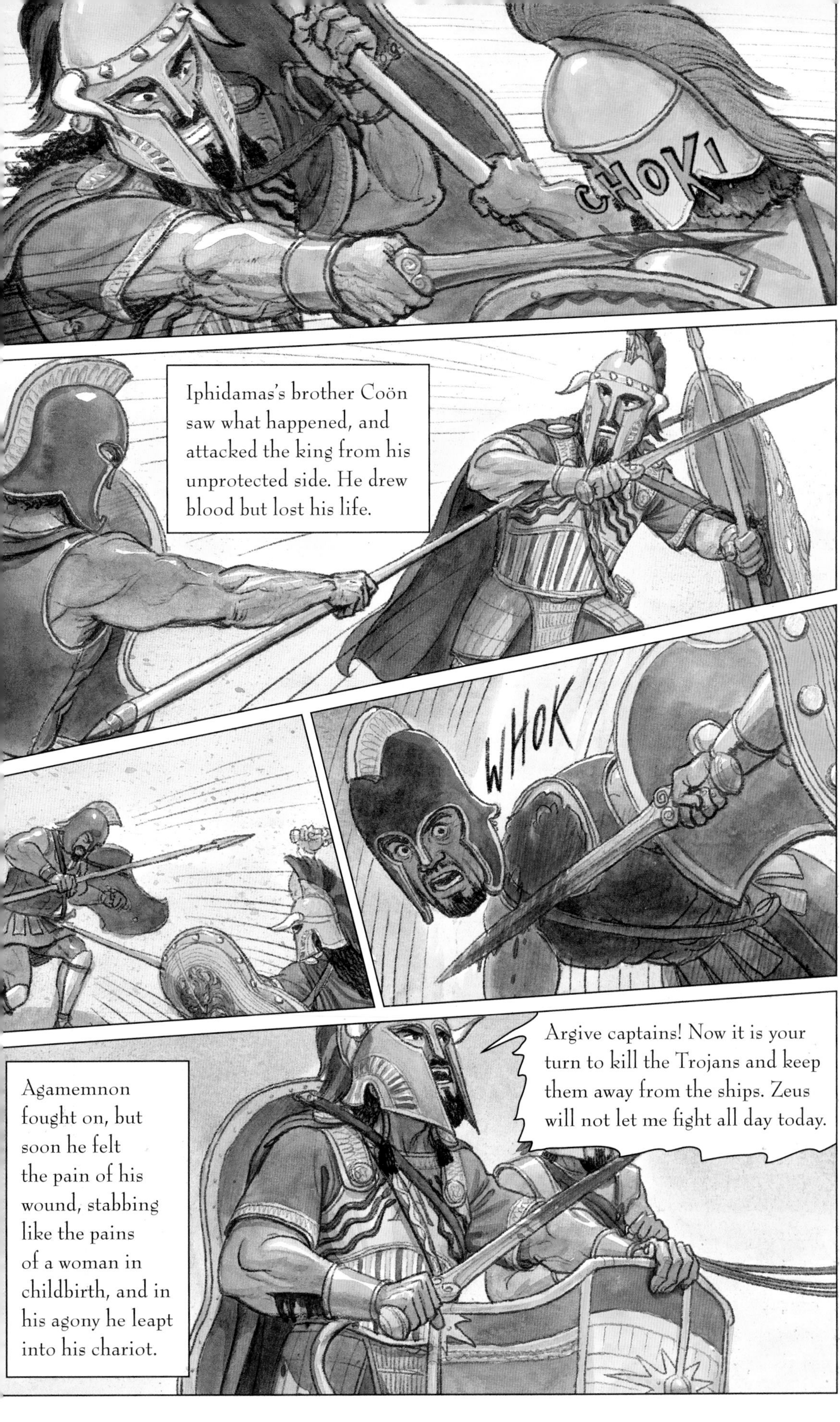
CHOK!
Iphidamas's brother Coön saw what happened, and attacked the king from his unprotected side. He drew blood but lost his life.
WHOK
Agamemnon fought on, but soon he felt the pain of his wound, stabbing like the pains of a woman in childbirth, and in his agony he leapt into his chariot.
Argive captains! Now it is your turn to kill the Trojans and keep them away from the ships. Zeus will not let me fight all day today.

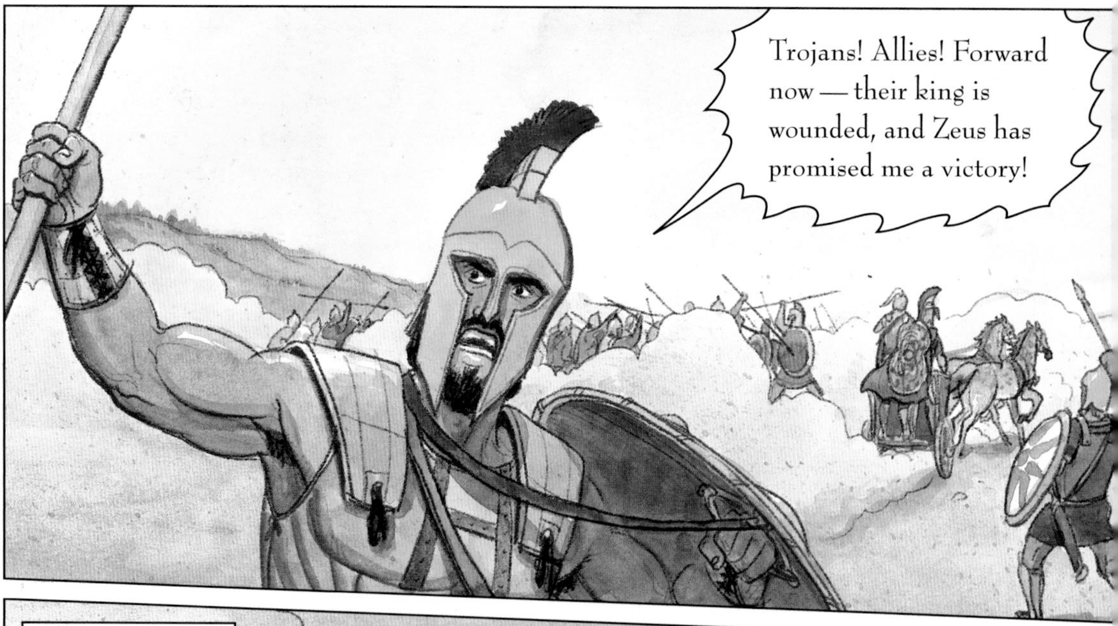
Trojans! Allies! Forward now — their king is wounded, and Zeus has promised me a victory!

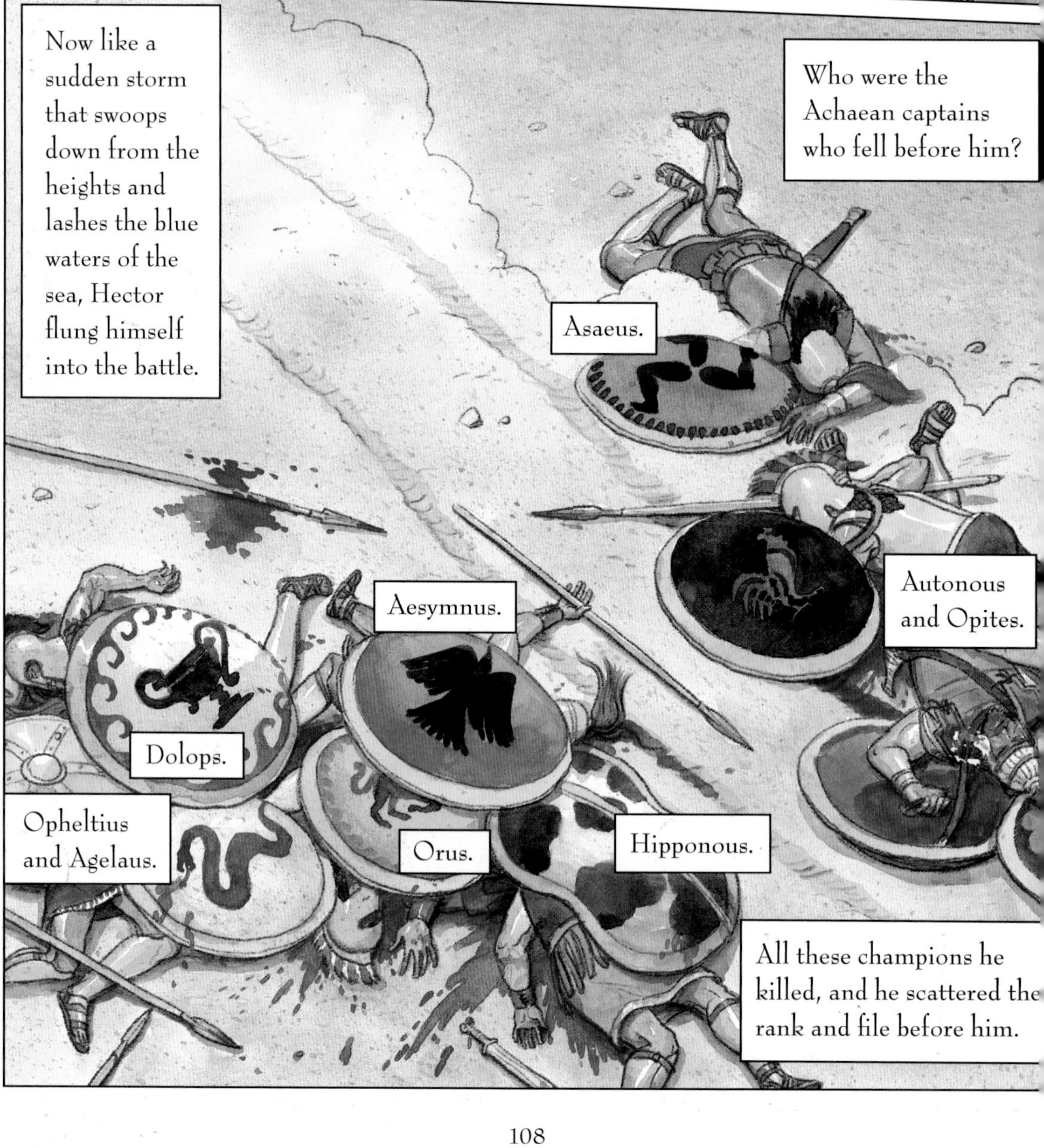
Now like a sudden storm that swoops down from the heights and lashes the blue waters of the sea, Hector flung himself into the battle.
Who were the Achaean captains who fell before him?
Asaeus.
Autonous and Opites.
Aesymnus.
Dolops.
Opheltius and Agelaus.
Orus.
Hipponous.
All these champions he killed, and he scattered the rank and file before him.

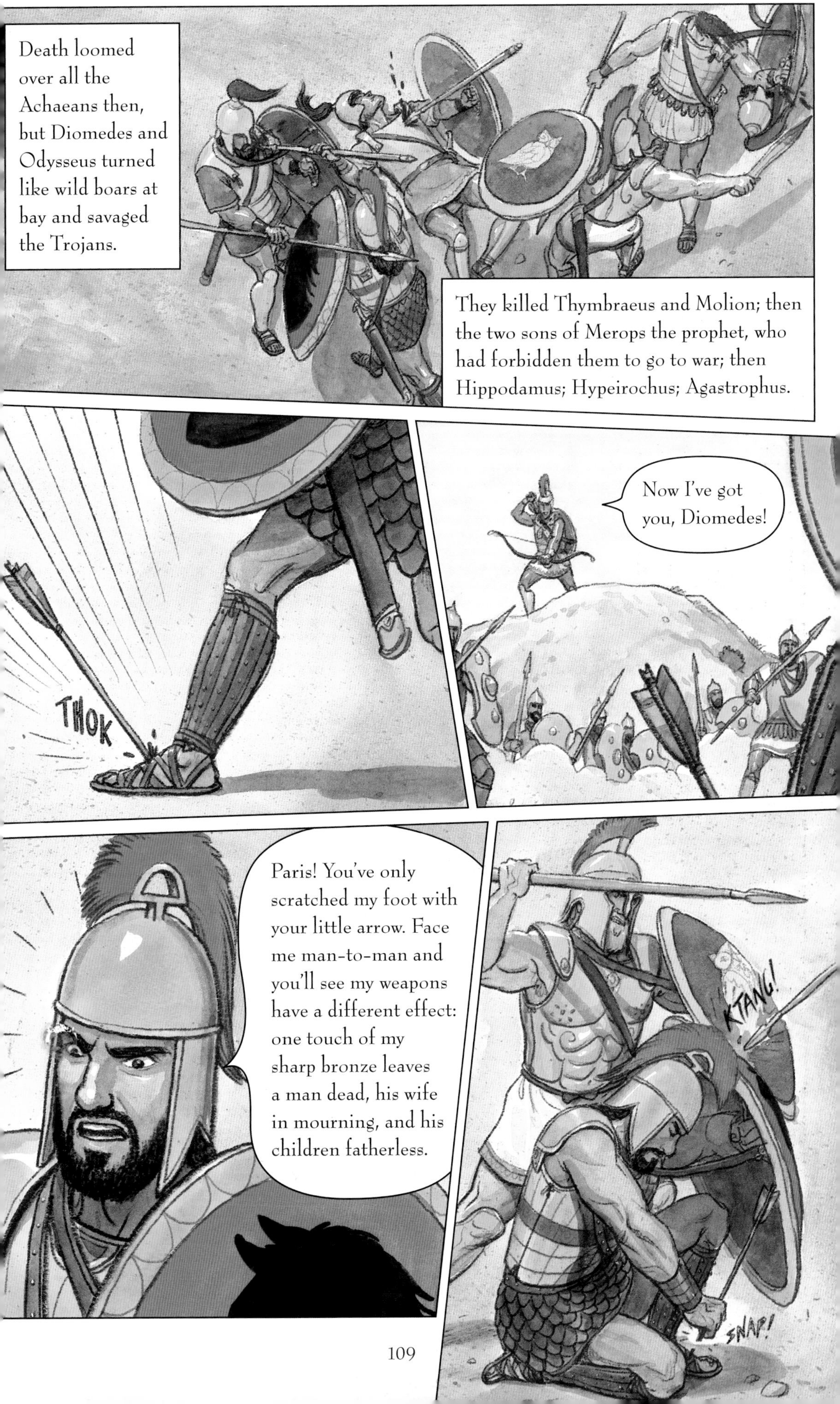
Death loomed over all the Achaeans then, but Diomedes and Odysseus turned like wild boars at bay and savaged the Trojans.
They killed Thymbraeus and Molion; then the two sons of Merops the prophet, who had forbidden them to go to war; then Hippodamus; Hypeirochus; Agastrophus.
THOK
Now I've got you, Diomedes!
Paris! You've only scratched my foot with your little arrow. Face me man-to-man and you'll see my weapons have a different effect: one touch of my sharp bronze leaves a man dead, his wife in mourning, and his children fatherless.
KTANG!
SNAP!

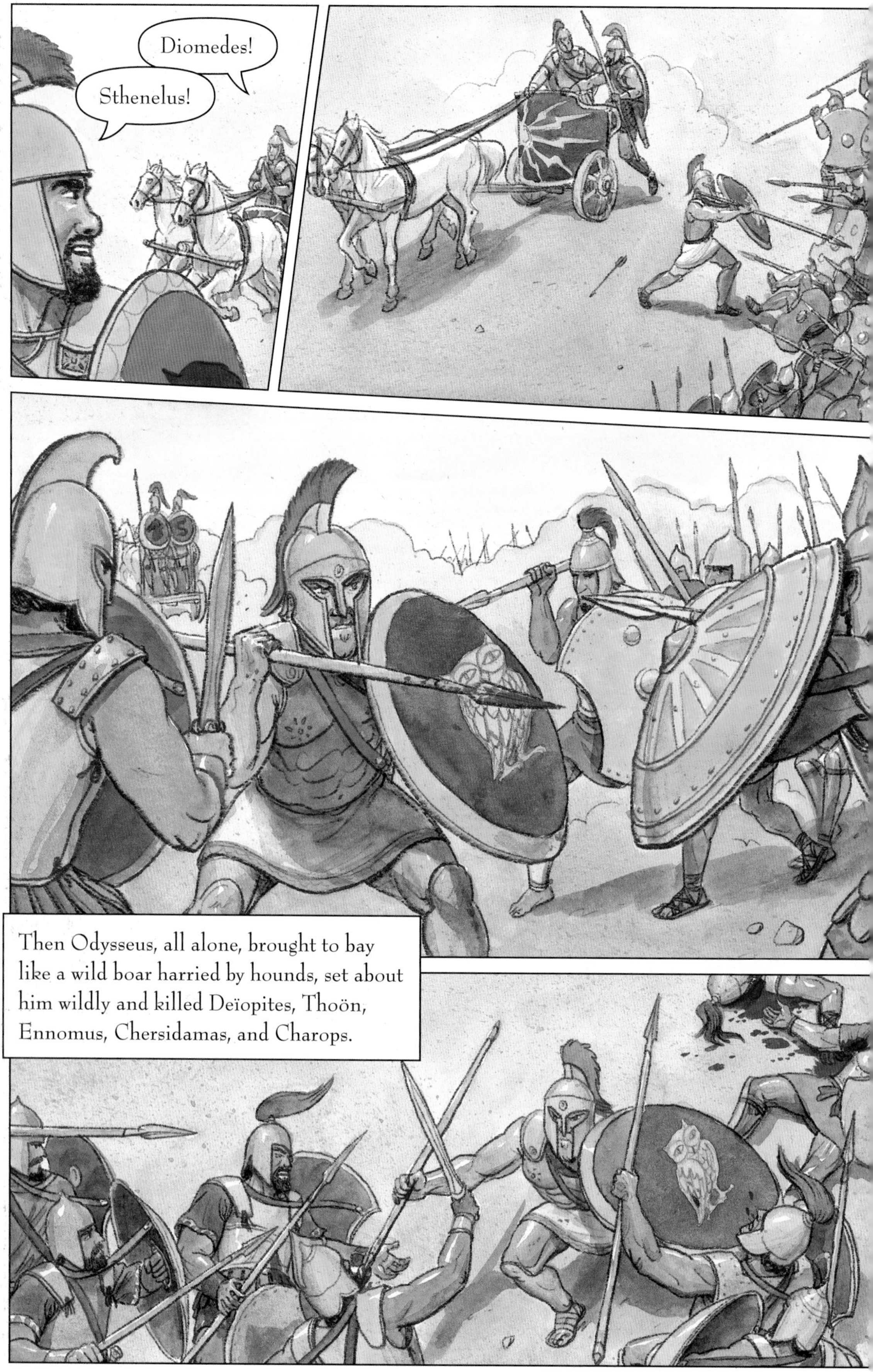
Diomedes!
Sthenelus!
Then Odysseus, all alone, brought to bay like a wild boar harried by hounds, set about him wildly and killed Deïopites, Thoön, Ennomus, Chersidamas, and Charops.

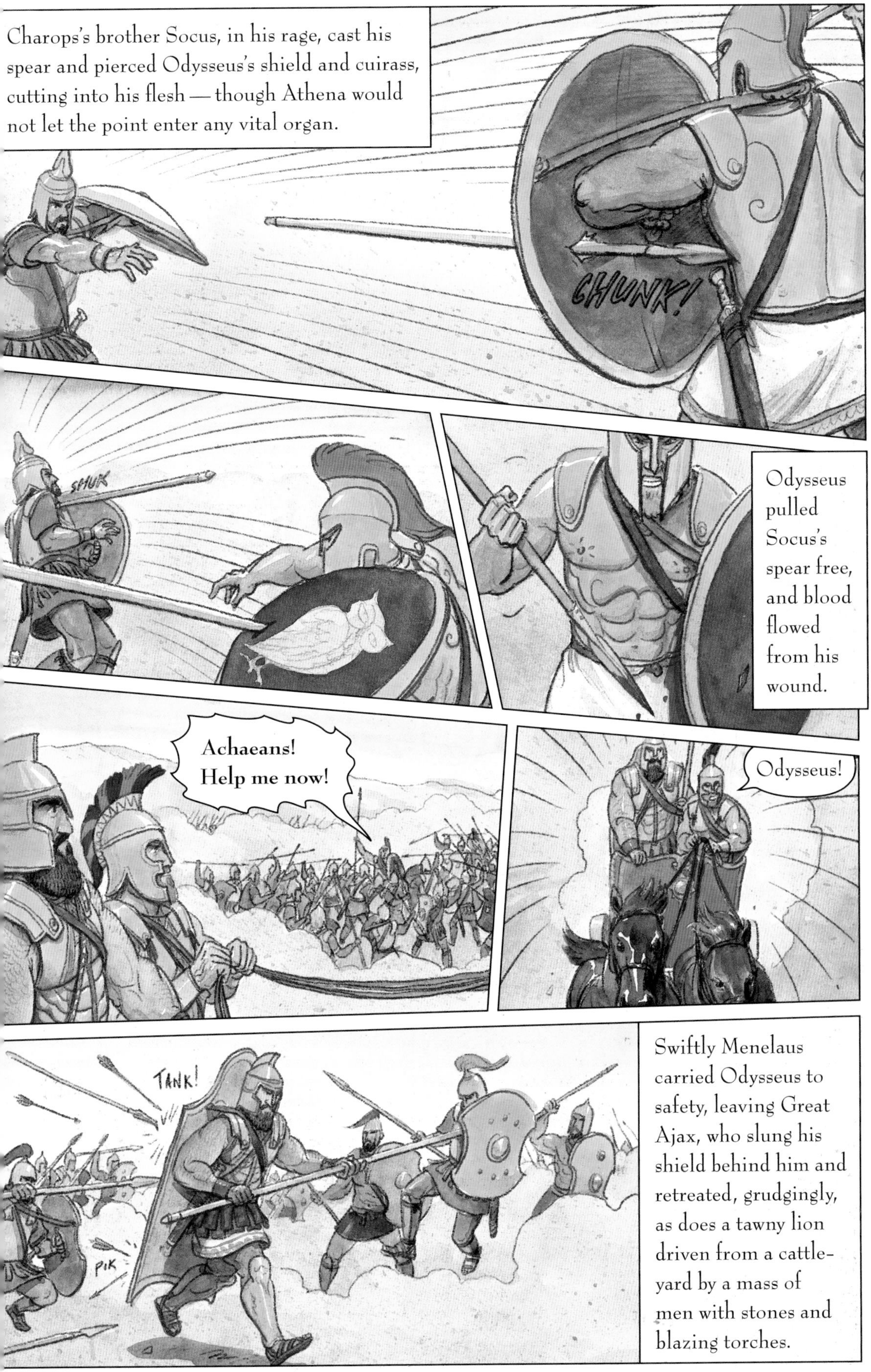
Charops's brother Socus, in his rage, cast his spear and pierced Odysseus's shield and cuirass, cutting into his flesh — though Athena would not let the point enter any vital organ.
CHUNK!
SHUK
Odysseus pulled Socus's spear free, and blood flowed from his wound.
Achaeans! Help me now!
Odysseus!
TANK!
PIK
Swiftly Menelaus carried Odysseus to safety, leaving Great Ajax, who slung his shield behind him and retreated, grudgingly, as does a tawny lion driven from a cattle-yard by a mass of men with stones and blazing torches.

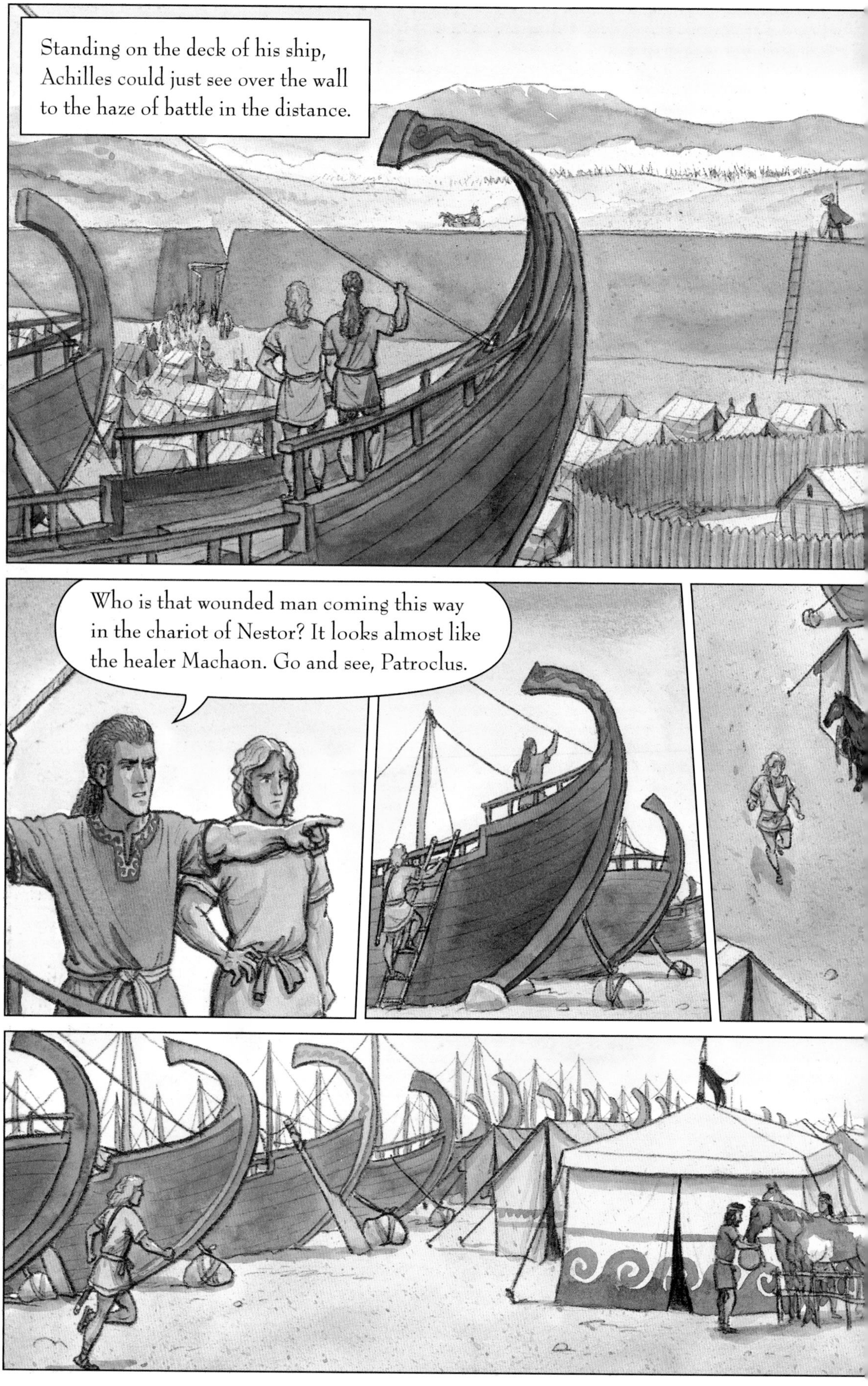
Standing on the deck of his ship, Achilles could just see over the wall to the haze of battle in the distance.
Who is that wounded man coming this way in the chariot of Nestor? It looks almost like the healer Machaon. Go and see, Patroclus.

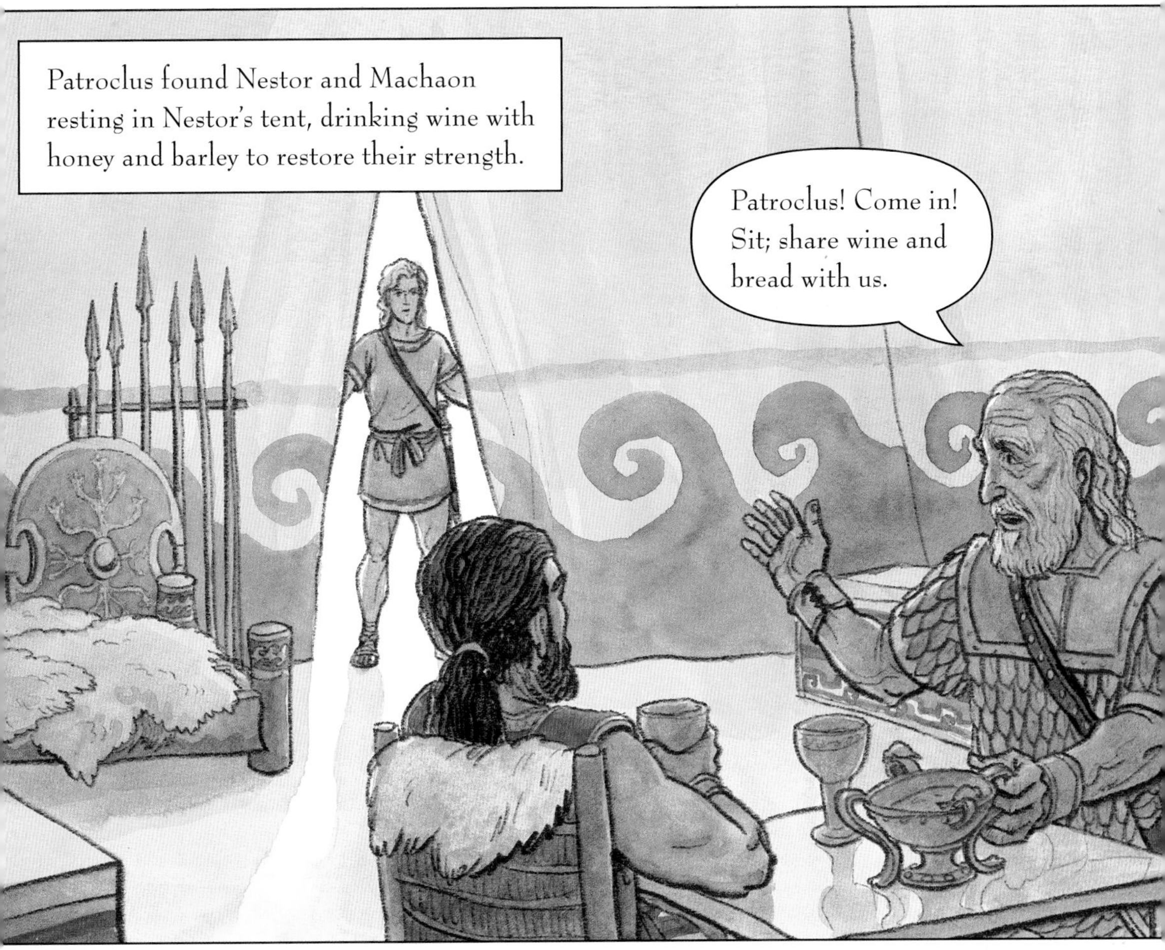
Patroclus found Nestor and Machaon resting in Nestor's tent, drinking wine with honey and barley to restore their strength.
Patroclus! Come in! Sit; share wine and bread with us.

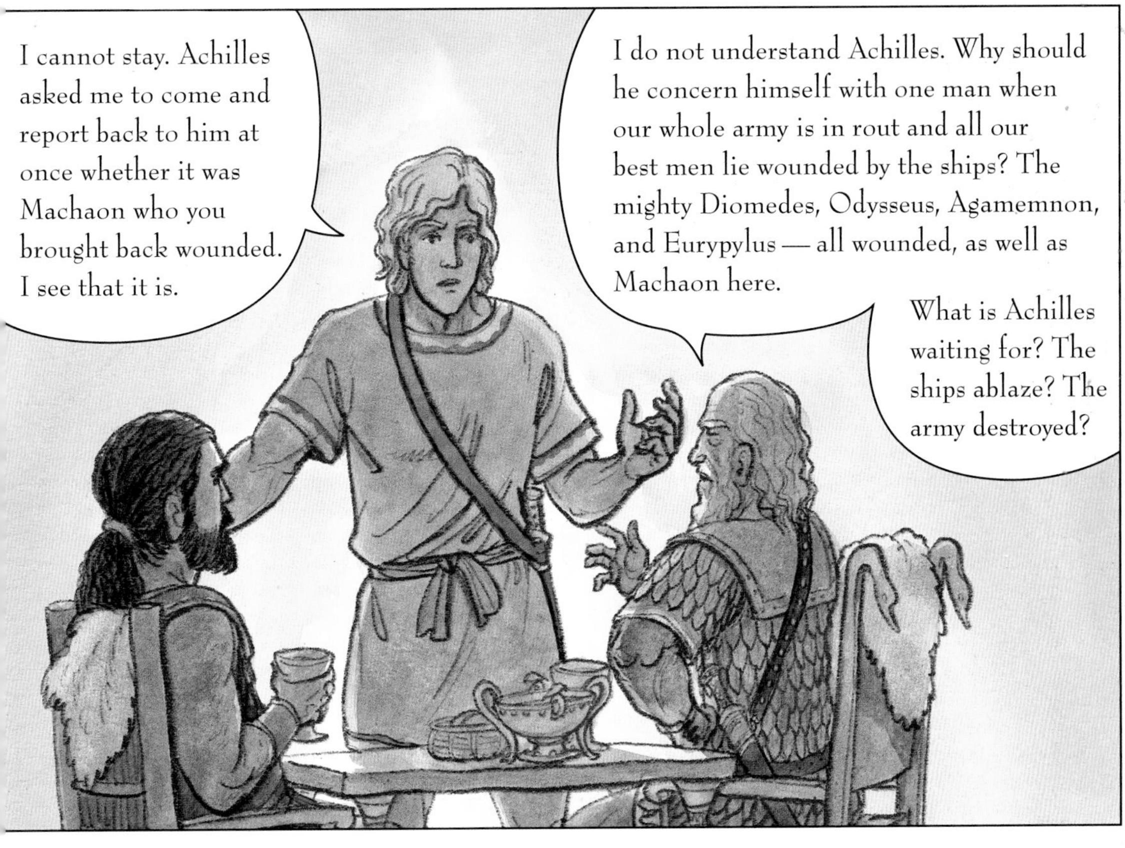
I cannot stay. Achilles asked me to come and report back to him at once whether it was Machaon who you brought back wounded. I see that it is.
I do not understand Achilles. Why should he concern himself with one man when our whole army is in rout and all our best men lie wounded by the ships? The mighty Diomedes, Odysseus, Agamemnon, and Eurypylus — all wounded, as well as Machaon here.
What is Achilles waiting for? The ships ablaze? The army destroyed?

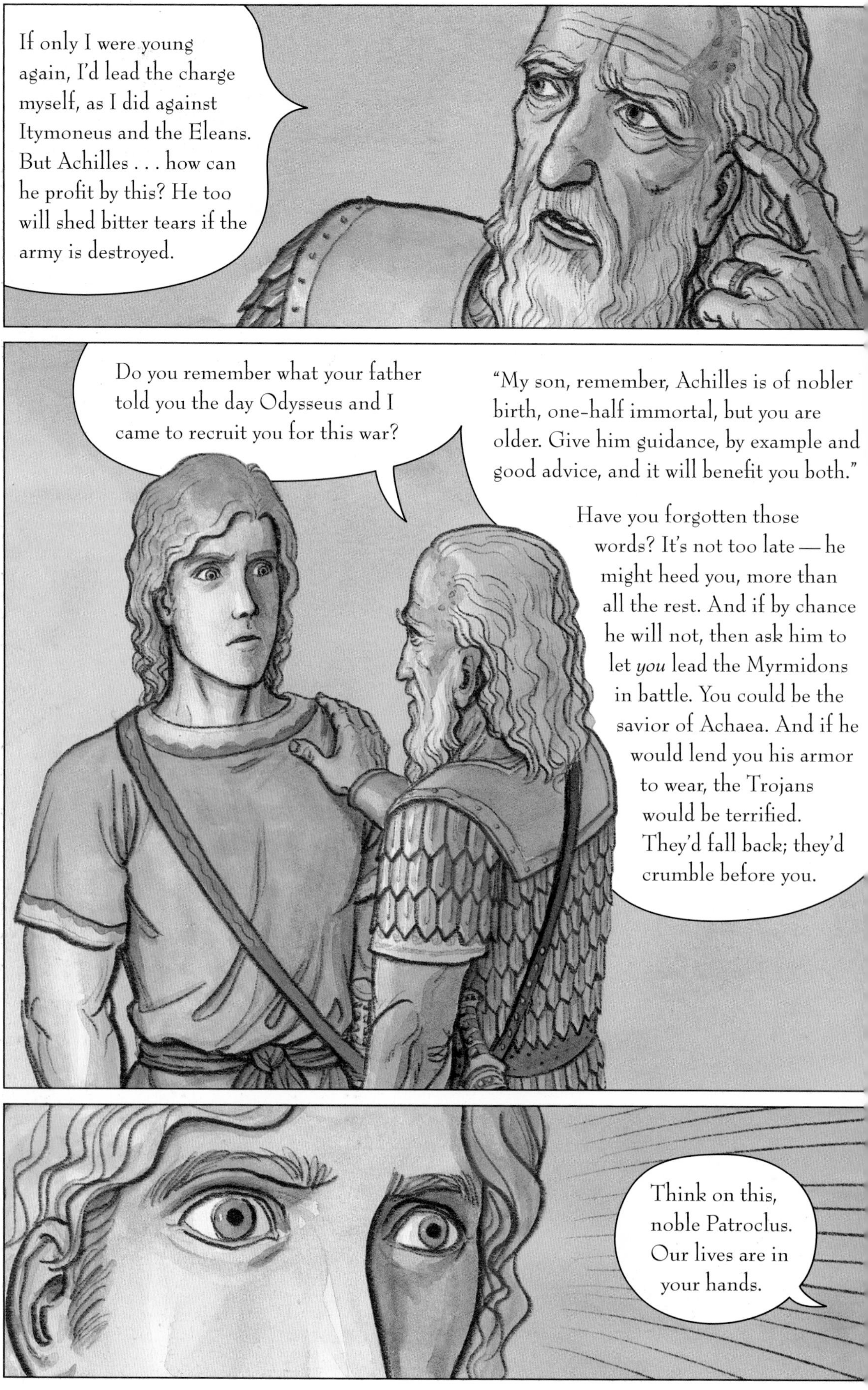
If only I were young again, I'd lead the charge myself, as I did against Itymoneus and the Eleans. But Achilles . . . how can he profit by this? He too will shed bitter tears if the army is destroyed.
Do you remember what your father told you the day Odysseus and I came to recruit you for this war?
"My son, remember, Achilles is of nobler birth, one-half immortal, but you are older. Give him guidance, by example and good advice, and it will benefit you both."
Have you forgotten those words? It's not too late — he might heed you, more than all the rest. And if by chance he will not, then ask him to let *you* lead the Myrmidons in battle. You could be the savior of Achaea. And if he would lend you his armor to wear, the Trojans would be terrified. They'd fall back; they'd crumble before you.
Think on this, noble Patroclus. Our lives are in your hands.

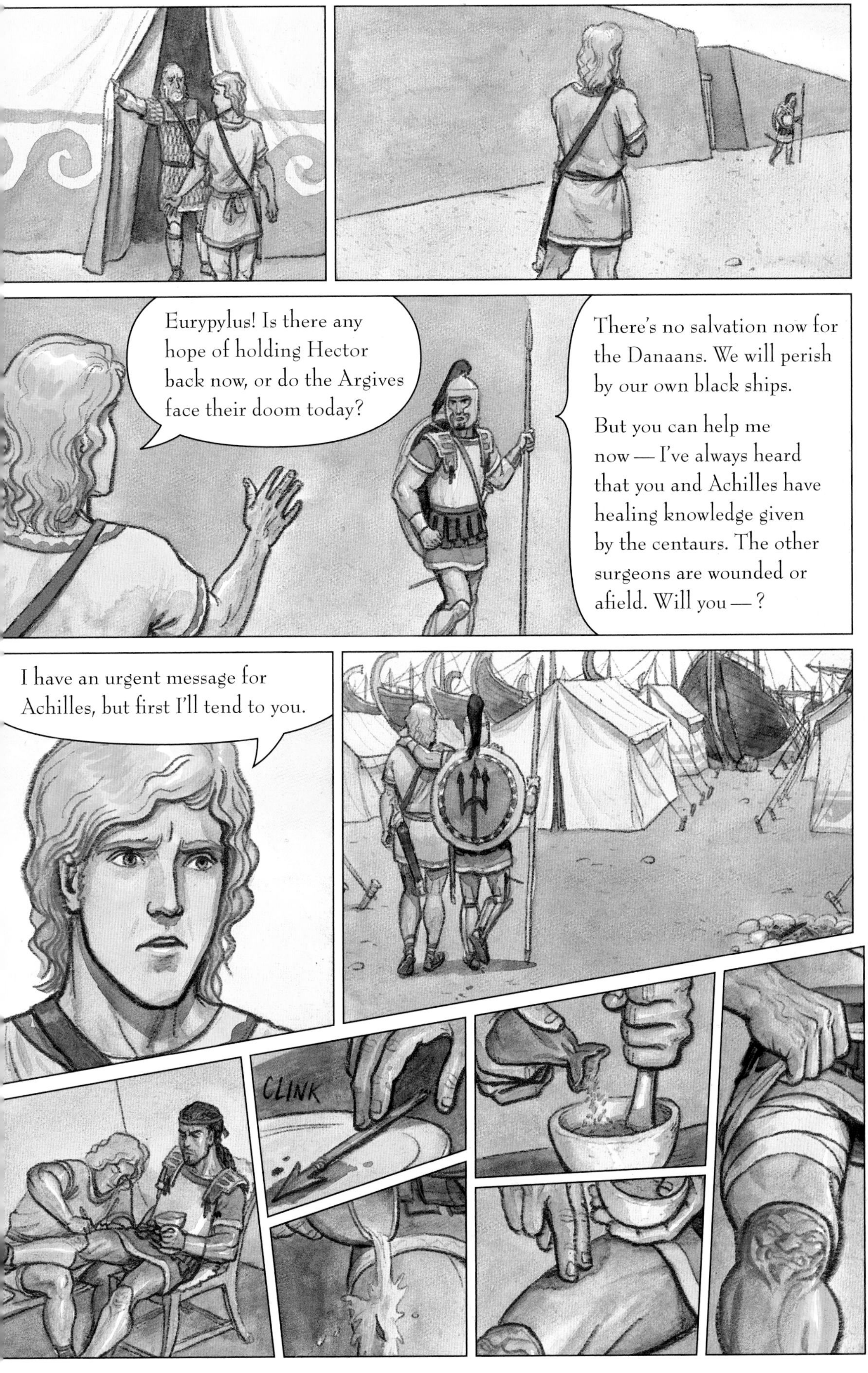
Eurypylus! Is there any hope of holding Hector back now, or do the Argives face their doom today?
There's no salvation now for the Danaans. We will perish by our own black ships.
But you can help me now — I've always heard that you and Achilles have healing knowledge given by the centaurs. The other surgeons are wounded or afield. Will you — ?
I have an urgent message for Achilles, but first I'll tend to you.
CLINK

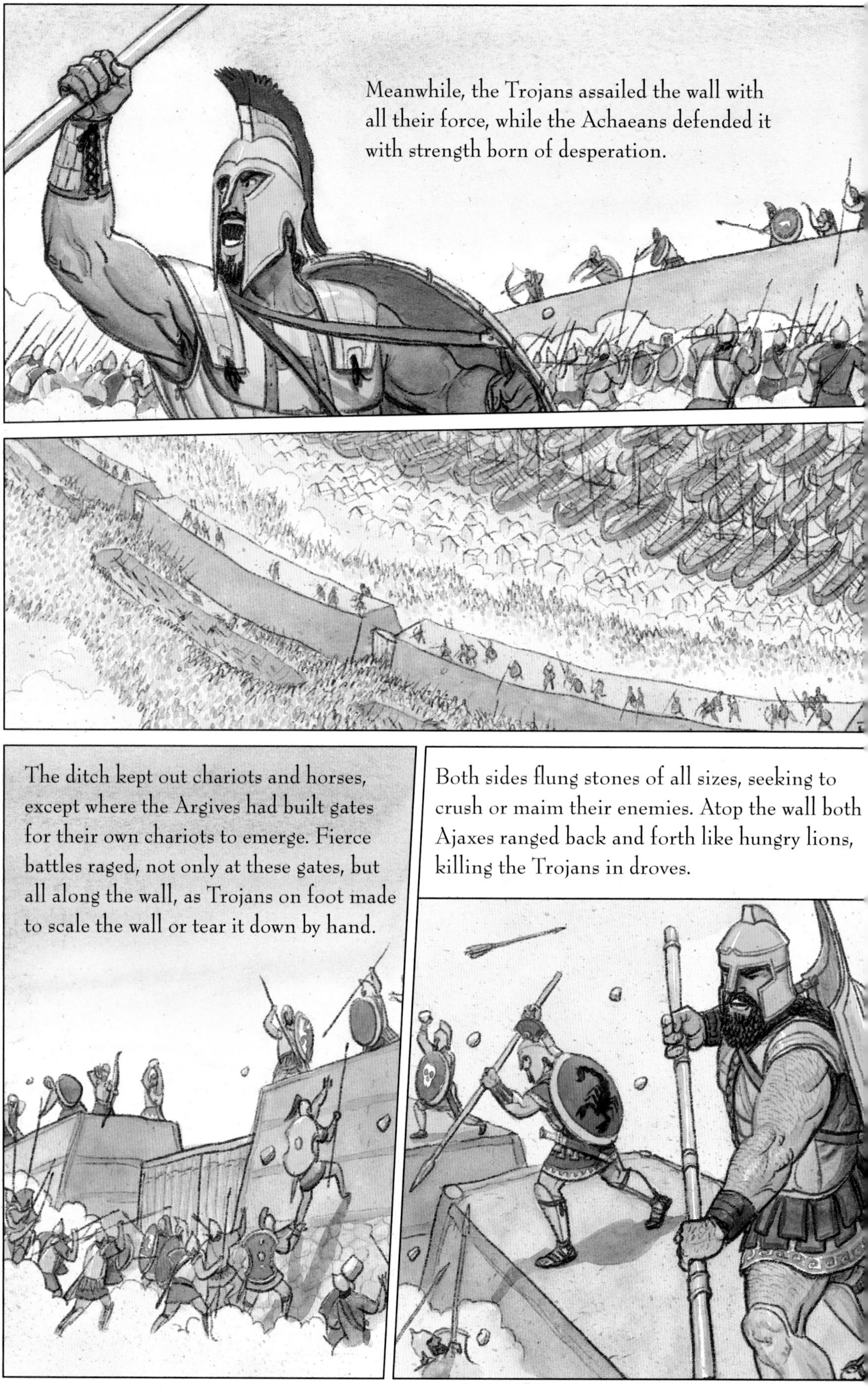
Meanwhile, the Trojans assailed the wall with all their force, while the Achaeans defended it with strength born of desperation.
The ditch kept out chariots and horses, except where the Argives had built gates for their own chariots to emerge. Fierce battles raged, not only at these gates, but all along the wall, as Trojans on foot made to scale the wall or tear it down by hand.
Both sides flung stones of all sizes, seeking to crush or maim their enemies. Atop the wall both Ajaxes ranged back and forth like hungry lions, killing the Trojans in droves.

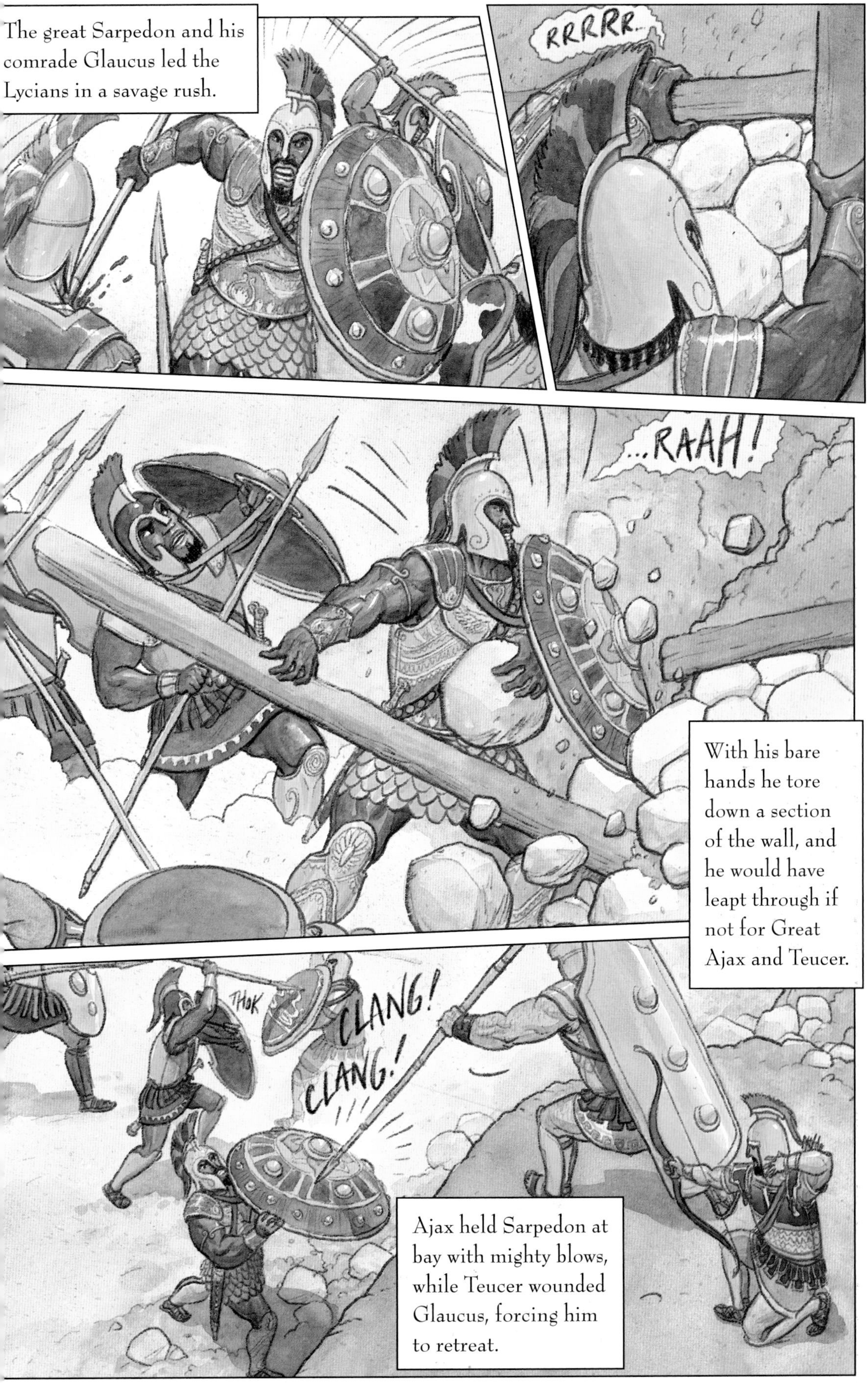
The great Sarpedon and his comrade Glaucus led the Lycians in a savage rush.
RRRRR...
...RAAH!
With his bare hands he tore down a section of the wall, and he would have leapt through if not for Great Ajax and Teucer.
THOK
CLANG!
CLANG!
Ajax held Sarpedon at bay with mighty blows, while Teucer wounded Glaucus, forcing him to retreat.

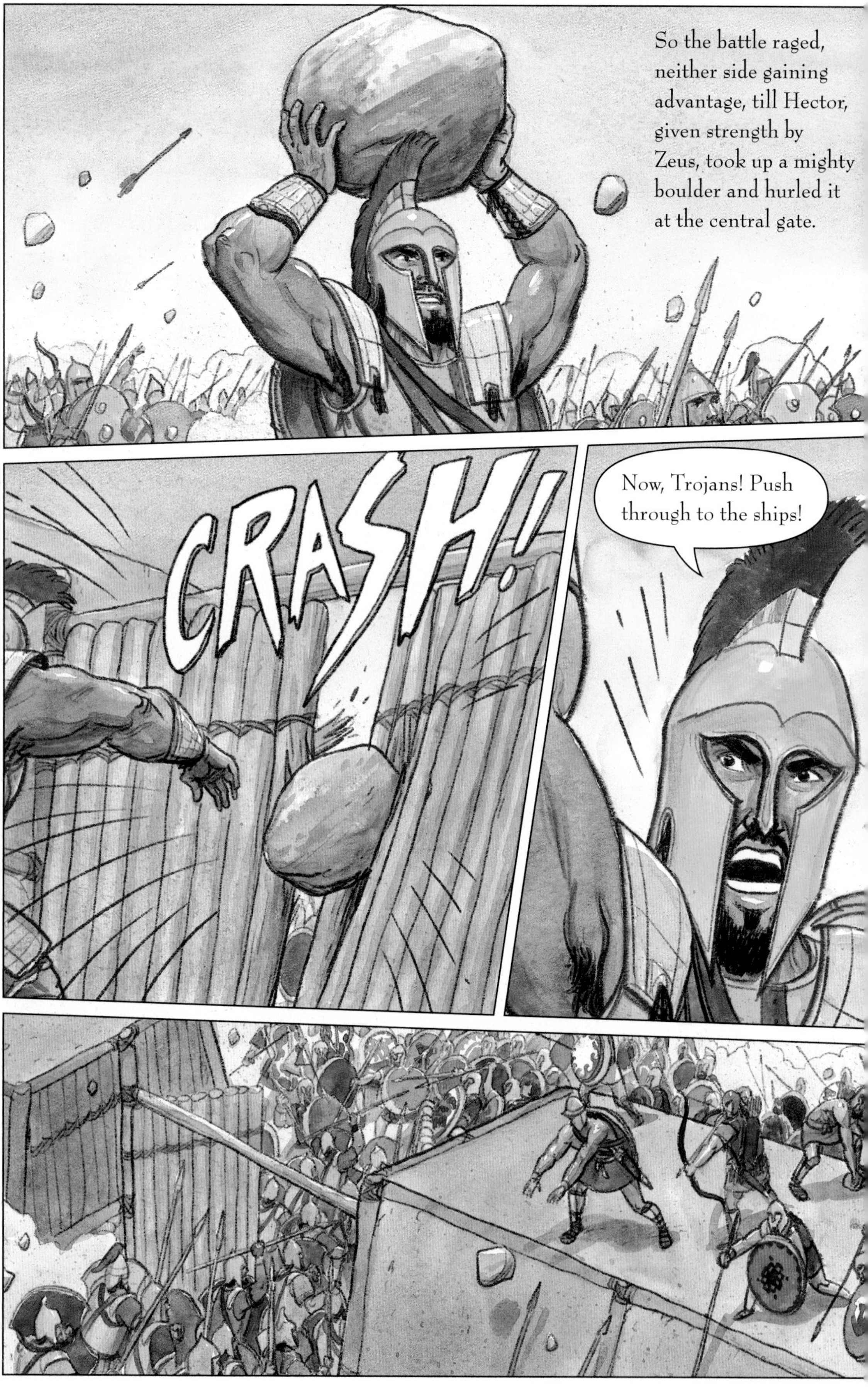
So the battle raged, neither side gaining advantage, till Hector, given strength by Zeus, took up a mighty boulder and hurled it at the central gate.
CRASH!
Now, Trojans! Push through to the ships!

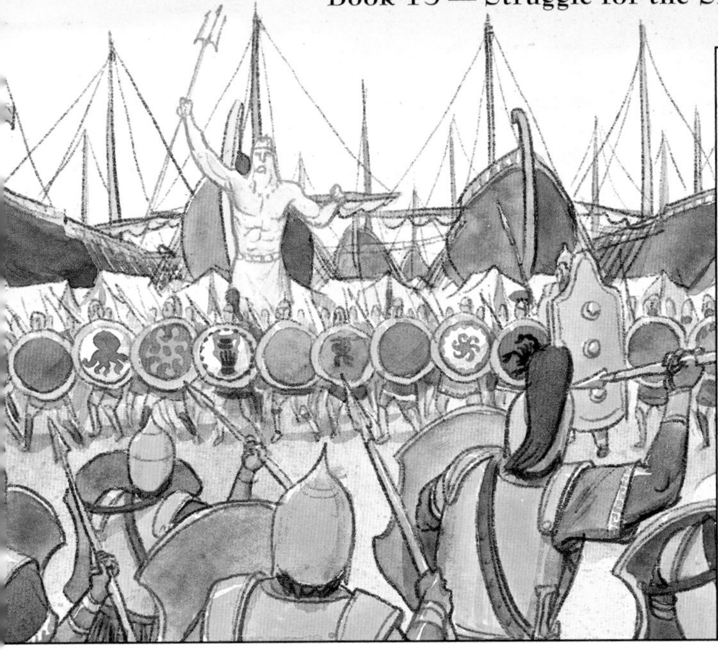

Zeus turned away from the battle then, confident that all was proceeding as he wished and that no other god would interfere.

But as soon as he was gone, Poseidon went among the Argives, rallying them and giving them divine strength.

Hector swept down the beach like a raging river in flood, but he was brought up short by the Achaeans who had gathered around the Ajaxes in a bristling shield-wall.

The battle roiled like a dust storm, lit by the glitter and clash of bronze as the armies strained with all their strength to gain an inch of ground, and every man sought to stab his enemy at close quarters.

Thus did the two sons of Cronus, Zeus and Poseidon, keep the rope taut in this deadly tug-of-war.

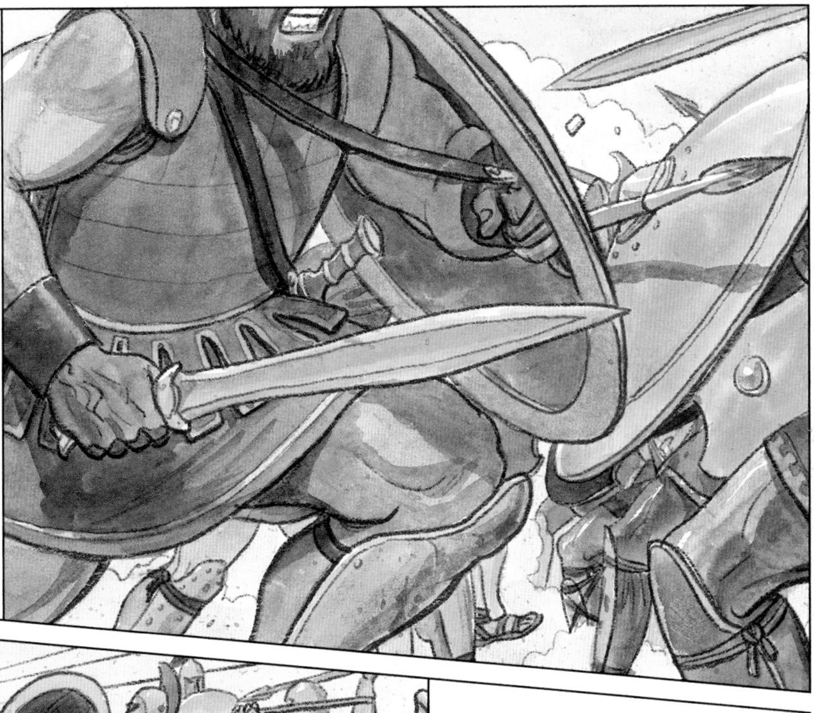

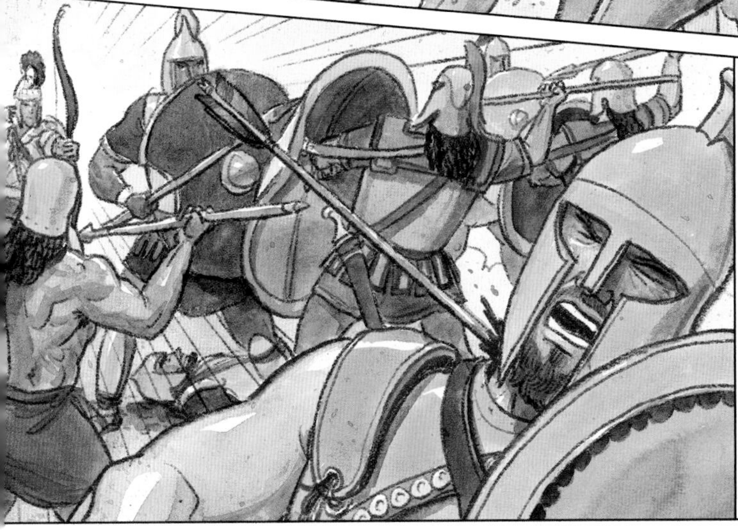

Thirteen heroes went down in that crush of men — among them Asius, Hypsenor, Ascalaphus, son of Ares, and Euchenor, son of the seer Polyidus. His father prophesied that he would either die of painful disease at home or be killed at Troy. He chose the swifter end.

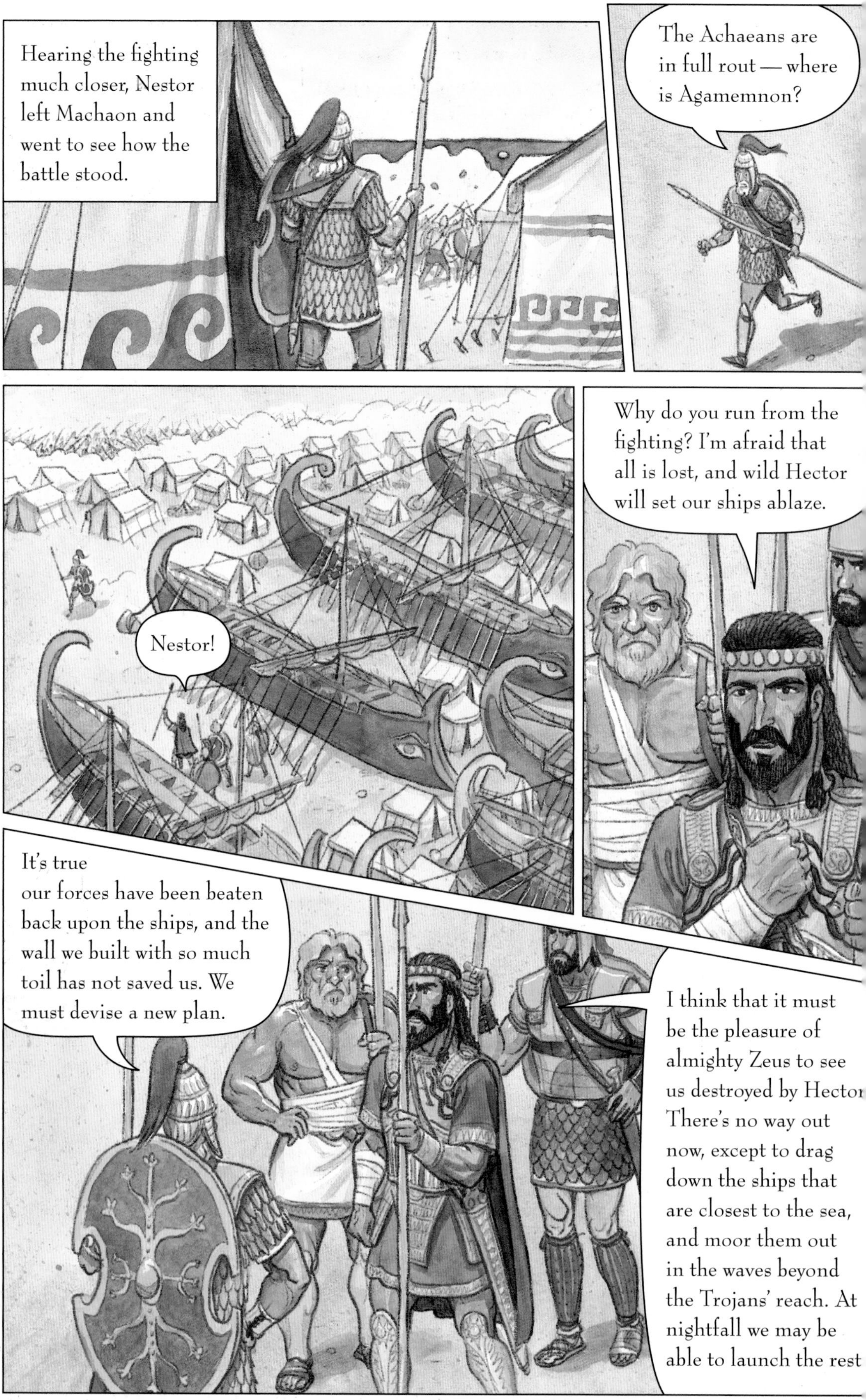
Hearing the fighting much closer, Nestor left Machaon and went to see how the battle stood.
The Achaeans are in full rout — where is Agamemnon?
Nestor!
Why do you run from the fighting? I'm afraid that all is lost, and wild Hector will set our ships ablaze.
It's true our forces have been beaten back upon the ships, and the wall we built with so much toil has not saved us. We must devise a new plan.
I think that it must be the pleasure of almighty Zeus to see us destroyed by Hecto There's no way out now, except to drag down the ships that are closest to the sea, and moor them out in the waves beyond the Trojans' reach. At nightfall we may be able to launch the rest

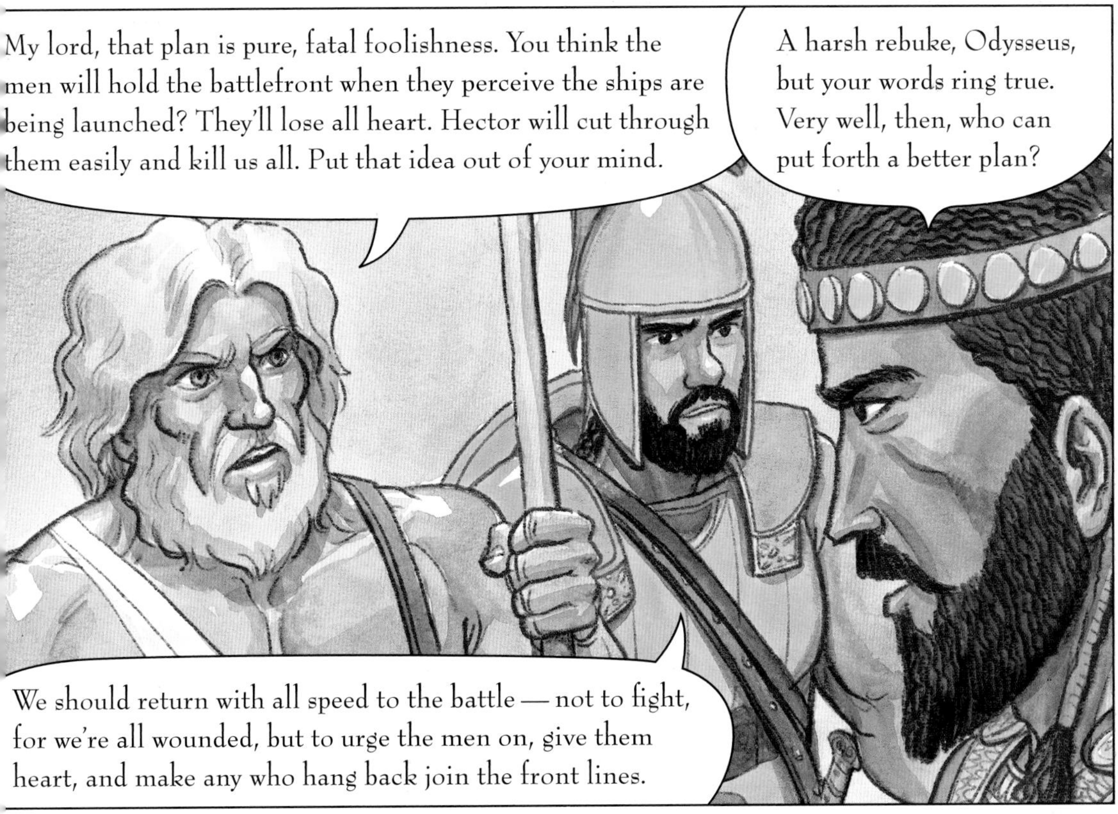
My lord, that plan is pure, fatal foolishness. You think the men will hold the battlefront when they perceive the ships are being launched? They'll lose all heart. Hector will cut through them easily and kill us all. Put that idea out of your mind.
A harsh rebuke, Odysseus, but your words ring true. Very well, then, who can put forth a better plan?
We should return with all speed to the battle — not to fight, for we're all wounded, but to urge the men on, give them heart, and make any who hang back join the front lines.

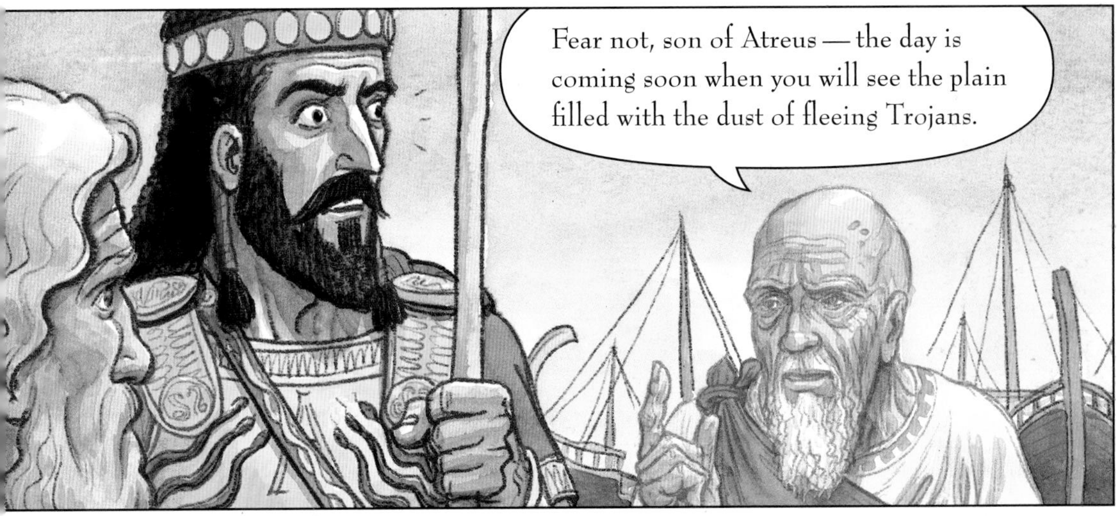
Fear not, son of Atreus — the day is coming soon when you will see the plain filled with the dust of fleeing Trojans.

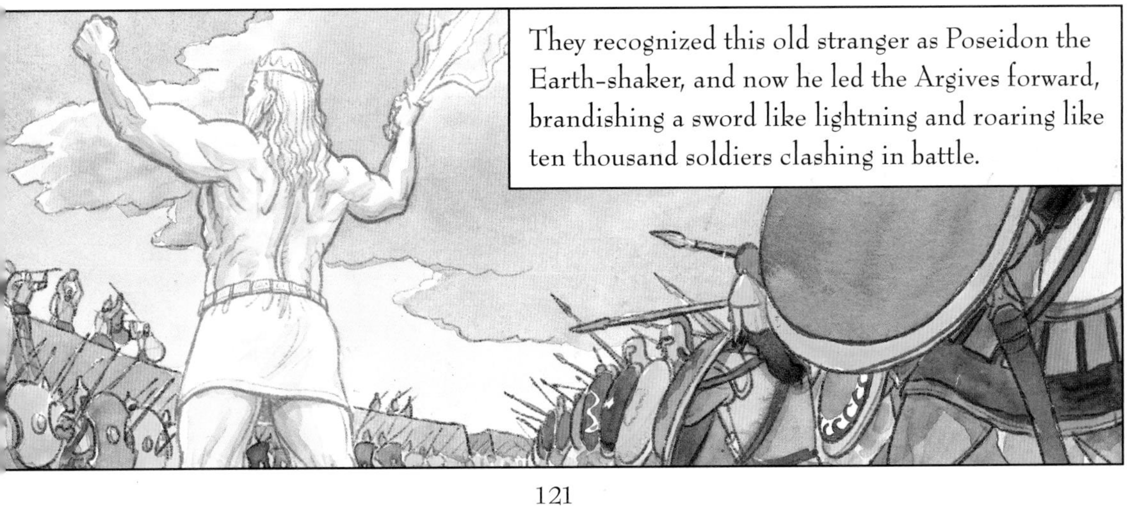
They recognized this old stranger as Poseidon the Earth-shaker, and now he led the Argives forward, brandishing a sword like lightning and roaring like ten thousand soldiers clashing in battle.

Book 14 — Zeus Tricked

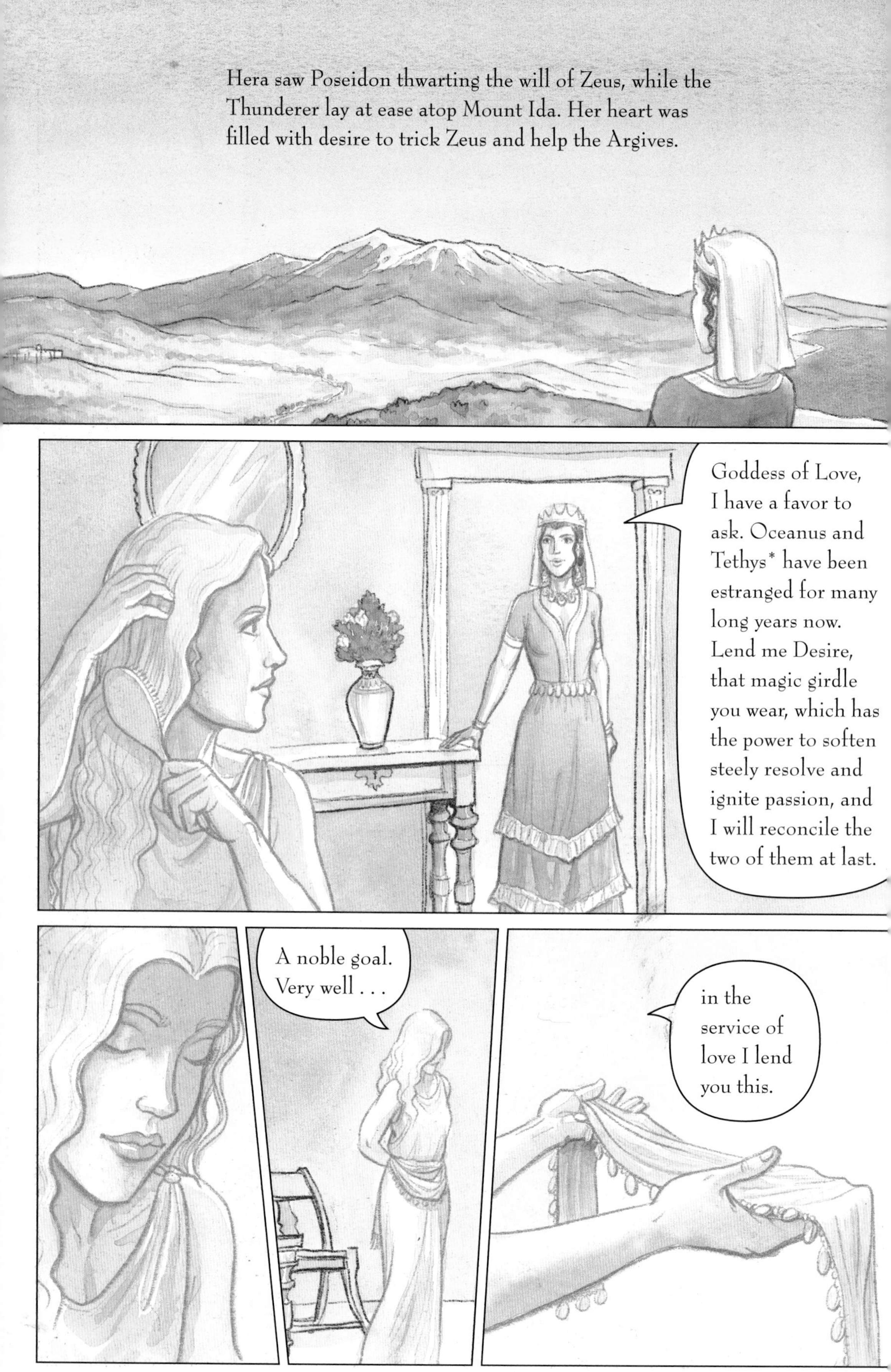
Hera saw Poseidon thwarting the will of Zeus, while the Thunderer lay at ease atop Mount Ida. Her heart was filled with desire to trick Zeus and help the Argives.
Goddess of Love, I have a favor to ask. Oceanus and Tethys* have been estranged for many long years now. Lend me Desire, that magic girdle you wear, which has the power to soften steely resolve and ignite passion, and I will reconcile the two of them at last.
A noble goal. Very well . . .
in the service of love I lend you this.

* Oceanus and Tethys are two of the Titans, son and daughter of Uranus and Gaia, parents of all the gods of rivers and oceans.

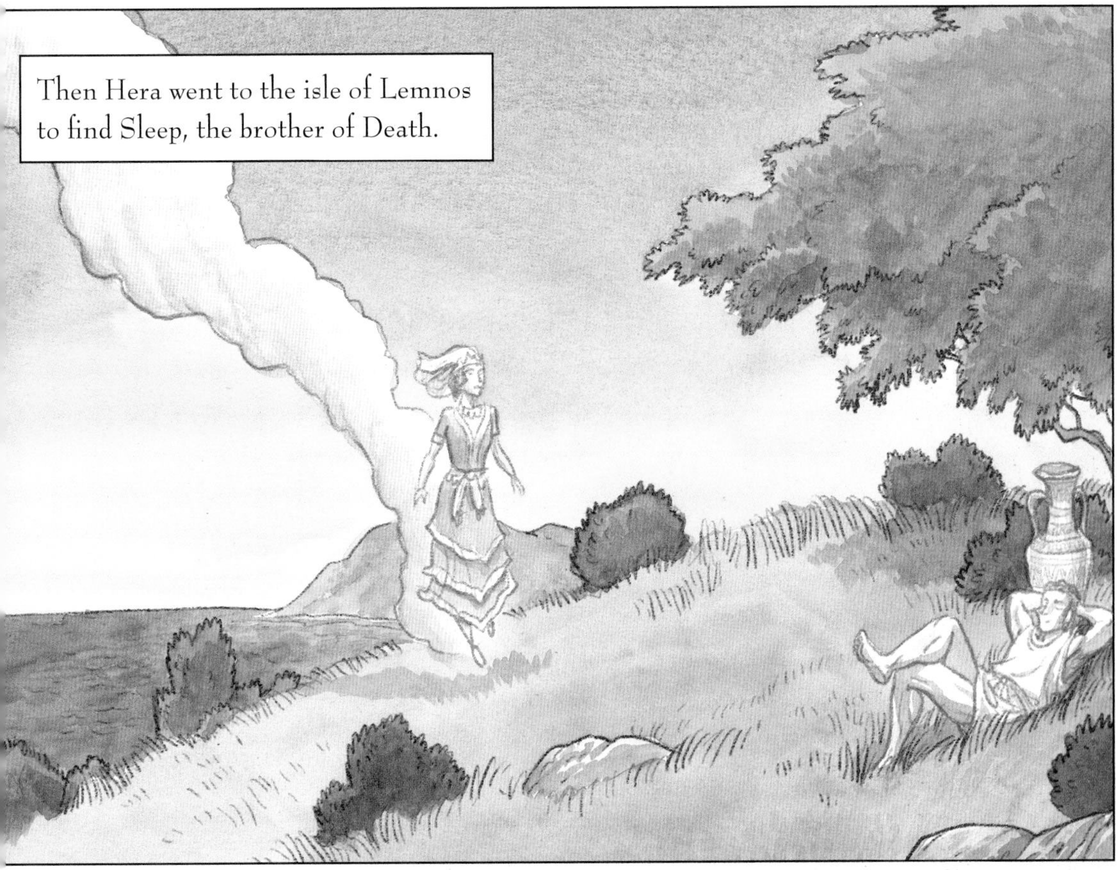
Then Hera went to the isle of Lemnos to find Sleep, the brother of Death.

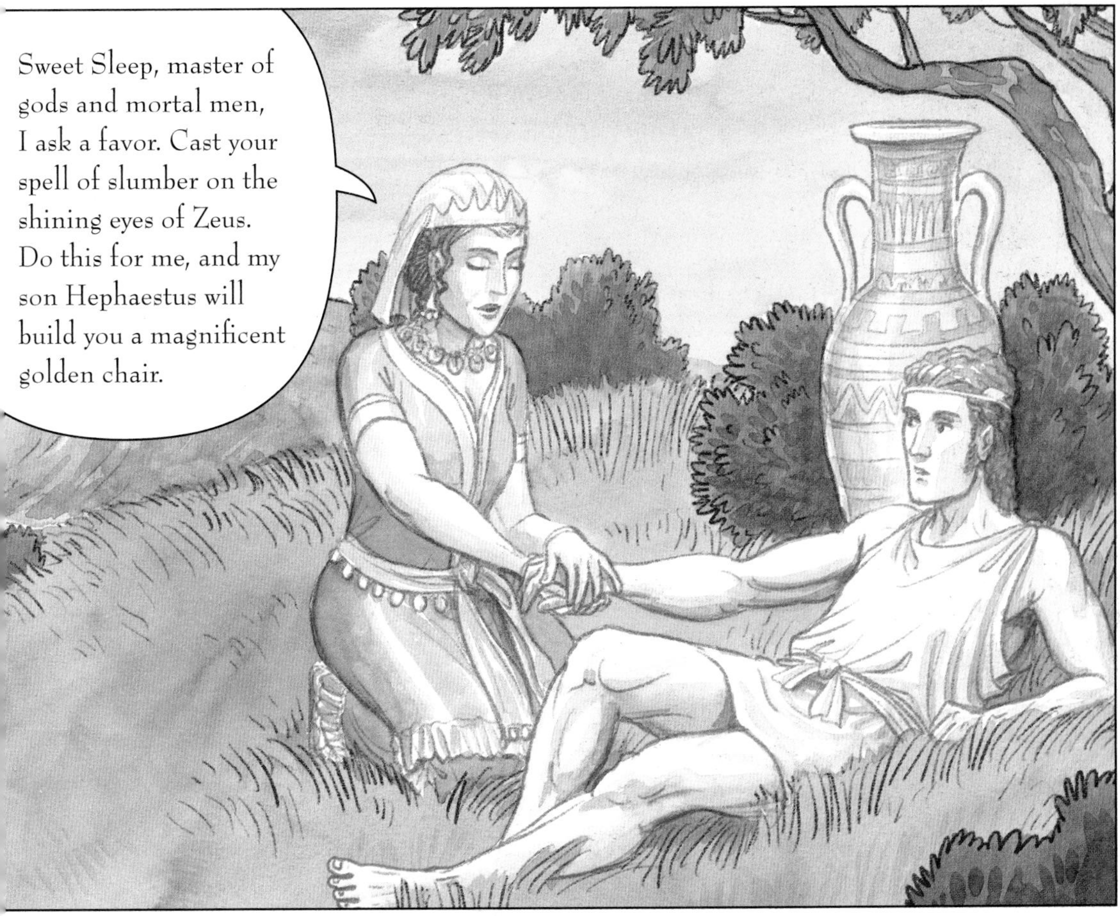
Sweet Sleep, master of gods and mortal men, I ask a favor. Cast your spell of slumber on the shining eyes of Zeus. Do this for me, and my son Hephaestus will build you a magnificent golden chair.

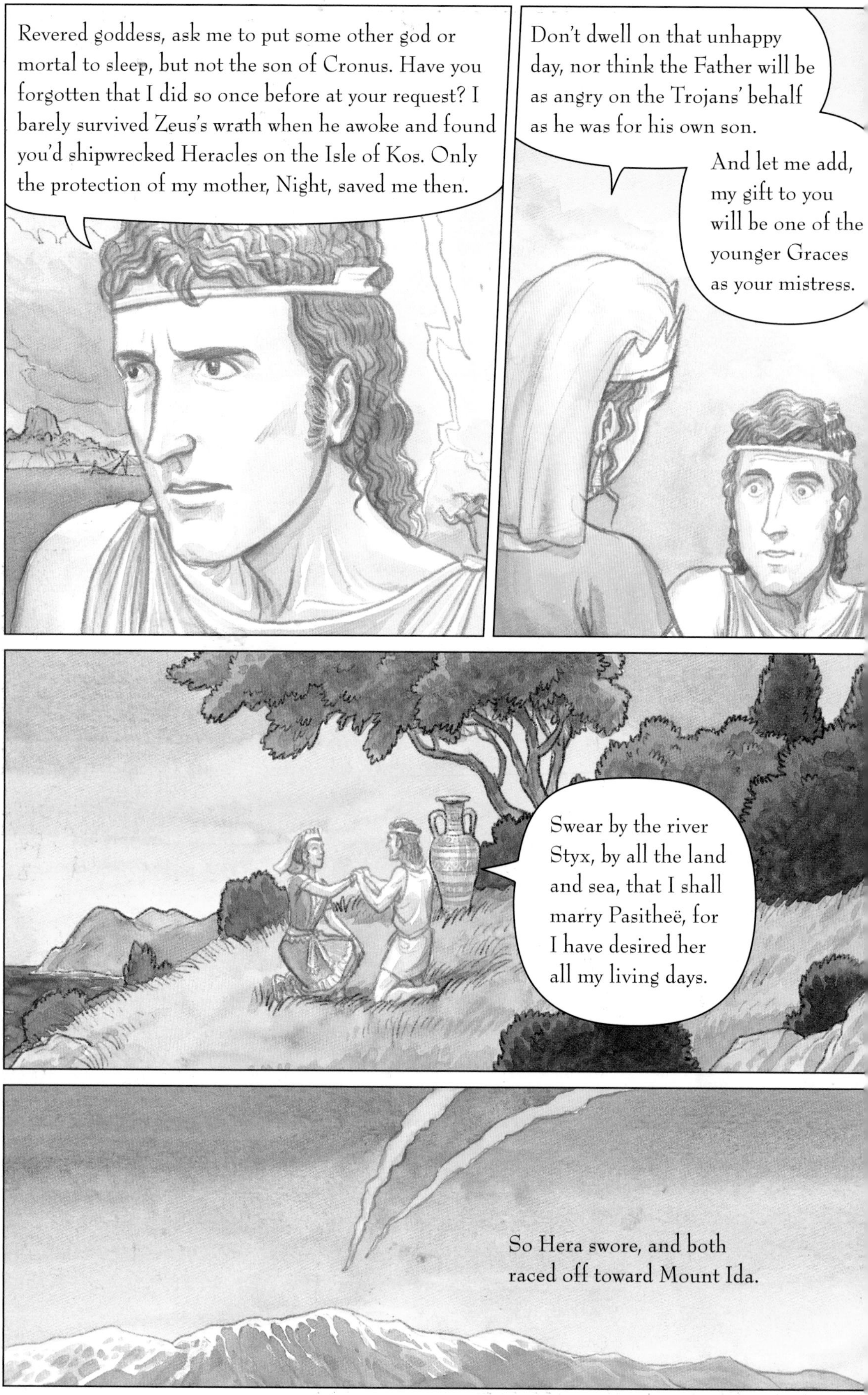
Revered goddess, ask me to put some other god or mortal to sleep, but not the son of Cronus. Have you forgotten that I did so once before at your request? I barely survived Zeus's wrath when he awoke and found you'd shipwrecked Heracles on the Isle of Kos. Only the protection of my mother, Night, saved me then.
Don't dwell on that unhappy day, nor think the Father will be as angry on the Trojans' behalf as he was for his own son.
And let me add, my gift to you will be one of the younger Graces as your mistress.
Swear by the river Styx, by all the land and sea, that I shall marry Pasitheë, for I have desired her all my living days.
So Hera swore, and both raced off toward Mount Ida.

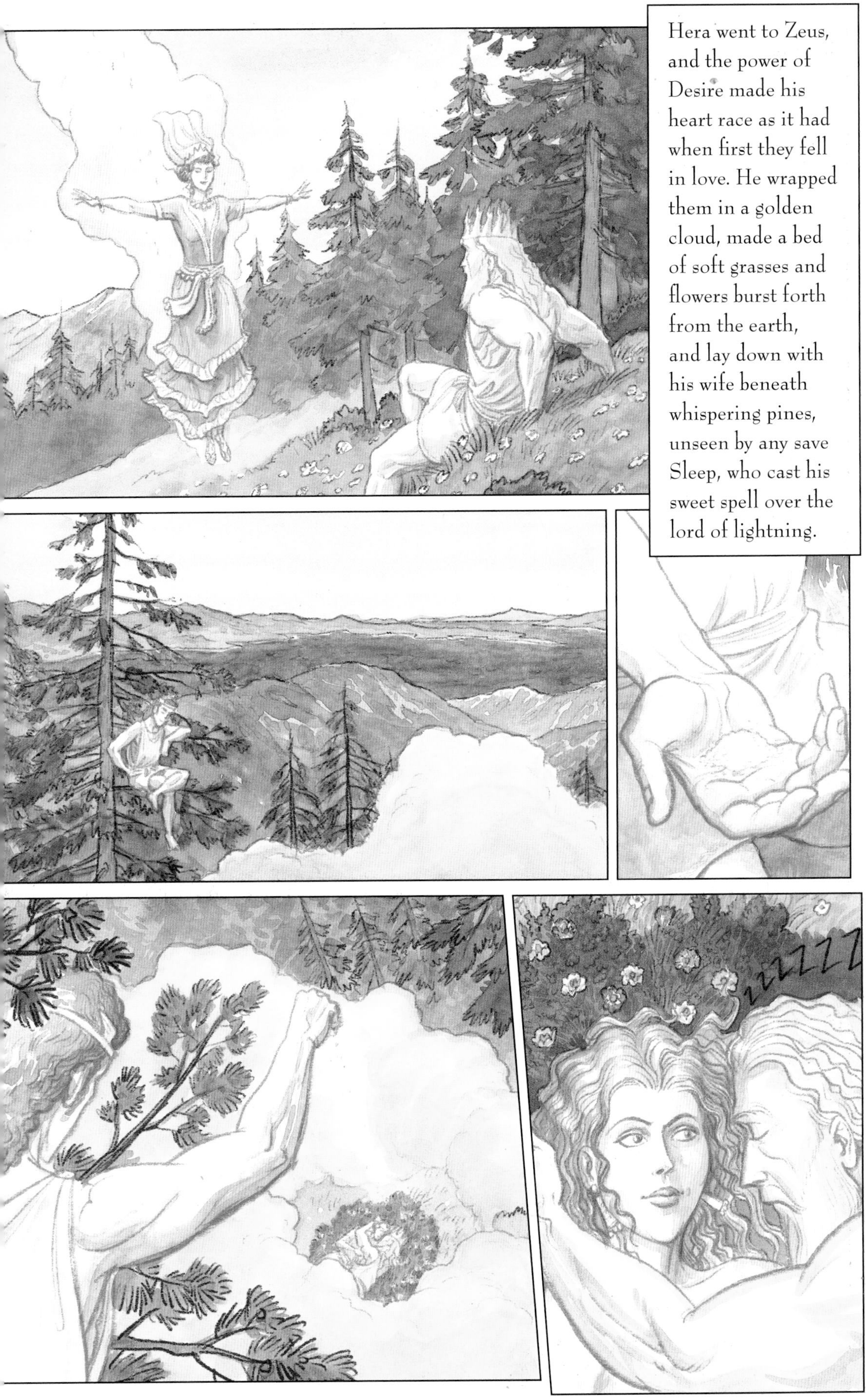
Hera went to Zeus, and the power of Desire made his heart race as it had when first they fell in love. He wrapped them in a golden cloud, made a bed of soft grasses and flowers burst forth from the earth, and lay down with his wife beneath whispering pines, unseen by any save Sleep, who cast his sweet spell over the lord of lightning.
ZZZZZZ

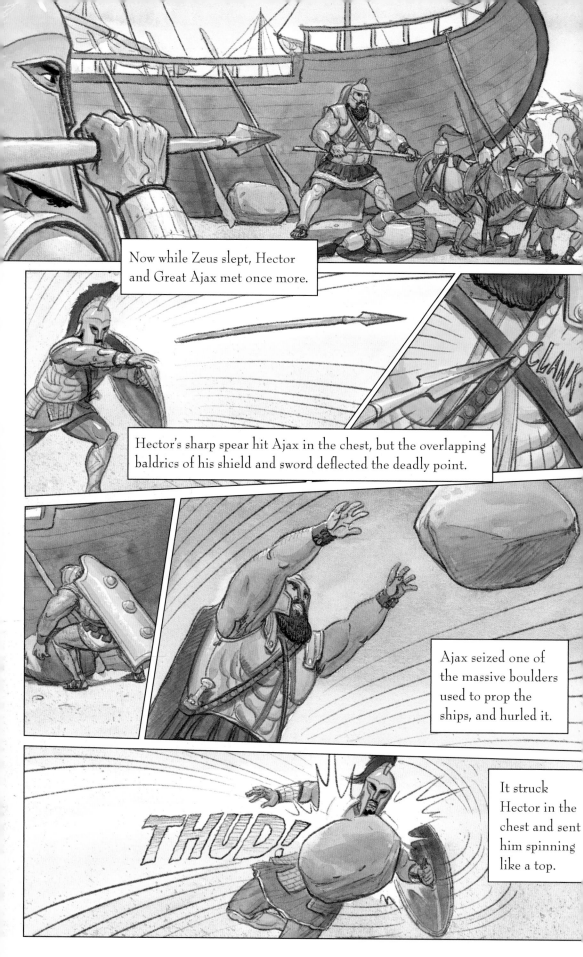

Now while Zeus slept, Hector and Great Ajax met once more.

CLANK

Hector's sharp spear hit Ajax in the chest, but the overlapping baldrics of his shield and sword deflected the deadly point.

Ajax seized one of the massive boulders used to prop the ships, and hurled it.

THUD!

It struck Hector in the chest and sent him spinning like a top.

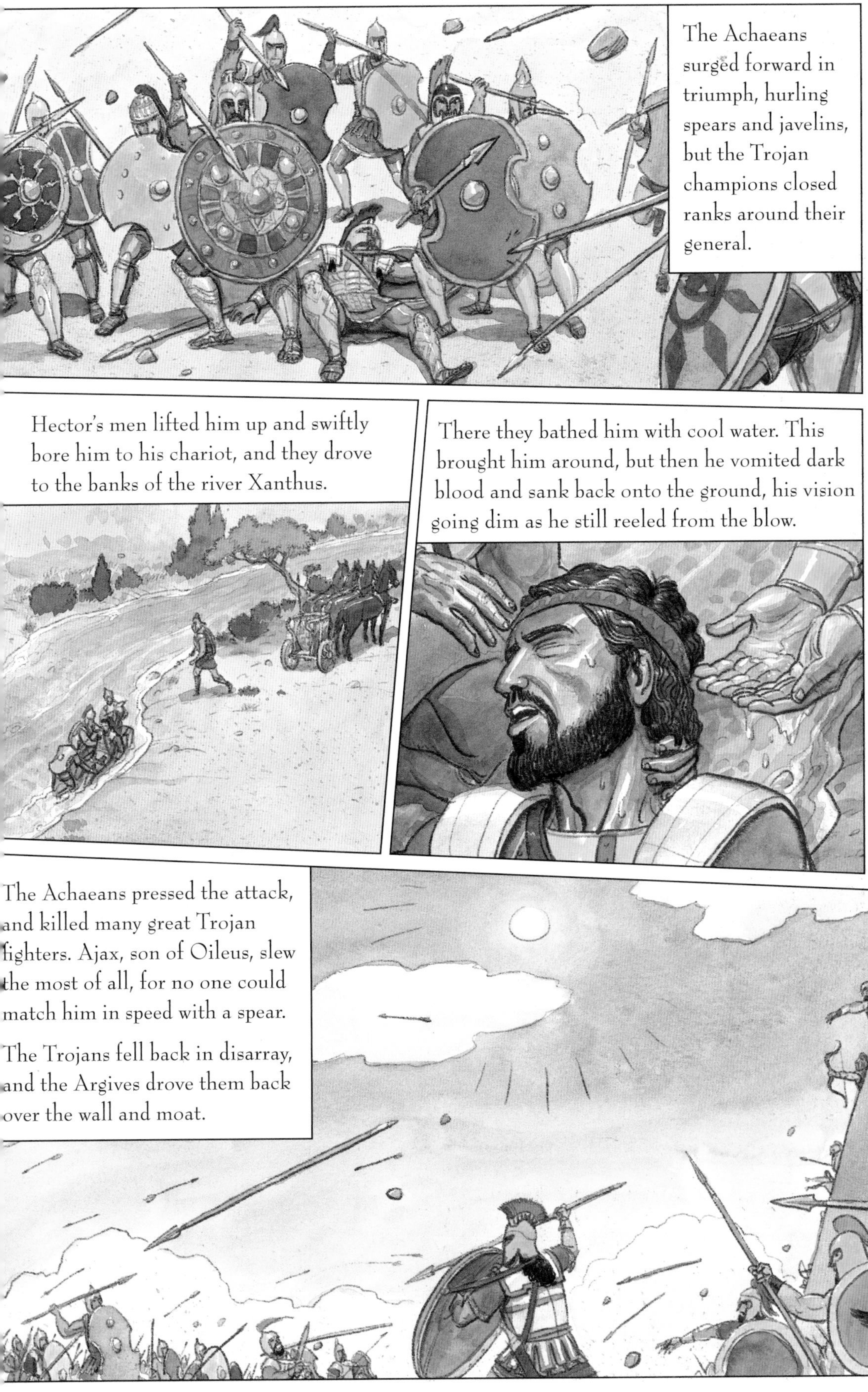
The Achaeans surged forward in triumph, hurling spears and javelins, but the Trojan champions closed ranks around their general.
Hector's men lifted him up and swiftly bore him to his chariot, and they drove to the banks of the river Xanthus.
There they bathed him with cool water. This brought him around, but then he vomited dark blood and sank back onto the ground, his vision going dim as he still reeled from the blow.
The Achaeans pressed the attack, and killed many great Trojan fighters. Ajax, son of Oileus, slew the most of all, for no one could match him in speed with a spear.
The Trojans fell back in disarray, and the Argives drove them back over the wall and moat.

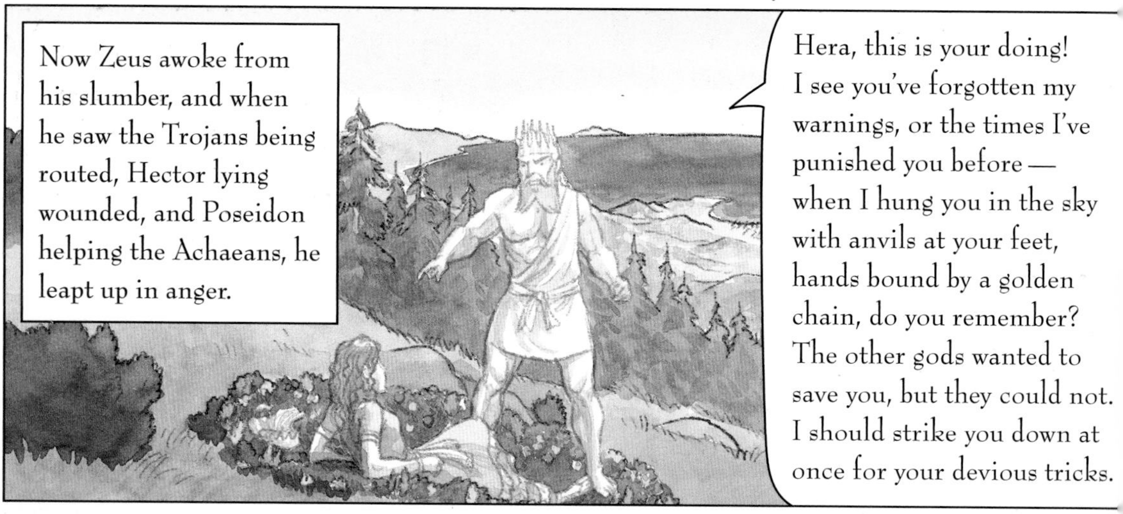
Now Zeus awoke from his slumber, and when he saw the Trojans being routed, Hector lying wounded, and Poseidon helping the Achaeans, he leapt up in anger.
Hera, this is your doing! I see you've forgotten my warnings, or the times I've punished you before — when I hung you in the sky with anvils at your feet, hands bound by a golden chain, do you remember? The other gods wanted to save you, but they could not. I should strike you down at once for your devious tricks.

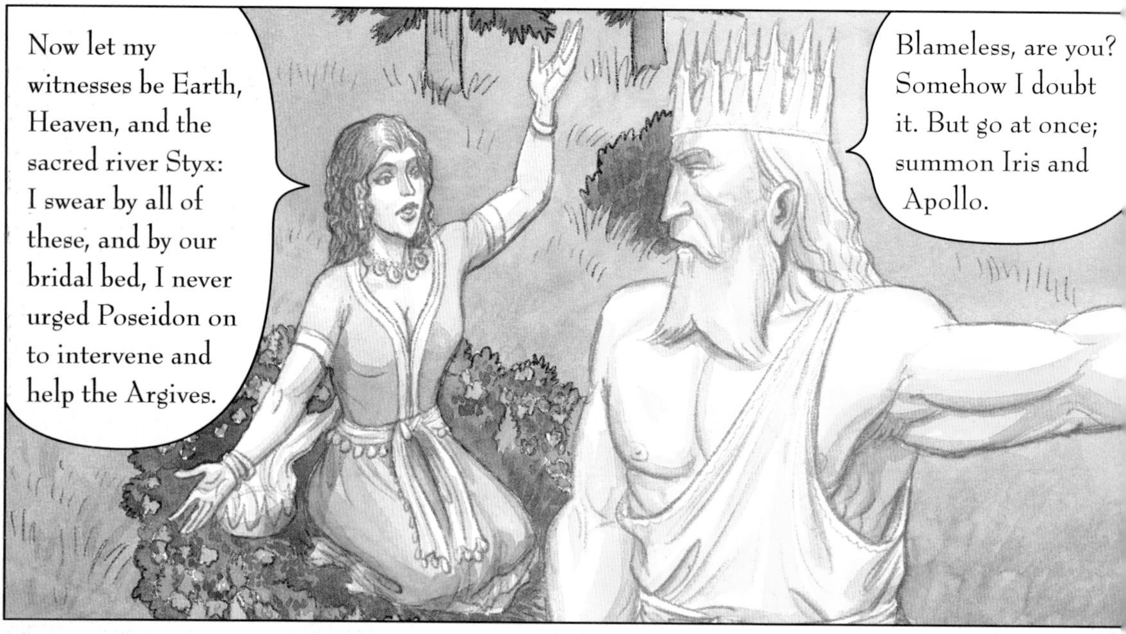
Now let my witnesses be Earth, Heaven, and the sacred river Styx: I swear by all of these, and by our bridal bed, I never urged Poseidon on to intervene and help the Argives.
Blameless, are you? Somehow I doubt it. But go at once; summon Iris and Apollo.

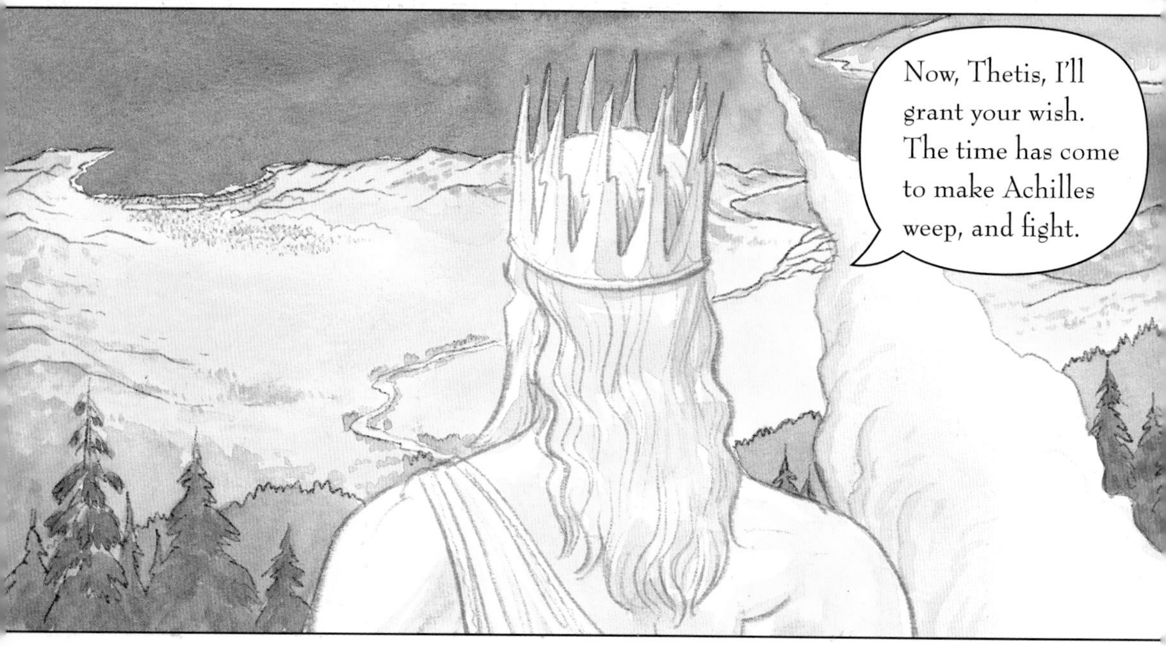
Now, Thetis, I'll grant your wish. The time has come to make Achilles weep, and fight.

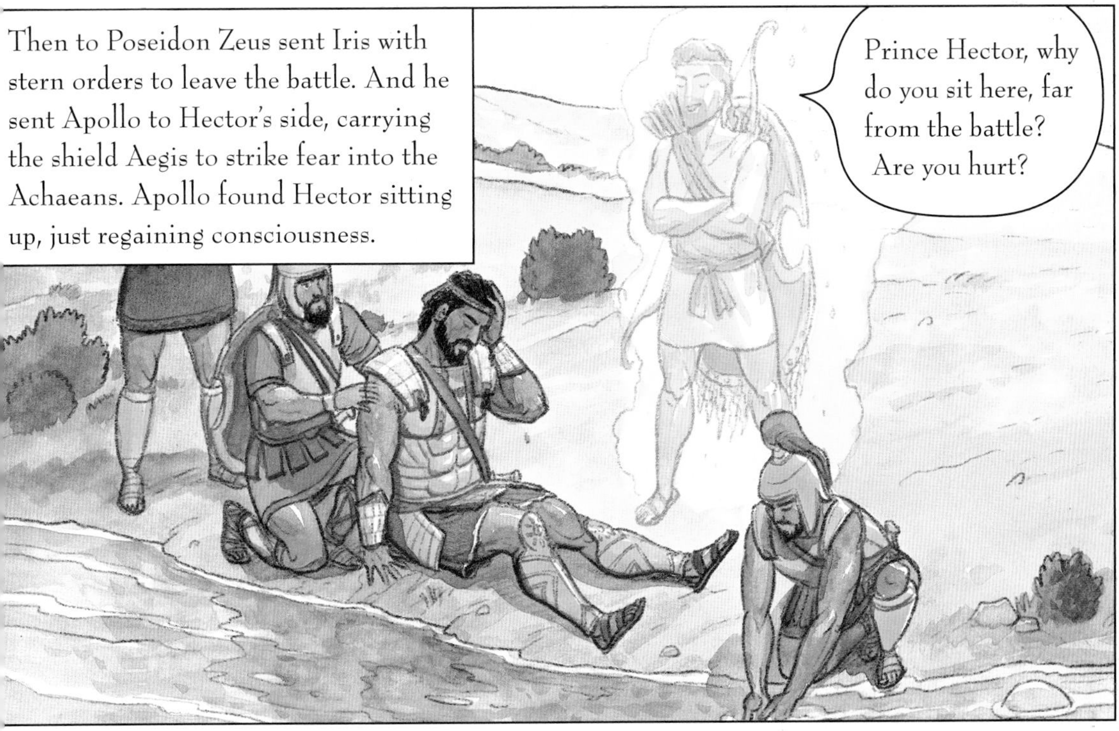
Then to Poseidon Zeus sent Iris with stern orders to leave the battle. And he sent Apollo to Hector's side, carrying the shield Aegis to strike fear into the Achaeans. Apollo found Hector sitting up, just regaining consciousness.
Prince Hector, why do you sit here, far from the battle? Are you hurt?

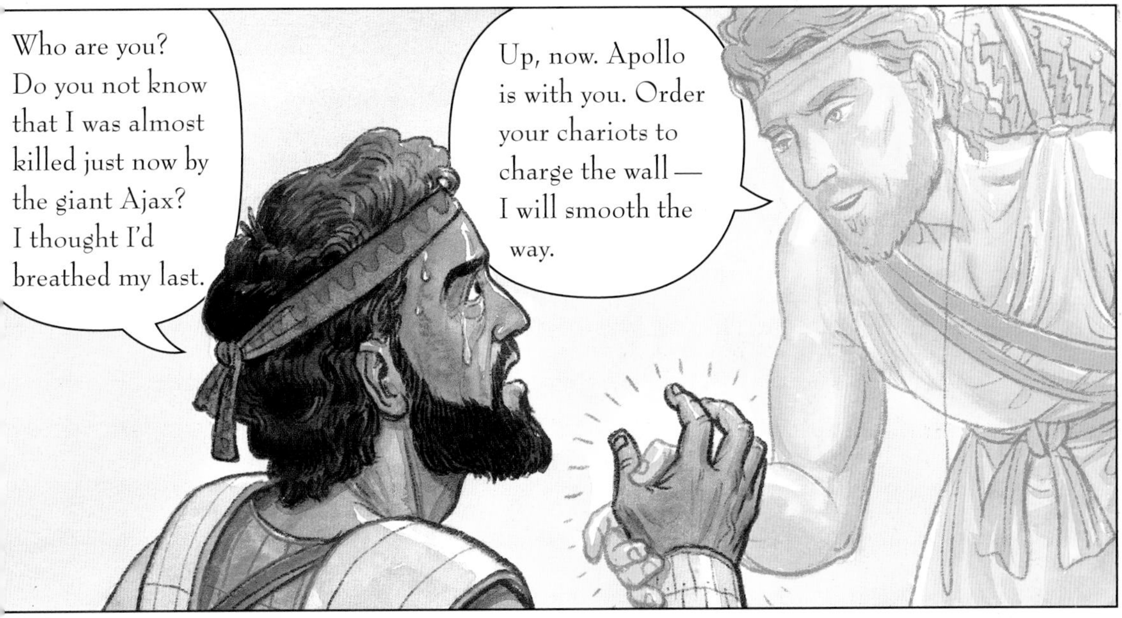
Who are you? Do you not know that I was almost killed just now by the giant Ajax? I thought I'd breathed my last.
Up, now. Apollo is with you. Order your chariots to charge the wall — I will smooth the way.

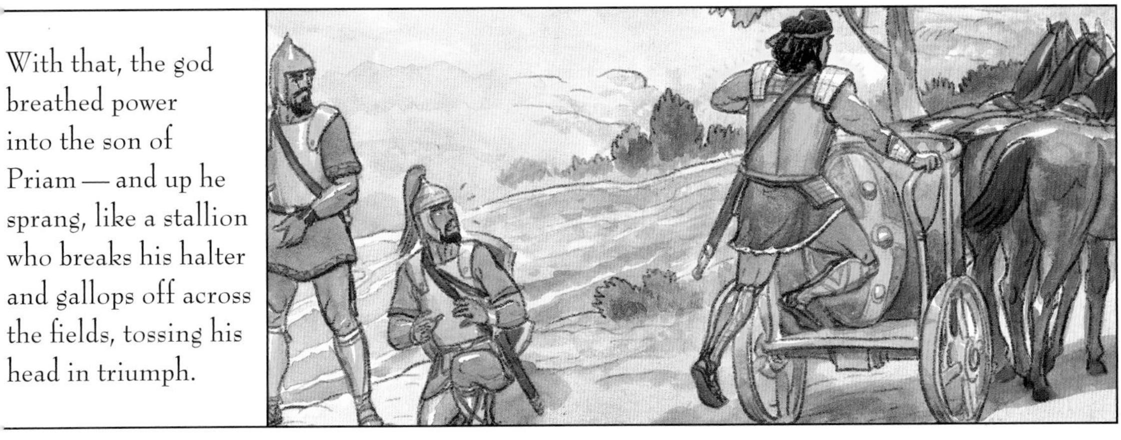
With that, the god breathed power into the son of Priam — and up he sprang, like a stallion who breaks his halter and gallops off across the fields, tossing his head in triumph.

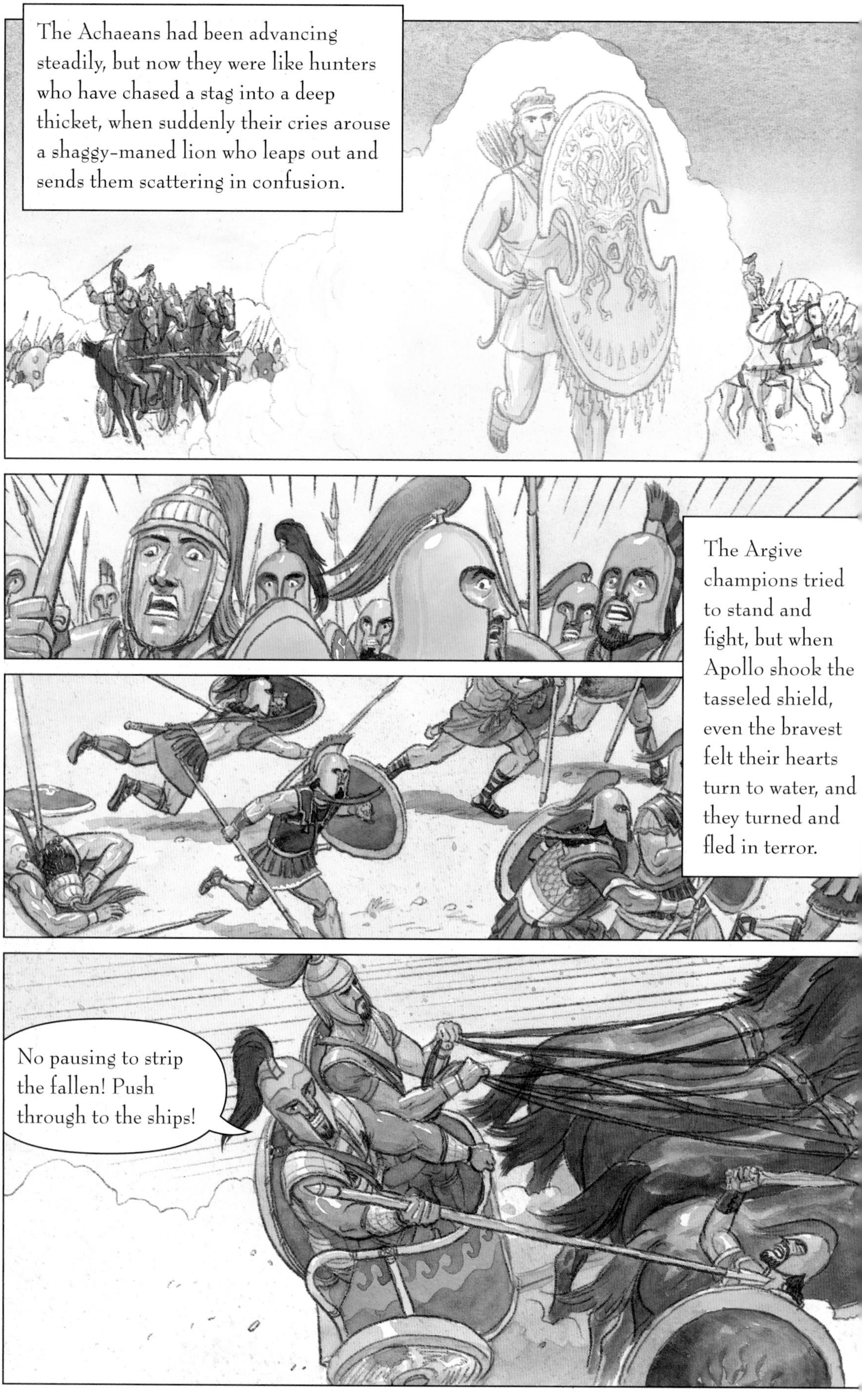
The Achaeans had been advancing steadily, but now they were like hunters who have chased a stag into a deep thicket, when suddenly their cries arouse a shaggy-maned lion who leaps out and sends them scattering in confusion.
The Argive champions tried to stand and fight, but when Apollo shook the tasseled shield, even the bravest felt their hearts turn to water, and they turned and fled in terror.
No pausing to strip the fallen! Push through to the ships!

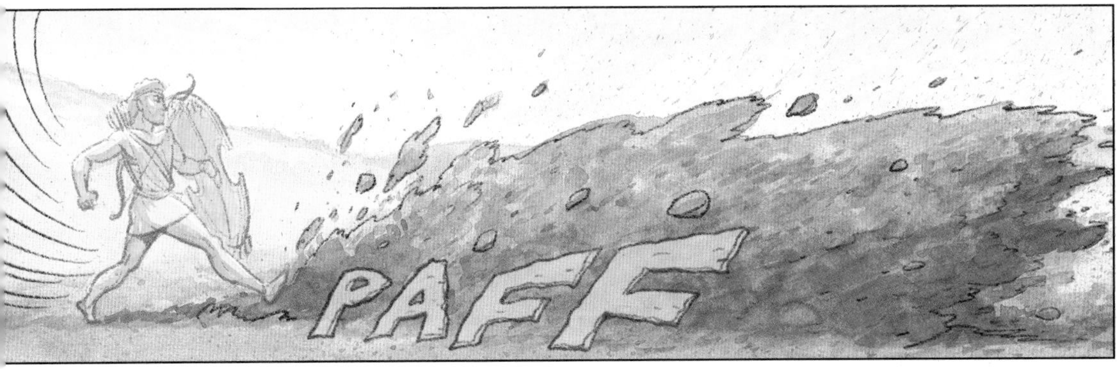
PAFF

Phoebus Apollo smote the center of the earthen wall and moat, easily clearing a path for Hector.

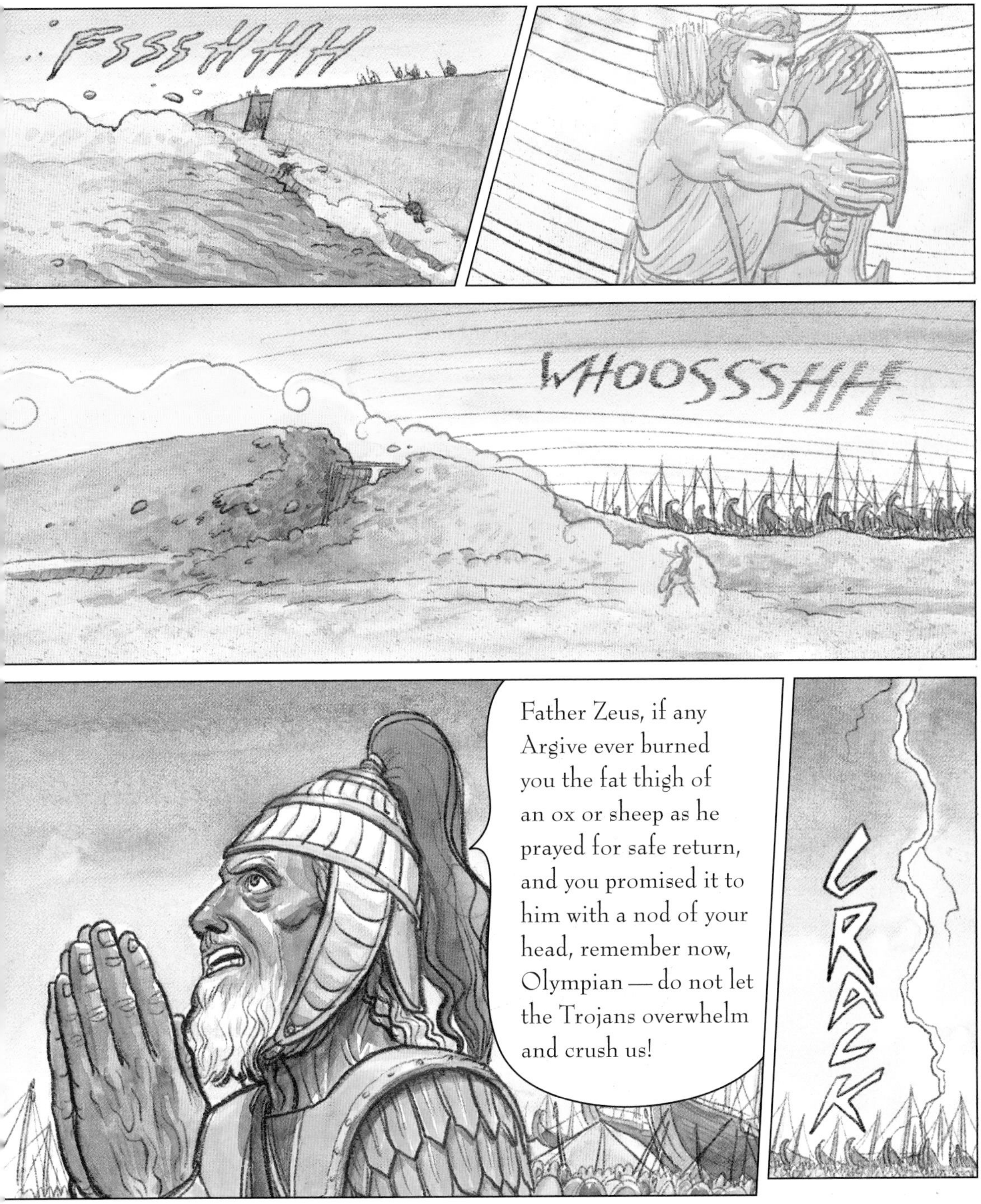
FSSSHHH
WHOOSSSHH
Father Zeus, if any Argive ever burned you the fat thigh of an ox or sheep as he prayed for safe return, and you promised it to him with a nod of your head, remember now, Olympian — do not let the Trojans overwhelm and crush us!
CRACK

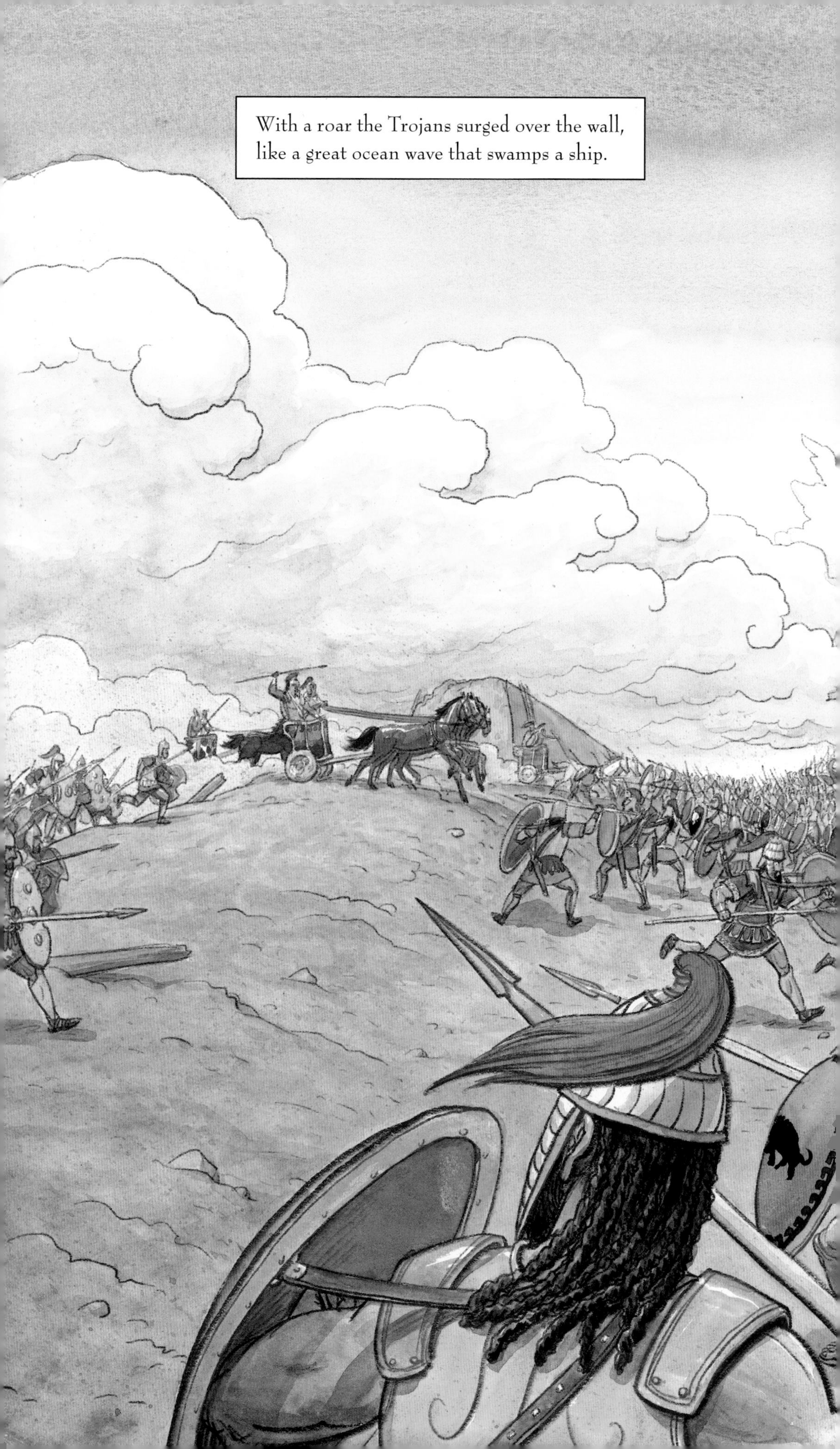
With a roar the Trojans surged over the wall, like a great ocean wave that swamps a ship.

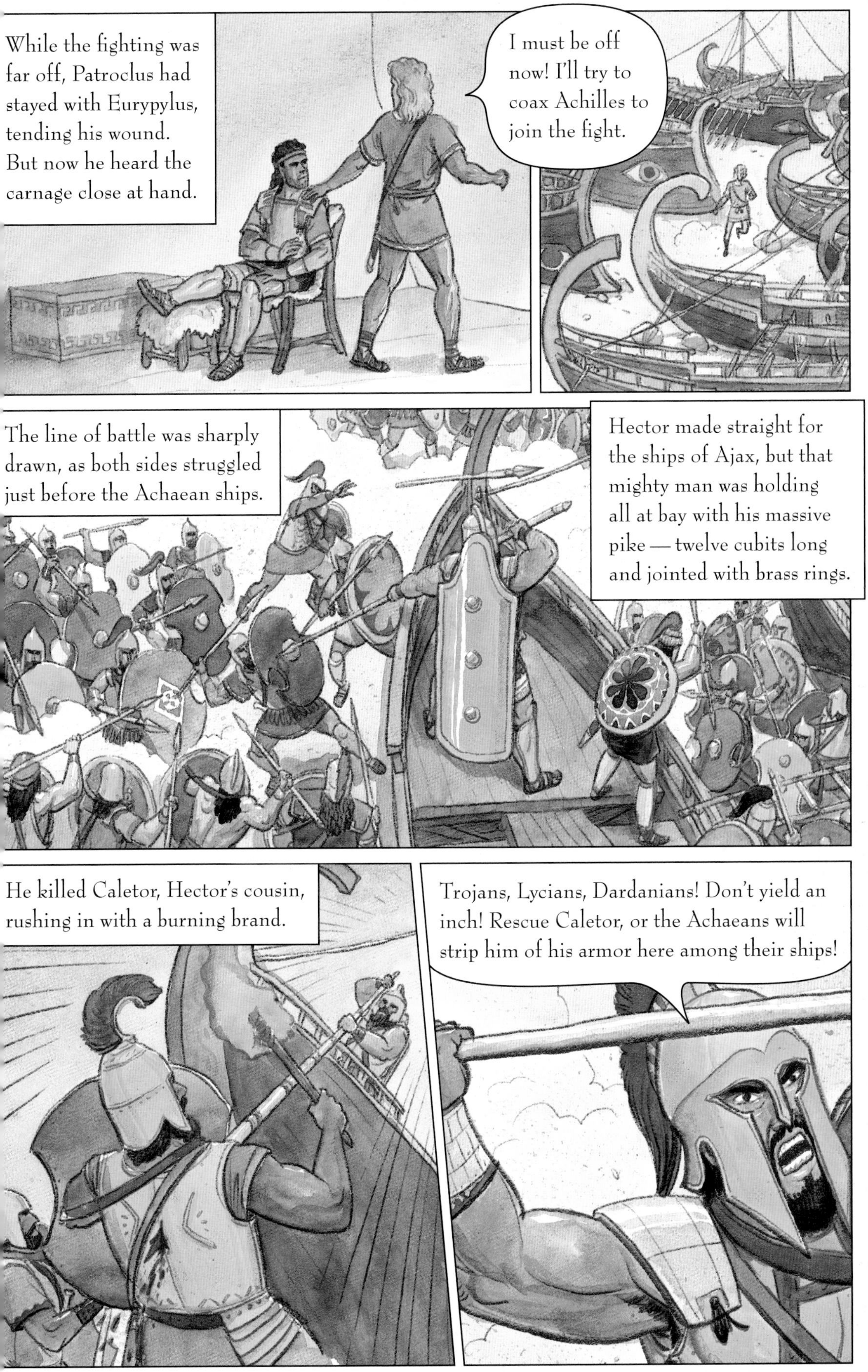
While the fighting was far off, Patroclus had stayed with Eurypylus, tending his wound. But now he heard the carnage close at hand.
I must be off now! I'll try to coax Achilles to join the fight.
The line of battle was sharply drawn, as both sides struggled just before the Achaean ships.
Hector made straight for the ships of Ajax, but that mighty man was holding all at bay with his massive pike — twelve cubits long and jointed with brass rings.
He killed Caletor, Hector's cousin, rushing in with a burning brand.
Trojans, Lycians, Dardanians! Don't yield an inch! Rescue Caletor, or the Achaeans will strip him of his armor here among their ships!

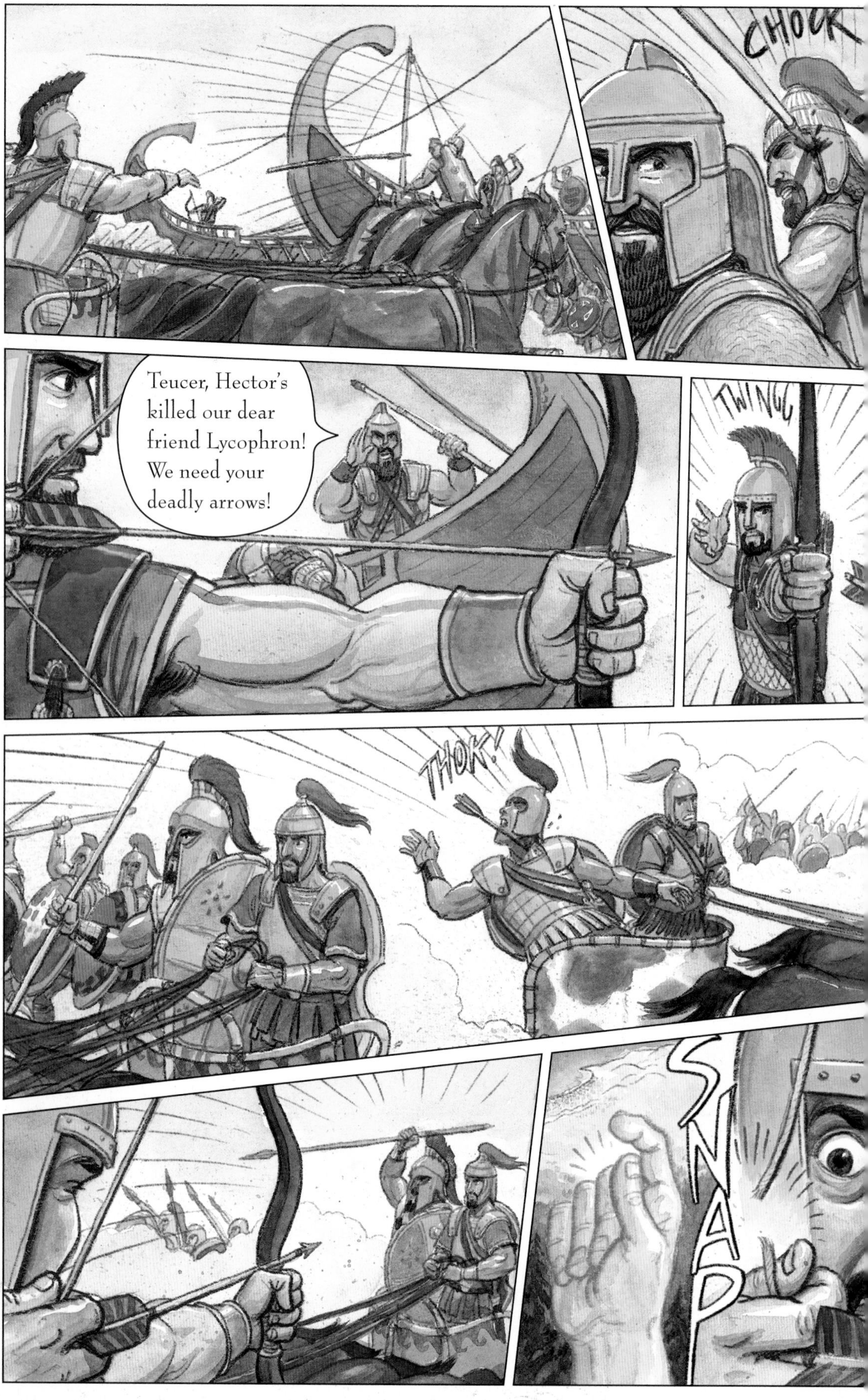
CHOCK
Teucer, Hector's killed our dear friend Lycophron! We need your deadly arrows!
TWINGG
THOK!
SNAP

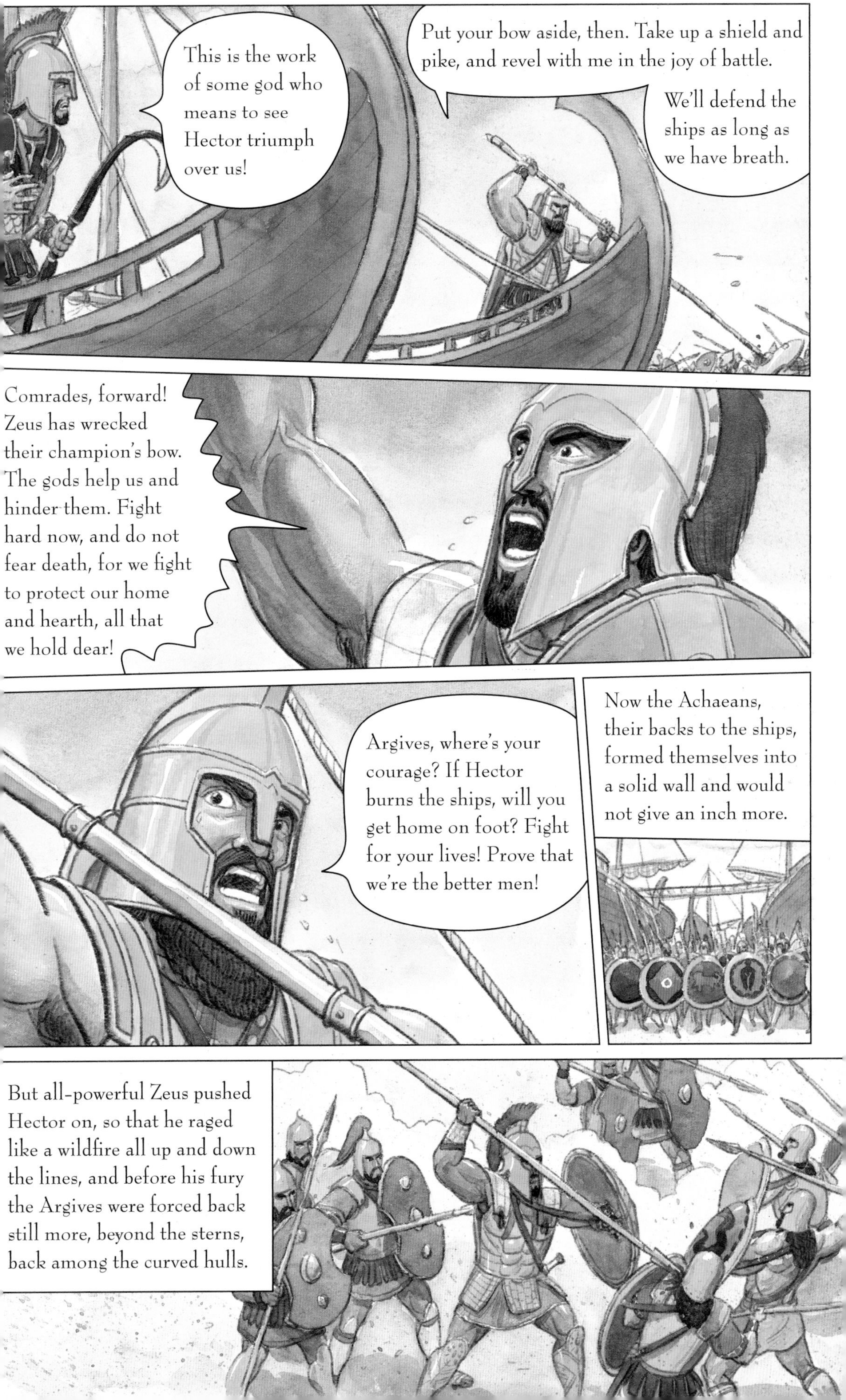
This is the work of some god who means to see Hector triumph over us!
Put your bow aside, then. Take up a shield and pike, and revel with me in the joy of battle.
We'll defend the ships as long as we have breath.
Comrades, forward! Zeus has wrecked their champion's bow. The gods help us and hinder them. Fight hard now, and do not fear death, for we fight to protect our home and hearth, all that we hold dear!
Argives, where's your courage? If Hector burns the ships, will you get home on foot? Fight for your lives! Prove that we're the better men!
Now the Achaeans, their backs to the ships, formed themselves into a solid wall and would not give an inch more.
But all-powerful Zeus pushed Hector on, so that he raged like a wildfire all up and down the lines, and before his fury the Argives were forced back still more, beyond the sterns, back among the curved hulls.

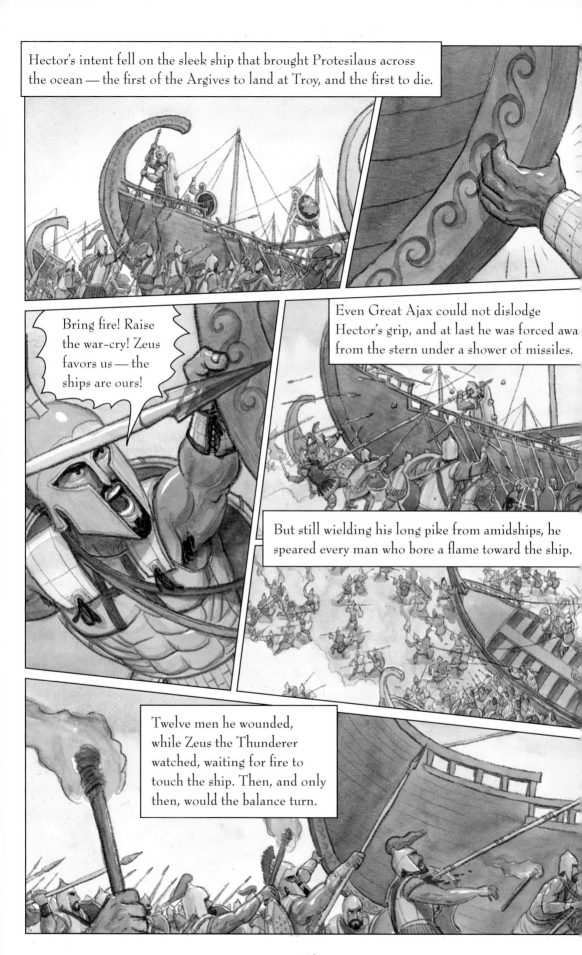

Hector's intent fell on the sleek ship that brought Protesilaus across the ocean — the first of the Argives to land at Troy, and the first to die.

Bring fire! Raise the war-cry! Zeus favors us — the ships are ours!

Even Great Ajax could not dislodge Hector's grip, and at last he was forced away from the stern under a shower of missiles.

But still wielding his long pike from amidships, he speared every man who bore a flame toward the ship.

Twelve men he wounded, while Zeus the Thunderer watched, waiting for fire to touch the ship. Then, and only then, would the balance turn.

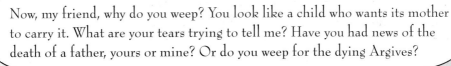

Now, my friend, why do you weep? You look like a child who wants its mother to carry it. What are your tears trying to tell me? Have you had news of the death of a father, yours or mine? Or do you weep for the dying Argives?

I weep for our *friends*, wounded and killed by the Trojans while we sit idle.

All the great champions have been wounded! Diomedes, Odysseus, Agamemnon, Eurypylus — all hurt with arrows or spears, being tended in their huts while Hector rages about the ships. Will you still do nothing? What glory will you get for this? Have you no pity? You cannot be a son of Thetis and gallant Peleus — only the cold sea and the jagged rocks could have fathered so hard-hearted a son.

Do you hold back in fear of some prophecy? If so, then at least allow me to lead the Myrmidons in battle. Lend me your armor too so that the Trojans will lose heart, break off the attack. Their men are exhausted, while we are fresh. We may be able to turn the day and save the Argives!

Well said, Patroclus. If only you knew you were praying for your own death.

137

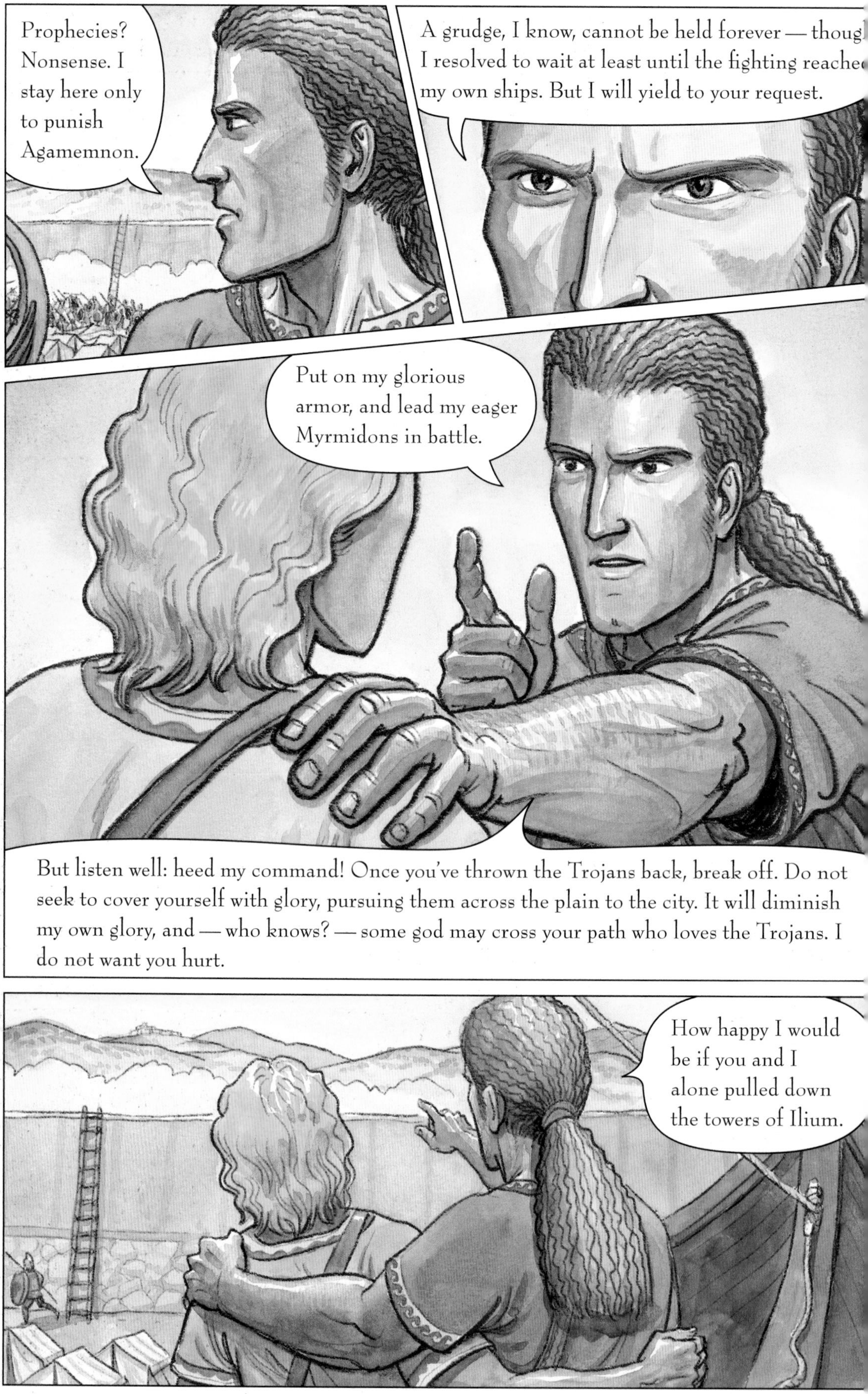
Prophecies? Nonsense. I stay here only to punish Agamemnon.
A grudge, I know, cannot be held forever — thoug I resolved to wait at least until the fighting reache my own ships. But I will yield to your request.
Put on my glorious armor, and lead my eager Myrmidons in battle.
But listen well: heed my command! Once you've thrown the Trojans back, break off. Do not seek to cover yourself with glory, pursuing them across the plain to the city. It will diminish my own glory, and — who knows? — some god may cross your path who loves the Trojans. I do not want you hurt.
How happy I would be if you and I alone pulled down the towers of Ilium.

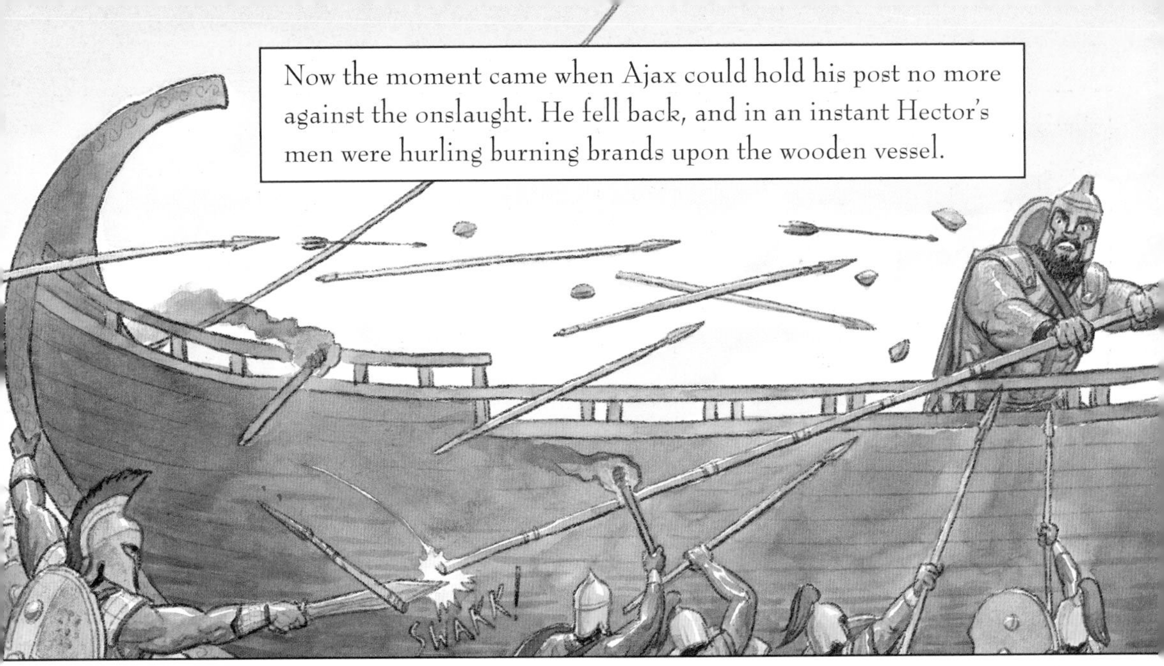
Now the moment came when Ajax could hold his post no more against the onslaught. He fell back, and in an instant Hector's men were hurling burning brands upon the wooden vessel.
SWAKK!

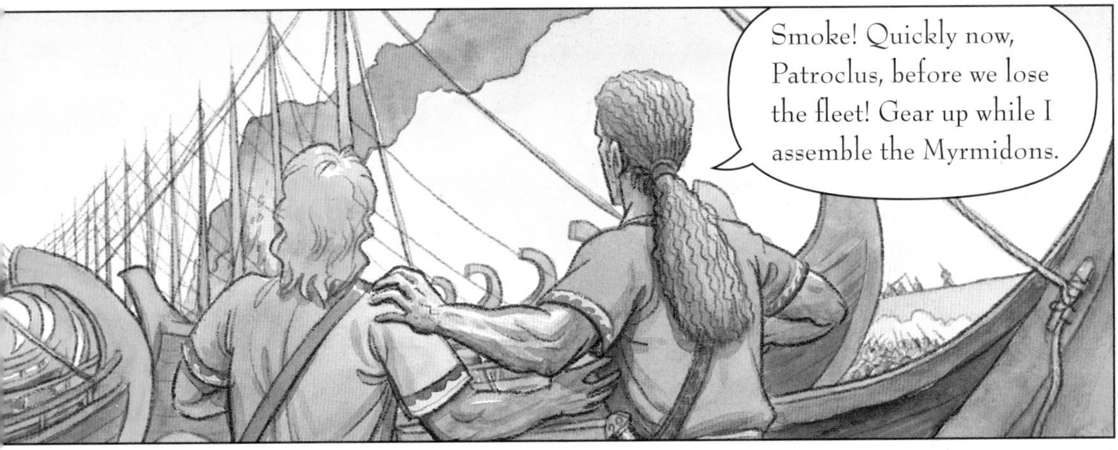
Smoke! Quickly now, Patroclus, before we lose the fleet! Gear up while I assemble the Myrmidons.

Patroclus donned Achilles's godlike gear, leaving only his massive spear — it was made from an ash tree atop Mount Pelion, and no Achaean could wield it in war save Achilles himself.

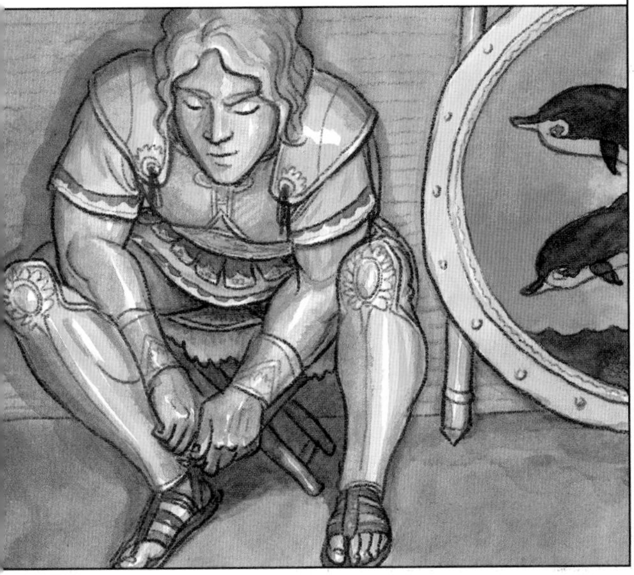

He sent Automedon to yoke the horses — Xanthus and Balius, offspring of the West Wind — and in the side-traces he put Pedasus,* a thoroughbred who was mortal and yet could keep up with the immortal pair.

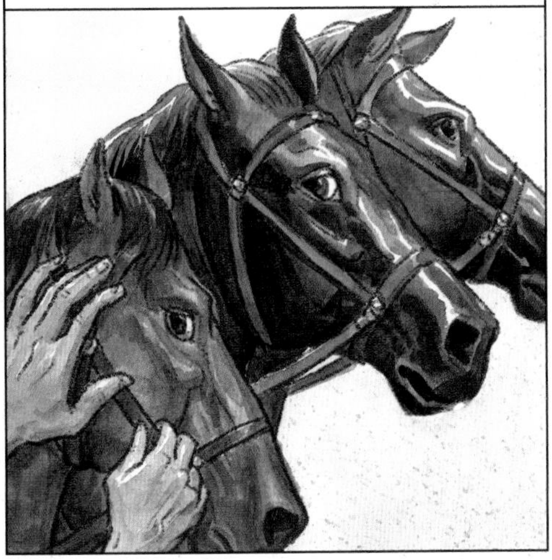

* Pedasus is not to be confused with Pegasus, the winged horse. The immortal horses Xanthus and Balius were one of the gods' wedding presents to Peleus and were supposed to be the best in either army.

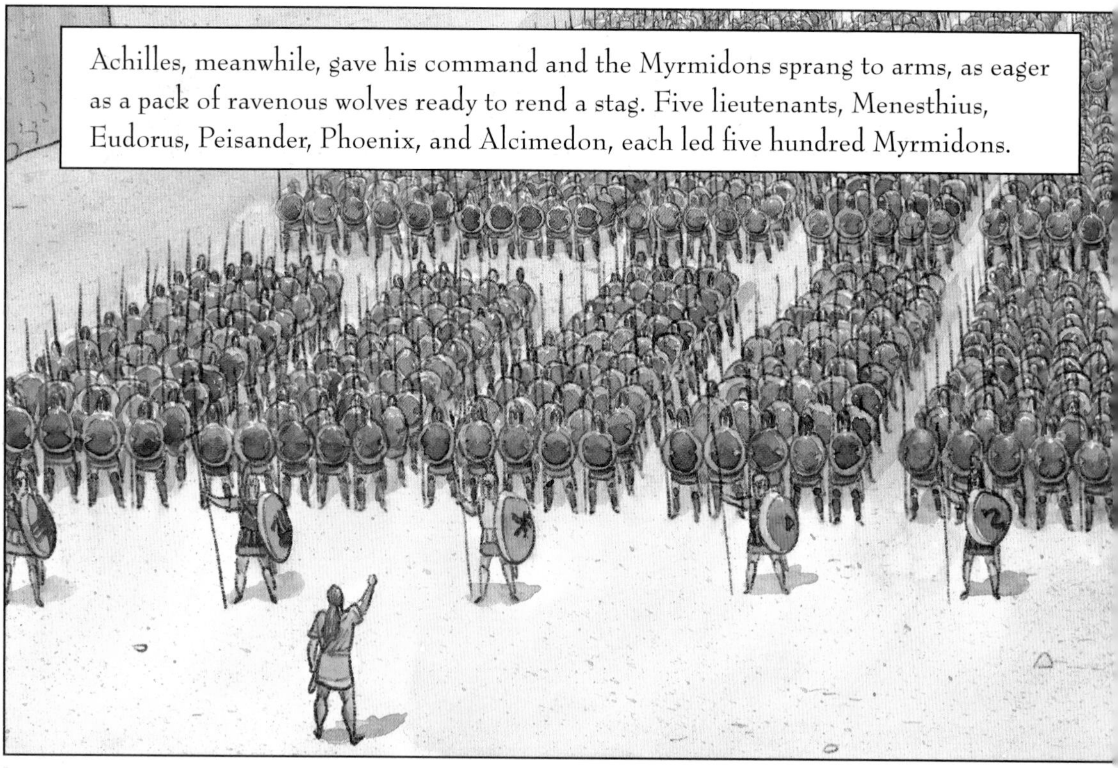
Achilles, meanwhile, gave his command and the Myrmidons sprang to arms, as eager as a pack of ravenous wolves ready to rend a stag. Five lieutenants, Menesthius, Eudorus, Peisander, Phoenix, and Alcimedon, each led five hundred Myrmidons.

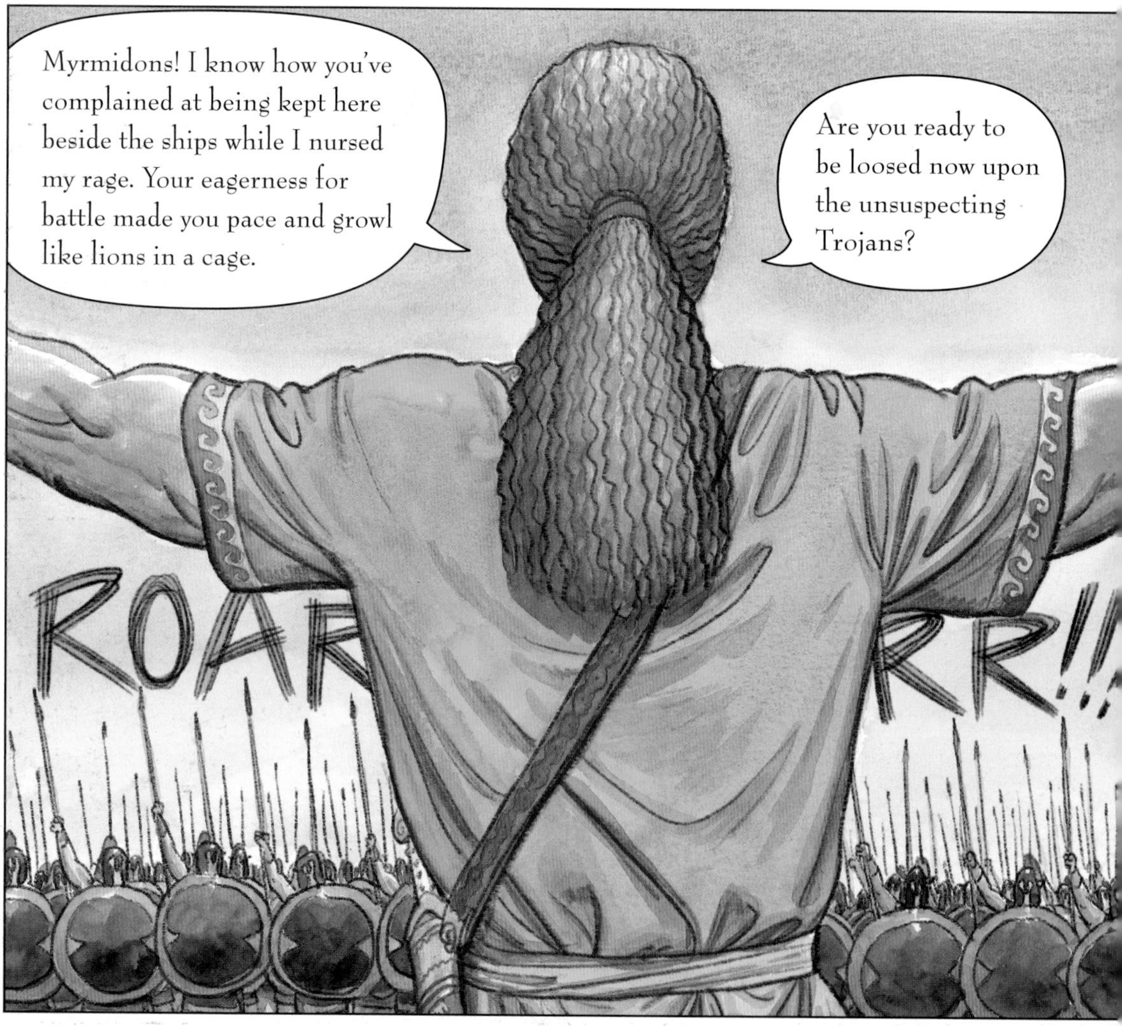
Myrmidons! I know how you've complained at being kept here beside the ships while I nursed my rage. Your eagerness for battle made you pace and growl like lions in a cage.
Are you ready to be loosed now upon the unsuspecting Trojans?
ROARRR!!

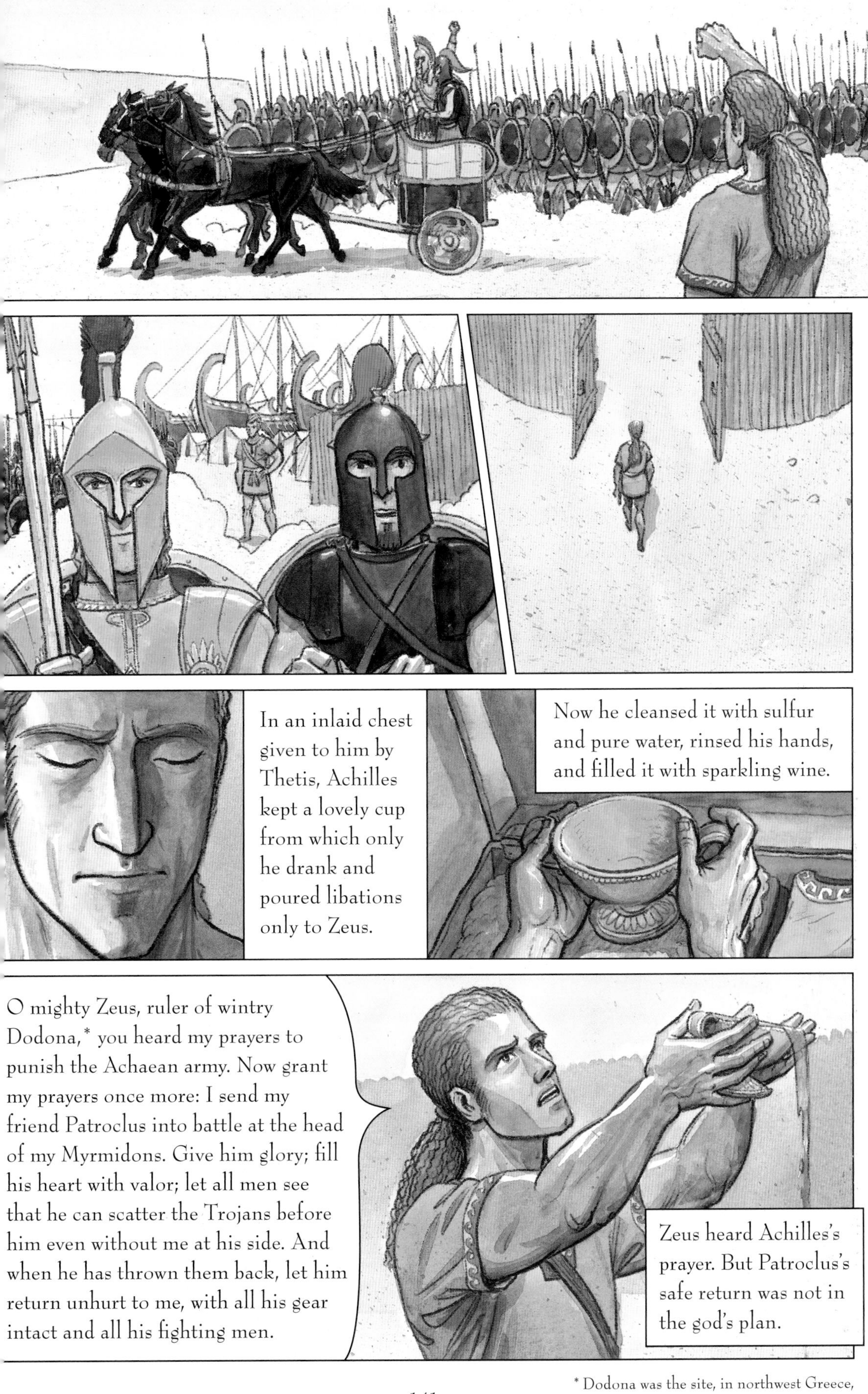
In an inlaid chest given to him by Thetis, Achilles kept a lovely cup from which only he drank and poured libations only to Zeus.
Now he cleansed it with sulfur and pure water, rinsed his hands, and filled it with sparkling wine.
O mighty Zeus, ruler of wintry Dodona,* you heard my prayers to punish the Achaean army. Now grant my prayers once more: I send my friend Patroclus into battle at the head of my Myrmidons. Give him glory; fill his heart with valor; let all men see that he can scatter the Trojans before him even without me at his side. And when he has thrown them back, let him return unhurt to me, with all his gear intact and all his fighting men.
Zeus heard Achilles's prayer. But Patroclus's safe return was not in the god's plan.

* Dodona was the site, in northwest Greece, of a famous oracle of Zeus.

Now the Myrmidons joined the battle, bursting forth in waves like hornets from a nest stirred up by foolish boys — they swarm out to attack anyone who passes unaware. Just so, they poured from the ships with a ceaseless din of shouting and fell upon the luckless Trojans.

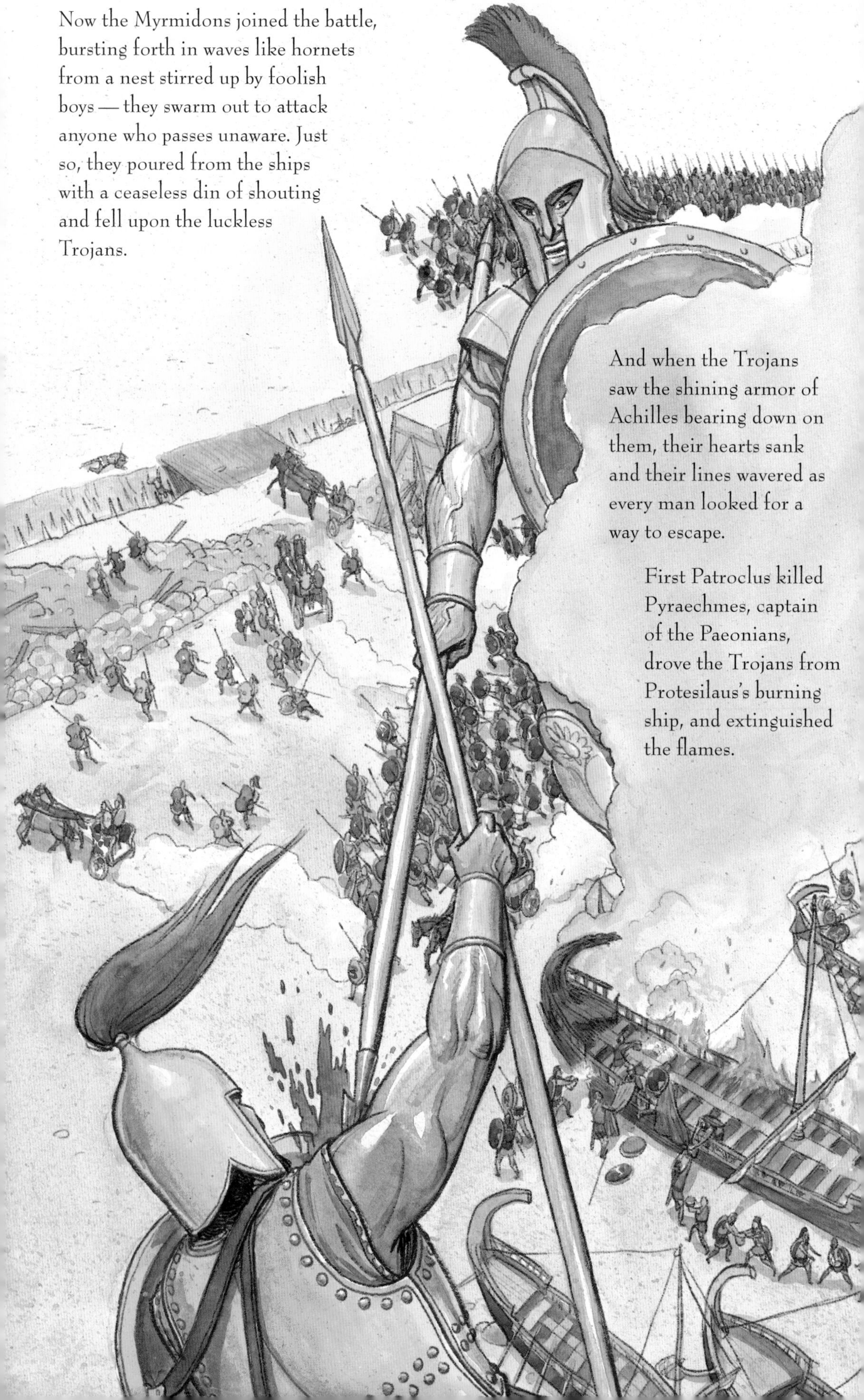

And when the Trojans saw the shining armor of Achilles bearing down on them, their hearts sank and their lines wavered as every man looked for a way to escape.

First Patroclus killed Pyraechmes, captain of the Paeonians, drove the Trojans from Protesilaus's burning ship, and extinguished the flames.

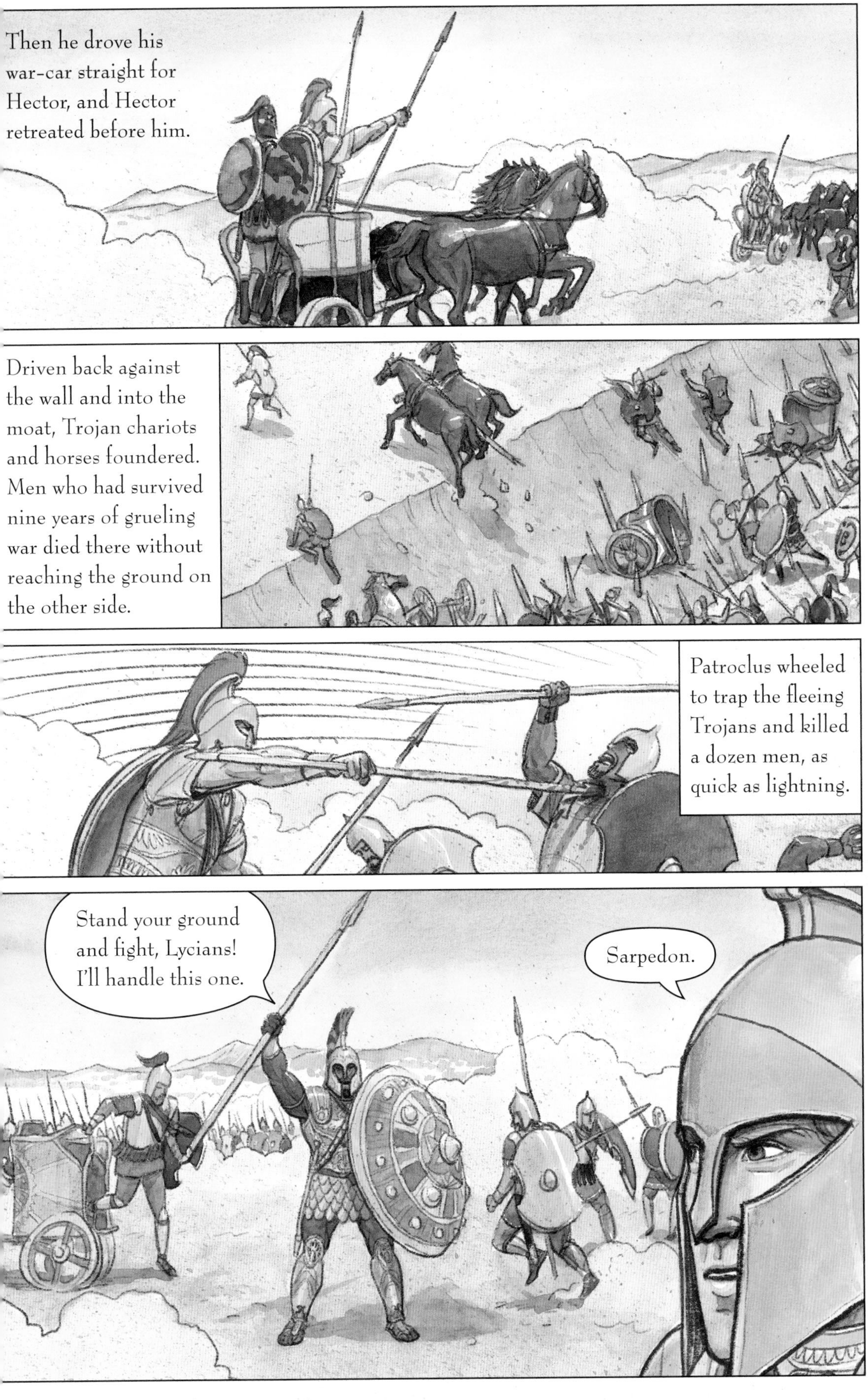
Then he drove his war-car straight for Hector, and Hector retreated before him.
Driven back against the wall and into the moat, Trojan chariots and horses foundered. Men who had survived nine years of grueling war died there without reaching the ground on the other side.
Patroclus wheeled to trap the fleeing Trojans and killed a dozen men, as quick as lightning.
Stand your ground and fight, Lycians! I'll handle this one.
Sarpedon.

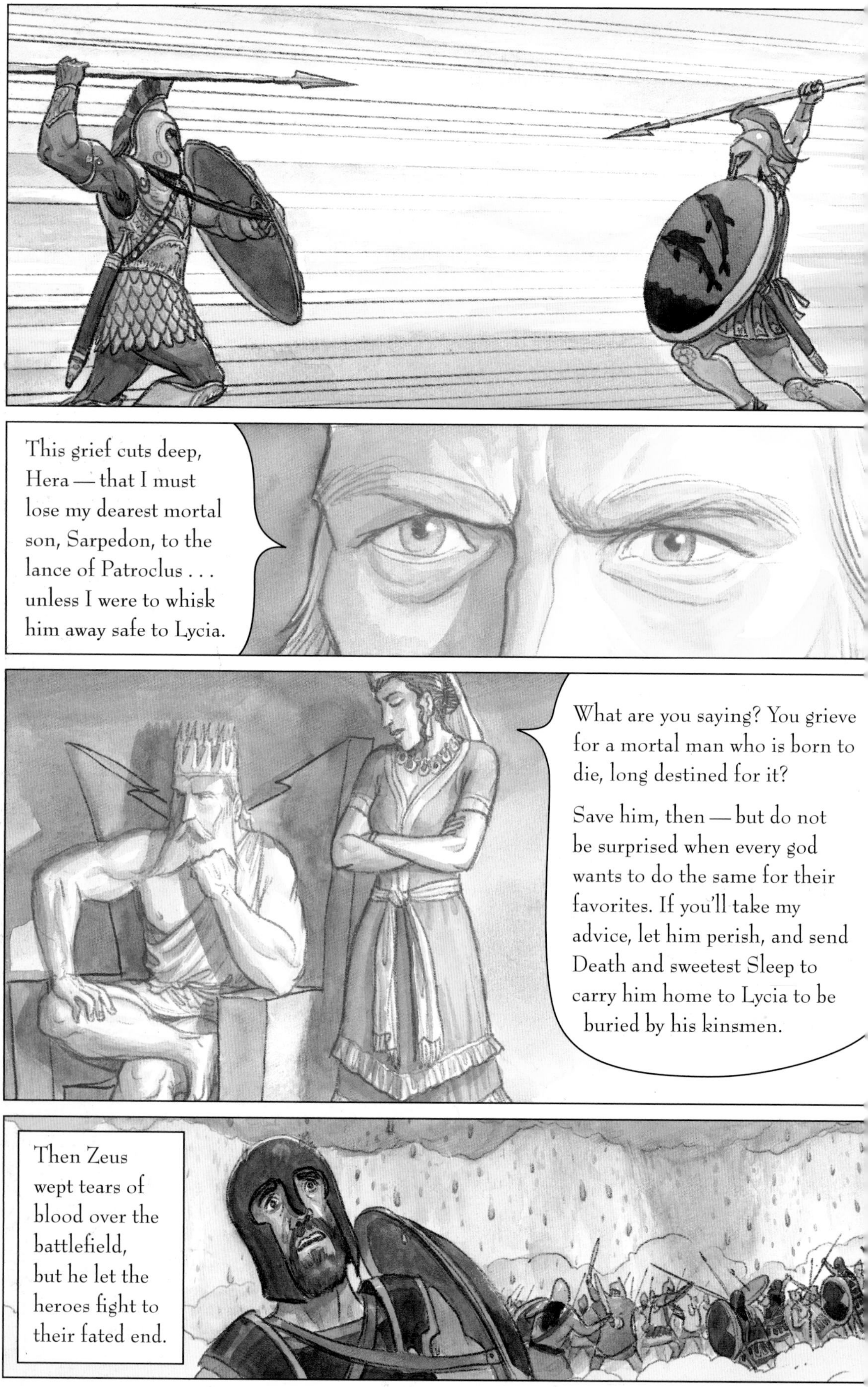

This grief cuts deep, Hera — that I must lose my dearest mortal son, Sarpedon, to the lance of Patroclus . . . unless I were to whisk him away safe to Lycia.
What are you saying? You grieve for a mortal man who is born to die, long destined for it?
Save him, then — but do not be surprised when every god wants to do the same for their favorites. If you'll take my advice, let him perish, and send Death and sweetest Sleep to carry him home to Lycia to be buried by his kinsmen.
Then Zeus wept tears of blood over the battlefield, but he let the heroes fight to their fated end.

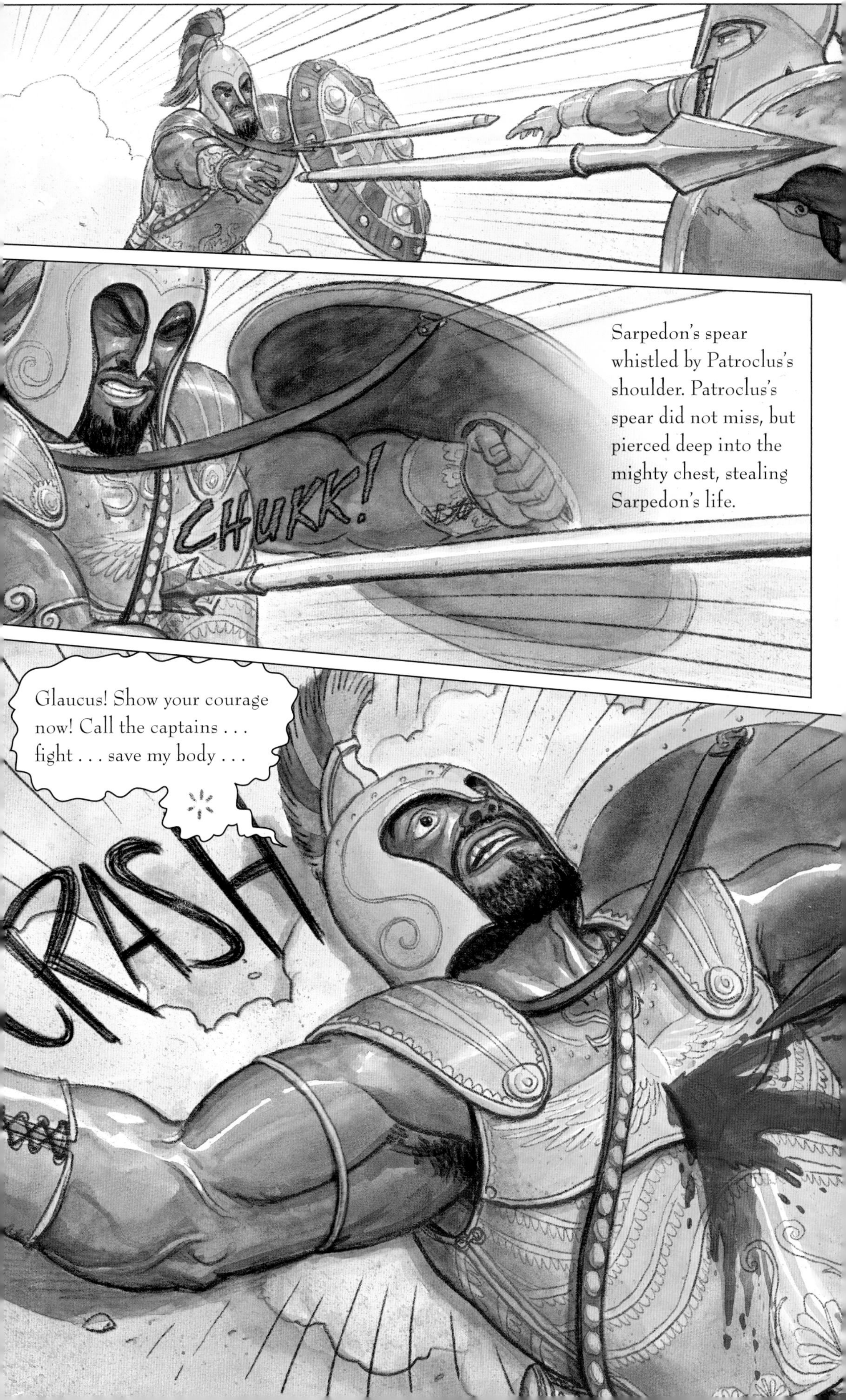
Sarpedon's spear whistled by Patroclus's shoulder. Patroclus's spear did not miss, but pierced deep into the mighty chest, stealing Sarpedon's life.
CHUKK!
Glaucus! Show your courage now! Call the captains . . . fight . . . save my body . . .
CRASH

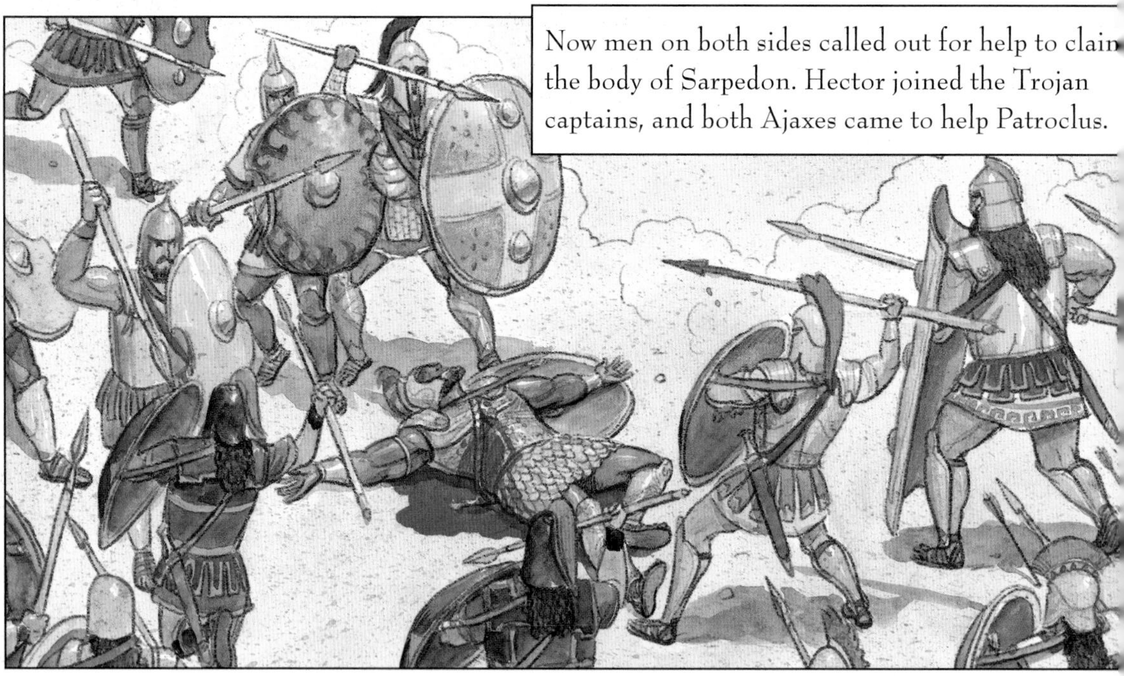
Now men on both sides called out for help to claim the body of Sarpedon. Hector joined the Trojan captains, and both Ajaxes came to help Patroclus.

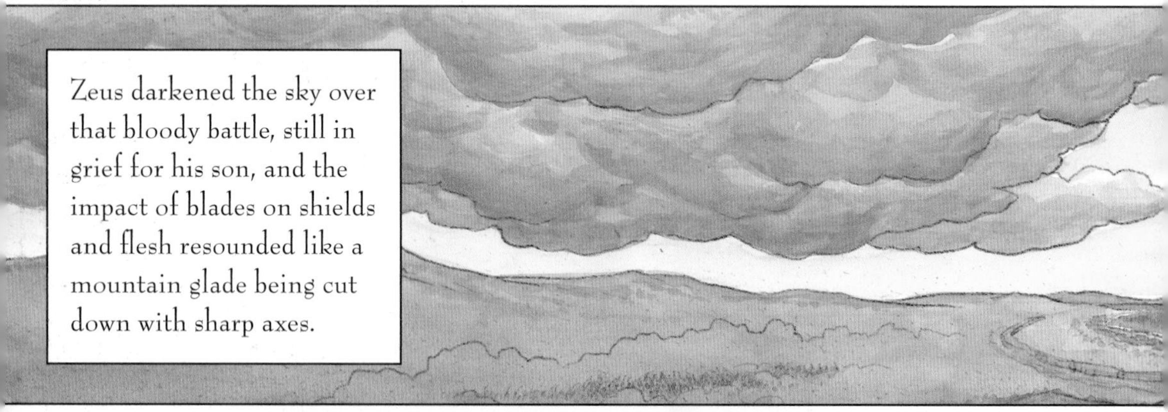
Zeus darkened the sky over that bloody battle, still in grief for his son, and the impact of blades on shields and flesh resounded like a mountain glade being cut down with sharp axes.

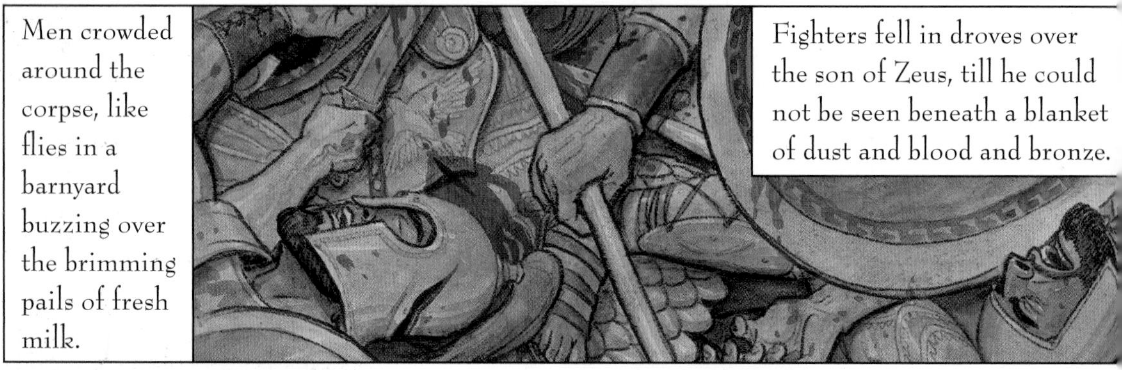
Men crowded around the corpse, like flies in a barnyard buzzing over the brimming pails of fresh milk.
Fighters fell in droves over the son of Zeus, till he could not be seen beneath a blanket of dust and blood and bronze.

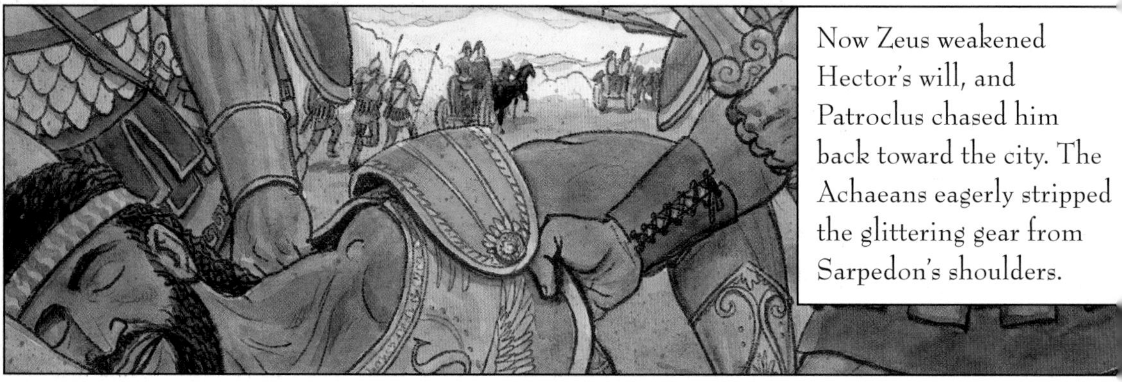
Now Zeus weakened Hector's will, and Patroclus chased him back toward the city. The Achaeans eagerly stripped the glittering gear from Sarpedon's shoulders.

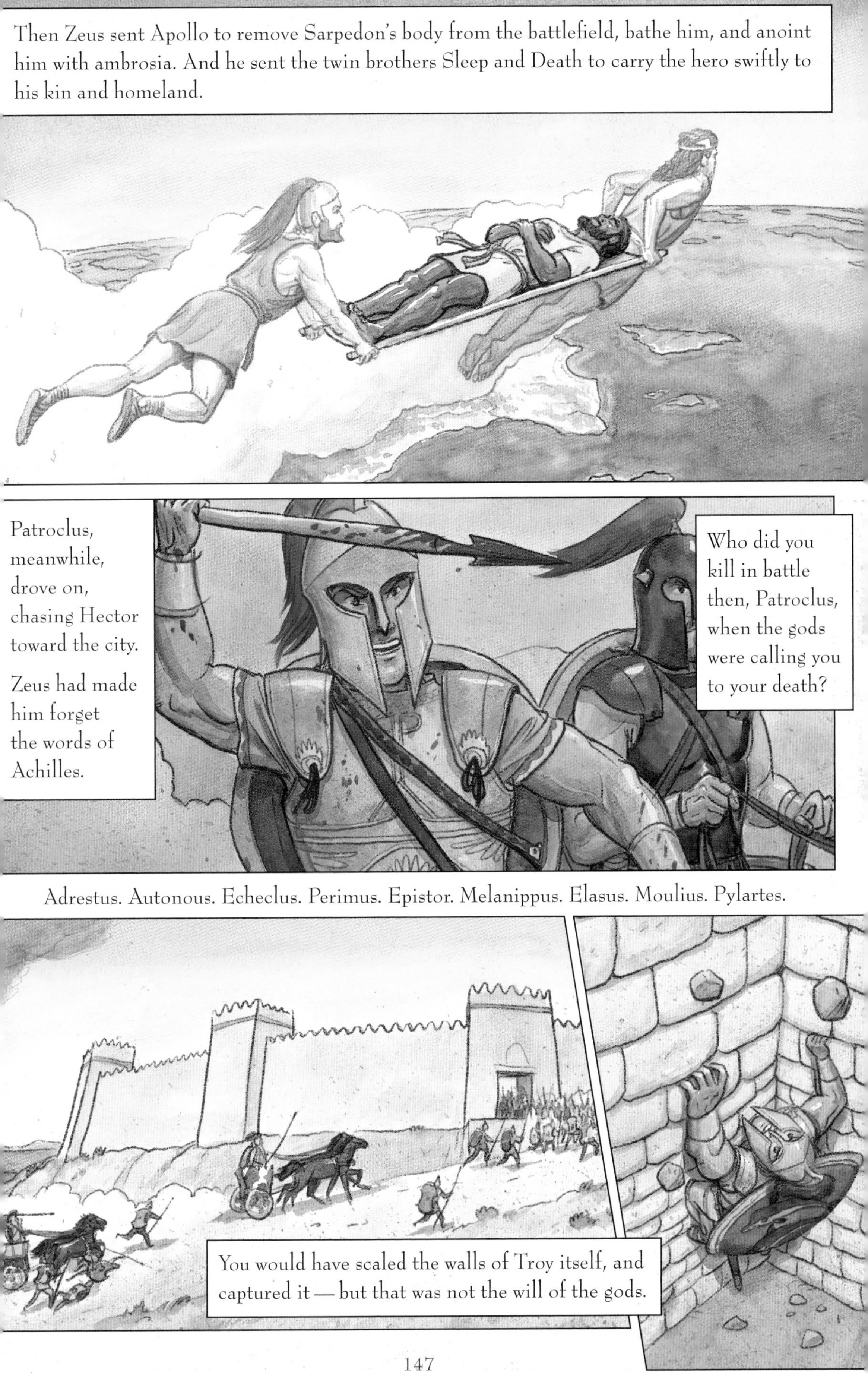
Then Zeus sent Apollo to remove Sarpedon's body from the battlefield, bathe him, and anoint him with ambrosia. And he sent the twin brothers Sleep and Death to carry the hero swiftly to his kin and homeland.
Patroclus, meanwhile, drove on, chasing Hector toward the city.
Zeus had made him forget the words of Achilles.
Who did you kill in battle then, Patroclus, when the gods were calling you to your death?
Adrestus. Autonous. Echeclus. Perimus. Epistor. Melanippus. Elasus. Moulius. Pylartes.
You would have scaled the walls of Troy itself, and captured it — but that was not the will of the gods.

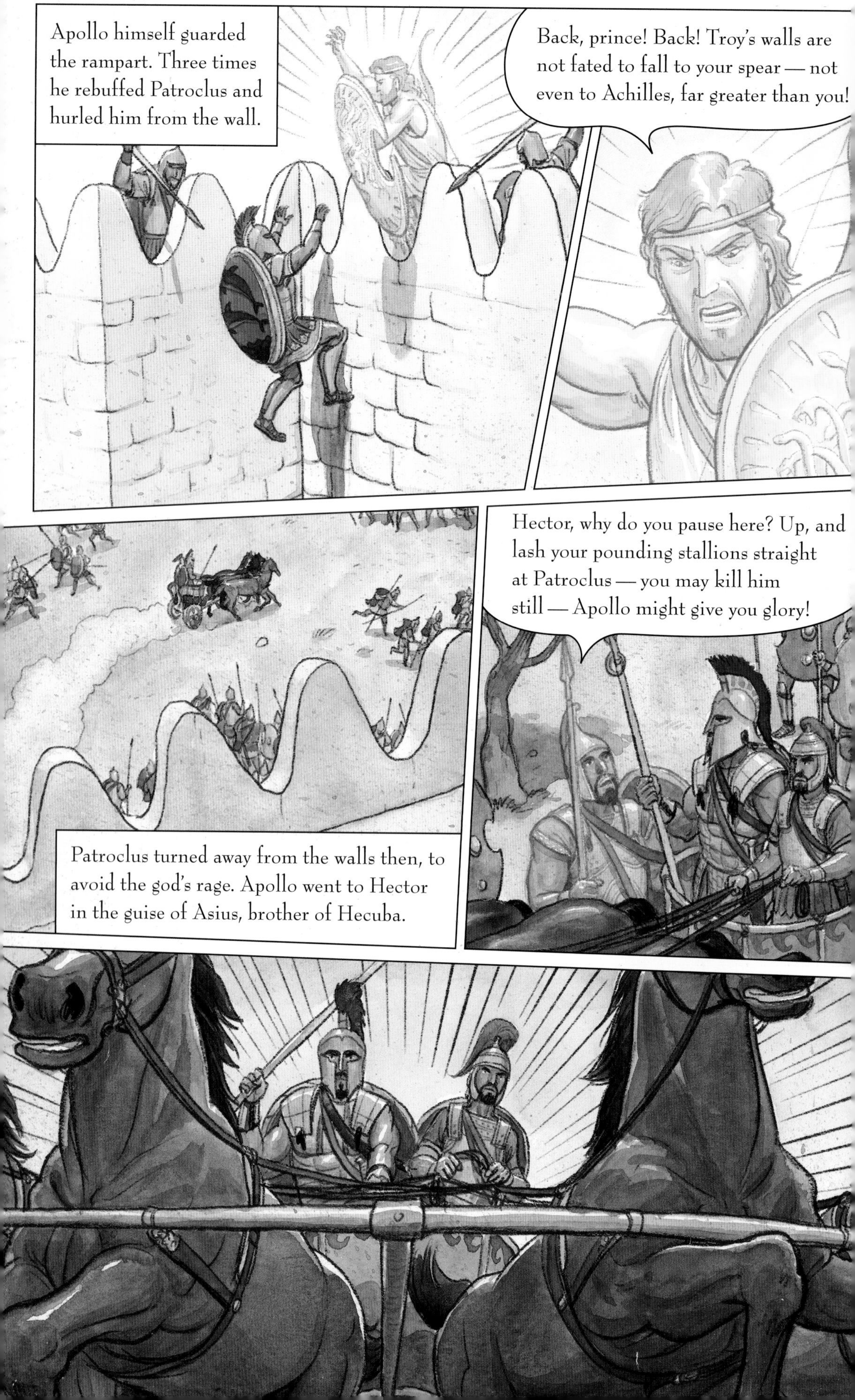
Apollo himself guarded the rampart. Three times he rebuffed Patroclus and hurled him from the wall.
Back, prince! Back! Troy's walls are not fated to fall to your spear — not even to Achilles, far greater than you!
Patroclus turned away from the walls then, to avoid the god's rage. Apollo went to Hector in the guise of Asius, brother of Hecuba.
Hector, why do you pause here? Up, and lash your pounding stallions straight at Patroclus — you may kill him still — Apollo might give you glory!

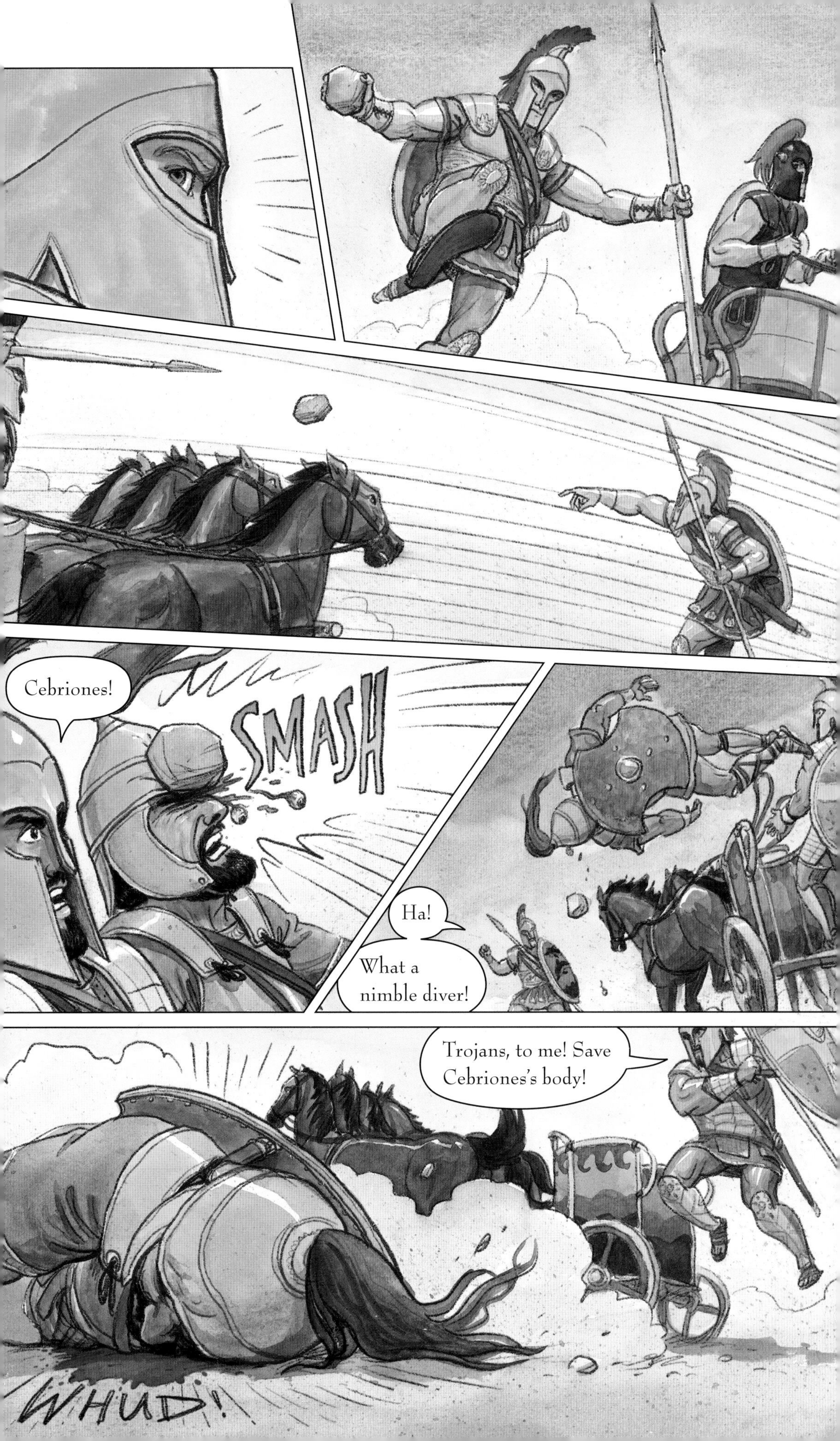

Cebriones!
SMASH
Ha!
What a nimble diver!
Trojans, to me! Save Cebriones's body!
WHUD!

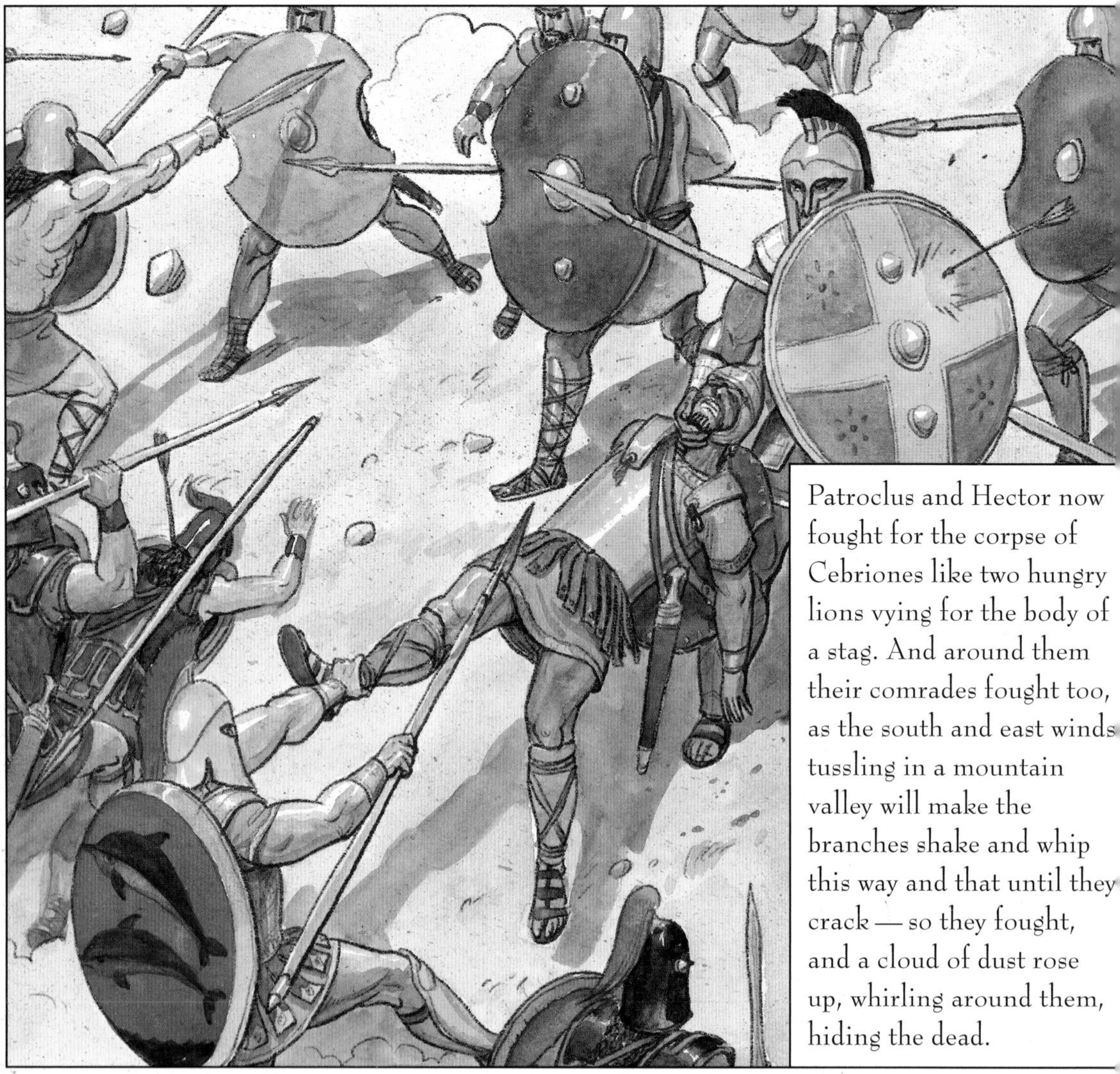
Patroclus and Hector now fought for the corpse of Cebriones like two hungry lions vying for the body of a stag. And around them their comrades fought too, as the south and east winds tussling in a mountain valley will make the branches shake and whip this way and that until they crack — so they fought, and a cloud of dust rose up, whirling around them, hiding the dead.

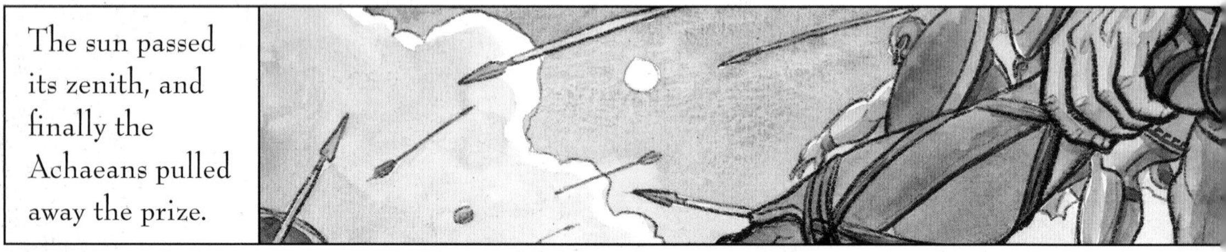
The sun passed its zenith, and finally the Achaeans pulled away the prize.

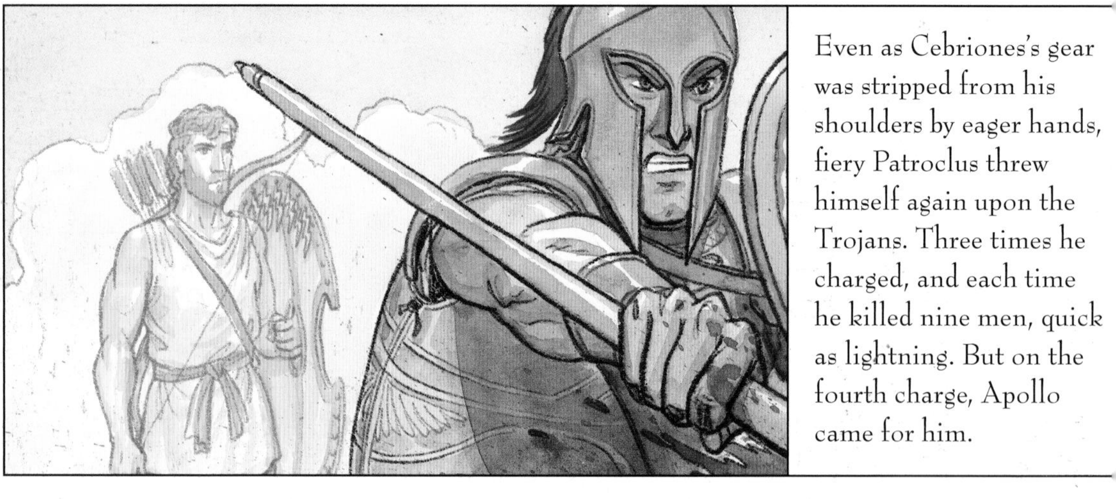
Even as Cebriones's gear was stripped from his shoulders by eager hands, fiery Patroclus threw himself again upon the Trojans. Three times he charged, and each time he killed nine men, quick as lightning. But on the fourth charge, Apollo came for him.

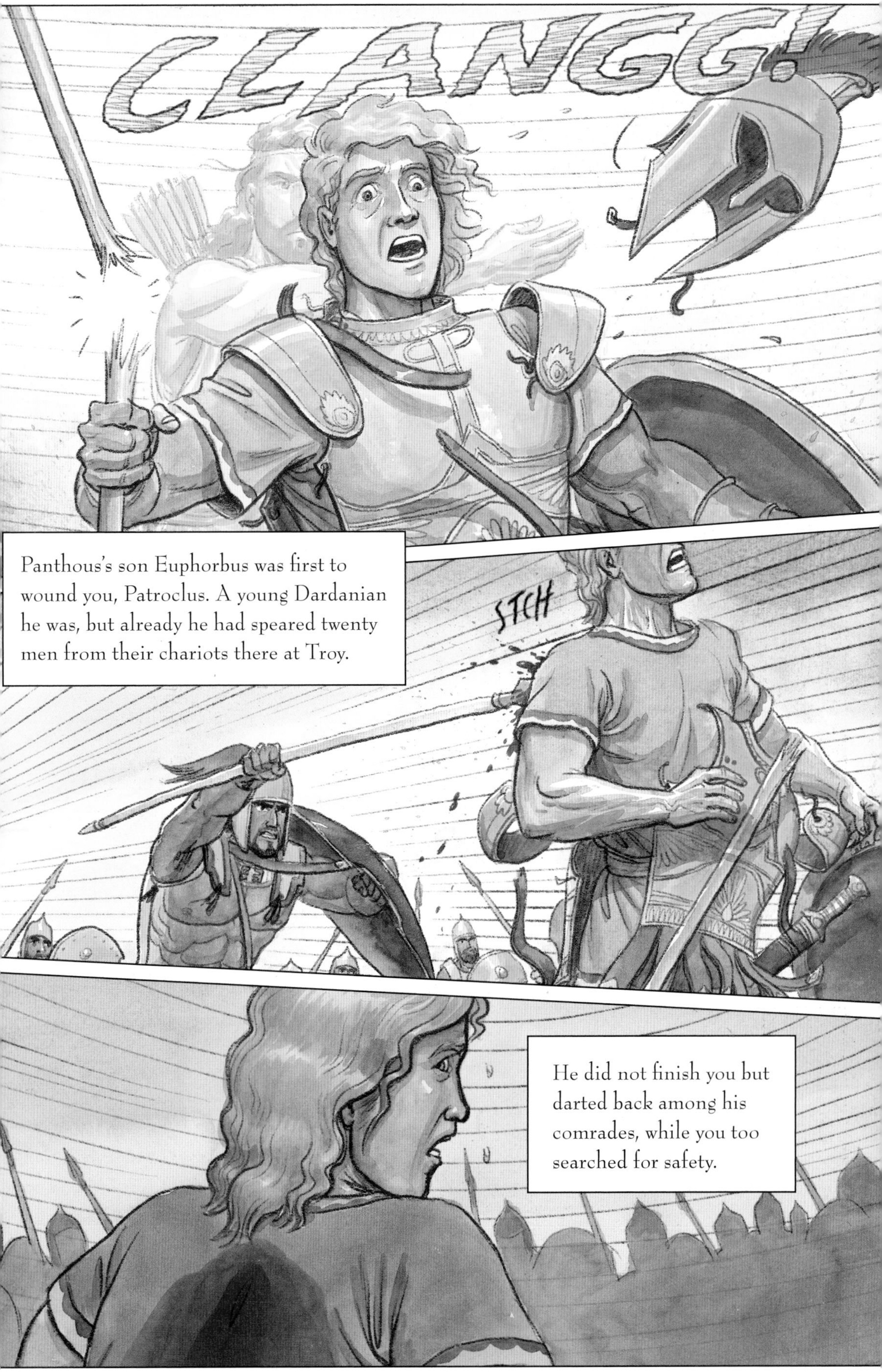
CLANGG!
Panthous's son Euphorbus was first to wound you, Patroclus. A young Dardanian he was, but already he had speared twenty men from their chariots there at Troy.
STCH
He did not finish you but darted back among his comrades, while you too searched for safety.

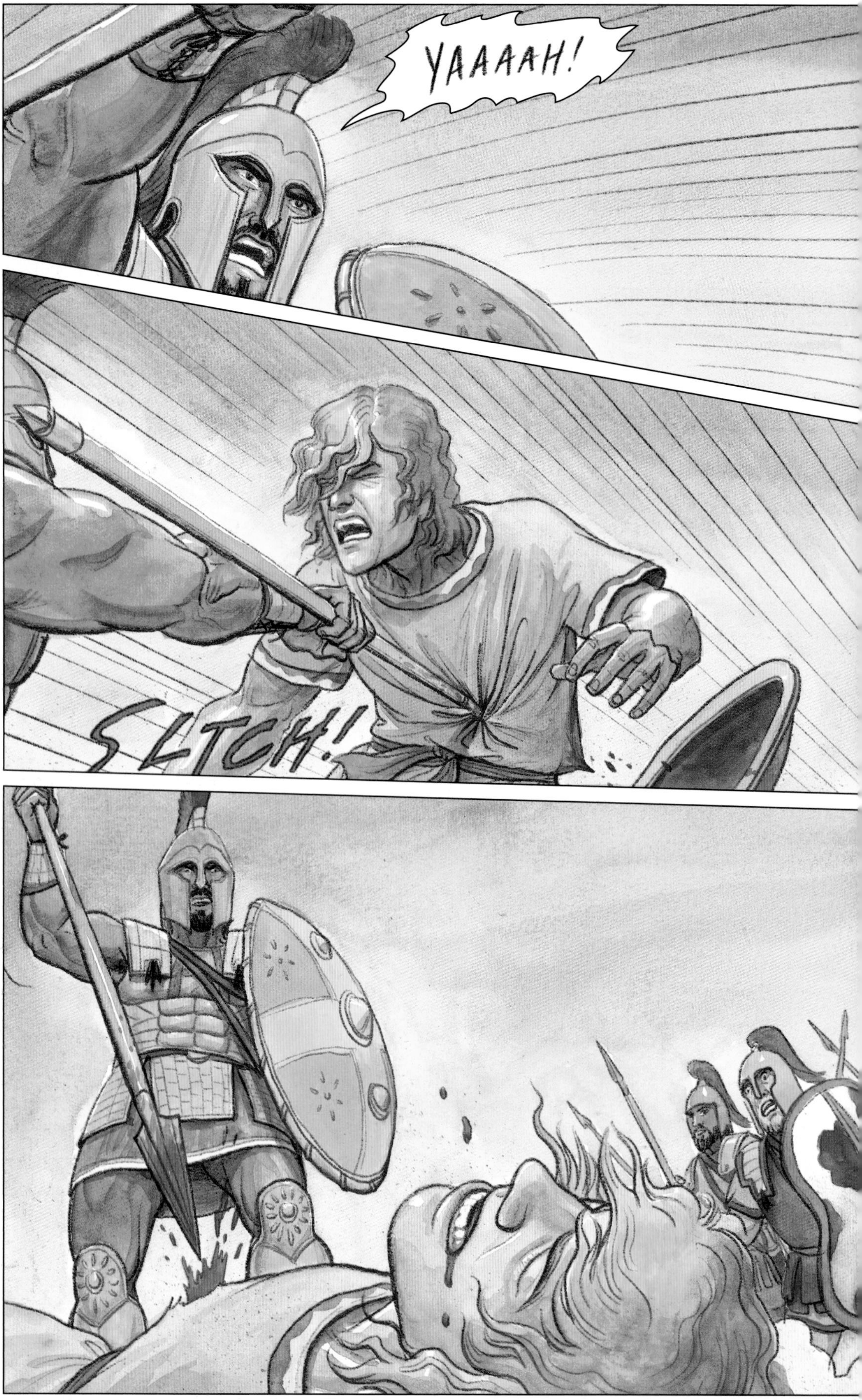
YAAAAH!
SLTCH!

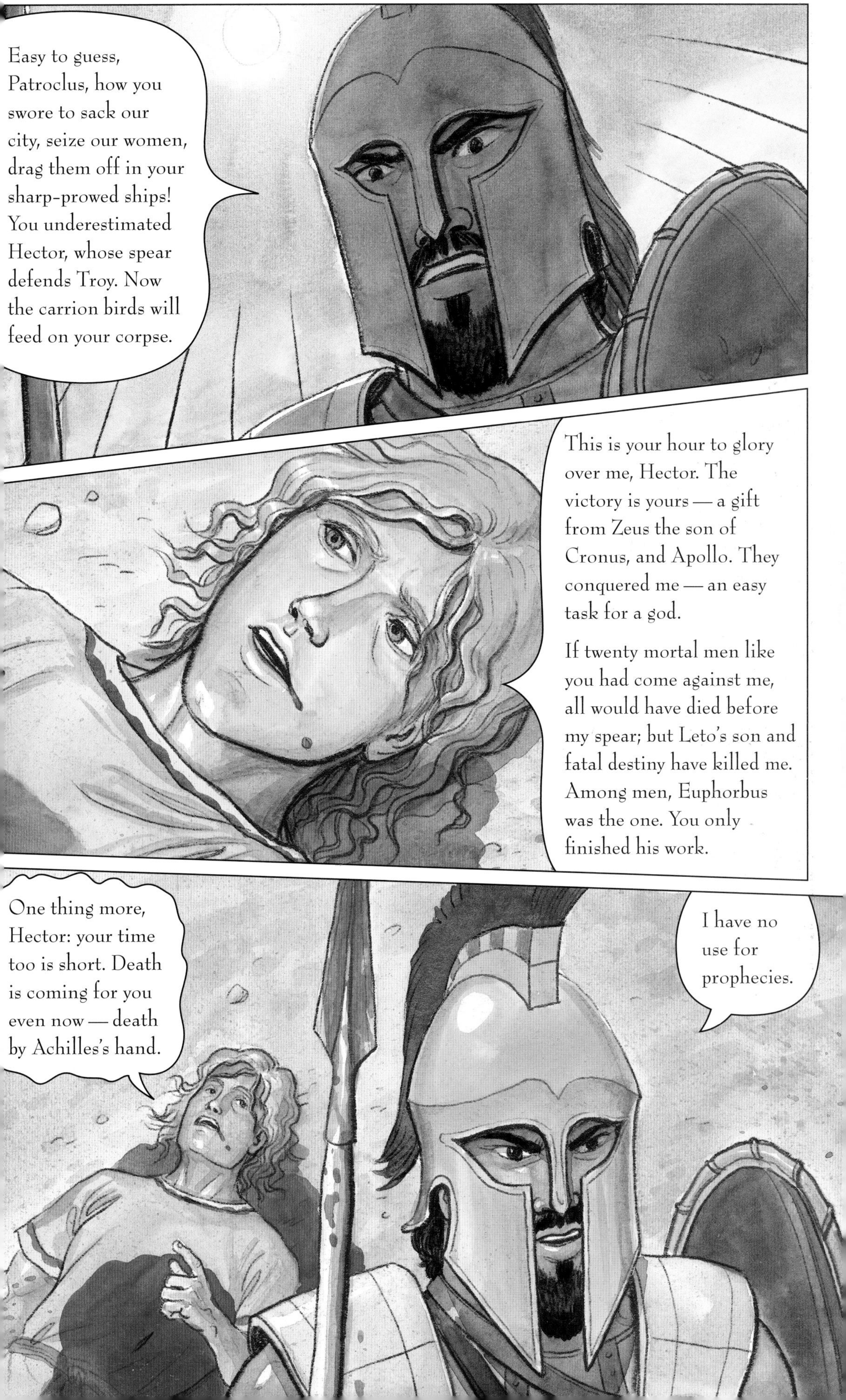
Easy to guess, Patroclus, how you swore to sack our city, seize our women, drag them off in your sharp-prowed ships! You underestimated Hector, whose spear defends Troy. Now the carrion birds will feed on your corpse.
This is your hour to glory over me, Hector. The victory is yours — a gift from Zeus the son of Cronus, and Apollo. They conquered me — an easy task for a god.
If twenty mortal men like you had come against me, all would have died before my spear; but Leto's son and fatal destiny have killed me. Among men, Euphorbus was the one. You only finished his work.
One thing more, Hector: your time too is short. Death is coming for you even now — death by Achilles's hand.
I have no use for prophecies.

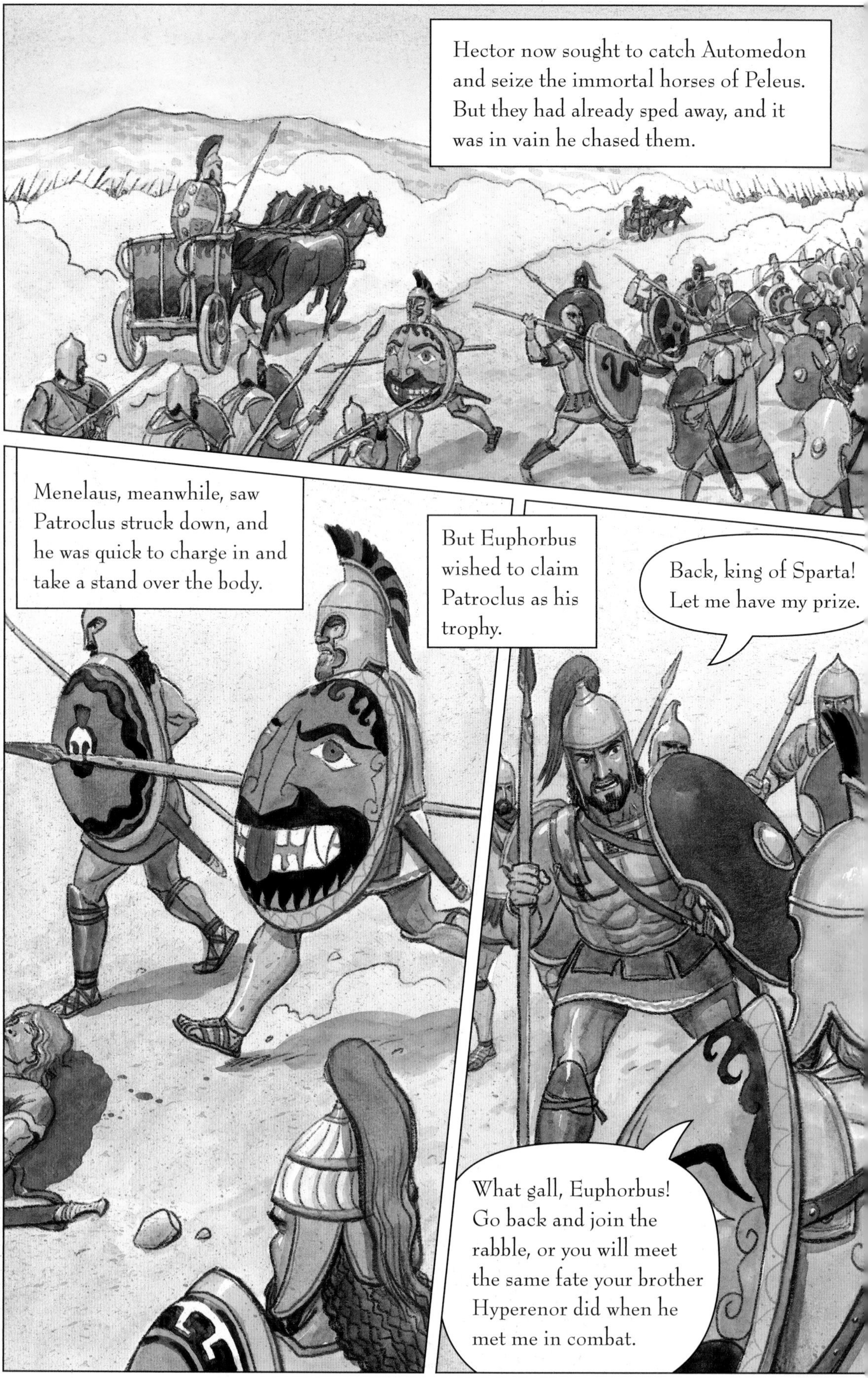
Hector now sought to catch Automedon and seize the immortal horses of Peleus. But they had already sped away, and it was in vain he chased them.
Menelaus, meanwhile, saw Patroclus struck down, and he was quick to charge in and take a stand over the body.
But Euphorbus wished to claim Patroclus as his trophy.
Back, king of Sparta! Let me have my prize.
What gall, Euphorbus! Go back and join the rabble, or you will meet the same fate your brother Hyperenor did when he met me in combat.

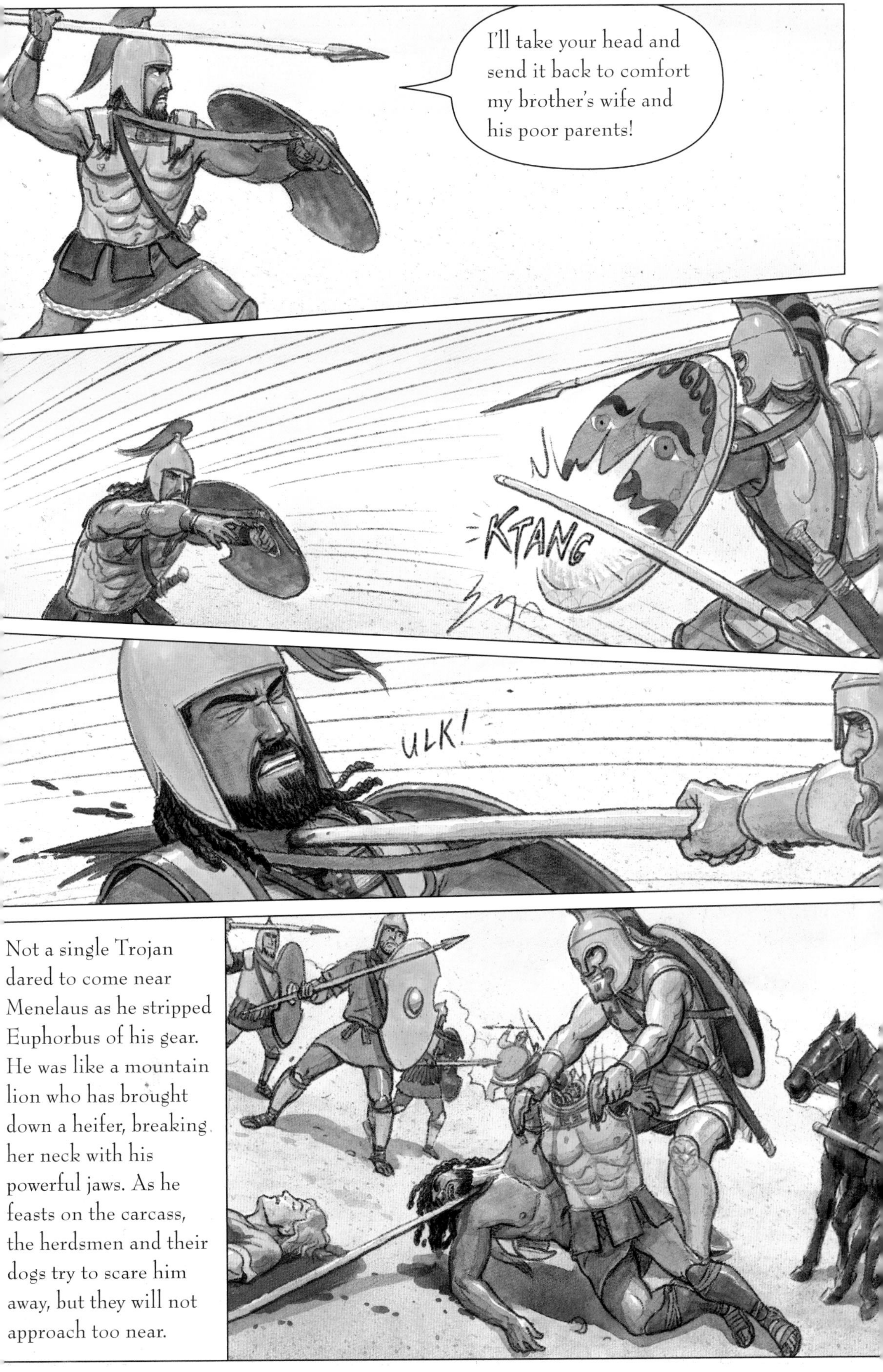
I'll take your head and send it back to comfort my brother's wife and his poor parents!
KTANG
ULK!
Not a single Trojan dared to come near Menelaus as he stripped Euphorbus of his gear. He was like a mountain lion who has brought down a heifer, breaking her neck with his powerful jaws. As he feasts on the carcass, the herdsmen and their dogs try to scare him away, but they will not approach too near.

So Menelaus might have taken his prize unmolested if Apollo had not convinced Hector to give up chasing Automedon and return to claim the armor of Achilles.

Menelaus heard Hector's war-cry and saw him coming, followed by a mass of Trojan warriors.

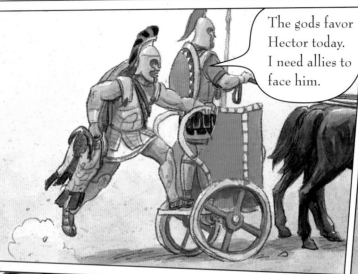

The gods favor Hector today. I need allies to face him.

Ajax! Patroclus is dead, and Hector has seized the armor of Achilles!

With Great Ajax at his side, Menelaus turned and sped back to challenge Hector.

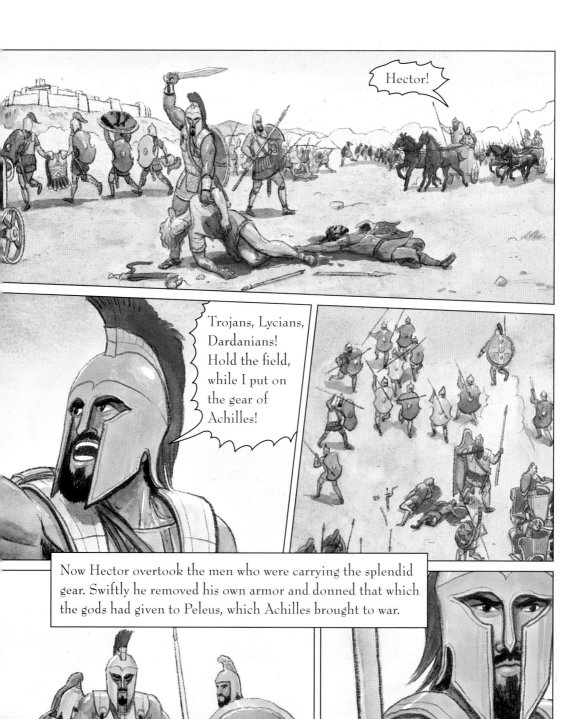

Hector!

Trojans, Lycians, Dardanians! Hold the field, while I put on the gear of Achilles!

Now Hector overtook the men who were carrying the splendid gear. Swiftly he removed his own armor and donned that which the gods had given to Peleus, which Achilles brought to war.

Zeus, looking down, pitied Hector, for his time was short. He made the armor sit easy on his shoulders.

And the savage spirit of the war-god entered Hector's heart too, filling his limbs with strength and vigor.

Allies of Ilium, hear me! I wanted not numbers but valor when I summoned you to Troy. My people starve to feed you and maintain your strength for combat. Repay us now; fight like heroes to defend the city! And to any man who forces Ajax back and brings Patroclus's body to our lines, I'll divide the spoils of battle equally with him.

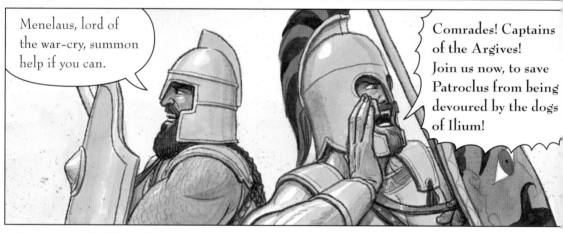

Menelaus, lord of the war-cry, summon help if you can.

Comrades! Captains of the Argives! Join us now, to save Patroclus from being devoured by the dogs of Ilium!

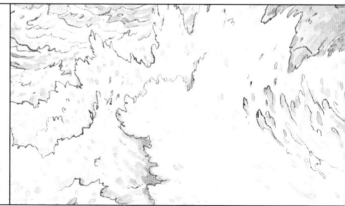

Idomeneus and Ajax, son of Oileus, heard that call, and they came, followed by a force of Achaeans too numerous to name, all rushing in to join the battle for Patroclus.

The forces met with a roar, like that of the ocean where it meets the headwaters of a mighty river swelled by flood.

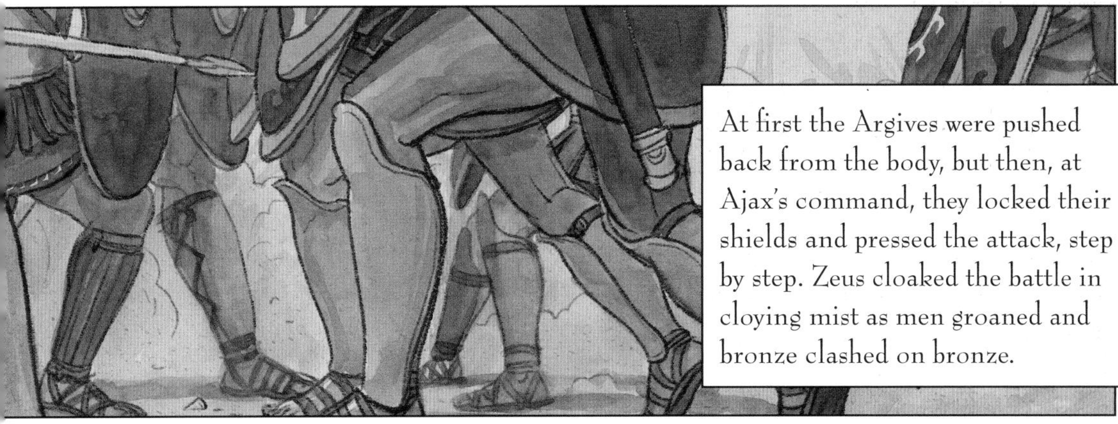
At first the Argives were pushed back from the body, but then, at Ajax's command, they locked their shields and pressed the attack, step by step. Zeus cloaked the battle in cloying mist as men groaned and bronze clashed on bronze.

They tugged Patroclus back and forth, muscles bunching, sweat pouring down — they were like tanners' men who stretch a great oiled oxhide, surrounding it and tugging it in every direction with all their force, till the moisture is squeezed out and the fat soaks into the hide.

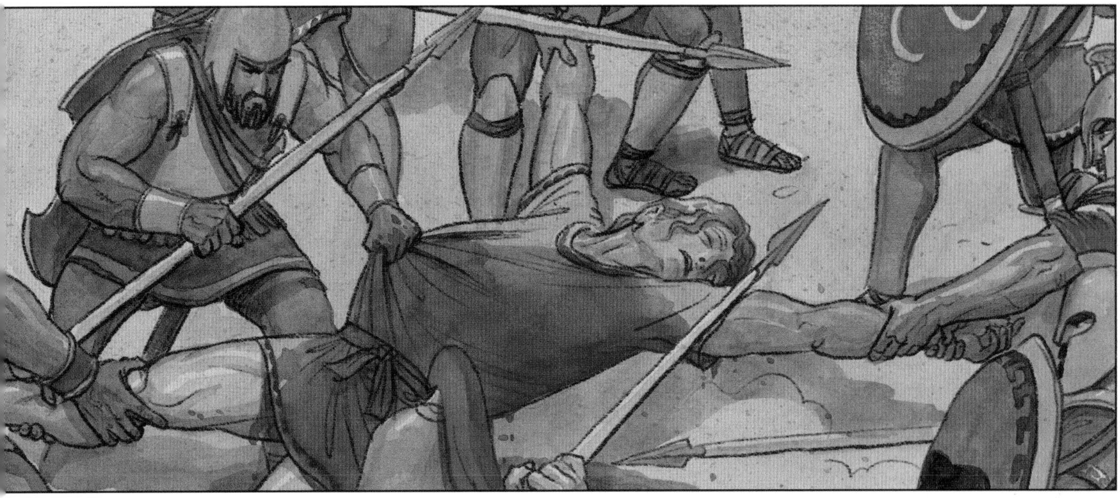

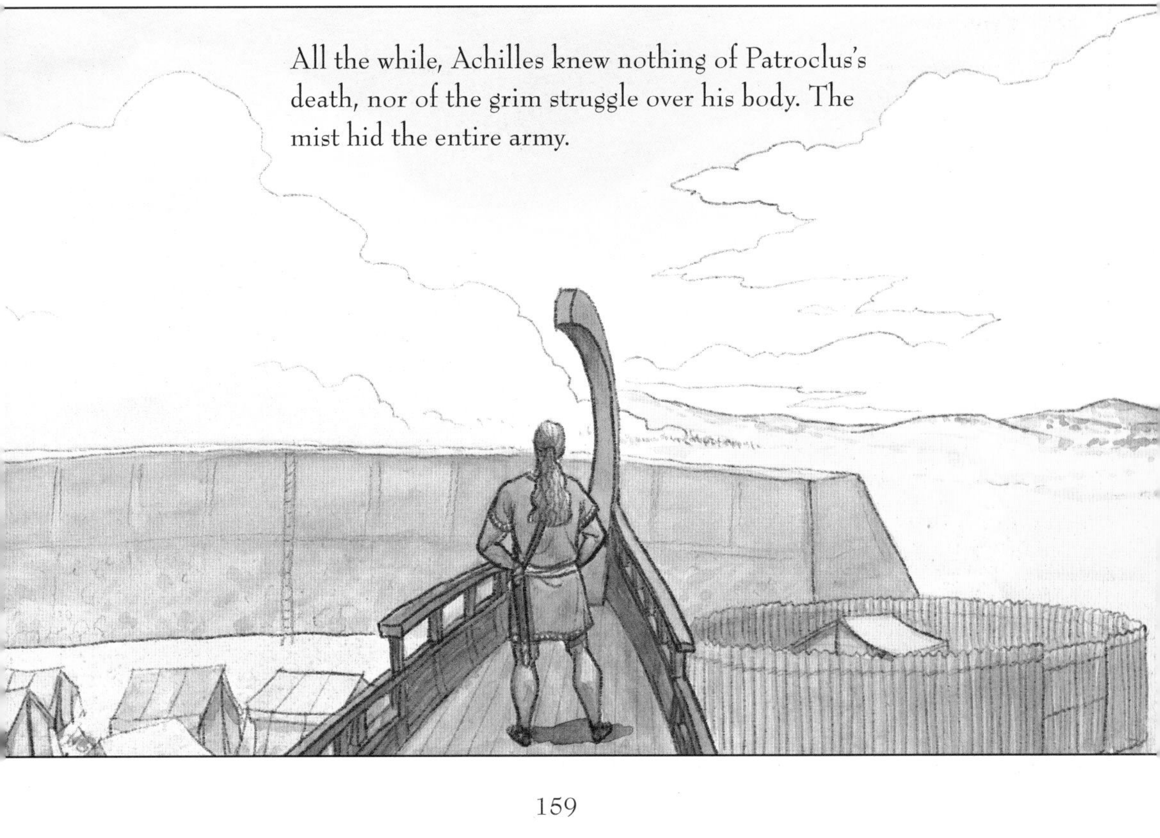
All the while, Achilles knew nothing of Patroclus's death, nor of the grim struggle over his body. The mist hid the entire army.

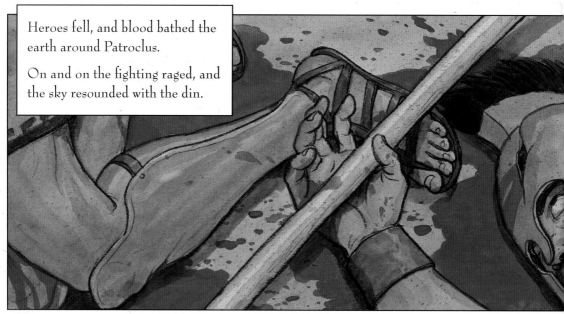

Heroes fell, and blood bathed the earth around Patroclus.

On and on the fighting raged, and the sky resounded with the din.

Great Father Zeus, hear me! Lift this fog! Let us live, or die if that is your will, in the sun!

Menelaus, we must send a runner to tell Achilles his friend is fallen!

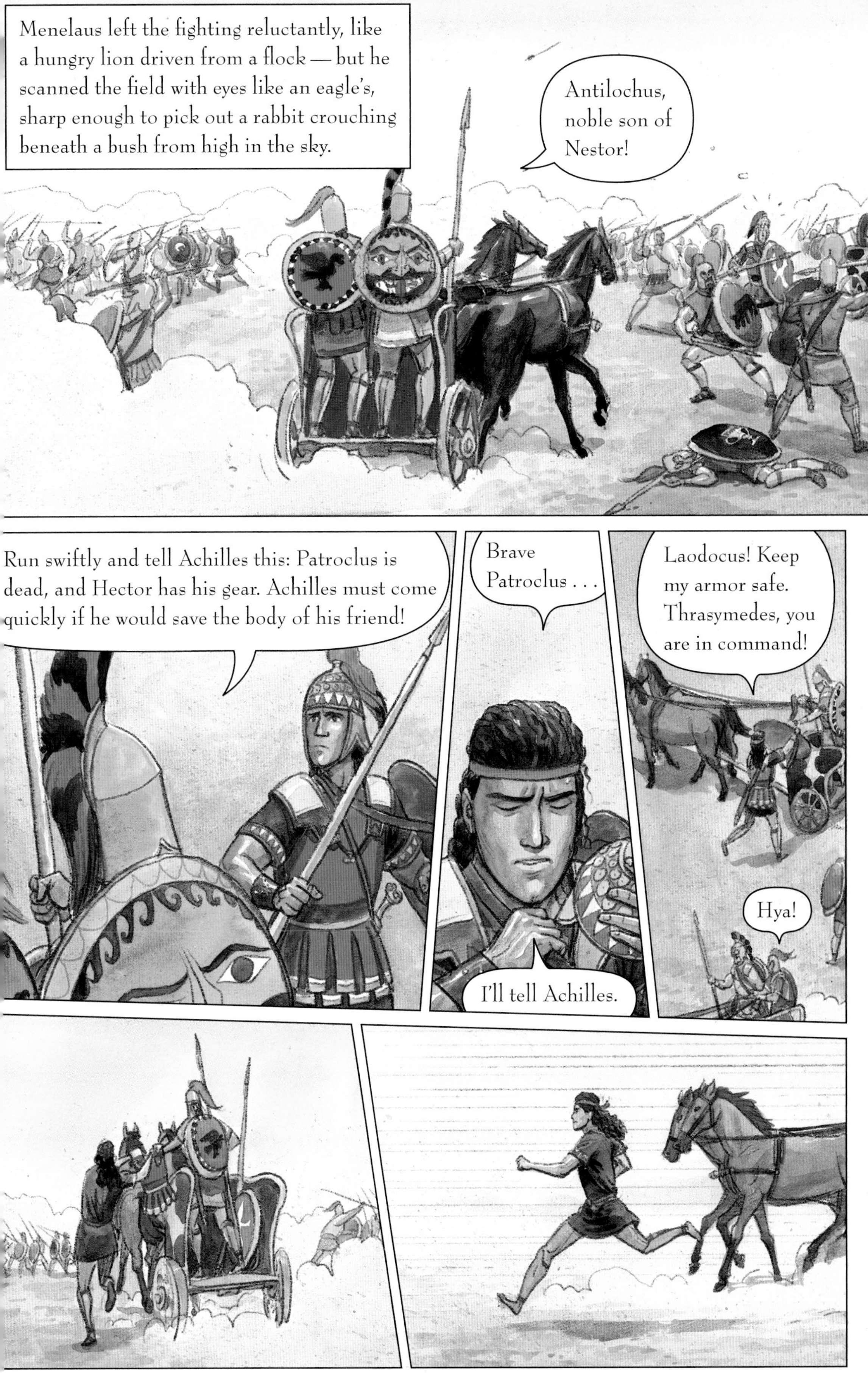
Menelaus left the fighting reluctantly, like a hungry lion driven from a flock — but he scanned the field with eyes like an eagle's, sharp enough to pick out a rabbit crouching beneath a bush from high in the sky.
Antilochus, noble son of Nestor!
Run swiftly and tell Achilles this: Patroclus is dead, and Hector has his gear. Achilles must come quickly if he would save the body of his friend!
Brave Patroclus . . .
I'll tell Achilles.
Laodocus! Keep my armor safe. Thrasymedes, you are in command!
Hya!

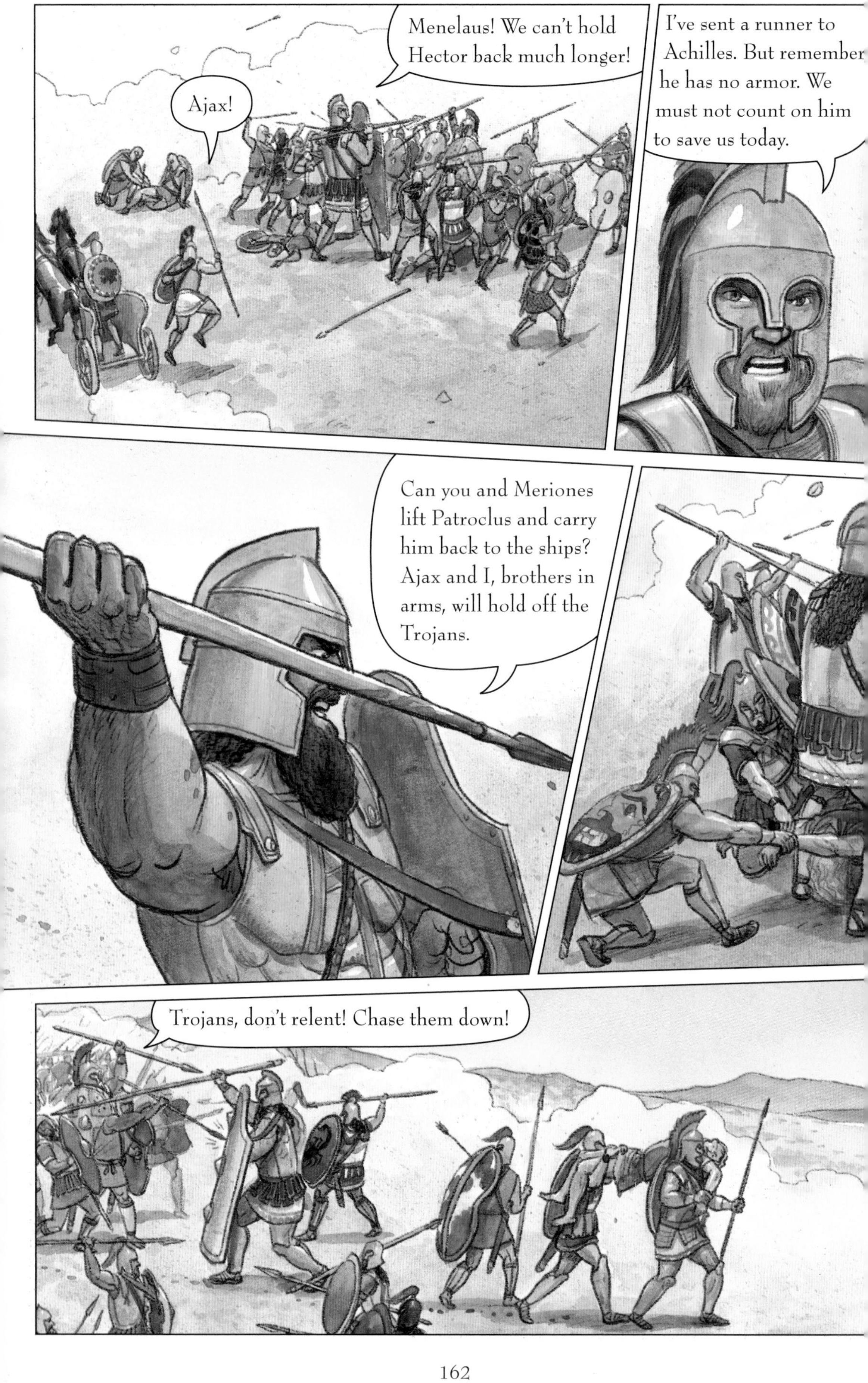
Ajax!
Menelaus! We can't hold Hector back much longer!
I've sent a runner to Achilles. But remember he has no armor. We must not count on him to save us today.
Can you and Meriones lift Patroclus and carry him back to the ships? Ajax and I, brothers in arms, will hold off the Trojans.
Trojans, don't relent! Chase them down!

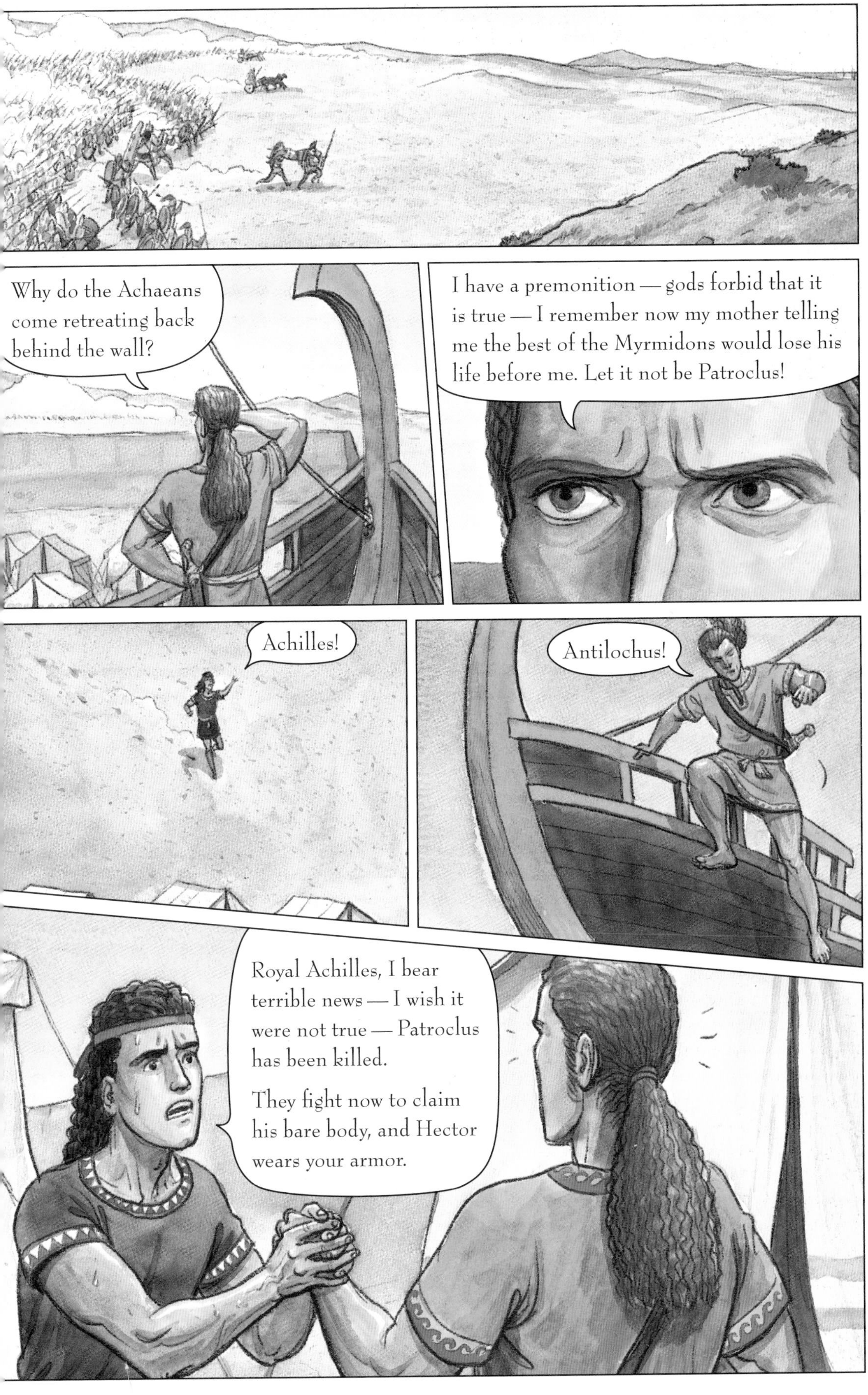
Why do the Achaeans come retreating back behind the wall?
I have a premonition — gods forbid that it is true — I remember now my mother telling me the best of the Myrmidons would lose his life before me. Let it not be Patroclus!
Achilles!
Antilochus!
Royal Achilles, I bear terrible news — I wish it were not true — Patroclus has been killed.
They fight now to claim his bare body, and Hector wears your armor.

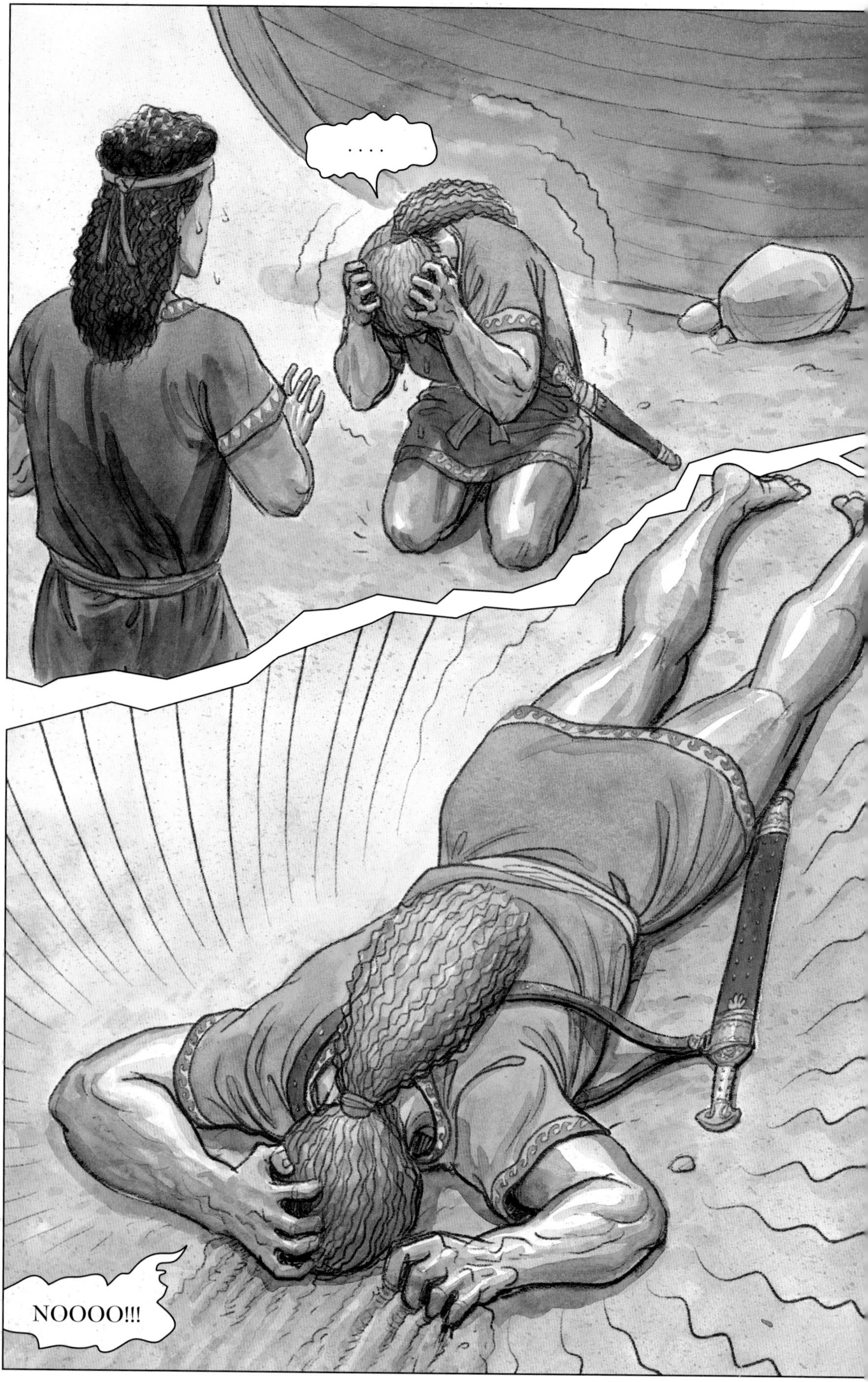
. . . .
NOOOO!!!

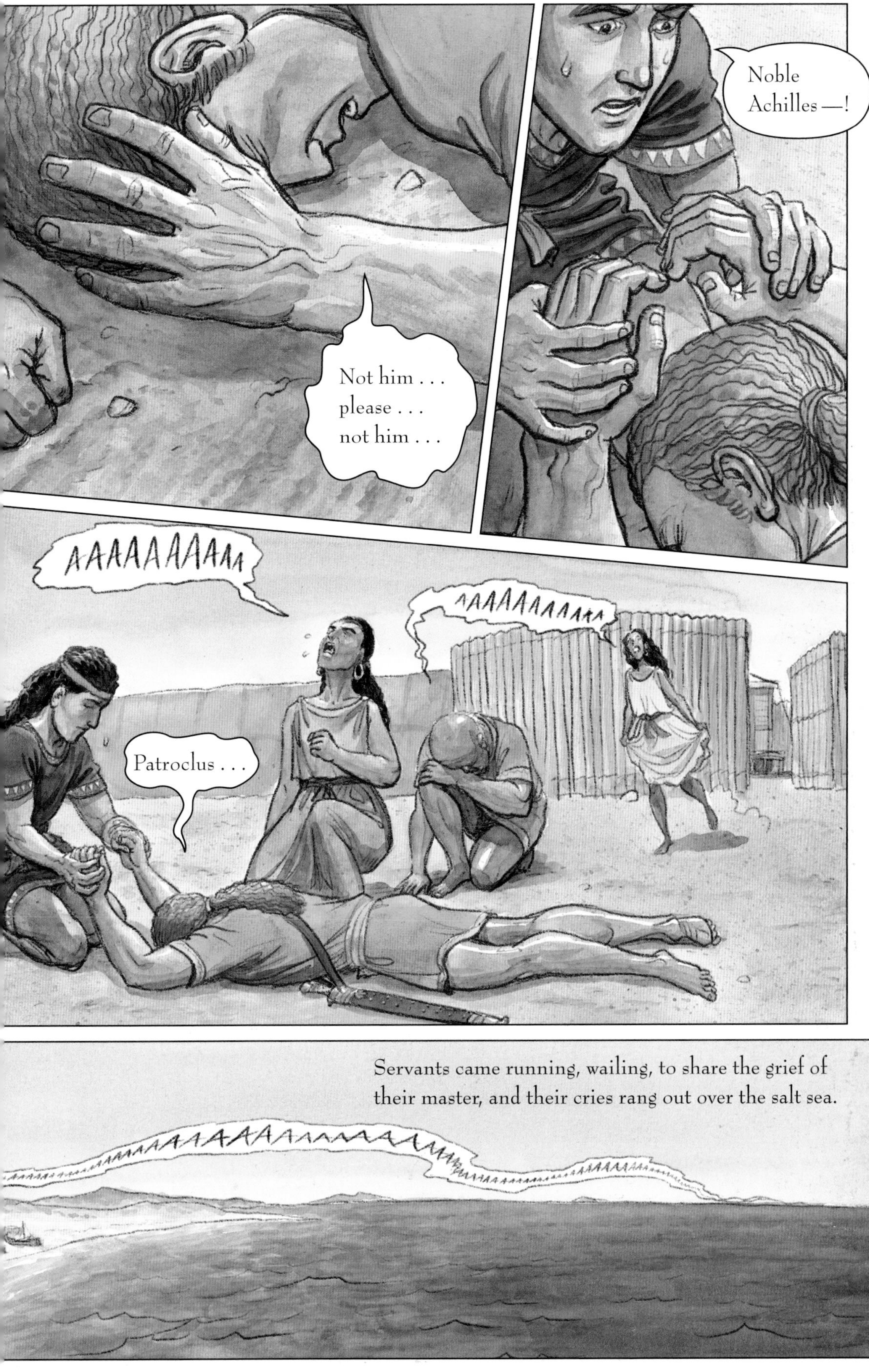
Not him . . . please . . . not him . . .
Noble Achilles —!
AAAAAAAAAA
Patroclus . . .
AAAAAAAAAAA
Servants came running, wailing, to share the grief of their master, and their cries rang out over the salt sea.

In a silvery cave beneath the sea, Thetis heard her son's grief, and she grieved with him. All the Nereids assembled around her joined their voices with hers.

AAAAIIIEEEEEEEEEEEEEEEEEEEEE

O sisters, listen to my misery! I bore a perfect son, who grew straight and strong, like a sapling into a mighty tree — strongest of all warriors. Then he sailed away to Troy, where he is doomed to die. Never again will I see him in the house of his father.

Nor can he enjoy his fame, but always he must suffer, every one of his remaining days under the sun. I can do nothing to ease his pain. But still I will go to see my son.

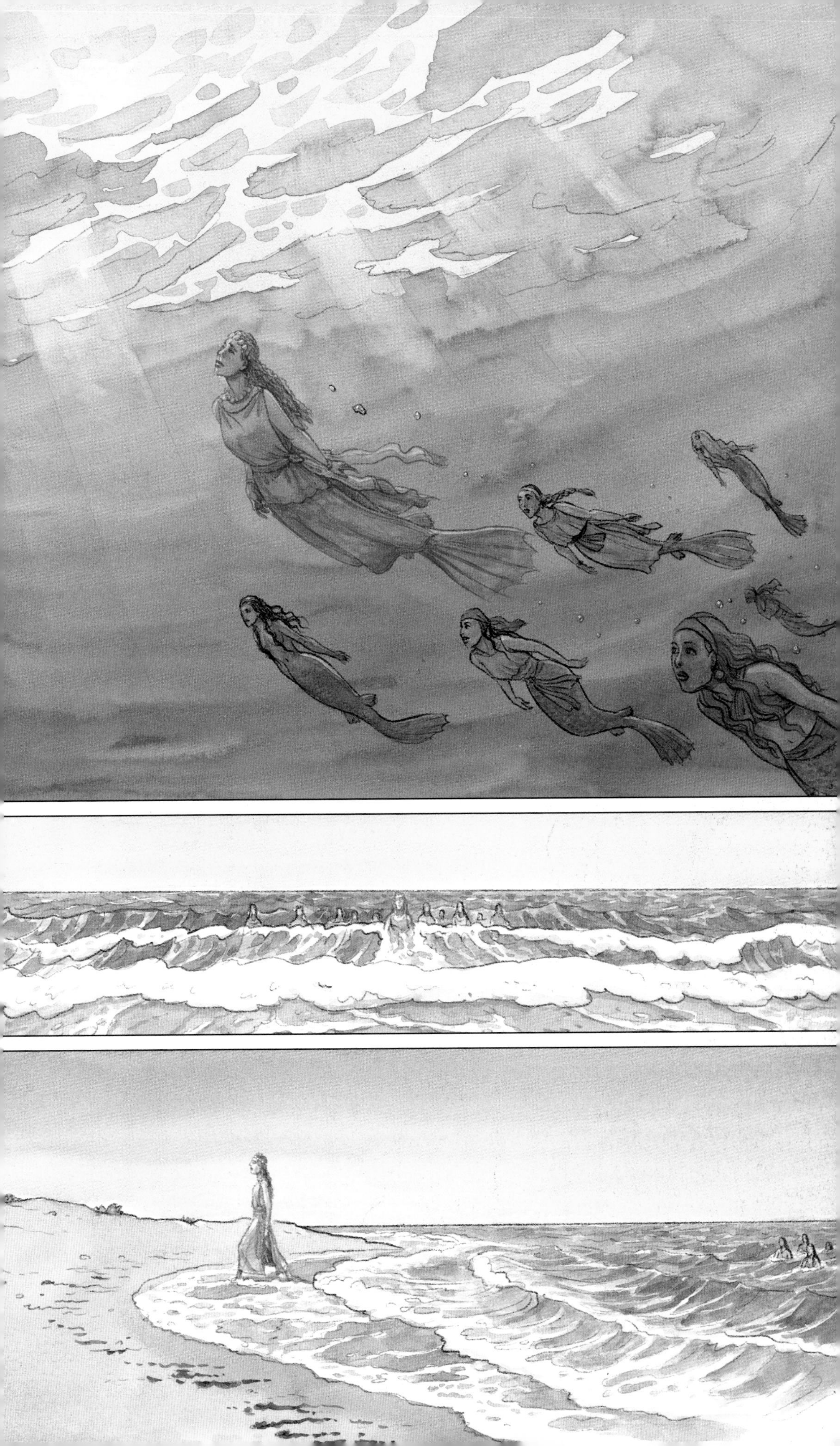

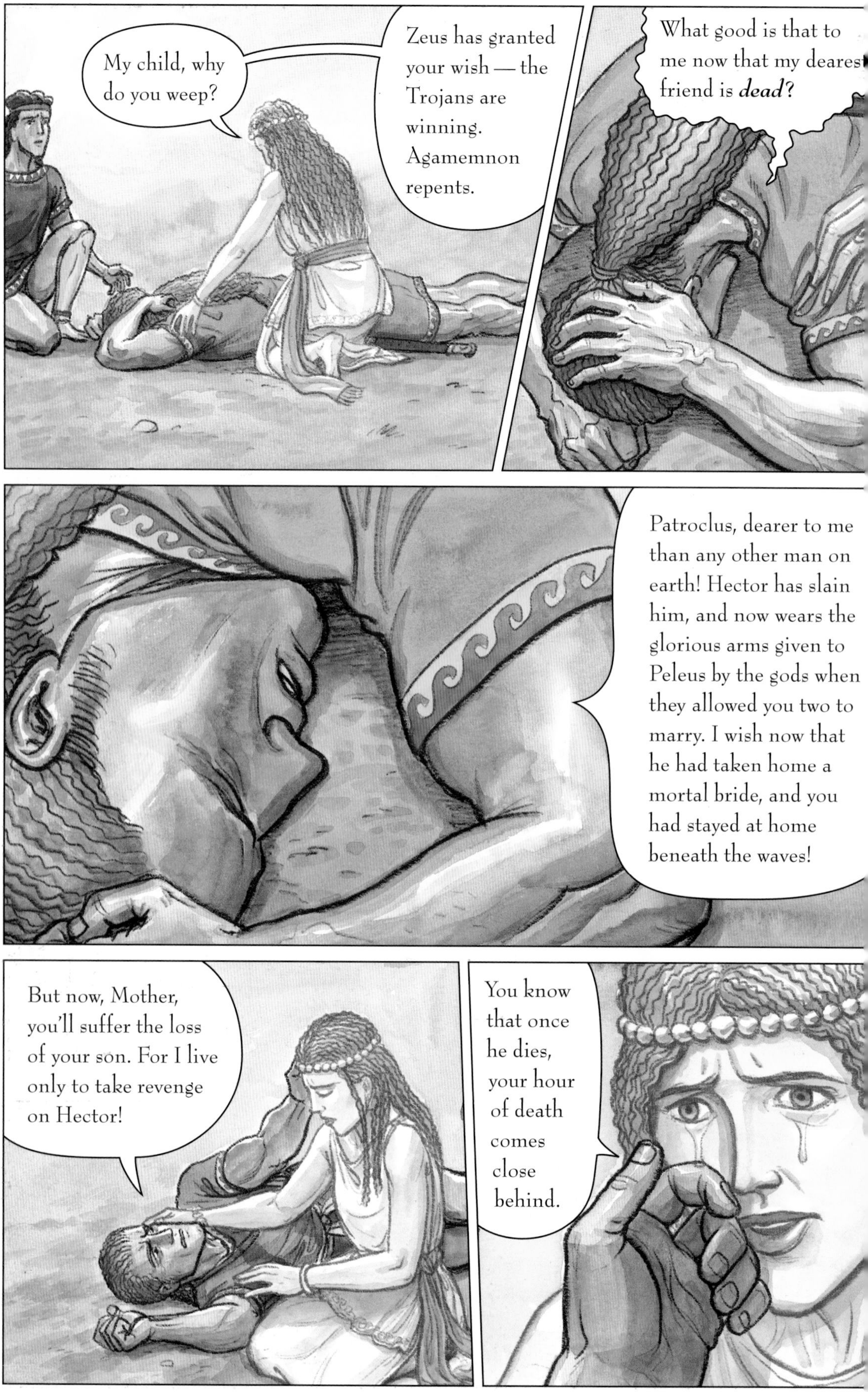
My child, why do you weep?
Zeus has granted your wish — the Trojans are winning. Agamemnon repents.
What good is that to me now that my dearest friend is *dead*?
Patroclus, dearer to me than any other man on earth! Hector has slain him, and now wears the glorious arms given to Peleus by the gods when they allowed you two to marry. I wish now that he had taken home a mortal bride, and you had stayed at home beneath the waves!
But now, Mother, you'll suffer the loss of your son. For I live only to take revenge on Hector!
You know that once he dies, your hour of death comes close behind.

What use is life, when I have failed Patroclus, and all my comrades? I, the best in battle, made useless by a clash of words . . . !

How I wish that Discord could be banished from the world — and with it anger, anger that billows up like smoke, filling the heart with darkness. So it filled me that day, anger at Agamemnon.

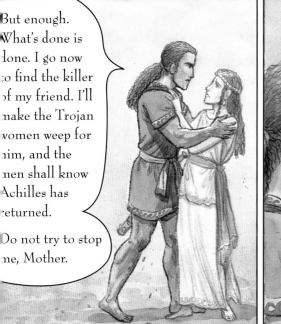

But enough. What's done is done. I go now to find the killer of my friend. I'll make the Trojan women weep for him, and the men shall know Achilles has returned.

Do not try to stop me, Mother.

I will not. But Hector has your armor. Do not go into battle until I return, I beg you. I'll come at sunrise — I go now to Hephaestus!

Meanwhile the Achaeans, carrying Patroclus, neared the moat, but Hecto[r] harried them close behind. He would surge forward and grab the corpse's feet, and each time, the Ajaxes would turn and drive him back — but they could not shake him off.

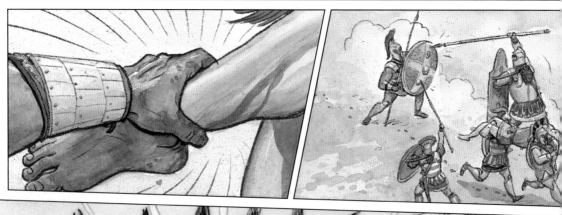

RAAAAAGGHH!

Hector would have prevailed, but swift-footed Iris summoned Achilles to the wall, unarmed though he was.

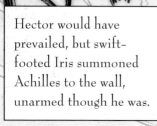

Athena cloaked him in her mighty Aegis, making his head glow with unearthly fire, and augmented his voice with hers. Three times their great shout rang out, and three times the Trojans felt their hearts skip an[d] their knees turn to water. Hors[e] turned and pulled for the city, some tumbling their riders dow[n] beneath the wheels or into the moat of spikes. A dozen good warriors lost their lives that wa[y]

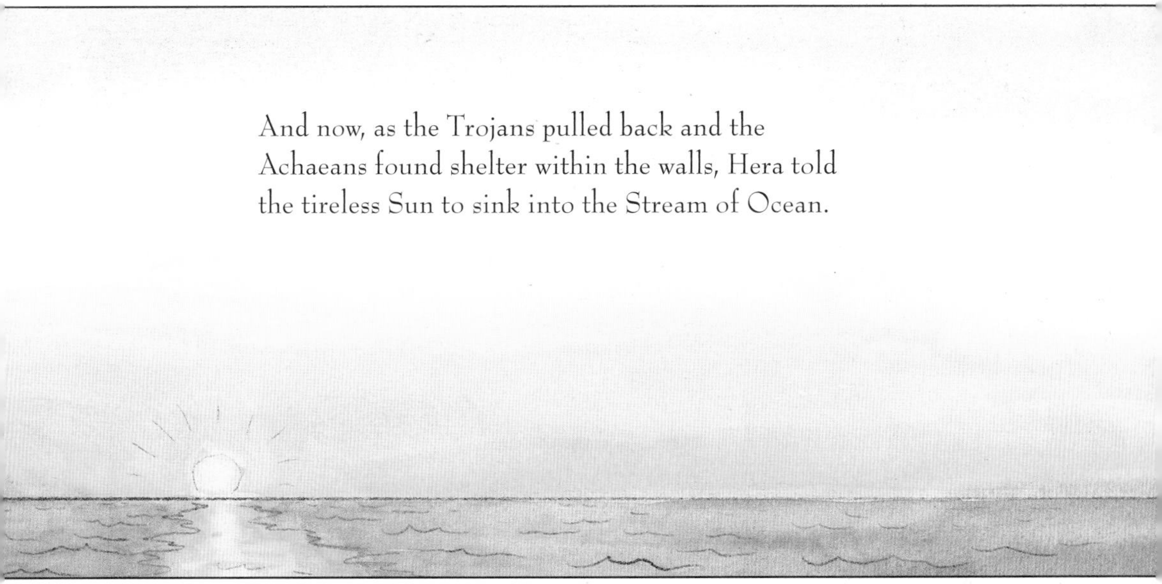
And now, as the Trojans pulled back and the Achaeans found shelter within the walls, Hera told the tireless Sun to sink into the Stream of Ocean.

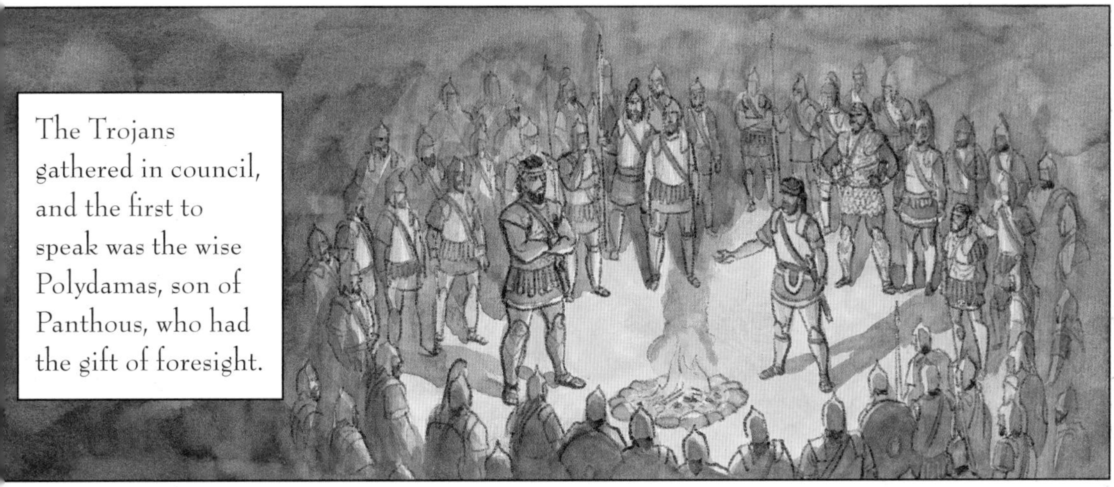
The Trojans gathered in council, and the first to speak was the wise Polydamas, son of Panthous, who had the gift of foresight.

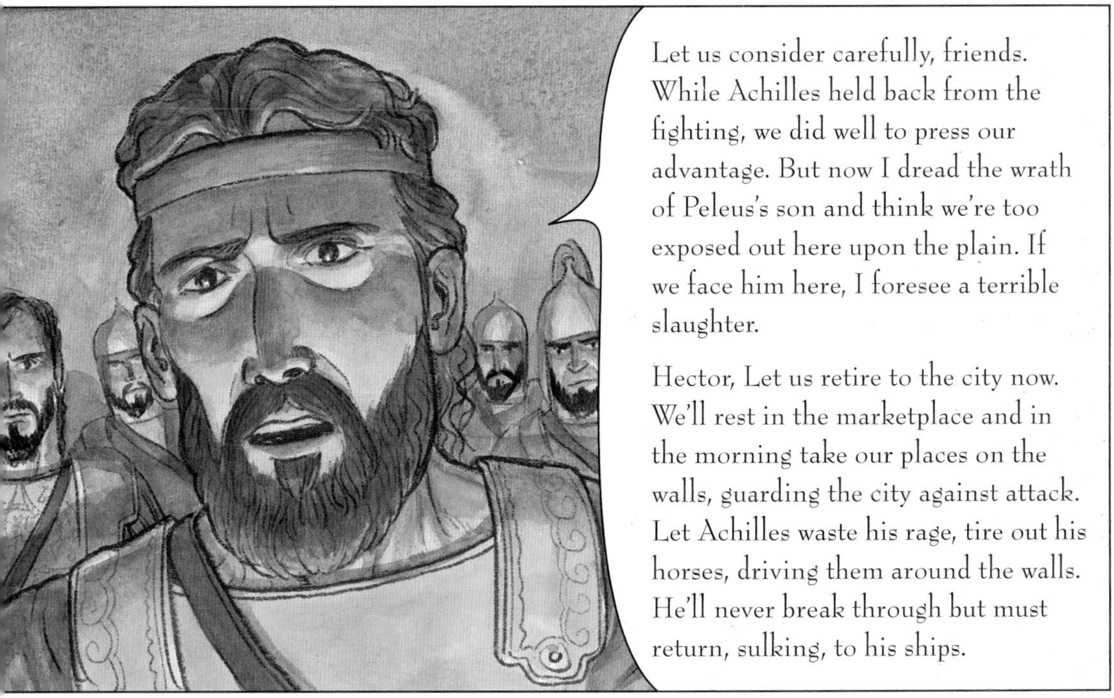
Let us consider carefully, friends. While Achilles held back from the fighting, we did well to press our advantage. But now I dread the wrath of Peleus's son and think we're too exposed out here upon the plain. If we face him here, I foresee a terrible slaughter.
Hector, Let us retire to the city now. We'll rest in the marketplace and in the morning take our places on the walls, guarding the city against attack. Let Achilles waste his rage, tire out his horses, driving them around the walls. He'll never break through but must return, sulking, to his ships.

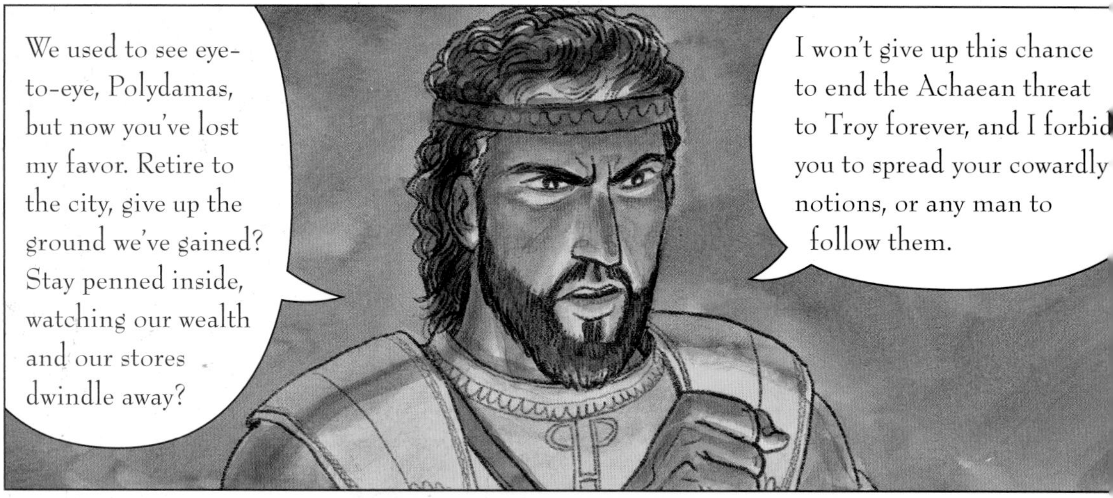
We used to see eye-to-eye, Polydamas, but now you've lost my favor. Retire to the city, give up the ground we've gained? Stay penned inside, watching our wealth and our stores dwindle away?
I won't give up this chance to end the Achaean threat to Troy forever, and I forbid you to spread your cowardly notions, or any man to follow them.

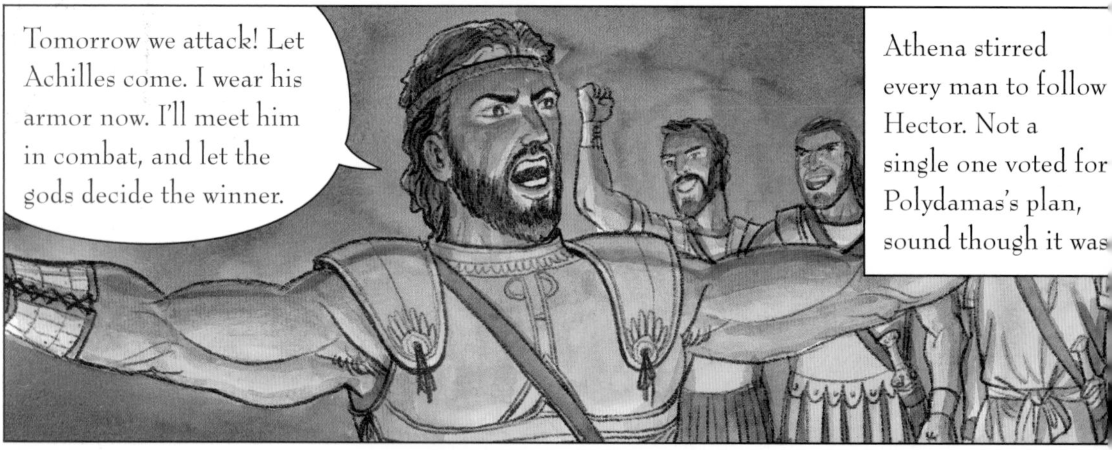
Tomorrow we attack! Let Achilles come. I wear his armor now. I'll meet him in combat, and let the gods decide the winner.
Athena stirred every man to follow Hector. Not a single one voted for Polydamas's plan, sound though it was

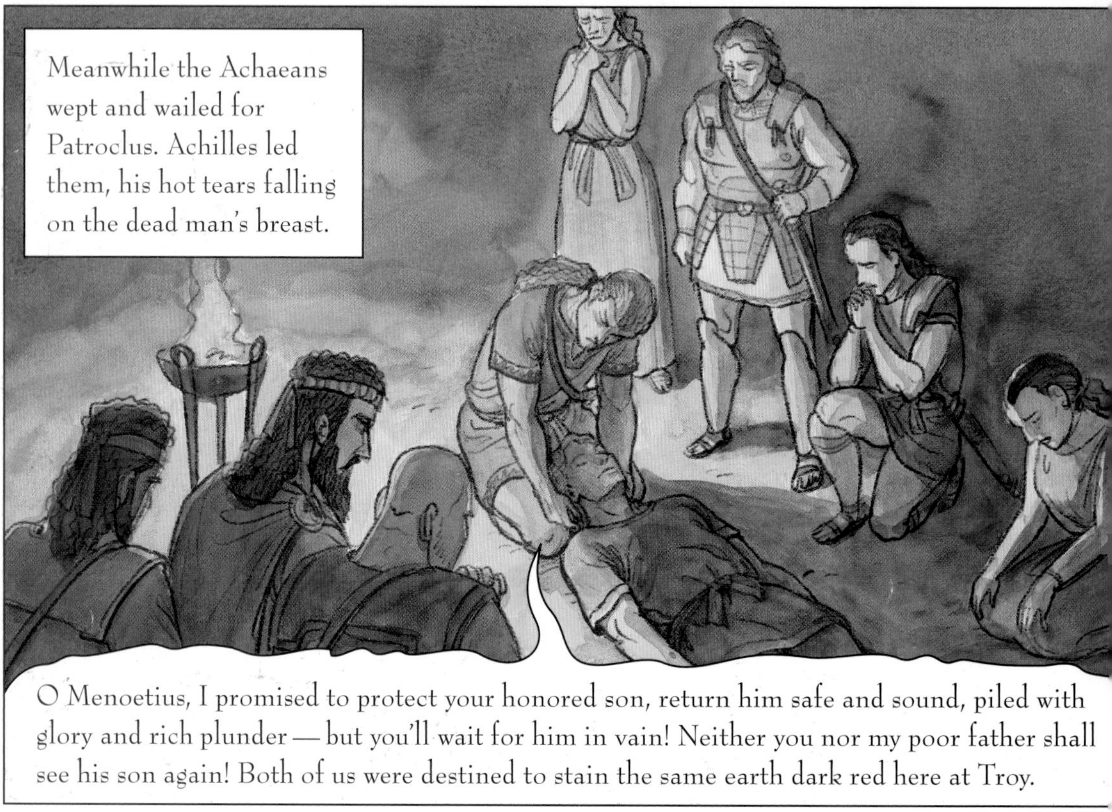
Meanwhile the Achaeans wept and wailed for Patroclus. Achilles led them, his hot tears falling on the dead man's breast.
O Menoetius, I promised to protect your honored son, return him safe and sound, piled with glory and rich plunder — but you'll wait for him in vain! Neither you nor my poor father shall see his son again! Both of us were destined to stain the same earth dark red here at Troy.

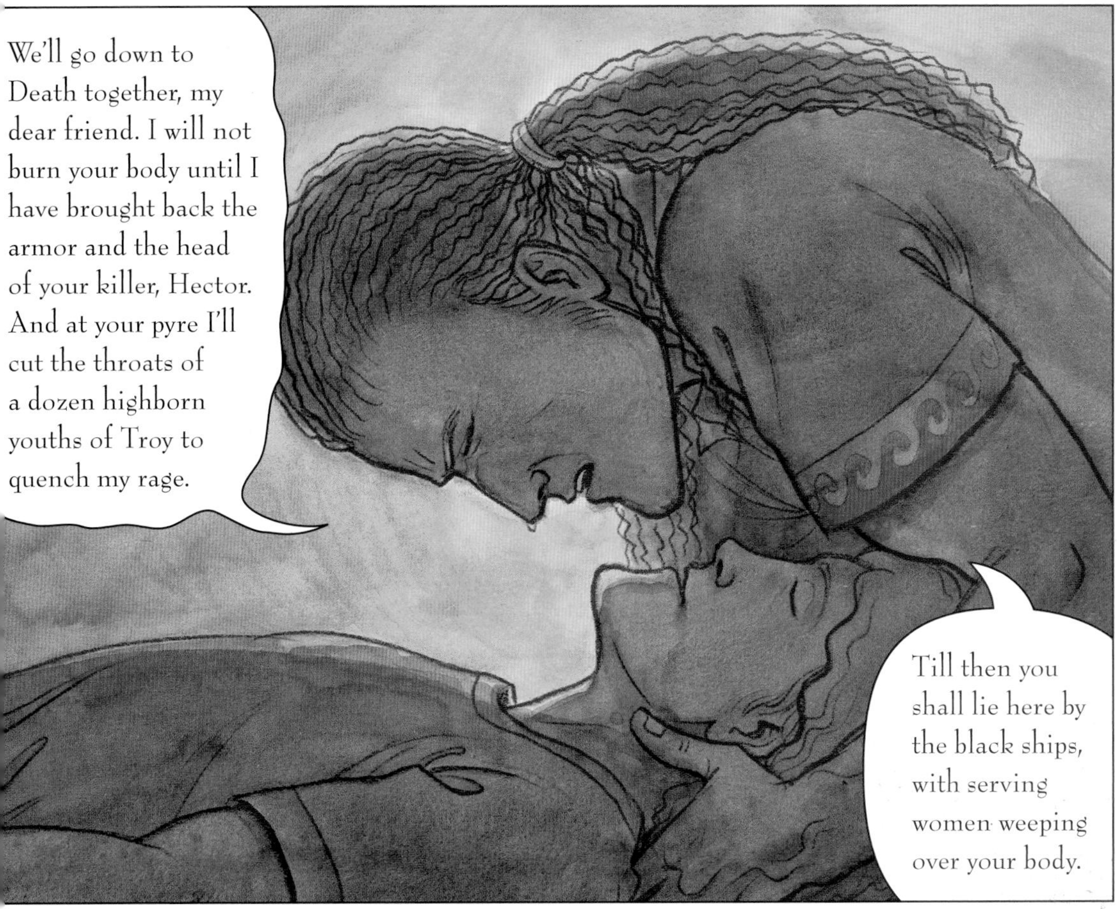
We'll go down to Death together, my dear friend. I will not burn your body until I have brought back the armor and the head of your killer, Hector. And at your pyre I'll cut the throats of a dozen highborn youths of Troy to quench my rage.
Till then you shall lie here by the black ships, with serving women weeping over your body.

Then, with heated water, the gore was washed from Patroclus's corpse, his skin was oiled, and his wounds treated with unguent. He was laid on a bier and covered with a pure white shroud.

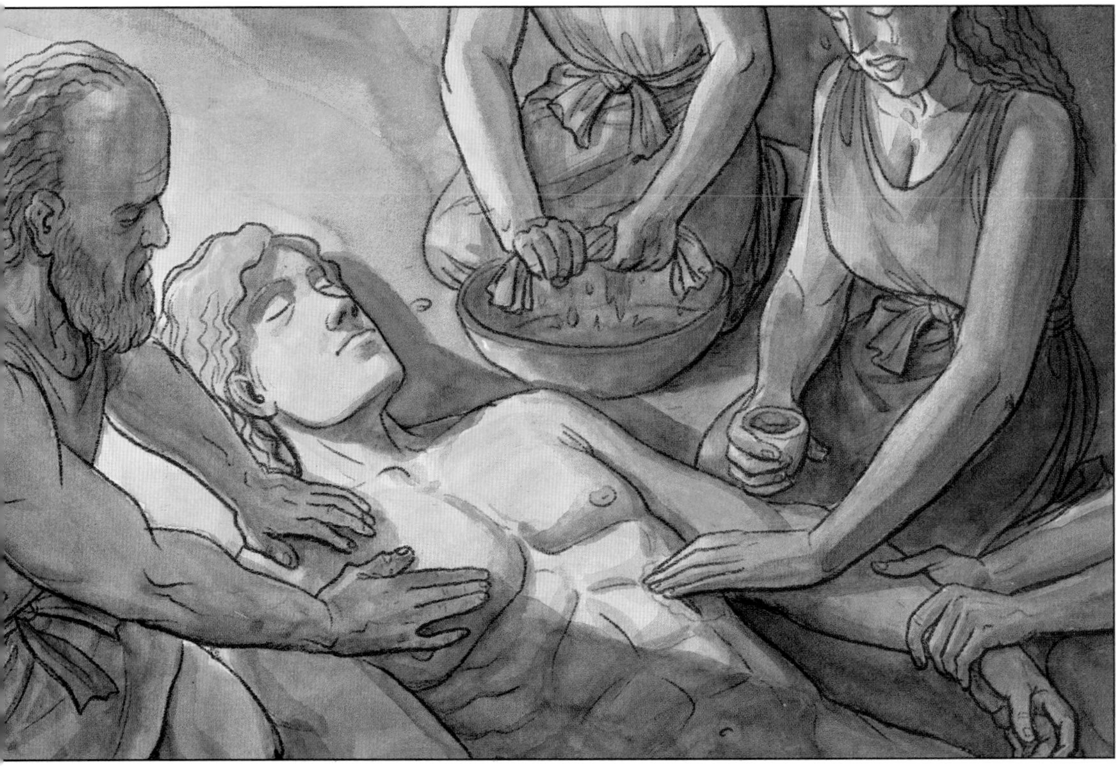

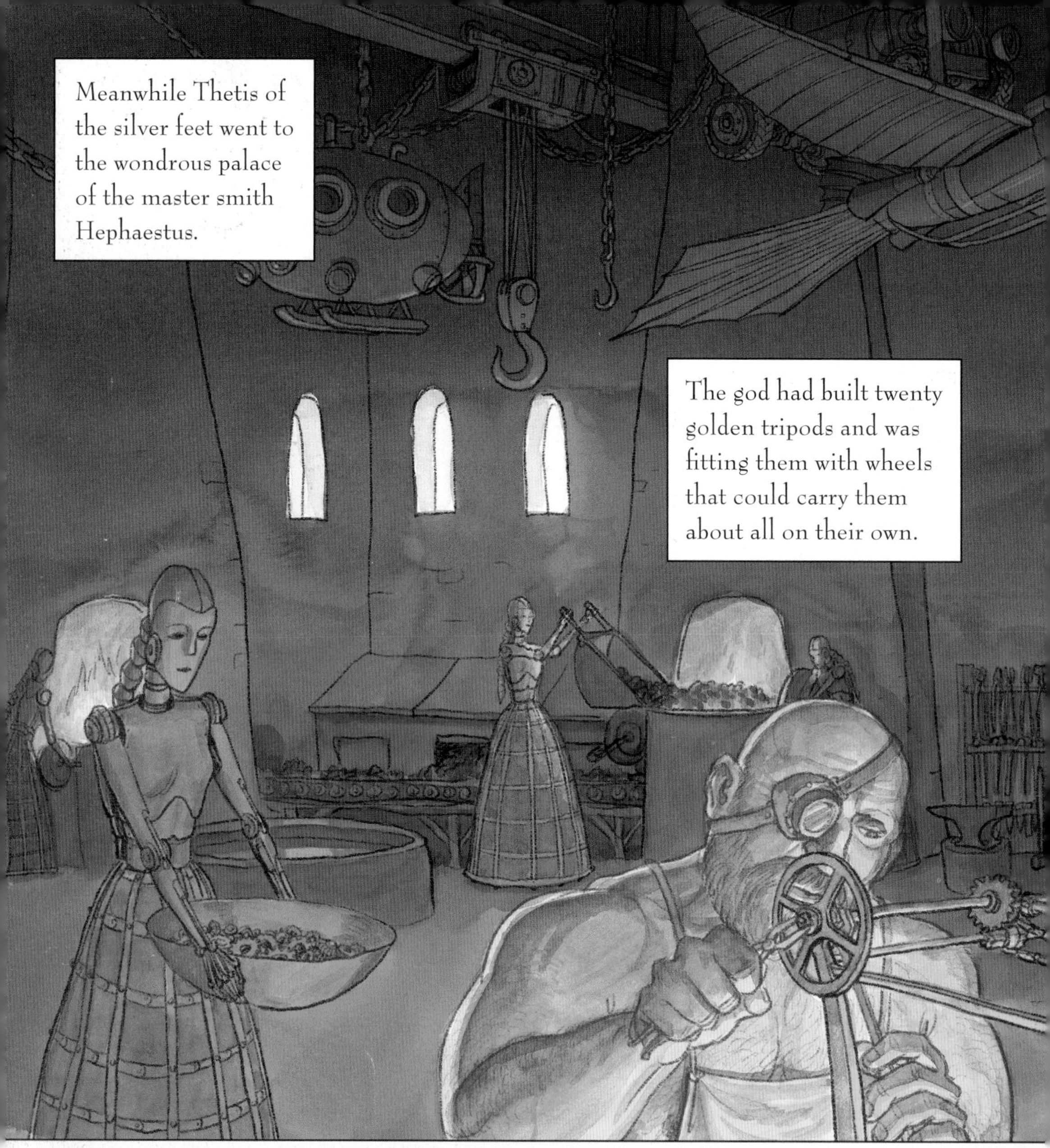
Meanwhile Thetis of the silver feet went to the wondrous palace of the master smith Hephaestus.
The god had built twenty golden tripods and was fitting them with wheels that could carry them about all on their own.

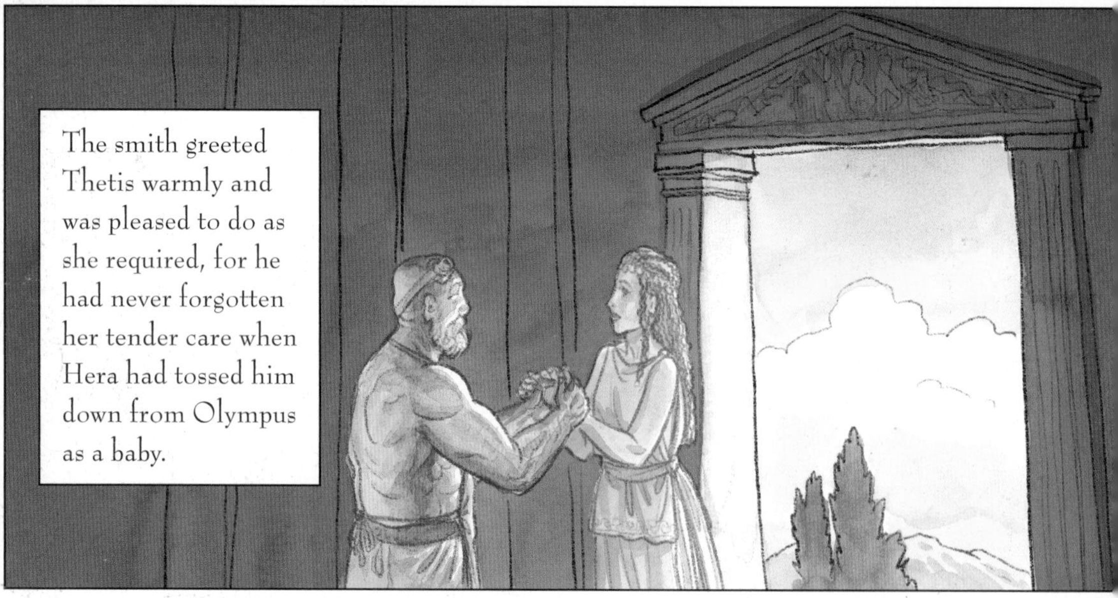
The smith greeted Thetis warmly and was pleased to do as she required, for he had never forgotten her tender care when Hera had tossed him down from Olympus as a baby.

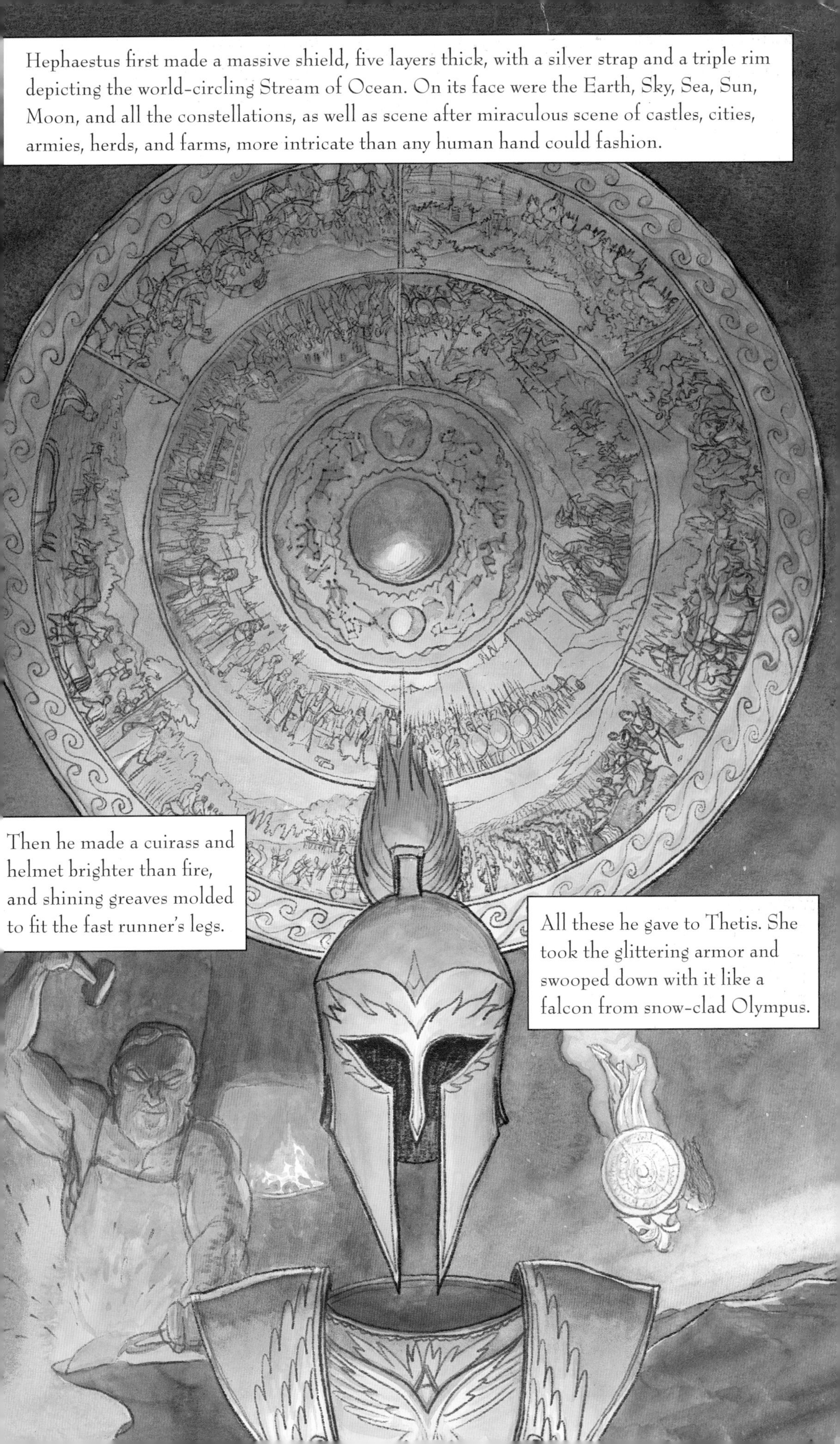
Hephaestus first made a massive shield, five layers thick, with a silver strap and a triple rim depicting the world-circling Stream of Ocean. On its face were the Earth, Sky, Sea, Sun, Moon, and all the constellations, as well as scene after miraculous scene of castles, cities, armies, herds, and farms, more intricate than any human hand could fashion.
Then he made a cuirass and helmet brighter than fire, and shining greaves molded to fit the fast runner's legs.
All these he gave to Thetis. She took the glittering armor and swooped down with it like a falcon from snow-clad Olympus.

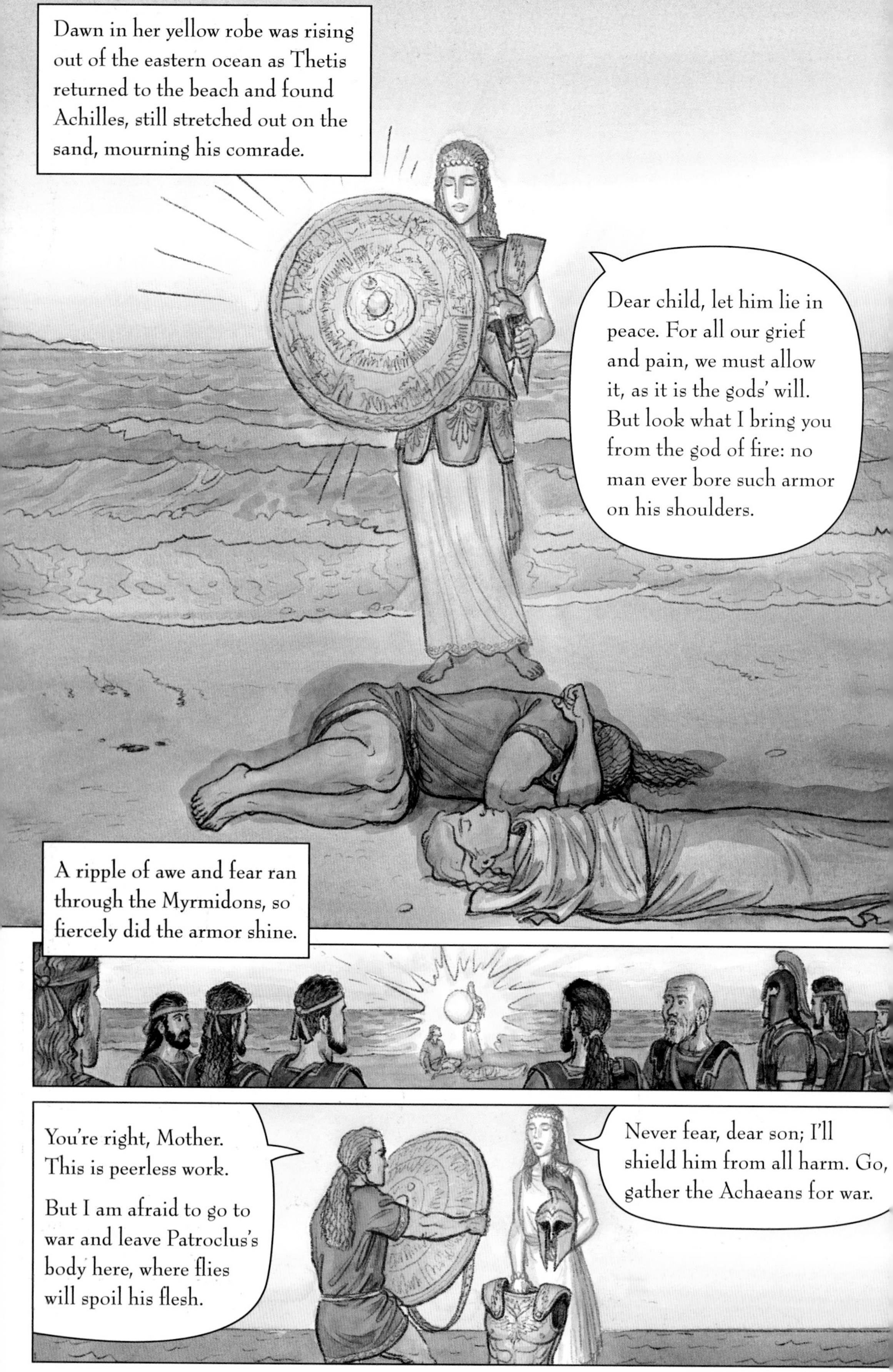
Dawn in her yellow robe was rising out of the eastern ocean as Thetis returned to the beach and found Achilles, still stretched out on the sand, mourning his comrade.
Dear child, let him lie in peace. For all our grief and pain, we must allow it, as it is the gods' will. But look what I bring you from the god of fire: no man ever bore such armor on his shoulders.
A ripple of awe and fear ran through the Myrmidons, so fiercely did the armor shine.
You're right, Mother. This is peerless work.
But I am afraid to go to war and leave Patroclus's body here, where flies will spoil his flesh.
Never fear, dear son; I'll shield him from all harm. Go, gather the Achaeans for war.

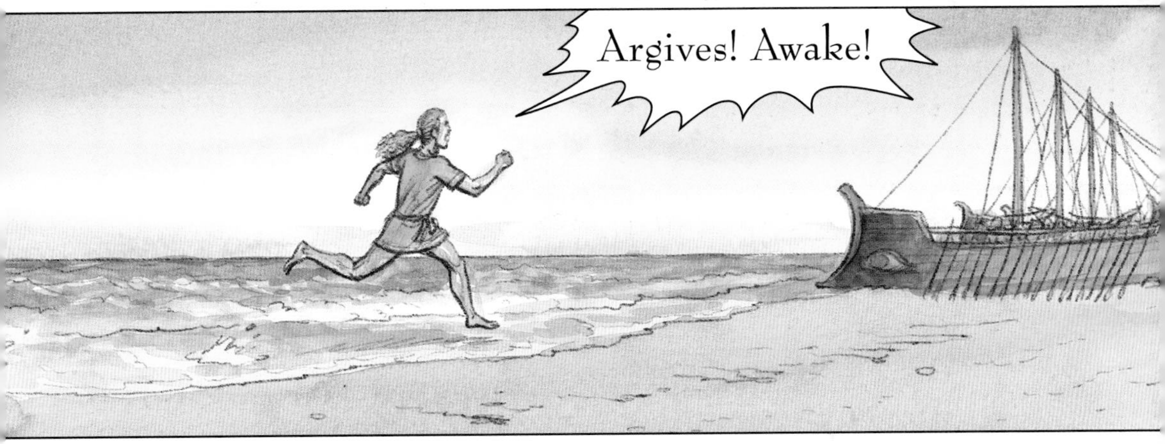
Argives! Awake!

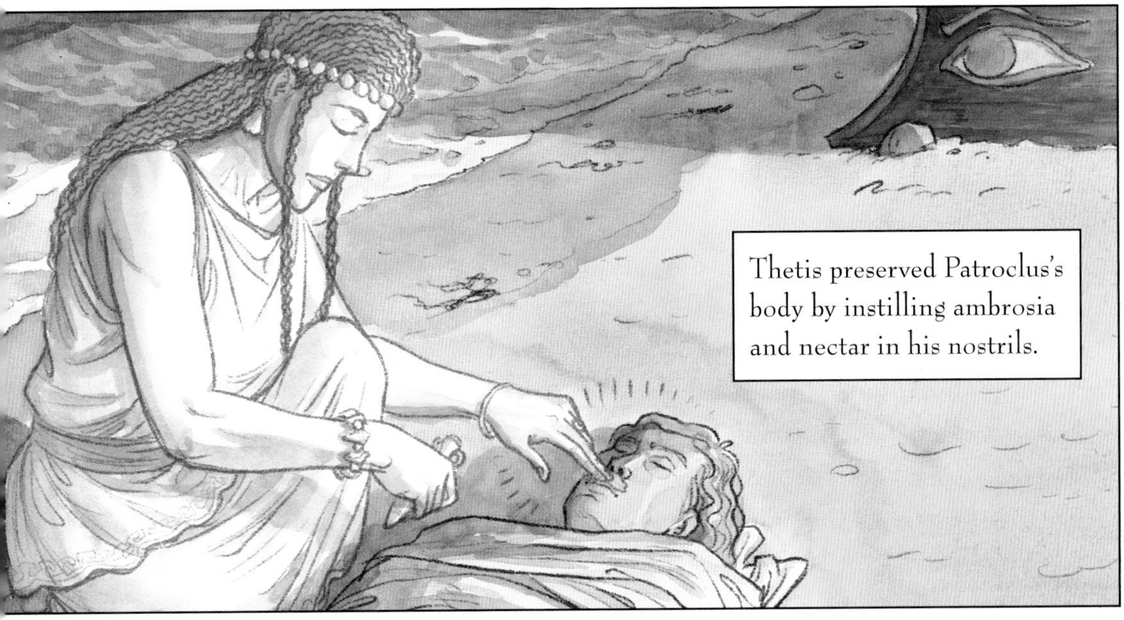
Thetis preserved Patroclus's body by instilling ambrosia and nectar in his nostrils.

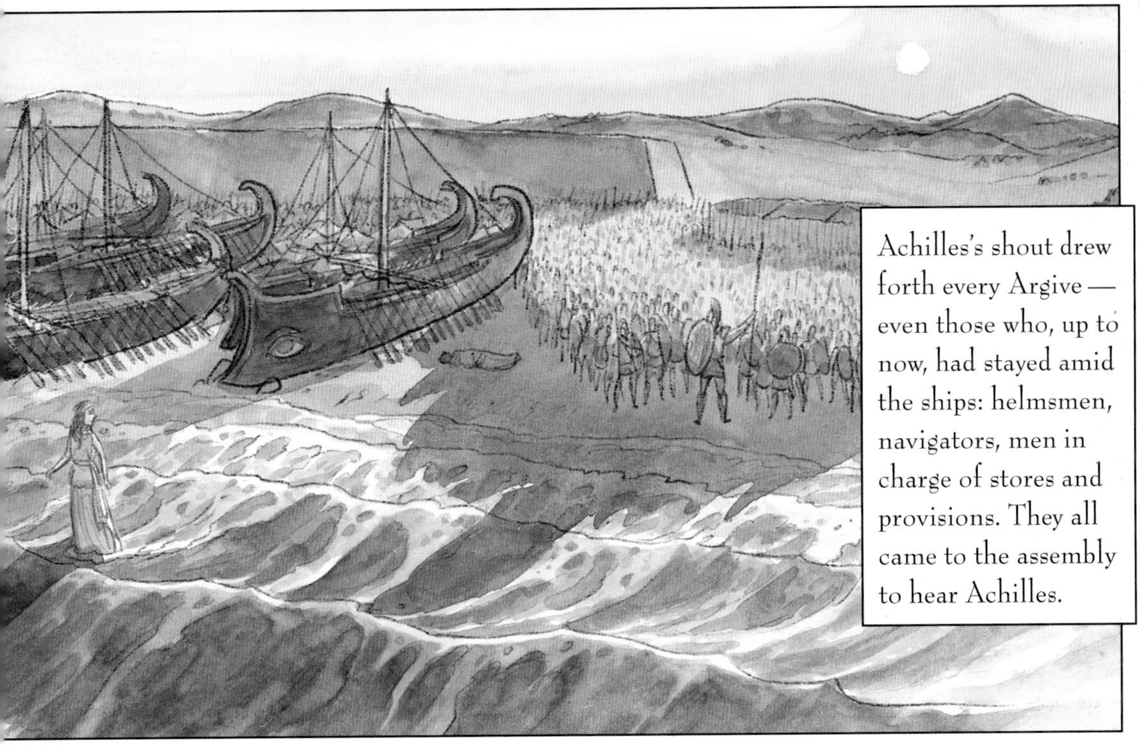
Achilles's shout drew forth every Argive — even those who, up to now, had stayed amid the ships: helmsmen, navigators, men in charge of stores and provisions. They all came to the assembly to hear Achilles.

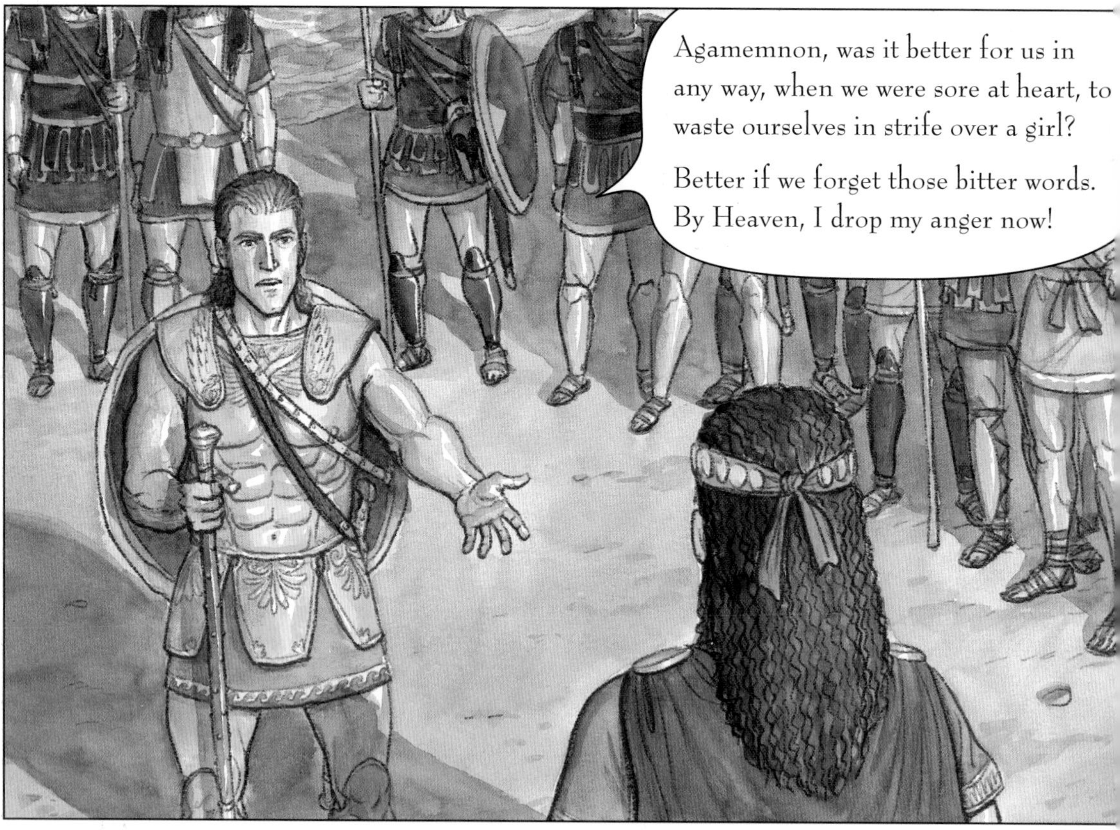
Agamemnon, was it better for us in any way, when we were sore at heart, to waste ourselves in strife over a girl?
Better if we forget those bitter words. By Heaven, I drop my anger now!

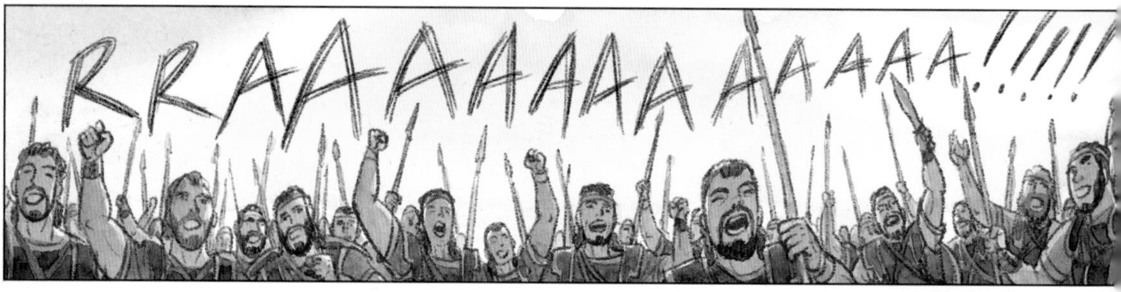
RRAAAAAAAAAAAA!!!!!

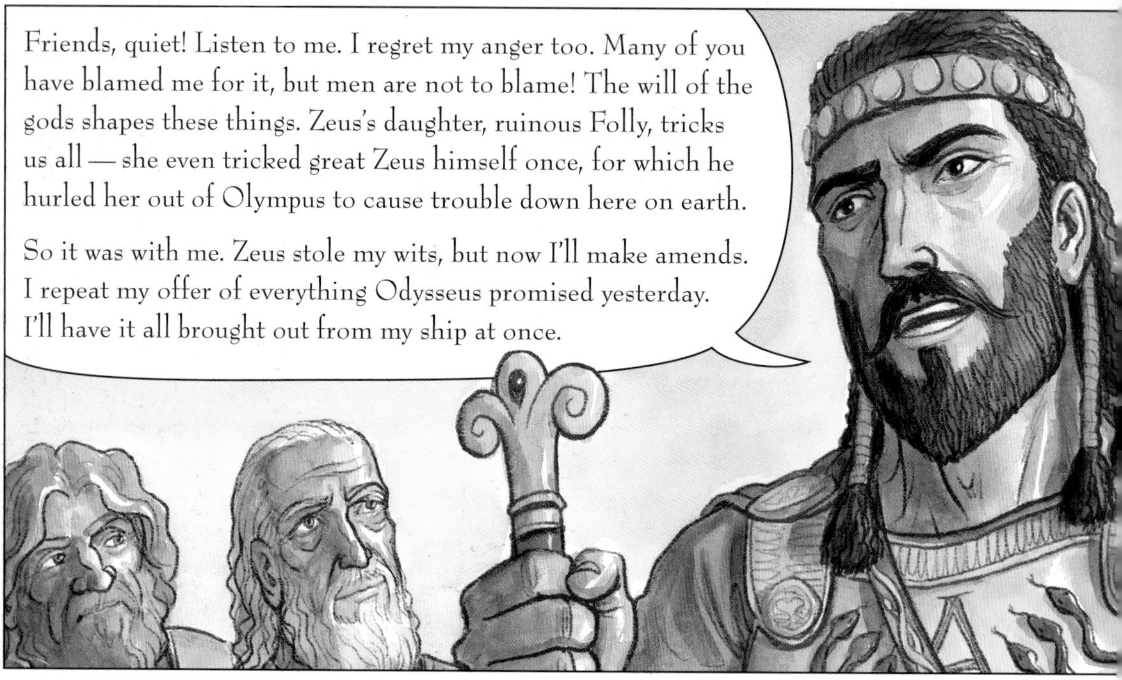
Friends, quiet! Listen to me. I regret my anger too. Many of you have blamed me for it, but men are not to blame! The will of the gods shapes these things. Zeus's daughter, ruinous Folly, tricks us all — she even tricked great Zeus himself once, for which he hurled her out of Olympus to cause trouble down here on earth.
So it was with me. Zeus stole my wits, but now I'll make amends. I repeat my offer of everything Odysseus promised yesterday. I'll have it all brought out from my ship at once.

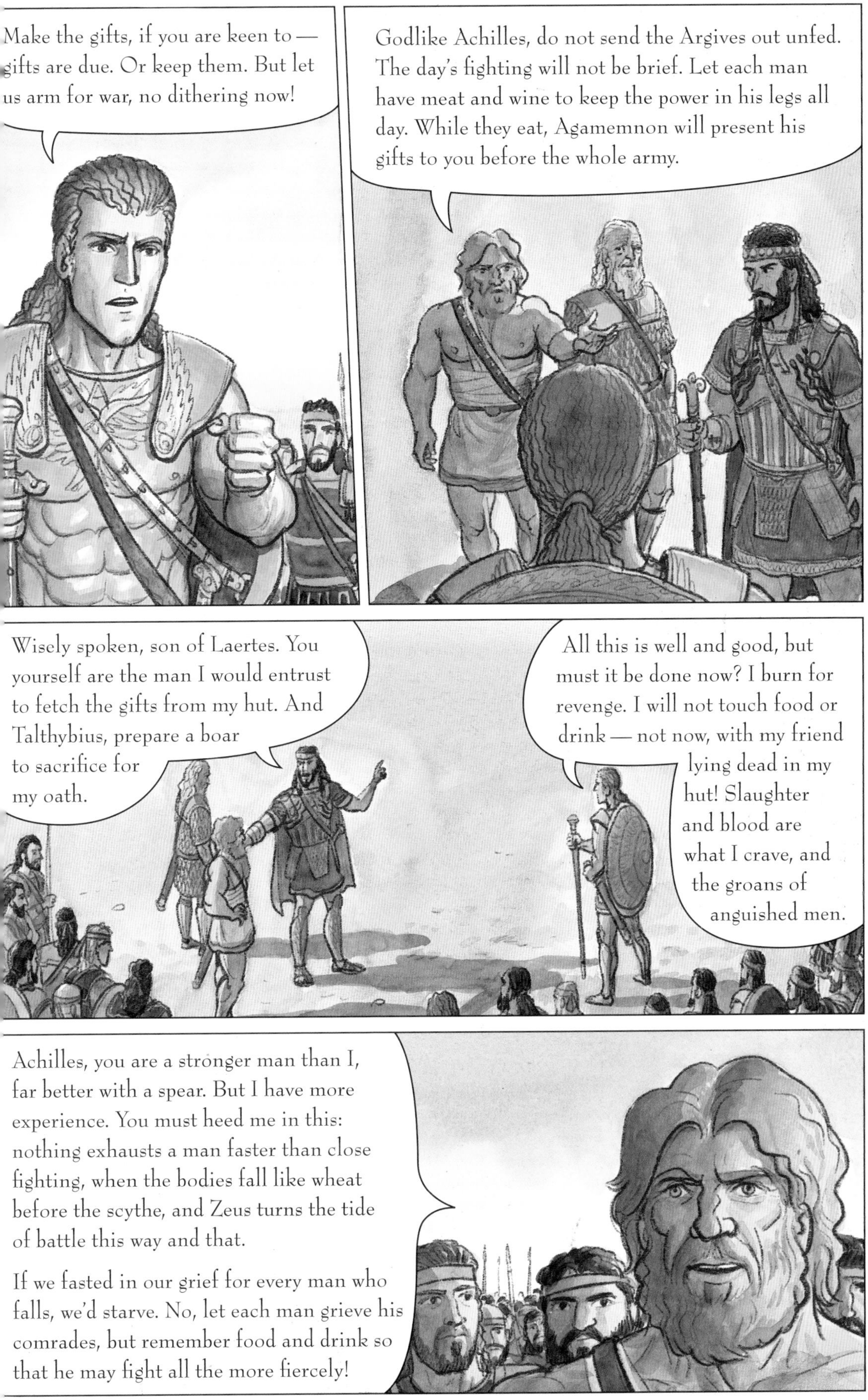
Make the gifts, if you are keen to — gifts are due. Or keep them. But let us arm for war, no dithering now!
Godlike Achilles, do not send the Argives out unfed. The day's fighting will not be brief. Let each man have meat and wine to keep the power in his legs all day. While they eat, Agamemnon will present his gifts to you before the whole army.
Wisely spoken, son of Laertes. You yourself are the man I would entrust to fetch the gifts from my hut. And Talthybius, prepare a boar to sacrifice for my oath.
All this is well and good, but must it be done now? I burn for revenge. I will not touch food or drink — not now, with my friend lying dead in my hut! Slaughter and blood are what I crave, and the groans of anguished men.
Achilles, you are a stronger man than I, far better with a spear. But I have more experience. You must heed me in this: nothing exhausts a man faster than close fighting, when the bodies fall like wheat before the scythe, and Zeus turns the tide of battle this way and that.
If we fasted in our grief for every man who falls, we'd starve. No, let each man grieve his comrades, but remember food and drink so that he may fight all the more fiercely!

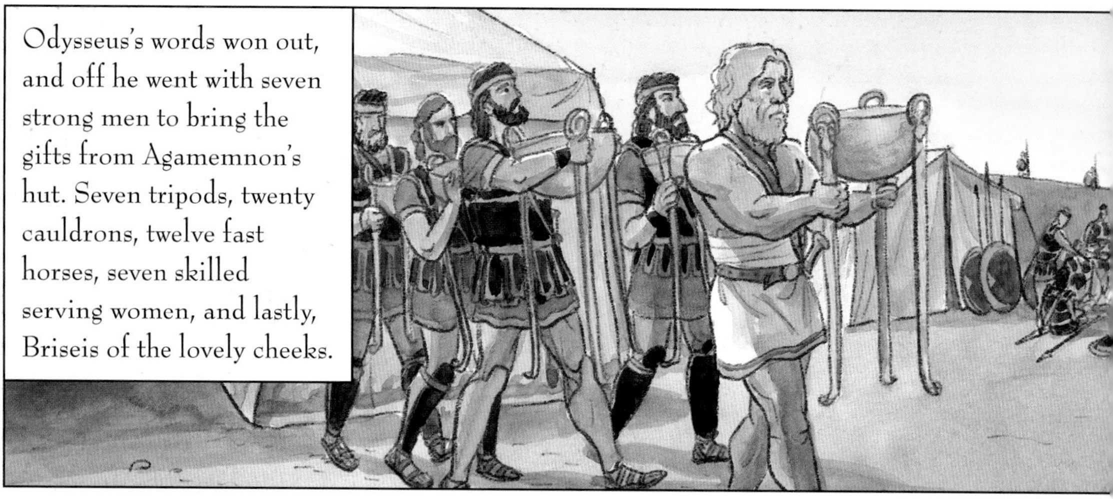
Odysseus's words won out, and off he went with seven strong men to bring the gifts from Agamemnon's hut. Seven tripods, twenty cauldrons, twelve fast horses, seven skilled serving women, and lastly, Briseis of the lovely cheeks.

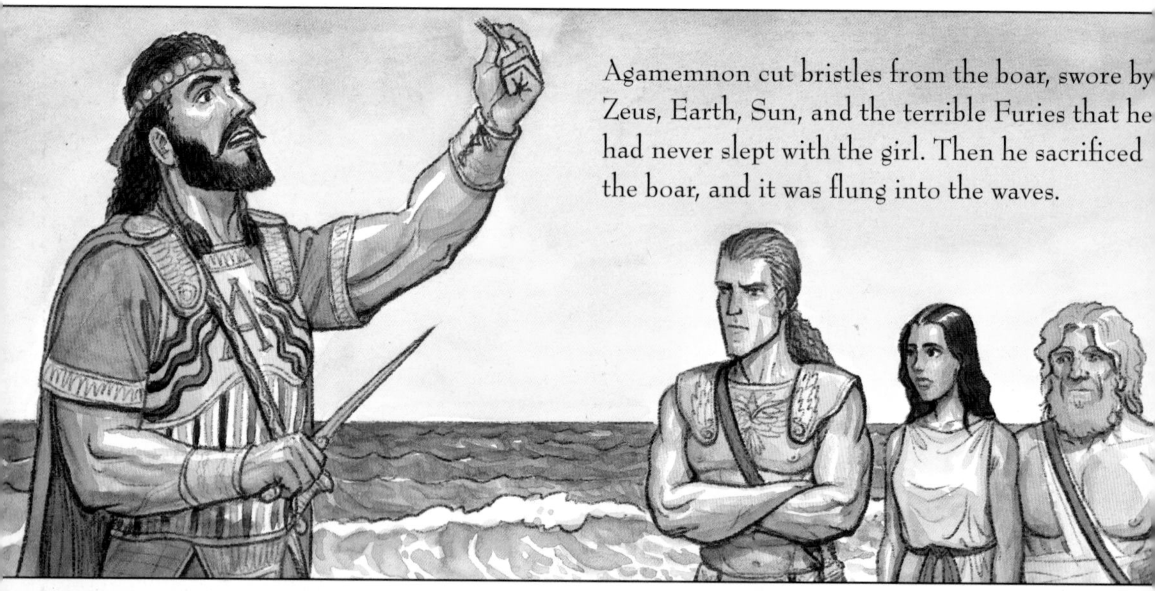
Agamemnon cut bristles from the boar, swore by Zeus, Earth, Sun, and the terrible Furies that he had never slept with the girl. Then he sacrificed the boar, and it was flung into the waves.

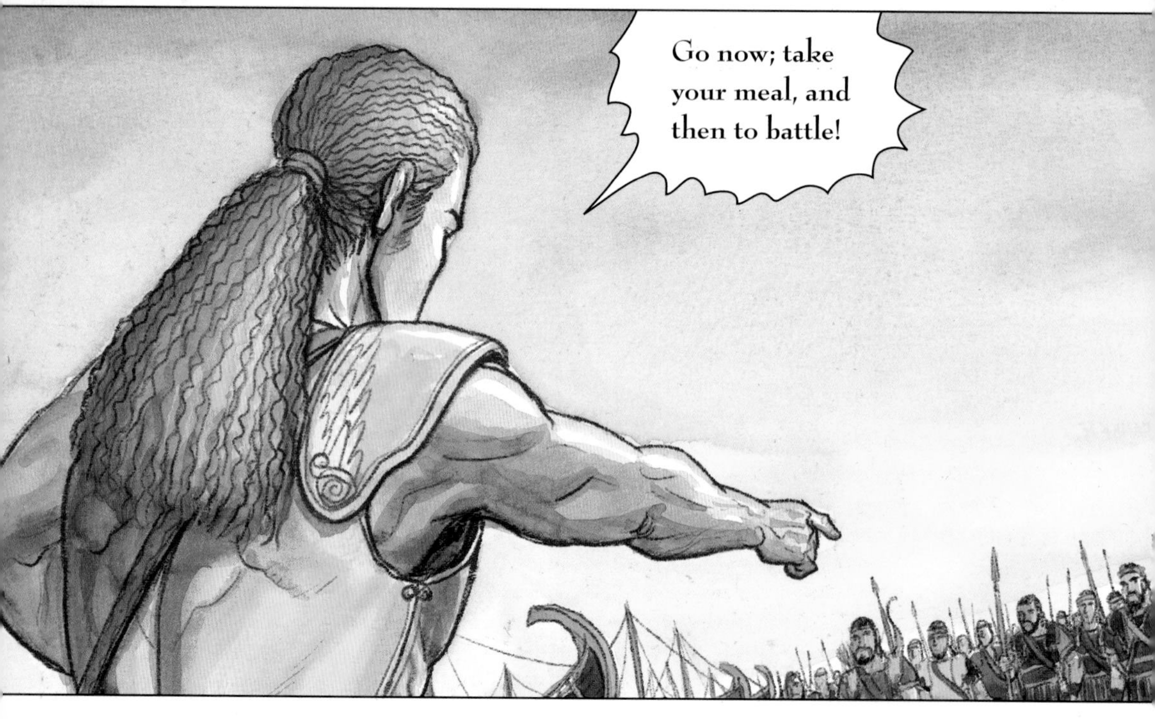
Go now; take your meal, and then to battle!

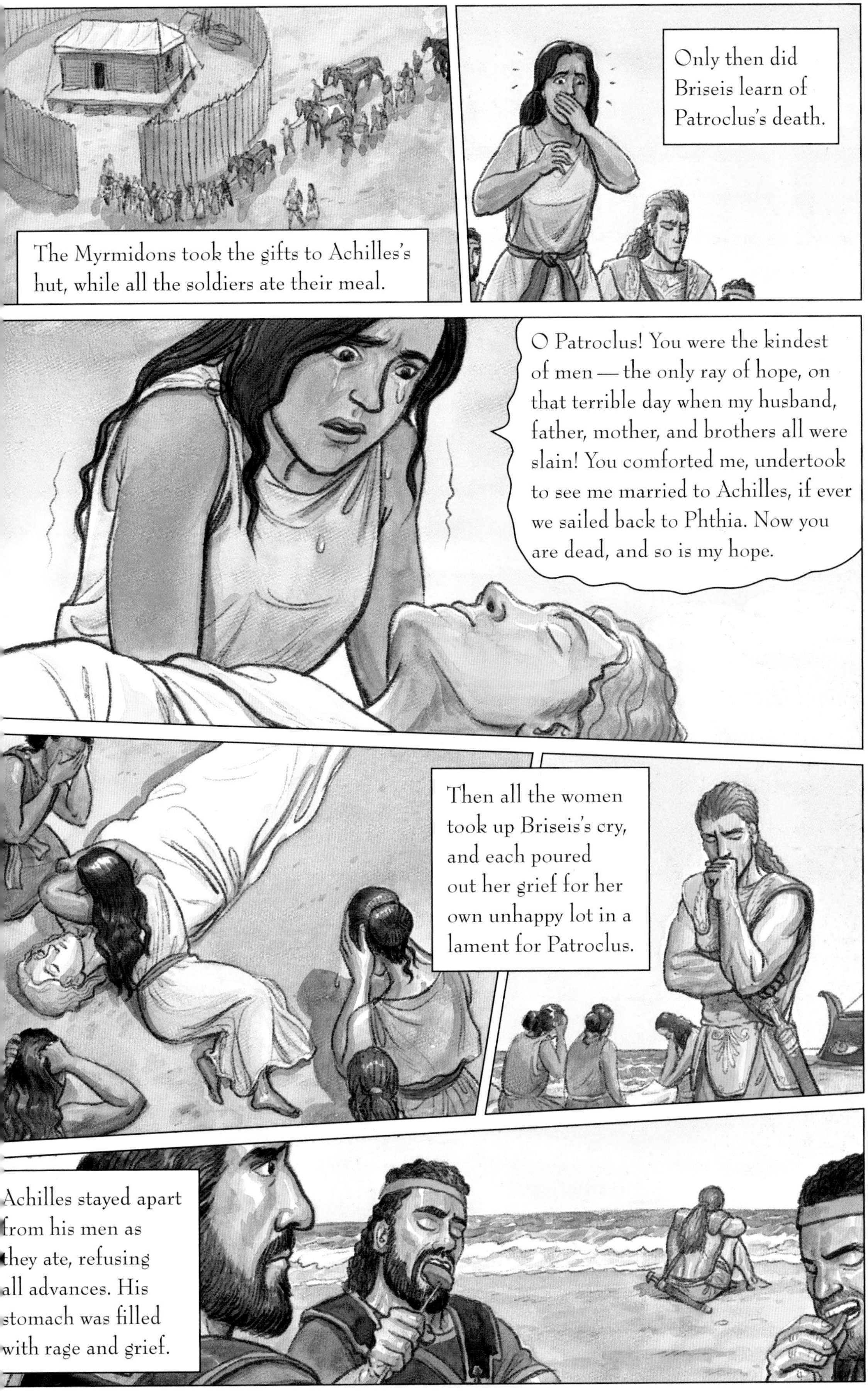
The Myrmidons took the gifts to Achilles's hut, while all the soldiers ate their meal.
Only then did Briseis learn of Patroclus's death.
O Patroclus! You were the kindest of men — the only ray of hope, on that terrible day when my husband, father, mother, and brothers all were slain! You comforted me, undertook to see me married to Achilles, if ever we sailed back to Phthia. Now you are dead, and so is my hope.
Then all the women took up Briseis's cry, and each poured out her grief for her own unhappy lot in a lament for Patroclus.
Achilles stayed apart from his men as they ate, refusing all advances. His stomach was filled with rage and grief.

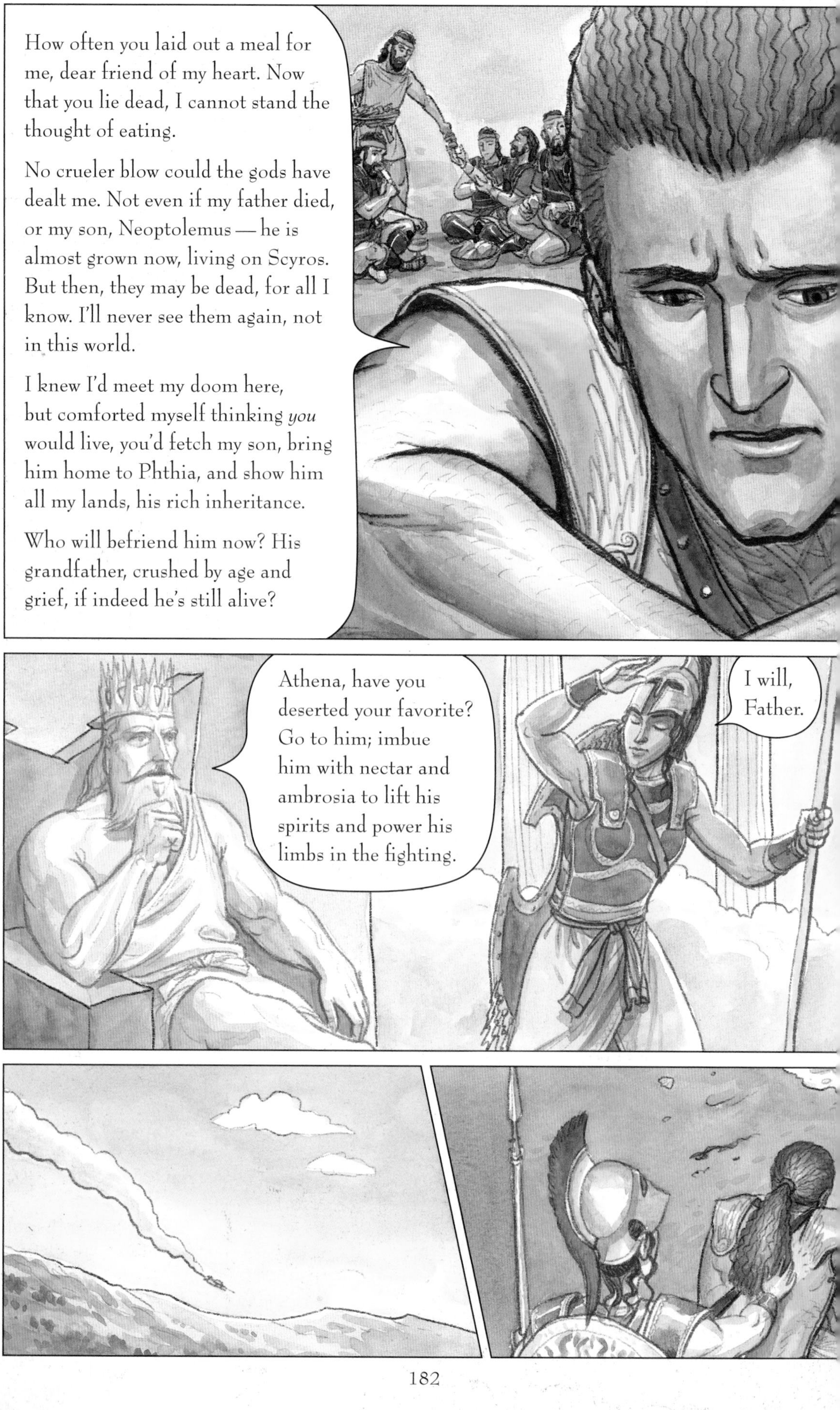
How often you laid out a meal for me, dear friend of my heart. Now that you lie dead, I cannot stand the thought of eating.
No crueler blow could the gods have dealt me. Not even if my father died, or my son, Neoptolemus — he is almost grown now, living on Scyros. But then, they may be dead, for all I know. I'll never see them again, not in this world.
I knew I'd meet my doom here, but comforted myself thinking *you* would live, you'd fetch my son, bring him home to Phthia, and show him all my lands, his rich inheritance.
Who will befriend him now? His grandfather, crushed by age and grief, if indeed he's still alive?
Athena, have you deserted your favorite? Go to him; imbue him with nectar and ambrosia to lift his spirits and power his limbs in the fighting.
I will, Father.

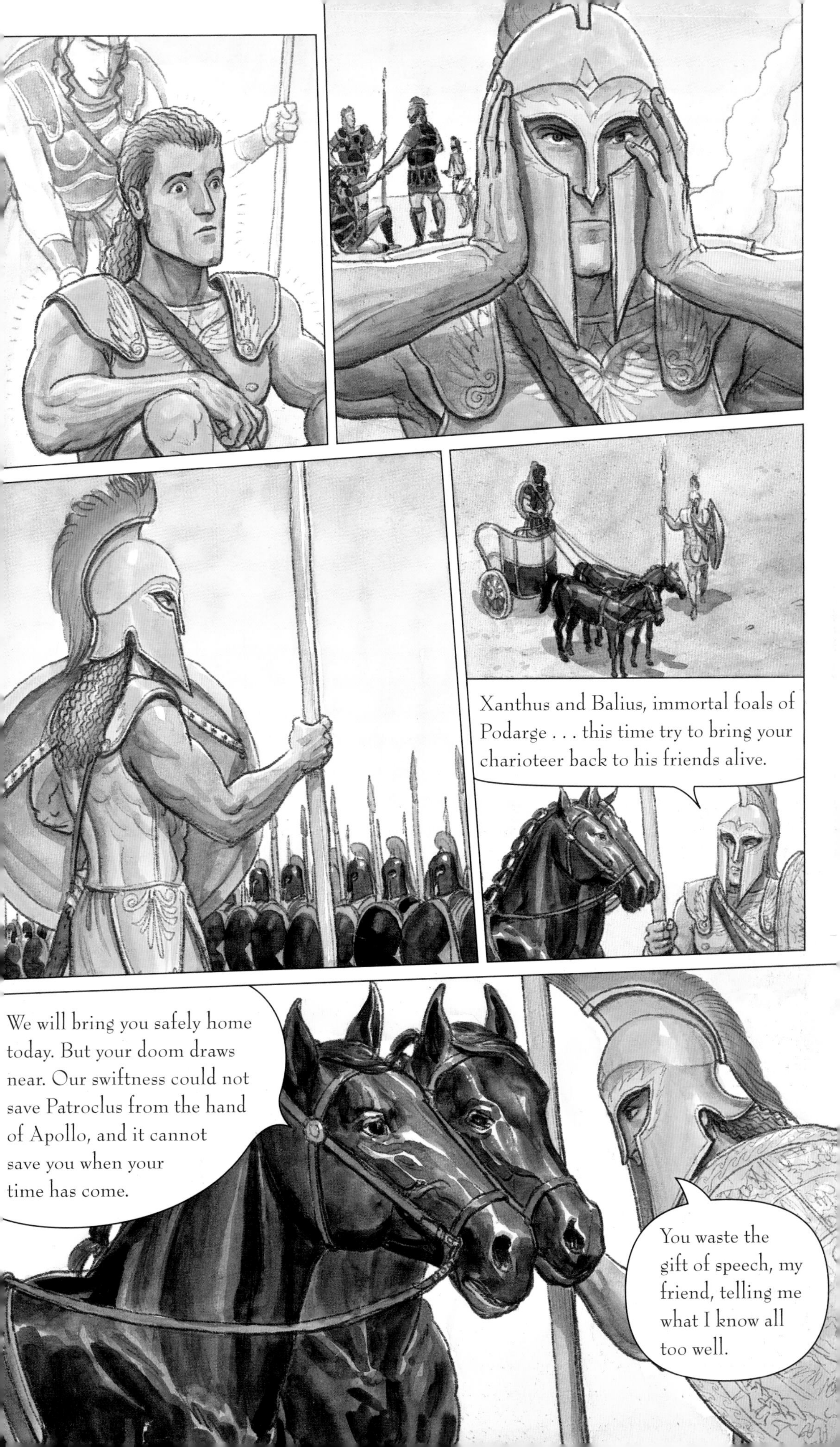

Xanthus and Balius, immortal foals of Podarge . . . this time try to bring your charioteer back to his friends alive.
We will bring you safely home today. But your doom draws near. Our swiftness could not save Patroclus from the hand of Apollo, and it cannot save you when your time has come.
You waste the gift of speech, my friend, telling me what I know all too well.

Book 20 — Battle of the Gods

All the Achaeans assembled for battle, and the glitter of bronze rippled like laughter over the plain.

Now Zeus told all the gods to help both sides as they wished. Hera, Athena, Poseidon, Hermes, and Hephaestus went to aid the Achaeans, while Apollo, Ares, Artemis, Leto, Aphrodite, and the river Xanthus (known to men as Scamander) took sides with the Trojans.

And Strife flew over all, feeding the violence of men and gods.

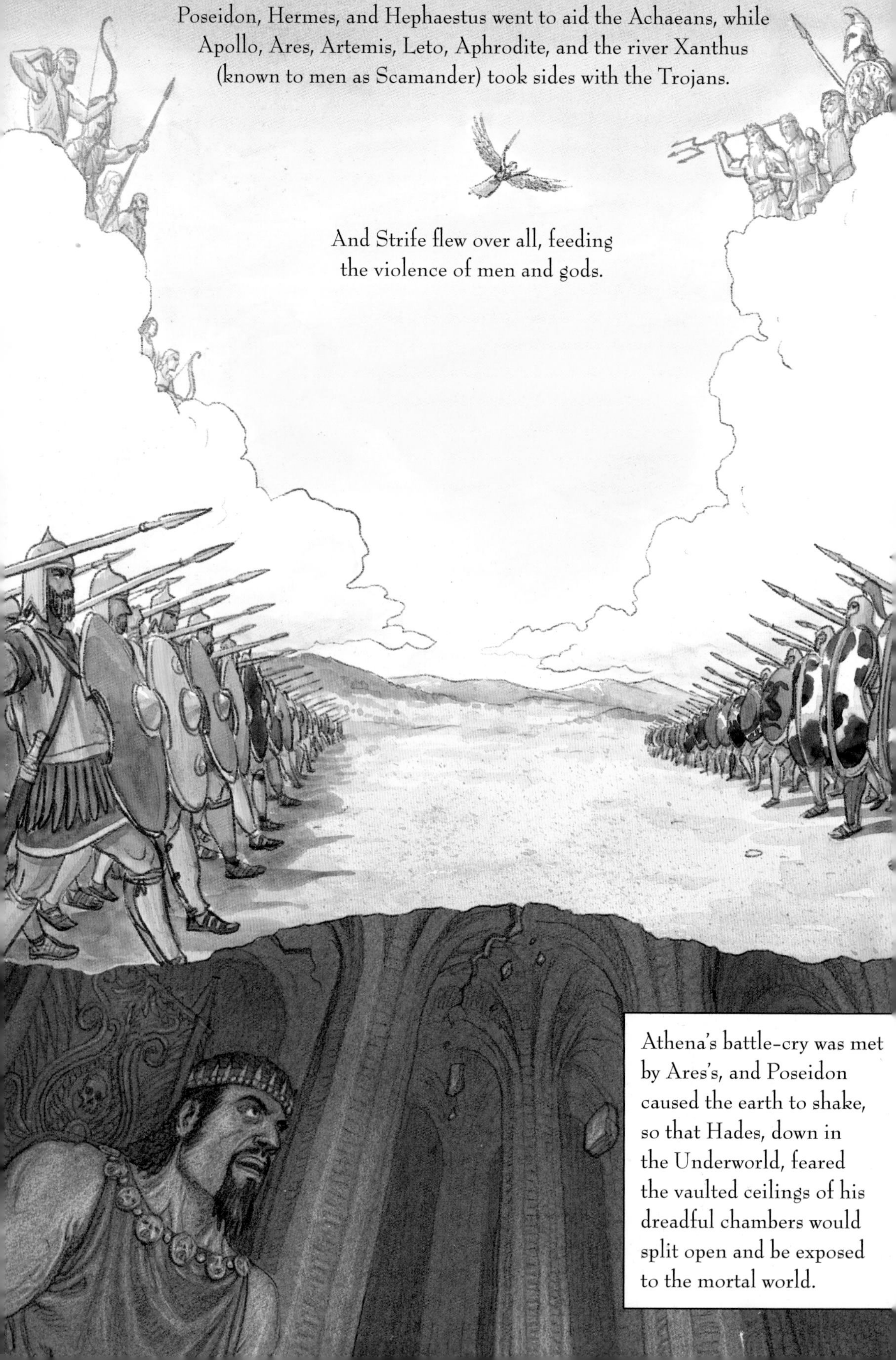

Athena's battle-cry was met by Ares's, and Poseidon caused the earth to shake, so that Hades, down in the Underworld, feared the vaulted ceilings of his dreadful chambers would split open and be exposed to the mortal world.

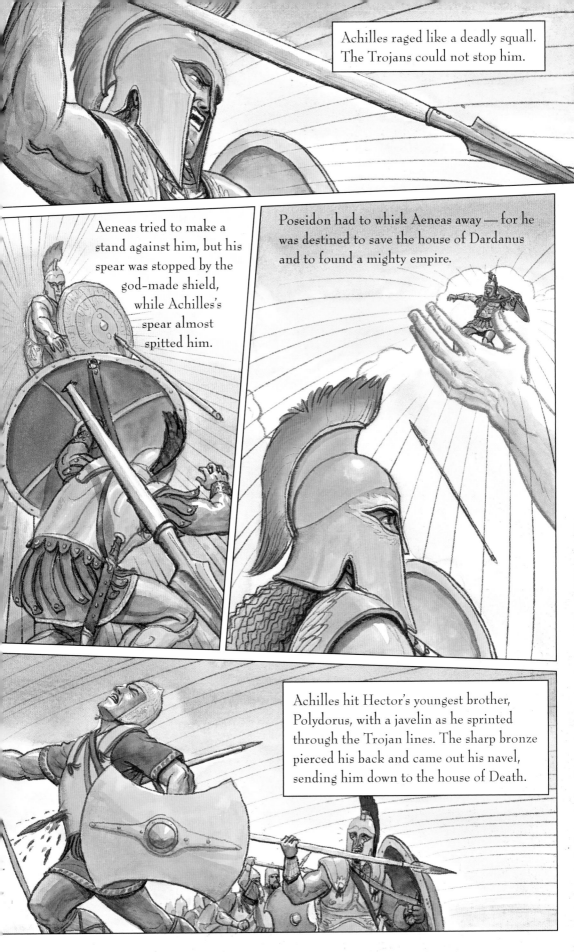

Achilles raged like a deadly squall. The Trojans could not stop him.

Aeneas tried to make a stand against him, but his spear was stopped by the god-made shield, while Achilles's spear almost spitted him.

Poseidon had to whisk Aeneas away — for he was destined to save the house of Dardanus and to found a mighty empire.

Achilles hit Hector's youngest brother, Polydorus, with a javelin as he sprinted through the Trojan lines. The sharp bronze pierced his back and came out his navel, sending him down to the house of Death.

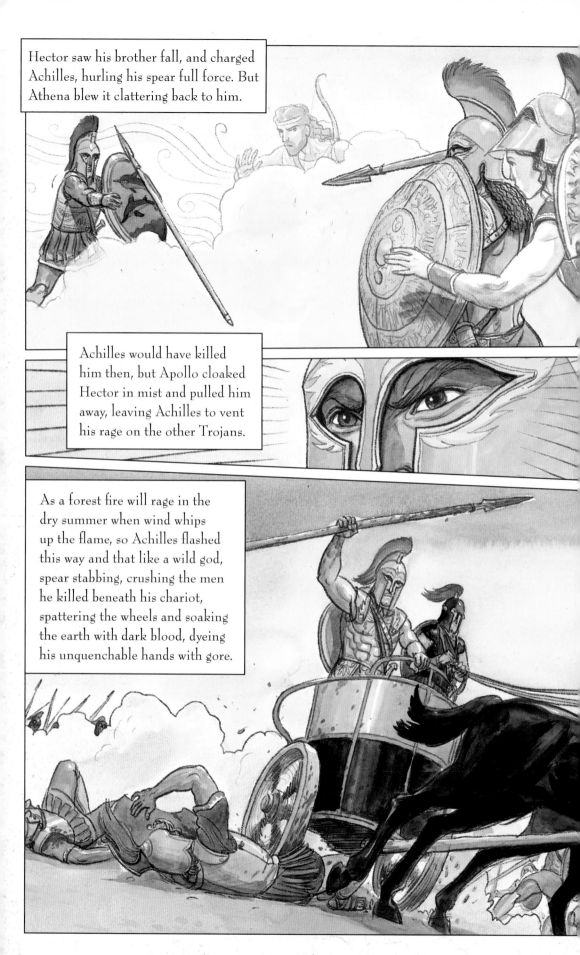

Hector saw his brother fall, and charged Achilles, hurling his spear full force. But Athena blew it clattering back to him.

Achilles would have killed him then, but Apollo cloaked Hector in mist and pulled him away, leaving Achilles to vent his rage on the other Trojans.

As a forest fire will rage in the dry summer when wind whips up the flame, so Achilles flashed this way and that like a wild god, spear stabbing, crushing the men he killed beneath his chariot, spattering the wheels and soaking the earth with dark blood, dyeing his unquenchable hands with gore.

Book 21 — Achilles Fights the River

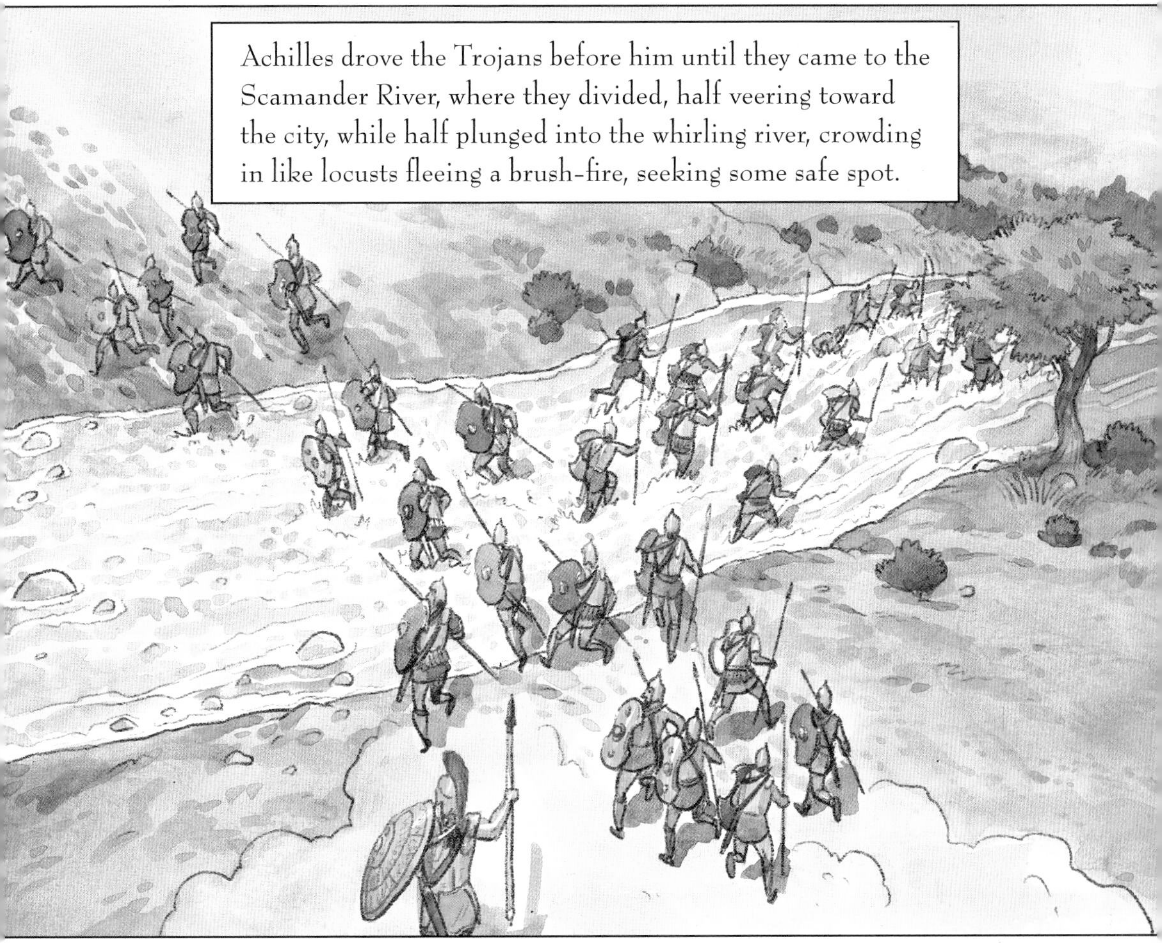
Achilles drove the Trojans before him until they came to the Scamander River, where they divided, half veering toward the city, while half plunged into the whirling river, crowding in like locusts fleeing a brush-fire, seeking some safe spot.

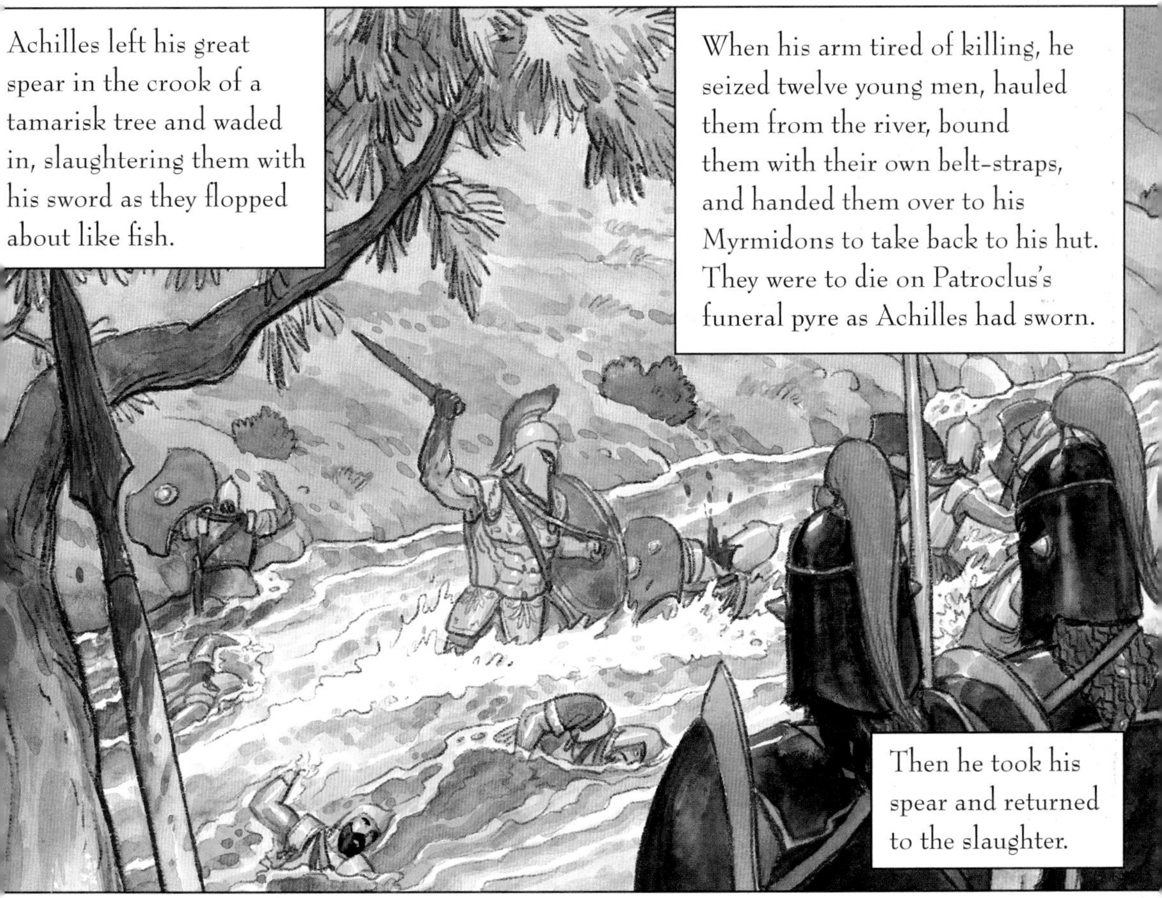
Achilles left his great spear in the crook of a tamarisk tree and waded in, slaughtering them with his sword as they flopped about like fish.
When his arm tired of killing, he seized twelve young men, hauled them from the river, bound them with their own belt-straps, and handed them over to his Myrmidons to take back to his hut. They were to die on Patroclus's funeral pyre as Achilles had sworn.
Then he took his spear and returned to the slaughter.

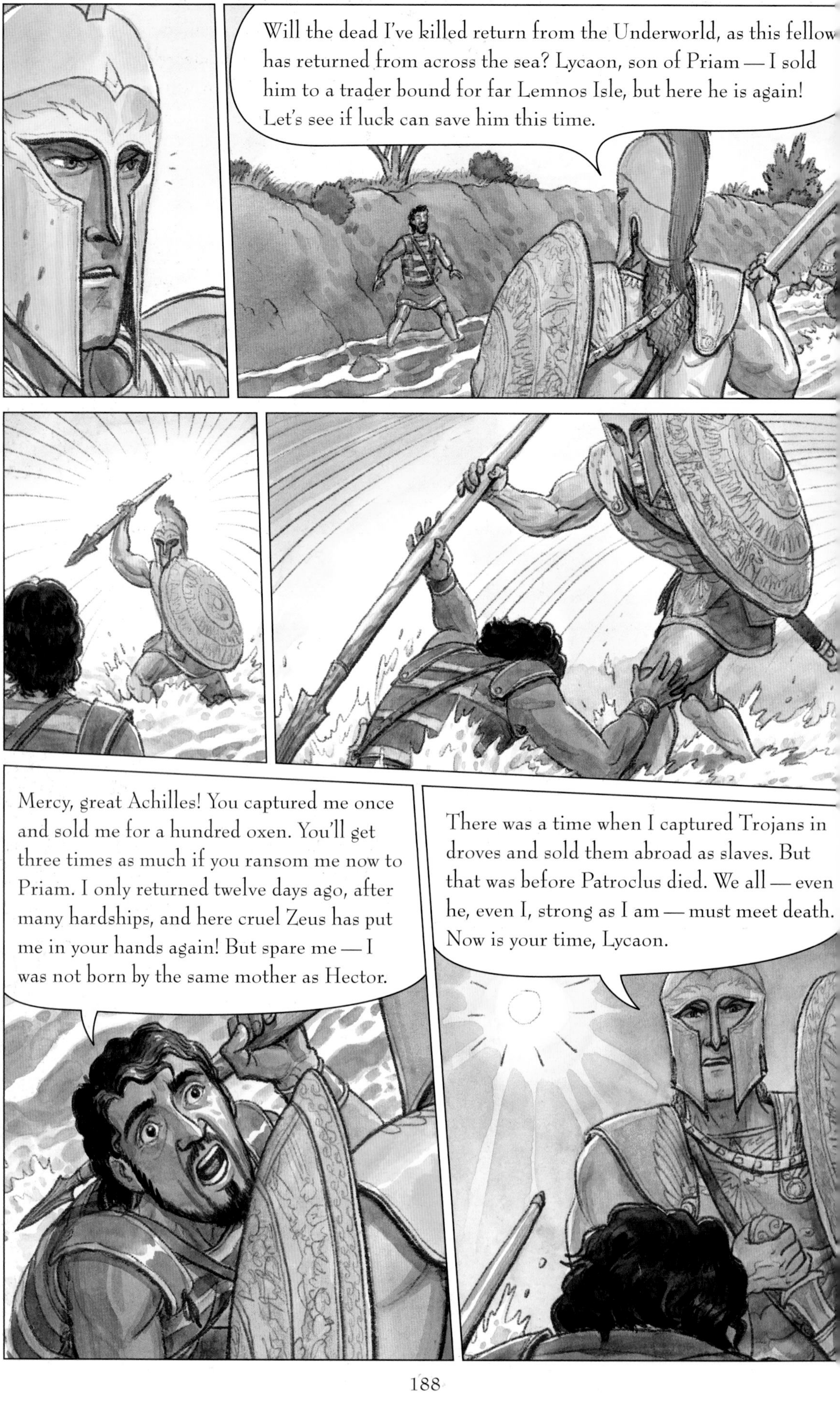
Will the dead I've killed return from the Underworld, as this fellow has returned from across the sea? Lycaon, son of Priam — I sold him to a trader bound for far Lemnos Isle, but here he is again! Let's see if luck can save him this time.
Mercy, great Achilles! You captured me once and sold me for a hundred oxen. You'll get three times as much if you ransom me now to Priam. I only returned twelve days ago, after many hardships, and here cruel Zeus has put me in your hands again! But spare me — I was not born by the same mother as Hector.
There was a time when I captured Trojans in droves and sold them abroad as slaves. But that was before Patroclus died. We all — even he, even I, strong as I am — must meet death. Now is your time, Lycaon.

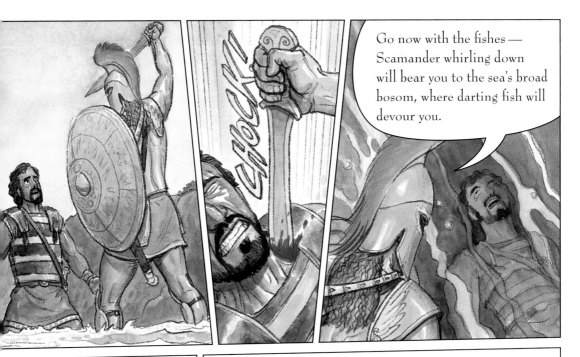

Go now with the fishes — Scamander whirling down will bear you to the sea's broad bosom, where darting fish will devour you.

Nothing will save you, Trojans! Not even Scamander of the silver eddies can save you, despite the bulls, the living horses you've sacrificed in his pools!

Hearing this, the river's anger against Achilles surged, so he gave strength to Asteropaeus. This man was the grandson of another river, Axius. He was ambidextrous, and held a spear ready in each hand as he faced his foe.

Who are you that dares to face Achilles? What is your homeland, your parentage?

I come from far Paeonia. I led my troops here to Ilium eleven days ago. My father is Pelagon, son of the broad river Axius. But let us fight, not bandy words.

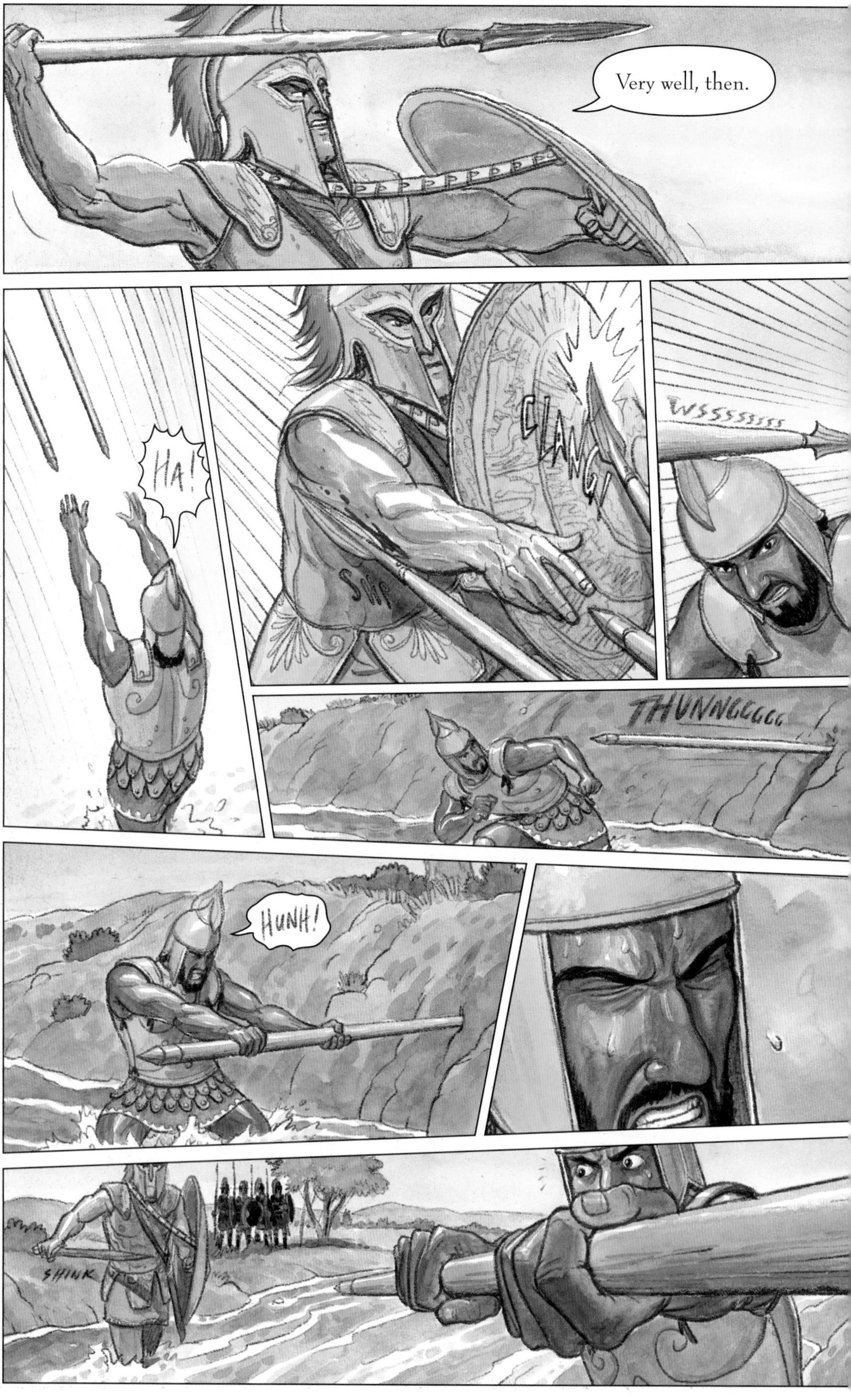
Very well, then.
HA!
CLANG!
SHP
WSSSSSSSS
THUNNGGGGG
HUNH!
SHINK

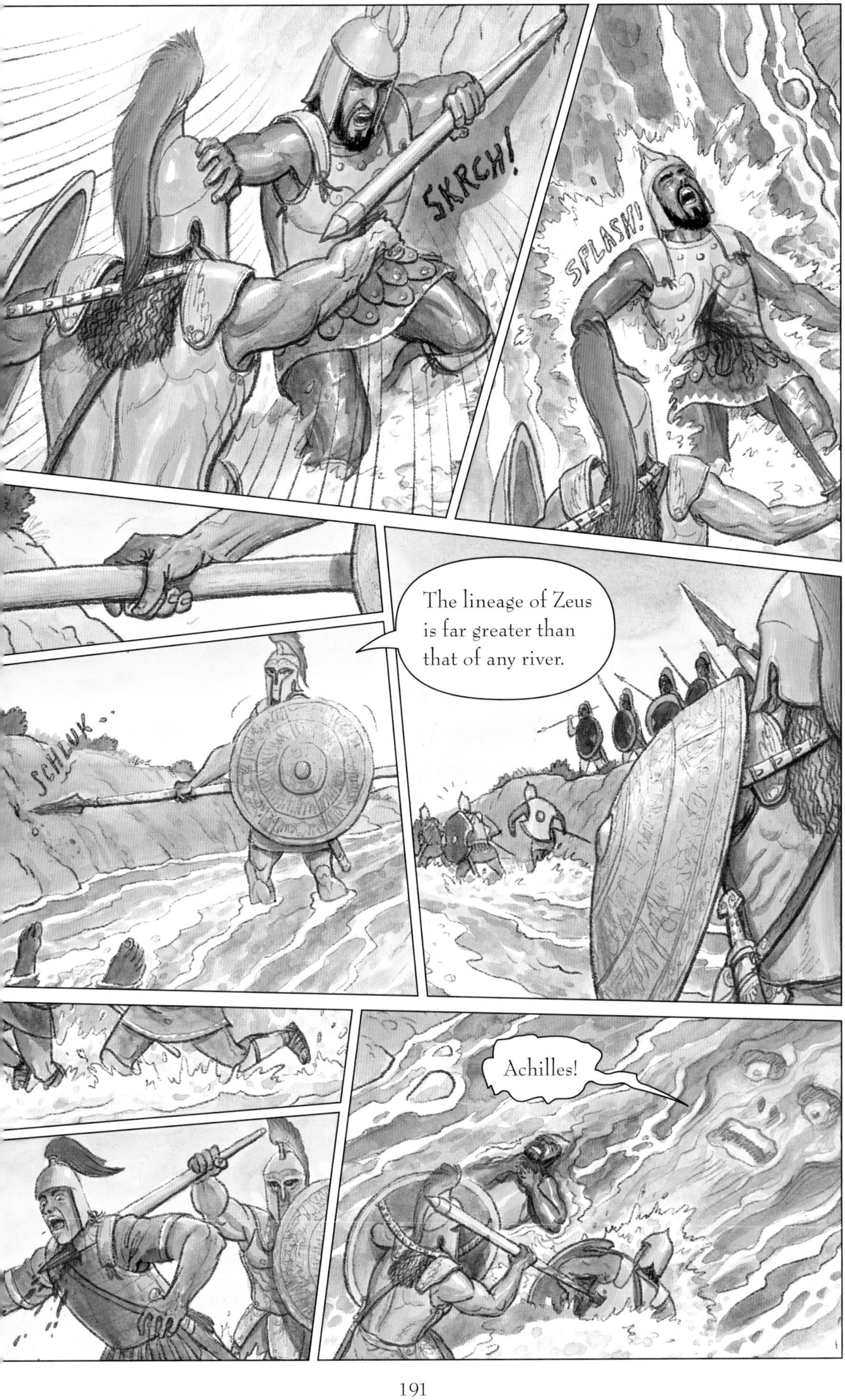
SKRCH!
SPLASH!
The lineage of Zeus is far greater than that of any river.
SCHLUK
Achilles!

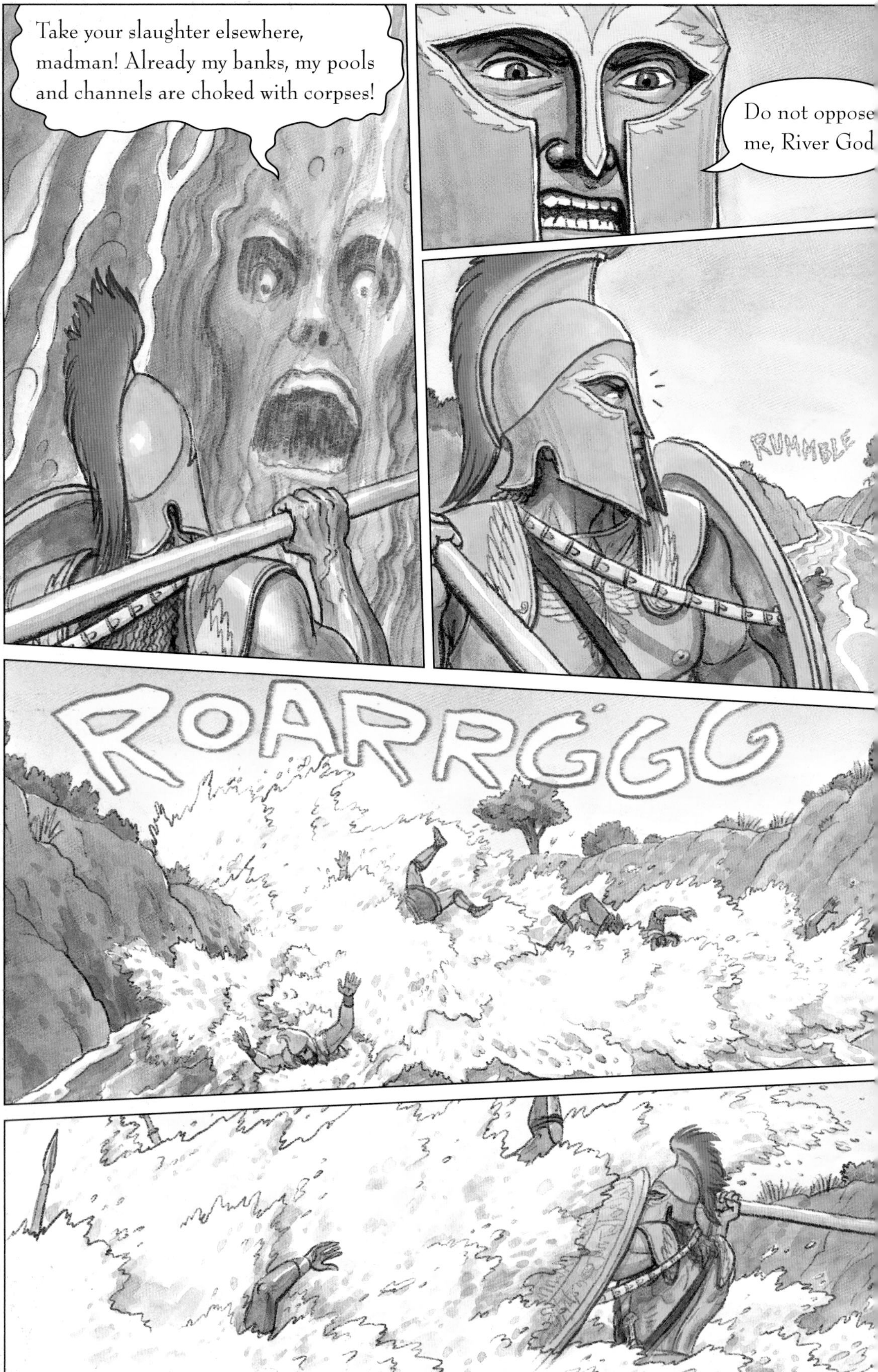
Take your slaughter elsewhere, madman! Already my banks, my pools and channels are choked with corpses!
Do not oppose me, River God
RUMMBLE
ROARRGGG

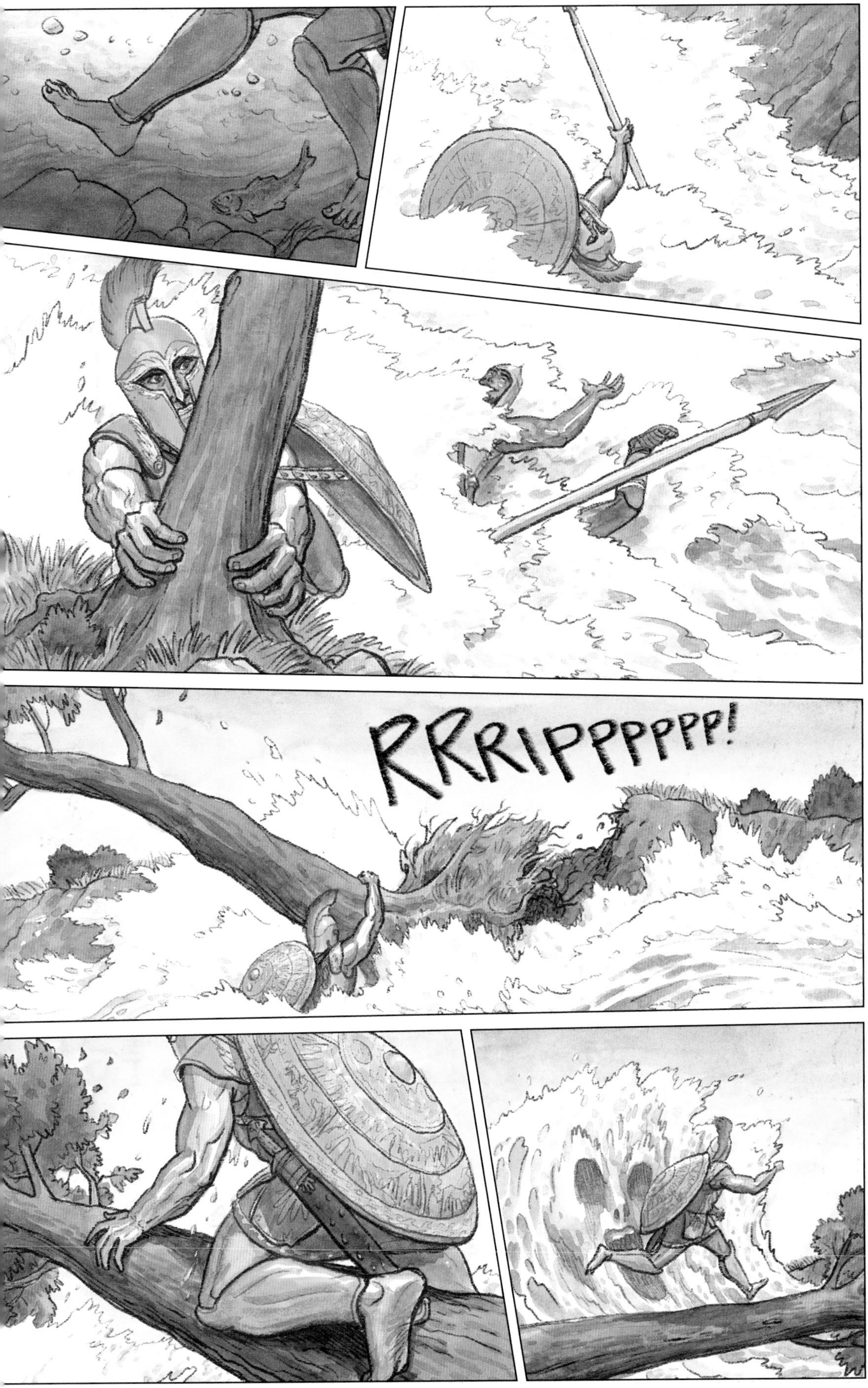
RRRIPPPPPP!

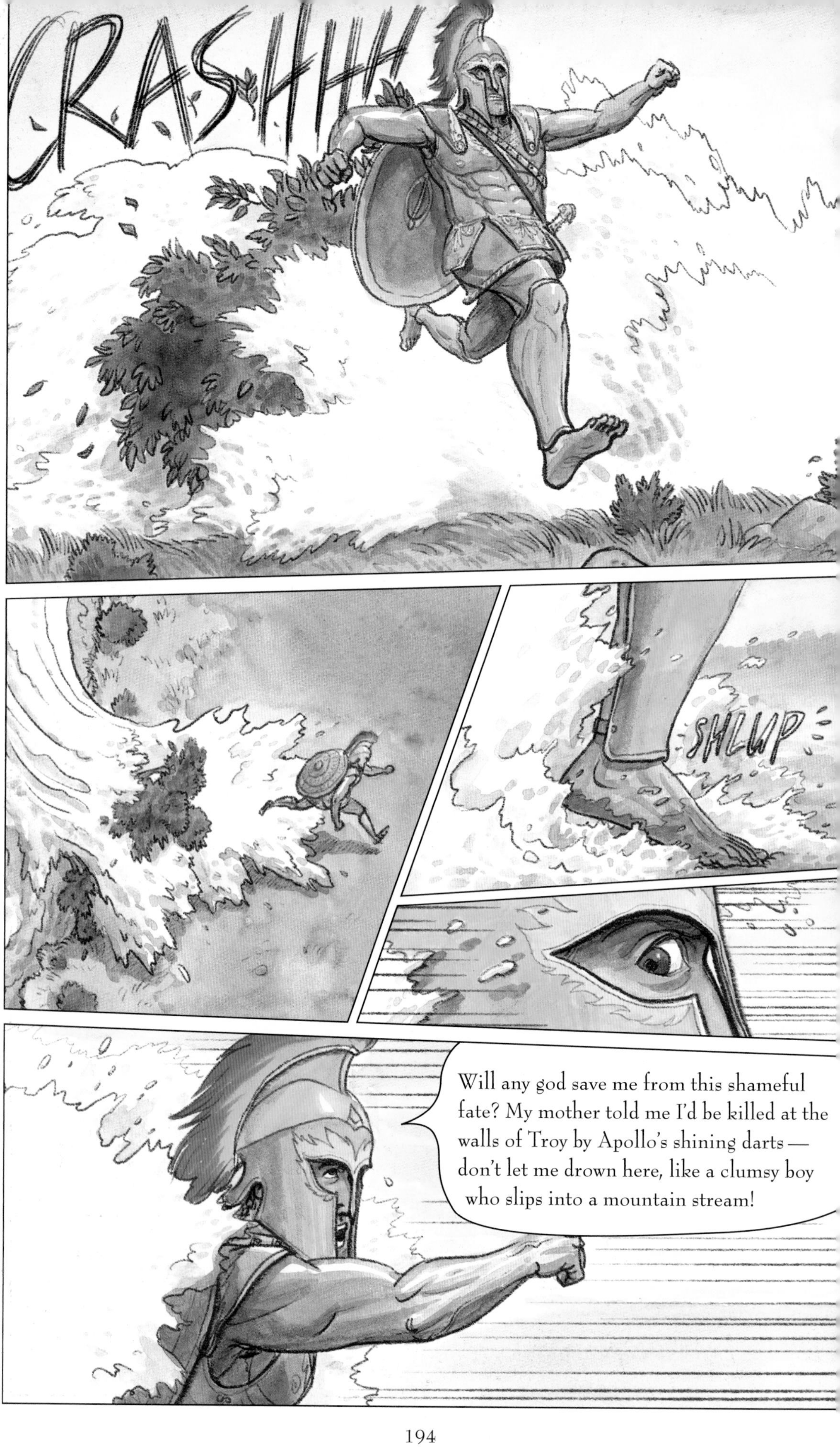
CRASHHH
SHLUP
Will any god save me from this shameful fate? My mother told me I'd be killed at the walls of Troy by Apollo's shining darts — don't let me drown here, like a clumsy boy who slips into a mountain stream!

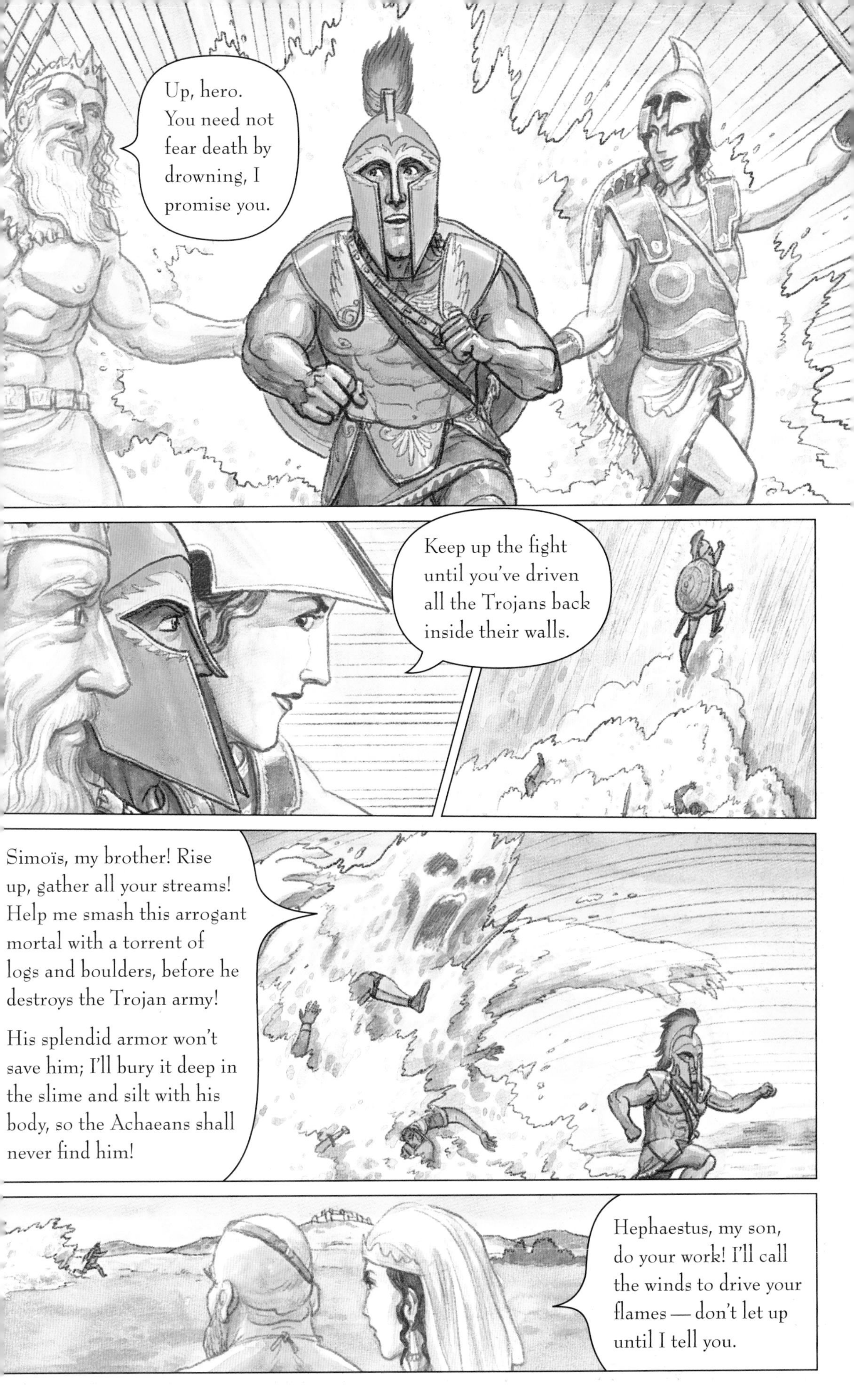
Up, hero. You need not fear death by drowning, I promise you.
Keep up the fight until you've driven all the Trojans back inside their walls.
Simoïs, my brother! Rise up, gather all your streams! Help me smash this arrogant mortal with a torrent of logs and boulders, before he destroys the Trojan army!
His splendid armor won't save him; I'll bury it deep in the slime and silt with his body, so the Achaeans shall never find him!
Hephaestus, my son, do your work! I'll call the winds to drive your flames — don't let up until I tell you.

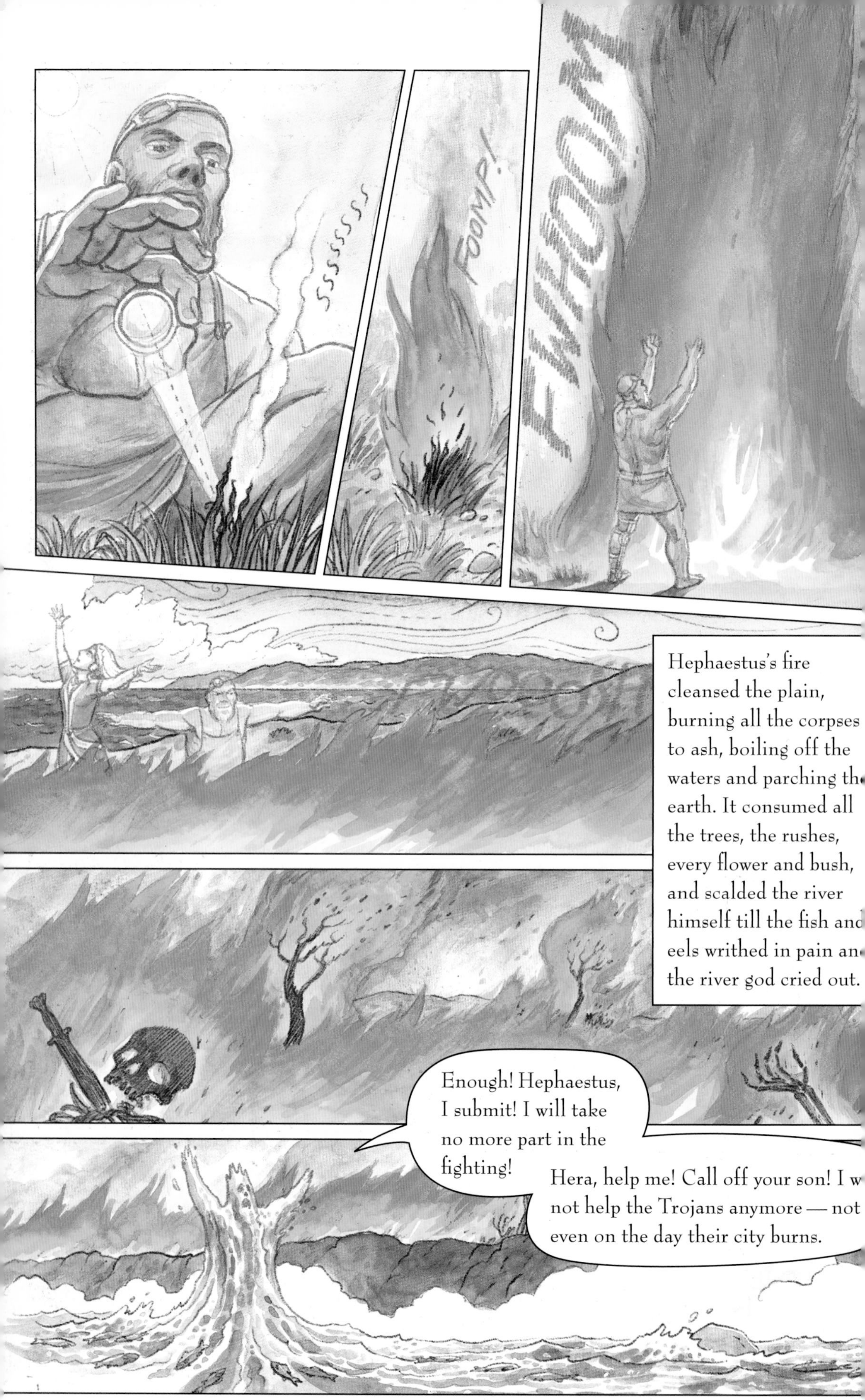
ssssssss
FOOMP!
FWHOOOM
Hephaestus's fire cleansed the plain, burning all the corpses to ash, boiling off the waters and parching th
earth. It consumed all the trees, the rushes, every flower and bush, and scalded the river himself till the fish and
eels writhed in pain an
the river god cried out.
Enough! Hephaestus, I submit! I will take no more part in the fighting!
Hera, help me! Call off your son! I w
not help the Trojans anymore — not even on the day their city burns.

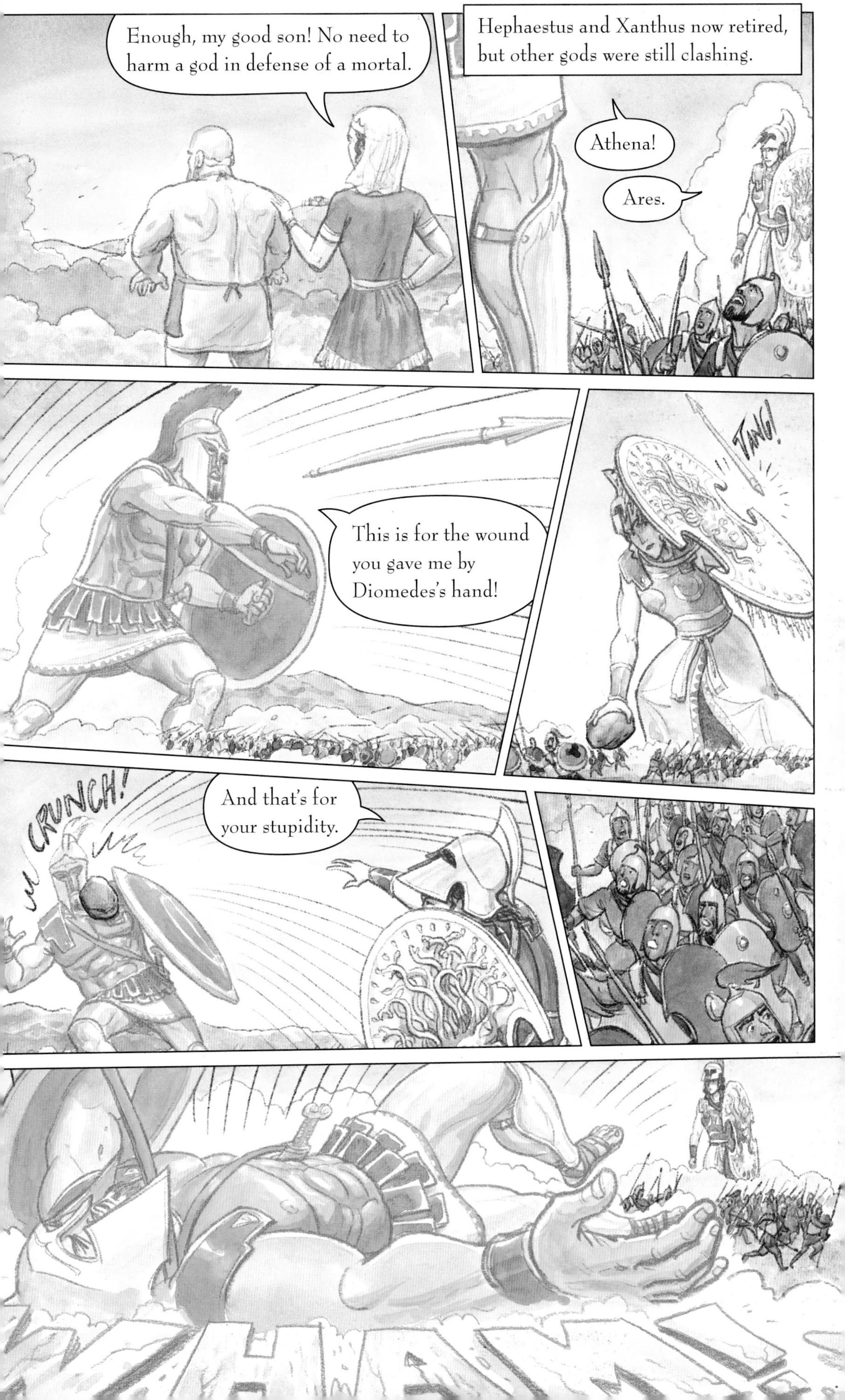
Enough, my good son! No need to harm a god in defense of a mortal.
Hephaestus and Xanthus now retired, but other gods were still clashing.
Athena!
Ares.
This is for the wound you gave me by Diomedes's hand!
TANG!
CRUNCH!
And that's for your stupidity.

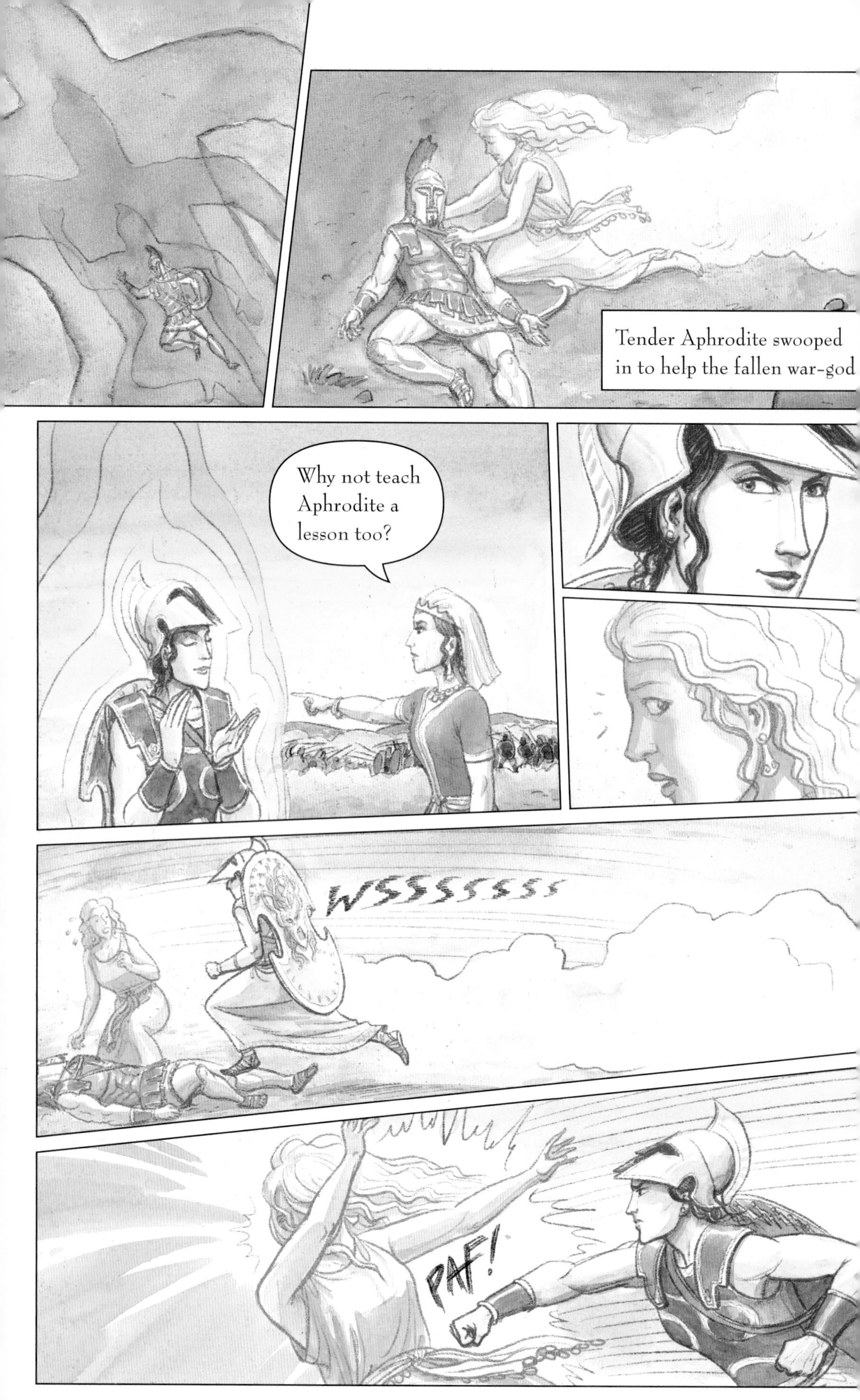
Tender Aphrodite swooped in to help the fallen war-god
Why not teach Aphrodite a lesson too?
WSSSSSSS
PAF!

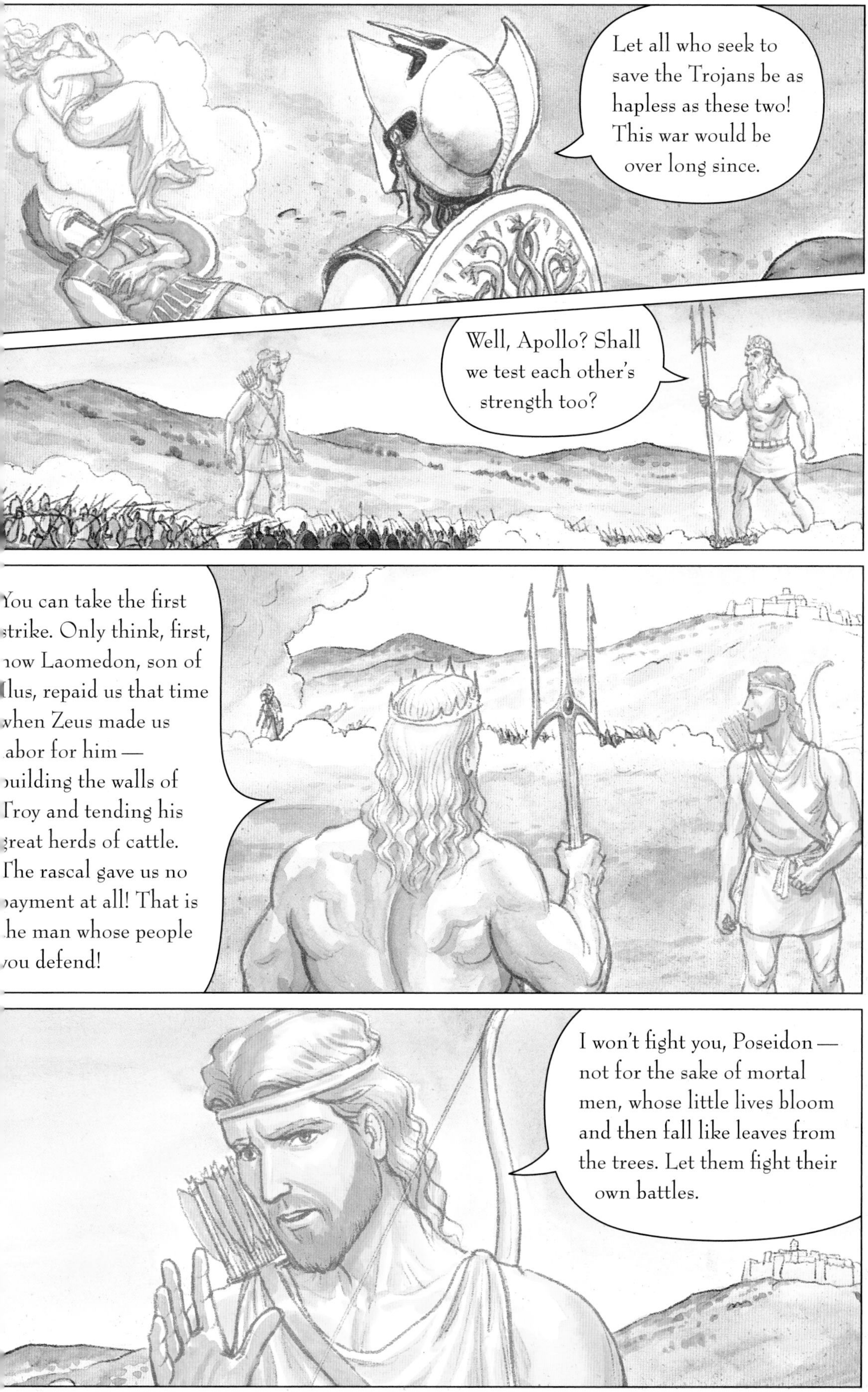
Let all who seek to save the Trojans be as hapless as these two! This war would be over long since.
Well, Apollo? Shall we test each other's strength too?
You can take the first strike. Only think, first, how Laomedon, son of Ilus, repaid us that time when Zeus made us labor for him — building the walls of Troy and tending his great herds of cattle. The rascal gave us no payment at all! That is the man whose people you defend!
I won't fight you, Poseidon — not for the sake of mortal men, whose little lives bloom and then fall like leaves from the trees. Let them fight their own battles.

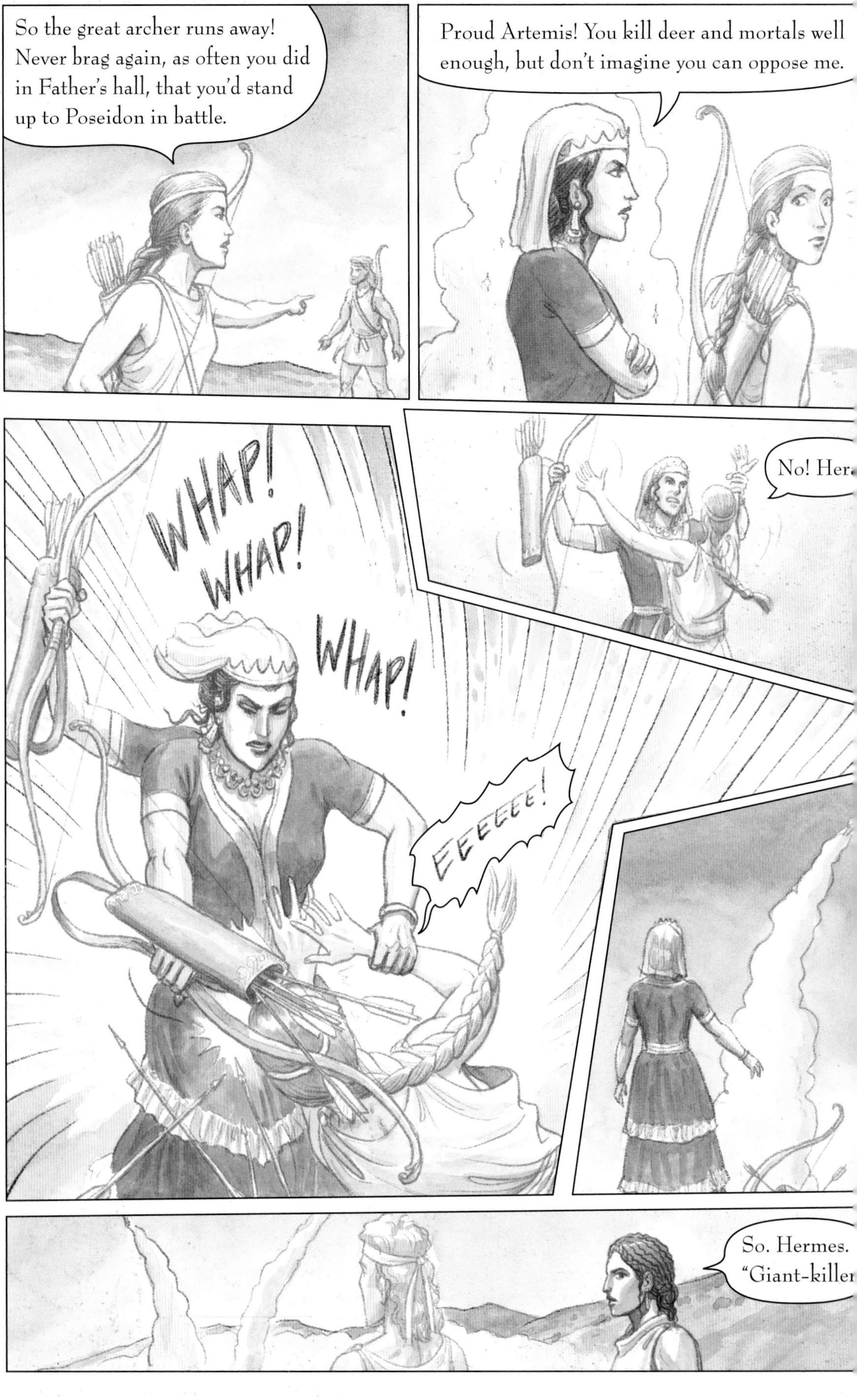
So the great archer runs away! Never brag again, as often you did in Father's hall, that you'd stand up to Poseidon in battle.
Proud Artemis! You kill deer and mortals well enough, but don't imagine you can oppose me.
WHAP! WHAP!
WHAP!
EEEEEE!
So. Hermes.

Aheh-heh . . .

Noble Leto,* I would not dream of fighting you, now that I've seen the wives of Zeus in action. You may boast to all the gods that you have beaten me.

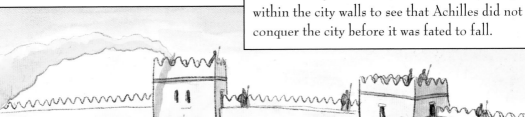

Now all the gods retired, save Apollo, who stayed within the city walls to see that Achilles did not conquer the city before it was fated to fall.

201

* Leto is the mother of Apollo and Artemis (by Zeus) and daughter of the Titans Coeus and Phoebe.

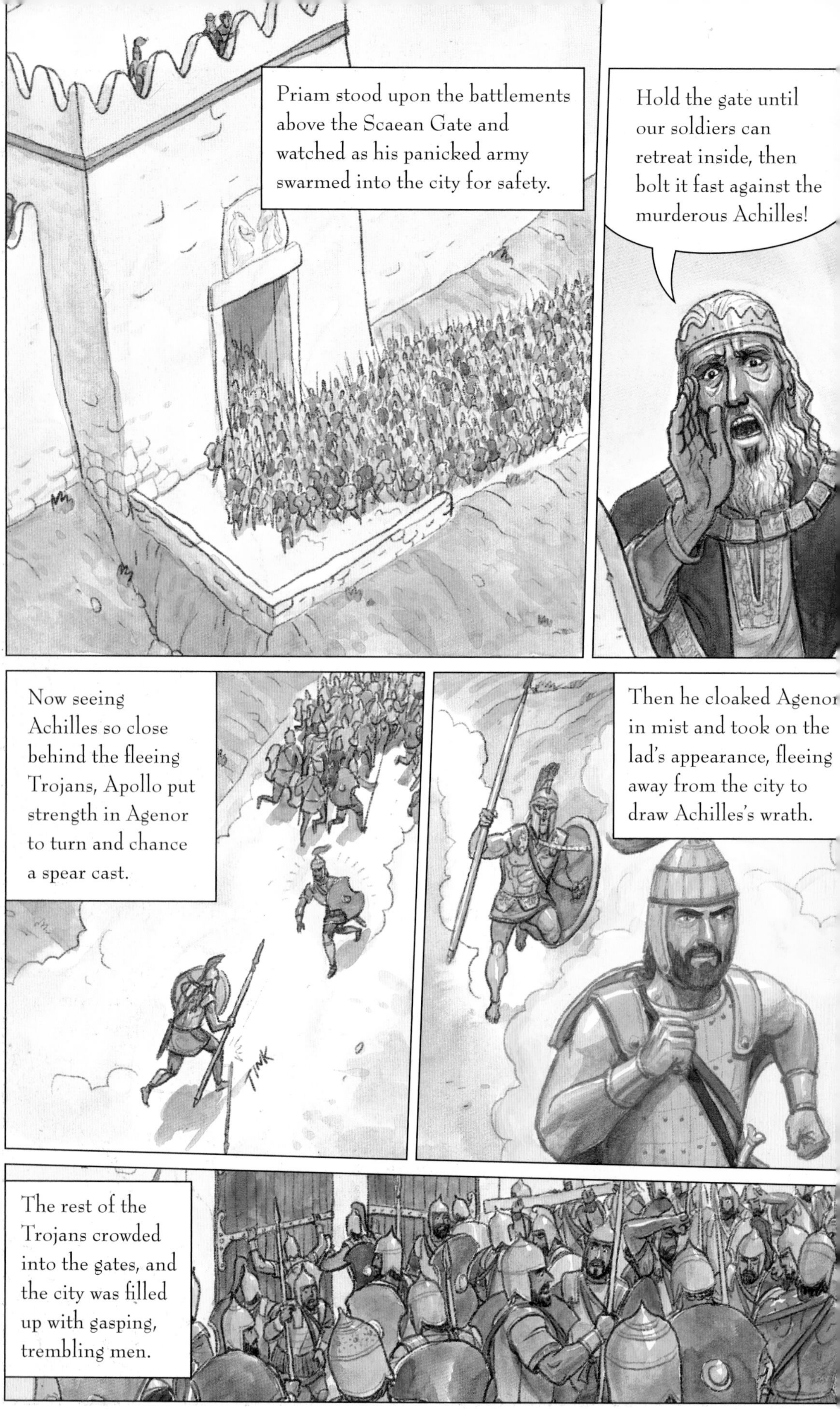

Priam stood upon the battlements above the Scaean Gate and watched as his panicked army swarmed into the city for safety.
Hold the gate until our soldiers can retreat inside, then bolt it fast against the murderous Achilles!
Now seeing Achilles so close behind the fleeing Trojans, Apollo put strength in Agenor to turn and chance a spear cast.
TINK
Then he cloaked Agenor in mist and took on the lad's appearance, fleeing away from the city to draw Achilles's wrath.
The rest of the Trojans crowded into the gates, and the city was filled up with gasping, trembling men.

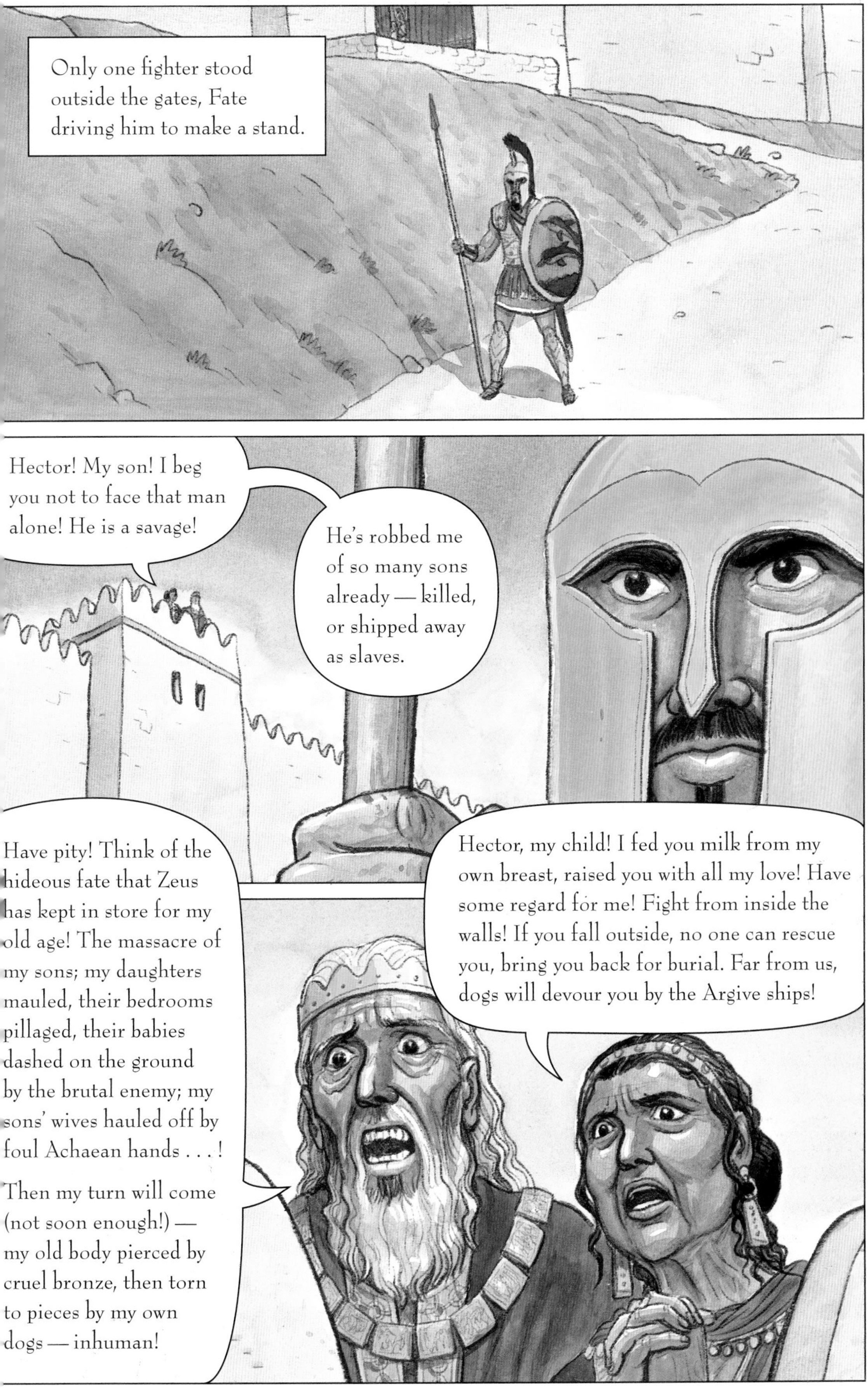
Only one fighter stood outside the gates, Fate driving him to make a stand.
Hector! My son! I beg you not to face that man alone! He is a savage!
He's robbed me of so many sons already — killed, or shipped away as slaves.
Have pity! Think of the hideous fate that Zeus has kept in store for my old age! The massacre of my sons; my daughters mauled, their bedrooms pillaged, their babies dashed on the ground by the brutal enemy; my sons' wives hauled off by foul Achaean hands . . . !
Then my turn will come (not soon enough!) — my old body pierced by cruel bronze, then torn to pieces by my own dogs — inhuman!
Hector, my child! I fed you milk from my own breast, raised you with all my love! Have some regard for me! Fight from inside the walls! If you fall outside, no one can rescue you, bring you back for burial. Far from us, dogs will devour you by the Argive ships!

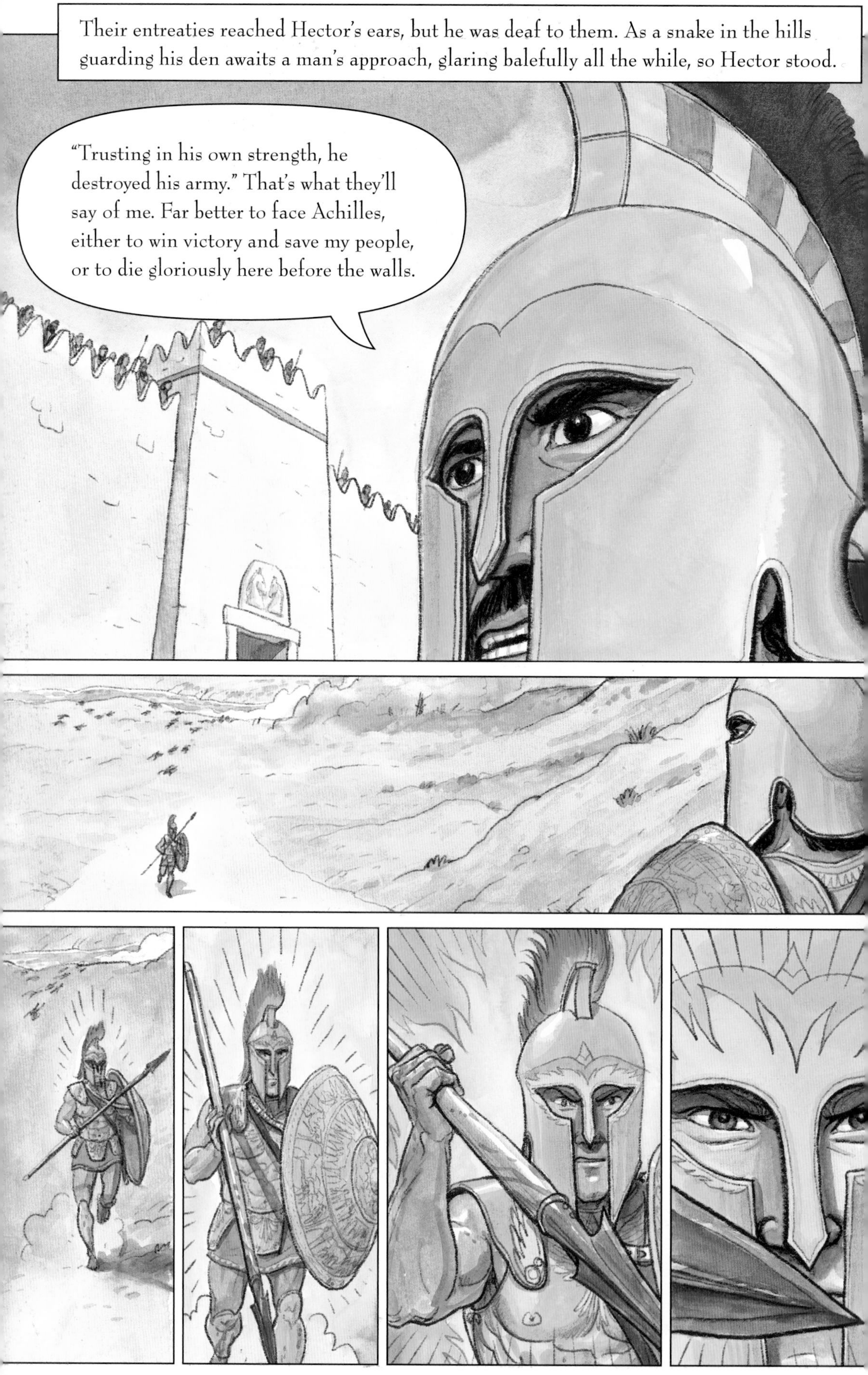
Their entreaties reached Hector's ears, but he was deaf to them. As a snake in the hills guarding his den awaits a man's approach, glaring balefully all the while, so Hector stood.
"Trusting in his own strength, he destroyed his army." That's what they'll say of me. Far better to face Achilles, either to win victory and save my people, or to die gloriously here before the walls.

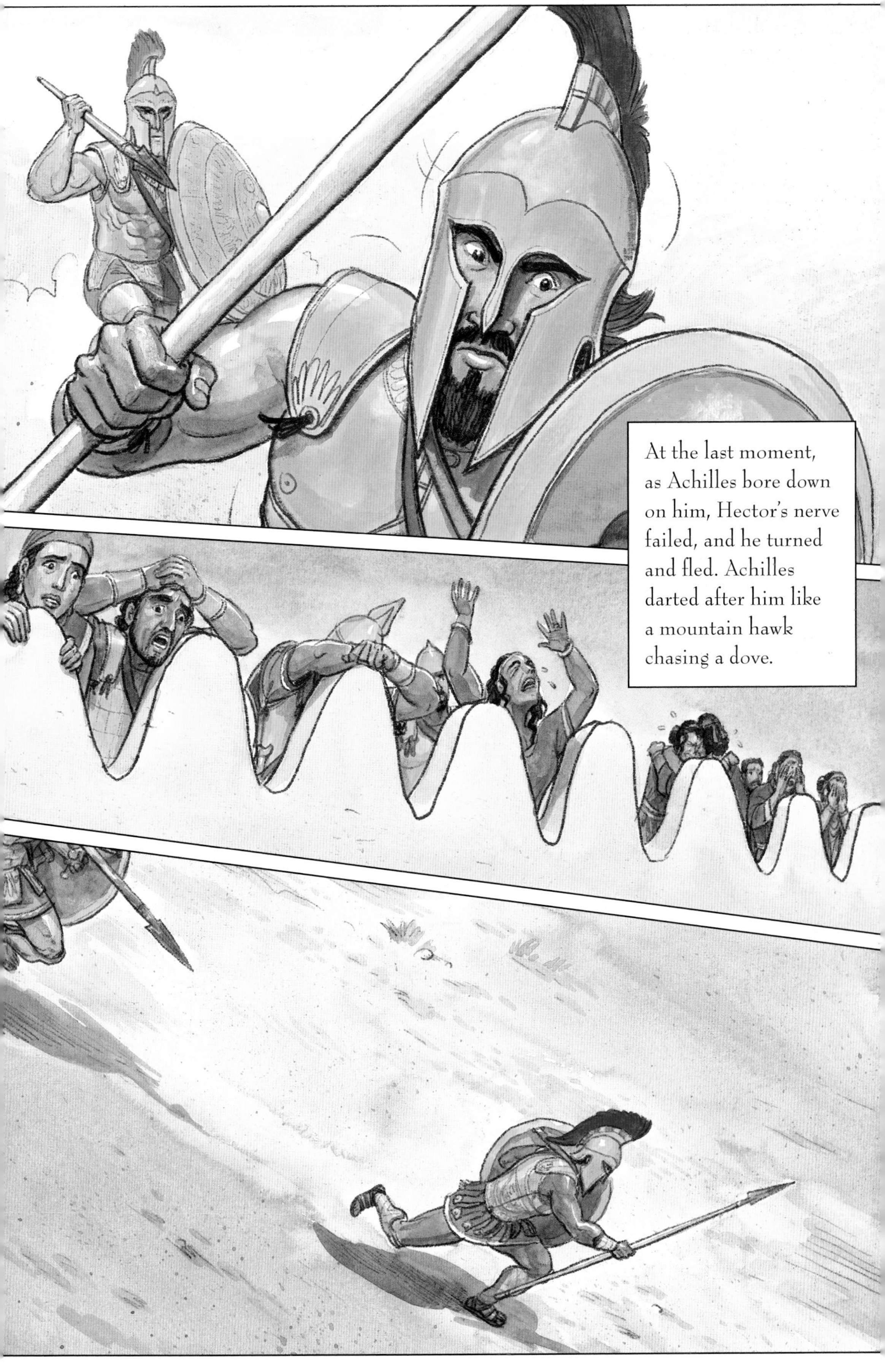
At the last moment, as Achilles bore down on him, Hector's nerve failed, and he turned and fled. Achilles darted after him like a mountain hawk chasing a dove.

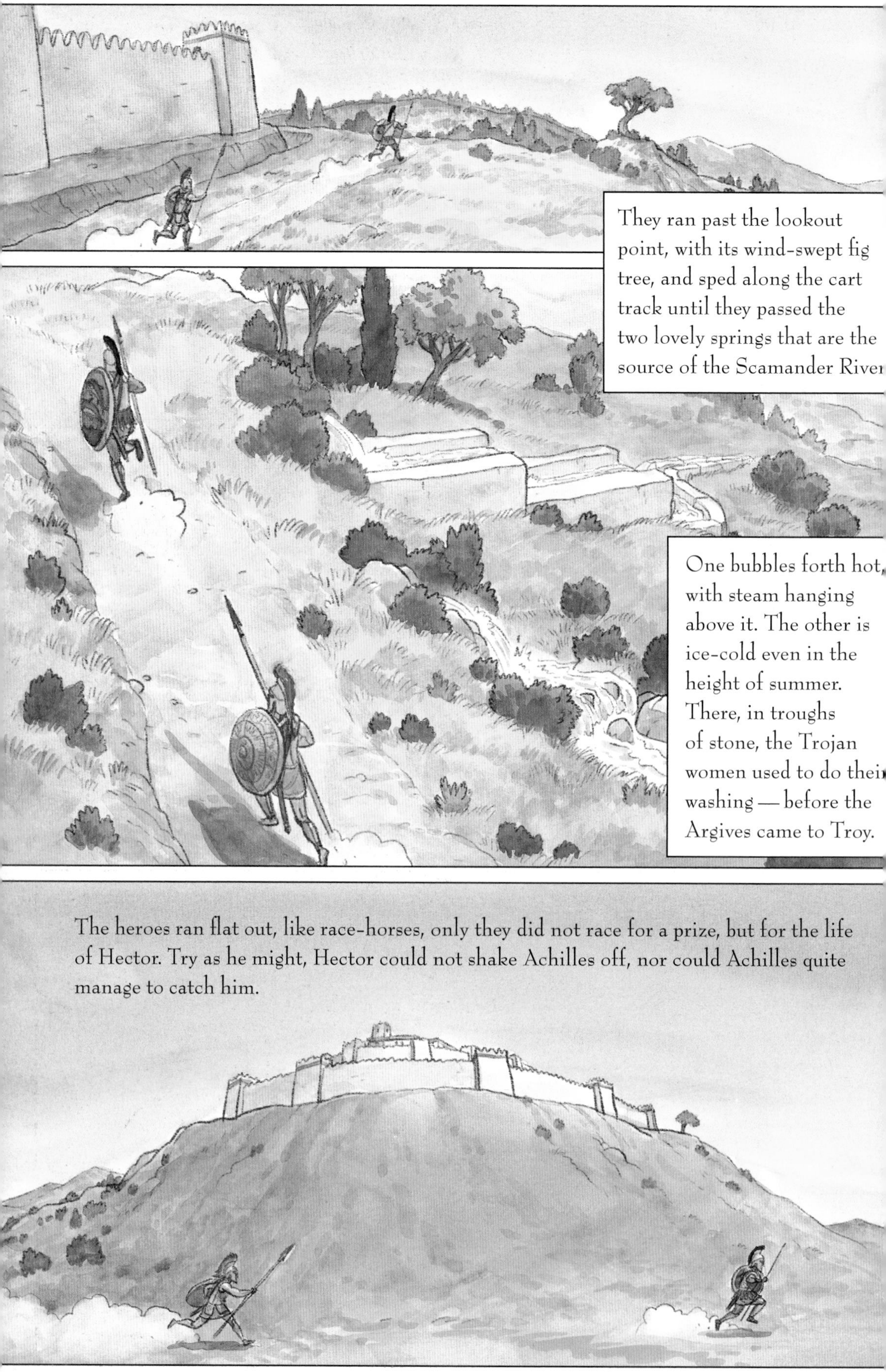
They ran past the lookout point, with its wind-swept fig tree, and sped along the cart track until they passed the two lovely springs that are the source of the Scamander River
One bubbles forth hot, with steam hanging above it. The other is ice-cold even in the height of summer. There, in troughs of stone, the Trojan women used to do their washing — before the Argives came to Troy.
The heroes ran flat out, like race-horses, only they did not race for a prize, but for the life of Hector. Try as he might, Hector could not shake Achilles off, nor could Achilles quite manage to catch him.

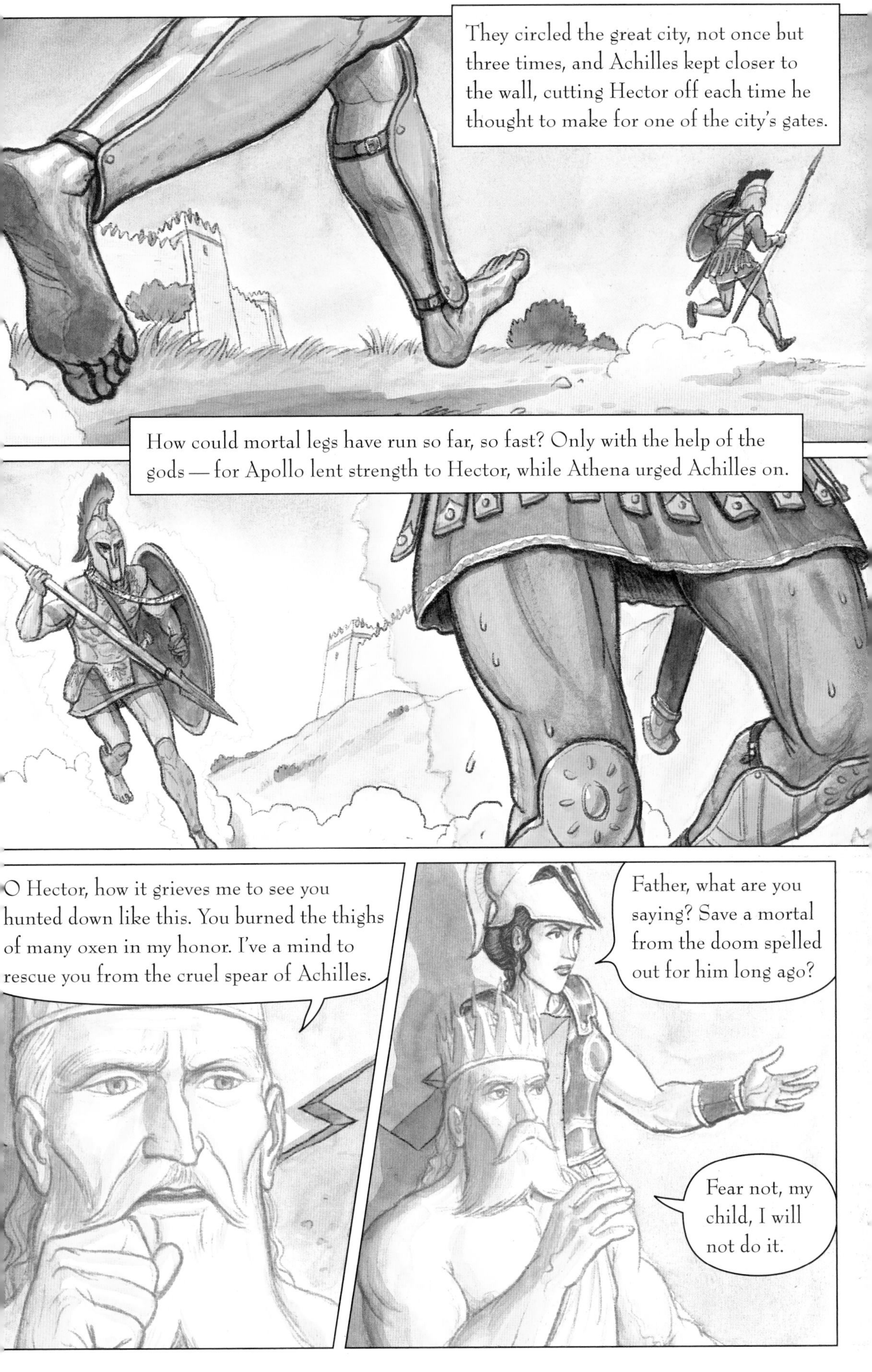
They circled the great city, not once but three times, and Achilles kept closer to the wall, cutting Hector off each time he thought to make for one of the city's gates.
How could mortal legs have run so far, so fast? Only with the help of the gods — for Apollo lent strength to Hector, while Athena urged Achilles on.
O Hector, how it grieves me to see you hunted down like this. You burned the thighs of many oxen in my honor. I've a mind to rescue you from the cruel spear of Achilles.
Father, what are you saying? Save a mortal from the doom spelled out for him long ago?
Fear not, my child, I will not do it.

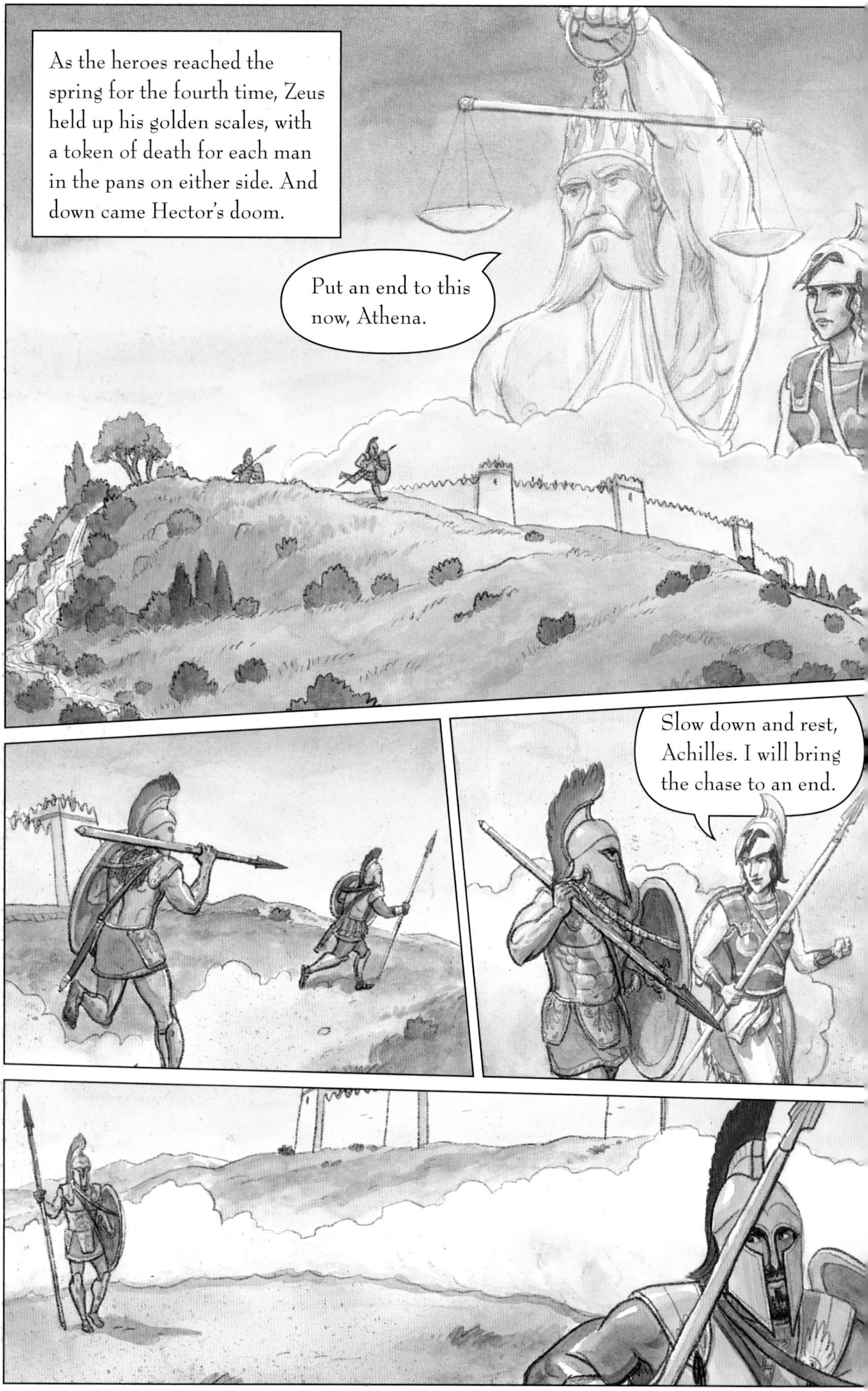
As the heroes reached the spring for the fourth time, Zeus held up his golden scales, with a token of death for each man in the pans on either side. And down came Hector's doom.
Put an end to this now, Athena.
Slow down and rest, Achilles. I will bring the chase to an end.

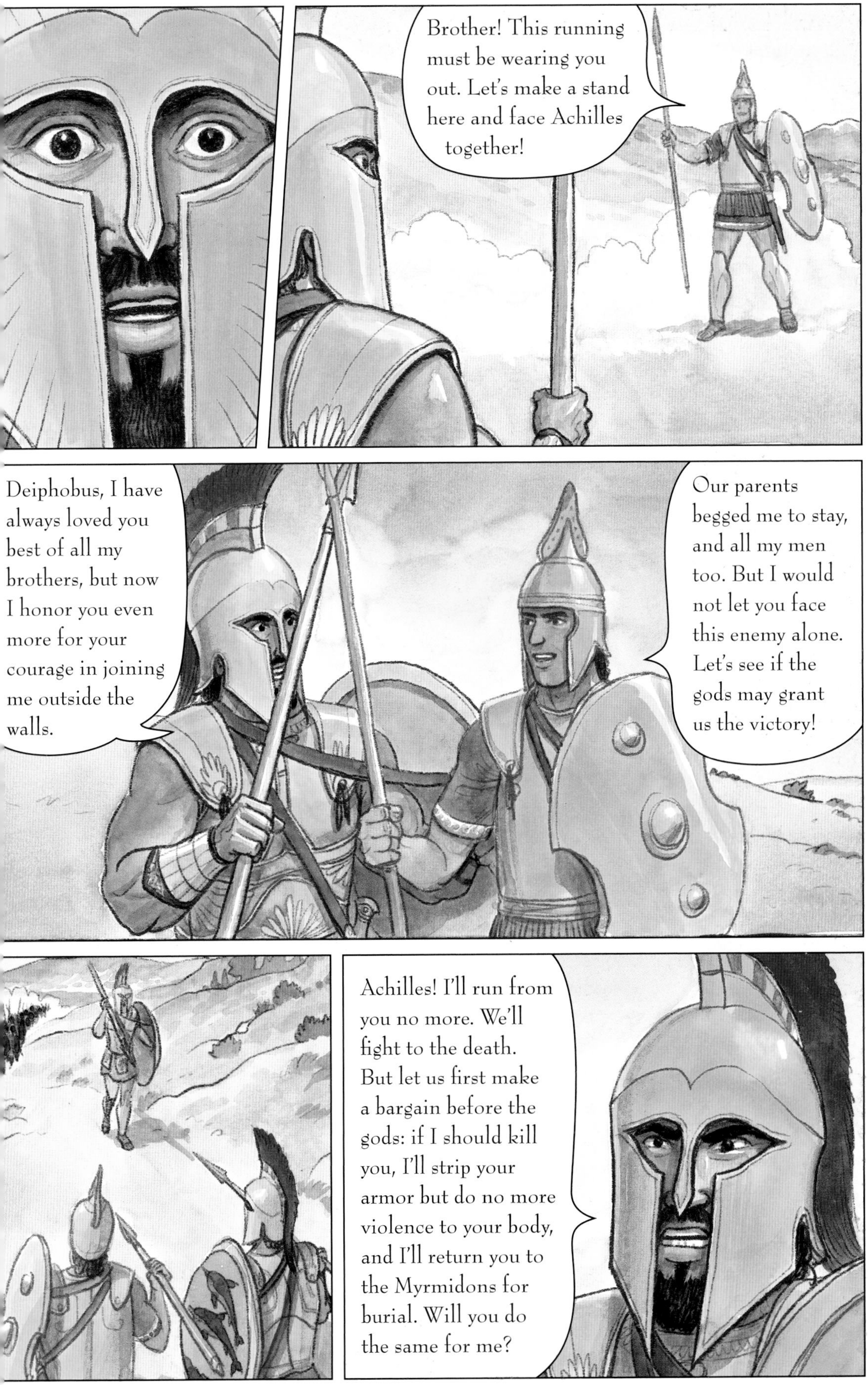
Brother! This running must be wearing you out. Let's make a stand here and face Achilles together!
Deiphobus, I have always loved you best of all my brothers, but now I honor you even more for your courage in joining me outside the walls.
Our parents begged me to stay, and all my men too. But I would not let you face this enemy alone. Let's see if the gods may grant us the victory!
Achilles! I'll run from you no more. We'll fight to the death. But let us first make a bargain before the gods: if I should kill you, I'll strip your armor but do no more violence to your body, and I'll return you to the Myrmidons for burial. Will you do the same for me?

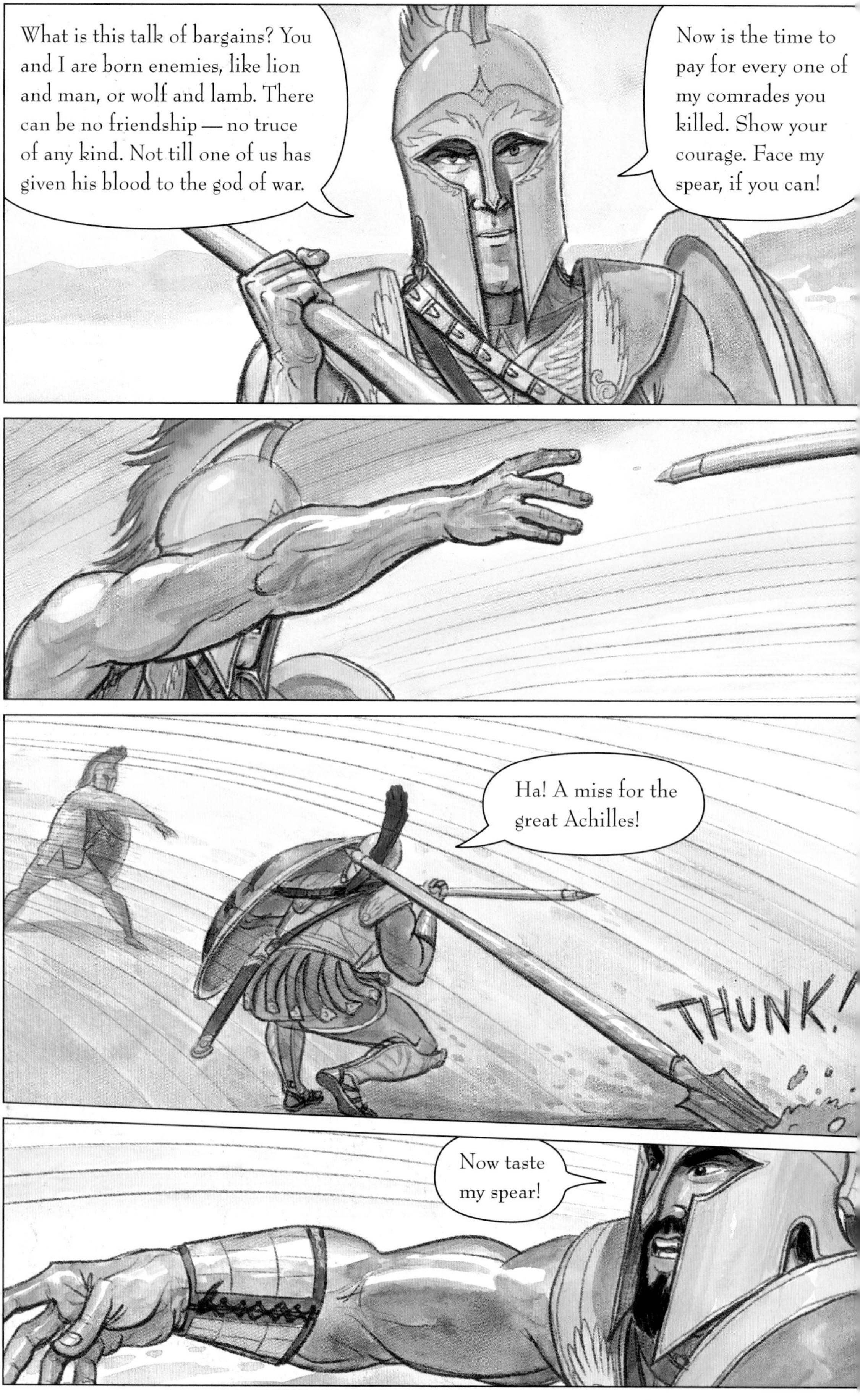
What is this talk of bargains? You and I are born enemies, like lion and man, or wolf and lamb. There can be no friendship — no truce of any kind. Not till one of us has given his blood to the god of war.
Now is the time to pay for every one of my comrades you killed. Show your courage. Face my spear, if you can!
Ha! A miss for the great Achilles!
THUNK!
Now taste my spear!

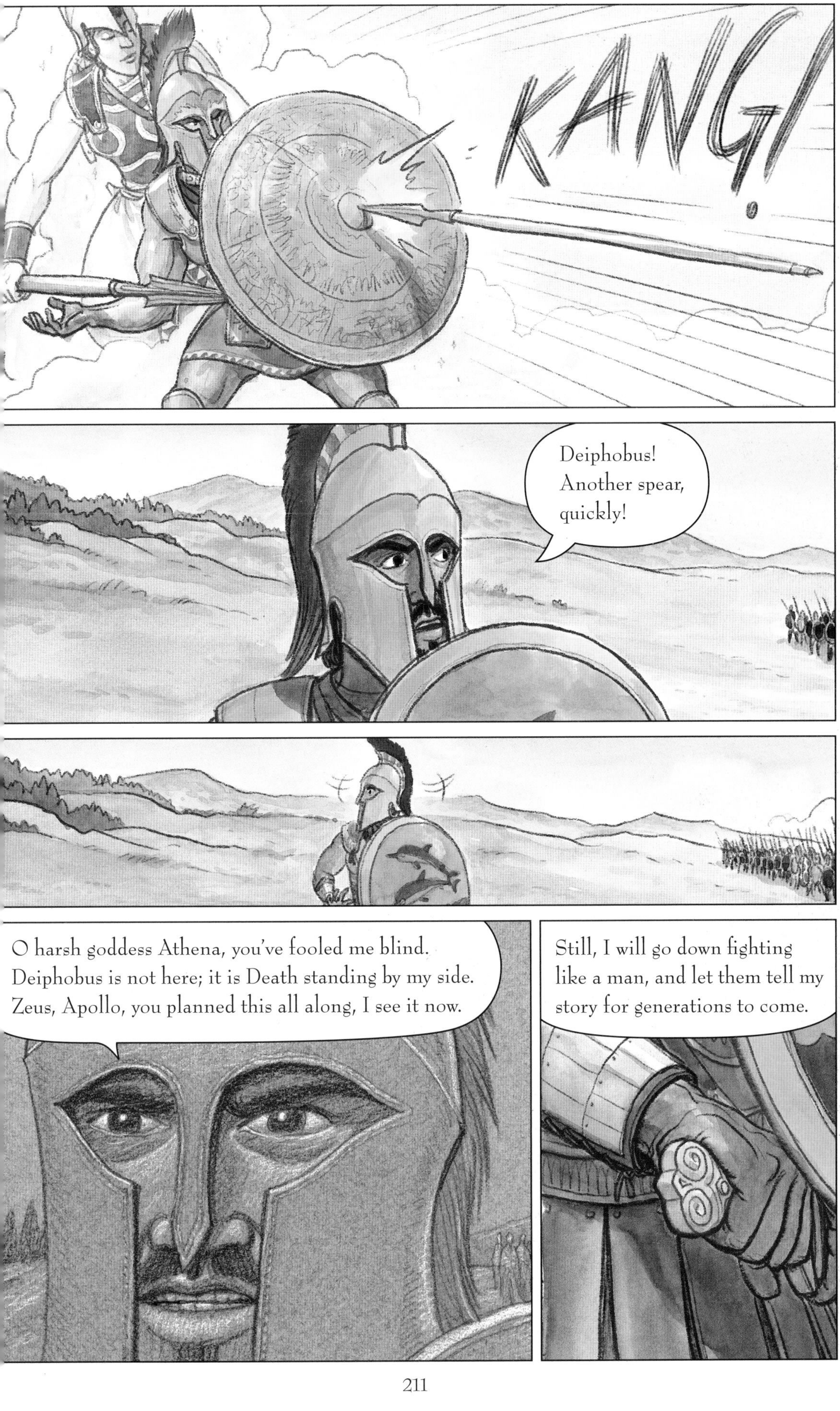
KANG!
Deiphobus! Another spear, quickly!
O harsh goddess Athena, you've fooled me blind. Deiphobus is not here; it is Death standing by my side. Zeus, Apollo, you planned this all along, I see it now.
Still, I will go down fighting like a man, and let them tell my story for generations to come.

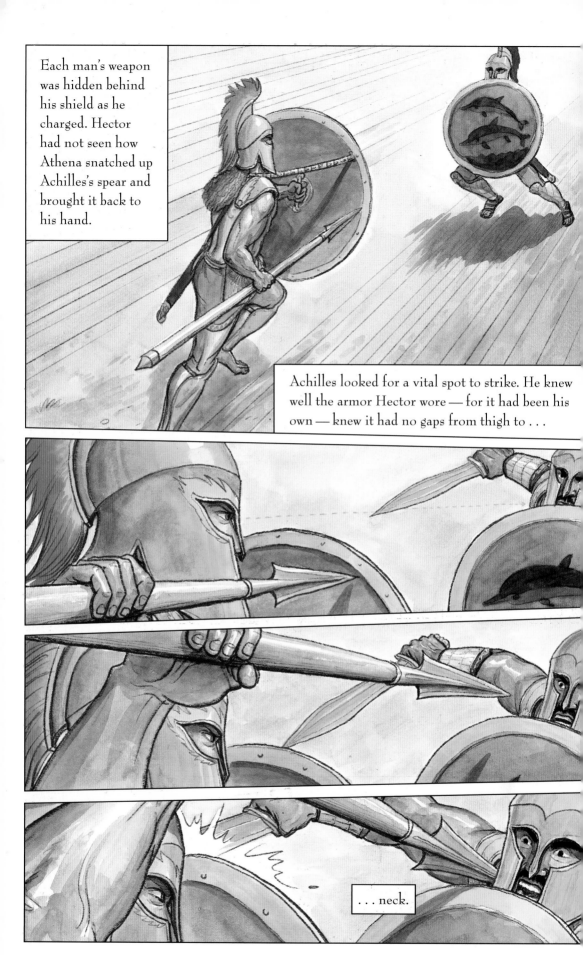

Each man's weapon was hidden behind his shield as he charged. Hector had not seen how Athena snatched up Achilles's spear and brought it back to his hand.

Achilles looked for a vital spot to strike. He knew well the armor Hector wore — for it had been his own — knew it had no gaps from thigh to . . .

. . . neck.

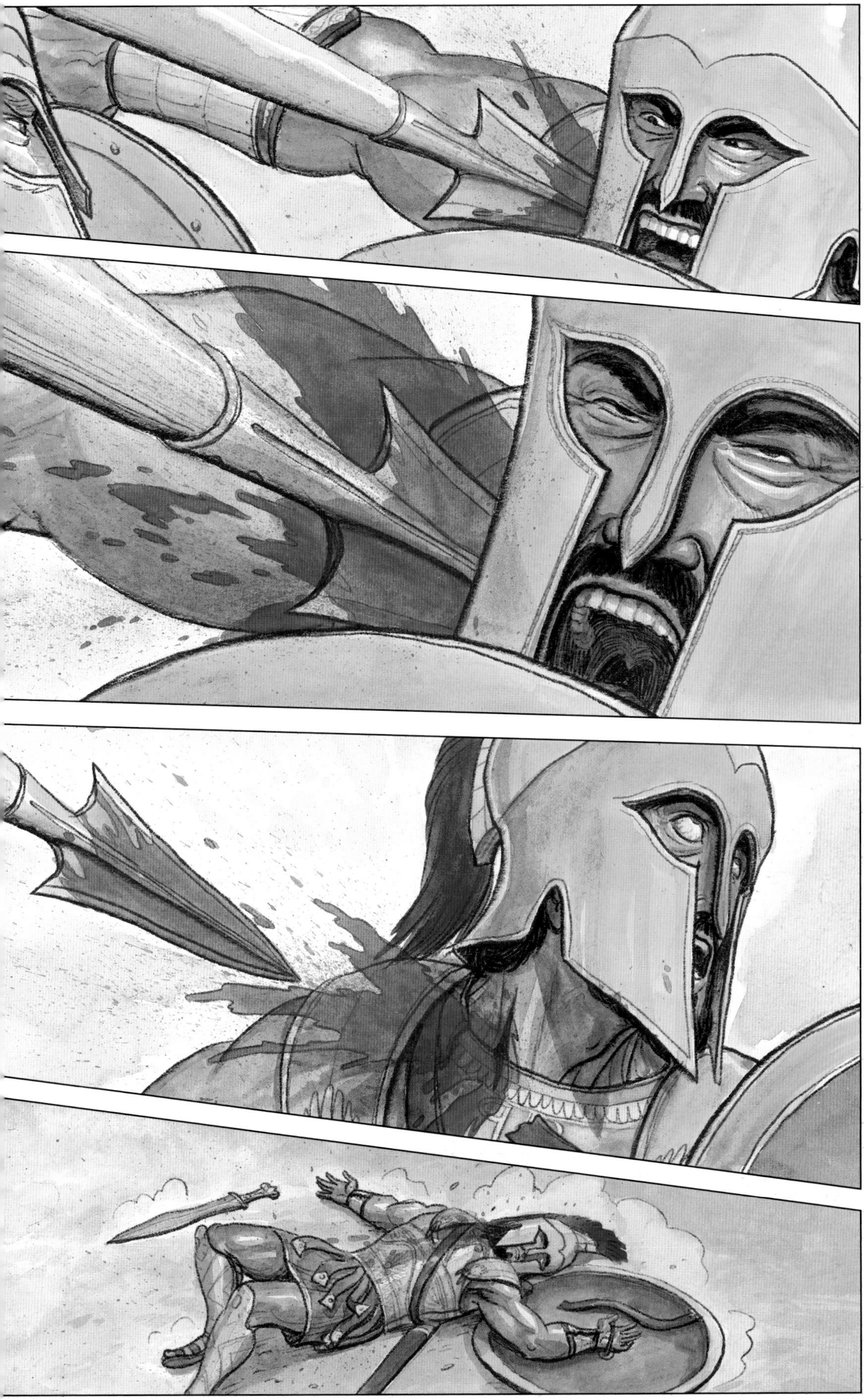

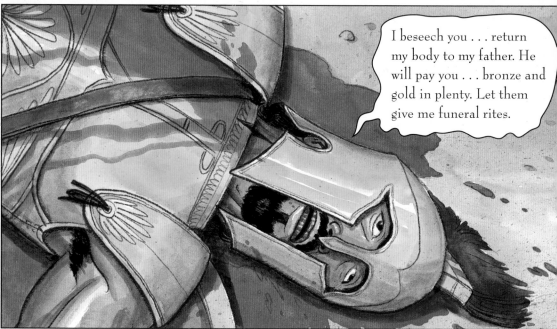

I beseech you . . . return my body to my father. He will pay you . . . bronze and gold in plenty. Let them give me funeral rites.

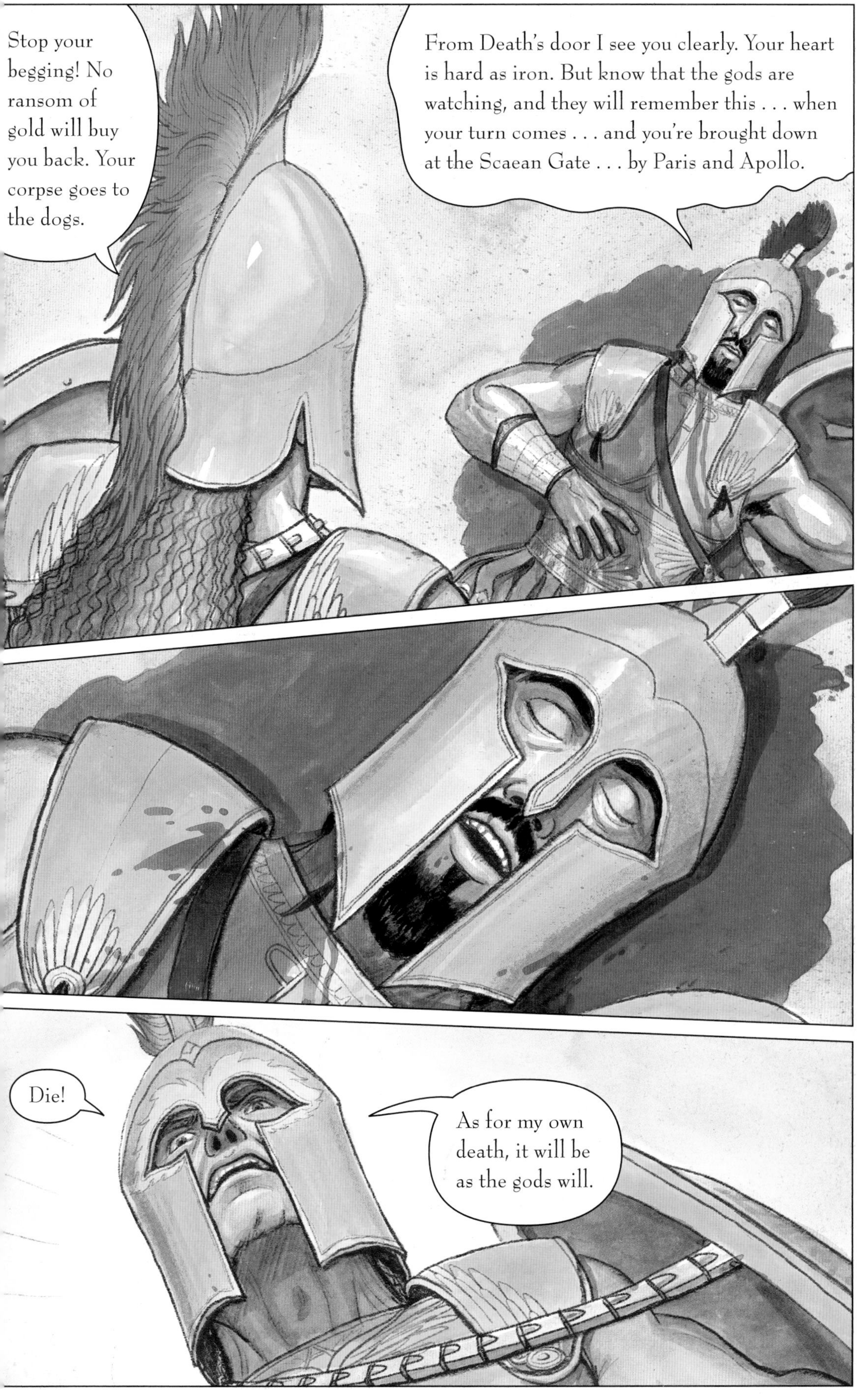
Stop your begging! No ransom of gold will buy you back. Your corpse goes to the dogs.
From Death's door I see you clearly. Your heart is hard as iron. But know that the gods are watching, and they will remember this . . . when your turn comes . . . and you're brought down at the Scaean Gate . . . by Paris and Apollo.
Die!
As for my own death, it will be as the gods will.

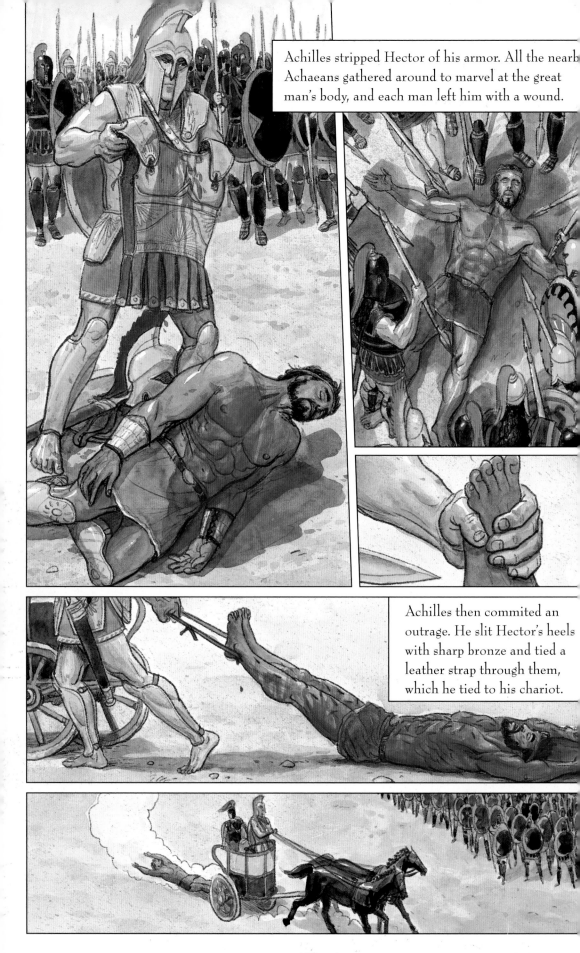

Achilles stripped Hector of his armor. All the near[b]
Achaeans gathered around to marvel at the great
man's body, and each man left him with a wound.

Achilles then commited an
outrage. He slit Hector's heels
with sharp bronze and tied a
leather strap through them,
which he tied to his chariot.

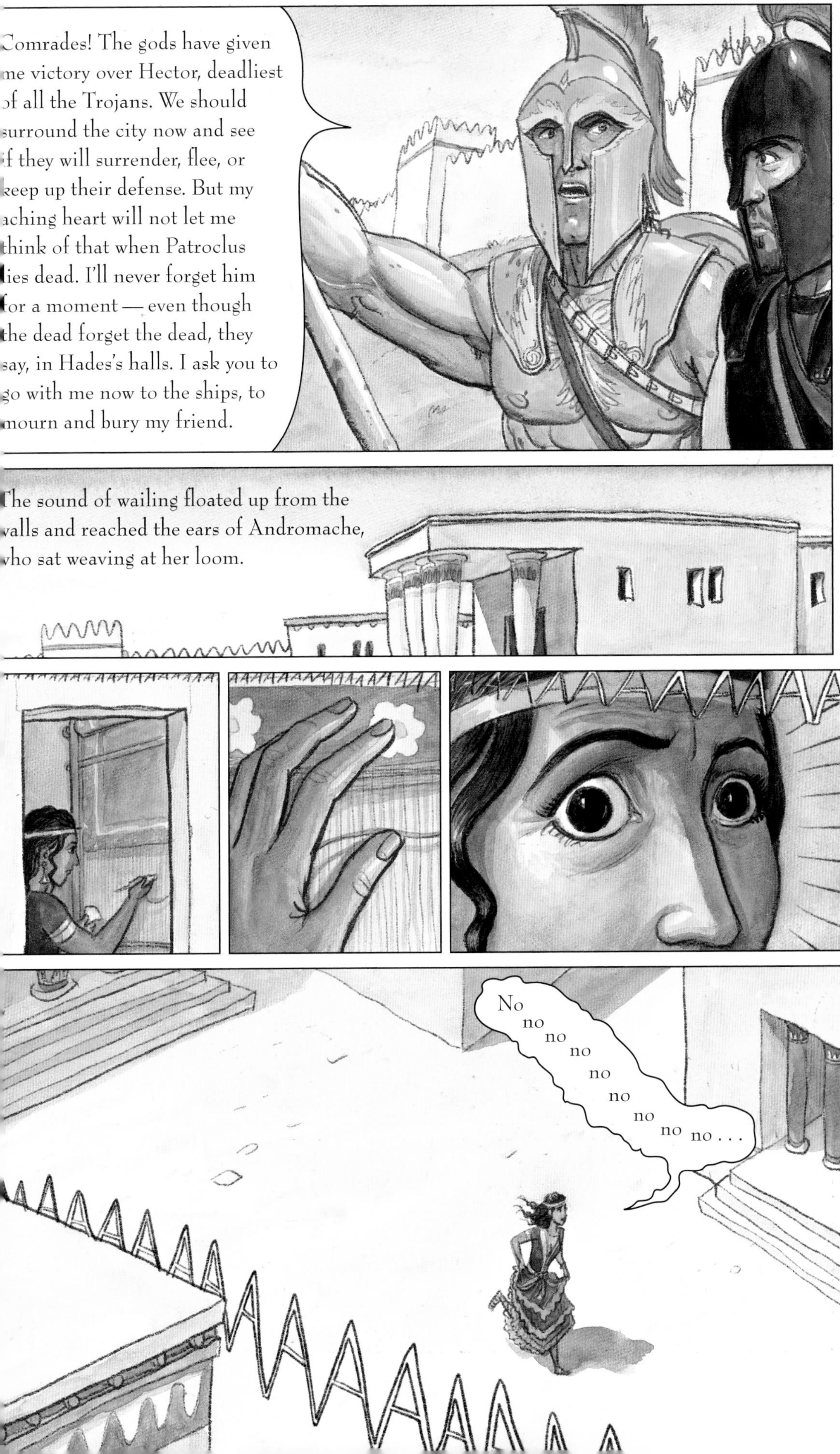
Comrades! The gods have given me victory over Hector, deadliest of all the Trojans. We should surround the city now and see if they will surrender, flee, or keep up their defense. But my aching heart will not let me think of that when Patroclus lies dead. I'll never forget him for a moment — even though the dead forget the dead, they say, in Hades's halls. I ask you to go with me now to the ships, to mourn and bury my friend.
The sound of wailing floated up from the walls and reached the ears of Andromache, who sat weaving at her loom.
No no no no no no no no no . . .

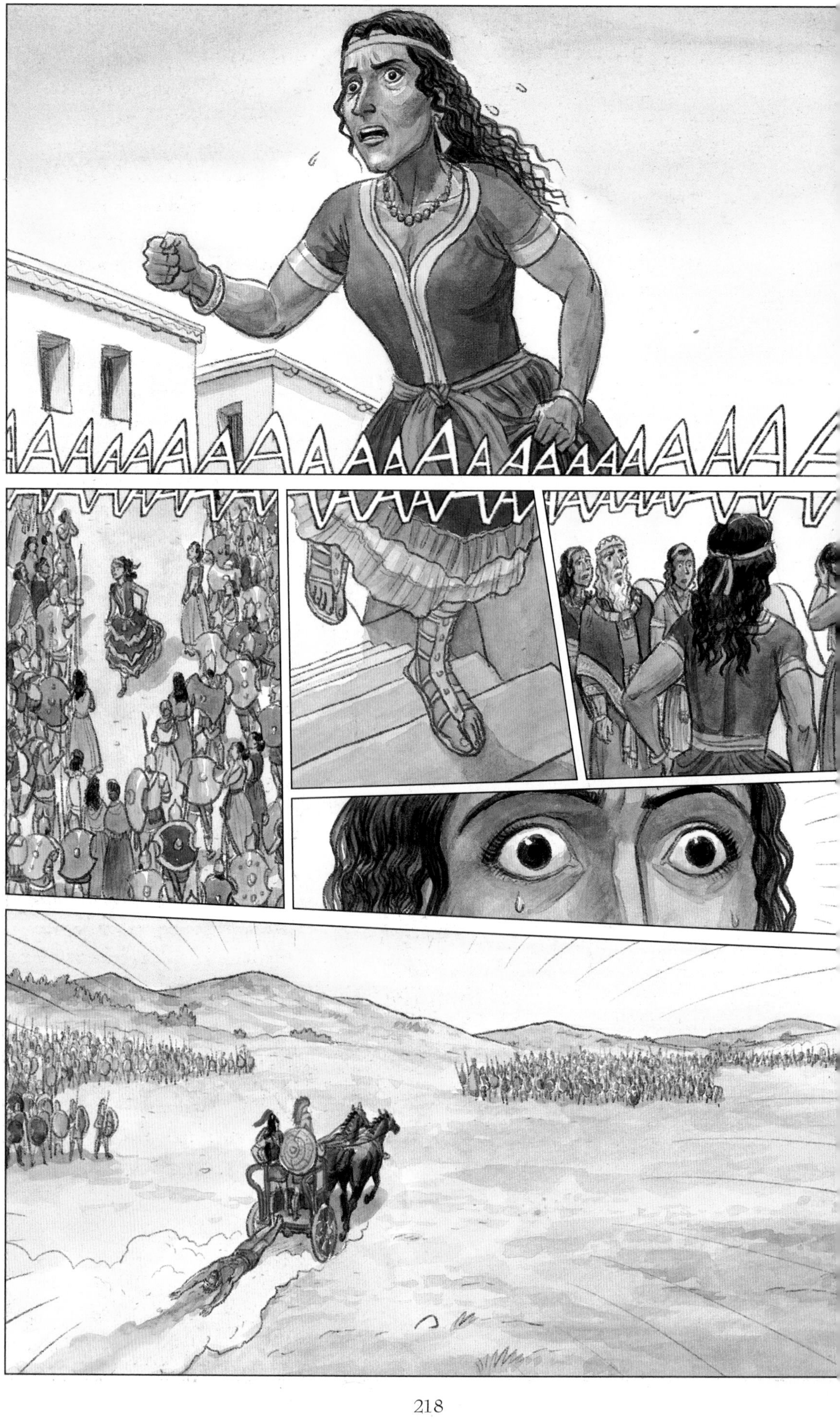
AAAAAAAAAAAAAAAAAAAAAAA

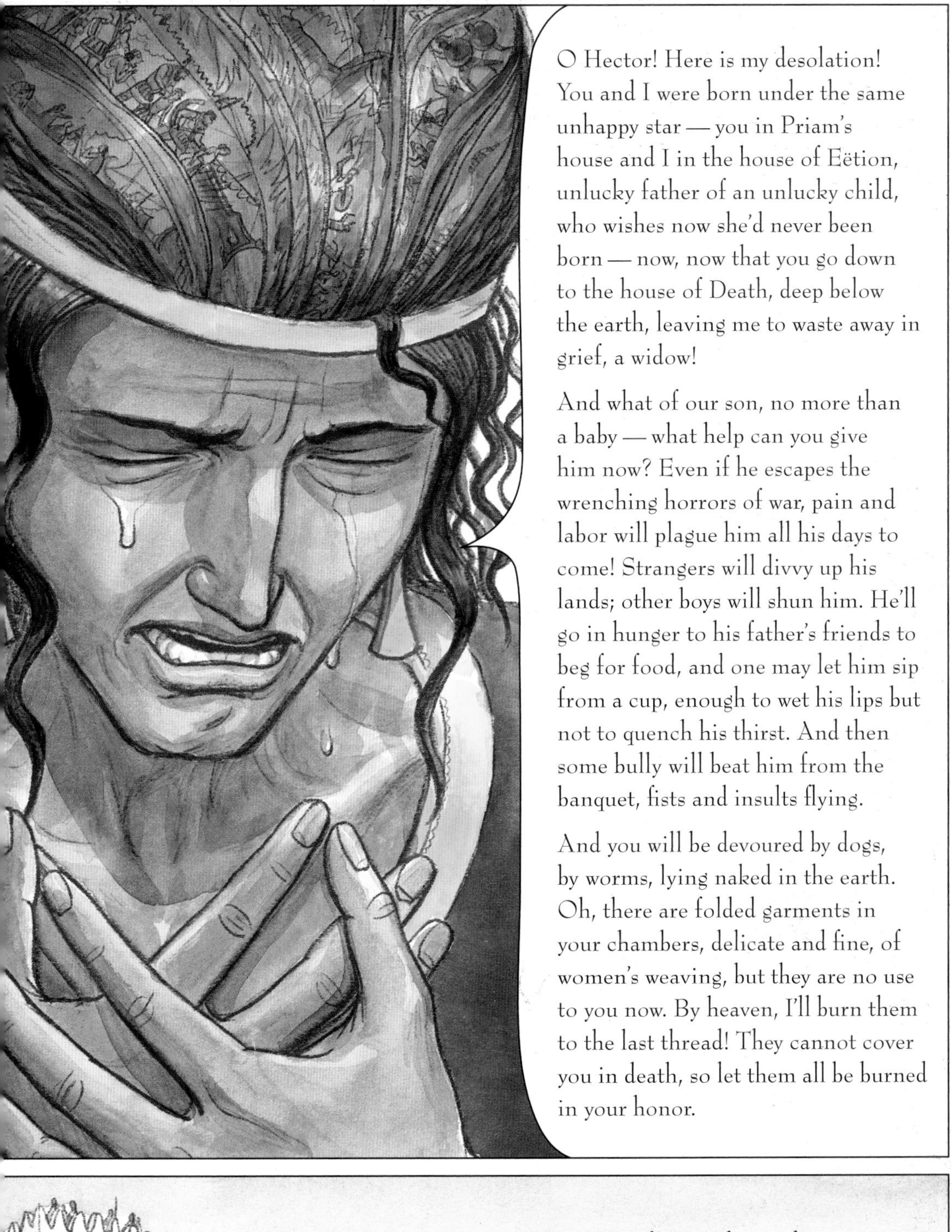
O Hector! Here is my desolation! You and I were born under the same unhappy star — you in Priam's house and I in the house of Eëtion, unlucky father of an unlucky child, who wishes now she'd never been born — now, now that you go down to the house of Death, deep below the earth, leaving me to waste away in grief, a widow!
And what of our son, no more than a baby — what help can you give him now? Even if he escapes the wrenching horrors of war, pain and labor will plague him all his days to come! Strangers will divvy up his lands; other boys will shun him. He'll go in hunger to his father's friends to beg for food, and one may let him sip from a cup, enough to wet his lips but not to quench his thirst. And then some bully will beat him from the banquet, fists and insults flying.
And you will be devoured by dogs, by worms, lying naked in the earth. Oh, there are folded garments in your chambers, delicate and fine, of women's weaving, but they are no use to you now. By heaven, I'll burn them to the last thread! They cannot cover you in death, so let them all be burned in your honor.

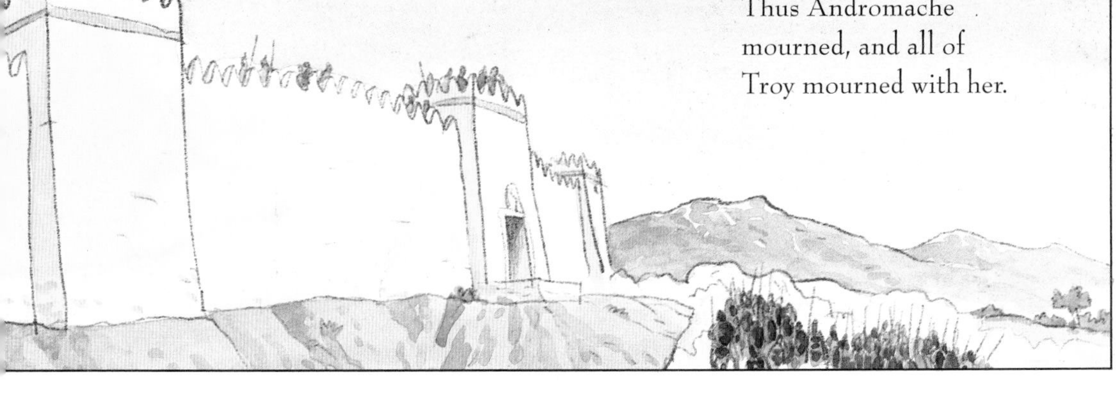
Thus Andromache mourned, and all of Troy mourned with her.

As the Trojans lamented Hector, so too the Achaeans lamented Patroclus, when they had returned to their ships. Three times the Myrmidons circled his body, wailing and shedding salt tears for the man they loved.

Achilles ordered a funeral feast, and by the body of Patroclus sleek oxen, sheep, and fatted pigs were sacrificed and roasted over open flame, and the fighters ate their fill.

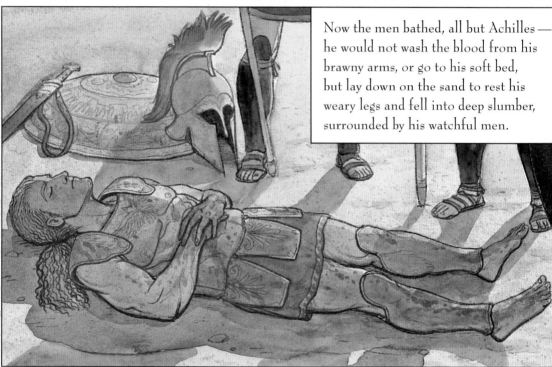

Now the men bathed, all but Achilles — he would not wash the blood from his brawny arms, or go to his soft bed, but lay down on the sand to rest his weary legs and fell into deep slumber, surrounded by his watchful men.

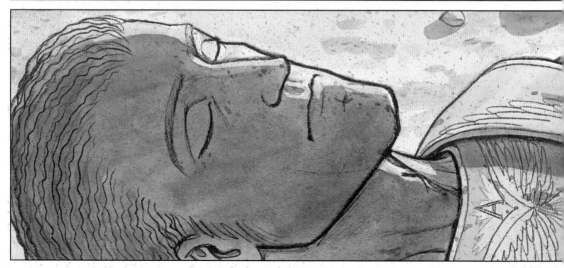

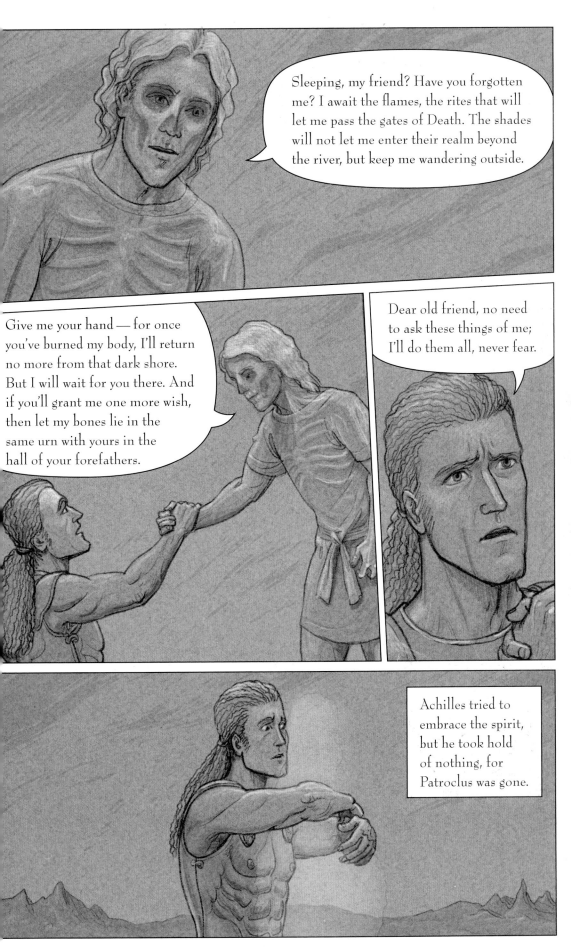

Sleeping, my friend? Have you forgotten me? I await the flames, the rites that will let me pass the gates of Death. The shades will not let me enter their realm beyond the river, but keep me wandering outside.

Give me your hand — for once you've burned my body, I'll return no more from that dark shore. But I will wait for you there. And if you'll grant me one more wish, then let my bones lie in the same urn with yours in the hall of your forefathers.

Dear old friend, no need to ask these things of me; I'll do them all, never fear.

Achilles tried to embrace the spirit, but he took hold of nothing, for Patroclus was gone.

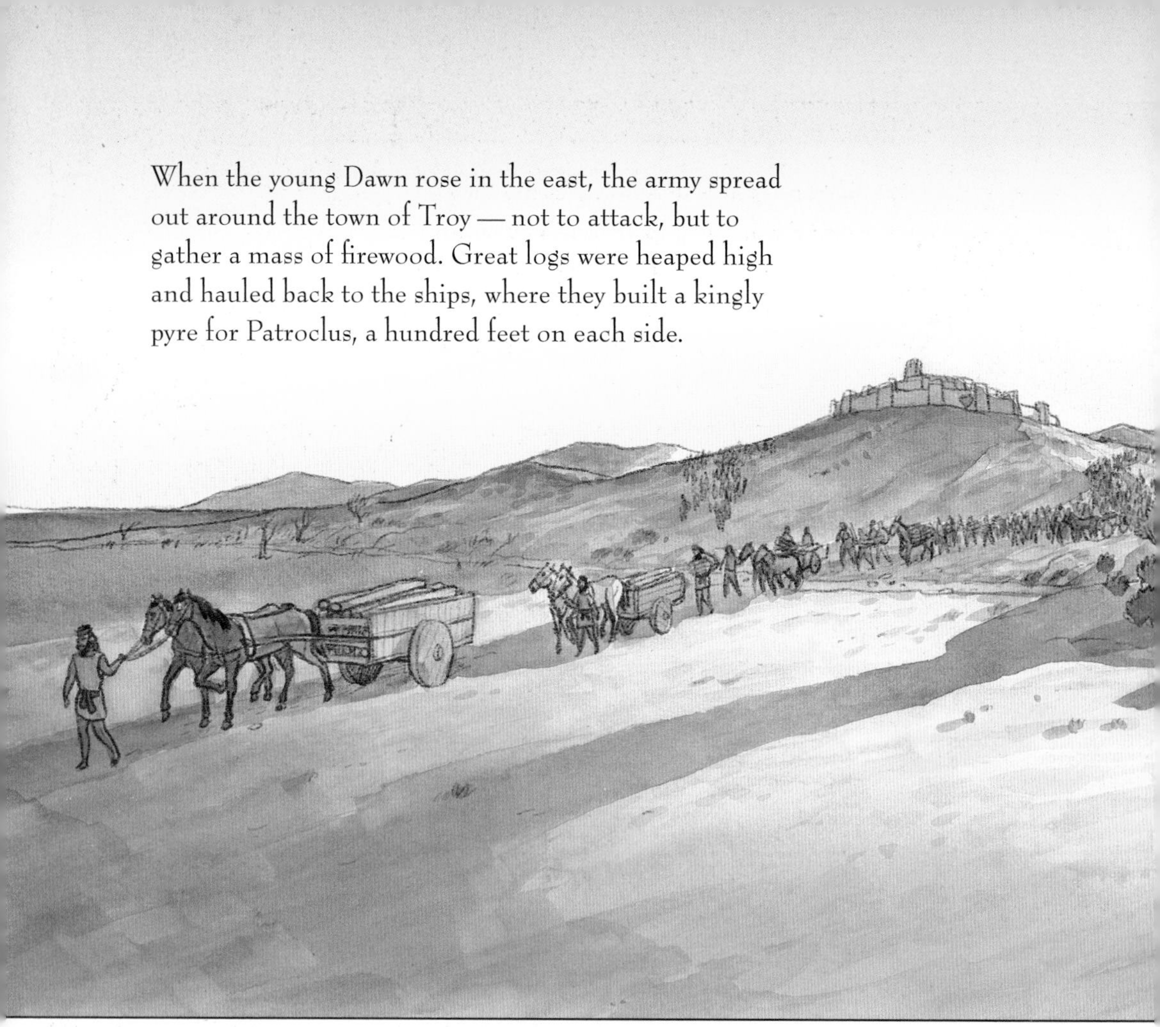
When the young Dawn rose in the east, the army spread out around the town of Troy — not to attack, but to gather a mass of firewood. Great logs were heaped high and hauled back to the ships, where they built a kingly pyre for Patroclus, a hundred feet on each side.

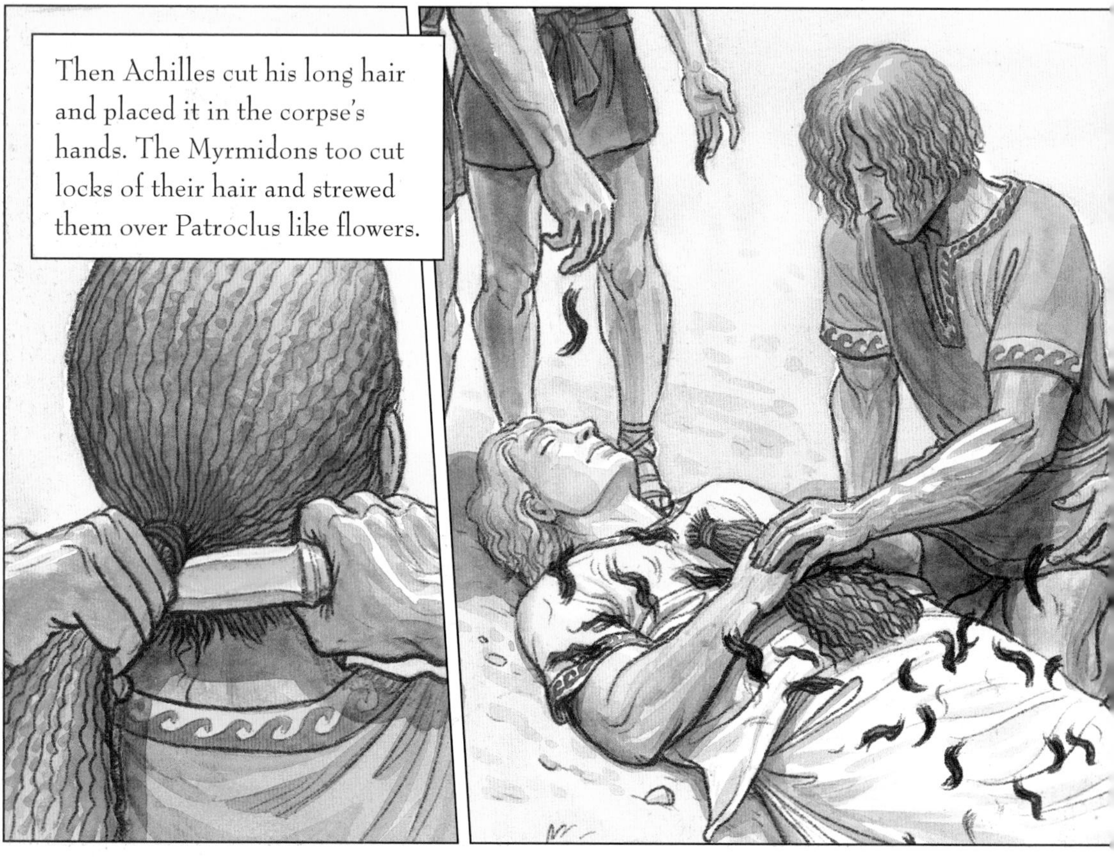
Then Achilles cut his long hair and placed it in the corpse's hands. The Myrmidons too cut locks of their hair and strewed them over Patroclus like flowers.

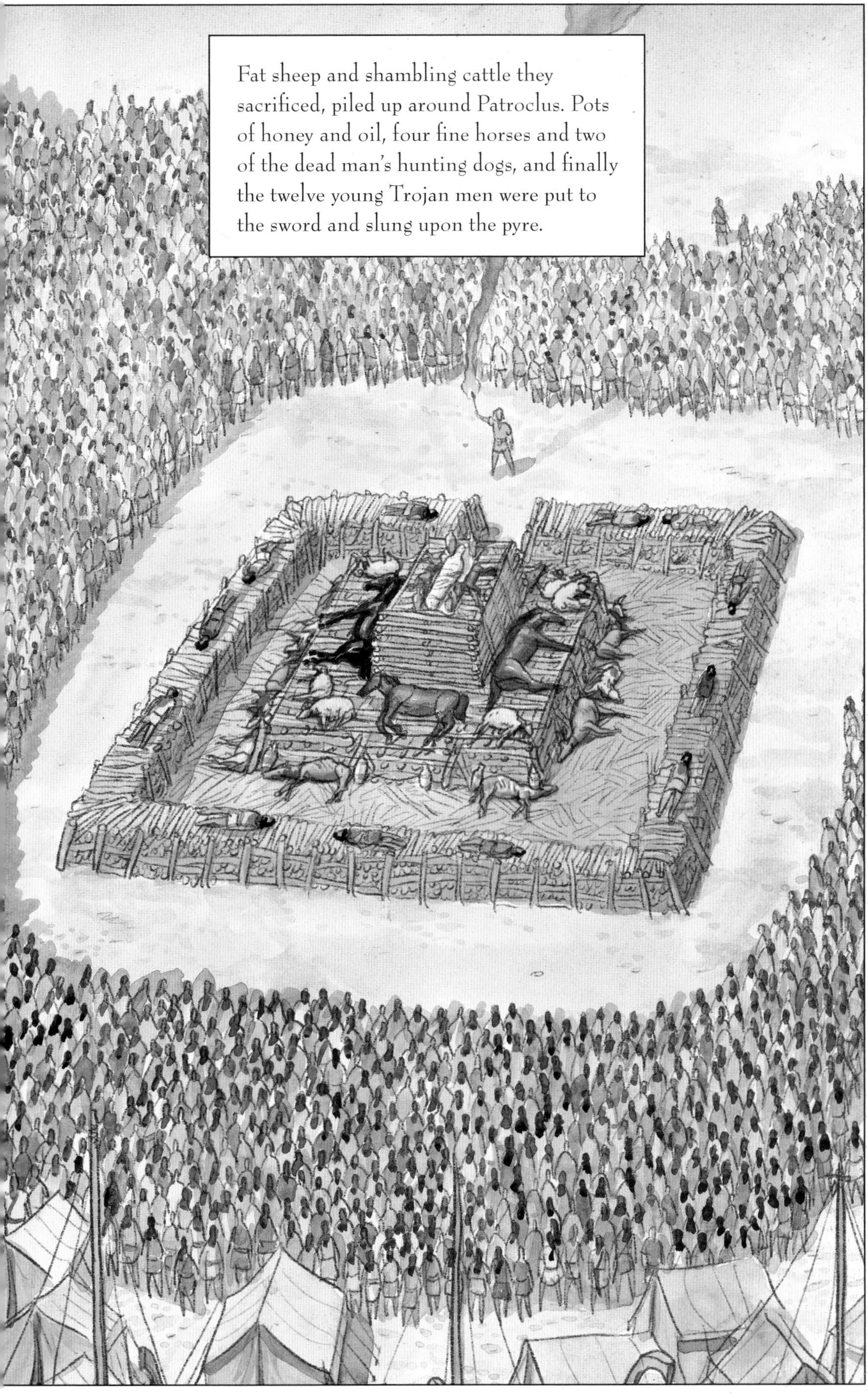
Fat sheep and shambling cattle they sacrificed, piled up around Patroclus. Pots of honey and oil, four fine horses and two of the dead man's hunting dogs, and finally the twelve young Trojan men were put to the sword and slung upon the pyre.

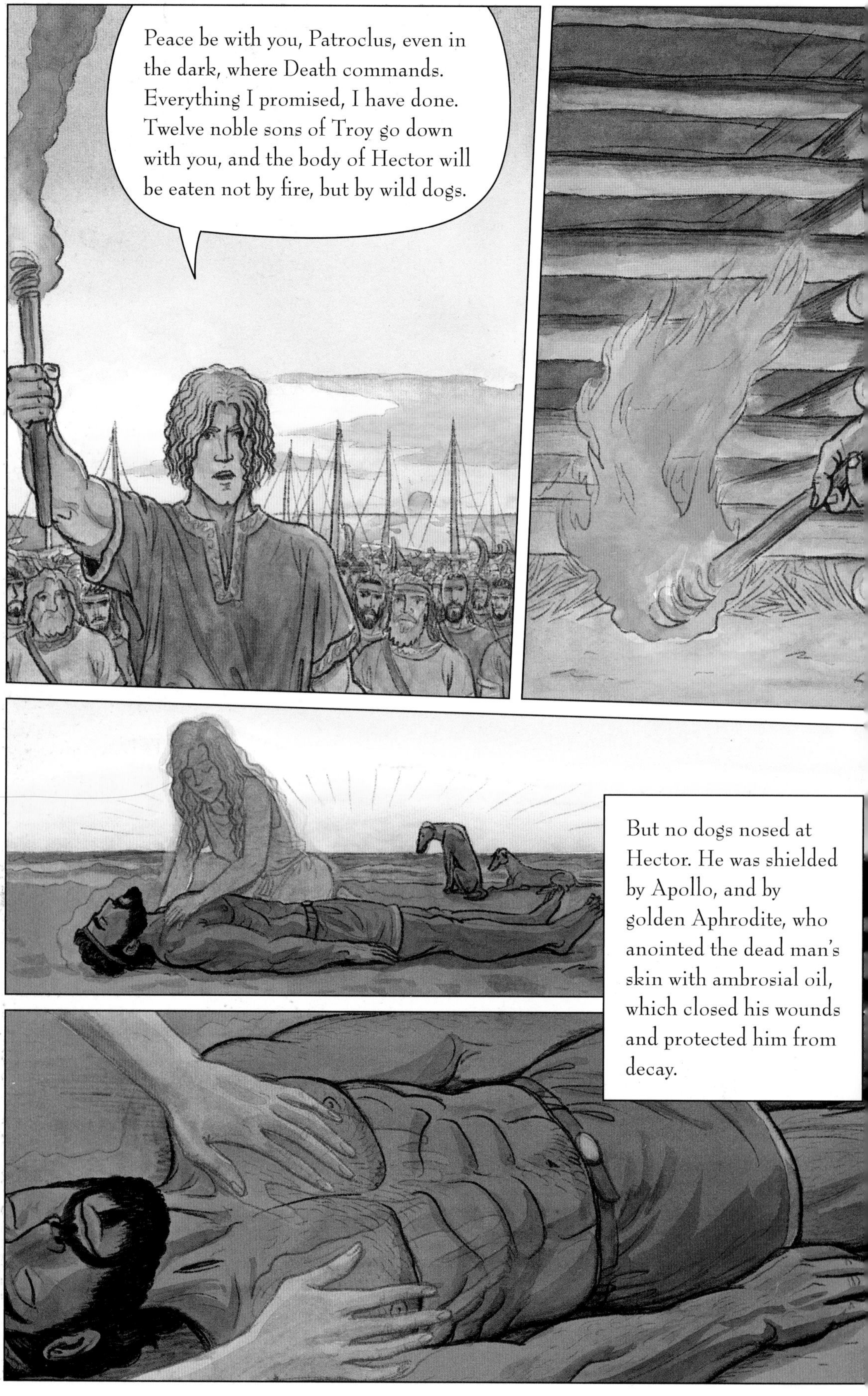
Peace be with you, Patroclus, even in the dark, where Death commands. Everything I promised, I have done. Twelve noble sons of Troy go down with you, and the body of Hector will be eaten not by fire, but by wild dogs.
But no dogs nosed at Hector. He was shielded by Apollo, and by golden Aphrodite, who anointed the dead man's skin with ambrosial oil, which closed his wounds and protected him from decay.

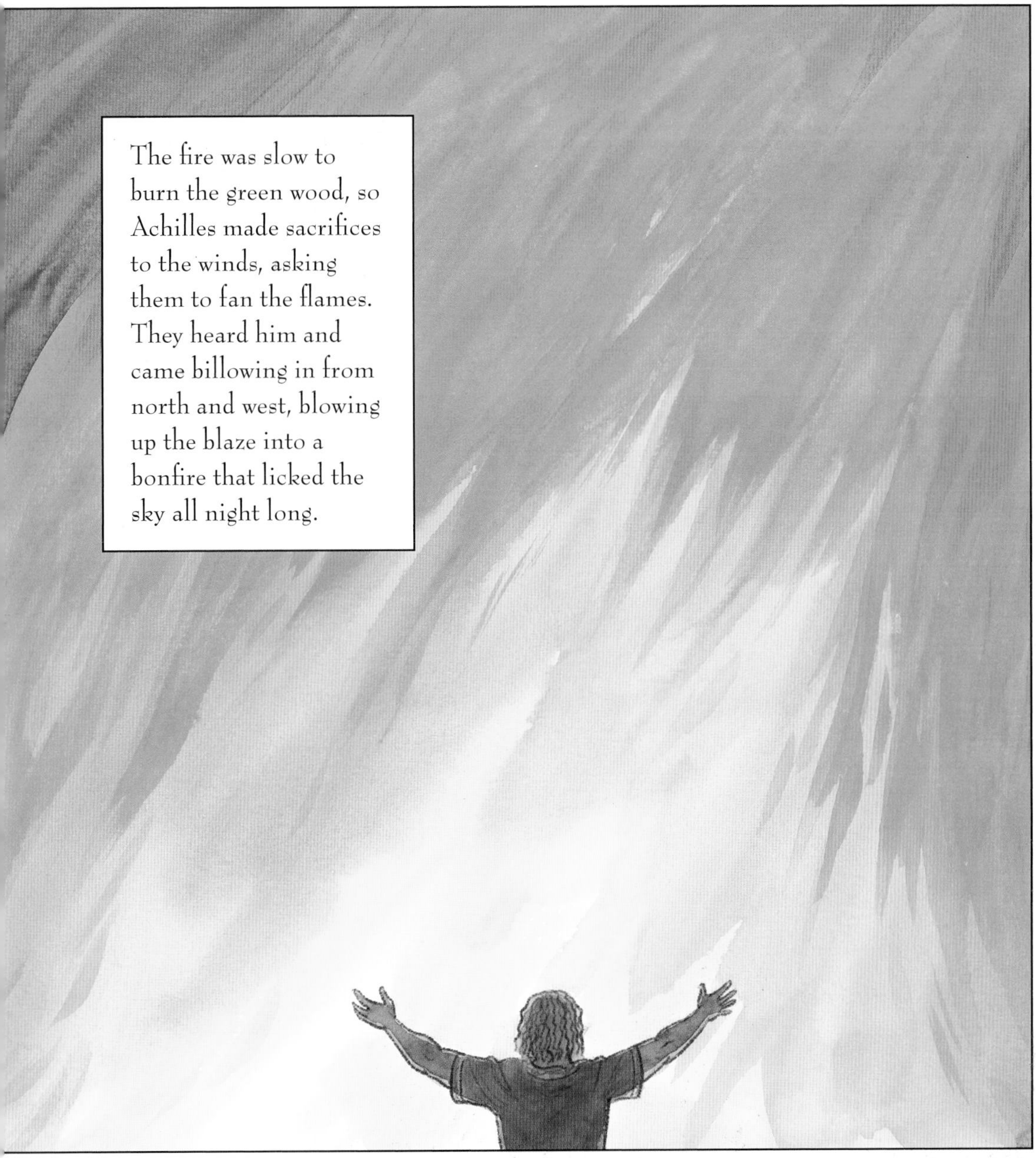
The fire was slow to burn the green wood, so Achilles made sacrifices to the winds, asking them to fan the flames. They heard him and came billowing in from north and west, blowing up the blaze into a bonfire that licked the sky all night long.

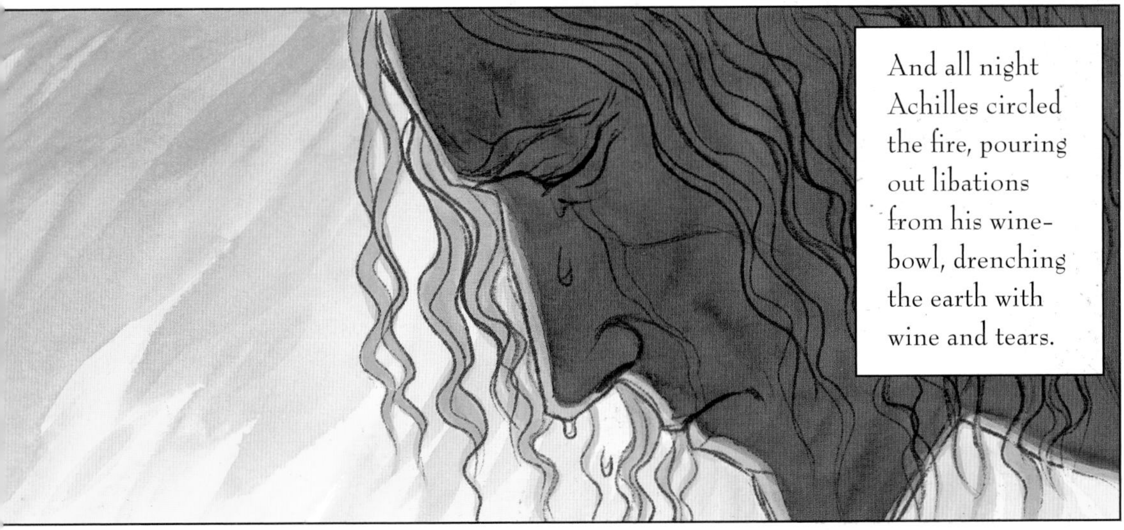
And all night Achilles circled the fire, pouring out libations from his wine-bowl, drenching the earth with wine and tears.

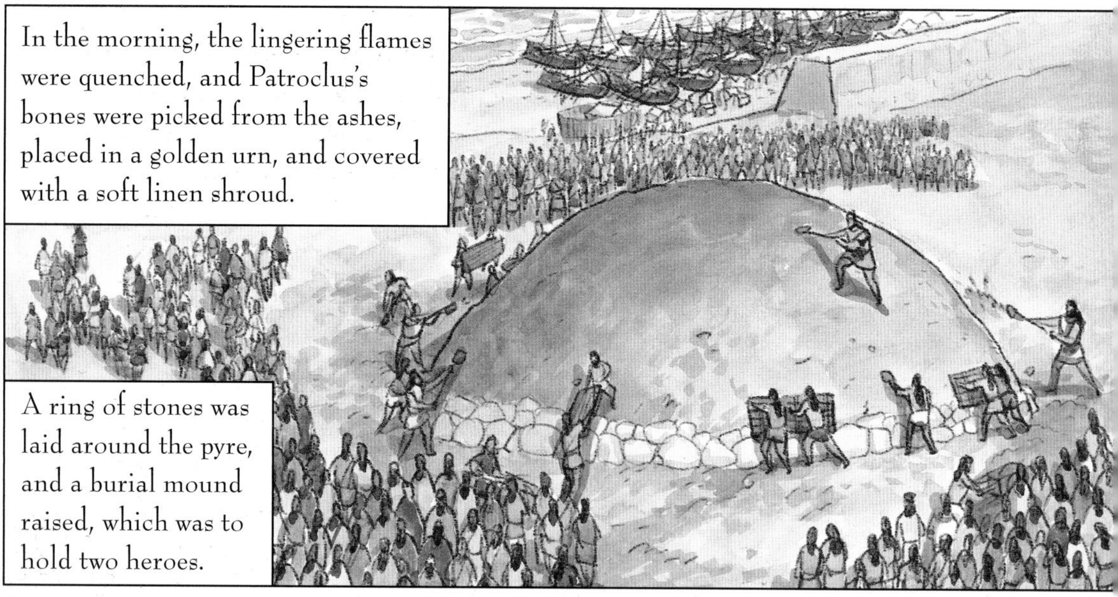
In the morning, the lingering flames were quenched, and Patroclus's bones were picked from the ashes, placed in a golden urn, and covered with a soft linen shroud.
A ring of stones was laid around the pyre, and a burial mound raised, which was to hold two heroes.

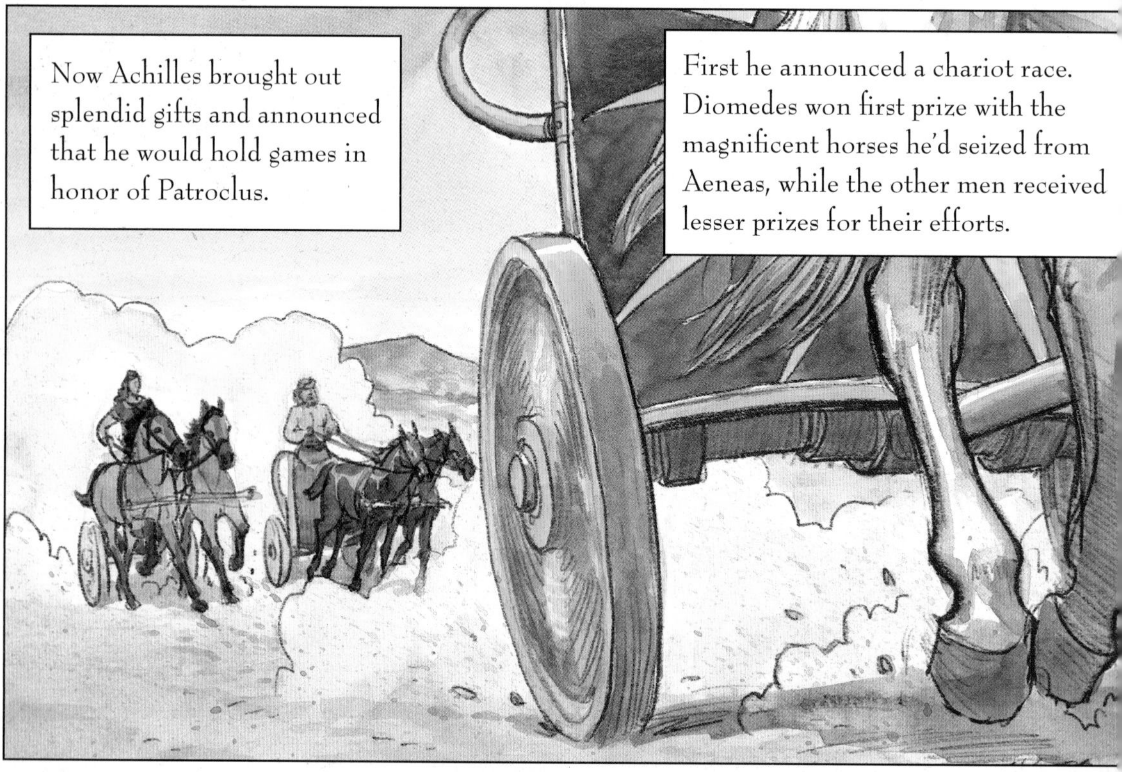
Now Achilles brought out splendid gifts and announced that he would hold games in honor of Patroclus.
First he announced a chariot race. Diomedes won first prize with the magnificent horses he'd seized from Aeneas, while the other men received lesser prizes for their efforts.

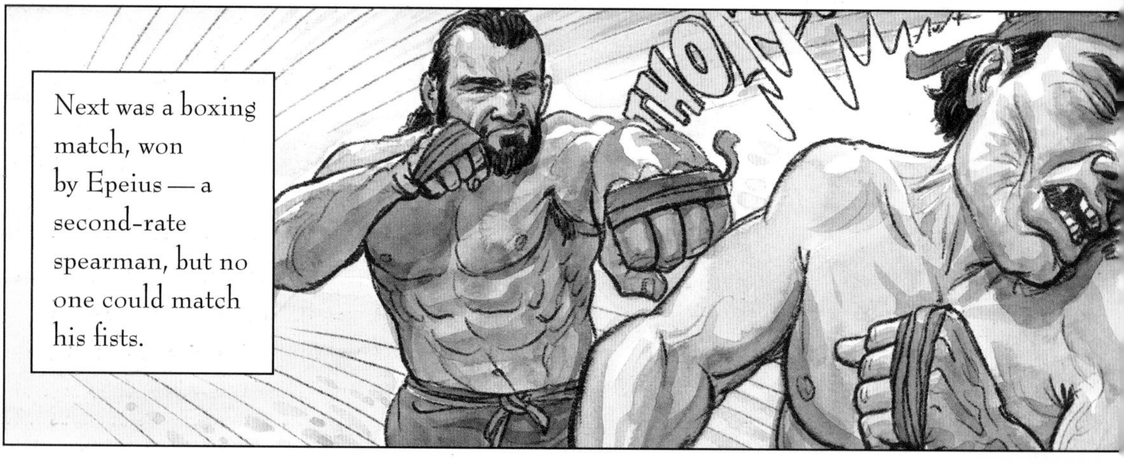
Next was a boxing match, won by Epeius — a second-rate spearman, but no one could match his fists.

Then Great Ajax and Odysseus wrestled to a tie. Odysseus could not lift the giant, but tripped him each time Ajax tried for a throw, so that they both fell together.

Odysseus also won the footrace, even though he was the oldest competitor — for the gray-eyed goddess stood by him as always.

Polypoetes, leader of the Thessalonians, won a lump of meteoric iron by throwing it farther even than Great Ajax could manage.

Achilles tied a pigeon to a tall pole and challenged the best archers to hit it. Teucer's arrow cut the cord that bound the bird, but Meriones swiftly shot it through the wing as it flew for freedom.

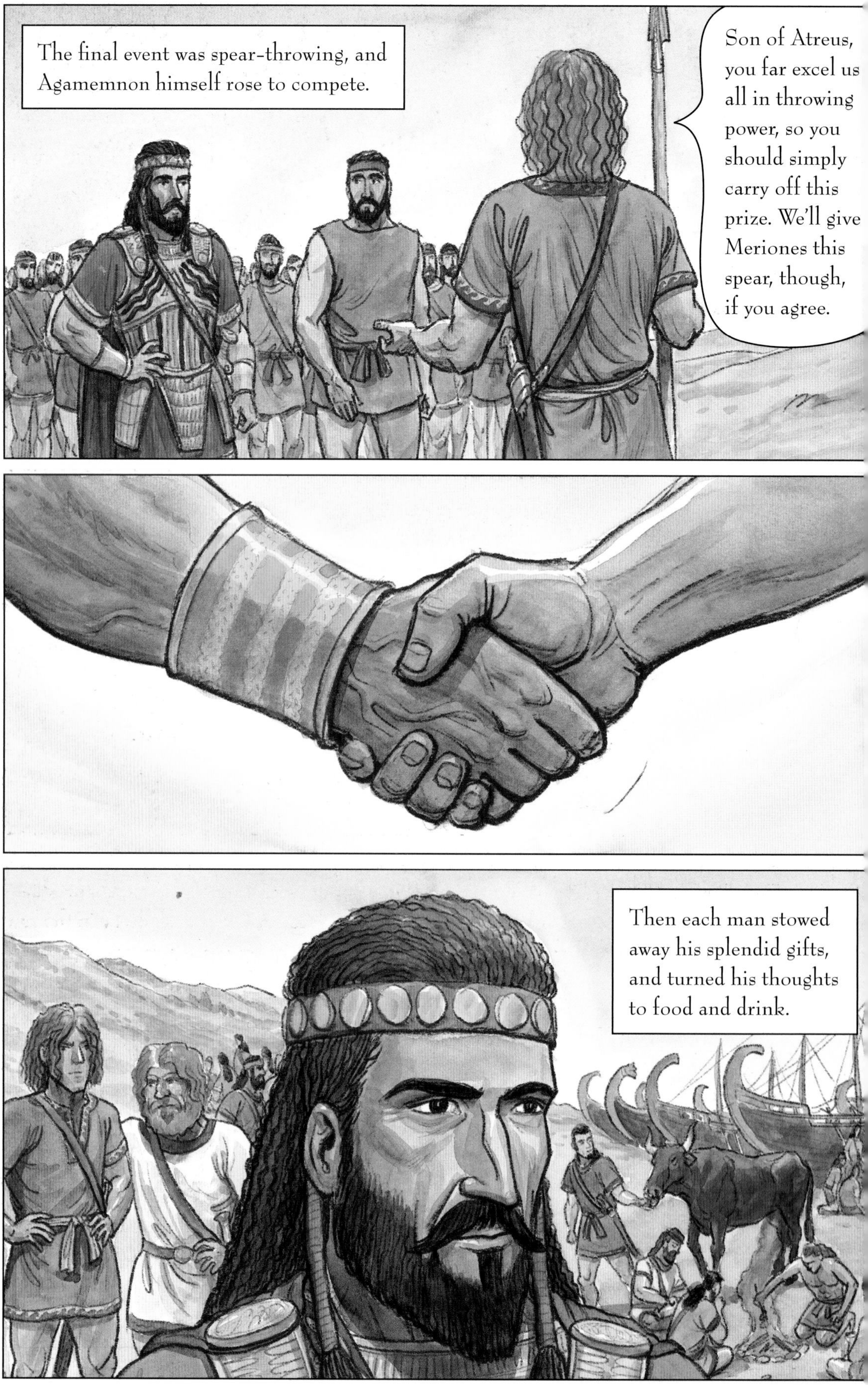
The final event was spear-throwing, and Agamemnon himself rose to compete.
Son of Atreus, you far excel us all in throwing power, so you should simply carry off this prize. We'll give Meriones this spear, though, if you agree.
Then each man stowed away his splendid gifts, and turned his thoughts to food and drink.

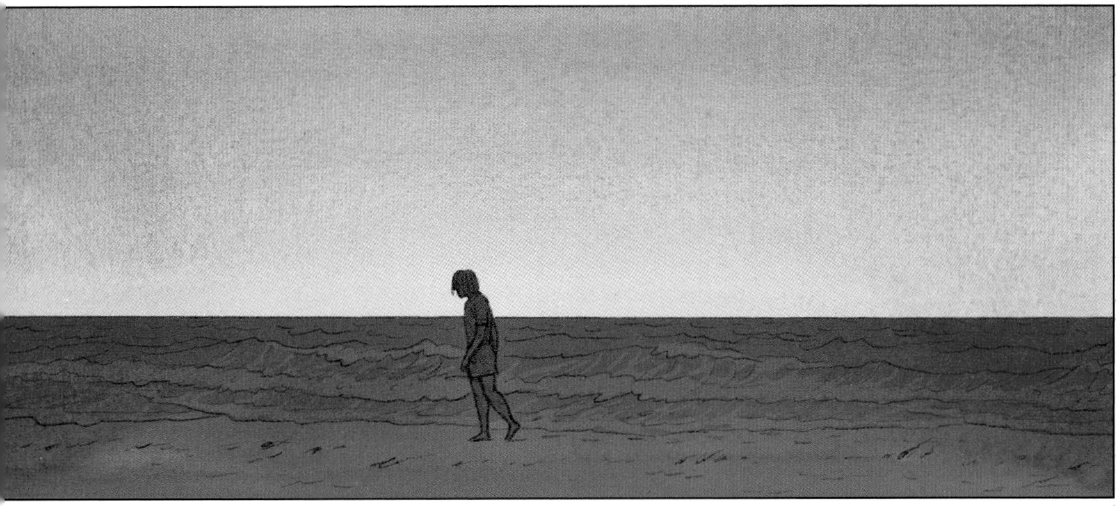

But no rest came to Achilles, that night or for ten nights thereafter. He'd toss and turn, then go out and pace along the surf until the sky began to pale with the approach of rosy-fingered dawn.

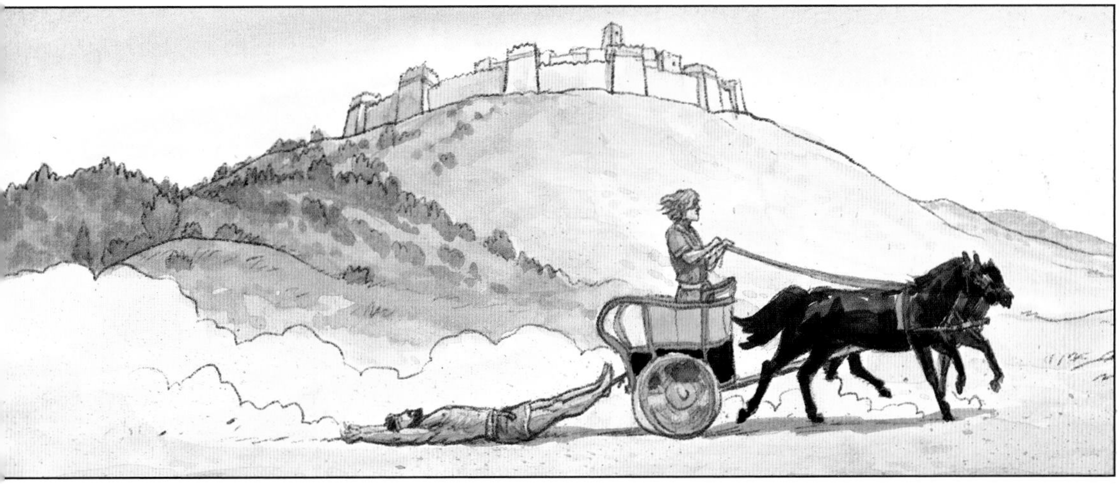

hen he'd hitch his team and drag Hector's body round and round Patroclus's tomb. Afterward, he'd ave the body lying in the dust while he flung himself down in his hut. But Apollo and Aphrodite ill protected Hector, never letting his skin be torn by the rough rocks, or his flesh decay in the sun.

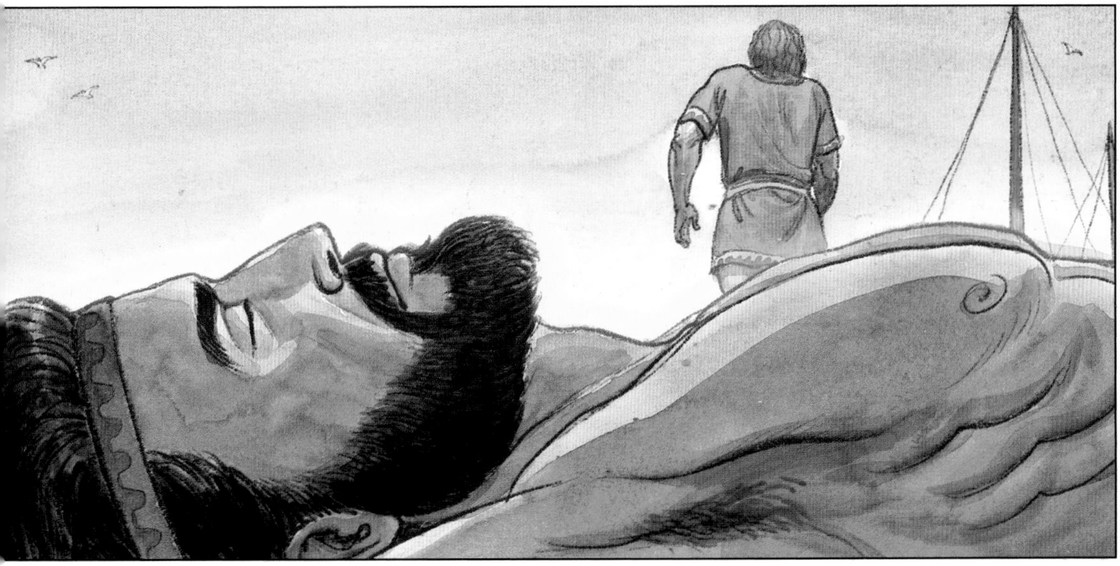

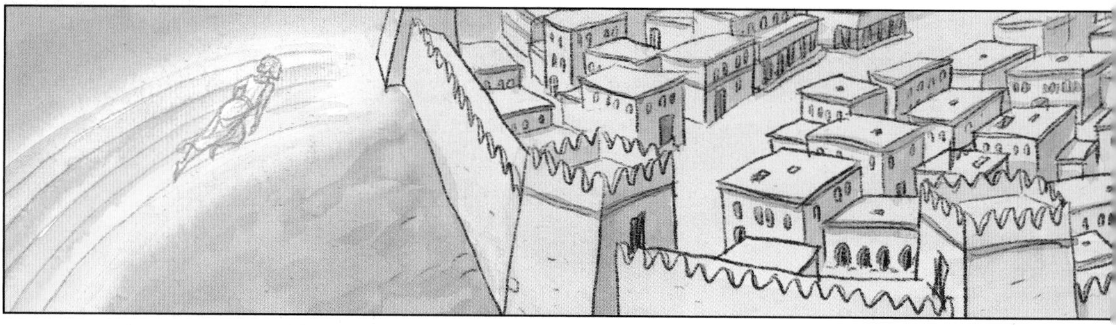

Now Zeus sent swift-footed Iris running on the rainy winds to Priam's palace courtyard, where the king sat, despondent, in the dirt, surrounded by his weeping sons and daughters.

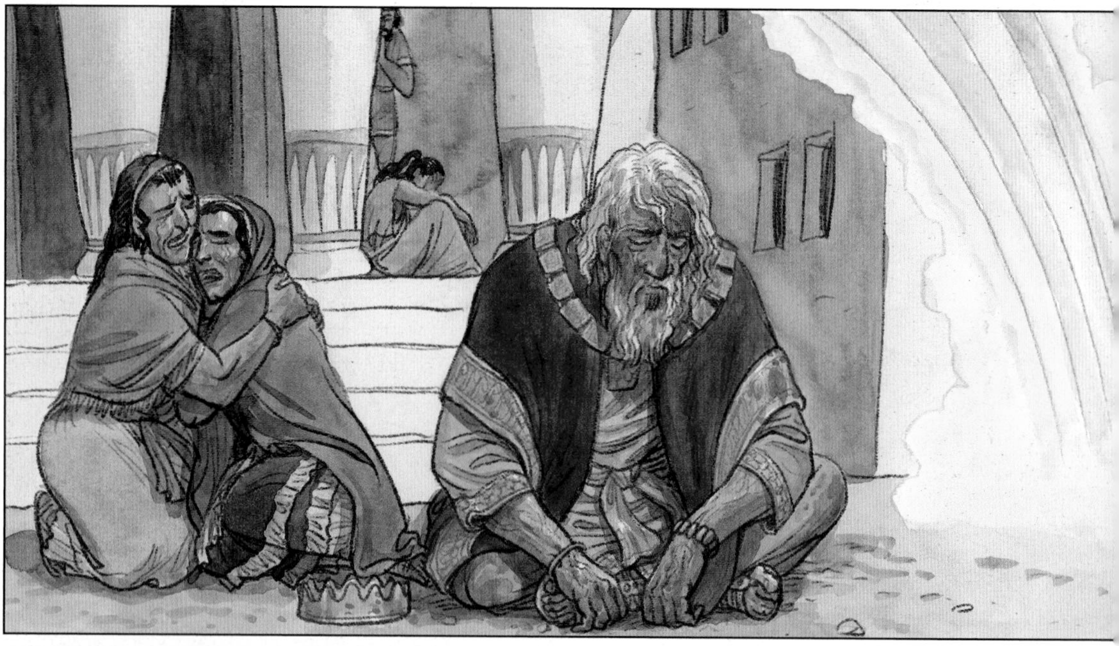

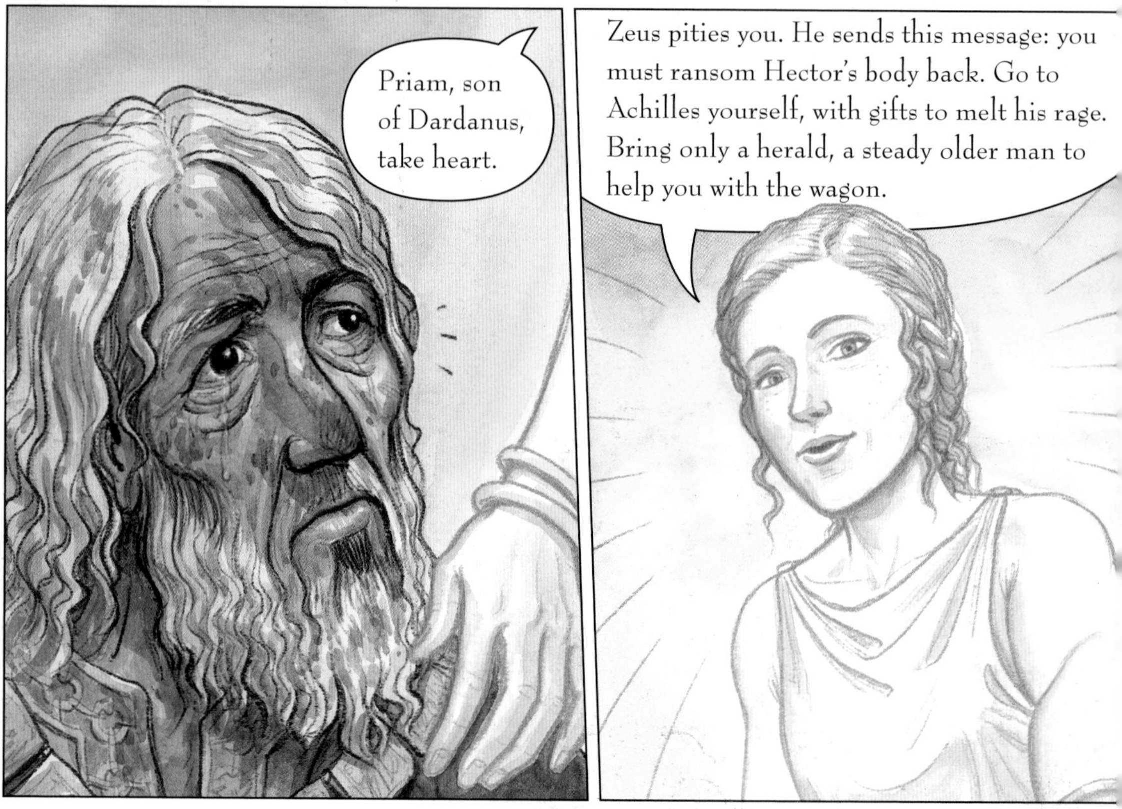
Priam, son of Dardanus, take heart.
Zeus pities you. He sends this message: you must ransom Hector's body back. Go to Achilles yourself, with gifts to melt his rage. Bring only a herald, a steady older man to help you with the wagon.

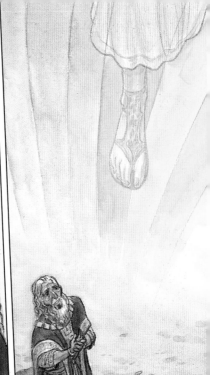

Have no fear, for you'll be guided safely through by Hermes, the Giant-Killer. Achilles will not harm you — he knows the will of Zeus.

Dearest Hecuba, a messenger came to me from Zeus on high. I am to go to Achilles and ransom back the body of our son.

Oh, sorrow! Grief has made you mad! How can you think of going to face the man who killed so many of your sons? He has no mercy and no shame!

My heart is set on going. If any man had urged this course, I'd call him mad, or a liar. But not now. I heard her voice, looked straight at the goddess, face-to-face.

The gods' commands must not be ignored. If I should die, so be it, but let me hold my son once more.

Call Idaeus! Prepare my chariot, and a sturdy wagon with a wicker box.

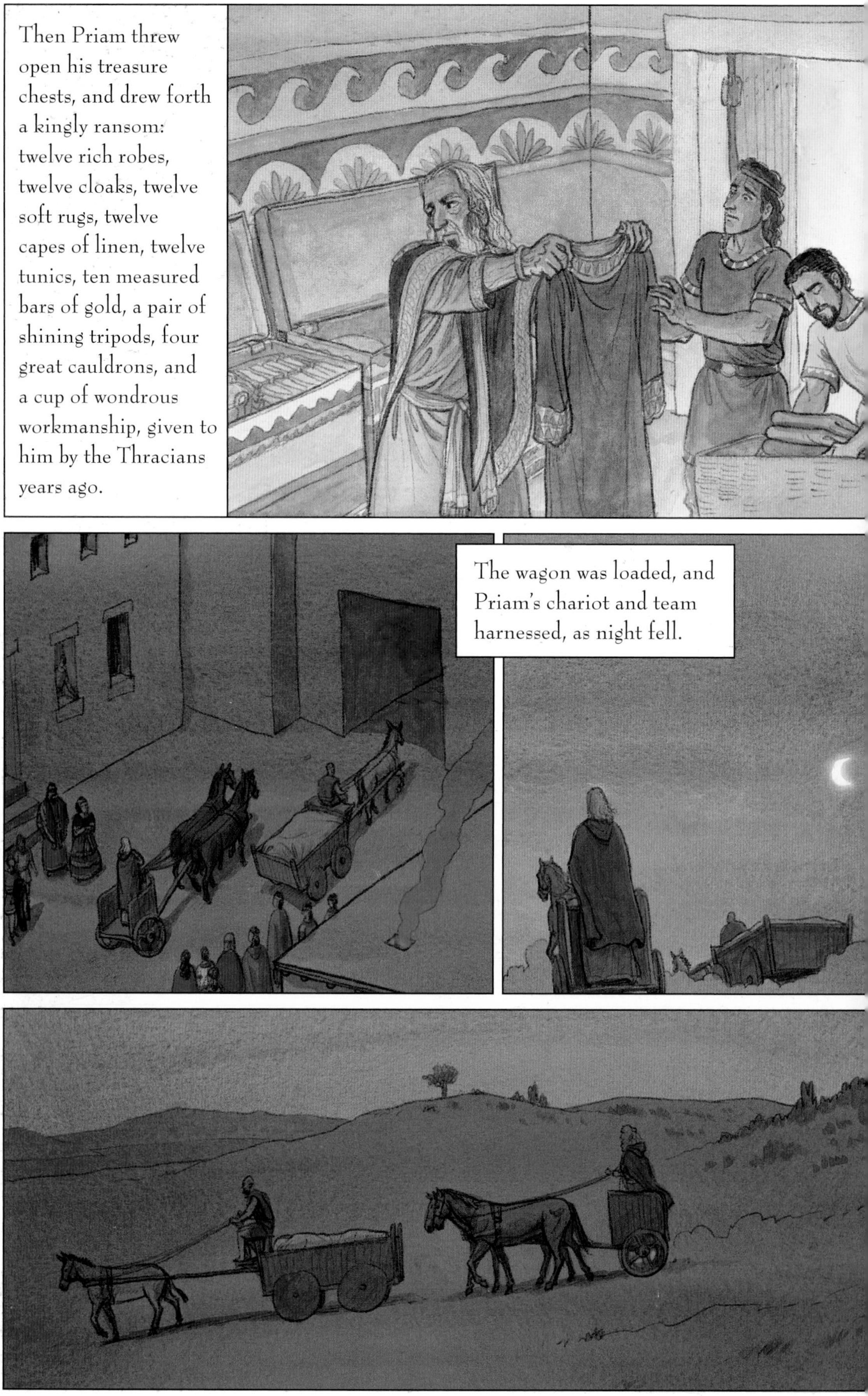
Then Priam threw open his treasure chests, and drew forth a kingly ransom: twelve rich robes, twelve cloaks, twelve soft rugs, twelve capes of linen, twelve tunics, ten measured bars of gold, a pair of shining tripods, four great cauldrons, and a cup of wondrous workmanship, given to him by the Thracians years ago.
The wagon was loaded, and Priam's chariot and team harnessed, as night fell.

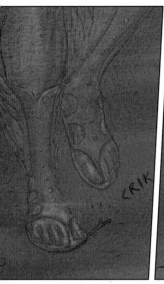

My king, danger! A man comes, an Achaean! We may be slaughtered. Let's flee in the chariot, or else grasp his knees and beg for mercy.

Old father, where are you going with mules and horses in the dead of night, when other men are all asleep? I won't hurt you, but do you not fear the fiery Achaeans, near at hand?

Should someone see you with such treasure out here in the dark, how could you defend yourselves?

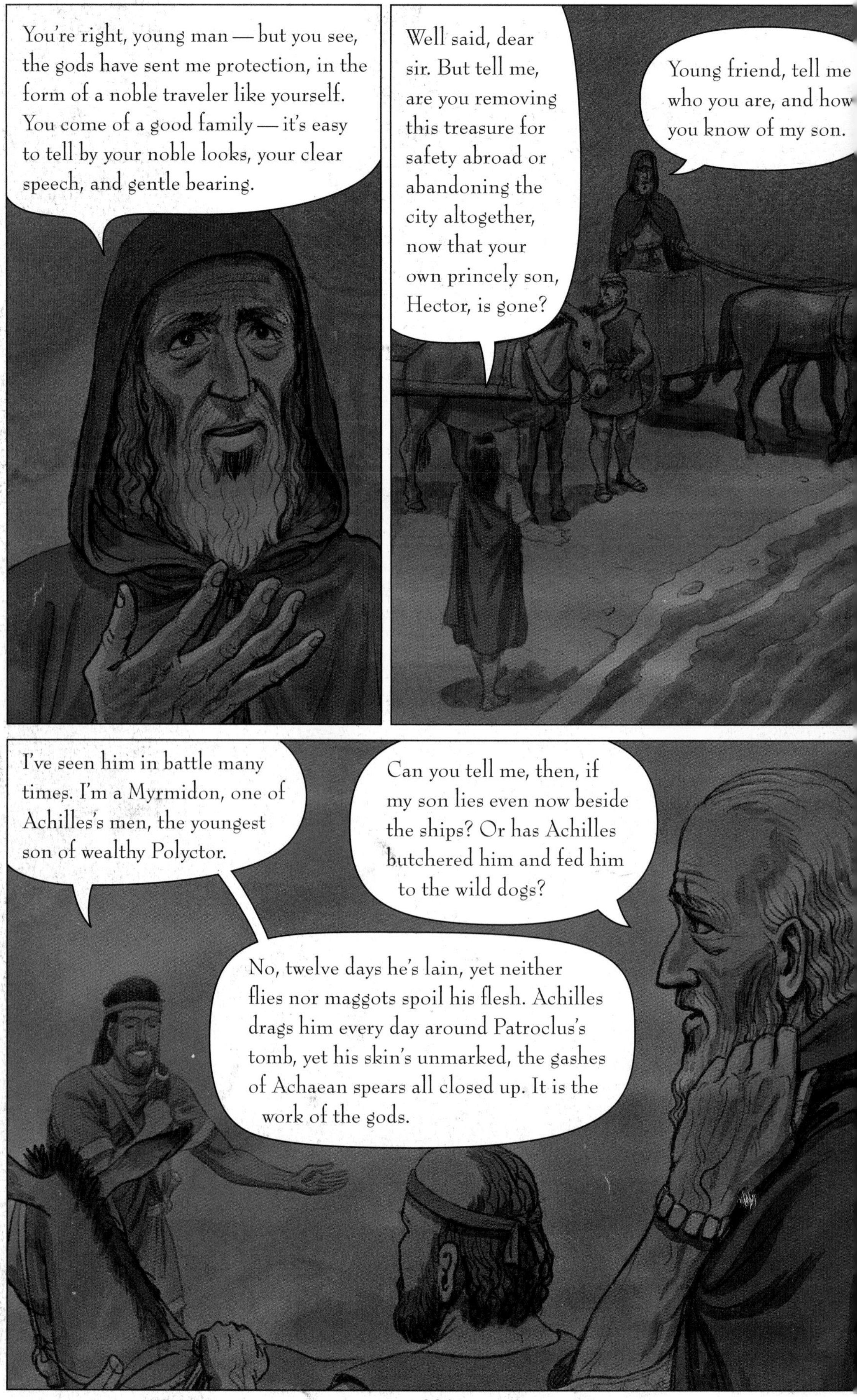
You're right, young man — but you see, the gods have sent me protection, in the form of a noble traveler like yourself. You come of a good family — it's easy to tell by your noble looks, your clear speech, and gentle bearing.
Well said, dear sir. But tell me, are you removing this treasure for safety abroad or abandoning the city altogether, now that your own princely son, Hector, is gone?
Young friend, tell me who you are, and how you know of my son.
I've seen him in battle many times. I'm a Myrmidon, one of Achilles's men, the youngest son of wealthy Polyctor.
Can you tell me, then, if my son lies even now beside the ships? Or has Achilles butchered him and fed him to the wild dogs?
No, twelve days he's lain, yet neither flies nor maggots spoil his flesh. Achilles drags him every day around Patroclus's tomb, yet his skin's unmarked, the gashes of Achaean spears all closed up. It is the work of the gods.

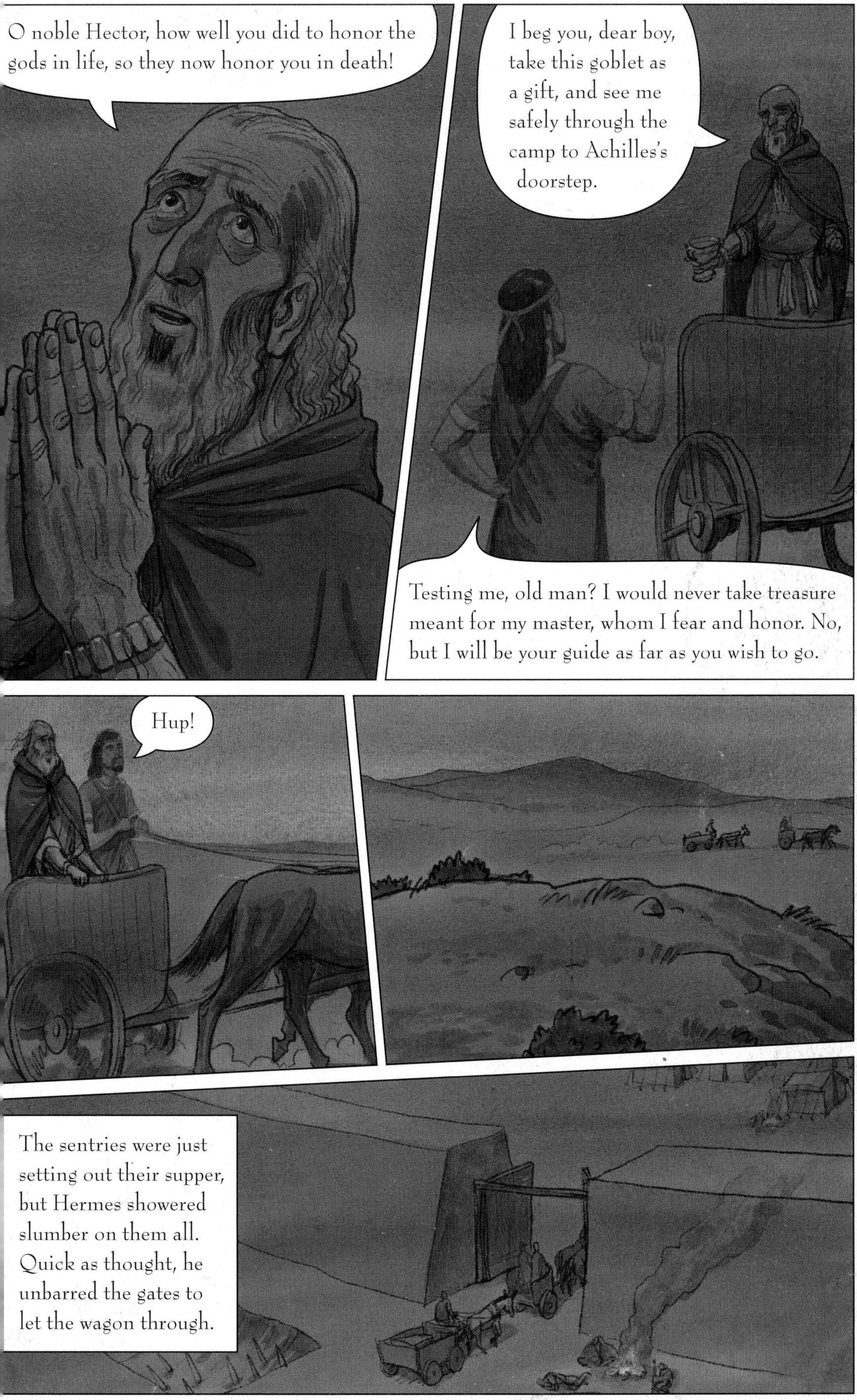
O noble Hector, how well you did to honor the gods in life, so they now honor you in death!
I beg you, dear boy, take this goblet as a gift, and see me safely through the camp to Achilles's doorstep.
Testing me, old man? I would never take treasure meant for my master, whom I fear and honor. No, but I will be your guide as far as you wish to go.
Hup!
The sentries were just setting out their supper, but Hermes showered slumber on them all. Quick as thought, he unbarred the gates to let the wagon through.

Around Achilles's hut, a palisade of posts marked off a courtyard. Its gate was barred with a massive beam of pine, which took three men to open or close — though Achilles could lift it alone.

TAP

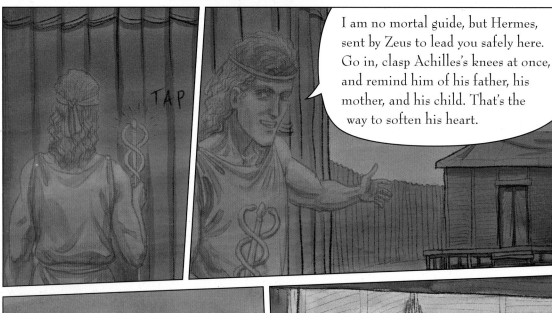

I am no mortal guide, but Hermes, sent by Zeus to lead you safely here. Go in, clasp Achilles's knees at once, and remind him of his father, his mother, and his child. That's the way to soften his heart.

O mighty Achilles, hear my prayer. . . .

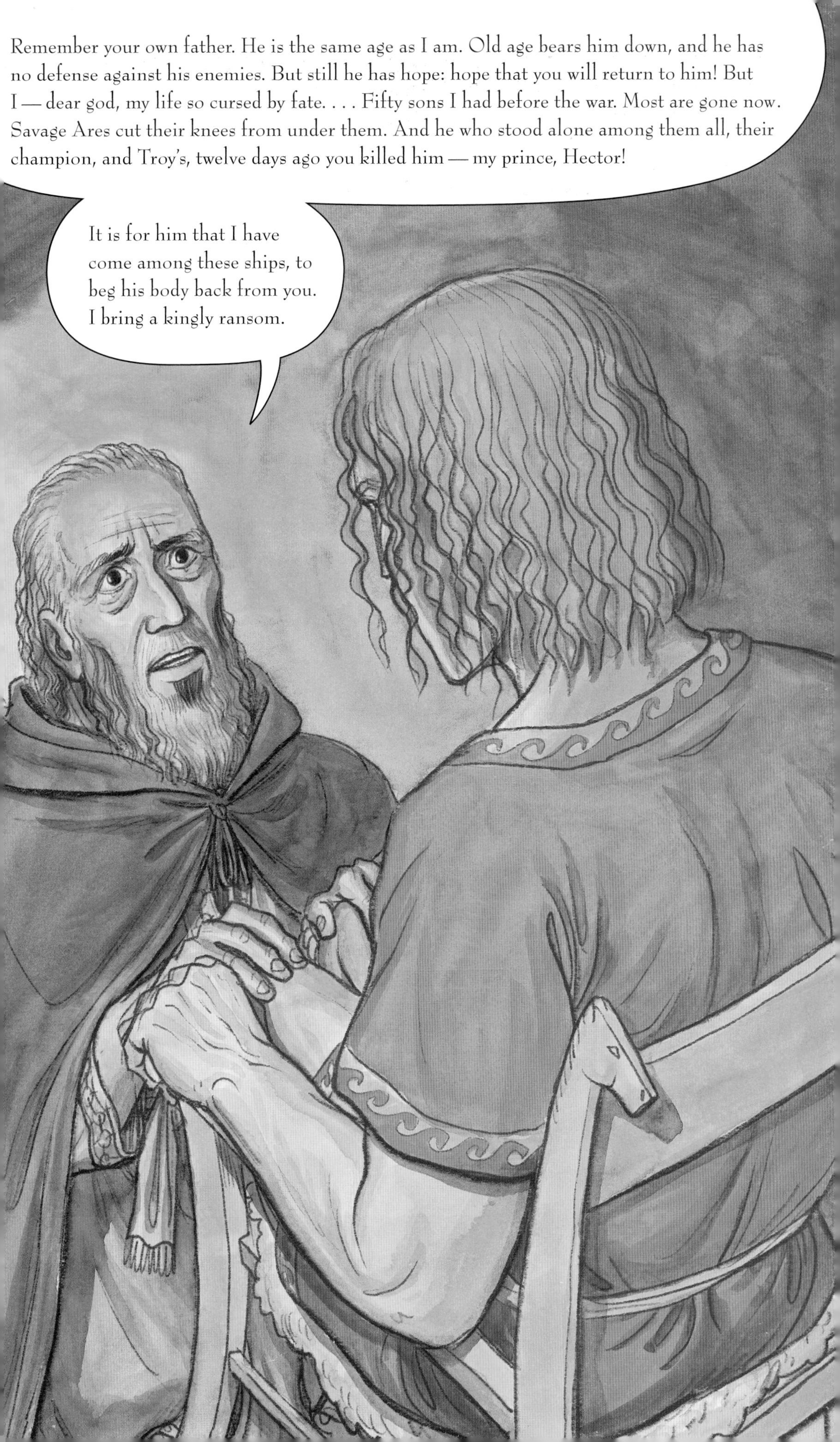
Remember your own father. He is the same age as I am. Old age bears him down, and he has no defense against his enemies. But still he has hope: hope that you will return to him! But I — dear god, my life so cursed by fate. . . . Fifty sons I had before the war. Most are gone now. Savage Ares cut their knees from under them. And he who stood alone among them all, their champion, and Troy's, twelve days ago you killed him — my prince, Hector!
It is for him that I have come among these ships, to beg his body back from you. I bring a kingly ransom.

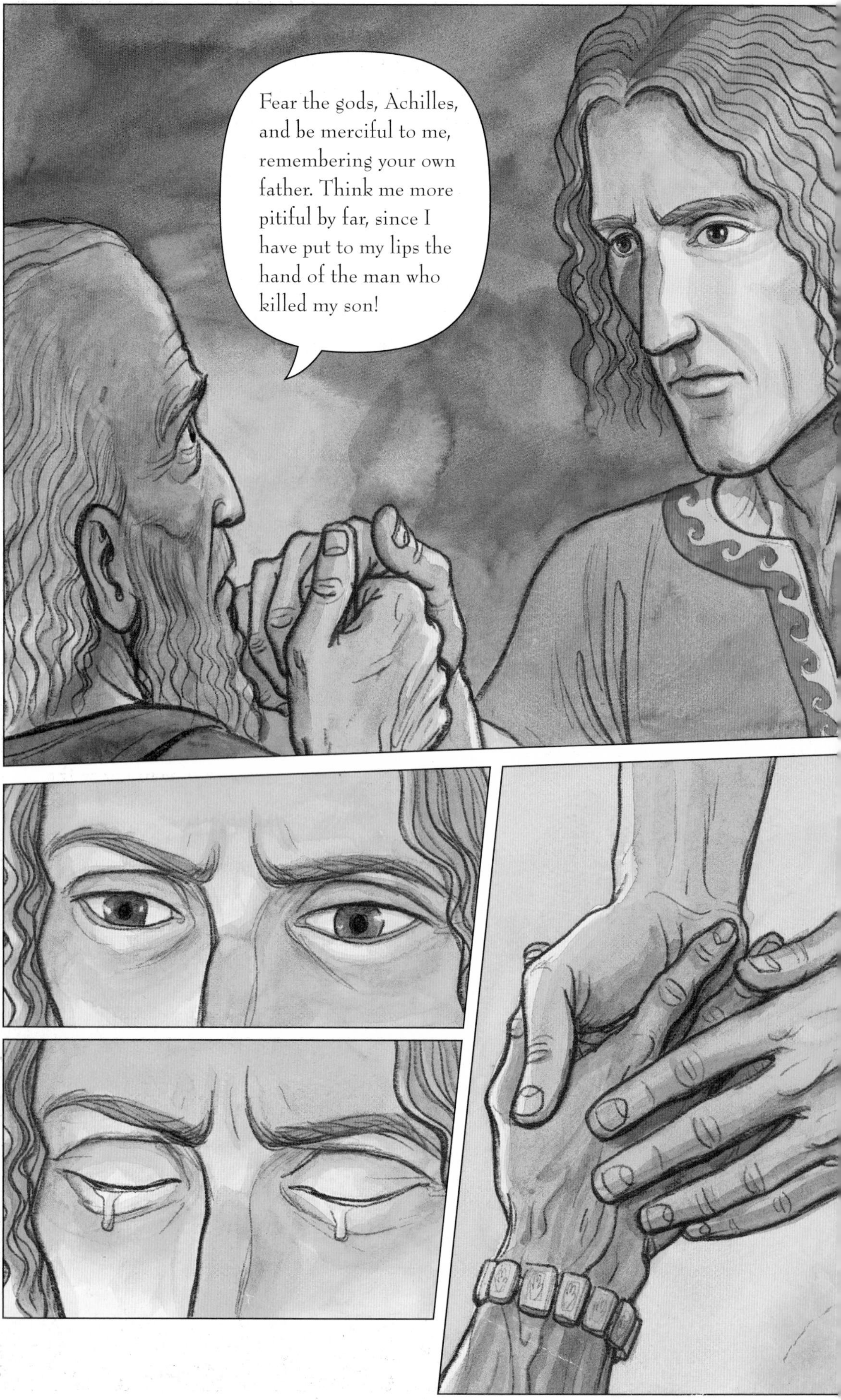
Fear the gods, Achilles, and be merciful to me, remembering your own father. Think me more pitiful by far, since I have put to my lips the hand of the man who killed my son!

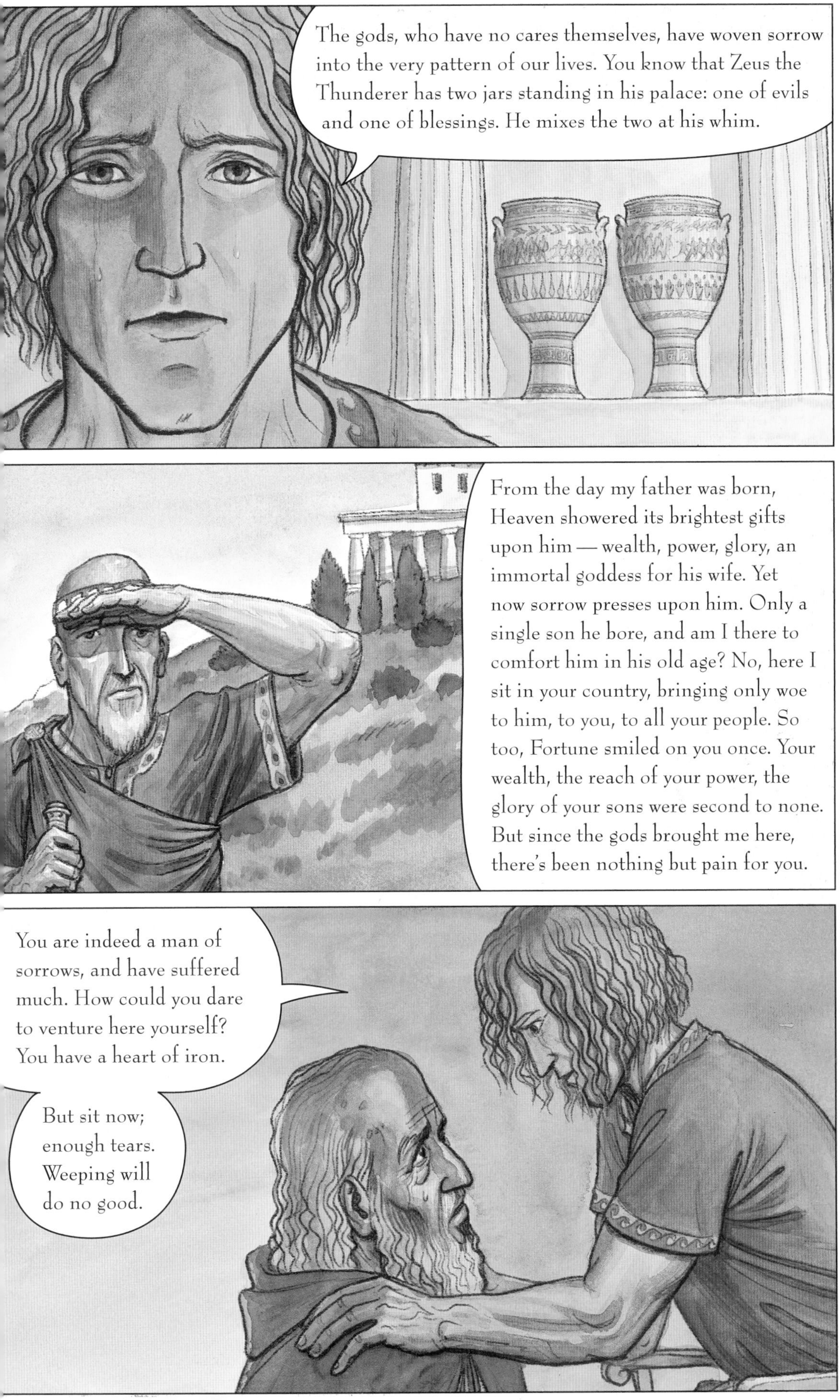
The gods, who have no cares themselves, have woven sorrow into the very pattern of our lives. You know that Zeus the Thunderer has two jars standing in his palace: one of evils and one of blessings. He mixes the two at his whim.
From the day my father was born, Heaven showered its brightest gifts upon him — wealth, power, glory, an immortal goddess for his wife. Yet now sorrow presses upon him. Only a single son he bore, and am I there to comfort him in his old age? No, here I sit in your country, bringing only woe to him, to you, to all your people. So too, Fortune smiled on you once. Your wealth, the reach of your power, the glory of your sons were second to none. But since the gods brought me here, there's been nothing but pain for you.
You are indeed a man of sorrows, and have suffered much. How could you dare to venture here yourself? You have a heart of iron.
But sit now; enough tears. Weeping will do no good.

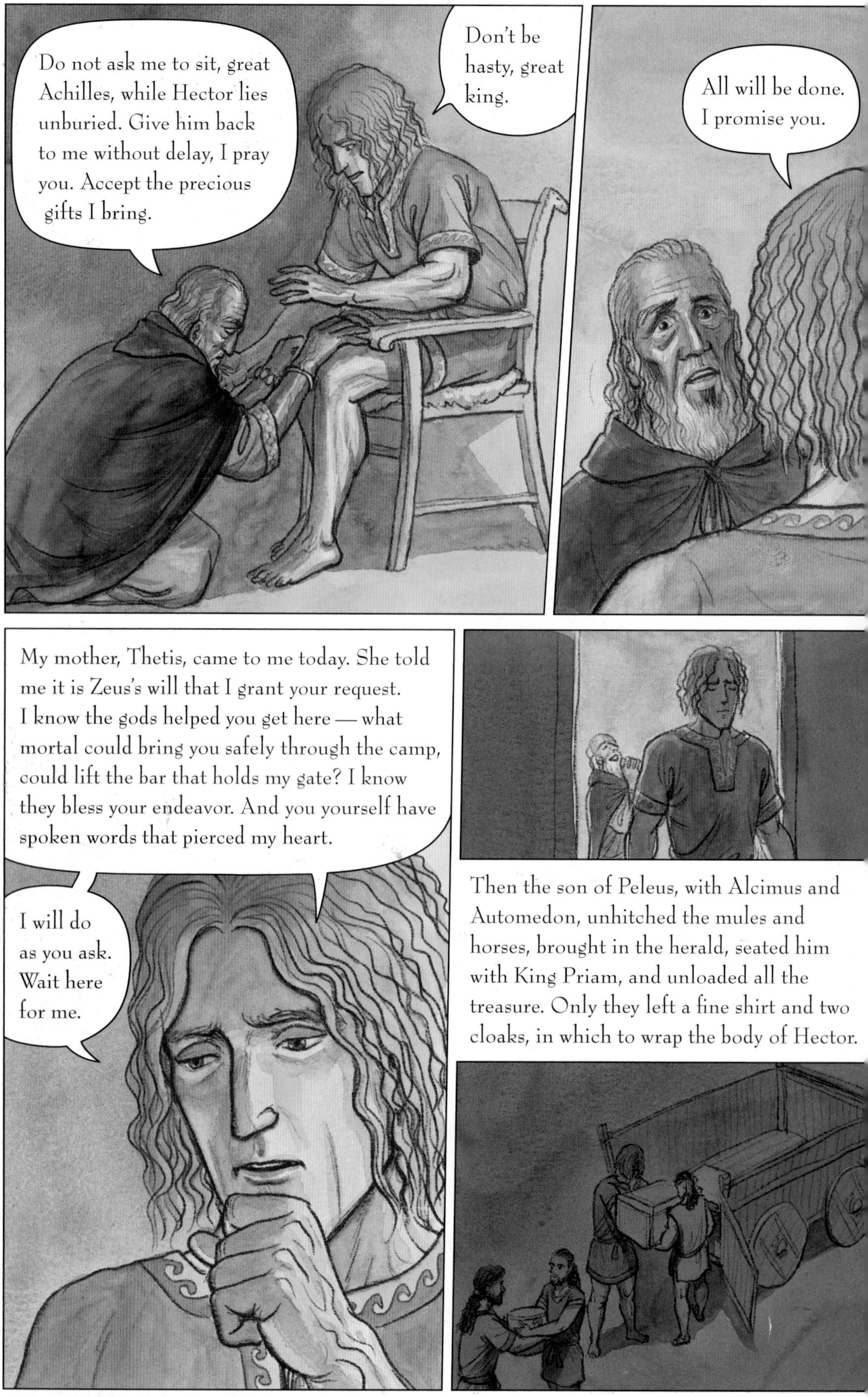
Do not ask me to sit, great Achilles, while Hector lies unburied. Give him back to me without delay, I pray you. Accept the precious gifts I bring.
Don't be hasty, great king.
All will be done. I promise you.
My mother, Thetis, came to me today. She told me it is Zeus's will that I grant your request. I know the gods helped you get here — what mortal could bring you safely through the camp, could lift the bar that holds my gate? I know they bless your endeavor. And you yourself have spoken words that pierced my heart.
I will do as you ask. Wait here for me.
Then the son of Peleus, with Alcimus and Automedon, unhitched the mules and horses, brought in the herald, seated him with King Priam, and unloaded all the treasure. Only they left a fine shirt and two cloaks, in which to wrap the body of Hector.

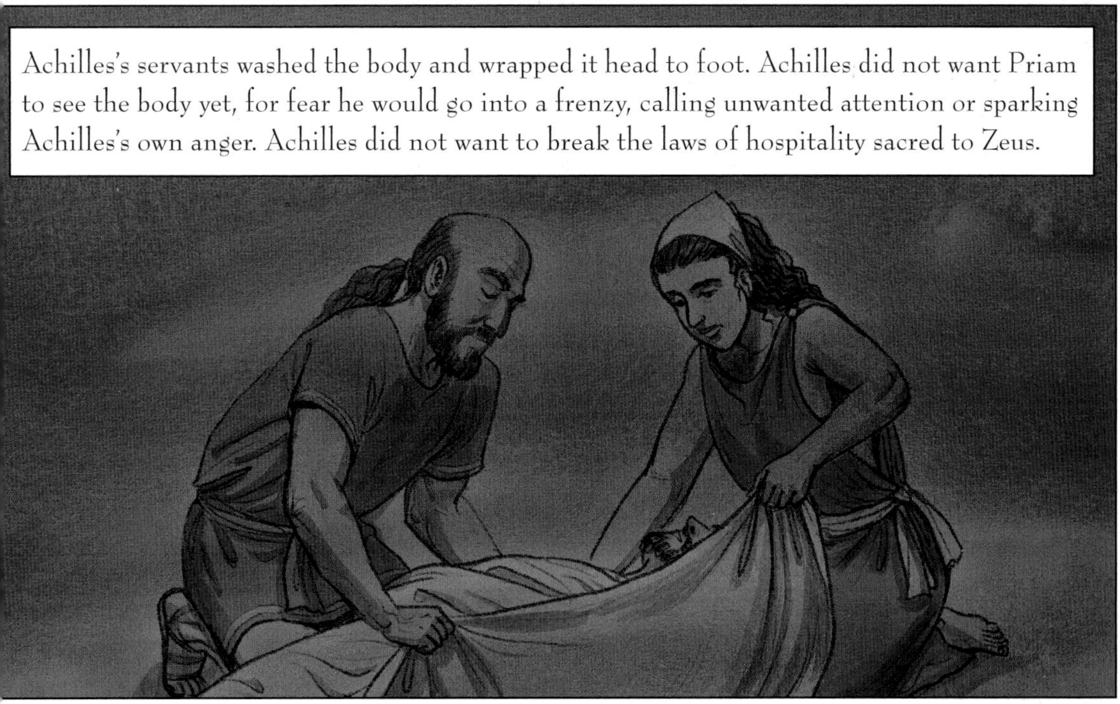
Achilles's servants washed the body and wrapped it head to foot. Achilles did not want Priam to see the body yet, for fear he would go into a frenzy, calling unwanted attention or sparking Achilles's own anger. Achilles did not want to break the laws of hospitality sacred to Zeus.

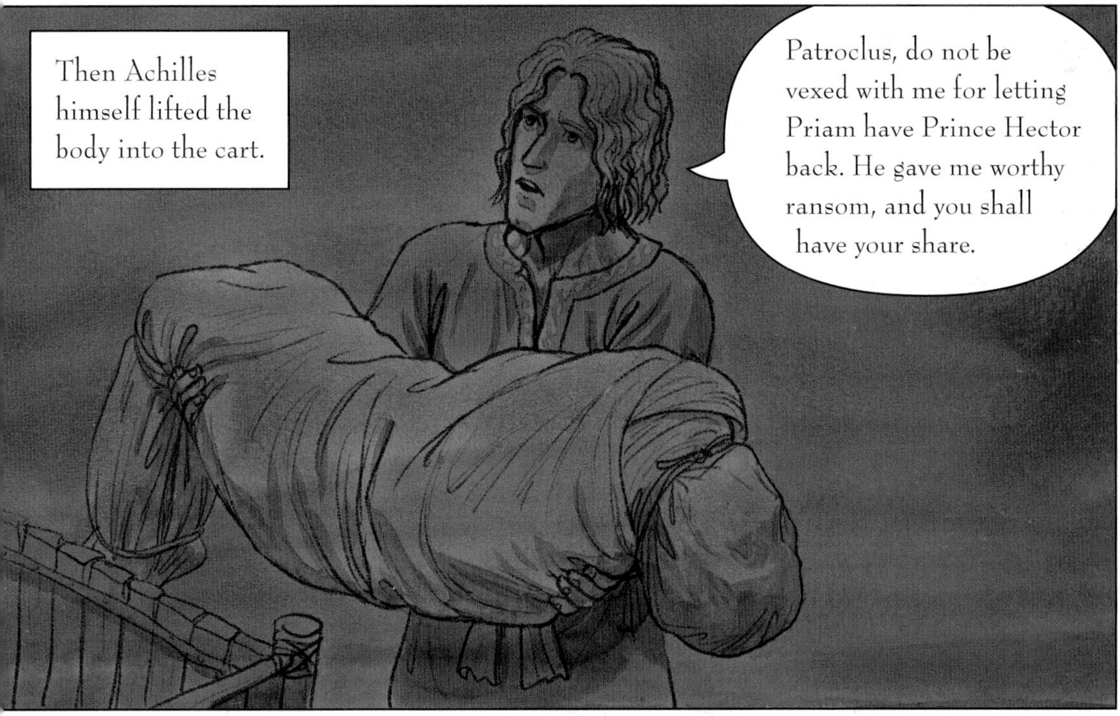
Then Achilles himself lifted the body into the cart.
Patroclus, do not be vexed with me for letting Priam have Prince Hector back. He gave me worthy ransom, and you shall have your share.

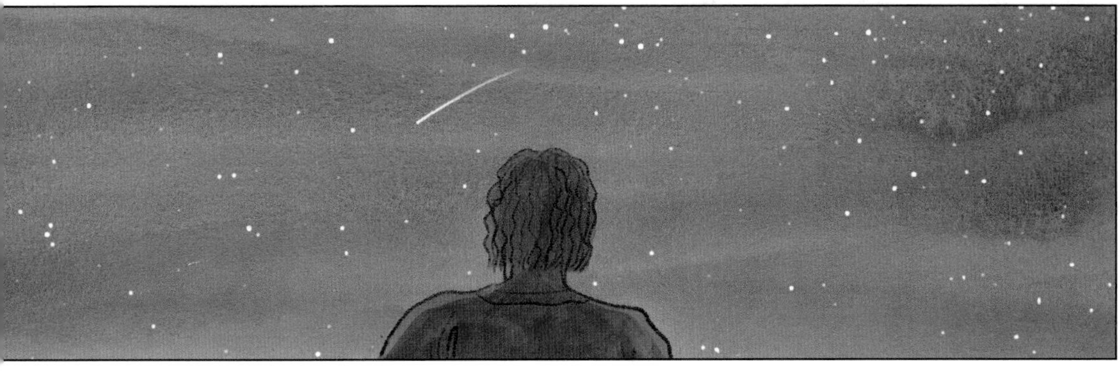

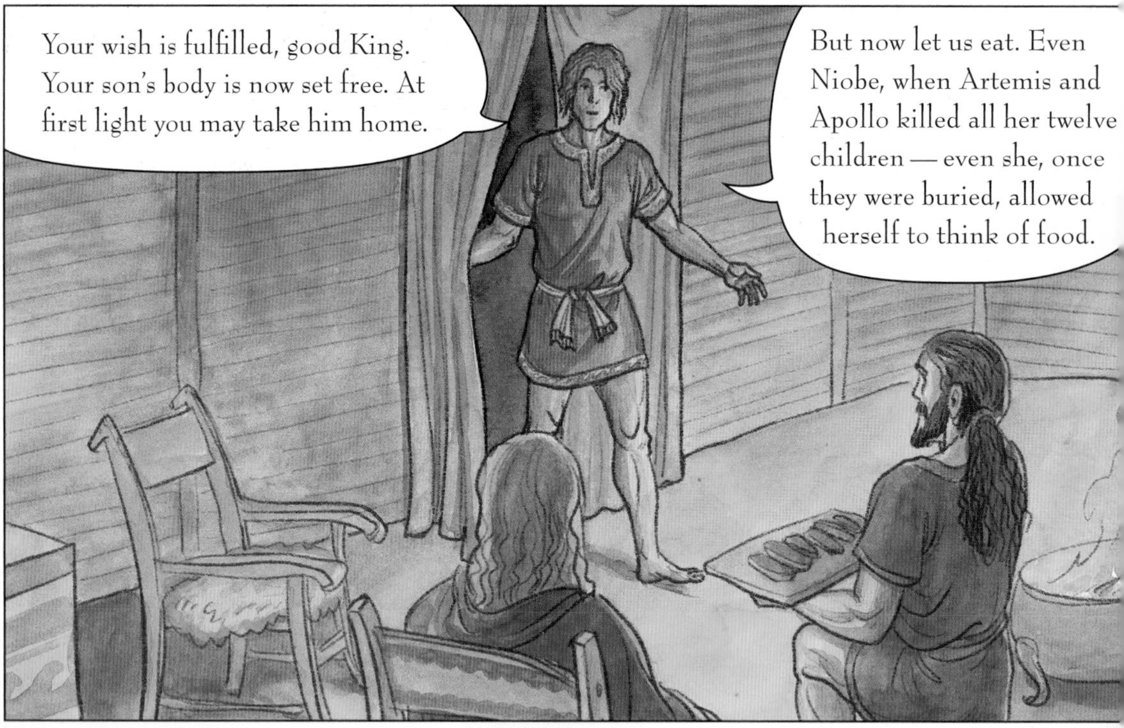

Your wish is fulfilled, good King. Your son's body is now set free. At first light you may take him home.
But now let us eat. Even Niobe, when Artemis and Apollo killed all her twelve children — even she, once they were buried, allowed herself to think of food.

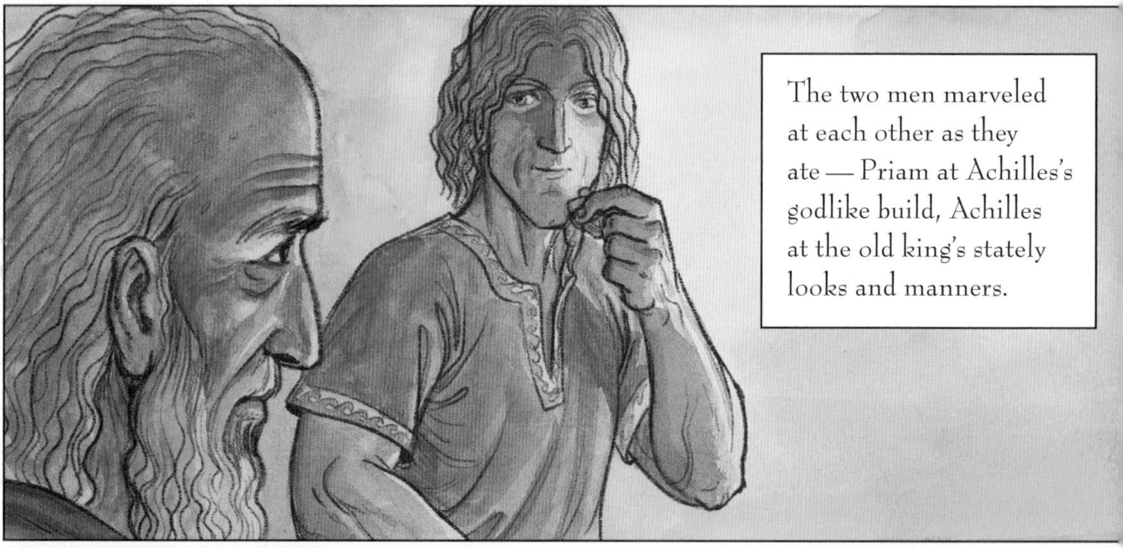

The two men marveled at each other as they ate — Priam at Achilles's godlike build, Achilles at the old king's stately looks and manners.

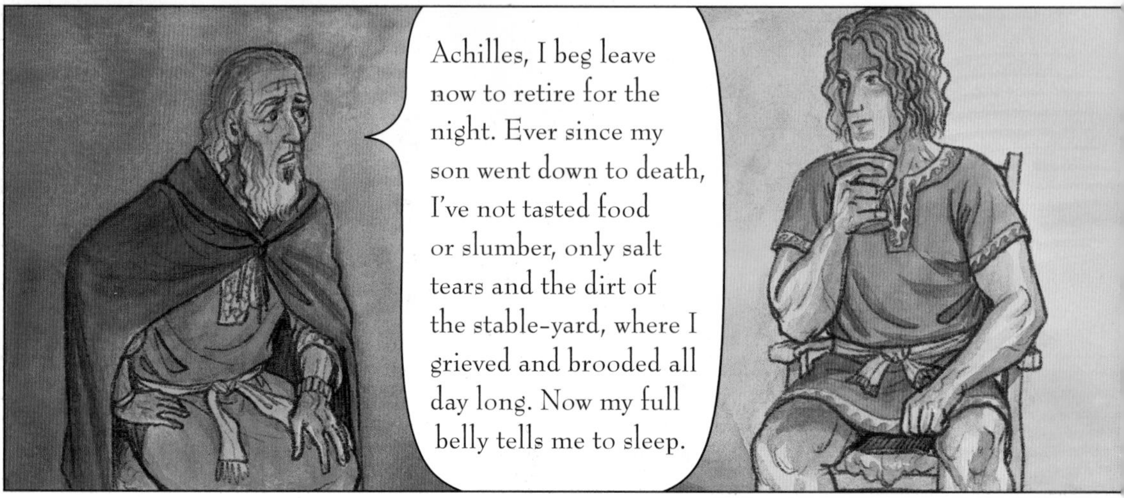

Achilles, I beg leave now to retire for the night. Ever since my son went down to death, I've not tasted food or slumber, only salt tears and the dirt of the stable-yard, where I grieved and brooded all day long. Now my full belly tells me to sleep.

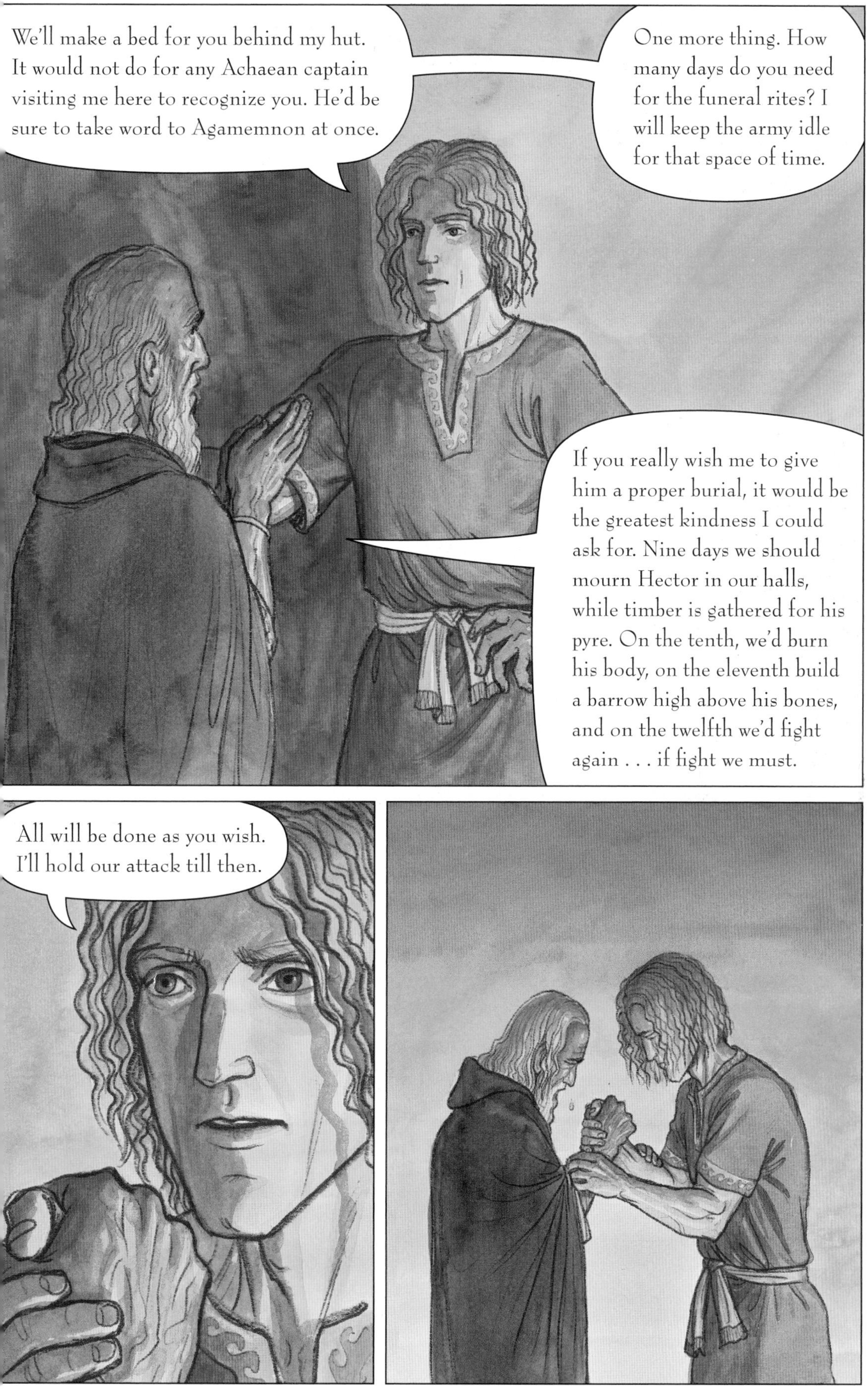
We'll make a bed for you behind my hut. It would not do for any Achaean captain visiting me here to recognize you. He'd be sure to take word to Agamemnon at once.
One more thing. How many days do you need for the funeral rites? I will keep the army idle for that space of time.
If you really wish me to give him a proper burial, it would be the greatest kindness I could ask for. Nine days we should mourn Hector in our halls, while timber is gathered for his pyre. On the tenth, we'd burn his body, on the eleventh build a barrow high above his bones, and on the twelfth we'd fight again . . . if fight we must.
All will be done as you wish. I'll hold our attack till then.

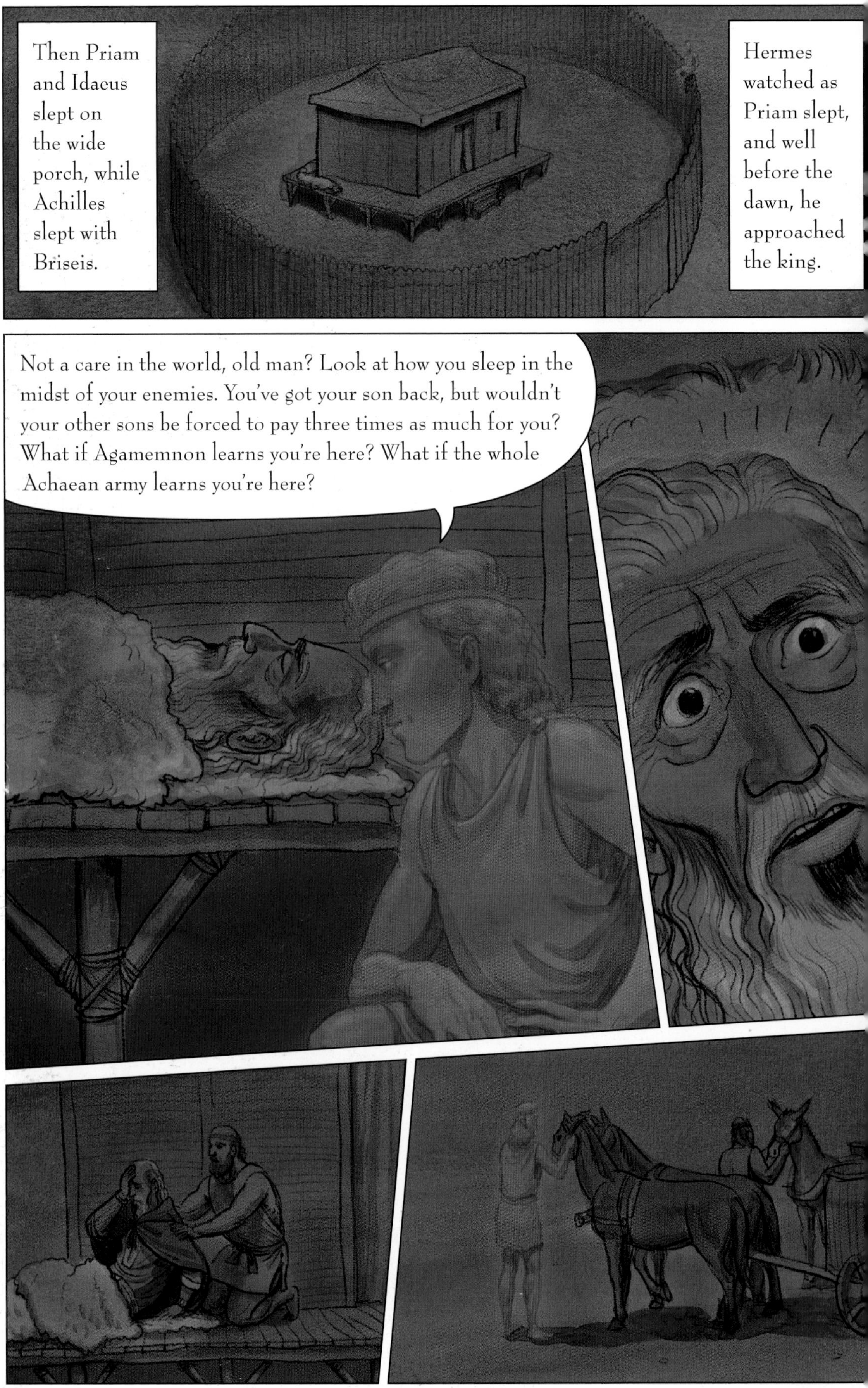
Then Priam and Idaeus slept on the wide porch, while Achilles slept with Briseis.
Hermes watched as Priam slept, and well before the dawn, he approached the king.
Not a care in the world, old man? Look at how you sleep in the midst of your enemies. You've got your son back, but wouldn't your other sons be forced to pay three times as much for you? What if Agamemnon learns you're here? What if the whole Achaean army learns you're here?

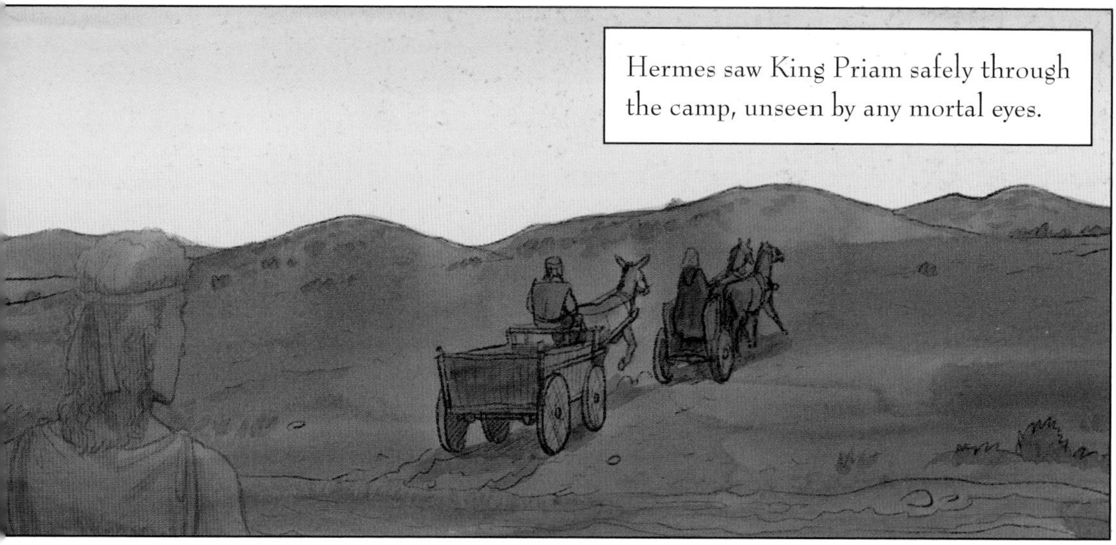
Hermes saw King Priam safely through the camp, unseen by any mortal eyes.

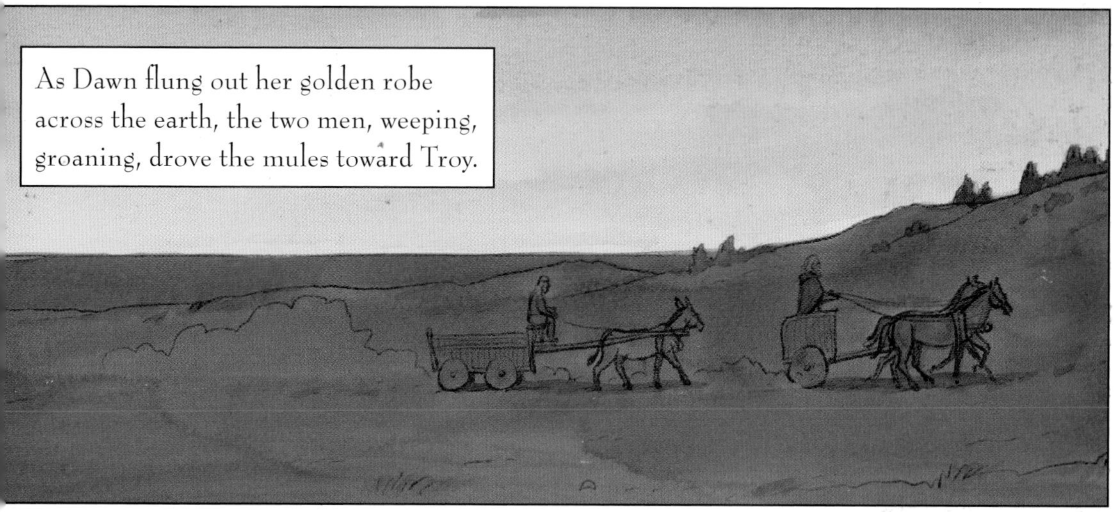
As Dawn flung out her golden robe across the earth, the two men, weeping, groaning, drove the mules toward Troy.

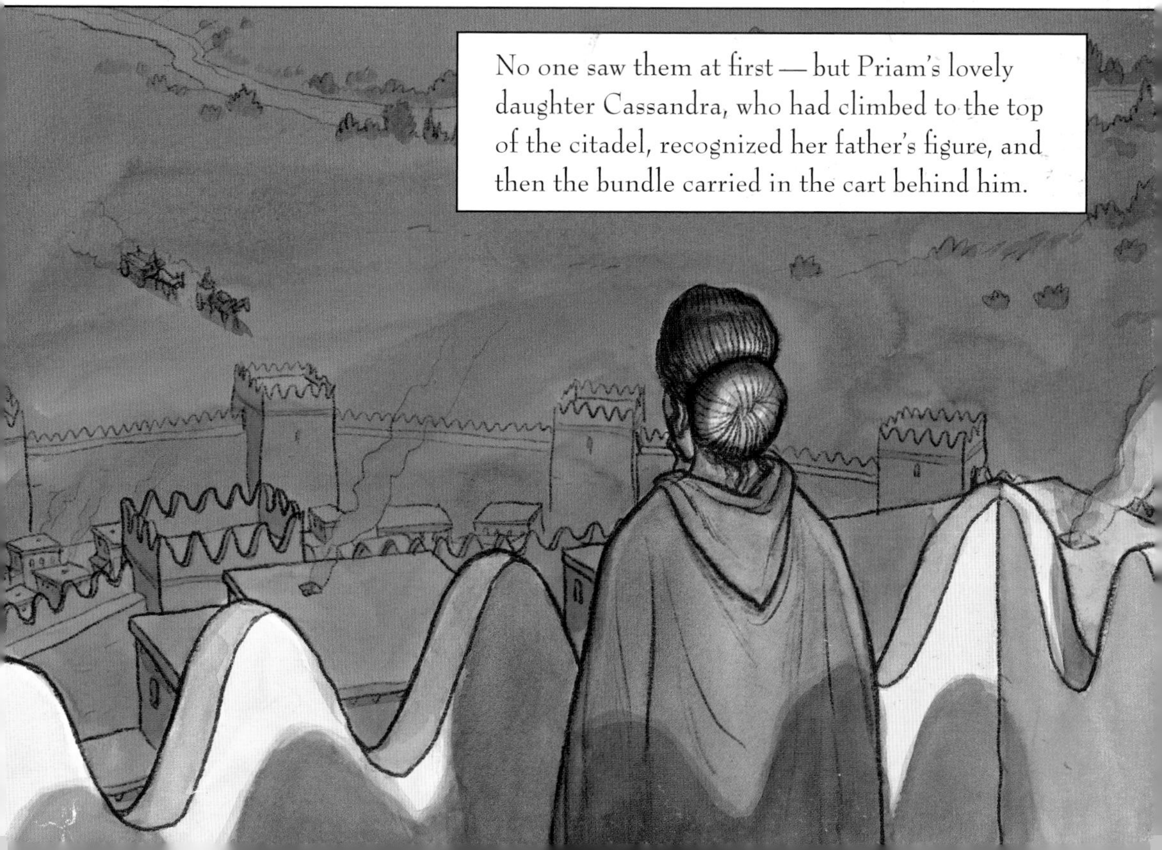
No one saw them at first — but Priam's lovely daughter Cassandra, who had climbed to the top of the citadel, recognized her father's figure, and then the bundle carried in the cart behind him.

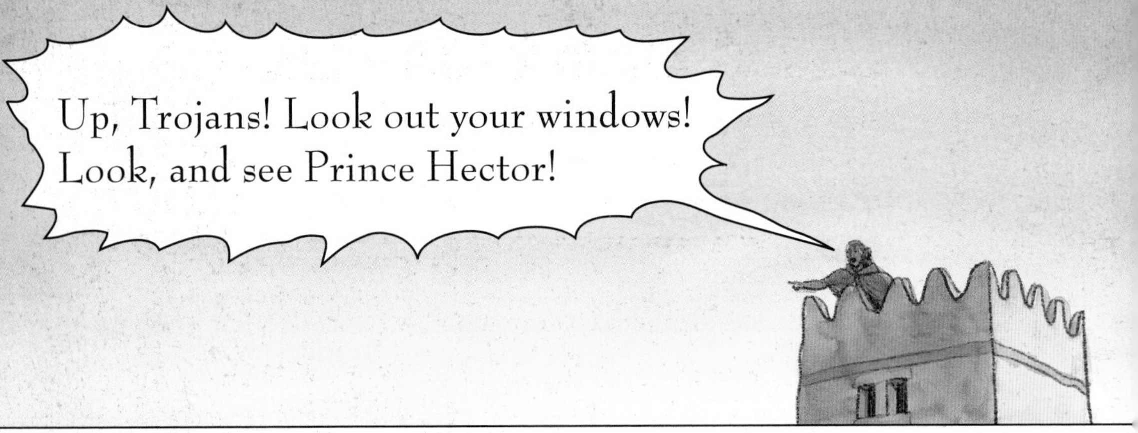
Up, Trojans! Look out your windows! Look, and see Prince Hector!

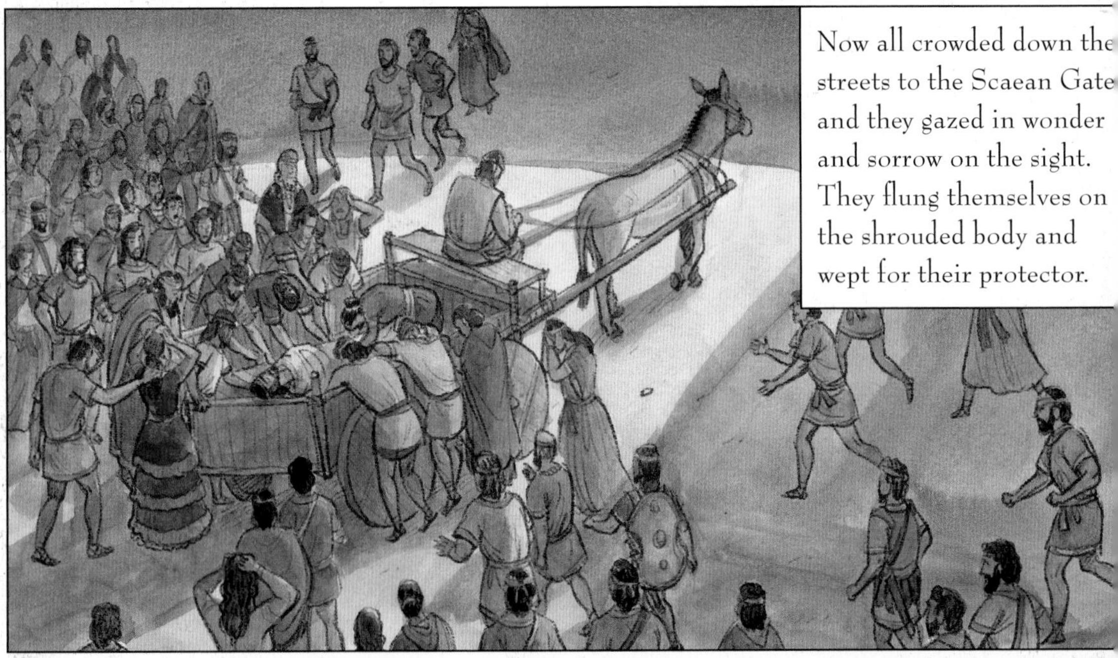
Now all crowded down the streets to the Scaean Gate and they gazed in wonder and sorrow on the sight. They flung themselves on the shrouded body and wept for their protector.

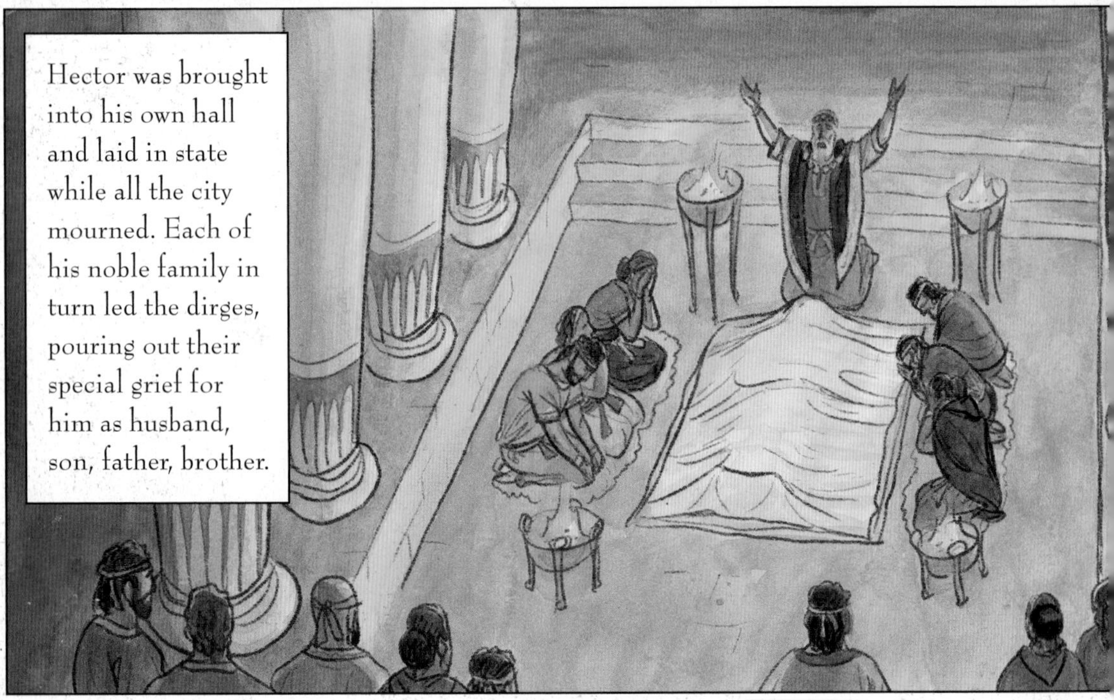
Hector was brought into his own hall and laid in state while all the city mourned. Each of his noble family in turn led the dirges, pouring out their special grief for him as husband, son, father, brother.

Nine days they mourned, while men of the city labored to haul in timber and build the pyre. On the tenth day, they placed the body high atop it, and lit the blaze.

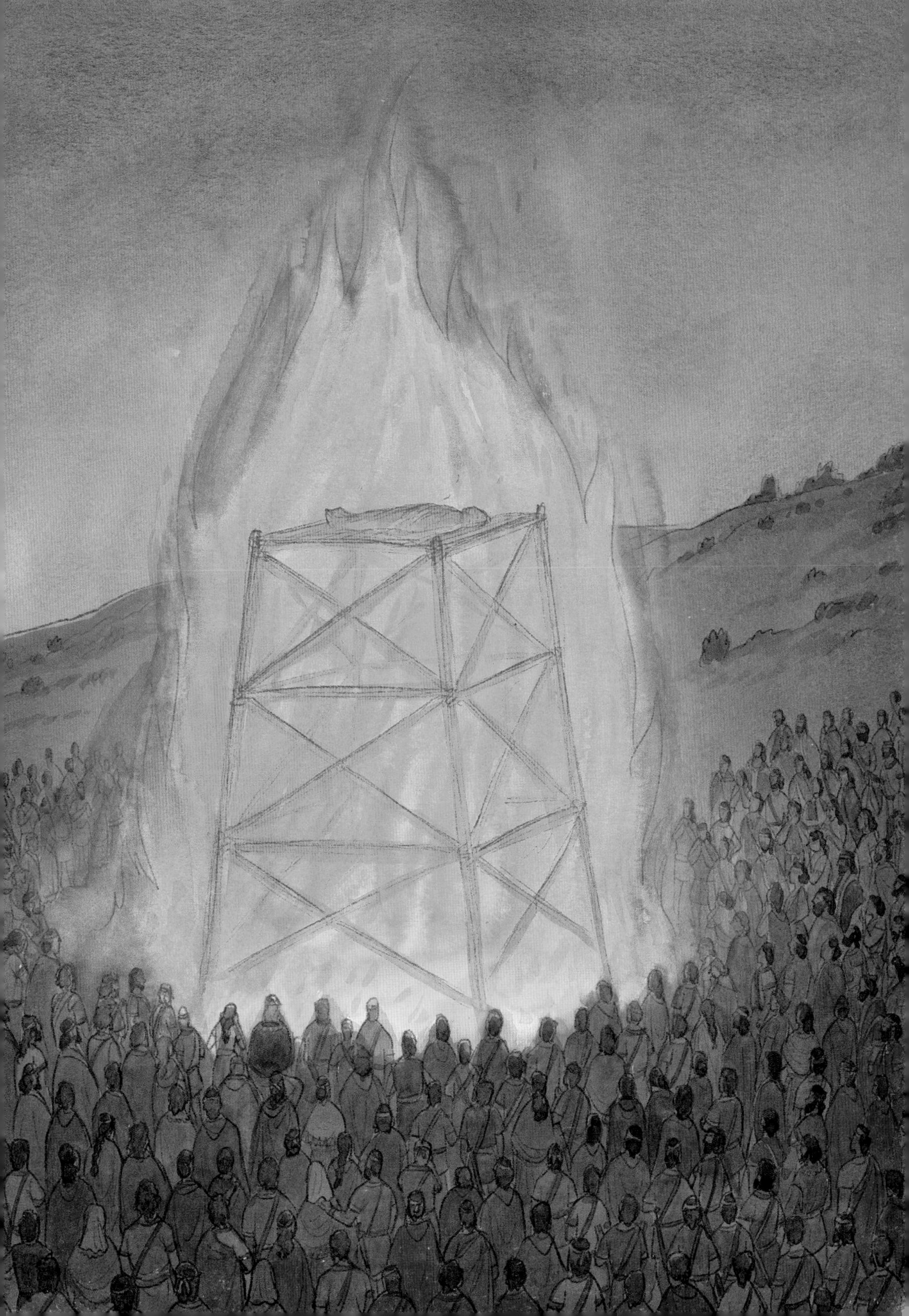

On the eleventh day, when the young Dawn with her fingertips of rose lit up the eastern sky, they quenched the pyre with tawny wine and gathered up the bones. They placed them in a golden chest and wrapped it in soft purple cloth.

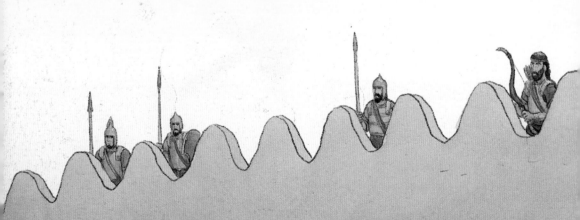

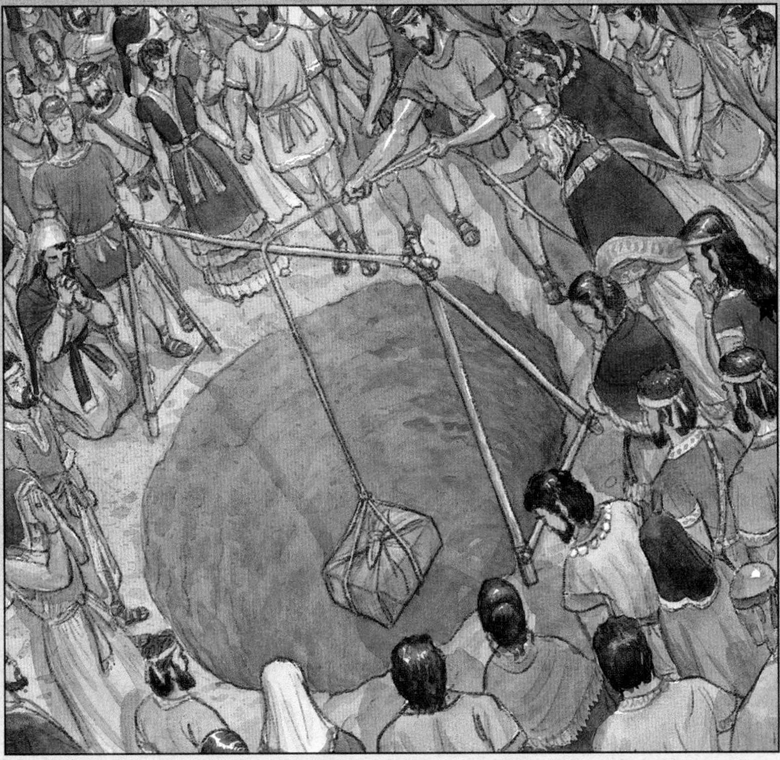

This they lowered into a deep hollow grave, and over it they laid stones and heaped up a barrow, while lookouts watched to warn them if the Argives should attack before the hour agreed.

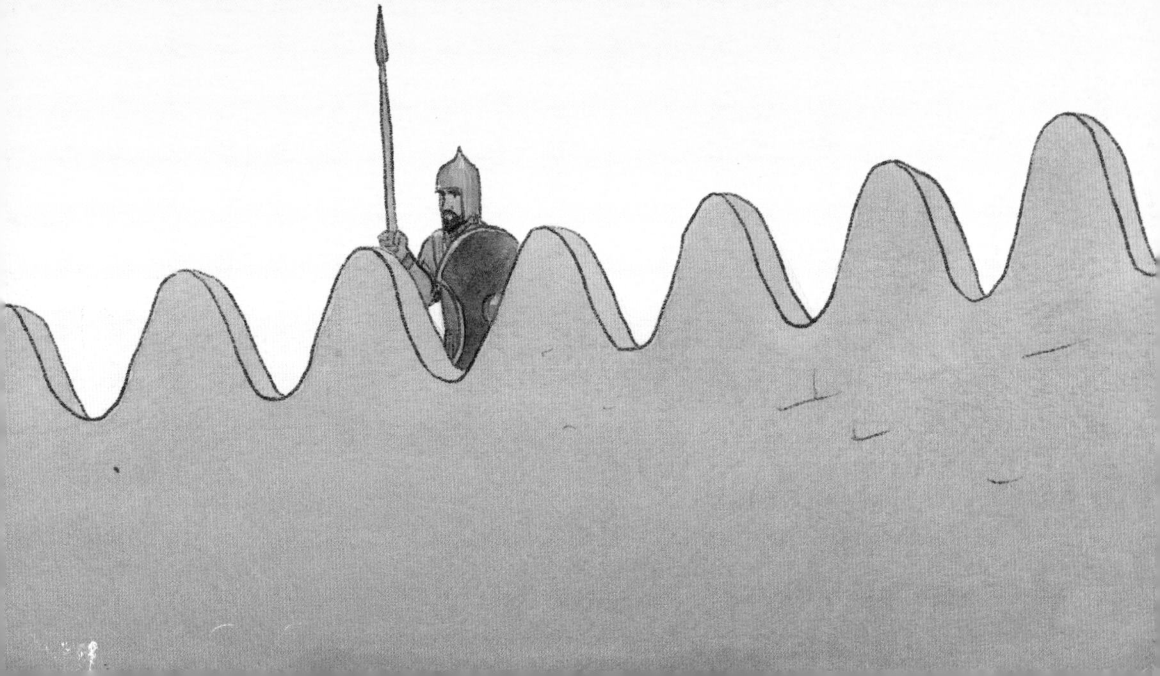

And once they'd heaped the mound, they turned
back home to Troy and shared a splendid funeral
feast in Hector's honor, there in the house of Priam.

This was how the Trojans buried
Hector, breaker of horses.

AUTHOR'S NOTE

WHAT HAPPENS NEXT?

Homer ended *The Iliad* here, with the powerful scene of Hector's burial, but this was not the end of the Trojan War. As I mentioned at the beginning, *The Iliad* is not a full account of the war—it tells only the story of Achilles and Agamemnon's quarrel, and the consequences for both sides.

What we know of events before and after *The Iliad* comes from other classical sources (see bibliography). The war continued for approximately another year after Hector's death. Achilles met his doom when Paris shot him through the heel with an arrow (this incident is the source of the term *Achilles' heel*). Then the Achaeans deployed the famous Trojan horse, Odysseus's strategic masterwork that allowed them to sneak inside the walls and finally capture Troy. The wooden horse was so big it couldn't be dragged in through the gates—the Trojans actually tore a hole in their own wall to bring the horse inside. Bits of that scene are depicted in *The Odyssey* (page 89 of my version).

Most of the Trojans were killed or enslaved when the Achaeans sacked the city. A few of the Trojan heroes escaped, most notably Aeneas, who stars in Virgil's epic poem, *The Aeneid*. Of the Greeks who survived the war, not all got home safely. We learn more in Books 3 and 4 of *The Odyssey*.

WHY DO WE STILL READ *THE ILIAD*?

First, because it is universal. As archaic or foreign as the world of *The Iliad* may initially seem, we quickly recognize the humanity in the characters portrayed by Homer. Angry arguments driven by pride turn into personal tragedies to which I think we can all relate. Humanity is on display in all its nobility and pettiness and violence and tenderness. It is, simply, a powerful story.

It's more than that, however. It is our earliest and best window into life in the Bronze Age, more than three thousand years ago. Homer's epics may not be history per se, but they are intensely rich in details that paint a vivid portrait of a period about which we otherwise would know very little. *The Iliad* is packed not only with features of ordinary life, but of the political and military events and culture that would survive and grow into Western civilization as we know it. From the warring Greek tribes that Agamemnon led to Troy sprang the intellectual flowering of Athens, birthplace of democracy. The Roman Empire, which spread its system of government across most of Europe and Asia, was supposedly founded by Aeneas after he escaped the sack of Troy. Throughout their history the Romans considered knowledge of *The Iliad* to be the single most essential element of an education. Most people who considered themselves intellectuals knew it by heart.

It's also an example of the saying that "every war story is an anti-war story." *The Iliad* glorifies courage and fighting prowess while simultaneously showing the grisly suffering inflicted on soldiers and civilians in war. Whenever a nobleman is wounded or killed, Homer tells us who he was and the exact nature of his wounds, in graphic detail. These details drive home the horror and tragedy of each death. I've tried to preserve some of that effect, though I didn't have room to include all the names and descriptions. Each death and each new twist of the war invites us to consider whether all this killing is justified.

We can experience *The Iliad* as a timeless tale of the courage, heroism, vanity, pettiness, and mortality we all share, *and* as a way to understand the history of Western civilization. Either way, it's a great story.

HISTORICAL ACCURACY

Scholars have been trying for centuries to figure out how much of *The Iliad* is strictly true, and there's a lot we still don't really know. It's generally (though not universally) agreed that there was really a Trojan War, that it happened in the late 12th or early 13th century BCE, and that Troy was located in what is now northwestern Turkey, in the town now called Hissarlik. There are ruins there of a large walled city, built up in multiple layers over centuries. The layers are called Troy I–IX; Troy VIIa is considered Homeric Troy. Many of the other cities mentioned by Homer definitely existed—Mycenae and Pylos are particularly well preserved. Beyond that it gets a bit hard to say with confidence how much of the story is factual. Because poems and myths are our main sources from the period, its history is practically inextricable from literature and mythology. Presumably Homer used poetic license in telling the story, even if it was an account of actual events.

The Iliad was recorded several centuries after the Trojan War, and there are passages that seem to describe technology of that later time. It seems likely that Homer (or each performer of the epic) used imagery that suited their vision of the story and made sense to their audience while doing their best to preserve the essential nature of the story. I've basically done the same. I did a lot of research into the historical period, but I've used artistic license to tell the story as clearly and dramatically as I can. For example, I've borrowed some designs from later classical Greek depictions of the characters (we have many examples preserved on pottery). I also gave myself a lot of latitude in helmet and shield designs, since these were the easiest way for me to help readers distinguish characters on the battlefield.

I've also chosen to give a somewhat uniform appearance to each army, so that the reader can quickly tell which side each warrior is on. This is not accurate. Each subgroup within each army would have been dressed and armored quite differently, and even within those groups there was probably very little uniformity.

It's likely that only the wealthy and the noblemen wore full armor. The costliest armor was made of bronze, but some armor was made of leather or layers of linen (called a *linothorax*—modern re-creations prove linen does a surprisingly good job of stopping weapons). Ajax Oileus is specifically described as wearing linen armor, and many vase paintings appear to depict warriors wearing the *linothorax*. Commoners might have only had the cheapest and most important pieces of equipment: a shield, spear, and helmet. This allowed the "heroes" to inflict a lot of damage among the commoners, just as knights in plate mail did in medieval European warfare.

Nobles were also the only ones who could afford chariots and horses to pull them. This let them travel quickly around the battlefield, picking their targets, or break through the enemy lines in a charge.

AUTHORSHIP AND TRANSLATION

We know almost nothing for sure about Homer. Classical tradition (folklore, poetry, and the claims of some later Greek and Roman historians) has it that he was a real person, a blind poet of great genius. More recently, scholars have tended to dismiss this idea and favor the theory that *The Iliad* and *The Odyssey* are the result of a long oral tradition. They were probably revised and expanded as they were sung to audiences over many generations, until someone eventually transcribed the versions we now think of as definitive. If that's the case, "Homer" is more the title of a tradition than a single person's name, though for simplicity's sake, I will generally refer to Homer in these notes as an individual and author of the epic. Any time Homer is mentioned, you can mentally add "or the bards of the Homeric tradition" (see Lord).

The Iliad and *The Odyssey* were recorded in the 7th or 8th century BCE, and were composed in dactylic hexameter. That means lines of six dactyls, units of one long and two short syllables (dum-ditty). Two long syllables (called a spondee) can be substituted for a dactyl, and there are other rules and exceptions, but basically each line is six dum-dittys. This makes for a melodic, musical sound. In Greek and Latin, dactylic hexameter was considered the ideal form for epic poetry/song. In English it doesn't sound quite as epic, and is pretty restrictive besides, so few translators adhere to it (for an exception, see Rodney Merrill). In my text I decided to dispense with any strict metrical form but keep a rhythmic feel to the language, loosely adhering to iambic blank verse (alternating stressed and unstressed syllables, as in Shakespearean verse, but without any line breaks). The translations I've used as a basis for my text are listed in the bibliography.

As in my other adaptations, I've tried very hard to keep the spirit and all the key events and themes of the original, but *The Iliad* is lengthy, dense, and complex, so I've had to cut huge amounts of material, including many powerful battle scenes and lots of dramatic dialogue. I hope that if you enjoy my adaptation of *The Iliad,* you'll seek out a good translation of the full text and experience it in all its glory.

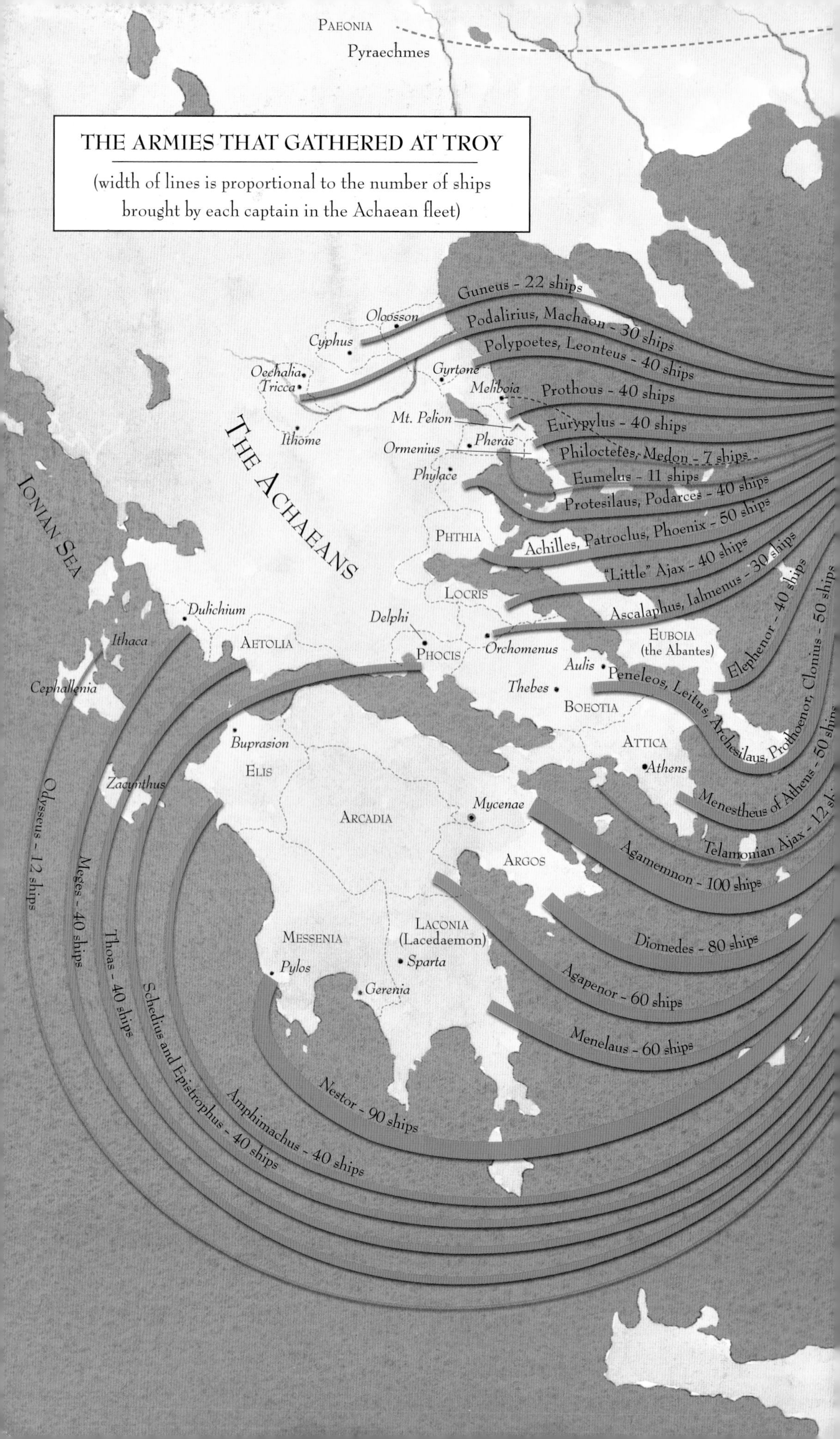
THE ARMIES THAT GATHERED AT TROY
(width of lines is proportional to the number of ships brought by each captain in the Achaean fleet)
PAEONIA
Pyraechmes
Guneus - 22 ships
Podalirius, Machaon - 30 ships
Polypoetes, Leonteus - 40 ships
Prothous - 40 ships
Eurypylus - 40 ships
Philoctetes, Medon - 7 ships
Eumelus - 11 ships
Protesilaus, Podarces - 40 ships
Achilles, Patroclus, Phoenix - 50 ships
"Little" Ajax - 40 ships
Ascalaphus, Ialmenus - 30 ships
Elephenor - 40 ships
Peneleos, Leitus, Archesilaus, Prothoenor, Clonius - 50 ships
Menestheus of Athens - 50 ships
Telamonian Ajax - 12 ships
Agamemnon - 100 ships
Diomedes - 80 ships
Agapenor - 60 ships
Menelaus - 60 ships
Nestor - 90 ships
Amphimachus - 40 ships
Schedius and Epistrophus - 40 ships
Thoas - 40 ships
Meges - 40 ships
Odysseus - 12 ships
Oloosson
Cyphus
Oechalia
Tricca
Gyrtone
Meliboia
Mt. Pelion
Ithome
Ormenius
Pherae
Phylace
THE ACHAEANS
IONIAN SEA
PHTHIA
LOCRIS
Delphi
PHOCIS
Orchomenus
EUBOIA
(the Abantes)
Aulis
Thebes
BOEOTIA
Dulichium
AETOLIA
Ithaca
Cephallenia
Buprasion
ELIS
ATTICA
Athens
Zacynthus
Mycenae
ARCADIA
ARGOS
MESSENIA
LACONIA
(Lacedaemon)
Sparta
Pylos
Gerenia

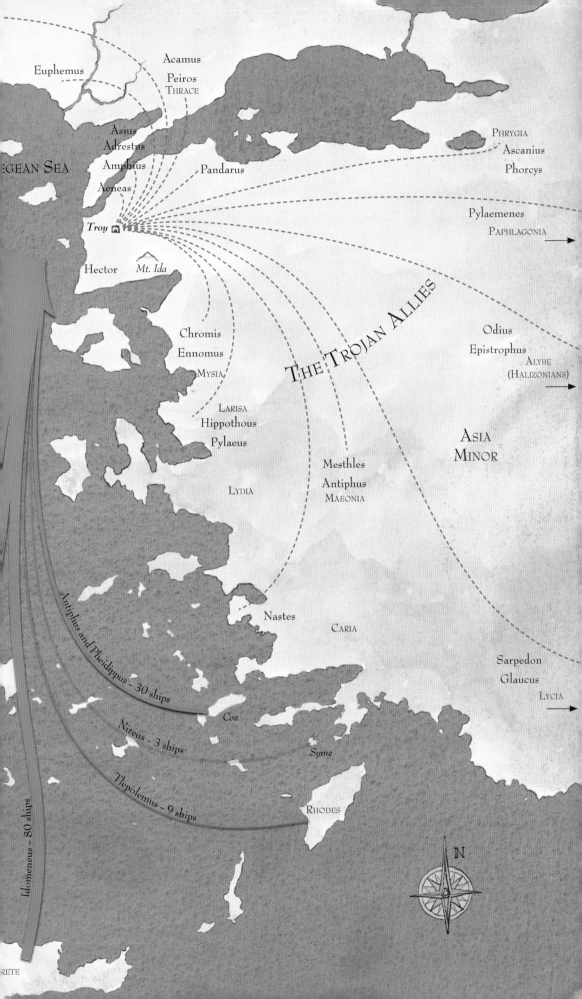

Euphemus

Acamus
Peiros
THRACE

Asius
Adrestus
Amphius
Aeneas

AEGEAN SEA

Pandarus

PHRYGIA
Ascanius
Phorcys

Troy

Pylaemenes
PAPHLAGONIA →

Hector

Mt. Ida

Chromis
Ennomus
MYSIA

THE TROJAN ALLIES

Odius
Epistrophus
ALYBE
(HALIZONIANS) →

LARISA
Hippothous
Pylaeus

ASIA
MINOR

Mesthles
Antiphus
MAEONIA

LYDIA

Nastes

CARIA

Sarpedon
Glaucus
LYCIA →

Antiphus and Pheidippus - 30 ships

Cos

Nireus - 3 ships

Syme

Tlepolemus - 9 ships

Idomeneus - 80 ships

RHODES

N

CRETE

PAGE-BY-PAGE NOTES

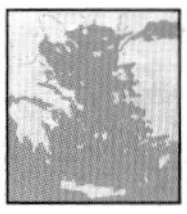

MAP: This map is based on an excellent map by Carlos Parada, author of *Genealogical Guide to Greek Mythology*. I added the ship numbers (from Homer's catalog of ships) and the fleet movements, which are simplified. The whole fleet went to Aulis before sailing for Troy (more on Aulis in just a moment). Note that many of the locations on this map are well established, but some are speculative.

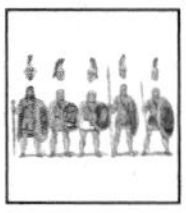

CHARACTERS: In my rough sketches, I drew the characters' initials on their chests and foreheads as a way to help my early readers tell them apart. They found this quite helpful, so I incorporated stylized initials into the final armor designs. Homer doesn't tell us what was on most of the shields, though in a few cases he does give detailed descriptions. For instance, he describes Agamemnon's shield in detail. For the shields Homer didn't describe, I tried to decorate each one with a symbol appropriate to that particular character. I gave Odysseus Athena's sacred owl; Menelaus a scowling face; Diomedes a stallion (he's king of "the stallion land of Argos"); Ajax a scorpion, since he's small but deadly at striking with a spear; and Nestor a stylized tree, since he's old and wise and multigenerational (he brought some of his sons to war with him, and he fought with the fathers of the other captains). Patroclus is wearing Achilles's armor here (we never see Achilles wear it, nor Patroclus wear anything else). It has both a *P* and an *A*, as well as an *H* since Hector wears it later. The shield has a dolphin, symbolizing Achilles's relationship to the sea via his mother, Thetis. I hid the front of Achilles's new shield here so as not to spoil the reveal on page 175. There are a number of points in the story where characters trade or borrow armor, and I have removed these to avoid confusion, except when they are particularly relevant to the plot.

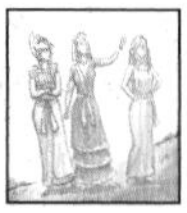

PROLOGUE: According to most sources, Thetis did not want to marry Peleus, but the sea god Proteus told Peleus how to capture her (a remarkably similar method to the one Menelaus uses to capture Proteus in *The Odyssey*). Thetis and Peleus supposedly had seven sons, but the first six died in infancy. The seventh was Achilles.

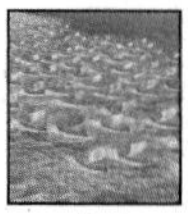

INVOCATION: *The Iliad* opens with the word *mênis,* which translates to "anger, rage, wrath, or fury," but has connotations of superhuman destructiveness that is usually only associated with gods. "Divine retribution" we might even call it, and it is the theme of the whole epic. Achilles is the only mortal to whom Homer ascribes *mênis.* [Lattimore]

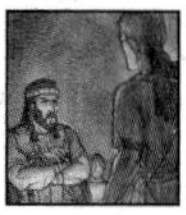

PAGES 3–5: The trigger for the events of *The Iliad* is basically a triple breach of contract, or at least breach of agreed-upon social norms in Greek society. First, Agamemnon refuses to ransom Chryseis back to her father. Then he seizes a lawfully given prize of war from Achilles. In retribution Achilles breaks his promise to honor Agamemnon as commander. One of the big morals of this story is that when men break their agreements, chaos and suffering ensue. The Achaeans probably saw these as more than just social contracts — essentially Agamemnon was breaking a cosmic order, thus inciting Zeus against him.

Before that, though, the Trojan War was started by Paris breaking proper guest etiquette as well as Helen and Menelaus's marriage contract.

At the very start of the war, Agamemnon sacrificed his own daughter Iphigenia to appease the wrath of Artemis, who had pinned down the fleet with unfavorable winds. The seer who told Agamemnon to make that sacrifice was Calchas. That's why Agamemnon is so angry and Calchas so afraid of him on pages 3–4, and it's this sacrifice that Odysseus is referring to on page 17. In some versions of the story, Artemis relents and saves Iphigenia. But Agamemnon's willingness to sacrifice his daughter is at least part of the reason his wife, Clytemnestra, plots to kill him when he returns home (as related in *The Odyssey*). The way he talks about Clytemnestra on page 4 might also have something to do with it, and she was also jealous of Cassandra, one of Priam's daughters whom Agamemnon claimed as a war prize and brought home with him.

When I say "prizes of war," I am of course talking about slavery. When the Achaeans conquered a city, they took captives, both men and women, as slaves. Women who were highborn, beautiful, or had domestic skills were the most valuable prizes of all, but anyone could suddenly find themselves enslaved (or killed) in a surprise raid on their city. Some of these men and women remained slaves for life. Others escaped, bought their freedom back through hard work, or were ransomed back by family members (like Lycaon on page 188). The awful prospect of being treated as property hangs over the heads of all the Trojan women, as Andromache and Hector discuss on page 68. It was a tough time for women, and Homer does not gloss over this.

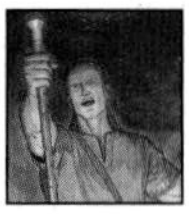

PAGE 7: Achilles says the staff is used to administer the justice of Zeus, but he also points out that it is dead wood that can never sprout again once it has been cut from the tree, which may be an insult to Agamemnon's power, as well as a warning that Agamemnon cannot undo the damage he has just done. By throwing the staff down, Achilles shows his contempt for the order and hierarchy that has been established within the army, and incidentally makes it a bit awkward for anyone else to speak in response, since they must first retrieve the staff. This doesn't stop Nestor, who can always be relied upon to speak up and share his wisdom.

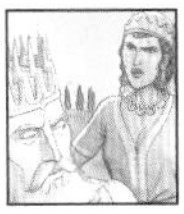

PAGE 13: I've removed Hephaestus from this scene. In the original, he intervenes between Zeus and Hera, offering her a cup of nectar, the drink of the gods. He mentions that the last time he stood up to Zeus in Hera's defense, Zeus flung him down from Olympus. Then he goes around pouring nectar for all the gods, who laugh at his awkward gait, caused by a crippled leg (another example of how petty and cruel the gods can be). Later, in Book 18, we are told Hera tossed him down (see page 174). The mythology seems to change according to the dramatic needs of the storyteller.

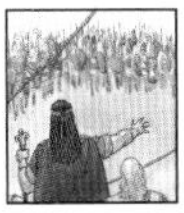

PAGE 16: Agamemnon's "test" of the army is clearly a dumb idea. In the original, Agamemnon mentions that such a test is customary, but either his timing or his method is wrong, and the test backfires. This strengthens the idea that Agamemnon is a bad commander, and that perhaps Achilles isn't just being sulky, he's actually standing on established social principle. Also, the scene is a great excuse for Odysseus to recap the prophecy about the war lasting ten years.

I left out a relatively minor character named Thersites, described as an ugly and sharp-tongued commoner who speaks up against Odysseus and gets beaten down for it. I mention him here because he's the only rank-and-file soldier who is ever given a name or any dialogue by Homer. This may reflect a general disinterest or even disdain for commoners that, perhaps, the poet shared with the Greek aristocracy.

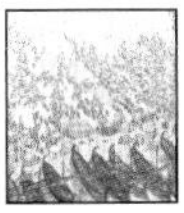

PAGE 19: Similes are a crucial part of *The Iliad.* There are almost twice as many similes in *The Iliad* as in *The Odyssey.* Many scholars believe that this was done to bring a deeper understanding of warfare to those who had not experienced it, especially to adolescent boys, who would soon be expected to go to war themselves. Most of the similes compare battles to scenes in nature — animals or agricultural settings — because that's what the rural Greek would have best understood. The imagery may also be intended to remind us of what peacetime looks like and of what is happening far from the bloody beach at Troy. While being told that fighting is *like* farming or cutting wood, we are simultaneously reminded of the contrast between these activities. [Guerriero]

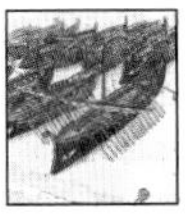

PAGES 20–25: In the original, Homer gives more information and a specific (though presumably rounded) number of ships for each contingent in a lengthy section often called the "catalog of ships." Instead of including every name, country, and ship count (which I included on the map), I focused here on information about the most important captains. The total number of ships according to Homer's account is 1,186, and each ship holds 50–120 men (the Greek ships of the period were known as penteconters, which means "50 oars," hence there would be at least 50 men to row each ship). So the total size of the Greek army was probably in the 70,000 to 130,000 range. Other ancient writers give the number of ships as between 1,000 and 1,200, but everyone agrees there were at least 1,000, hence Helen is said to have the "face that launched a thousand ships."

Troy is both the name of the city and of the country, and the area around Troy is called the Troad, after Priam's great-grandfather Tros. The city of Troy was founded by Ilus, Priam's grandfather (hence it is also called Ilium). Priam's father was Laomedon, who supposedly directed Poseidon and Apollo in building the walls of Troy (more about that in the note for page 82).

This is a very approximate reconstruction of Troy. The site believed to be Troy has been extensively excavated, but since the city was sacked and several layers of new city have been built on top in the centuries since, not much detail of Bronze Age Troy survives intact. The exact layout of the buildings and location of the Scaean Gate are not known.

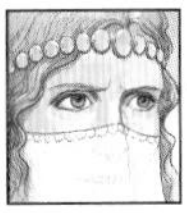

PAGE 30: Helen had two brothers, Castor and Polydeuces, and a sister, Clytemnestra (who married, and later killed, Agamemnon). Their mother was Leda, queen of Sparta and wife of Tyndareus. According to legend all four children were born at the same time, but only two of them were fathered by Tyndareus. The other two were fathered by Zeus, who had seduced Leda while disguised as a swan. Different versions of the story disagree about important details such as which of the children belonged to Zeus. Some legends say Polydeuces was immortal, and when Castor died, Polydeuces wished to share his immortality with Castor. Zeus agreed and turned them into the constellation Gemini. In *The Iliad,* Homer simply says that the two brothers have been killed, and in Book 11 of *The Odyssey,* Odysseus says that Zeus allows them to live on alternating days. Incidentally, both brothers went with Jason on the famous quest for the Golden Fleece.

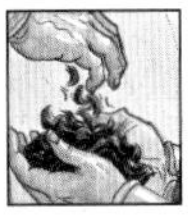

PAGE 31: Distributing bits of fleece from a sacrificial animal seems to be a symbolic way of involving all the leaders in the decision and the formalities of the duel.

Homer tells us that Paris borrows armor from his brother Lycaon, perhaps because he normally fights at long range with a bow and doesn't wear strong enough armor to protect from a spear thrust.

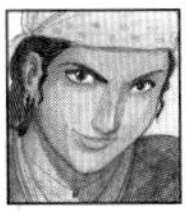

PAGES 40–41: Aphrodite takes the form not just of any servant, but of a spinning-woman from Lacedaemon, Helen's homeland.

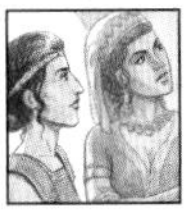

PAGES 42–43: Hera and Athena still hold a grudge against Paris for choosing Aphrodite in the beauty contest. By extension, they hate all the Trojans. One might ask why the gods are so petty. And indeed, why are

the "heroes" such as Agamemnon and Achilles so petty? This is one of *The Iliad*'s many great topics for discussion, but it is worth noting that the issue is not just who gets the prizes, but which god gets the most worship and which leader achieves everlasting fame as the hero of the epic.

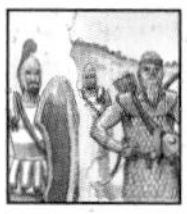

PAGE 44: Pandarus is somewhere between a tragic figure and a villain. He breaks the truce in an attempt to win glory, but in the process dooms many more men to die (if we assume the truce would have held otherwise) and fails to kill Menelaus. Since Apollo is the god of archery, Pandarus promises Apollo a ritual sacrifice if the god will help him hit his target. Unfortunately for him, Athena is literally calling the shots here, in the service of Zeus. Pandarus's other claim to fame is acting as a go-between to arrange an illicit marriage between his niece Cressida and the Trojan warrior Troilus (dramatized by Shakespeare in the play *Troilus & Cressida),* which is the source of the word *pander*—not a very flattering legacy.

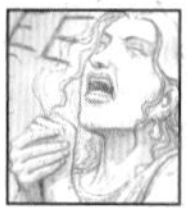

PAGE 55: How is it that Aphrodite, a goddess, can be wounded by a mortal? Presumably it has to do with the fact that Diomedes has Athena on his side. Homer tells us that Aphrodite runs home to her mother, the Titan Dione. Dione tells her that even the gods must suffer pain, giving several other examples: Ares chained by Otus and Ephialtes in a cauldron until Hermes rescued him, and both Hera and Hades shot with barbed arrows by Heracles.

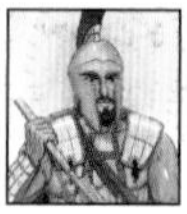

PAGES 56–59: In the original, more happens here: Apollo creates an illusion of a dead Aeneas, over whom both armies fight. The real Aeneas is healed and returns to the fighting, killing many Achaeans. Menelaus and Antilochus force him back. Zeus's son Sarpedon kills Heracles's son (Zeus's grandson) Tlepolemus, but is wounded in the thigh with a spear. And more! Almost every battle scene you see is more detailed in the original and trimmed for brevity and pacing.

Warriors tried whenever possible to seize the armor of their fallen opponents. This armor was often elaborate and costly. It was treasure in its own right, and it proved who you had killed *and* that you were skillful enough to strip it and carry it to safety. Generally speaking, the greater the warrior, the nicer his armor, and the nicer the armor, the harder both sides would fight to claim it.

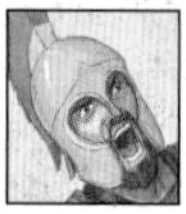

PAGE 59: The word *stentorian* (meaning "loud") comes from the name Stentor, the warrior whose guise Hera assumes here. Being able to yell at exceptionally high volume was a great advantage for issuing commands in the noise of battle, so characters who had this ability (like Stentor, Menelaus, and Diomedes) were often famous for it as much as for their rank or their fighting prowess.

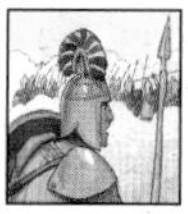

PAGE 62: Helenus is another of Priam's many sons. Some legends say Cassandra taught him the gift of prophecy (see the note for page 245). Certainly he's very good at making predictions. Had Paris heeded his warning not to go to Sparta, the whole war could have been avoided. And in *The Aeneid,* he predicts Aeneas's founding of Rome.

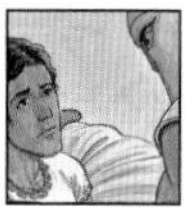

PAGES 64–65: Priam has many offspring, but only a few are by his wife, Hecuba, and those (e.g., Hector and Paris) have the highest status. Hector and Paris are the only sons who have their own separate houses. Paris built his house next to Hector's, employing "the finest masons of his day," which seems to reflect his belief that he's in the same league as the mighty Hector, even though his actions seem much less heroic.

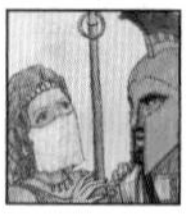

PAGE 66: Here and in Book 3 Homer adds more of a sense that Helen feels guilty about being the cause of the war. I left this out because although her feelings are understandable, she clearly *isn't* the cause of the war. The war is the work of angry gods and angry men. Rage, as the first word of the poem emphasizes.

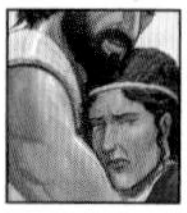

PAGE 68: Thebe (not to be confused with Thebes) was one of the cities raided by the Achaeans—the same raids Achilles talks about on page 5 (and indeed Thebe is where Chryseis was captured). According to *The Aeneid,* after the fall of Troy, Andromache is forced to marry Achilles's son Neoptolemus, but he dies young, and then she marries Hector's brother Helenus and becomes queen of Epirus.

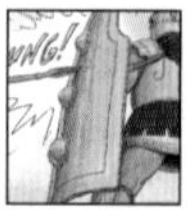

PAGE 76: A tower shield is a tall shield, often rectangular, large enough that a man can rest it on the ground and hide entirely behind it. It is probable that the Greeks used tower shields in parts of the Bronze Age, though there is debate about whether that includes the time of the Trojan War. Ajax is often described as a tower, and while this refers to the giant himself rather than his shield, I theorized that he might have used such a shield, since he was strong enough to carry it and large enough to need it. Also, Teucer is later described as being able to hide effectively behind the shield with Ajax, suggesting it was very large.

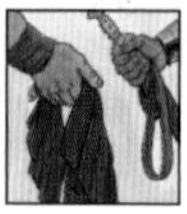

PAGE 79: The purple loin-guard may seem like a poor gift, but it would in fact have had great value. Purple dye was extremely expensive and difficult to produce because it was made from a tiny gland in a sea snail called the spiny dye-murex, and thousands of snails had to be caught and dissected to make a batch of dye. Usually only kings could afford purple-dyed goods. This was later codified as a rule, in the Roman Empire and others, that only royalty could wear purple [Pliny].

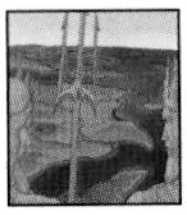

PAGES 82, 199: Supposedly Poseidon and Apollo offended Zeus, who then commanded them to work for Priam's father, Laomedon, who asked them to build mighty walls around Troy, and that is what Poseidon is referring to here. Laomedon promised them a reward but then went back on his word, so Poseidon sent a monster to ravage Troy, and Apollo sent a plague. Heracles killed the monster, but again Laomedon went back on his word, withholding the reward he had promised Heracles (the horses of Tros, from whom Aeneas's horses are descended). Heracles sacked the city in retaliation, killing Laomedon and all his sons except Priam.

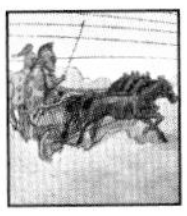

PAGE 86: Hector has four horses in his team, whereas most chariots were pulled by only two horses, occasionally with a third as a spare. Only very special horses would be fed. We have no idea if it was a common practice to feed wheat and wine to special horses instead of oats/barley and water, but the point is that Hector's horses are treated more like humans.

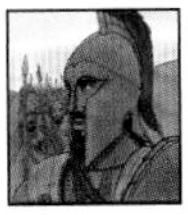

PAGE 91: Sometimes mortal characters are called "godlike" by Homer or by their comrades, but any time someone compares *themselves* to the gods, they are displaying hubris, fatal pride, and you can be pretty sure they are doomed from that point on. Even Hector isn't a perfect hero: his pride here and on page 172 shows him at his most flawed, and invites the wrath of the gods.

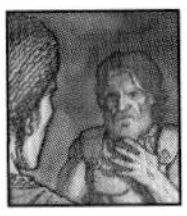

PAGES 94–95: Odysseus and Achilles represent two radically different types of war heroes. Achilles is straightforward, says what he thinks, and wins by superior prowess in battle. Odysseus is wily and perceptive and uses whatever methods it takes to win, including diplomacy, trickery, or outright lying. I've skipped over the repetition of gifts, but Odysseus repeats Agamemnon's entire offer verbatim, *except* for the part where Agamemnon says Achilles must submit to him. Odysseus replaces this with a more diplomatic appeal for Achilles to consider his comrades and his reputation.

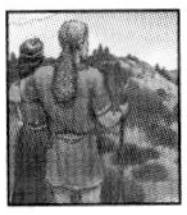

PAGE 96: I wanted to show a vision of the happy ending Achilles is picturing here, though it's doubtful that he truly knows what he wants.

Professor Gregory Nagy describes another interesting contrast between Achilles and Odysseus—these two heroes have very different fates and relationships to death and glory as relayed to them by the gods. According to Thetis, in order to win everlasting fame—Homer uses the Greek word *kleos,* "glory"—Achilles must die in battle, giving up on a homecoming, or *nostos.* Odysseus, however, will win fame precisely for the manner of his homecoming, according to Athena. His *nostos* is the source of his *kleos.* They both achieve this fame, and we are still telling their stories thousands of years later.

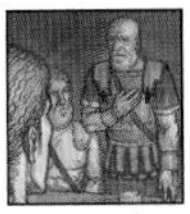

PAGE 97: Phoenix also tells Achilles the myth of Meleager—a story with parallels to Achilles's situation, the moral of which is that a warrior will never win glory if he allows his allies to be destroyed. This, Stephen Guerriero explains, is an example of the way storytelling was used as the primary teaching method of this culture. *The Iliad* itself would have been used in the same way. However, I left the story out because it's very long and because it fails to convince Achilles.

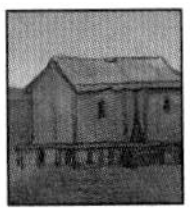

PAGE 99: Just in case we thought that Briseis was Achilles's only slave woman, at the end of this scene Homer tells us that Achilles and Patroclus go to bed with two of Achilles's *other* slave women: Diomede, captured from Lesbos; and Iphis, captured from Skyros.

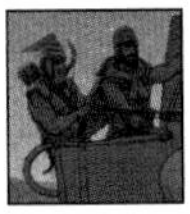

PAGES 102–104: I've omitted most of the details of Odysseus and Diomedes's night raid. The unfortunate spy is Dolon, an ambitious fellow who volunteers to scout the Achaean camp if Hector will promise him the immortal horses of Achilles as a war prize. It's quite a demand, but Hector agrees. Odysseus and Diomedes catch Dolon almost immediately and interrogate him, which is how they learn that the newly arrived Thracians are camped on the fringes of the army with no defenses (essentially Dolon throws the latecomers under the bus). It doesn't save him, though—Odysseus and Diomedes don't trust him at all, and they behead him. This is not the first or last time a surrendering enemy is killed (in fact there's another example in the very next scene).

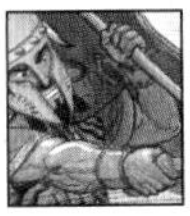

PAGES 106–107: The distinctive sword and figure-eight-shaped shield I show Agamemnon wielding are particular to the Mycenaeans. It's a rare example where we can tie a particular design to a specific subgroup, so I wanted to associate it with the king of Mycenae, though there is some question about whether they used the figure-eight shields in this particular time period.

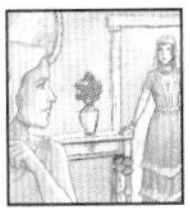

PAGE 122: I moved the chapter break for Book 14 here because it made more sense to me in terms of the flow of the story and the page layouts. Since *The Iliad* was an oral epic, there were originally no chapter/book divisions in it. These were introduced after it was written down. And since it was first written on scrolls, and probably took up at least twenty scrolls, one popular theory is that the "books" were actually the different physical scrolls.

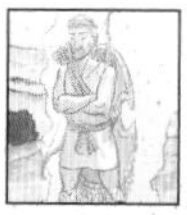

PAGE 129: The word *aegis* means "shield" or "protection," and usually refers to a magical shield or protective cloak that belongs to Zeus and is often worn by Athena. I have chosen to interpret it as a shield. It has tassels that make thunder and lightning when shaken, and the head of Medusa mounted on it to strike terror into all who look at it.

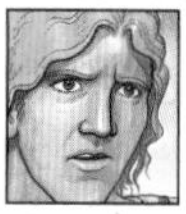

PAGE 137: Homer occasionally uses second-person narration in *The Iliad,* but only directed at two characters: Menelaus and Patroclus. Some scholars believe this is because they are the most blameless heroes in the story. I chose to omit the bits addressed to Menelaus, but keep those addressed to Patroclus, because I think they subtly impart a more tragic air to the scenes leading up to his death.

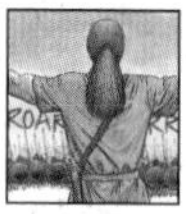

PAGE 140: The name Myrmidons comes from the Greek word for ant, *myrmex.* They took the name from mythical soldiers created by Zeus from ants. Homer extends the metaphor to hornets. The Myrmidons are the proverbial hornets' nest riled up by mischievous boys so that they will attack the next person to walk by. Hornets fight to defend their nest and their offspring, which might be a more apt comparison to the Trojans, but we can also imagine the Achaeans as hornets who have hung their nest outside the home of Priam and will not be dislodged.

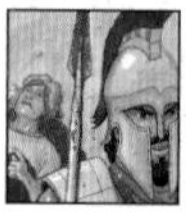

PAGE 153: Hector says birds will feed on Patroclus's corpse. This is a standard taunt, as it implies the warrior will not get a proper burial — pretty much the worst thing imaginable in a Bronze Age warrior's worldview.

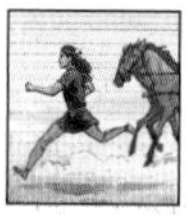

PAGE 161: Why does Antilochus run on foot to tell Achilles? Wouldn't it make more sense if someone went in a chariot? It's possible that over uneven terrain, a fast man *might* have actually been able to run faster than a chariot, but more likely Homer wanted to give Antilochus something heroic to do for dramatic reasons. Antilochus later (after *The Iliad*) becomes a sort of emotional and narrative replacement for Patroclus — Achilles becomes attached to him, and when Antilochus is killed, Achilles again flies into a rage and chases the Trojans all the way into the Scaean gate, where Paris kills him with an arrow.

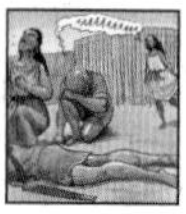

PAGE 165: Slaves and servants were expected to share in their master's grief. If their master lost a loved one, the servant had to put on a truly dramatic show of wailing and mourning (whether or not they actually liked their master or the deceased). In this case, there may have been some genuine grief for Patroclus, since there is evidence that he may have been more gentle and civilized than many of the other leaders (Briseis in particular says that he treated her kindly).

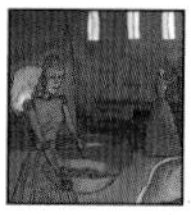

PAGE 174: Homer tells us that Thetis is met by Hephaestus's wife, Charis, one of the three Graces (goddesses of charm, grace, beauty, and charity). In most other stories, including the one recounted by the bard in Book 8 of *The Odyssey,* Aphrodite is Hephaestus's wife. Also, Hephaestus is usually said to employ Cyclopes in his forge, but here Homer instead tells us that he employs robots: golden women he presumably built himself to help out around the shop.

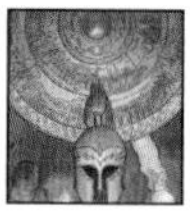

PAGE 175: The designs Homer describes on Achilles's shield are intricate and staggering in scope and execution. They are (arguably) impossible to replicate, since each contains incredible amounts of detail and depicts a span of time rather than a single instant. Homer's description of the shield takes up four full pages and is fascinating for its depiction of Bronze Age life. It is almost a graphic novel in its own right, showing the breadth of human civilization. By zooming in to the minute details of the shield, Homer simultaneously zooms out from the events of *The Iliad* to give us a wider view of war, peace, and the rhythms of life, as well as echoing important themes of justice, marriage, contracts, work, and celebration. However, it feels very long and it pulls the reader away from the story's action at its emotional peak. I decided to show the shield in all its glory, but to omit the lengthy text description.

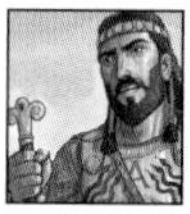

PAGE 178: Note that Agamemnon says he regrets his anger, but also that the gods "stole his wits." For the Greeks there was a delicate balance between personal responsibility and divine influence, and both could be in operation at once. Agamemnon promises to make amends but doesn't admit he was to blame. Likewise, Achilles drops his grudge but doesn't want to formally accept the gifts as an apology—he just thinks Agamemnon should give them because they "are due." He is preoccupied now with taking revenge on Hector—and with the knowledge that he is fated to die soon after.

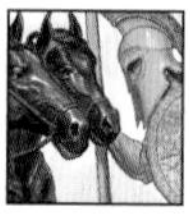

PAGE 183: Yes, Achilles's horses can talk. They were a present from the gods, remember. They also weep when Patroclus dies, a detail I left out.

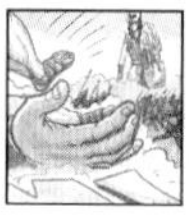

PAGES 197–199: The gods seem to change size at different points in Homer's narrative. Sometimes they are roughly human-size, but at other times they are gigantic. In this scene Homer tells us that when Ares falls, his body covers seven acres! My interpretation is that one of the gods' powers is the ability to grow larger when they want to be extra impressive, but then when they relax (or lose consciousness) they shrink back down to a more human size, as shown on page 198.

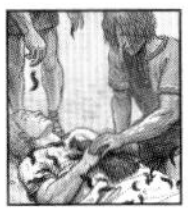

PAGE 222: Achilles had promised to grow out a lock of his hair until he returned home, when he would cut it and sacrifice it to the river Spercheus. Having chosen revenge, he symbolically sacrifices his homecoming on Patroclus's pyre. I chose to have him cut all his hair, as it was much more dramatic.

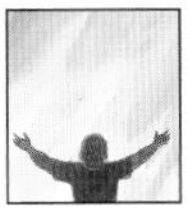

PAGES 224–228: Proper burial rituals were extremely important to the Greeks and Trojans. Stephen Guerriero explains that they believed the deceased needed these rituals to ensure their passage to Hades, while the living needed the rituals in order to grieve and say good-bye in a communal way.

The funeral games of Patroclus may have been an early inspiration for the Olympic games. Homer's descriptions of the funeral games are vivid, action-packed, and detailed, but I had to condense them down to a brief summary. It's well worth reading the whole thing. The chariot race is particularly contentious. We get another lesson in how easily the Achaeans get into fights, and how those disagreements are smoothed over with words and gifts. Actually, Achilles ends up giving prizes to all the charioteers, and to Nestor, who is too old to compete. The wrestling match between Odysseus and Ajax foreshadows events after *The Iliad:* after Achilles is killed, the two men compete for his armor. In that contest too they are tied, but Odysseus convinces the chiefs that he should have the armor, and Ajax is so enraged that he slaughters a bunch of innocent sheep and then commits suicide.

Epeius appears only on page 226, but he is notable because in addition to being a great boxer, he was supposedly in charge of building the Trojan horse.

The significant handshake on page 228 is my own addition. It seems clear from Achilles's words to Agamemnon in the original text that he has either lost some of his anger at Agamemnon, is willing to set it aside to honor his friend, or at the very least is willing to pretend to be on good terms with Agamemnon and get on with the war. The handshake seemed the best way to symbolize this.

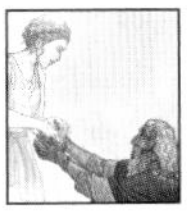

PAGE 231: I'm not sure why, but I find the moment when Priam says "I heard her voice, looked straight at the goddess, face-to-face" very powerful. I think it captures the feelings of a human who has had a direct encounter with the divine, and explains why Priam is intent on putting himself in such danger. It's also true that, having lost Hector, he and his city are doomed, and all he has left is honor and righteousness, both of which demand that he seek the proper burial for his son.

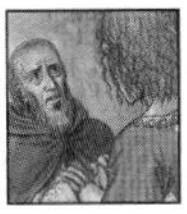

PAGES 237–243: Guerriero points out that this intense, climactic encounter between Priam and Achilles is a moment that's parallel to the meeting of Hector and Achilles outside the walls. There, Achilles was motivated only by his rage and violence. In this instance, Achilles recognizes Priam as a fellow man—a sufferer like himself, deserving sympathy. This is the great epiphany of Achilles. It is the key moment in the epic. Here also Homer gives us the closing of the frame that began with the failed attempt of Chryses to ransom back his daughter, a ransom denied by the injustice of Agamemnon. Here, the father's ransom is justly accepted by Achilles—even though he knows he will be dead soon and has little use for the gifts themselves.

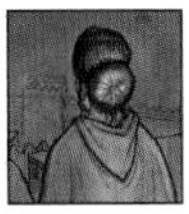

PAGE 245: Cassandra was a daughter of Priam who was said to have the gift of prophecy, but her gift was more like a curse because no one ever believed her prophecies. They thought she was crazy, and indeed she may have become so from the stress of knowing all the bad things that were going to happen to her people, and being ignored when she tried to warn them.

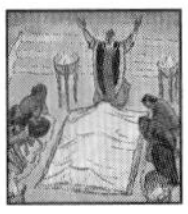

PAGE 246: Homer gives us many of the funeral dirges for Hector in their entirety. They are powerful, but I abridged them here because they repeat a lot of what's already been said on pages 203 and 219. Of note is that the final dirge is Helen's, and she speaks of Hector's kindness. He is a third type of hero, as contrasted with Achilles and Odysseus: one who is kind and generous and who fights primarily to defend his family.

While most of the Greek and Trojan champions are known for their talents in war, Homer names Hector "breaker of horses," meaning he was famed for his skill at taming wild horses so they would accept a harness or rider. This was generally done during peacetime, and Homer may be using it as a metaphor for kingship: a good king was expected to impose and protect order, law, and civilization (by force when necessary). Because Hector has the skill and temperament to excel at this, and his people clearly love him, we can speculate that he would have been an effective king if he had not been killed by Achilles. Then again, who is good or bad is at least partly a matter of perspective—the Achaeans call him "Man-killing Hector" because he's their deadliest enemy.

One final note on the funeral dirges: Albert Lord posits that they can be interpreted as a prototype or kernel of the Homeric epics themselves. By singing about the greatness of their fallen heroes, the Greeks, Trojans, and those who came after them have kept those heroes alive—all the way to the present day.

BIBLIOGRAPHY

Age of Bronze. http://age-of-bronze.com/CartoonistinTroy.shtml.

Gill, N. S. "Death and Dying in the Iliad." https://www.thoughtco.com/deaths-in-the-iliad-121298.

Greek Myth Comix. https://greekmythcomix.wordpress.com/comic/deaths-in-the-iliad-a-classics-infographic.

Guerriero, Stephen, MA, MEd. Discussions by e-mail, 2017.

Herodotus. *The History of Herodotus.* Translated by G. C. Macaulay. New York: MacMillan: 1890.

Homer. *The Iliad.* Translated by Samuel Butler. New York: Longmans, Green, 1898.

———. *The Iliad.* Translated by Robert Fagles. New York: Viking, 1990.

———. *The Iliad.* Translated by Robert Fitzgerald. Garden City, NY: Anchor Press, 1974.

———. *The Iliad of Homer.* Translated by Richmond Lattimore. Chicago: University of Chicago Press, 2011.

———. *The Iliad.* Translated by E. V. Rieu. London: Penguin Books, 1950.

———. *The Odyssey.* Translated by Robert Fagles. New York: Viking, 1996.

———. *The Odyssey.* Translated by Robert Fitzgerald. Garden City, NY: Anchor, 1963.

———. *The Odyssey.* Translated by Rodney Merrill. Ann Arbor: University of Michigan Press, 2002.

———. *The Odyssey.* Translated by E. V. Rieu. New York: Penguin, 1946.

Howard, Dan. *Bronze Age Military Equipment.* South Yorkshire, UK: Pen & Sword: 2011.

Lord, Albert B. *The Singer of Tales.* 2nd ed. Edited by Stephen Mitchell and Gregory Nagy. Cambridge, MA: Harvard University Press, 2000.

Luce, J. V. *Celebrating Homer's Landscapes: Troy and Ithaca Revisited.* New Haven: Yale University Press, 1998.

Muellner, Leonard, *The Anger of Achilles: Mênis in Greek Epic.* Ithaca, NY: Cornell University Press, 2005. https://chs.harvard.edu/CHS/article/display/6380.

Myth Index Greek. http://www.mythindex.com.

Nagy, Gregory. "Homer and Greek Myth." In *The Cambridge Companion to Greek Mythology,* edited by R. D. Woodard, 52–82. Cambridge: Cambridge University Press, 2007. https://chs.harvard.edu/CHS/article/display/2486.

Ovid. *Metamorphoses.* Translated by Horace Gregory. New York: Signet Classics, 2009.

Pliny the Elder. *The Natural History.* Edited and translated by John Bostock and Henry Thomas Riley. London: Taylor & Francis, 1855.

Quintus Smyrnaeus. *The Fall of Troy.* Translated by A. S. Way. Cambridge, MA: Harvard University Press, 1913.

Shanower, Eric. Discussions by email, 2016.

Warr, George C. W. *The Greek Epic.* New York: E. & J. B. Young, 1895.

Willcock, Malcolm M. *A Companion to the Iliad.* Chicago: University of Chicago Press, 1976.

Virgil. *The Aeneid.* Translated by Robert Fagles. New York: Penguin Audio, 2006.

ACKNOWLEDGMENTS

I hope you have enjoyed this timeless story. I would like to offer my deepest thanks to the Muses, both the immortal ones and the many wonderful humans who helped me bring this truly epic project to fruition.

To Carter Hasegawa, longtime friend and assistant editor on several previous books, who stepped into the role of editor smoothly and skillfully. To art director Sherry Fatla and designer Lisa Rudden, who work hard to make my books beautiful, along with the wonderful production team at Candlewick: Gregg Hammerquist, Andrea Corbin, and Amanda Bellamy. To my copyeditors, Pam Marshall and Maggie Deslaurier, and proofreader Emily Quill. To Jamie Tan, Andie Krawczyk, Anne Irza-Leggat, and all the other marketing and sales folks at Candlewick who send my books far and wide and are always great company at trade shows.

To my early readers for excellent feedback: Alison Morris, Judith Hinds, Steve Hinds, Mara Kanari, Stephen Guerriero, Mat MacKenzie, Paul Crook, Dianne Cowan, Barbara Harrison, Barbara Scotto, and Alexis Frederick-Frost. Stephen's speed and expertise were especially appreciated, and I used several of his ideas in the page notes. He, in turn, credits professors Ann Koloski-Ostrow and Stephen Esposito, as well as Gregory Nagy and Leonard Muellner at the Center for Hellenic Studies, who have authored many important works on Homer and Bronze Age Greece. I made several rewarding visits to the Center for Hellenic Studies myself, and my gratitude extends to all the staff and research fellows.

To Children's Literature New England and The Examined Life for bringing me as an artist in residence on two truly spectacular trips to Greece (www.teachgreece.org). I highly recommend their program, as well as the fantastic tour guide Mara Kanari.

To Eric Shanower for sharing his sources and opinions, and for his excellent work studying and illustrating the Trojan War.

To Betty Carter for answering bibliographic questions, and to Pamela Turner for awakening me to the value of well-cited author notes.

To Margaret Ryding and Wes Carroll for letting me continue to use your likenesses for Helen and Menelaus.

Enormous thanks to Jay Carpenter and his family for providing studio space, encouragement, and welcome support during the eight months it took to color this book.

For Alison, with all my love.
You inspire my greatest endeavors.

First edition 2019

Library of Congress Catalog Card Number pending
ISBN 978-0-7636-8113-5 (hardcover)
ISBN 978-0-7636-9663-4 (paperback)

18 19 20 21 22 23 APS 10 9 8 7 6 5 4 3 2 1

Printed in Humen, Dongguan, China

This book was typeset in Bernhard Modern.
The illustrations were done in pencil, watercolor, and digital media.

Candlewick Press
99 Dover Street
Somerville, Massachusetts 02144

visit us at www.candlewick.com